ARIEL

Ariel

No Name Under Heaven

R A HERKES

First published 2023

Copyright © Richard Andrew Herkes 2023

The right of Richard Andrew Herkes to be identified as the author of this work has been asserted by him in accordance with the Copyright, Designs and Patents Act 1988.

All rights reserved. With the exception of short extracts for the purposes of review, no part of this publication may be reproduced or transmitted in any form or by any means, electronic or mechanical, including photocopy, recording, or any information storage or retrieval system, without permission in writing from the author.

richard.herkes@gmail.com

Although most of the places in this book are real, the characters are fictional, and any similarity to persons living or deceased is accidental.

Cover design by Peter Smith and Chris Jackson.

ISBN-13: 979 8 3980 7270 9

CONTENTS

Prologue 7

PART ONE: LOST AND FOUND

1. The Stranger 11
2. The Storm 31
   Lapse 48
3. Tests 49
4. Secrets 58
5. Awakening 82
6. Arrivals 95
7. Enigmas 112
   Life 132
8. Connections 133
9. Rumours and Reports 150
10. Watching and Waiting 163
11. Suspicions 176
12. Elements of Surprise 196
13. Lies and Accusations 209
14. Disappointments 225
15. Emotions 256
16. Questions 273
17. Closing In 302
18. Conversations 332

PART TWO: THROUGH MANY DANGERS

19. Review	401
20. Puzzle	431
21. Taken	457
22. Capture	479
23. Degradation	498
24. Trauma	517
25. Intelligence	544
26. Temptation	570
27. Gathering	591
Light	604
28. Investigation	605
29. Intimidation	629
30. Revelation	652

PART THREE: LIFE ENDURES

31. Publicity	671
32. Believers	690
33. Unknown	714
Epilogue	731
Poems of Ariel	735

Prologue

A stone hits the water.
The waves ripple out some forty days
And more.

A story based on the accounts of those who rode the waves.

The years pass relentlessly, and we are aware that we shall not be here indefinitely. As we move towards the close of a century that has almost forgotten how to let a story unfold, the time has come to tell what really happened after human beings first stood on the surface of Earth's troubled sister, when a few of us were privileged to a second mysterious Window of unexpected opportunity.

MF/MF

PART ONE

LOST AND FOUND

Die Welt ist mir zu eng,
der Himmel ist zu klein:
wo wird denn noch ein Raum
für meine Seele sein?

Ich weiß nicht, was ich bin,
ich bin nicht, was ich weiß:
ein Ding und nicht ein Ding,
ein Pünktchen und ein Kreis.

Angelus Silesius

Too strait for me the world,
too small the open sky:
where now will be a room
still for this soul of mine?

I don't know what I am,
I am not what I know:
a thing and not a thing,
a dot and circle both.

CHAPTER 1

The Stranger

1

The rocky gorge spread out below in a blaze of splintered orange. Jack Forrester set one foot on a conveniently placed ledge and gazed at the alien landscape. He'd always thought orange a garish colour, but this had a robustness, a rightness, quite unlike anything he'd seen before. Above him the sky repeatedly flashed red and green, though each time the brightness was quickly subdued by his intellivisor. He shifted his position, enjoying the relative comfort of having one foot slightly higher than the other. Behind him his colleagues were busy burying probes and shovelling samples, but right now he told himself it was time to stop. To gaze and wonder. He remained standing for several minutes, until the concerned tones of the Captain broke through on his helmet intercom.

'You okay, Jack?'

'I'm fine, Jim,' he returned. 'But you can't come all this way and not stop to smell the roses.'

Jim had become used to Jack's softly Scottish tones and caught the hint of embarrassment. 'Don't apologise – you've been busy enough getting us down here. Take five and look around.'

Jack straightened up and turned away from the cliff edge – that valley deserved better than five minutes. Perhaps he could return later. Almost too late he had come to realise that his mind had been standing on even higher ground than his body, at the top of a mountain of training, and if it didn't come down soon everything he did here would be little more than going through the motions, running system checks and equipment checks before checking the checks. How easy it was to measure without really looking.

He headed back towards the rest of the crew of the Endeavour. The ship's captain, Colonel James Adamson, was standing a few metres away, alert as ever. His white suit was an angry orange now, covered in dust whipped up by the intermittent winds that felt more like sea currents, and his face was hidden behind a convex reflection of rocky outcrops which, from this short distance, looked for all the world like claws curled around his face.

Away to the left stood the World Space Agency's youngest astronaut, Ryan Chase. He was fiddling with one of the gadgets he had helped to design for this mission, an atmosphere analyser. He was struggling – rather pathetically, Jack thought – to operate the unit within the confines of his space suit, the special garb they had been given for extra-vehicular activity, or EVA as astronauts loved to call going outdoors. The gloves, actually extensions of the sleeves, were the thinnest design yet made for a space suit, but they were still not best suited for fine work. Just a few layers between human skin and several times normal atmospheric pressure, not to mention two hundred degrees of asphyxiating heat and the occasional cloud of sulphuric acid. And this was a good day. For they were standing on the surface of Venus, an impossibility before the strange phenomenon that had triggered their mission – a sustained and unexplained drop in temperature and pressure here in the Nightingale corona.

The dramatic change in conditions had opened a window of opportunity, turning the WSA's sights away from Mars, for now at least, and towards Earth's twin sister. Not that they were identical twins – Venus was almost exactly the same size as Earth, but there the similarity ended. Volcanic activity had served to make her the hottest planet in the solar system, trapping the sun's heat below thick layers of carbon dioxide and mixing in generous doses of burning sulphur. But a few months ago a small area of less hostile conditions had beckoned, and intrigue grew with each passing week. Recent advances in suit technology had served to bolster the arguments to go and investigate in person, for if the conditions persisted when the astronauts finally arrived in orbit, they might even have the chance to land, to walk on its surface and explore its rocks and ridges. Utterly unthinkable until now. Even so, such a mission would still be hugely perilous.

There was no shortage of astronauts on the volunteer list.

As Jack watched Ryan working he allowed his thoughts to dwell a while on the riddle of human technology. The wonders of these increasingly fantastic solutions and devices so often ended up separating him from the very environments he had come to explore. Yet he was utterly dependent on them, never more than here, where every second they saved him from being poisoned, fried and squashed. But there it was. You needed the barriers to cross the borders. The human frame was just too frail for it to be otherwise.

He thought of home, the earth, where a fragile atmosphere allowed him and billions of others to exist in what still seemed to be the rarest comfort zone the universe had to offer. If he were there now he could be doing something sensible, like flying fighters, or fishing, or sharing a take-away with Melody.

His eye was caught by a movement to the right – it was the mission's planetary geologist (whom one over-zealous journalist had insisted on calling a venerologist), Natasha Koroleva. Because she had a Russian military background yet went on to train with NASA, there had been a half-serious debate back at the training centre over whether she was a Russian spy or an American one. Nor did it go unnoticed that she was the only woman to join a crew of White males. But now, here, where human beings trod the surface of Venus for the first time, it was neither a Russian nor a woman Jack was watching, but a fellow human being. He found it hard to believe he could have lived for over forty years on Earth and remained so ignorant of how incredibly alike human beings were, separated only by subtleties of culture and politics. But back on Earth that's just what you were. Ignorant.

He pushed back a feeling of guilt as he indulged his reverie. Since the unexpected 'Window' had opened a few months before, he had been trained at great expense and breakneck speed to ensure Venus was visited in person for the first time, and yet here he was using the sixty-million-mile round trip to waste time reflecting on the quality of human existence. He recalled feeling the same when, as a young RAF pilot, he had seen the sights of the Far East on his first long-distance mission. 'Perks,' his training officer had said. He smiled to himself now. He'd expected this trip to bring such complimentary extras, of course, but he had not been prepared for the reflective mood that had mushroomed since they had arrived. And yet wasn't that really the point of it all? To pause, to reflect, to try to understand what all the facts and figures really meant?

Certainly out here you had a change of perspective. In the month or so it took to get here he had experienced human fellowship at a level almost impossible back on Earth, except perhaps in some remote desert or hundreds of metres below the ocean surface, the very environments in which their training had taken place. Yet out here the closeness seemed less exclusive somehow. Their shared humanity was way stronger than their elite professional bond.

He watched Natasha now as she chipped away at a piece of yellow rock. There had been great excitement after their first EVA when she had made a totally unexpected discovery. Near the top of a large escarpment her attention had been caught by a small circular depression in the rock. A few quick tests strengthened her impression that this was not the usual volcanic kind but an impact crater. In the centre, just below the surface, she had found treasure in the form of a layer of purple, melted rock that concealed a silvery-white, translucent crystal about the size of a cricket ball, though Jim had insisted it was like a baseball. It had very quickly been given pride of place on board ship, ceremoniously mounted on a ledge between the main flight control panel and the communications console.

Jack turned his thoughts to this last 'member' of the team, the Endeavour herself, which stood out of sight beyond his fellow crew members, just over a low ridge. Sleek and classically shaped, looking like a rocket yet built like a submarine, she was the landing craft of a larger vessel that had been their home for the five-week journey across space, and on and off for two weeks before that. The Resolution had been built in space and represented the second generation of nuclear-powered spacecraft which were revolutionising humanity's exploration of the solar system.

And so they had come to Venus. Once they had set the craft in orbit and confirmed that the relatively 'favourable' conditions were sustained, they had transferred to the Endeavour and Jack had flown them down. They knew it would still be the most challenging environment ever faced by human beings, with a murderously inhospitable climate; but you didn't turn your back on the opportunity of a lifetime – quite possibly of many lifetimes. In each EVA all four astronauts had disembarked, making the most of both the time and the high-tech environmental suits that had been tailored especially for them.

As Jack trudged back now through the clear but strangely thick atmosphere towards his friends, it occurred to him that they had gathered as many questions as they had samples. The variations in light, temperature and atmospheric pressure, as well as the types of rock, had mystified even Natasha, their resident expert on all things environmental. And a storm on their second outing had produced some real surprises. The normally sedentary atmosphere of ground-level Venus had become inexplicably agitated. And, for this crew at least, 'inexplicable' was just another word for 'inviting'.

Even now the weather looked set to provide another of those dramatic changes in the lighting conditions. Noticing the shift, Jack pulled himself out of his reverie. His visor data screen told him that the temperature had gone up by twenty-five degrees since they had left the ship just two hours before. Particularly unnerving was the fact that, as the temperature climbed, the light level dropped; once again Venus was reminding him how alien she was.

A message from the Captain confirmed that it was time to get back to the ship. But Ryan was not ready.

'Hey Cap, this is just the kind of atmospheric change I've been waiting for!'

'Can't you analyse it from the ship?'

'You know Endeavour's sensors are clumsy next to this baby,' Ryan pleaded. He held up his box of tricks close to his visor and stroked it like a favourite pet.

'Okay. But at least come back with us over the ridge so we can see you.'

Jack imagined that this fatherly concern would be lost on Ryan, or at the very least be a source of amusement to him; but then the world could be tumbling down around him and Ryan wouldn't care, or even know, so long as there was an opportunity to extend the boundaries of human knowledge. Or, at least, Ryan's knowledge.

He checked himself for his cynicism. What would Mel say? There she was again, his 'fiancée', as his father insisted on calling her. It brought him a welcome dose of earth-sickness. He turned to see Natasha already disappearing over the ridge. Ryan and Jim followed, still locked in a discussion that was crossing the airwaves.

A strong wind was starting up now, buffeting them more like an angry sea, as dark red clouds billowed overhead and the light faded yet again. In these conditions, as they came over the ridge, the Endeavour looked like something out of an old sci-fi movie: an enormous silver cigar upended on sturdy legs, its smoothly pointed nose reflecting the flashing of the alien sky, as though some giant below were inhaling deeply.

Jack sighed. 'I wonder what Venus smells like,' he said to himself, as thick dust began to swirl past him like mini-tornadoes in slow motion. His visor could give him wind speed, atmospheric content and temperature in fine digital detail, but all of that couldn't match a simple physical sensation. Still, he had no complaints. To breathe out here would be to breathe your last.

He made his way past Ryan, who was busy punching in new instructions to his analyser, and soon reached the foot of the Endeavour. Grabbing hold of a handrail, he pushed a large green button and started to ascend the automatic ladder that stretched out from the ship, glad to be carried for a while. The ladder worked on the same principle as an escalator, the rungs moving slowly up one side of the structure, across the middle in front of the hatch, and down the other side. As he rose above the huge rockets clamped to the side of the vessel, he thought of the days when chemical power was the only kind that carried you across the heavens. The Endeavour acknowledged those pioneering days by making use of a rocket biofuel to grapple with Venusian gravity. By contrast they had made the journey across space by nuclear power alone, direct from Space Station Alpha in Earth orbit, stretching the limits of their capacity to withstand multiple Gs as they rammed on the brakes and allowed Venus to pull them in close.

Jack studied the rockets as he glided towards the hatch. Although they had been adapted for use in the Venusian climate, and were of modest size, they were really not that different from the Saturn V beasts from the earliest days of interplanetary space flight a century before. He shivered as it crossed his mind that these particular engines had not yet had a chance to prove themselves in leaving a planet's surface. They had got them down here without a hitch, of course, but still the fear lurked, irrationally perhaps, that they would fail at lift-off.

As the ladder drew level with the ship's EVA hatch he brought it to a halt by pressing a red button that sat next to another green one on the side of the spacecraft. He took a last look down towards the surface, needlessly checking that the other handrail was now in position for the last man in. The swirling atmosphere, more like dark water up here, made the shapes of the rocks twist and shift. He turned back to the hatch and yanked the heavy door catch downwards before pushing the panel open and stepping into the airlock. As soon as he was in he secured the sturdy metal door behind him. There was no sudden change in sound level as he shut the storm out, since his airtight helmet had its microphone switched only to his colleagues, not to the environment. Even so, as the seals clamped shut he felt safe, almost cosy.

Once the chamber was filled with breathable air and repressurised to the ship's standard level, he carefully removed his helmet, twisting it sharply to undo the seal, and stepped out of the EVA suit. This was the outer shell that resisted the phenomenal pressures on this implacably hostile world. New developments in metals and polymers had forged a masterpiece of suit engineering. They might look like humanoid armadillos, but the rewards were huge, cancelling the need for pressurisation or a special breathing mix and allowing them precious extra hours in the toxic cocktail of the Venusian atmosphere.

Now that he stood free of the heavy life-support rucksack his shoulders instantly relaxed and he straightened up. Donning the regulation soft shoes for inside the craft, he opened the inner door into a corridor. In their current vertical landing position this looked more like a lift shaft: to reach the cockpit meant a fairly long climb up a ladder fixed to one of the walls. When he reached the flight deck, Jim was already on the radio to Mission Control back at SS Alpha. It was a strange kind of discussion, awkwardly punctuated by the inevitable delays that were part and parcel of a conversation across so many millions of miles of space. Right now those delays had peaked at well over two minutes.

'It looks like we've got more fireworks on the way, guys. Ryan's staying out for a while, taking readings. But we have him in view. Over.'

While they waited for the response, Jim and Jack compared notes on what the changing conditions might mean. It was clear neither wanted to bail out until it was absolutely necessary. This might simply be a very intense fluctuation.

A few minutes later the radio crackled into life: 'Okay, Jim. We'll catch you later. Out.' The voice sounded a long way away.

'See you too,' returned Jim. 'Aphrodite Base out.'

Jack decided this was a good time to sleep. There seemed little point in staying on the flight deck when he was this tired. He climbed down through a round hatch back into the ship's main corridor which gave access to the separate sleeping quarters and single toilet. Listlessly now, he released the catch and opened his cabin door. He could hear some kind of folk music coming from Natasha's cabin further down the passage below him. He craned his neck to look down. Her door was ajar, signalling she was disturbable, but right now he needed sleep more than company.

He stepped off the ladder into the small room – still a novel manoeuvre, after so many weeks of floating around the mother ship in zero-G. But at least the gravity on Venus was the same as on Earth, and that almost made it seem like they were back in training, if you didn't think about what was outside. He let the metal door of his quarters swing behind him, and it bounced noisily on the catch, remaining half-open. Impatiently he pulled off his soft shoes. Next came the inner flexisuit, a continuous high-tech overall from his neck to the tips of his fingers and toes, complete with its own cooling and venting system. He hung it up for now, knowing he wouldn't be stashing it until the last EVA was over. Then he flopped onto the cushioned ledge that was his bed, and drifted into welcome sleep.

He dreamed of smoke, red smoke swirling around a large silver cigar lodged between giant teeth. Faces flashed before him in the tumult: Ryan shouting with glee; the Captain – or was it his father? – calling him in for dinner; other faces, obscured by the smoke, crying out to each other. Perhaps it was because the wind was deafening, or because they spoke a strange language, but he couldn't tell the meaning of their words. But he could sense fierce aggression. Then he heard Mel scream. No, it was Natasha. Suddenly he was wide awake and Natasha's urgent words were coming in from somewhere outside his half-open door. 'Jim, Jack, come quickly!'

He scrambled to his feet and clambered down the ladder.

Something made him hesitate, despite the urgency in her voice. As though still in a dream he realised that he was dressed in only his underpants. ('Pants' versus 'trousers' had been the subject of yet another transatlantic debate with Jim.) Regulations dictated that the crew must be dressed decently outside their personal quarters at all times, and Jack had been the first to remind Ryan of this when the mission was barely a week old. He shook off the memory as he continued climbing. If there was one person not normally given to excitability it was Natasha. Following the sound of her voice, he climbed down the remaining wall rungs, past her cabin and the airlock, into the lounge below. As the name implied, this was the one common room afforded by the landing craft.

In the weightlessness of space, on the few occasions when he had needed to board the Endeavour, entering this room had been a simple manoeuvre, but now it was all he could do to prevent himself falling the seven feet from hatch to floor. Down the wall he climbed, bare feet slapping against the cold hardened plastic of the ladder. Where was Jim? Was Ryan back on board yet? How long had he been asleep?

Natasha looked up as he descended. Not the view she had expected, but no time now for the comment that flitted across her mind.

As Jack looked down he tried to read the expression on her face. Certainly there was more emotion in those cool Slavic features than he had seen at any time during their training. He stepped off the ladder.

'Oh Jack, quick, come over here!'

In the corner at the bottom of the lounge lay a man. From the apparently white clothing Jack guessed it was Ryan, still in his undersuit. But had Jack really been asleep that long? And why was Natasha so disturbed?

He moved closer. The clothing was loose – more a boiler suit than a flexisuit, not unlike the overalls Natasha was currently wearing, except there was no Aphrodite mission logo on these, and the colour was all wrong. What Jack realised in the next instant hit him like a slap in the face, as confusion gave way to an ice-cold fear that was supercharged by an almost reckless excitement. This was not a member of the crew.

'Here, help me get him onto the chair,' he breathed, forcing himself to act. Carefully they lifted the stranger and tried to sit him up. Questions flooded Jack's mind, but he pushed them back, only too happy to climb Mount Training once more. 'No bones broken, as far as I can tell. Or blood lost – at least, not externally.' He continued to make his way through first-aid procedure. He thought he could detect a pulse, though he wasn't sure.

'What the...?' Still in his flexisuit, Jim clambered down the ladder to the extraordinary sight below him.

'I thought it was Ryan,' said Jack slowly and deliberately.

'I don't understand,' said Jim. 'How...?' He broke off as he stared at the stranger. 'But... but I've been in the cockpit the whole time. The hatch indicator has been off. How on earth did he get in here?'

'Well, one thing's for sure,' put in Natasha, making an admirable stab at looking composed, 'on Earth it must have been.' She lifted the man's face towards Jim. 'But where have you been hiding?' Even as the question was out, they all knew how stupid it was. There was nowhere to hide. There were only four cramped cabins, a small lounge with four swivel-chairs bolted to the floor, and an even smaller cockpit. True, the middle of the lounge floor contained a hatch with emergency access to the engine maintenance area, but Jack and Jim had both been down there since they had landed, and there were no hiding places.

Jim shook his head. 'He must have come down from the Resolution when we left her in orbit,' he mused. But again, the idea evaporated in the heat of common sense. He would have needed a separate ship, not to mention a space suit. And there had been no sign of either.

'I'm gonna get Ryan in.' Jim turned back to the ladder, concern for his missing crewman now outweighing curiosity. 'It's getting pretty rough out there.' And without another word he began the long climb back up to the cockpit. Once there, breathing heavily, he punched the radio switch. 'How ya doin', Ryan? Have you gathered enough data?'

There was no reply. Unfamiliar panic rose, but he beat it back down. *He's probably too busy to notice me. Let's try another tack.*

'Ryan, we're gonna need your help in here, buddy. I need to run some climate simulations through the flight computer so we can decide when to lift off.' *That should do it. Don't show him you're worried; show him you need him.*

When there was still no response, Jim switched the radio channel through to the lounge. 'Jack, Natasha, I can't raise Ryan. I'm patching you through to my helmet radio. Keep an eye on... and stay in touch. I'm going EVA.'

'Hold on Jim!' said Jack. 'You're hardly likely to find him if the storm's getting worse.'

'Jack, you know I'm not one to pull rank, but... I'm going, and you're staying with Natasha. Okay?'

'Okay.'

Five long minutes later Jim's voice came back on the speaker mounted on the wall close to the lounge door. 'I'll maintain contact. I'm exiting the airlock now. How's our guest?'

'Alive. There's a little movement behind the eyelids, but not much else going on.' Jack sat back down in one of the chairs, and noticed to his surprise that Natasha was smiling.

'Really, Jack, so informal. I'd never have thought it of you!'

Jack looked down at his state of undress. 'Oh, er...' He hesitated. No way was he going to leave her now.

She seemed to read his thoughts. 'It's okay,' she smiled, 'I don't think our friend has any immediate plans.'

'Well, we don't know he is a friend,' Jack remarked. Natasha's untypically soft smile and soothing tone were meant to reassure him, but even that was unnerving and he stayed in his chair. So she tried scowling. 'Honestly Jack, it's fine. I mean, how long does it take to get dressed?'

He returned to his cabin.

Back in standard relaxation attire, he checked himself in front of the mirror and smiled. Here they were, with an impossible stowaway on board, Ryan missing in a Venusian storm, the Captain gone too, and he was enjoying a glimpse into a new side of Natasha's personality. What a strange thing the human psyche was.

2

Down in the lounge, Natasha knelt beside the stranger and felt for his pulse. It was weak, though fairly regular. He was still slumped in the chair, though his head was fairly upright. She put her hand on his forehead, then gasped and pulled away as he suddenly opened and closed his eyes, moaning something unintelligible. She surprised herself by whispering to her new-found patient. 'All right. It's going to be all right.' English remained the language of all international space flight, but she repeated herself in Russian, just in case.

He tossed his head back and forth, then let out a deep sigh. His eyes were open again, and this time he didn't close them. They were deep blue, and when Natasha looked into them she saw pain and confusion.

She stood up and took her first proper look at the newcomer. He had nothing on his feet and must have been over six feet tall. His age was not easy to tell, maybe mid-thirties. His skin was a pale beige, not as white as his suit, and maybe with a tinge of yellow? Or light brown. Yes, that was it. His hair was fair – a deep bronze, she decided. No, it was basically brown but reflected the light at times with an almost metallic gold. She sighed. Her eyes couldn't settle, but the most noticeable thing about him, if you didn't look into those eyes, was his suit. It looked white most of the time, although from some angles it was more silver. As she looked at it, it became dazzling, and so she returned to those pools of deep blue to find what refuge she could.

'Well, my friend,' she whispered, 'whoever you are, I think you are in deep trouble. But you're safe here. We'll look after you.'

Jack was surprised to hear Natasha's voice as he climbed back down into the room. 'Is that Jim on the blower?' he asked.

'What? Oh, no, just talking to myself, I suppose.'

Jack gave her a doubtful look and then asked how the mystery man was. He had closed his eyes again and, before Natasha could answer, Jim's voice suddenly came crackling out of the speaker on the wall, barely audible over the background cacophony.

'Jack, Natasha, I think I've found him. It's hard going in these conditions, so I'll have to get closer. I'll let you know.'

'Okay Jim,' Jack shouted back. 'Be careful.'

'I will.'

3

Out in the storm, some forty metres from the ship, Jim approached a hazy figure that appeared to be facing away from him. It was sitting down, or slumped, hurt perhaps. He couldn't see it clearly and stumbled forward as the elements came at him relentlessly. His intellivisor overloaded his eyes with information, and the noise in his ears was deafening because he had switched on his environmental microphone. Not that he expected to hear Ryan that way, as their direct radio channel should be sufficient, but with the advent of the stranger he needed to be ready for more surprises – perhaps more visitors.

Venus had never felt friendly, and that was no surprise, but now it was as though everything was against him. He called Ryan's name. The only answer was a flash in the billowing clouds above. He lost his footing. Over he rolled, and over, pushed on by the dense, swirling wind. Instinctively he put his hands over his helmet to stave off the kind of damage that could be lethal. The storm howled, and it sounded for all the world like voices.

Then darkness.

4

Inside the ship's lounge, Jack was giving the impossible stowaway a closer examination. While Natasha looked on, he searched for weapons and rechecked for any sign of wounding.

'Jack,' she whispered, 'Jack, don't you notice anything strange about his clothes?'

'They're certainly an odd choice for space flight, if that's what you mean.'

'No. Take a look at the material. It's like nothing I've ever seen. What's it made of?'

As Jack completed his examination, Natasha wrestled with her feelings. Why hadn't she told Jack that the stranger had opened his eyes? Why did she feel so protective towards him? At that moment he stirred and opened his eyes again. Jack seemed not to notice, as he had switched his attention to the suit. It looked like a synthetic fibre, silvery white, not unlike like their own flexisuits, but every time he tried to focus on it he found he couldn't see anything clearly at all. Finally he blinked a few times, then looked away.

'Well,' he said at last, 'he seems to be in some state of shock.' Natasha felt relieved at this shared diagnosis. 'I'm not sure there's a lot we can do for him, Natasha, and he's clearly not going to be answering any of our questions just yet, though there's a whole stack of them building up. But right now I'm more concerned about that storm out there, and the guys. Let's call Jim.'

He stabbed at a switch on the wall. All he got was a noise that sounded like static. 'Funny – he said he was going to leave his channel open.'

'Something wrong with the radio?' suggested Natasha.

'No,' said Jack slowly, 'but listen! That's not radio noise – it's the storm. There's all kinds of sound in there. He must have switched to environment.'

'Then why can't we hear him?' said Natasha uneasily.

'I presume,' said Jack slowly, 'because he's not saying anything.'

5

Jack was sitting in the cockpit, peering out of the window. All he could see was dust swirling around the ship in some kind of crazy dance. What to do? Radio Alpha? And what would he tell them? Survivable conditions deteriorating fast, two crew members missing (including the Captain), and alien personnel on board? (And what sense was he to give to the a-word?) He didn't need advice right this minute, yet there was clearly little point in going out after them either. Apart from the distinct possibility that he too might become lost, it would mean leaving Natasha alone with the stranger for much too long. Even so, he had decided to don his flexisuit once more, just in case he needed to suit up fast.

His eye caught the ball-like crystal next to the radio, and he picked it up. It didn't look natural. He always knew this would be a mission like no other, possibly the only chance human beings would ever get to explore in person the infernal regions of the Venusian atmosphere, right down to the surface. He revelled in the soul-wrenching wonder of seeing another world, especially this one. But he knew that wasn't all that was pumping through his veins right now. What was this heightened appreciation of the other crew members? It was more than the usual bonding that came from intense training together. This was unexpected and, he had to admit, outside of his control. It felt like his emotions were doing impressions of the swirling dust storm outside. And to cap it all, he was in the position he hated the most. Responsible and powerless.

'Are you okay?' He turned to see Natasha climbing into the cockpit in her usual noiseless fashion. 'Our friend is out for the count, so I thought I'd check up here.'

He nodded, still unable to throw off his reflective mood. 'You know, it's ironic. This ship is named after James Cook's historic vessel of exploration. I was reading an account of Cook's exploits just before we flew out, refreshing my memory of those key observations he made of the transit of Venus, giving us the kind of information we would need one day when we went into space – like how far we'd have to fly to get here!'

Natasha sat down and let him continue.

'But yesterday I finished the book.'

'And you found out how he died?' Seeing Jack's surprise, she continued. 'I read up about him before we began the mission,' she explained. 'I wanted to find out more about the first Endeavour and Resolution. Names are important to me, as you know.'

Jack nodded. Almost the first thing he'd learned about Natasha Koroleva was that when she had come of age she had changed her adopted name and taken a new surname, after the universally acknowledged father of Russian spaceflight, Sergei Korolev. It was this passion for astronomy and space exploration, coupled with her geological training and flair, that had won her a place on the first manned flight to the surface of Venus. And, of course, she had seen to it that everyone choked on the term 'manned'.

Captain James Cook had died in 1779 at the hands of a few indigenous people on a far-away island. Did life go in cycles – meaningful cycles, in terms of human history, not just physical cycles on an astronomical scale? Was their captain, James Adamson, solid and lovable explorer, now also to fall at the mercy of some unfriendly alien environment?

'Listen,' said Natasha, adopting a back-to-business tone, 'I've been thinking. We can't go out there after them, as you say, but we can use the trigs to help locate them.'

'What? Those crazy binoculars you use?'

'That's right. They don't just compute size and distance. They have other wavelength settings, including infra-red. I have one pair which has been specially adapted to filter out many of the local atmospheric conditions and extreme temperatures. The high-sensitivity range isn't much, but within thirty metres they might be able to distinguish the heat of a human body.'

Jack was grateful to be given a practical focus for his thoughts, but he couldn't share his colleague's optimism. 'Aren't you forgetting the suits?' he objected. 'They don't allow heat to pass through.'

'Ah, but don't you see? In a way they do. The cooling system has to offload body heat. I've seen you all through these during training back on Earth, and if your back's turned you do give a distinctive trace on infra-red. They may not be as sensitive as an exo-planet telescope, but they do show some differential. It may be enough.'

'Okay,' said Jack, placing the crystal he had been cradling back on the ledge. He stood up, but then almost immediately sat back down.

'What about our visitor? We can't very well leave him here.'

'Why not?' she said. 'After all, we already have.'

'Well, I suppose you have a point there. Right again, Natasha. But it looks to me like he could come round any minute. You know what I think? I think we are not the first people on Venus. I think someone got here before us. What other explanation can there be?'

'I don't know,' she shrugged. 'But where's his breathing equipment? And that suit he's wearing – that wouldn't keep out a Siberian breeze, never mind a Venusian acid bath.'

'Oh well, one mystery at a time,' said Jack, making his way towards the ladder down to the airlock. 'I'll take a wee wander with these fancy field glasses of yours. I'll not go far, and I'll not be long. I don't want to leave you here alone with... but I don't want you going out there either.'

'Jack!' Her eyes flashed.

'I know – don't patronise you. Believe me, I'm not. I'm trying to make the best decision in the light of all the options. Okay? How's that for brutal logic?' He concluded with a grin, and she granted him a faint smile in response.

Just as he was about to climb onto the ladder out of the cockpit he hesitated.

'Call home?' said Natasha.

'Aye,' said Jack. He crossed to the communications console that would route his message via the Resolution to Space Station Alpha, and proceeded to spell out the situation in the simplest terms he could muster: an unconscious man had been found on the Endeavour, while Jim had gone looking for Ryan in a storm, and both were now out of contact. He didn't wait for the reply.

'But Jack,' said Natasha. 'What if they tell you to stay inside the craft?'

'Why do you think I'm going?' he grinned. 'Shan't be long.'

She followed him down to the airlock antechamber, where she took out the trigs from the EVA cabinet. He suited up, but before he put on the helmet she came and stood just behind him and hung them round his neck. With her lips close to his ear she described the controls he would need to use and those he could safely ignore.

'There,' she said softly, 'I've set it for infra-red vision. All you have to do is point and focus.'

'Fine,' he breathed, but the word didn't quite make it to his larynx. Funny, he hadn't noticed that she had such slender hands before. He felt her closeness, which suddenly seemed more intimate than functional, and took a sharp intake of breath.

'Jack?'

'Right, that's great. Thanks, Natasha. I'll stay in radio contact.' And with that he grabbed his helmet and almost dived into the airlock.

6

Natasha watched the airlock display as it indicated the drastic change of pressure that confirmed the airlock was ready for EVA. Seconds later the hatch indicator told her Jack had opened the outer door and closed it. He was gone.

She closed her eyes. What was going on here – all these strange emotions? She didn't have time for emotions. She was a highly trained professional in a completely unexpected situation which called for heightened readiness and cool thought.

But she couldn't think. She returned to the cockpit and waited for Alpha's response to Jack's message. It was mercifully brief. 'Understood. Stand by.'

She'd done enough of that. With her thoughts now returning to the stranger, she quickly climbed back down to the lounge.

She was surprised to find him stretched out on a padded bench the crew had affectionately dubbed the chaise longue. 'You've been on the move, my friend.' She felt no fear as she sized him up again. He groaned. She went over to the cabinet and half-filled a cup with water from a faucet, smiling as she recalled Jack's insistence that it was a tap.

'Here,' she whispered, pulling the stranger into an upright sitting position. 'Take this.' She sat next to him and held the cup to his lips, tipping it gently. He spluttered, then drank deeply.

'Good. Good. That's better.' His eyes half-opened as she whispered words of reassurance. 'What are we going to do with you, my friend?'

He lifted his head. Those eyes seemed vacant now, yet they were trying to focus, struggling to make sense of what they saw.

Instinctively Natasha put her arm around his shoulders, and drew his head close to her. She laughed at the idea that popped into her mind, but then as her patient began to cough and moan once more, she followed her intuition and began to sing. It was a lullaby, one that someone had sung to her as a disturbed and lonely twelve-year-old, a young woman who longed to be the child she could not remember.

Chapter 2

The Storm

1

Mission Control was not living up to its name. The news that the Endeavour had two crew members missing had charged the air with an electricity that must have recalled the first landing on the Moon a century before. Or maybe it was more like the fated third attempt at landing there, when Apollo 13 had caused more collective breath to be held in the world than ever before in human history. Only this news was not public.

It was now three hours since Jack had radioed Mission Control on Space Station Alpha. When the Aphrodite mission to the surface of Venus had originally been announced, Alpha was the natural venue for the command centre. The station, speeding around the earth fifteen times a day, had been developed for the Mars, Moon and asteroid missions that had come to characterise manned spaceflight in the twenty-first century, as well as providing a launchpad for the endless stream of robotic probes destined for the solar system and beyond. A massive spinning wheel with a central hub and four giant bubbles in the outer rim, it was the largest human construct in space and spanned more than two hundred metres. Each bubble was home to a separate zone of activities, linked by the giant wheel's curved corridors that allowed people to move from one zone to the other without leaving artificial gravity. The central hub was home to zero-G labs and four docking stations. But perhaps most important of all was the station's role in bringing nations together in an effort to reduce the proliferation of weapons in earth orbit, a project that so far could claim only small successes.

Jack's words had been few, simply warning that this was a Code 1 message. At that point the feed to the loudspeakers and monitors was killed and the channel re-routed to the Mission Controller. Shortly after that came an announcement that Adamson and Chase were missing.

Some of the staff were not satisfied that the whole story was being told. Clearly, in asking for Code 1 procedure, Jack Forrester had thought his message hyper-confidential, yet it was unlikely he would keep this kind of information from his colleagues on Alpha. And, sure enough, here was Mission Control sharing the news with them just a few minutes later. So why the initial secrecy? It didn't add up. There must be a missing ingredient that would explain the situation. Dark matter indeed.

In addition to the scientists and commercial mining operators elsewhere on the space station there were a few select members of the media present. One of these was Melody Grantley James, though unlike the others she was staying in the crew family quarters. It was here on Alpha, little more than a month earlier, that she had kissed Jack goodbye, more in the role of astronaut's girlfriend than journalist. But now, with rumours spreading across the station faster than a rocket fuel fire, she was unmistakably a freelance columnist – or reporter, as the Americans insisted on calling her.

When Jack had come on the radio, Melody the girlfriend had been one of those in the room. But when the Code 1 status brought the shutters down and she was asked to leave, her concern quickly gave way to inquisitiveness, before dissolving in frustration. Perhaps Sam would have some answers.

Sam Braithwaite was the Deputy Station Controller, and with more than forty years of missions behind him not much went on that he didn't know about. His current role was acting liaison officer between the Aphrodite mission and the rest of Alpha. Melody now approached his office, her immaculately brushed long fair hair bouncing with every step. She paused to pull back the sleeve of her crisp white blouse and access her eband, the wide yet thin device that served as recorder, information store and communicator on the forearms of nearly 80% of the planet's inhabitants (so they said). Setting it to record, she covered it back up and went into Sam's office.

'I'm sorry, Mel,' Sam drawled in rich Tennessee, 'but I can't tell you anything else.'

'Can't?' Melody sang back in perfect Kensington. She flicked back her hair with a short toss of her head. 'Oh come on, Sam, be fair! I've a right to know. Jack must be in some kind of danger. Does he know why Jim and Ryan are missing? Give me some details!'

'There you go, asking for information like you're after a story.'

The hurt look on Melody's face seemed genuine, and Sam relented.

'Look, I really am sorry, Mel. I know you're worried. We all are, dammit. But what can I say?'

Just then the door opened abruptly behind Melody, and she turned to see Station Controller Brad Shepperton striding in.

'Oh, excuse me, I didn't realise... Sam, I need you now please. Dan wants to see us right away.'

'That's all right,' Mel got to her feet. 'I was just going anyway, wasn't I, Sam?'

He dropped his eyes as she left the room. As she stepped outside the small office, she conveniently tripped over some invisible object and lost her shoe, which slid several inches across the floor. As the two men filed past on their way to the mission control centre, she detected a knowing smile on Sam's face. Was she that obvious? Still, he didn't say anything.

They were going to see Dan Marshall, the Aphrodite Mission Controller. She couldn't follow, so she waited. There were few others this close to the restricted area and, in the minutes that followed, the few who did come by were in too much of a hurry to notice that she wasn't actually going anywhere herself. After a while she slipped into an adjacent observation chamber, one of two such areas on the station where there was more window than wall. Like every other human being that had been up here, she never tired of watching the earth roll in and out of view. She looked up and out across the breadth of the station, past the giant bubbles containing Zones 2 and 4, homes to an assortment of mining missions and laboratories. These were situated either side of the central hub which loomed over her head, hiding from view the last remaining bubble at the other end of the enormous structure, Zone 3, where people lived and enjoyed what recreation the station afforded. She still found it disorienting to see the centre of the station above her head and not under her feet. In her head she understood the reason – that the gravity effect she currently felt was actually the centrifugal force of the station's relentless spin – but somehow that never quite translated to her unconscious perspective, according to which the station's centre ought to behave like the earth's core and lie below her feet, not above her head. Such was life in space.

After about twenty minutes she heard Sam's unmistakable voice coming near, so she hurried to hide behind the wide-open door of the chamber. He and Shepperton were in the middle of a lively conversation. She pressed her ear to the space between the door and the wall as they sped past. She couldn't catch everything they said, but what she did hear was enough. 'But we were *sure* we were the first there!' And then, after more words she couldn't make out, 'What kind of alien?'

They had been gone several seconds before she noticed she wasn't breathing.

She gave a loud gasp. Shepperton had used the a-word. With unrestrained excitement he and Sam had chattered away like a pair of schoolboys sharing an illicit secret. But this was the secret of a lifetime. Of a career.

What kind of alien? An unauthorised crew member? A foreign power? Or could it really be something extra-terrestrial?

'Come on, girl, compose yourself!' She took another deep breath and lost no time in returning to her quarters. It was time to contact London. But what to say? It's not as though she had a lot to go on.

She drank a glass of water and sat down. Feverishly she began to dictate a report to her eband. 'Yesterday Space Station Alpha forgot itself, throwing composure to the ether as it came to terms with a top-secret message from the Endeavour on Venus.' She pressed the edge of her eband and said, 'Insert background file 2a.' This would incorporate text she had prepared for a brief history of Alpha and a reminder of the sudden decision to go to Venus in the cause of advancing our understanding of global warming – a decision that was made after the detection of an unusually favourable set of conditions on the planet. ('For "favourable" read "slightly less deadly".') A second file explained how this decision was cemented by the coincidental development of a new material that had made space suits thinner and tougher, especially the ones needed on Venus, which were more like diving suits, engineered to withstand immense pressures rather than shield against the vacuum of space.

Now for the finale. After adding a brief description of the four crew members, she applied the fuse for the explosion. 'The word "alien" has been used in at least one corridor conversation. Has someone arrived on Venus outside of the Aphrodite mission? Or could it be that our valiant crew have discovered something – or someone – that will change the way we see ourselves for ever?'

She smoothed back her hair and took another sip of water. A picture of Jack came into her mind, causing her to hesitate, but she quickly pushed it down as the exclusive of a lifetime beckoned. The whole Code-1-message thing obviously meant this was not for public consumption, not yet anyway, but as a journalist she could hardly be expected to exercise Jack's level of discretion. In fact, didn't professional integrity and duty demand she break the story? Not that there was a story – just a word overheard, close to the action. No, it was time to go with her intuition. She asked her eband to call the office. Two seconds later a voice came through with an English accent almost as impeccable as hers. 'Good morning, The Times. May I help you?'

'Hello. This is Melody James. I'm uploading a file for Mr Stewart, and it's urgent.'

The fuse was lit. She hadn't given them much, but it was enough, as the Times website and news bulletins soon revealed. Mel's report was worked into a piece by the editor, who cited 'a reliable source' for his information about 'someone from Venus'. It was only a preposition – 'from' rather than 'on' – but it made all the difference. It was a world scoop, flashed around the globe online – and, of course, read eagerly in space.

As soon as Brad Shepperton caught up with the news he called the errant reporter into his office.

'Do you mind explaining this? I don't want to believe what I'm thinking.'

'I'm sure I don't know what you mean.' But her eyes contradicted her words.

'Come on, Mel, don't give me that! This is off the record. Okay?'

'Okay.'

'So what do you know?'

'Know? I don't know anything. Do you?' The eyes were now positively mischievous.

Shepperton told his desk to accept no calls, eyed the walls warily for a moment, as though they had ears, and leaned forward across the desk.

2

The noise coming though Jack's environmental microphone showed no sign of abating. He raised a hand over his brow, as if he might see

THE STORM

more that way, but all he was shielding was orange darkness. The swirling cloud was impenetrable. He peered through Natasha's trigs, turning round as he did so, changing the spectral views, watching the numbers at the edges of the image. Nothing – nothing that stood out to him, at least. Not for the first time he wished they'd had more time for training, but when the Window had opened and recruitment began, flying hours had seemed more important than a full set of skills. And Jack Forrester had the hours.

The storm was wild now. People had long said that the surface of Venus would be like hell, yet even now he could not agree. For a start, there were no other people. No demons either, as far as he could tell, although the howling winds were chilling enough. He had always liked being out in a storm, and even with the hi-tech shielding he revelled in the buffeting of the elements.

After a few minutes he turned off environmental sound. The silence was welcome to begin with, until his own heavy breathing started to annoy him.

'Come on, man,' he said to himself, and to Natasha if she was listening. 'This is not the time to panic.'

Ignoring his earlier promise to stay close, he decided to move away from the ship in the direction of Ryan's last known whereabouts. The way was paved with misshapen boulders. He kept an eye out for fissures, just in case the ground beneath him started to become as unstable as the atmosphere. Something Natasha had said during training came to mind: 'The planet's crust is a fluid... just a more solid one.' It seemed to him now that this fact was almost visible to his confounded eyes, as the ground appeared to fold in front of him. Some of the stones were larger now too, and stepping over them taxed his balance. He was getting nowhere.

For a while determination to find his colleagues drove him on. How could he give up if there was a chance he might find them? But when he cleared the ridge and there was still no sign he decided to go back to the ship. Only, which way was back? He had turned so many times he couldn't tell, and the ridge itself appeared distorted. After another self-reprimand, he switched the microphone to Natasha's com-link. 'Natasha, I can't find them. Hello? Natasha?'

For a moment there was silence. Then that lovely soft click, and she was there. 'Hi, Jack. Sorry, I was busy. They're back! I'm just helping them de-suit now.'

He let the sense of relief wash over him. Disaster averted. 'Excellent!' he said. 'I'm on my way. Only, there's just one thing...'

'Yes?'

'Er, can you guide me in? I lost my way a wee bit there.' He hoped embarrassment didn't travel by radio.

'Surely. Leave your microphone on. No, wait, I've got a better idea. Are the trigs in standard view mode?'

'I have absolutely no idea. But hold on... there. They're in standby now.'

'That's good enough,' came the reply, and Jack thought he detected a grin in the voice. 'Leave them that way and I'll find you. I have a cradle for them which can send out a paging signal, and I should be able to locate your position and give you directions.'

It sounded easy enough, and his intellivisor indicated all the directions Natasha gave him, but soon the going became even tougher. After five minutes he concluded his eyesight was definitely being affected, as his left arm appeared to be melting. It took another minute to realise that part of his sleeve actually was melting, at which point the truth hit him like a cold shower in a hot bath. He peered at his arm. The familiar fine lines that criss-crossed every section of the sleeve were starting to disappear, and now he recognised this as the indicator developed by the manufacturers to signal when the material was degrading. Once again panic had to be told in no uncertain terms to lie down quietly. His visor told him the temperature was rising fast, and with lines starting to disappear all over the suit, he knew that the outer layer didn't have long before its integrity was compromised. Yet if he quickened his pace, he risked stumbling and doing worse damage, not to mention presenting the rest of the crew with yet another hazard as they came to rescue him.

There was only one thing for it.

'Jack,' said Natasha over the radio. 'Jack, are you singing?'

It was 'My love is like a red, red rose'. It had always calmed his nerves. He smiled at the thought that a red rose wouldn't actually show up in these conditions. But a song survived anywhere.

'Till all the seas gang dry, my dear, and the rocks melt with the sun...' The song was gaining new layers of meaning.

And suddenly there she was. The unmistakable outline of the Endeavour signalled the safety of home.

Five minutes later he was dusting himself down in the airlock, or rather gently picking at the lead fibres that had alerted him to the critical rise in temperature. They had done their job where the numbers in his visor had somehow passed him by. It had been a near thing, but in the end the tough outer layer of the suit had held.

He climbed out of the suit and into Natasha's arms. The hug was not unexpected, though it seemed to last a second or two longer than the usual colleague's welcome. 'Well done,' she whispered, and led him down into the lounge.

His remaining crewmates were sipping tea. He didn't know whether to laugh or cry at such a domestic scene. Questions filled his head as he flopped onto a chair. The new visitor was on the chaise longue, apparently asleep.

'Nice to have you back,' said Jim.

'Nice to be back,' said Jack. 'Almost got a little cooked out there. You guys okay? What happened? Ryan, did you find anything interesting?'

'Not really, just a bump on the head.'

Jim cut in. 'He's not speaking literally. We can't find a mark on him. Nor me either. When I came to, Ryan was already on his feet.'

'Why didn't you radio in, both of you?' Jack couldn't disguise the anger in his voice.

'I'm sorry, Jack,' said Jim. 'It's a bit disorienting out there. As I believe you know.'

Jack decided to leave it there, although he couldn't believe that neither man had followed standard procedure, especially his stickler captain.

His thoughts were interrupted by Ryan. 'But guys, come on, what are we going to do with the intruder?'

3

Mel sipped her Earl Grey gently. She was in Brad Shepperton's grey, functional office as she listened to his few but earth-shattering words. Jack had phoned home with a report about a stowaway, one who must have come on board after they had landed on Venus. Brad was reluctant to say more.

'Oh come on, Brad, I've a right to know! Jack could be in great danger!'

'That he could, and I know you're worried. Hell, we're all worried! We don't know what's going on here.' He fiddled with his coffee mug, and Mel noticed his eyes look away for a moment, before he added, 'You know as much as we do.'

She could sense the lie, but now wasn't the time to push her luck. Instead, she offered an apology. 'Brad, I'm sorry about the article. I honestly didn't think they'd go that far. And as for the rest of the press, well, I just didn't think—'

'You've got that right! If you'd have *thought*, we wouldn't be having this conversation! And now I have to decide what I'm going to do with you.' His fingertips turned a whiter shade of brown as they clenched the mug.

'But Brad, you need me here. For better or worse, there's no way you'll be able to keep the press off now. Far better to have me here, someone you can trust—' Brad tried to interrupt, but she kept going. 'Someone you *can* trust. Someone who has a right to be here, as an astronaut's partner, and who can also represent the interests of the press.' She was thinking just two seconds ahead of speaking, which was not her favourite scenario, but she was getting into her stride. As her eyes widened, Brad leaned back in his chair, clearly on the point of capitulation. She pressed home. 'Let me follow up my first report with something that's not anonymous, and that chimes in with any official statement you make. I've already got Level 2 clearance, so Washington and Westminster will prefer me to some other characters I could think of... characters who will be on the line to you already, I've no doubt.' She closed with a smile, and finished her tea.

'Mel, I gotta hand it to you,' he sighed, 'you are one class act. Okay, let me talk to the boss, and I'll get back to you. Meanwhile, go back to your quarters. And, Mel...'

'Yes, Brad?'

'For all our sakes – for your own sake – stay there!'

4

Natasha and Ryan were arguing. Jack had never seen anything like it. Natasha, normally so cool, so collected, had instantly objected to Ryan's use of the word 'intruder' for her patient. Ryan had responded with insinuations bordering on an outright accusation that Natasha had somehow been in on the whole thing.

'What, you think I'm a spy? You... you've never liked me, have you Ryan?'

'I don't trust you.'

'You don't trust anything east of the Atlantic seaboard!'

'Hold on, guys!' Jim cut in. 'This is not helpful. Granted, Ryan, we have a problem with our friend here.' He raised a hand to stop Ryan cutting in. 'But whether he be friend or foe, we obviously can't leave him here. Now, Jack has already told Mission Control the situation, and I've sent in my own report. I fully expect them to call us home early–'

'No!' said Natasha, raising her voice more than she intended. 'We've got so much work to do in the little time we have!'

'For once I agree,' said Ryan. 'We shouldn't let this... incident put us off our main objective. We have to collect more data and run more tests.'

'Er, hello everybody,' said Jack, 'but would you care to go take a look at my space suit? If things get much worse, it won't be long before the ship's hull looks the same. We have to go.'

'Then that will be it,' said Natasha, resignation in her voice. 'We don't have enough fuel for a second landing and lift-off.'

Jack shrugged. 'What can I say? I'm sorry.'

'Well, there's no point talking ourselves to death,' said Jim. 'I'm going back to the cockpit. Should anyone care to join me, we have tests on the ship's sensors to run. And I need to get back to mission control. I'm afraid the decision will be out of our hands.'

5

Dan Marshall didn't get to become Controller of the Aphrodite Mission by being indecisive. He had told Colonel Adamson that with the worrying change in atmospheric conditions the risk was too high for more than a few hours' delay. Added to that, no one knew how long this stowaway would remain unconscious, and the crew were not fitted for security measures.

This much Jim expected. But the sting in the tail made him wince. 'Jim, you remain the Captain in terms of the flight home, but the mission has changed. Jack will be in charge of our John Doe.'

'What? Why would you do that? Don't you trust me?'

The whinge was untypical. Jim was one of Dan's most seasoned and mature astronauts. He decided to ignore it for now and mentally file it away under 'odd things that may be important but probably aren't'. The delays in conversation by radio made an argument a clumsy thing anyway. 'Now then, Jim, we've known each other a long time. Our mutual trust remains secure. But this one's out of my hands. Geneva, Washington and London are all singing the same tune: Forrester is in charge of security.'

As Jim climbed back down to the lounge, he muttered to himself grimly. He knew Jack had been with British Intelligence before becoming an astronaut, but stupidly he'd thought that was all in the past. 'Ha! Once a spook...! Seems all of a sudden I have a ship full of spies to ferry home.'

He climbed down the lounge wall. Ryan and Natasha had gone back to their quarters. The stowaway was still out of it. Jack looked up expectantly.

'Well, my canny little friend, it seems you've got what you wanted.'

'I'm sorry, I don't understand,' said Jack.

'Oh don't give me that! You're in charge now. The old Washington-London alliance kicks in again, huh? Kick's the word.'

'Jim, are you okay? What's happened? What did Mission Control say?'

'Okay, you want me to spell it out? Commander Forrester, it is my duty to inform you that, due to your higher level of security clearance, you are now in charge of our intruder here. He is a prisoner of the US government... I think, or is it the British government? Whatever. Let me put it this way: he's all yours.'

6

In the few days they had been there, Venus had moved slightly further away from planet Earth. Like an athlete or racing driver on the inside track, she had pulled away in her closer orbit of the sun. This alone would not have added more than a day to their journey, but the crew knew they also faced another delay. Some of the funding for their adventure came from the owner of a deep-space telescope and asteroid detector that orbited the sun between Earth and Venus. That company had lucrative contracts waiting to be signed as soon as new electronic filters were installed, and it was down to the Venus crew, specifically Ryan, to get the job done. Like it or not, they were going to have to make a detour, and take their stowaway with them.

Once they had all accepted they were leaving the surface they began to focus on the tasks before them. They donned their space suits as take-off procedure dictated, the crystal was duly stashed and all personal items made secure. Jack was relieved to be able to take his mind off the quick-shifting emotional climate, and the rifts between Jim and himself, and Ryan and Natasha, stopped widening. The business of take-off was tense enough, and the seemingly endless checks of launch procedures and calculations buried everything else for now. Soon all eyes were on the ship's external sensors and their sorry tale of increasing temperature, pressure and hull corrosion. When they found they could not retract the rotary ladder that had carried them down to walk on the surface, they decided to jettison it, thankful for the nameless engineer who had had the idea of providing that option. Still haunted by the sight of his own suit, Jack began to imagine what was happening to the ship's hull. Pre-flight checks looked good, however, and it was a relief when the landing supports retracted correctly. These had drilled down into the Venusian crust on arrival, to hold the ship steady in its thick, swirling atmosphere.

The standard checks weren't quite complete when several sensors finally failed after a sharp rise in atmospheric acidity. Jim lost no time in giving the order. 'Punch it, Jack. We gotta get out of this place before it eats us alive!'

The rockets fired, and with the sensation of lift-off everyone breathed more easily. The altimeter was still working, sending its radar pulses in various downward directions, and before long they registered several miles above the surface. The next challenge came in the form of thick, swirling clouds, where the conditions rapidly deteriorated. 'I'll have to duck and dive a wee bit,' Jack spoke into his helmet microphone. 'Not sure where we'll come out.'

'That's okay,' said Jim. 'We can get our bearings in orbit.'

Ryan chipped in. 'Hatches nominal. Ready to release UAPs on your command, Cap.' These were six small Upper-Atmosphere Probes which Endeavour was to leave behind and which would carry out vital experiments, adding to the wealth of data they had already amassed. At thirty miles high where the pressure was one-G they were expected to last several hours, floating on the currents and transmitting readings to Earth via a relay station in orbit around Venus, before finally succumbing to gravity and falling to a hot and sticky end. And during that time they would release bacterial cultures that might just possibly help in the bid to save planet Earth.

The Greenhouse Smash project had been five years in the making. Several companies had been developing microbes that would digest and neutralise the carbon dioxide in Earth's atmosphere. The problem was, they all promised a dizzying array of nasty side-effects that might very quickly mushroom out of control, which meant no one dared let them loose. Not over the Earth. But Venus was a different matter. Where better to study the effects of these micro-air-cleaners than over a world that didn't have life to protect – certainly not life as we could recognise it?

Ryan counted his way through the release sequence. All but one of the probes launched without a hitch through a series of small hatches in the ship's hull. The one that jammed served only to emphasise the need to continue their hasty retreat from the hostile environment.

But Venus wasn't ready to let them go just yet. Ryan hit the console in front of him and let out a long sigh. 'People, we have two hatches remaining open. Jammed tight. Absolutely no response to multiple pressing of this button in front of me.' He scratched his head and grinned. 'Shouldn't be a problem, I guess, once we're back inside the Resolution.'

Jack frowned. He was monitoring the fuel level, already concerned by the effect of an extra passenger. Now there would be additional drag on the spacecraft caused by the open hatches. The fuel might be more dense than the rockets of yesteryear, and therefore more efficient, but they had a small tank and no reserves.

He decided not to share his concerns, and when the booster rockets jettisoned without any trouble he breathed a little more easily. They reached orbit with the fuel gauge flashing its alarm, but no one else seemed to notice. He smiled at the thought that his own quiet confidence had drawn a veil over it.

No one was there to see the Stranger writhe and moan down in the lounge.

The next challenge was to link up with the Resolution. Jack gave this job to a programmed autopilot, and the Endeavour duly homed in. Once they had drawn close, he retook the controls and guided the ship round to the docking position, reversing into the module that would provide them with the extra space and speed they needed to make the journey home swiftly and comfortably. Happily, the small amount of fuel for this manoeuvre came from separate tanks connected to the directional jets. Sensors and auto-clamps made the final fit.

Jim led the way through the main airlock into the mother ship. There was no slap on the back for Jack, no 'Nice work, buddy,' as there had been on the way down. Everyone moved silently. With the return of weightlessness it was a fairly simple matter to transfer the semi-conscious stowaway. While Jim headed for the bridge and Ryan disappeared into a toilet, Jack and Natasha steered their patient to the sleeping quarters where they settled him in a large container which looked like a cross between a medical scanner and a bunk bed. Medbeds were where the crew slept and where Mission Control could check various functions, from blood pressure to circadian rhythms. The Resolution was originally designed for a larger crew bound for Mars, so there was a choice of four spare medbeds where the Stranger could be safely strapped in and connected up. This would provide him with both rest and nutrition while he remained in his more or less comatose state. It would also protect him from the worst effects of the increased G-force they were soon to undergo as the ship made its detour via the space telescope on their way home. They themselves would use their pressurised suits to help keep blood to the brain as the ship rammed on the brakes and then sped up again.

Jim radioed Alpha with the call sign 'Resolution', confirming the fact they were back in interplanetary mode now that the Endeavour was securely reintegrated with the orbital ship. Then he set about initiating the drive protocols that would get them home, once Alpha had transmitted the course correction made necessary by their early departure.

He was about to initiate the nuclear drive when Natasha suddenly shouted, 'Wait! Shouldn't we look for another ship?'

It had been impossible to detect anything down in the thick, hostile atmosphere, but now, as they considered their lone passenger, it seemed the least they could do. He was unlikely to have come to Venus alone. The rest of his crew might still be out there, waiting in orbit. Ryan initiated a radar sweep as they circled the planet twice more. There was nothing.

'Time to go,' said Jim, only too aware that a thorough search was beyond their remit. Reluctantly Natasha made her way back to her patient, while Jim turned to the console and pulled on a large green lever to engage the nuclear drive that would get them home in a matter of weeks. Then he called Mission Control again. 'This is Resolution, en route to Lagrange L1. Alpha, we're on our way home.'

With the Stranger out of sight, they tried their best to settle into the routines that were meant to characterise their journey, but awkwardness was in the very air. Once Natasha had checked the settings on the Stranger's medbed she moved into the ship's one laboratory and threw herself into cataloguing Venusian rock samples. Jack checked the calculations for the bursts of deceleration and acceleration that would be required for the detour, while Ryan rehearsed the work he would need to do once they got there.

About an hour later Jack headed for the kitchen to make himself a 'cup of tea', in reality a sealed dispenser designed for use in space. The ship was picking up speed, but gravity was still low. He found Jim heating up the coffee version. They tried conversation, but it sputtered and failed at the first attempt.

'I just don't get it,' said Jim as he made for the door. 'How could you not tell me about this?'

'Tell you about what?' said Jack. 'We're talking about a bolt from the blue here. I'm as surprised by the whole thing as anyone.'

'Why do I find that hard to believe?' said Jim, turning back to the door without waiting for an answer. The last thing Jack heard as Jim retreated was a surly muttering about needing some sleep.

Lapse

Down and down he flew, falling fast in fear and fury. Eight became four became two became one, then fractioned over two, over four, over eight. He was slowing. Closing. Landing. Bright light shifted into dark matter.

He froze. In two hundred degrees of boiling sulphur he lay cold as a corpse. Swirling clouds of angry orange licked his limbs and fingered his face. Yet he knew nothing of it. He dreamed.

In the thick of battle comrades cried, cheered by the scent of victory, bracing themselves as one for the onslaught to come. We're going to push forward. We're going to push back the enemy. Today will be a day to remember.

To remember... Remember the sound of fear in your enemies. Remember the look of dread in their eyes. Remember what you do. Remember who you are.

Location.

A new face. She looks worried. Questions crease her brow. Compassion crowns her eyes. Beautiful eyes.

New voices. Angry.

Must sleep. Sleep and remember.

Remember.

Chapter 3

Tests

1

Melody was in her quarters, compliant but not idle. She had no direct access to Jack while he was on the mission, but Sam had become a conduit for information ever since she had agreed to become the station's tame news correspondent. So she was one of the few who knew that the Endeavour would be docking today, several days earlier than originally scheduled, and that security would be, in Sam's typically inappropriate words, 'tighter than a Scotsman'. But at least she knew that her very own Scotsman would be right in the middle of the story.

The time for docking came and went. She decided to go to the newsroom. To walk the full length of the station would do her good and stop her feeling she was in everybody's way. Donning a pair of sensible slacks and trainers, and a light jacket to ward off the pesky drafts of the controlled air system, she stepped out into the corridor. Her route took her up the never-ending slope that was the challenge of every trip between zones, before the floor levelled off and opened out, with rooms on either side. She had entered Zone 4, where sick bay was situated together with those laboratories that did not require zero-G.

She crossed the zone, about fifty metres of level walking, before entering the next curved corridor to Zone 3 and the press briefing room. Here she found various of her fellow correspondents, some of whom looked up expectantly when she came in. It was becoming common knowledge that, if any story were going to break, it would be via the astronaut's aristocratic girlfriend. But just then a Chinese journalist picked up that the Resolution had been left in a lower orbit, which meant that the Endeavour must be close by – possibly even docked by now. This got the rumour machine up and running, though everything remained guesswork.

Melody needed facts. She left the room and made her way back across the station along the curved corridor which was, against all intuition, still uphill even though she was retracing her steps. As she crossed Zone 4 she messaged Sam from her eband. The immediate response surprised her. 'We're just finishing up, and I'll be with you in five.' She only just made it back to Zone 1 and her quarters in time.

At the sound of the doorbell, hoping Sam would put her breathlessness down to anxiety, she threw off her jacket, flicked her hair and opened the door. Sam had an odd look about him, not so much worried as mystified.

'Come in, sit down, and let me get you a drink.'

'Thanks, Mel. I think you may be needing one too.'

'Don't tease, Sam. That's my job.'

Unnervingly, he said nothing in response.

Once he had downed the bourbon, he took a deep breath and

launched in. 'What I'm about to tell you can't go to press – no, wait a minute, can't go to press today. I'm only here because Jack says you should be trusted... and I know you can be. The time will come to go public, but right now there's a twenty-four hour embargo while we run a few tests.'

'Tests? What kind of tests?'

2

Back in Zone 4 an elevator door opened and Brad Shepperton emerged, followed by a small party of men and someone stretched out on a gurney. Jim followed first, then came Jack on one side of the patient and a white coat who had been introduced as Dr Schlesinger on the other. Mission controller Dan Marshall served as rearguard. Jack eased the trolley along the floor, pushing it a little too hard as he hadn't yet fully adapted to the artificial gravity of the outer rim.

They filed into a white room and Dan closed the door behind them. The place oozed sterility. Jack helped to get the Stranger transferred to what looked remarkably like an operating table, not a difficult task in a quarter of Earth gravity. He watched as Schlesinger, now revealed as the station's Chief Medical Officer, wordlessly clamped the unwitting patient's wrists and ankles to the table, taking care not to touch the silvery suit he wore. He proceeded with a visual inspection of the patient, which amounted to little more than the head, hands and feet. Finally he gently lifted first one eyelid then the other. When he spoke, his voice was husky.

'Has he shown any signs of being more than half-conscious?' He threw his question out for anyone to catch.

'No,' said Jim. 'Some ramblings at first, but nothing that made any sense. And once we were on board the Resolution we used the medbed – where he spent most of his time.'

'Ah,' said Schlesinger. 'Yes, well, I haven't seen any medical records beyond the crew.'

'Well no,' said Jim, not concealing his irritation. 'That would be because he was, shall we say, unexpected. Only the crew's medbeds were set up to be monitored from Mission Control.'

'Yes, yes, of course,' said Schlesinger, brushing off Jim's comment. 'Doubtless others more worthy than I will be examining his data in due course.' The irritation bug seemed to have been caught by the doctor already, though it was apparently fighting a losing battle with his curiosity. He peered down at the pearl-white face, blinked, and then decided it was a light brown face. The same thing happened when he checked the patient's hands and feet. He shrugged – perhaps it was an after-effect of looking too long at the suit, even though he'd been trying not to look at it. 'Well, gentlemen,' he croaked, 'I don't think he'll be answering any questions for a while yet. He's not in a coma as such, but patently he isn't fully conscious either. I suggest you leave me to see what a preliminary scan can tell us – I can't do much more with the equipment I have here – and I'll call you when there's more to be done.'

Jack studied the doctor, trying to place his accent, which he decided was that transatlantic combination of Englands New and Old. He thought he detected an eager look in the doctor's eyes. He clearly couldn't wait to take a closer look.

'Very well, Doctor,' said Dan. 'Let's leave him in peace for now, and start again tomorrow, unless there's any change before then. Right now the Colonel and I need to complete our debrief, and then the crew needs to get some sleep.'

3

Sam was on his fourth bourbon. He knew Mel wanted him to blab, but he was keeping it brief, if only because he himself knew so little. He had confirmed what he knew she knew already, that they had found someone on Venus, though her look of surprise was genuine enough, as up to now she had had next to no detail. A stowaway. How was that possible?

'I really don't know what to make of it,' said Sam as he set the glass down firmly on the table. 'We have him in quarantine. They're going to check out his vital signs, do a standard infection sweep, and take a good look at what he's wearing.'

'What he's wearing?' Definitely a surprise.

'Ah, well, the less said about that the better. Shoot, is that the time? I need to go.' He stood up a little too quickly, steadied himself, headed for the door, and was gone.

Melody remained in her chair, her head quite still but her mind racing. She had barely got used to the idea of an LGM (the 'little green men' of twentieth-century sci-fi legend, whose handle had somehow stuck) when all of a sudden there was interest in his space-wear. She recalled just how much this mission had depended on a recent breakthrough in textile technology which had provided the attire necessary to explore the surface of Earth's hotter-than-hot twin sister. (She had made a lot out of that metaphor in her first article on the mission.)

Where was Jack? Could she get to him? She knew it wasn't likely to happen any time soon, so she decided to take another walk.

4

Dr Schlesinger took a long look at his patient. Then he walked around the operating table and tried to describe the odd changes that were happening to the suit's aspect as it shifted and hinted its way through a variety of colours. It was like looking through a prism as you turned it in your hand. Most of the time it was a silvery white, but as it caught the light from different angles its vague shimmering suggested purples, blues, greens, yellows and reds. 'Well, Mr Rainbow Man,' Schlesinger whispered, 'just what have they kitted you out in? Let's take a look, shall we?'

As the hand-held body scanner gently whirred into life, Schlesinger added his own variety of humming, vaguely working his way through some half-remembered medley of songs. The Stranger's even stranger garment kept tickling his mind. In the end he left the scanner idle in the corner and took a small hand-held camera, walking round the patient once again, trying to catch the various colours that danced off the shimmering suit. He took a second and third tour, filming by infra-red and ultra-violet light. Then, holding a pair of scissors in one hand and one of the Stranger's cuffs in the other, he tried to cut up into the sleeve of the suit. The scissors jammed. Repeated efforts got him nowhere. Intrigued, he tried a scalpel, but it slipped off the material like a pen on paper, only narrowly missing the man's hand. This sent him off to a cupboard to find something with a bit more bite. 'Okay, my friend,' he said with his back to the sleeping patient, 'let's see how tough this stuff is.' And, with that, he pulled out a burner – a kind of miniature blow torch not unlike the old Bunsen burners that were used for heating various concoctions. He had not found a use for it until now.

He turned back to the patient. What was different? He couldn't have moved. Schlesinger walked round, and that's when he realised the suit was no longer reflecting all the colours of the spectrum. It was still silvery white, but now had a flatness, almost a normality, about it. He tried to cut it one more time with a scalpel, but that much at least had not changed.

He turned on the fuel supply and approached the patient. 'Well, this may wake you, but I promise to be careful, okay?'

He fired the thing up and levelled it at a sleeve, near the shoulder, wondering what sort of discolouration or damage it would do. But there was no change. 'As I thought,' he whispered. 'Fire-resistant. I wonder, how much?'

He needed a sample for more rigorous testing, so he went back to the cupboard and pulled out a small circular bone-saw, the most powerful cutting device available to him. When had he last known such intrigue? Or had this much fun? After checking the saw was charged up, he applied it to the cuff that had so obstinately resisted the scissors. It squealed as the spinning blade tried to cut in, but there was no purchase at all. He pushed harder, but then his hand slipped and ran the saw right off the sleeve and onto the patient's bare hand.

In an instant the room rang with a sudden cry that echoed unheard down the corridor outside. But it was not the Stranger who had found his voice – it was Dr Schlesinger. He could not believe what he was seeing.

5

Melody's wandering had turned into a march to Dan Marshall's office. She had decided this was the most likely place for Jack's debriefing. She found Sam sitting restlessly as he played guard dog in the small outer office that was his current base as liaison officer for the Aphrodite mission. He was about to tell her to turn round and go back when the inner door opened and Brad Shepperton emerged from Dan's office, followed swiftly and silently by Jim and Jack, both now dressed in what passed for casual attire in space, short-sleeved shirts and jeans.

'Mel!' Jack's arms were round her before she had chance to say a word. Finally he put her down, smoothed her hair from her face, took a good look at her, and kissed her.

Sam broke the silence. 'Well, this is nice. But, when the lovebirds are ready... There are some things going on, as you both know.'

'Well, that is most certainly true,' said Jack. 'But some things won't wait, even though the whole world be in peril!'

'Don't joke,' Shepperton cut in. 'We really don't know what we're dealing with. Or who.'

Mel took this statement as another gesture of trust towards her and promptly assumed her professional air. 'So how are we going to handle this?'

'*We* are not going to handle anything, Miss James,' replied Shepperton. 'You are going back to your quarters, while we plan a press conference – don't interrupt, please. You already know more than anyone, beyond a very few, and you'll doubtless be privy to some details that don't come up at the conference. But you'll appreciate that we can't hold back any longer. There are things the world needs to be told properly.'

She felt the slap, but for a second time there was no opportunity to respond, because at that moment a flustered Dr Schlesinger rushed past them and dived into Dan's office. With a nod to Sam, Shepperton followed.

'Okay, people,' said Sam. 'Time to break up this happy reunion. Jack, Jim, you'd best wait here with me. And Mel–'

But she was already marching down the corridor.

6

Inside the small chamber that served as his office, with Brad, Jim and Jack just gone, Dan Marshall took time to think. Laid out all over his e-desk stretched a maze of perplexing and therefore exciting data, courtesy of his protégé Ryan Chase who had been sending it to him throughout the return trip. On the non-live part of his desk, next to a framed photograph of his wife and grown-up kids at their home in Vancouver, was a crystal from the surface of Venus, more or less spherical, though with flat faces that allowed it to sit there quietly, guarding its secrets. But what was exercising Dan's mind even more were reports from Jim and Jack Forrester, both verbal and written, which made it very clear the two men had had a significant falling-out. Jim's account of the journey home was peppered with comments about Jack's security status which bordered on the paranoid. Jack's account was more considered but confirmed the two men were now at odds. And last but not least was the Stranger, the proverbial elephant in the room, so large that Dan couldn't step back far enough to see properly. Who was he? And, even more pressing, what were they going to do with him?

It was certain, of course, that he wouldn't be Dan's problem for long. Already emissaries were on their way from the six bodies both he and Shepperton reported to. He looked up at their emblems on his office wall: the space agencies of the USA, Europe, Russia, China, India and Australasia, all of whom had clubbed together to build Space Station Alpha, crucially undergirded by commercial enterprise.

And Dan was sure the military wouldn't be far behind them, knowing only too well that, in some of those organisations, the distinction between space agency and military was blurred at best. And then there was the business with Jack's girlfriend. Thanks to her they had all but lost control of the story to the world's media before the crew had even returned. He liked Mel, but he had seriously considered prosecuting both her and The Times, until he had discovered that this situation was not clearly and unambiguously covered by international law.

He eyed the crystal. It was beautiful, catching the light in different ways as if it were moving. Yet there it sat, still as a stone. What forces had formed it? And what made it so shiny and polished?

His silent reflection was broken by the door bursting open to reveal Dr Schlesinger, flustered and out of breath. 'Colonel Marshall,' he exclaimed, 'I think you had better come to the lab.'

'What is it?'

'I, I... think it's best you come. Maybe just you at first.'

Dan's mind was suddenly clear. 'I think, Doctor, that anything you have to show me will sooner or later have to come out anyway. Let's gather up those in the know as we go.'

'Maybe it's for the best,' said Schlesinger, scratching his head. 'Only what I have just seen is not really possible.'

Chapter 4

Secrets

1

At the last count Hugh Coates was only worth $50 billion, or £40 billion in his native Britain, but his mega-corporation Infostructure was worth trillions, to say nothing of his investment in new technologies. His conscience was at ease, for he had earned every penny and ploughed most of them back into his business interests. He was the one who had had the ideas, and he the one with the tenacity to believe in them come what may. At base his fortune had been made by identifying a fundamental building block for an edifice everyone had come to rely on: electronic communication. Oneness with the other. But this was not oneness with the divine, which seemed in most cases to rely far too heavily on the Other's terms; this was oneness with whomsoever, whensoever, under your own control. Whoever you were.

And how did this convert to trillions? By providing the synapses and bridges in a global network, all the while keeping his head down, letting others be the big names, and simply taking a fraction of a fraction of a percent every time someone communicated. It was like building the railways all over again, while leaving the trains to others. And running the signals with faultless efficiency.

At first the income had been modest, and it took hard work to gain the few necessary backers for the slowest growth forecasts since the new technologies late last century. But that just made it easier to weight the contracts in his favour, since no one really believed such a business was going to take off. And, in one sense, it didn't. It slid slowly and silently into the air, like an old polythene bag that took time to catch enough of the breeze to inflate before it could fly. So it was always easy to ensure there was a slice for him, for Infostructure – the company that provided infrastructure for information-sharing. A tiny share of a humble transaction, every time.

And so, one by one, the satellite-makers and social media platforms, the VR gamesters and the eband engineers, and eventually the military, turned to the friendly new company that eschewed the fast buck for the sake of a long-term future. They came to believe its tagline, 'Here for you today and tomorrow – and the day after,' and like eager new converts they spread the word. Within ten years the entire planet had been rewired, from ocean floor to mountain top, from Manhattan high-rise to Shanghai house-boat. A true 'ether net' – global and orbital, wired and wireless. No one could say they owned the internet, but this had to be the next-best thing.

Today was a day that promised much, though first he would be meeting, discreetly here in his New York office, the pioneer of the textile technology that had made possible the first manned flight to Venus. His intercom bleeped on cue.

'Mr Coates, Mr Box has arrived.'

'Bring him through. Coffee too.'

The two men knew each other a little, courtesy of the recent mission to Venus, but they had never actually had a meeting on their own before. Even though he was due to travel later on, Hugh was smartly dressed in suit and polo neck, eager as ever to make a statement to the work force – we're relaxed but totally together, on top of all that must be done. Conway Box was smart too but definitely occupied the casual category, sporting a dark blue jacket, light brown trousers and boots that put Hugh more in mind of a rodeo than a business meeting.

'So, Hugh – what's the biz? Have you picked up something about the Aphrodite mission? Only Alpha's closed its doors to mere mortals like me. Do you have something of interest?'

'I believe I may.' Hugh drained his tiny cup of espresso. Conway presented as the full-blooded American, his voice loud and his accent deep south, unlike Hugh whose dual British-American citizenship ensured he was a bit of an outsider on both sides of the Atlantic. And insider, of course. 'You don't get to install the wires of communication without, shall we say, picking up the vibrations.'

Conway made no comment, though his eyes gave no hint of surprise. He knew that Hugh was taking a risk if he was admitting to any form of interference or surveillance on his customers' private channels; but then, for all he knew, Mr Coates had come by the information the old-fashioned way, through a spy. After all, it was widely rumoured he had people in every part of the globe, as well as above it.

'I see,' said Conway. 'Well, I'm intrigued. I guess it has something to do with the unidentified guest, or should I say prisoner, on the Endeavour. But then, you don't need to be a rocket scientist to work a few things out.' He chuckled at his own attempt at humour.

'Go on,' nudged Hugh, eager not to divulge too quickly.

'Well, anyone who comes back unexpectedly from Venus has to have made it there first, and presumably survived for some time. And since we know that it's my space suit that finally got us there, I take it you're assuming we kitted this guy out.'

'I appreciate your directness,' said Hugh, 'but actually that's not it. Not exactly. What I have "picked up", as you so delicately put it, is that enquiries are not being made in your direction. That is to say, the Stranger seems to be decked in different technology.'

'You mean, I have a competitor?'

'It would appear so.'

Conway almost dropped his cup into its saucer. 'Well I'll be... Do they have any clues? Where are they looking?'

'Well now, those are two different questions, aren't they? Where they are looking is not so surprising – if you exclude the Big Six within the WSA, you are pretty much left with South America, South Africa, the Gulf, and Israel. But as for clues, there don't seem to be any.'

Conway mentally bookmarked this last statement as a surprisingly obvious lie. 'Mm, well, my money is on the last in your list. The Israelis have never gotten over being denied membership of the big boys' club.'

'Ah, so. You think it's the men who still make the rules, eh?'

'It was a figure of speech. There are some fine women in the industry.'

Hugh's intercom made its second entrance right on cue. Just as well, he thought, as the conversation was going nowhere. The man clearly knew nothing, even if he believed Hugh knew something.

'Mr Coates, I need to remind you of your next meeting.'

'Yes, thank you. We're just finishing here. Tell Miranda I'll meet her on the plane.'

2

Dr Schlesinger unlocked the door to his lab and led Dan Marshall inside. They were followed swiftly and silently by Brad Shepperton, Jim and Jack. The five men approached the table where the Stranger lay unmoved and unawake.

'Well, what is it, Doctor?' asked Shepperton. 'He looks fine to me.'

'Yes, yes... that's the point. He's right as rain – not a mark on him. Which is extraordinary, amazing, when you consider what just happened – and, trust me, "amazing" is not a word usually in my vocabulary.'

'Why don't you start at the beginning?' said Dan, and they all sat as comfortably as two chairs and two ledges would allow. Schlesinger proceeded to relate in heightened tones how he had been testing the Stranger's suit, only to make a startling discovery quite by accident. Barely containing his excitement, but eager to relate the events in the correct sequence, he pointed out to them how the suit's shimmering effect had grown dull, finally dissolving into a silvery white.

'Well, that is interesting,' said Shepperton. Jack sensed the impatience in his tone.

'Yes, yes,' puffed the doctor. 'But that isn't all. When I applied the burner, it got nowhere. Not a mark – no discolouration at all.'

'We need to test this garment thoroughly,' said Jack. 'Forgive me, Doctor, but I think we're going to need a bit more than a Bunsen burner.'

'Quite, quite. Absolutely. But there's more!'

'Go on,' said Shepperton with a sigh.

'Let me show you.' Schlesinger picked up the small bone-saw and set it whirring.

'Whoa!' said Jack. 'Be careful with that thing.'

'I will, I will... this time.' He approached the prone figure on the table, but as he leant forward wielding the saw, the patient stirred.

At this four voices chimed in unison. 'Wait!'

3

Back in her quarters, with her wounded pride from Shepperton's rebuke already healed by the sheer relief and joy at seeing Jack, Melody considered her questions for the press conference. Her room communicator signalled an incoming message. It was Jack.

'Hello, my lovely. I'm really sorry about all this cloak-and-dagger stuff. But don't worry, we'll be going public pretty soon. We've just got a couple of things to get clear on.' He paused.

'Jack? What are you not telling me?'

'Oh, there's plenty I'm not telling you. You know that. But I can tell you this, as it will be in our first official statement to the press.' The adjective stung a bit, but she knew she deserved it. 'He wasn't in great shape when we found him, but it looks like he may be on the mend. Anyway, I was calling to ask you to dinner, and we can catch up a bit more then.'

'You mean, they're letting me out?'

'Och yes, that's fine – so long as you're with me, of course.'

An hour later Jack and Melody were sitting at a table in *The Panorama*, Space Station Alpha's more expensive restaurant which made a brave attempt at luxury through tablecloths and silverware. It was situated next to the press room, face-out in Zone 3. The couple had dressed for dinner, both revelling in the chance to wear the only glad rags they had brought on board. Jack sported an open-neck pale blue shirt under a dark blue suit, while Melody had chosen a long green dress, remembering how Jack had more than once commented on the classy combination of the emerald fabric and her golden hair.

They sat by a window, not the most difficult seat to get, as the normally awe-inspiring spectacle of the earth passing by every minute was not quite so popular with those busy digesting their Panorama Paella. But for most of those who had undergone astronaut training this was no great challenge, and anyone in love with an astronaut very soon learnt to feel the same way. More than that, as an investigative writer now established as one of the more readable astro-journalists, Mel was no newcomer to space anyway, and she had decided not to leave the station after the Endeavour had launched. When the drama on Venus had emerged, five weeks soon turned to ten. It was the longest she had ever been away from planet Earth, and her space legs were now fully formed.

They talked a while about life on board Alpha. For Jack, one-quarter of Earth's gravity was clearly a luxury after weeks of mainly zero-G flight across space. Mel had come at it from the opposite direction, from planet Earth, and it had taken her a while to remember not to make any sudden moves. Not unless you particularly wanted to leave the floor for several unnerving seconds. 'Most disconcerting.'

When the food arrived they tucked in, before the conversation naturally turned to Venus. It wasn't long before Mel's antennae were twitching, as she began to sense that Jack was holding back on more than details about the Stranger. Eventually she surmised – more from what he didn't say – that it was to do with the crew. But she knew better than to ask searching questions. Not now. So she turned to what was, ironically, the more legitimate area of discussion.

'How's our visitor? Earlier on you talked about him recovering from something.'

'Well, he's fine. He's not saying anything, and he's, er, shall we say a little indisposed. But he's making good progress. You'll get to hear a bit more in the press briefing. And actually, that's one favour you did us.'

'How so?'

'As we now have to include the discovery of our stowaway in the first briefing, we're limited to the press already on the station while the security implications are sorted out.'

'Just the elite, you mean? And no live-link with Earth?"

'Precisely. That way, we can decide what goes out, should any of the questions prove... difficult.'

'I don't think I like the sound of that,' said Mel.

'No, I'm sure you don't,' said Jack with a sigh.

'And nor do you!' she said, pointing a silver fork in his direction. 'I know you.'

He shrugged, and they continued eating, watching the lights of some vast city wheel past them three hundred miles below. After several minutes Jack could stand Mel's uncharacteristic silence no longer.

'Look, you know I can't breach security...'

'Of course you can't.'

'Okay,' he relented. 'I'll tell you this much. We found the guy in our ship. He'd not been on board before. He had no EVA equipment. And he wasn't conscious.'

She choked on her last penna. 'So, so... how did he get there?'

'My love, I haven't got a clue.'

4

Dr Schlesinger had a lot to prove. He had sworn – both to himself and his colleagues – that he had inadvertently sent a powered saw into the Stranger's flesh. Only it hadn't gone into the flesh. It had bounced off like a child's toy. Clearly the extraordinary nature of such a claim, from an individual whose carefulness normally bordered on tedium, needed testing. And so the two controllers Brad Shepperton and Dan Marshall sat, flanked by Jim and Jack, awaiting the demonstration.

The Stranger himself had returned to his apparently comatose state. It had been agreed that to carry out the experiment with the bone-saw would be too drastic, unnecessarily dangerous, so the doctor approached his patient with a hypodermic needle. Carefully he placed the sharp point on to the patient's forearm. His own hand shook, from fear or excitement none could tell.

He thought he could feel some resistance as he began to press the needle home, but his grip gave way at the sound of an alarm. It was the tell-tale siren of a collision warning blaring out across the station, and it called for immediate action from the Station Controller. Brad now had to drop everything and oversee the change in orbit that might be required to avoid damage to Alpha's hull or external equipment. He duly disappeared, and Dan and Jim were only two seconds behind him.

'Well, Doctor,' said Jack, 'it looks like we're going to have to wait a little longer. You know the drill. We all need to suit up in case of pressure loss.'

The crestfallen doctor found a space suit, and together he and Jack put it on the Stranger. They decided to leave the helmet off until such time as he actually needed it. Jack then scuttled off to Zone 1 to find his own suit, leaving Schlesinger to suit up and wait for the all-clear.

5

A grey room with dull walls, bright lights and a large shiny black table played host to the first formal meeting of interested parties since the Endeavour had returned to Earth orbit. The station had successfully avoided a collision with a cloud of space junk, a crisis the station's builders had clearly anticipated but never expected to be so frequent at this distance from the earth's surface. This particular event had come with no prior warning, a fact that propelled Brad Shepperton to the radio as soon as the danger was past. His protests were heard but no one was claiming responsibility.

Brad had thrown himself into the task of navigating the station clear of the debris, which in the end meant dropping a few miles before resuming standard orbit. The tech team couldn't help noticing that he was actually enjoying himself in what turned out to be a straightforward crisis with reassuringly familiar parameters. Unlike the situation that faced him now.

There were no windows in the meeting room. Jack felt the overhead lights bore into him, despite the white ceiling that diffused them. Around the oval table were twelve chairs, steel frames shining. So much grey, black and silver shouted its aggression at the soft orange tones of Venus still lingering in his memory.

He sat down nearest the only door, with Jim on his left and Dan on his right – the three of them dressed in their two-tone-grey, WSA-logoed overalls, representing the Aphrodite mission. At the far end of the room, in what clearly functioned as the head of the table, stood Brad Shepperton, in collar and tie, already welcoming the august gathering to his space station. Normally he would be addressing these people, or more likely their underlings, on issues to do with space tourism, or planetary exploration, or space telescope maintenance, or the mining interests that used Zone 2 to launch their hardware to the Moon or the latest promising asteroid. Today he felt both thrilled and completely out of his depth.

On Brad's immediate right was an empty chair; on the left, some kind of assistant or official Jack did not recognise. The remaining six chairs were occupied by the six heads of the members of the WSA, the World Space Agency, who oversaw – and part-funded – the operation of Space Station Alpha. Brad was making it clear to Dan, Jim and Jack that these were not just representatives of the governing organisations, they were the chiefs of staff – just in case anyone thought this was not being treated as anything other than huge. 'So, ladies and gentlemen, this is no ordinary mission debrief, as you will appreciate. You here today are not only responsible for the funding and development of all the exploration that comes out of this space station; you are in direct contact with the governments of the world's most developed nations. At this meeting we have two very specific goals: to clarify just what happened on Venus; and to agree precisely what we are going to say at the press briefing tomorrow.

'Now, I appreciate there are scientific findings that we'll also need to report on, with regards to the Venusian atmosphere and surface, but for once those initial reports can wait a little, which I'm sure will be good news to the scientists in the various project teams supporting the mission. We know how much they love to explain findings to the general populace when they've scarcely had time to absorb the initial data themselves!' A ripple of laughter went across the centre of the room. 'We will of course be meeting with the project co-ordinators in due course. But for now,' and with that he let his gaze circle the entire table, 'we need to turn to our Big Surprise.'

And so the mission report began. Brad's comments notwithstanding, Dan began by rehearsing the reasons for the fairly hurried mission in the first place – an unusual dip in atmospheric pressure in a small region of the planet which, once new advances in protective clothing were factored in, meant that we had the wherewithal to do the unthinkable: to mount a manned mission to the surface of Venus. 'As you will appreciate, no one knew how long these conditions would last, so we moved as quickly as we could. I remind you of this now as it may have a bearing on why we found someone else had beaten us to it. And I think we'll have to address this at the press conference.'

Jack watched the official sitting next to Brad make his first note.

At this point Jim took up the story, as he proceeded to relate how a fascinating ('you could hardly say routine') survey of the surface of the planet had been brought to a rapid end by a change in atmospheric conditions, 'too close to the kind of weather you normally get on Venus'.

Jack looked around the room, trying to read the body language of the six esteemed visitors. If Brad sat at twelve o'clock at the top of the table, and Jack at six, then you could say eight and nine o'clock were starting to show more obvious interest. At eight sat Mia Caitsby, head of ASA, the Australasian Space Agency, already in the process of looking for a new name now that it had been joined by Japan. Next to her, at nine o'clock, was Lena Bergstrom, head of ESA, the European Space Agency with the UK Space Agency. Each had her gaze fixed firmly on Jim. At ten o'clock and two o'clock the heads of America's NASA and the Russian Federal Space Agency sat looking at each other. As Jack's gaze completed the circle, it passed over the Chinese and Indian directors, both of whom were looking down.

But it wasn't long before every eye in the room was fixed on Jim, as he came to the discovery of the Stranger on board. Only now did Jack realise how little the visitors had been told about the stowaway. How was Jim going to tell it?

'There was a lot going on all of a sudden. With Ryan Chase still out in the storm that was upon us, I took the decision to leave Commander Forrester and Dr Koroleva with our new guest while I headed out to bring him in.'

'Why was Dr Chase not already inside?' It was Lena Bergstrom who asked the obvious question.

'Well, Ma'am, Ryan gets a bit focused when he's excited. The rapid change in atmospheric conditions was just the kind of thing he'd come to see. Now, we wanted him to make the most of our in-person presence on the planet, but I also knew he'd push things to the limit to get what he wanted – and none of us knew for sure just how well our suits were going to perform.' The Chinese and Indian directors exchanged a whisper.

'The going wasn't easy out there. Even with enhanced visor

controls I could make out very little. Then I saw what I took to be Dr Chase, slumped in a heap on the ground. It's at that point I must have lost my footing, because the next thing I knew Ryan was standing over me telling me we had to get back to the ship! Which we did, only to discover Commander Forrester – Jack here – was out looking for us.'

Brad cut in, and asked Jack if he wanted to add anything at this point.

'Not exactly,' said Jack. 'I could mention a rather fascinating crystal we'd found earlier, but I guess we can come to that in due course.' Another note by the official. 'However, I would like to ask a question, if I may. Where is the WSA's Director? Should she not be in that chair next to you, Brad?'

A flash of annoyance in Brad's face quickly gave way to a smile. 'I'm sorry, I should have explained earlier. Ms Bridlington can't be with us today because she's away on retreat. We've only recently got a message through to her. She told us to go ahead, given the urgency of the situation.'

Given the urgency of the situation, thought Jack, she should be nowhere else right now. But he kept his thoughts to himself. 'Right,' he said out loud. 'As for the Stranger, I must underline what Jim said just now, that a lot was going on all at once. We had injured crew, a hazardous storm looking uglier by the minute, and an impossible stowaway. I had come uncomfortably close to a sticky end myself out in the storm, and it didn't look like conditions were going to improve any time soon. That had implications for the ship's hull integrity, so Jim made the decision to leave. As for the security aspect, when the directive came through from Mission Control that I should assume responsibility for the stowaway, I was as surprised as anyone.' He decided this was not the time or place to mention Jim's out-of-character reaction.

'But gentlemen, what if there were other... unexpected personnel nearby, unaccounted for?' It was the Chinese director.

Jim offered to respond. 'That's a good question, Dr Li, and one of course that I had to consider. But really, there was no other choice. We couldn't leave the ship and go looking for anyone. As Jack has intimated, the pressure was going up, the temperature too, and we needed to get the ship out of danger. I didn't know if there were any other "personnel" out there, of course; and as for any other spacecraft, we had neither the time nor the means to go looking for it – at least, not from the surface.'

'But I don't understand.' It was Lena Bergstrom again. 'Forgive me if I'm missing the obvious, but how could this "Stranger", as you call him, come to be in your ship without the EVA equipment needed to take him from his ship to yours?'

'Ma'am, that really is the obvious question,' Jim replied. 'Lightning from the storm seemed to have taken out some of our systems, and that unfortunately included the outside video recordings, which meant we couldn't see the actual moment he came on board. So, really, we're none the wiser than you right now. Pretty much.'

'Pretty much?' It was the Russian chief, Alexei Nargarov. 'What are you not telling us?'

'Let me take it from here,' put in Brad. 'As you know, we've only had our guest with us for a few hours. He's still unconscious – "pretty much" – but we have run a few tests on him, including his clothing. These tests are far from conclusive, but it would appear that the suit he is wearing is unusually resistant to damage, possibly the highest form of resistance we have ever encountered.'

'All this happened five weeks ago,' said Lena Bergstrom. 'Has he been like this the whole time?'

Brad looked to Jim and Jack to respond. 'Well,' said Jack, 'at first we thought he was coming round. In the first hours of the trip home we tried to get him on his feet. We managed to get some fluids into him, but we weren't getting anywhere. And you all know how tricky toilets can be in a weightless environment.'

Some of the directors chuckled at this, while others kept their eyes fixed on the table.

'So we soon decided to keep him in his medbed for the entire trip.

As you may know, these were developed for the Mars missions for cases of medical emergency. We got him out of his suit and into the space nappy, and then plugged him in.' Jack looked around the room, and got the distinct impression no one wanted details, though he himself could not forget the relief he had felt once they had tucked the Stranger in, leaving the business of feeding and waste disposal to the machine.

After this, the discussion rambled on for another half-hour, with speculations over whether the Stranger had had time to jettison some of his space suit before he had collapsed on board the Endeavour. At last it was agreed that his existence should be confirmed to the press (there was little alternative anyway after the initial leak), but that the properties of the suit should be kept secret for now. It would be sufficient to say that someone else got there first, though it was decided not to go with the Russian proposal that suspicion be laid at the door of the Israelis. While everyone knew that Israel was intent on a space programme without reference to the WSA, there was simply no evidence.

The meeting broke up. Jack left the room with a familiar feeling of 'cover-up in progress', only this time it was not only the press who were being denied the full story but even the people who were supposed to be running the show.

'Jack, you got a minute?' It was Dan. 'We need to talk.'

6

Three hundred miles below Space Station Alpha, on the eastern seaboard of North America in the twilight of a busy day, Hugh Coates boarded one of his private jets. It was the smallest and the most secure. With a single voice command he withdrew the steps into the cabin and sealed the door. Leaving his bag on a table, he walked towards the cabin door at the front of the plane, where the pilot stood waiting.

'Miranda.'

'Good evening, sir. Where to?'

7

Jack looked around Dan Marshall's office while he waited for him to appear. Actually 'office' was too grand a word for any of the pokey, windowless rooms given over to senior personnel aboard the station, but there was an e-desk, with its inbuilt communication and computing power, and even three chairs that weren't bolted to the floor, all of which served to keep the epithet 'cupboard' at bay. There was almost nothing to reveal whose office it was, but then since Dan would be on board only for the duration of the mission to Venus, that was not so unusual.

Jack had a lot of respect for the colonel who had joined the UN from the Canadian air force while still finding time to take a degree in planetary sciences. He was a thoughtful guy, naturally consultative but not afraid of making the hard decisions when these were called for. Not unlike me in fact, Jack mused.

He spotted the crystal on the desk and felt an unexpected delight in handling it once more. He peered into it, and the longer he looked the more the light played games with his vision. He broke off when Dan came in.

'Sorry to keep you waiting.'

'That's fine,' said Jack, as he fondled the seductive object in his hands. 'You know, we really should get this to the lab as well.'

'Yeah, I know,' Dan sighed. 'Somehow the Stranger has taken over everything. But you're right. Ryan was pretty excited about it too. He said his initial results led him to an interesting conclusion.'

'Oh?'

'That the crystal was not native to Venus.'

'A meteorite?'

'I guess. It would have to have been a pretty hefty chunk of rock to leave something like this behind. It's clearly melted and crystallised, but it's not like any meteorite I've ever seen. It's too rounded for a start, too symmetrical, though I guess that could just be an accident of formation.' He held out his hand and Jack passed it back over the desk. 'But right now we need to talk about what we do with our number one mystery. What's your view of Schlesinger?'

Jack recognised the implication in the question. 'That he's not up to the job, you mean? Oh aye, not much doubt about that. He's here to look after your personnel. Doubtless he's fine in that regard, but this is a bit beyond your average bout of space sickness.'

'Exactly right. I think we need a different approach. And, well, the boss agrees with me.'

'Our missing Director, you mean?'

Dan nodded. 'Ms Bridlington has made it very clear that we should move the Stranger away from here asap, to a safe place, where he can take his time to recuperate and we can take our time to monitor him. After all, Schlesinger says there are no broken bones, his blood pressure is stable, breathing normal, muscle tone good.' He grinned. 'Better than yours, in fact.'

Jack gently shook his head. 'And she's organised the move over the phone?'

'What can I say? You know our beloved leader. She doesn't like to travel if she can control her empire from her throne. Anyhow, I used my personal eband to bring her up to date.'

'But Dan, you must know that even that level of encryption's not totally secure.'

'Sure. But we couldn't wait. And, really, how many people are there who could hack into the kind of communicators you and I have?'

'It's not likely, I agree,' said Jack. 'Unless they were already monitoring us.'

8

'Go to autopilot.' As soon as the flight control deck complied with Miranda's simple command, she closed the cockpit door quietly behind her and walked down the cabin to where Hugh Coates sat dozing at a table by a window. She stood for a moment, studying the one she had devoted her life to for sixteen years, ever since she had left college and joined Infostructure on a scholarship programme as a young and eager software designer. True, her first few months had been fairly routine, but then she got to meet the man who would turn her aspirations into achievements. She hadn't been the one to spill coffee on him that day, but she had moved faster and fairer than anyone to clean it up and call his secretary. Within minutes his new shirt had been brought downstairs. Within weeks she had moved upstairs and into his entourage. It proved to be a fiercely loyal circle – not that the temptation to disloyalty could ever get much traction when you worked for the man who, sooner or later, knew everything.

She made her way now down the cabin of the electronically screened Gulfstream 1000X that served as Hugh's most private office. 'Mr Coates... Hugh!'

He started and broke into a rare smile. 'Ah yes. Where are we?'

'Right now we're 40,000 feet above the middle of the Atlantic, as requested. Can I get you anything?'

'Ah Miranda – my confidante, my pilot... and now my stewardess? No, come and sit down, and take a look at this.' He activated a tablet that lay on the table and turned it towards her as he told it to 'play most recent video file'.

It took a moment for her to understand what she was watching. She was looking down from a ceiling in the corner of a room. There was a man in a white coat in a laboratory, and he looked like he was filming an unconscious patient. A number of other men were there, though it was not clear why. 'What am I looking at?'

Hugh's response was to ask for another file to be played. The screen now showed the same room, only this time she could hear the man in the white coat talking to the men, explaining what he had witnessed earlier – a shimmering suit of some kind that was apparently changing in some way. Then he began to wield some kind of burner. 'Stop file.'

Miranda didn't move a muscle. The aircraft continued to purr as it made its way across the sky.

'One of the many qualities I appreciate in you, Miranda, is your cool approach to the job in hand – to life, in fact. Now listen. Play most recent audio file.'

> 'Bridlington here. What is it, Dan?'
> 'Well, we have what we call a Situation. I need you here.'
> 'That's not possible right now.'
> 'It's about the Code 1 message from Venus.'

There was a pause.

> 'I'm really sorry, but I can't get to you until after the UN meeting. You know how important that is. Our funding may depend on it.'
> 'Very well. Then we're going to have to do this remotely. I'm sending you a couple of files that will demonstrate that the guy we picked up during the mission has been equipped with technology unknown to us.'
> 'What kind of technology?'
> 'Some kind of super-resistant suit. But that's not all.'
> 'Go on.'
> 'There is some evidence... no, there is a suggestion, that the subject himself has been enhanced in some way.'
> 'Dan, stop right there.'

Hugh then played a second audio file, in which Miranda heard the unmistakable British English tones of Ms Bridlington give the description, complete with geographical co-ordinates, of some kind of monastery in Switzerland.

She looked at Hugh with just the hint of a knowing smile. 'I think it's time I got back to the flight deck.'

9

The small press room in Zone 3 of SS Alpha remained unusually quiet as the few journalists and presenters aboard began to file in. Melody had decided to take a back seat, literally, and let her colleagues in the industry have their moment. The Aphrodite Mission Controller, Dan

Marshall, was already seated at the speakers' table at one end of the room, together with the four astronauts who had made the journey, each one already a global celebrity, each one dressed in the bespoke grey overalls that signified the Aphrodite mission. At the last minute Dan turned to Jack and whispered that he need make no mention of his security role.

At the appointed time Brad Shepperton made his entrance, occupying the seat between Ryan and Natasha before welcoming everyone. He began with an announcement that they were not being joined online by other news agencies due to antenna damage in the recent incident.

Jack's eyes opened wide, though he quickly covered his raised eyebrows by sweeping a hand through his hair. This was the first he had heard of any damage to the station. Cover-up continues.

Brad explained that the mission had been a qualified success, albeit limited by the rapidly changing climate conditions that had signalled a premature end to what they could do on the surface. Much of the data they had collected had already got the fifteen teams of scientists around the world working day and night, ready for what must surely prove to be a whole new volume in our library on the solar system, with new insights already emerging on the Venusian lithosphere and lack of magnetosphere. This, together with data from the probes left in the upper atmosphere, was already promising to make a giant contribution to our understanding of Venus and, it was hoped, global warming. He then listed some of the business corporations whose generous financial backing had made the whole mission possible.

People shuffled. No one spoke.

'However, I appreciate that that's not why you're here.' He held up his hand. 'Yes, of course, some of you are eager to fill your columns with new scientific facts... but I realise that all of that — and some of us had been preparing ourselves for that with great excitement — all of that has been eclipsed by the news of our stowaway.'

'Are we going to hear from him?' One journalist clearly could not contain himself. Brad simply took a glass of water and raised it to his lips as he looked in the opposite direction.

'What I'd like to do now is hand you over to Dan Marshall, who as you know was in charge of the mission, and let him and his team address this issue. There will be a chance for questions after that.'

Dan rehearsed the events surrounding the mission, before handing over to Jim. The minutes ticked by as the agreed plan was followed. It was going well. The time came for questions.

Dan got to his feet and looked straight at the journalist who had spoken earlier. A sea of hands went up, but to everyone's surprise and annoyance he gave the floor to the offender. 'Go ahead, ask your question.'

After a moment's silence the young journalist gathered his thoughts. 'Noah Willington, Washington Post. I'd like to know if we'll be getting the opportunity to speak with the stowaway... the Stranger, as you seem to be calling him. But,' and now he spoke rapidly, 'if that isn't possible, I'd love to ask Dr Koroleva for her impressions of the Stranger.' As he sat down, the mood of the other journalists appeared to soften. Jack observed the New York Times journalist turn to his neighbour in the front row and distinctly whisper, 'Great question!'

Jack sensed trouble. Had some instinct told this guy that Natasha had more to say? Why hadn't they let her speak for longer earlier on, when she had more control, especially as they had so carelessly revealed that she had been alone with the Stranger when the storm first hit? But almost before those questions had taken shape in his mind, he knew they really couldn't have done anything differently.

The room was looking at Natasha. 'Well, there isn't a lot to say, Mr Willington. I'm afraid the Stranger has not regained consciousness since whatever trauma affected him and led him to the Endeavour.'

Jack's shoulders dropped a little and he breathed more easily as he saw the old Natasha, formal and businesslike, then direct the question away from the Stranger, away from her, and back towards the storm they were all tussling with at that time. But soon the questions turned towards the medical state of the Stranger, which prompted Brad to take back the meeting and report that he was under careful observation while they waited for him to regain consciousness. All they knew was that he was a male, possibly of mixed race, though they had no clue to his nationality, and DNA-testing was not possible on board the station. Further updates would be released. 'Thank you all for coming.'

As the people dispersed Jack remained seated, drumming his fingers on the table as he asked himself what it was that had scared him when Natasha had the floor.

10

'Natasha, can I have a wee word?'

Jack's face looked innocent enough on Natasha's eband, and his tone was relaxed, but she sensed that he was worried about something. 'Okay,' she said. 'When?'

'How about now? I'm standing outside your door.'

She appeared within seconds, having already exchanged the mission overalls for a loose-fitting khaki top and white baggy trousers cropped to mid-calf length. She ushered him to a seat. 'So, how can I help?' Her eyes danced around the room, giving him no chance to catch them with his own.

'Well,' he began, 'we haven't really been able to talk privately since the EVA on Venus, what with all the monitoring that goes on over the airwaves.' He took a deep breath. 'I don't suppose you have anything to drink around here?'

'No single malt, I'm afraid,' she said. 'Will vodka do?'

'Admirably.'

She disappeared into the galley before returning with a glass of clear liquid and a steaming cup from which she began to sip. 'So?' she said, sitting upright, and this time her gaze was locked on. To Jack's surprise, it made things easier. For a brief moment he studied her face, barely framed by her blonde hair which was, as usual, tied back tight. It was a pale, almost rectangular face with high cheek bones not too pronounced, as if whoever did the chiselling made sure they had sanded the edges afterwards, and a wide bridge between bluish-grey eyes, above a straight nose with its relatively short distance from the mouth, ending with a very slightly narrowing chin. All in all, a face he had come to admire and to trust implicitly.

He took a sip of vodka. 'Okay. To the point. Why do I get the feeling that there's more to that time you had with our friend, right at the beginning?'

'You think I've not told you everything?'

'No one ever tells anyone everything.'

'Now Jack, you're sounding like a skilful interrogator.' She raised her hand as he started to respond. 'But don't worry. I have nothing to hide. It just hasn't seemed right to say anything... at least, not until now.' She put her cup down. 'When Jim was out looking for Ryan, and you were back in your quarters getting dressed,' and with that her lately-found wicked smile brought the whole scene vividly to his mind, 'our friend, as you call him... and I believe he *is* our friend... stirred from his slumber. Just for a moment.'

Jack took another sip, not wanting to interrupt the flow of new information.

'It wasn't much, and yet... I know this sounds stupid, but I saw no malice in his eyes.'

This time Jack choked. 'His *eyes*? You mean, he opened them?'

'Just for a moment. And he spoke – well, rambled, but I couldn't make out the tongue.'

'The language, you mean?'

'That's right. I only speak Russian, English and American, as you know.' They both relaxed at the joke. 'He was basically unconscious, but not completely. He rambled, as I say, and he was obviously confused. I admit I calmed him down a bit.' Her eyes dropped. She didn't mention the lullaby, and Jack didn't ask. 'Anyway, he was soon asleep again, which, as you know, is more or less how he's been ever since.'

Jack eyed her directly, but said nothing, waiting to see if there was more. There was.

'On the journey home,' she continued, 'it fell to me to check in on him more than most, as you know. But as far as I could tell, no one else heard a squeak out of him.'

'That's true. Go on.'

'Well, every time I went to see him, I'd, er, sing a little... and he would stir, open those deep-blue eyes, and try to speak again. But it didn't last long.'

Jack sighed. 'Natasha, why didn't you say anything at the time?'

'I'm sorry – I don't know. No, that's not true. I think I was protecting him.'

In his mind Jack was now back on the Resolution, recalling only too clearly how frayed tempers had become, especially between himself and Jim, and between Ryan and Natasha. He decided not to press her any further.

Natasha picked up her drink. 'What are you going to do?'

'Ah well,' said Jack. 'What you don't know is, we're moving him off-station very soon. So what I am going to *do* is ask Brad and Dan to let you come along.'

11

Outside Dan Marshall's office Sam Braithwaite was checking something on screen. Jack approached. 'Still on guard, Sam?'

'Aw no... well, I guess. He's got Brad Shepperton in there, and Jim. Telling them something important, I think. Anyways, he asked me to look busy out here for a while.'

'Sure, I think I know what he's telling them. I'll come back later.'

Jack had barely finished speaking when the door opened, and Jim and Brad filed out. Seeing his chance, and with a nod from Sam, Jack went in.

Dan was at his desk, crystal in hand. 'Oh, Jack. Good timing. I've just been bringing Brad and Jim up to date with our travel plans.'

'Aye, I guessed as much. Tell me, do we have room for one more?'

'What, Ryan? I hardly think he's going to let himself be drawn away right now, with so much data to analyse.'

'No, not Ryan.'

'You can't mean Natasha. Why would we do that?'

'Because our Natasha, cold and clinical as we thought, has developed some kind of bond with our mysterious guest. It seems she's had it right from the start. I think she may prove a significant help in the process of getting him to speak.'

Dan smoothed back his hair – the grey ones far fewer than Jack's, thanks to the bottle in his shower. 'Well, okay... if you're sure. We weren't wanting too many people questioning him once he wakes up, though – assuming he does.'

'Then I suggest we start with one. And that one should be Natasha.'

12

The corridor in Zone 4 was empty, but for two men walking purposefully towards one of the lab doors. It was officially night-time on Alpha – an artificial reality of course, but absolutely necessary for normal human life. Dr Schlesinger keyed in the code to unlock the door. 'After you, Commander Forrester.'

Jack walked in, but after two steps he came to an abrupt halt. 'Well, well.'

Schlesinger brushed past him. 'What is it?'

Before them, sitting on the edge of the makeshift bed, was the Stranger. He was sitting up and looking directly at them.

Chapter 5

Awakening

1

For an out-of-the-way part of the world, the alpine foothills to the west of Lake Lugano were surprisingly well serviced by road, rail and air. Miranda held the controls steady as she lowered the private jet into the compact airport at Agno. Spread out before her was an array of contrasts, as cars streamed along a busy motorway, dark green trees nestled in the shadows of the hills, and sunlight danced on the lake below.

Once they were down she made the necessary arrangements for the plane to be housed safely away from the terminal, before escorting Hugh through a VIP immigration zone and out to the pound where their car awaited. He felt like driving, but decided against. There was work to do on the short drive ahead.

They made their way ever higher into the foothills towards the small mountain village aptly named Montagnola. As they came off the autostrada Miranda switched off the autodrive and guided the car smoothly around the many bends that inevitably came with mountain driving, while Hugh took out a small box he had taken from his case and proceeded to remove his contact lenses. On went the dark-rimmed glasses he had chosen for this assignment. Spectacles and lenses were still the preferred option over surgery for some people his age, and they would certainly prove useful now in the disguise department. Next came the beard – short and trim and highly realistic. Finally some splashes of grey applied to his long sideburns and short hair which, ironically, were denied such honesty most of the time.

Miranda smiled. She loved it when she and Hugh went off grid on some tangent that even left the inner circle in the dark. Hugh may not have had a face that was known across the world, but these days you couldn't be assured of anonymity anywhere. And you could hardly say they were leaving civilisation in Switzerland.

Miranda had long admired her boss and mentor for the careful attention he paid to his own reconnaissance work. As CEO of a multi-national company he relied on thousands of dedicated men and women; as a man always one step ahead, he kept his own counsel. And seemingly closest of all to that counsel was Miranda. She was there to make sure his more secret plans turned to reality; but increasingly she felt she was counsellor too. Maybe.

They drove along clean roads, past neat lawns and trimmed trees, to what appeared to be the centre of the village, where the car indicated their hotel in front of them. They checked in as a businessman and his personal assistant. He changed only his surname. 'Never lie more than you have to.' After booking an evening dinner they retired to their rooms.

Ten minutes later Miranda stepped out on to her small balcony, her pilot's shirt and skirt exchanged for a plain green top and denim shorts. She watched the sunlight play through a pleasing mix of green and gold as she peered through the trees in the general direction of the monastery. Hugh had said he had no idea how long it would be before the Stranger arrived, but all being well they would have time to visit the place first and plant some listening devices. Sound would almost certainly be easier than video, and more important. A site visit was essential because he had discovered that the entire place was protected by some kind of electronic screen.

To most men that would be a barrier. To Hugh Coates it was an invitation.

2

Tiredness crashed in on Dan Marshall like the waves of a stormy sea, wearing him down till he succumbed to its soothing chorus. He thought he heard Sam rifling about somewhere in the room, but he paid no attention. He dreamed about a pair of hands, more like claws, grasping the crystal on his desk. He tried to call out, but all he could manage was a low moan. This turned into a buzzing in his head which gradually settled into a low humming sound. Then a brief surge of white gold and he was awake.

He looked around. Everything appeared normal. There was no sign of a light, no sound in his head. He shrugged, put it down to the vagaries of half-sleep and stepped outside.

Sam was just returning to his desk. Dan thought about asking him if there had been any kind of power surge on the station, but before he could say a word a bright light came from behind him. Both men rushed into his office. The crystal had come alive. It was emanating a yellowish-white light which quickly fell into a soft glow before finally disappearing. For a moment they could both hear a gentle humming. Then nothing. The whole episode had lasted less than sixty seconds.

Neither man moved. Gingerly Dan approached his desk, only to leap back suddenly when a loud sound erupted from it. It was his intercom. With a nervous laugh he turned back to Sam. 'I suppose I'd better answer that!'

Jack came on, talking too fast to make much sense.

'Slow down, Jack!' His Scottish accent had gone into hyperdrive. 'Who's awake and speaking *pairr-fect* English?'

'Our man, of course!' Jack replied. 'Schlesinger and I have just found him, sitting up and saying hello to the world as bright as a button.'

Within a few minutes Dan had joined them in the lab. He was about to ask a question but hesitated. Now that he knew the Stranger could speak, he felt he couldn't talk about him in the same way. He found himself staring, until Jack broke the silence.

'Let me introduce our Mission Controller, Dan Marshall.'

'Hello, Dan Marshall.'

The voice was even, though not flat. In fact Dan was surprised how bright it was. 'Er, hi there. Pleased to meet you properly at last. Tell me – who am I addressing?'

'Ah.' It was Jack again. 'Thereby hangs a tale. It seems our visitor doesn't know the answer to that question.'

The Stranger looked down at his hands. 'I regret that is true. I have no memory of how I came to be here.'

'Okay,' said Dan. 'So what *do* you remember?'

'Nothing.'

3

Dan was back in his office. Dr Schlesinger was at a loss. 'I'm sorry, Colonel, but right now I can't throw much light on this. Initial scans are... inconclusive.'

'Why do I find that word so troubling right now?'

Schlesinger began to defend himself, saying that he'd not yet had chance to do a proper brain or body scan.

'Okay, okay,' said Dan. 'Let me think a moment. The tests can wait. We need to talk to this guy. We need to do it as soon as possible, and we need to do it away from the public eye. And the military. He seems physically fit, no obvious sign of any infection, so we don't need to keep him up here a day longer.'

He called Sam in. 'Sam, we need to accelerate the transfer. Our friend, if he is a friend, needs to move on sooner rather than later.'

Sam had not been idle. 'That's not a problem. I've found an available shuttle and it will be docking in three hours. It'll have room for a pilot and up to four passengers.'

'Very good. And thanks, Sam, as always.'

Next Dan called the lab. 'Jack, I need you, Jim, Natasha and our guest to be ready for flight in two hours. And Jack... are you okay with being our security here? I'm in no hurry to call in extra help, but if you'd rather not–'

'No, no. Let's not add any more than we need. Our guest is quite docile.'

Dan ended the call and sent Schlesinger back to Zone 4. Then, breathing more easily, he turned once more to his trusty aide. 'There are just a couple of things I need you to do for me, Sam, before I leave the station myself. First off, I want Ryan to take a closer look at this crystal.'

'Of course,' said Sam. 'Though I don't think there's much more he can do with the equipment he has here on Alpha.'

'Exactly. So I need Ryan on the next scheduled flight back to Earth, to give him some time before we open this thing up to the world.' He sighed. 'I need to talk to Bridlington before I go.' He hoped she would honour a request that the crystal be removed from the station as soon as possible. It didn't feel safe.

'Sure thing,' said Sam. 'Is that the couple of things?'

'Not quite.' Dan smiled. 'I need you somehow to convince the press that they'd be better employed back on Earth now.'

4

The ESS Herschel slipped away from the vast clamps and seals that had been its moorings for only a matter of hours and turned silently away from the central hub of Space Station Alpha. Destination Earth. It was part of the small fleet of shuttles owned and operated by the European Space Agency, and right now you could be forgiven for thinking that it was making a standard return trip after delivering cargo and passengers.

Jim sat alone in the cockpit, dressed in his mission overall, apparently monitoring the autopilot settings, but actually mulling over the momentous events of the last few weeks. His return to a flight deck brought to mind the journey home from Venus. In many ways it had gone smoothly, with the Resolution's new nuclear-powered engines efficiently fighting the sun's gravitational pull and bringing them home in record time. 'Endeavour returns on angel-wings' was one headline.

But it had been a difficult journey. Difficult because of the Stranger, the crew, the already emerging politics and the need for secrecy. And of all those challenges, which had been the most difficult? He didn't need to think about that for long. It was the crew. A crew he thought he knew. He had enjoyed sketching all of them during training, in his beloved manner of caricature – Jack the cool Brit, tall, dark and handsome (if not quite as dark as he must once have been). He'd drawn him with a chiselled chin, riding an old bike with wings. A man with a past, but with enough vigour yet for a promising future. He'd decided against a kilt, as Scottish was not the first thing you thought of when you saw Jack, nor even the second. Ryan had a baseball cap, obviously, but with a microscope stuck to the peak, on a head too large for his slight frame. Both men had happily displayed the sketches in their quarters. Natasha's he had held back, and she didn't ask.

He thought about the three of them now. Jack's flying credentials were solid, of course. A pilot in the air arm of Britain's Royal Navy, he was not an unusual choice for an astronaut. They had not flown together before, yet he had become a good friend during the hurried training for their unscheduled mission. But had it all been too cosy? The man had been a British spy! Why on earth was he assigned to the mission? Dan Marshall had never made much of it, and Jim had trusted that because he trusted Dan. But in the cold light of space it was suspicious.

As for Ryan, he was scarily clever, which was never reassuring, but he was Dan Marshall's protégé and that was surely a plus. And his rare combination of skills and experience – organic electronics and environmental physics – had fitted him perfectly for a mission that added telescope repair to atmosphere analysis. But here again things no longer seemed so straightforward. When they had said their goodbyes on Alpha just an hour before, Ryan had looked distracted. Dan had met with him separately. What was that about?

And then there was Natasha, holed up with the Stranger in her new self-appointed role as guard – or was it guardian? True, no one else had wanted to keep an eye on him, but what was it with this woman? And what was she doing here on this particular trip?

A heatshield alert came on, momentarily pulling him back to the task at hand. Then he looked back over his shoulder into the small cabin where his four passengers sat. Dan, Jack and Natasha, also back in their mission overalls, were readying themselves for re-entry to the earth's atmosphere. Jim turned his brooding attention to their mysterious ward, now dressed in civvies and sitting perfectly calm, his odd suit doubtless packed off for testing. The press were starting to call him Icarus. He knew who'd come up with that name, of course: Melody Grantley James, the spy's girlfriend. In her second exclusive she had referred to the ancient myth about the hapless fellow who had flown on artificial wings too close to the sun, whereupon the wax in his father's latest invention had melted and sent him crashing into the Aegean Sea. Well, that's not where they were headed now, and Ms James was not coming with them either... though Jim couldn't help wondering whether, if there had been another seat, she'd have been on board as well. And that brought him back to the politics of all this. He shook his head and turned his attention back to the instrument panel.

The extra heatshield had just been deployed, and their angle of descent had altered slightly. He switched on the intercom. 'Hold tight, everybody. We're beginning re-entry.'

Natasha looked at the Stranger. His eyes were closed and hands open. She fought the urge to hold one of them and gazed out of the window instead. No stars, no black either; just a bluish blur turning to white. It would be good to step again on *terra firma*, though she had been informed that their first landing was going to be on an aircraft-carrier somewhere in the Atlantic Ocean. From there they would be transferred to a secret location. Not the welcome home she had expected, though that didn't matter now. She was where she needed to be. Where she was needed.

When it came, the transfer was surprisingly brief. They were escorted from the Herschel directly into a plane which took off without delay. Not so much as a comfort break. The seatbelt light came off not a moment too soon, and Natasha made for the washroom. Somehow Venus had seemed much simpler.

5

Melody was enjoying a bear hug in Zone 1's communal kitchen. 'I'm going to miss you, Sam.'

'Aw, get outta here. You've barely seen your guy since he got back. You need to go.'

She straightened up and checked her hair, pinned up in a bun ready for the spacesuit she was soon to don. 'I know. But I do want you to know how much I appreciate all you've done. And that's not just professionally. You're a real friend, Sam.'

He scratched his head and leant back on the worktop. 'So, where are you off to next? Back to London?'

'Not quite. The press shuttle I'm on is going to London, but as the space dock is in Kent I thought I'd go see a friend in Canterbury.'

'That's nice. But what about Jack? When's he likely to get out of wherever it is they're going?'

Sam appeared to know as little as Mel did about the next stage in the proceedings, possibly even less. Was he pumping her for information? 'That depends on when he calls me to come and see him,' she said, 'wherever that might be!' She smiled, the familiar sparkle still shining in her eyes.

The truth was, Melody had no idea when she would see Jack again. The transfer of the Stranger had happened so fast that they had had no more than a few minutes to say goodbye. 'I'll see you soon – wait for my call' was all she had got from him.

She left the kitchen and finished packing the few items of carry-on luggage in her quarters. Half an hour later, dressed in tank top and shorts with her bag strapped to her back, and accompanied by a member of station personnel who took her suitcase, she entered one of the lifts that transferred travellers from the rim to the central hub. This meant leaving artificial gravity, so as they ascended she braced herself for the change. The first time she had done this she had been caught out, expecting it to happen gradually, forgetting that the lift was providing its own G-force while it bore them up. As soon as it came to a halt, nearly all sense of gravity was gone.

She took hold of one of the many handles in the spacious cubicle, while her companion pressed a button to open the door. That had been the second surprise on her first trip. When travelling off-station the exit door was the ceiling. Following her guide's lead she gently pushed off from the floor and drifted out of the lift into a suiting-up area. Using the ever present handles she landed on her feet. Next she took off her rucksack and stepped into a decidedly second-hand-looking space suit – a large and dumpy affair – before carefully making her way towards an airlock door, bag in hand. She was not yet completely weightless, as there was still some velocity in the station's rotation, but the feeling of lightness coupled with the awkward suit made an elegant walk impossible.

Some flashing lights caught her eye and she looked up at the sign overhead: 'You are now entering the differential collar. Pressurised suits must be worn at all times.' She pulled an expensive-looking version of a shower cap over her pinned hair, donned the helmet and clicked it into place, giving a thumbs-up to her guide, and proceeded alone into the airlock where her suitcase was already waiting. A few seconds after the door closed she heard the tell-tale hiss of air rushing away. In her helmet a loud voice now broke in, warning her of the need to step with care when she exited the airlock. Amber warning lights flashed. The tension of the moment served to lessen the sensation of lightness, almost as if the commotion was causing its own kind of artificial gravity.

A door on the other side of the airlock now opened, where a short staircase automatically extended, much like those on small jet aircraft. Carefully she hung onto its banister, finally yielding her carry-on bag and leaving it with her case for an attendant to collect, and made her way down the steps which rather unnervingly ended a few inches short of the floor. With little grace and a muted yelp she made the tiny leap, congratulating herself on bouncing only once before she came to a halt. Here, while one assistant went to fetch her luggage, another took her by the hand and led her to a seat where she strapped herself in.

She looked around. She was in a small cabin-like room. It was the spin shuttle, part of the giant collar that separated most of the station from the hub. She watched as the attendant secured her baggage and the staircase from the airlock retracted. A door then sealed them in. Within seconds more flashing lights heralded another alarm that sounded in her helmet speakers. A vibration in the seat and the floor told her that the room had begun to move, though with no windows it was hard to tell by how much. After a few moments it felt like some of her internal organs were shifting. Automatically she tried to shake her hair, as if that might shake off the sensation, but soon wished she hadn't. Her head was still contained by a heavy helmet. She groaned.

A couple of minutes later the guide stood up and unfastened Melody's safety belt, advising her to get up carefully as they were now in zero-G. She had made it to her docking gate.

She paused as her brain adjusted its perspective to make sense of what had just happened. She knew full well of course that it was the rest of the station that moved incessantly around the core: she had actually been transferred from a moving environment to a stationary one, even though at the time it had seemed to be the other way round.

A memory surfaced. She was sitting on a train waiting at a station. Outside the window was another train. Suddenly it looked like her train was pulling out of the station, because she could see the neighbouring carriages moving past her window. But who was really moving? Was it her train or the other one, or both? The only way to find out was to turn her head and look across to the other side, where a stationary platform obliged by suddenly wrenching her perception back from motion to stillness.

Right now she was in Space Station Alpha's central hub which contained the four docking stations used by incoming spacecraft. The hub remained motionless, relative to approaching vessels. This arrangement meant that they could fly in and dock without having to match the spin of the station. Inside the collar she had just spun down from one revolution a minute to zero. And her perspective had shifted. What had seemed solid and unmoving in the outer rim – if you didn't look out of a window – was now revealed to be in a perpetual spin. Not for the first time Melody thought about the significant, even subversive, role played by perspective in human perception.

At a signal from her guide she retrieved her hand luggage and boarded the earthbound shuttle, a large people-carrier, where she quickly grabbed a window seat and waited as the remaining passengers arrived in ones and twos. In the end there were about a dozen other journalists and TV presenters on board. Once the cabin was pressurised, she stashed her helmet under her seat, detached the life-support system, and made herself as comfortable as her suit would allow.

The craft was more like a small plane, its main bay designed to be fitted out for people or cargo as required. In its current configuration there were ten rows of four seats each, with a central aisle. As it turned out, only a few people chose window seats. Some evidently wanted to file reports rather than be reminded they were flying through space in a tin can which was about to reach over a thousand degrees on the outside. Others, meanwhile, were content to take their last opportunity to chat with the competitors who had been a part of their lives for the last few days, perhaps sensing the imminent end of the unity that comes with outer space. Back to business as usual.

At the sound of giant clamps being released Melody looked outside. She could see they were slowly backing away from the hub. Craning to see as far forwards as she could, she marvelled not for the first time at the wonder of engineering that had been her home these past eleven weeks. The ship started to bank, and she turned her gaze upwards, revelling in the smooth transition of black to deep blue to light blue. The earth's atmosphere seemed just a meteor-throw away, a tenuous veil that somehow proved sufficient to ensure life could thrive down on the surface.

The view was short-lived, as suddenly the window shields came down to protect them from the glare of the unfiltered sun. She smiled, as it made her think once more of Icarus and his fabled brush with the sun's merciless heat. Why had she thought of that in connection with the Stranger? Was it just that Venus was closer to the sun than the earth? Or was there another reason, buried somewhere in her subconscious, something to do with the stowaway himself? Could he be in trouble? Might he have come crashing down in his own version of the Aegean Sea?

How she would love to meet him! Yes, to get the scoop interview, but that wasn't the only reason. He was now going to become the biggest thing in Jack's life, and that meant he was personally important to her too. And maybe there was something else. What if this man of mystery really was an alien from another world? What knowledge might he bring with him? What answers might he have to life's biggest questions?

She surprised herself by thinking along these lines, but it was a reminder that millions of others would be doing the very same thing. She took out a tablet from her rucksack and started to catch up with what the world below was saying about the man from Venus. Up to this point she hadn't really been interested, but she knew that all too soon social and mass media would become two (or was that one?) of the most important factors in what happened next. There were going to be some wacky ideas out there, while serious journalism would have to wait till more information came to light.

And for that, at the very least, Melody Grantley James needed Commander Forrester. Though the Stranger himself would be even better.

She sat back in her seat. There was nothing to be done until she regained access. And with that thought she swapped the tablet for her make-up bag. There were other issues to sort out, more personal if not more pressing. And right now she could think of only one person she could discuss them with. David.

CHAPTER 6

Arrivals

1

The smooth, pale façade of the *Palais de Nations* had been the pride of Geneva for around a hundred and fifty years. Still fronted by the *Allée* with its steel avenue of national flags, it had recently become the world's largest base of the United Nations. None could compute the outcomes of the deals struck in its many rooms, still less those in its busy corridors.

For most of this time the International Atomic Energy Agency had maintained a dogged presence here, working hard for the peaceful use of such hazardous energy. A loud collective cheer had gone up when space engineers finally found a way to apply nuclear fusion to speed human beings to Mars, more than halving the journey time. The note of celebration did not drop when the Mars programme was suddenly interrupted by Venus. In fact the drama of it all gave human-crew space travel an unexpected boost.

All this served to swell the ranks of the World Space Agency and to strengthen the arm of its formidable Director. At sixty-two years of age, nearer the end of her career than the beginning, Constance Bridlington now found herself at the head of a revitalised organisation. Space travel was back in the news. New links were being forged between national governments and private enterprise.

Ms Bridlington didn't have to keep telling herself she had handled things rather well – she was quite comfortable with the knowledge. When the Window on Venus opened, the data coming in provided all the leverage and incentive this skilled operator required to gather the world's best, and she had taken only weeks to spin her complex web of scientists, business tycoons and diplomats.

She had been but two years into the job when a Russian-built WSA probe made its first startling report as it circled our bright but shy sister planet. For decades astronomers had made do with blurred photographs and radio images of the surface of Venus, blanketed as it was by thick clouds of carbon dioxide and sulphur. Even the probes that had landed bore limited fruit. For the Venusian atmosphere was not just a dead-end for visible-spectrum astronomy; it was an effective barrier to direct human exploration, threatening all comers with its deadly cocktail of pressure, heat and acidity. Venus was stand-offish in the extreme, which was why Mars was the natural place to pursue the adventure of planetary exploration. While scientists searched for signs of life long past, entrepreneurs focused on life that might thrive in the future. No one denied that Mars should be the first major planet to be colonised by the human race.

That view had not changed. The Mars programme had slipped only a little way down the priority listing. But the spotlight was certainly on Venus for the time being. When data from the Venus 2 probe revealed what amounted to a hole forming in the hostile atmosphere – the now famous 'Window' – the level of excitement soon eclipsed everything else, far surpassing the last time Venus went to the top of the bill, when phosphines had been detected in the atmosphere decades before.

Yet if there hadn't been much excitement over Venus, there had been no lack of attention. This had grown alongside Earth's own global greenhouse problems. Unmanned probes had set out on a steady stream of short-lived suicide missions to investigate the planet's surface, where the carbon dioxide was first generated, sending back data on the complex relationship between crust and atmosphere. But at no time was a personal visit ever entertained as a possibility. Until now. What might this Window of opportunity do for the cause of global cooling back home?

The reason for the sudden drop in lethal conditions remained unknown, but the opportunity was too good to miss. First a probe that was already in orbit was sent down to the surface where the strange phenomenon was taking place. This confirmed that, when the crew were ready, the Endeavour should survive for several hours, maybe even days. There was no assurance of a long stay, but Constance felt sure that the growing drop in pressure, temperature and acidity would allow a meaningful expedition to the surface. A human team might even exceed what an unmanned lander could achieve. But even if they didn't, to walk on such a world... How could we not?

Her immediate challenge had been to convince the various member states of the Agency. Enter Messrs Coates and Box who provided the speedy journey and the space suits that would make it all possible.

She had already met Hugh Coates, a man of similar age to her own. Although his work in telecommunications was legendary, she hadn't put much store by his forays into nuclear power until it emerged that he was designing and developing a new generation of even faster and more efficient nuclear-powered spacecraft. It seemed that, for Mr Coates, the world was not enough. So it was that Nuclear Aerospace became a real player and soon provided the necessary acceleration – both political and physical – to get us to Venus while the Window remained open. How long that would be, nobody knew.

So much for getting us there. It was Conway Box who had provided the solution to the survival problem facing the chosen few who would finally get to step outside the ship. Box Industries had been developing polymers for more than twenty years, specialising in exploration suits for hostile environments. And nothing would be more hostile than Venus, even a Venus off the boil.

The mission was finalised in record time, and the new engines provided both the acceleration and the braking power needed to cut the trip to a record-breaking thirty-five days. On Venus itself initial conditions had proved acceptable, if not welcoming, and the mission soon proved to be an unqualified success. A highly skilled crew were able to gather bucketloads of data in the interests of understanding global overheating. Everything was working smoothly and without incident.

All that had changed with the arrival of the Stranger.

Constance moved to a small meeting room near her office. Brushing off a passing colleague's 'Hi, Connie!' with a shiver and a forced grin, she took up her position by a window to await Dan Marshall's arrival. Dan had proved himself more than able in this crisis, but she couldn't say the same about the Endeavour crew. What was going on with them? Was all the emotional unrest down to the mysterious stowaway? Or had the mission got to them in some other way? Her instinct told her finding the answer to that question should be her priority, even if everyone else was focusing on the new star of the show.

The glass door of the meeting room clicked open. Her assistant, an eager young man yet to complete his thirtieth year on this planet, was clearly excited. 'Colonel Marshall, Ma'am.'

'Thank you, Petroc. Coffee, Dan?'

'Thank you, no – I don't think we have time. My, er, colleagues are waiting downstairs.'

She raised an eyebrow. 'Yes, of course. But a word first, if you would. Thank you, Petroc, that will be all.'

The crestfallen aide withdrew. Constance and Dan sat at the end of the meeting table (more glass) and looked at each other. With her light floral jacket-cum-cardigan, short straight hair, wide-rimmed glasses and no-nonsense tones, the Director reminded Dan of his old school headmistress.

'Downstairs?' she quizzed.

'A figure of speech – they're safe enough, in the Old Town. The medics have only just left them, under some duress. They've hardly readjusted to normal gravity.'

'They'll have time enough for that. I'm more concerned about their psychological state. Have you formulated any ideas yet? What do you think is going on?'

He sighed. 'It's hard to say, it really is. Ryan and Natasha hadn't met before training, of course, and Jim and Jack hadn't actually been on a mission together.'

'Yes, and don't say it – the training was unforgivably short.'

'Hardly unforgivable,' said Dan. 'No one knew how much time we had, and if we'd waited any longer we'd have missed our chance, as we now know. Still, if I'm honest, I'm most concerned about Jim. In all the years I've known him I've hardly ever seen him get riled – not by anything or anyone. Yet since his return – in fact, since the incident on Venus, as far as I can make out – he's really had it in for Jack.'

'How much of that do you think is due to Jack being given custody of the Stranger?'

'Well, it's all of it and none of it. What I mean is, it's the presenting reason, but it's not enough to make the Jim I know lose his equilibrium – or his professionalism.'

Constance gazed towards the window, though she wasn't really looking beyond the glass. 'You talk about "the" incident, as if finding the Stranger is all that happened. But you and I both know that some strange things were going on outside the Endeavour as well.'

Dan nodded. 'Jim went out into the storm in search of Ryan, only to black out and have no recall of what went on for about an hour. Yet his report amounts to little more than "I found Ryan on the ground, I blacked out, we both came to and made it back to the ship". A masterful exercise in telling me next to nothing.'

Constance sighed. 'You know I have people on my back wanting the stowaway put in a secure facility right away?'

Dan looked at her while she stood motionless by the window with her back to him, her tall figure reflected in the glass table. 'I don't doubt it,' he said. 'The Russians, of course.'

'Yes, and the Chinese, and the Americans.' Her shoulders tightened.

Suddenly she turned on her heels and crossed the room to the door. 'Right, Dan, I think it's time for you to complete your journey – that is... you, Jack, Natasha and our guest. You can send Jim up here.'

Dan opened his mouth to say something, but he knew that look and left the room.

2

A late sun streamed through the open window as Miranda checked the clock by her bed. She must have dozed off. After a quick lick and a change of top she checked her eband for messages and alerts, made a couple of notes and then left the room. She took a few steps down the hallway and was about to knock on Hugh's door when she heard his voice inside. He was on a call, either via his tablet or, more likely, his ridiculously secure eband. As she hesitated it struck her as ironic that the oldest way of overhearing a conversation was still the best – by occupying the same physical space.

'No, no, it's good to keep contact. As soon as I have more I'll let you know. And I take it you'll do the same for me.'

Miranda heard no reply, but then she knew that Hugh would be wearing an earpiece. She knocked.

'Good. Have to go.' The door opened, and Hugh ushered her in.

'Wow,' she intoned as she stepped past him. 'Don't often see you in shorts. Did you get to speak to Conway Box?'

'Yes, I did. He's cool – at the moment, at any rate. He's decided the best way to gain any intelligence, considering the routes available to him, is to ask for all the Aphrodite mission space suits to be sent to him for testing... in the interests of R and D.'

'Makes sense.' She crossed to a small table close by the balcony window. It was empty except for a bowl of olives and she popped one in her mouth as she sat down. 'What about *our* available routes? Are you picking up anything on the monitor?'

'Well, it's working, if that's what you mean. We have a clear signal. But whether we'll get any intelligence is, of course, a completely different matter.'

The day after they had arrived Hugh and Miranda had walked up to the monastery, which happily turned out to be a public retreat centre as well, and played tourist. With Hugh's show of interest backed up by the offer of a handsome donation, the Abbot was happy to show them around, and Miranda had been able to conceal five super-sensitive recording devices in various parts of the building and in both courtyards. Once activated, these would work together to pick up most of the movements and conversations that would go on. The final piece in the set had been to install a relay in the perimeter wall, a necessary extra due to the formidable electronic screen that covered the place.

Hugh joined her at the table. 'Juice?' She nodded. 'The fact is,' he continued, 'all we may have by this time next week is a detailed understanding of the workings of a monastery – if that's what it really is. If all the business happens on the upper floor, we're going to have to rely on open windows and some very fine tuning to get anything from the array at all.'

She nodded, though she wasn't worried. The whole enterprise thus far had been exhilarating, and that was worth it whatever the final outcome.

3

Spartan Laboratories may not have been kitted out with the latest in all things geotech, but it suited Ryan Chase perfectly. It was a world of electronics – his first love – yet also sported some of the latest gear in environmental analysis. After each field trip he would return to his own corner of the independent lab complex and subject his finds to a wide range of tests and analysis. Spartan had given him what he needed to achieve a doctorate by his mid-twenties, through which he had laid the path for a new level of electronics using insights from what he called living-cell technology. Before long he moved into a small apartment adjacent to the facility in California. Today, after what was surely the wildest 'field trip' he would ever undertake, he was heading back home, leaving the airport and instructing his hire-car to pick its way across the ever-widening skirts of LA towards the eastern edges of Orange County. The vehicle was conventional, aerocars being as impractical in built-up areas as they were in mountainous regions.

Back on Space Station Alpha the man who had done so much to open doors for the young scientist had given him a piece of Venus with the words, 'Go home and play with that.' Colonel Marshall had spied the young UN army cadet very early on in his career, soon realising that the great outdoors was pulling him in a different direction from the military route. Ryan's flair for all things electronic, coupled with his passion for environmental physics, seemed to Dan to make him a timely fit for the latest satellite-clearing programme. They had talked it all through, and within a year Ryan was working on Space Station Alpha. 'Colonel Marshall' soon became 'Dan' as the young scientist's brilliance was steered into a career that took him all over the globe in the cause of healing the environment.

Of course, no one was sure the crystal really was a piece of Venus, and after the light show in his office it seemed to Dan that it might just as well be treated as an artificial device of some kind. An ideal project for the new field of electronics his protégé had pioneered.

Ryan sat back in the driving seat, allowing the car to find its way home. His eye roamed carelessly over the dashboard – such a simple affair after the Endeavour. He wouldn't disengage the autodrive till he was well away from the suburban sprawl that now filled most of the county. As he motored along the freeway he looked through the darkened windows across the lanes of traffic at the arid desert around him, and reflected how it was a cool, clear paradise compared with where he had just been. Everyone knew the world was in trouble, but even now he couldn't help clinging onto the belief that there was still time to avoid a global environmental catastrophe. Venus must never be a model for our own future.

He took the silvery-white ball out of a box and turned it over in his hands, polishing it lightly against his unbuttoned check shirt. It was a once-in-a-lifetime find, that was for sure, and maybe never to be repeated after he was gone. For even now data was coming in from two Venus orbiters confirming the suspicions they had had while on the planet. Pressure levels were rocketing back to normal, and with them the temperature. The Window was closing.

In the handful of hours he had had for field trips on Venus he had taken in-situ readings and bagged loads of samples from various locations within the bubble of less horrific conditions that marked out their exploration zone. But it was the Russian's find that had eclipsed all the treasures he had unearthed (or was that unvenused? unvenerated?). Koroleva had decided to concentrate her excavation on one small area instead and had come back with what they were loosely naming 'the crystal'. Somehow she had convinced Jim that it need not be stashed in a box on the journey home, and so it had been afforded decorative status in the cockpit of the Endeavour. Even Ryan had had to admit that it looked the part, and it was no great surprise when he saw it on Dan's desk on Alpha.

What was a surprise was that he was holding it now. Koroleva was the undisputed expert on Venus. So was this a case of the Colonel giving special treatment to his own? Maybe. But he knew that wasn't Dan's style – he would never favour Ryan to the detriment of others. But he had always given him room to prove himself, so that must be what was happening now. And, besides, the Russian had business elsewhere, with the real star of the show – Mr Freaky in his curious outfit. Once Ryan was done with the crystal, maybe he could get a look at the enigmatic suit of the space man. Maybe. One mystery at a time.

The crystal was a smooth spheroid with rounded edges and corners, whitish in colour yet translucent, though less heavy than solid glass. He might even catalogue it as a dodecahedron, as the twelve pentagonal faces were remarkably equal in size. If the even, polished effect wasn't artificial, it had to be down to erosion, but by what? It had been pulled out of a piece of rock that had caught Koroleva's attention by being much darker than its immediate surroundings – an island of purple in a sea of yellow, she had called it. That had been intriguing enough, never mind the later reports of glowing and buzzing. It made no sense.

He peered at it. It was totally inert. How could it be anything else? If only he could have studied it in Dan's office when it had come to life for a few brief moments. Maybe something there had affected it, or it had reacted with something on the station in some kind of resonance. Maybe it wasn't inert but dormant.

If that were true, he felt his best bet would be to try to recreate the conditions on Alpha. But first things first. He would begin by examining its structure at the microscopic level. He punched the dashboard and called Dan to let him know his plan. Somehow he felt that now was not the time to take a piece out of it.

Not yet.

4

David Carter was a man on a mission. Ever since leaving university more than twenty years earlier, he had committed his life to building a church like the one he had encountered during his studies. Impacted by an experience that had been inconveniently mystical in nature, he had nevertheless driven a straight course ever since: a life of faithfulness to 'the word' (as he had learnt to call the Bible) and to the calling he had sensed to 'build My church', a church where people counted for more than bricks or stone. Over the years he had played a pivotal role in establishing a small but vibrant congregation that was committed to systematic Bible study, to gathering for prayer and worship, and to reaching out to the wider community, working for their good and inviting them to respond to the claim that Jesus had died for their sins.

That community was situated just a few miles from the symbolic seat of the national church in Britain, Canterbury Cathedral. David had no truck with major denominations, but whenever he could he soaked in the sacred space of this ancient building, taking pains to avoid both tourist and congregation in his search for peace and quiet.

His own church was a small and unpretentious shell of a building on a not-so-new industrial estate on the edge of the city. Funding his own salary through his work as a print and web designer, he had managed to secure ownership of the building through mortgaging the all-too-splendid house that he and his wife Alice had been gifted by her parents.

He was in that house now, looking out of his study window to the garden that still amazed him every time he really looked at it. Alice proved to have the same effect on plants as she did on people: in her presence they came to life, somehow feeding off the belief she clearly had in them and the attention she wholeheartedly gave to them.

Alice. People talked of soul mates far too glibly. But you knew when it was for real. They had never been blessed with children, but such pain as she had she bore with a lightness that bore no grudge, finding in the church a needy family she could tend with love and practical care.

He looked at himself in the small mirror that hung on the only piece of wall not lined with books. Somebody had recently described his wife's hair as mousy. If it was, it was the only mousy thing about her. His was a similar shade of brown, apart from flecks of grey distributed across the top and down the sides. His hairline hadn't receded appreciably, granting him the boyish looks that ensured the ladies of the church mothered him mercilessly.

And then there was Melody. She was coming to see them today. Nearly a year with scarcely a word, and now here she was, apparently ready to re-enter their lives.

The doorbell rang as if on cue. He heard Alice answer it, bright and positive, as if she had somehow packed away all the angst from the hours of counselling and coaching they had both poured into the young journalist. Mel was back, doubtless on her own terms as always.

He fluffed his wiry hair with his fingers and applied his practised pastoral face before going through to join them.

5

Glass doors at the front of the UN building slid quietly open for a tall figure dressed in US Air Force uniform who confidently approached the security point. 'Colonel Adamson for Ms Bridlington.'

The duty officer called upstairs and then directed Jim through security. 'Go through and you'll be met by one of her aides.'

Jim walked through the scanner and crossed the wide, polished lobby to an elevator where a young man was already waiting.

'Colonel Adamson? My name is Petroc Naismith. May I say what an honour it is to meet you? Please follow me.'

Another Brit.

They made the ascent to the third floor and Petroc ushered Jim into Ms Bridlington's office before retreating to his own, where he poured himself a coffee and switched on his eband. The device looked like one of the many models on the market, but this one had an added extra all its own, courtesy of his benefactor and secret employer, Hugh Coates.

He had met the multi-billionaire at a technology fair shortly after graduating at Oxford. He was of course not the only person with a first in their renowned PPE degree (Philosophy, Politics and Economics), but he was one of the few that day to impress the entrepreneur. Petroc had been taking an Infostructure employee to task about the horrific number of nanosatellites in orbit around the earth, and the legal nightmare surrounding what to do with them when their orbits degraded. Hugh was always on the lookout for new talent that would address weaknesses in his complex line of work, and when he saw it he wasted no time. Before the day was over he had offered the young graduate funding for further training in space treaty law and a placement at his Manchester facility in Britain. This was the nerve centre for the socio-political analysis that Infostructure pursued as part of their drive to keep up with cultural trends. Stints in the New York and Adelaide offices followed before a brief spell in the top secret facility in Bruges in Belgium. Brief but career-changing.

During these early years he had familiarised himself with the complex web that was Infostructure, but only in Bruges did he learn that there were other ways he could help them keep one step ahead. After signing an even more intense version of the company's confidentiality agreement, an apparently casual chat with 'the Chief' (as Hugh was universally known in-house) opened a new door. Within a month he found himself working incognito at the European headquarters of the United Nations. He had to land the job on his own merits, but the whole process cemented his view that he was working close to where real power operated. That was not in the United Nations of course, which had always had to pursue negotiation over control, but in the microscopically fine global network that was Infostructure.

And so here he was in the offices of the World Space Agency, an eye and an ear for the man who had eyes and ears everywhere. As he sipped his coffee he switched his discreet wireless earpiece to what his eband was receiving on a heavily encrypted channel. He was surprised how far they had already got into the conversation. Bridlington was not one for small talk, but this was fast even for her. She was demanding that Jim tell her just what was going on with his crew.

'Well, that's just it, Ma'am – they're hardly *my* crew.'

'What do you mean? With the global dimension of the project, you could hardly have expected to be given your first choice of pilot, let alone pick your own scientists.'

'No, that's true. But a spy on the team? I'm beginning to wonder whether I was ever really Captain of the ship.'

There was a pause, followed by a scrunching sound and then silence. Petroc quickly switched channel. He had noticed only that morning some serious deterioration in the gilt design on her personalised coffee mug – the design that housed the paper-thin electronics that was receiving and transmitting right now. He could control a lot of things in her office, but not the ferocity with which her assistants scrubbed the dishes.

A second bug now kicked in. He was particularly pleased with this one: a piece of duct tape containing the same kind of device, stuck to the underside of her desk alongside a few other bits of genuine tape. Should the desk ever be turned over, they would look perfectly innocent, like something left over from the factory.

The sound was less clear, but good enough. '–your research engineer lost consciousness, you lost consciousness, your pilot nearly died, and I have nothing to begin to explain any of it! No, let me finish. I'm not blaming you for the conditions – we knew they were never going to be friendly. But I see nothing in your report about what actually happened to Chase, or why you should black out when you did.'

'Well, that's because we don't know. I'm just giving you the facts – what actually happened.'

There was silence for several seconds.

'All right. But what about this animosity between you and Jack? I thought you'd become best buddies! What did he actually do to upset you? Apart from follow orders?'

At this point a fellow aide knocked at the door and quickly entered Petroc's office. He had to leave the earpiece running and do his best to ignore it, knowing the eband would continue recording anyway. In fact he was pretty sure it was transmitting to Infostructure's secret hub in Bruges as well. He'd be surprised if it wasn't. He turned his attention to the girl at his door.

'Hey, Petroc – do you have a spare tablet charger?'

It took a while to sort her out – this particular aide seemed to take a special interest in him. While three years ago he would have put that down to his own natural charm, now he found it suspicious. Truth was, he found everyone suspicious. He shrugged. Such was the life of espionage.

When she was gone he switched off the earpiece, deciding to listen to the recording later on. And when, just minutes later, Adamson strode past his office, he switched his eband and himself back to normal. He was a keen, green aide once again.

6

'Are we not nearly there yet?'

It was impossible to ignore Natasha's slight misfire at humour, and Dan and Jack looked squarely at the way ahead as they suppressed their laughter. Dan was driving a spacious hire-car up the road to Montagnola, with Jack riding shotgun. Natasha was in the back with the Stranger who appeared to be asleep. They had just heard that Jim was on his way back to the States. Jack couldn't deny he was relieved.

'It's not far now,' said Dan, allowing himself a chuckle. 'I guess we'll all be glad of a good night's rest. Hold on, though... what's this?' The car's navigation console, which had been preset for them back in Geneva, was telling him to turn off the main highway into an unmarked road. 'Okay... clearly we're not going into the village.'

The evening twilight quickly succumbed to the shadows of the forest. For a while the car headlamps showed nothing but tarmac between the trees, then something more like a dirt track, until they came to another turning which they were instructed to take. After five more minutes they reached a high stone wall in which was set what appeared to be a large solid gate. It was closed.

'Looks like it's the tradesman's entrance for us,' Jack said. He got out of the car and immediately felt the cool mountain air on his face. Closing the car door behind him, he strode over to what turned out to be a pair of large wooden doors. He tried a handle and pushed, but without success. 'They're locked!' he shouted. 'Wait a minute... there's something here.' On the right of the doors was a small metal panel.

After a moment's pushing and pulling it flipped open, revealing a solitary button. 'Okay,' he said to himself. 'Looks like there's a doorbell.' He pressed the button and waited. As he looked around he saw a small red light overhead in the trees. A live CCTV camera? He decided to watch it for a while – maybe someone was on the other end, someone who might be expecting them.

Dan was just getting out of the car to join him when Jack heard the distinctive sound of sliding bolts. He watched as the doors swung open, half-expecting to see some becowled monk appear out of the darkness beyond. But there was no one there.

He got back into the car, and Dan joined him. 'A bit flashy for a monastery, don't you think?' Dan commented as he moved the car slowly forward. 'I mean, remotely activated doors? What exactly is this place?'

'I assumed Bridlington let you know,' said Jack.

'All she said was that it's some kind of monastery. I wasn't expecting high-tech security.'

'Ah,' Jack replied, 'then you should have been. You know Constance Bridlington – not a lady to leave anything to chance.'

They drove on. The doors closed behind them and the road twisted through more trees for what the dashboard console told them was half a mile, before they came into an open area in front of a single-storey building, although Jack surmised it was the rear of the place. The dusk was supplemented here by a diffuse glow from lamps on the wall. And there at the door stood the anticipated monk, habit and all. Dan and Jack got out.

'Welcome, gentlemen.' The accent was Italian. 'And lady?'

Natasha got out of the car, went round and opened the other rear door. The Stranger was out before she could lift a finger, apparently wide awake now. His eyes sparkled in the lamplight.

'And this must be...'

Jack cut in. 'We'd like to go in, if you don't mind. It's been a long journey – longer than you know, I'm guessing.'

'Of course,' said the monk, who now pushed back his cowl to

reveal a full head of silver-grey hair. Jack guessed he was in his late sixties, maybe older. The man continued: 'But first, allow me to introduce myself. I am Abbot Leonardo, and I have in fact been fully briefed. Well,' and at this his eyes seemed to catch the light, 'perhaps I should say adequately briefed!'

'For sure,' Jack responded. 'I'd expect nothing less – and nothing more – from our Miss Bridlington. Lead on!'

They gathered up their luggage and followed the Abbot through a fairly narrow corridor, across a small courtyard, another corridor, then under a covered way to a larger building, and eventually via a cloister to some stairs. These delivered them, at last, to their rooms and long-awaited beds.

Five miles away Miranda switched off her tablet and left the cool of her balcony to retire for the night. Clearly nothing was happening yet.

CHAPTER 7

Enigmas

1

Melody closed the bedroom door behind her and slumped into a chair, tired and troubled. The adjustment to full earth gravity after so many weeks in the space station explained why her body felt so weary. She had only been down a matter of hours and everything felt weighed down, not least herself. But she knew that didn't explain the heaviness in her heart. She tried to sift through the conversations of the past evening. Alice had welcomed her warmly, if perhaps at a distance. Did she know something? Something even Melody herself couldn't yet put into words?

And then there was David. What was he feeling? What lay hidden under the not-so-easy banter and the downcast eyes? Was it regret? Did they not share something incredibly special when she allowed him to lead her on her spiritual journey? And hadn't they all three been together on the road?

It had been five years since she had first met David in the quiet of an almost empty cathedral, a man with no dress sense, above forty but with boyish features. There in the shadow of the shrine of

Thomas à Becket they had talked together about history, about politics, about suffering. It had all flowed quite naturally. When he gave her his contact details at the end of his conversation, it seemed only natural to say she might actually get in touch.

But then things moved on apace with Jack. Their careers provided a rare overlap which allowed them time to explore the world together, and each other. So it was nearly six months before she and David met up again. Despite the likelihood that he'd forgotten all about her, she messaged him to say she'd be in the area. Might they continue their conversation? She turned up at the house, only to be greeted by Alice, whereupon she let herself be enveloped in a blanket of warmth and sisterly affection.

It was during the second cup of tea that she had unfolded before Alice some of the many complications that featured in her psyche – her fascination with people, her wit and charm, unapologetically feminine, that so often became slaves to her need for affection and attention. And, with all that, a longing to know what really makes us human, and whether there might be some kind of cosmic reason for us being here – perhaps a task we must perform as caretakers of our planet and its immediate surroundings, especially now we were moving out into space. Her chosen form of journalism, human exploration and environmental issues, provided just enough satisfaction to pacify her more metaphysical angst, most of the time. But maybe now was the right moment to look into other avenues of knowledge. Even faith?

When David came home he naturally joined the conversation, delighted that Alice had made more progress in two hours than he had in two afternoons. And so began three years of what some might call counselling but what Melody recognised as a growing friendship. Although her job sent her far away at times, her London base was close enough for further meaningful cups of tea in Canterbury.

She looked at a pair of photographs framed on the wall above a chest of drawers. One showed Alice with a woman of similar age, the other Alice and David. No children.

Why had she connected with David so easily? And why was Jack so hostile to her association with this couple, accusing them (from a safe distance) of being little more than a religious cult? Once she'd put these two questions together, she saw the answer with a clarity so sudden it almost stung her eyes. Jack was jealous. Jealous of a couple – no, of a man – who could understand her at a depth he himself had not yet fathomed.

Maybe she had always understood this at some subconscious level, and maybe that was why she had stayed away for so long. And now, as she let the domestic air around her seep into her pores, she could see she had made a mistake in coming here. This was hardly the time for philosophical conversations, when the story of a lifetime was waiting less than two hours away.

She opened her valise, suddenly resolved to leave the very next morning. She told her eband to book a call with Bridlington. Enough of waiting. It was time to move closer to the action.

2

The sun was shining from a clear blue sky as Miranda stepped out on to her balcony. The sound of church bells came drifting across the village below. Hugh was standing on the next balcony along the hotel's flower-strewn front, sipping coffee.

'Good morning, Miranda. Sleep well?'

'Always. Any news?'

'Yes. You'd best come round.' He eyed her somewhat inadequately tied bathrobe with the quickest flick of an eye. 'When you're ready. Perhaps you could bring croissants?'

Thirty minutes later – dried and dressed and armed with a light breakfast – she joined Hugh in his room. They sat at a small table away from the open balcony door while he finished snipping his false beard, holding up his eband in selfie mode to function as a shaving mirror. His own sideburns needed attention too as they were longer than the provider of the disguise had anticipated. When he had finished she poured more coffee.

He lifted a croissant to his nose and took a deep breath, absorbing the freshness of the bakery that still lingered at this early hour. 'Good,' he began. 'I've had a brief report from Bruges, but Petroc filled me in with a few more details... you know, those emotional facts that get left out of written reports and secret recordings. It seems picking up the unexpected visitor wasn't the only strange thing that happened on Venus.'

Miranda sat back, ready to receive. She never tired of the confidence this man placed in her. 'What do we know?'

'Well, to be honest, it sounds like it was mayhem. When the storm hit they lost Chase, and when the Captain went out after him, they lost him. And both lost consciousness!'

'Could it be a suit failure?'

'That's possible, of course... yes, I suppose that's the most likely explanation. Probably something to do with the life support system. Maybe our Mr Box can fill us in on that score at some point. But the thing Petroc picked up concerns Adamson and Forrester. It seems they've had a falling out – apparently over Forrester turning out to be the on-board spy. Or one of them, at least.'

'Forrester's a spy?' Miranda leaned forward and broke open a croissant.

'Well, an agent for British Intelligence. Which we knew.'

'Oh.'

'I don't tell you everything, Miranda.'

'No, of course.' She took a swig of orange juice. 'Do you think maybe Forrester wasn't surprised to find someone on board?'

Hugh reached for his coffee, apparently considering her words. 'You know, Miranda, one of the things I like about you... one of the things... is the speed with which your alert mind moves to the really important questions. And this last question opens the door to a whole network of possibilities. But now, it's time to do some listening ourselves.'

'Sorry? You mean – ?'

'Yes. It seems our small party, minus the good captain, arrived last night under the radar.'

Hugh fetched his tablet from the bedroom and Miranda set about accessing the files that would soon yield a harvest from their recent fieldwork.

3

Natasha awoke with the sound of a bell, though whether it had been in a dream or come from outside she could not be sure. She was surprised to find it was still dark, and even when she opened the blind she saw only the hint of a new day. She looked around the room as her eyes adjusted. She could spy no clock, but her eband told her there was more than an hour to go before the breakfast time they had hastily arranged the night before. She decided to go for a walk.

She washed and dressed quickly, choosing her trusty cream-coloured tracksuit which sported a dark line down the arms and legs. As soon as she stepped into the corridor she halted. She had spent much of her life in institutions, latterly in the Russian armed forces, but this was different... somehow redolent of a happier time. She shrugged. Doubtless it would come back to her. Pressing on, she glided silently down the stairs and slipped into a courtyard. It was a larger one than they had come through the night before, faintly lit by reflected moonbeams filtering down from the walls above. She shivered.

She was standing in a corner of a cobbled square. There was an arched corridor all the way round, which she instantly recognised as a cloister. And with that a host of memories began to surface.

She decided to walk right round. She turned right and walked slowly. Half-way along the first side of the square she could just make out an alcove in the wall. With so little light coming through the arches behind her, she turned on the torch in her eband. It was a drinking fountain.

She pressed on, round the next corner to the left, with a closed door on her right. Half-way along the next wall was another alcove. This time she decided to let her hands do the looking, but when she traced them round the hollow she felt nothing at all. The torch confirmed that the alcove was empty.

She approached the next corner more slowly, as the door here was ajar and there was a faint glow. But there was no light on the other side of the door. Hearing and seeing nothing, she turned the corner in silence with just a touch of caution. As she entered the third side of the square she discovered the source of the light. At the half-way point, in the expected alcove, something was flickering. To get to it she had to pass an open corridor and then another door. There in the alcove was a small oil lamp, burning gently

One more corner and she was in the final side of the square. She approached the alcove with mounting anticipation. Again she gave her hands the task of initial exploration. There was a bowl, and something in it that ran between her fingers, generally soft but a bit gritty in parts. Once more the torch. It was soil.

Time to explore the courtyard. She turned and walked out into the open space and crossed the cobbles to a statue in the middle. Round it, quite low, ran a wide stone sill that served as a bench, so she sat down and faced the side with the oil lamp. The minutes went by. She started to imagine someone behind her, so she turned and looked up at the statue silhouetted against the lightening sky. It was a human figure, but more than that it was impossible to say.

She sat in the stillness and considered her surroundings. They could not have been more unexpected, and she wasn't sure even Jack had known where Dan had been taking them after they left Geneva. This was a place of stone walls and open spaces, where it felt like time could be made for reflection. And conversation, something that would begin in earnest today with the first formal interview with the Stranger.

That thought changed her mood. It was too cold to stay put anyway, so she got to her feet. As she was in no hurry, she decided to treat herself to the feel of the stone one more time before leaving the statue. Slowly she walked round the statue, running her fingers along the smooth underside of the sill. Instantly she recalled something she'd done as a child in a place that had been tapping gently on her memory these past few minutes. The Orthodox orphanage in Siberia had become a happy home for several years before convent school had set about reclaiming and subduing the creative spaces that had begun to flourish in her mind. There too the early morning had been the quietest time. She shivered, recalling the discipline she must endure if the nuns caught her outside before the day had officially begun.

The chill that settled on her now had little to do with the cold, and she turned to go back inside. She was just about to withdraw her hand, which was now trailing along idly, when the smoothness of the stone suddenly became rough. She stooped down for a better look, but she couldn't make out any reason for the change in texture. Switching on the light of her eband one last time, she peered underneath. It was a kind of tape, stuck onto the stone. It seemed this curious place just grew curiouser. As her eband was pointing right at it she popped up the lens and captured an image. Then, taking a moment to work out which corner was her way back, she left the courtyard.

4

Ryan pushed back on the white bench and let his favourite old swivel-chair roll a while. He was trying to make up his mind whether he was intrigued or annoyed, but he was too tired to tell.

The crystal had given up a few secrets, but each one led to new questions. The rock had turned out to be straightforwardly crystalline, its molecules in a state of alignment. The molecules themselves, however, were unknown.

Unknown.

The thrill had kept him up all night, firing lasers from all angles as he mapped his way across the strange substance.

By 6.00 am he had compared his results with other bits of Venusian rock and satisfied himself that this was quite different. Probably not from Venus. Almost certainly.

By 8.00 am he had examined a sample of the purple rock where it had been embedded. This showed all the signs of Venusian weather that he had expected.

By 9.00 am, back with the crystal, he had tried to freeze it, melt it and, finally, break it.

There was no visible change.

Time to sleep on it, literally. He would keep it under his pillow, for it seemed so much more in need of protection now that he knew it was indestructible. He laughed out loud at the paradox. Yet nothing was indestructible, even though this thing, whatever it was, was behaving badly.

He was determined to get to the bottom of it, but he knew that determination was not enough to get the job done. Right now his brain definitely needed some distance from the concoction of discoveries that he had plied it with. Whatever else it was, this crystal was not like anything he had seen before, not even the ones that had come to us from the earliest days of the solar system.

In his next session he would treat it less like a natural object and more like a device. Maybe X-rays and magnetic field detectors would yield answers. There was much still to be done.

He left the lab, walked over to his apartment, threw off his white coat and crashed onto the bed.

5

Breakfast was in the refectory. It was a simple affair, amounting to little more than fruit juice and croissants. Today the Brothers were eating in silence, so Dan, Jack, Natasha and Abbot Leonardo followed suit. The Stranger wasn't talking anyway. Jack didn't know if silence was the rule for every day, but he was glad that, for now at least, there would be no opportunity for anyone to ask questions about their presence.

After a few awkward smiles, Jack was surprised how enjoyable the whole process was. With the burden of conversation lifted, thoughts kept bobbing up to the surface of his mind like corks in water, where he could let them float a while as he considered them from a safe distance.

This was the first time he had had chance to draw breath since they had docked on Alpha. In fact the whole sequence of events since his return to the Endeavour back on Venus remained perplexing. Jim's frostiness on the trip home had not thawed, while conversely Natasha's steely approach to life had somehow become more supple. He glanced at her now as they ate. She seemed so much freer in herself.

Across the table Dan was clearly enjoying the warm, fresh bread that must have been baked on the premises. Abbot Leonardo was engrossed in his reading. Jack noticed he had chosen a tablet over one of the many books that seemed to litter the place. The Stranger seemed to be enjoying the food immensely, relishing each mouthful, almost as if he'd not tasted food before.

Jack watched one or two of the Brothers out of the corner of his eye. They all wore habits which were basically grey affairs with splashes of brown for cuffs, collar and hem. Just what kind of monks were they? And what kind of monastery was this? Of course it had never been part of his original briefing to come to such a place, either as astronaut or as agent, but Ms Bridlington clearly had some kind of connection. That surprised him, as he was fairly sure she wasn't religious. Still, she did have the governments of the WSA member states on her back, doubtless hotly pursued by their respective security services, and that could drive a person almost anywhere – even the formidable Constance Bridlington. Jack had little doubt she had fought hard to let her people be the first to talk to the Stranger. And this did seem an ideal way to keep him out of the spotlight for a while.

His thoughts returned to their strange and secret charge. He had hardly said two words since they had returned to Earth. Though, to be fair, no one had been ready to engage him in conversation, struck, it seemed, by a reticence that was as curious as it was universal.

Still, the guy was at least fully conscious now and seemingly alert, which was just as well, as today was the day Jack had to begin questioning the man with no name. He had settled on his first line of approach: Natasha.

There she was now, still in her tracksuit, collecting the Stranger's dish and taking it over to the refectory bar. He downed his fruit juice and joined the others as, silently, they followed Leonardo to the place of interrogation.

6

Miranda powered down the tablet with a sigh. All the recording devices seemed to be working, but none of them carried anything of interest. She was still in Hugh's room, where she had listened to some Italian, some broken English, and a language she couldn't quite place, though it did put her in mind of one of their trips to China, specifically the region of Xizang, for a meeting about laying cables across the Himalayas. She had become accustomed to saying *Tashi delek* every time she greeted someone, and she thought she had heard it again now. At one point she was fairly sure she could discern the targets' arrival, as there were more people about and they were walking quite fast. But they hadn't lingered near any of the recording devices. There was shuffling in the refectory, and before that there was a very strange sound in the larger courtyard, perhaps an animal brushing past the super-thin, sensitive audio tape she had put on the base of the statue.

The tape, of course, was nothing like the material of the same name from an earlier century, which only played back sound. This was a highly durable sheet of micro-electronics, developed by Infostructure for several security organisations around the world. It could receive sound and convert it to a signal before encrypting and transmitting it to a receiver.

The door opened as Hugh returned from a walk. 'Any joy?'

'No. Are you sure they arrived last night?'

'Yes. Petroc has confirmed.'

'Well, in that case, I think I can say *when* they arrived, but nothing much was said.' She told him about the muffled sound in the courtyard earlier that morning and the shuffling in the refectory.

'Muffling and shuffling, eh?' he chuckled. 'In what way muffled?'

'Difficult to make anything of it, but I'd say it was tactile. Probably an animal.'

Hugh sat down next to her at the table. 'Did you see any animals?'

She got up and went to the window. She hated being anything less than one hundred per cent on the ball, especially when she was with Hugh. She opened her mouth to speak but didn't know what to say.

'Not to worry, though,' Hugh interjected in a reassuringly relaxed tone. 'It's still functional. It's not as if we can ever be sure when someone's clever enough to know we're monitoring them. We'll carry on. We are, after all, just listening.'

'Yes.'

She stopped biting her lip and returned to the tablet.

7

Softened by a patchy mist, the morning sunlight was drifting across the faintly yellowing leaves of the forest, and probing the half-open shutters on the monastery walls, as Natasha peered out through a shaded window to the suggestion of trees beyond the perimeter walls. She realised she must be facing west, with the sun behind her. Her eband clock, which had switched to manual as there was no signal here, told her it was five past nine. She had found her own way to what had been called the meditation room when Dan had asked her to go ahead while he went over 'a few final details' with Jack and the Abbott, with the Stranger in tow.

As she turned from the window she was surprised to see a glossy brochure on a coffee table in the centre of the room. She hadn't seen this kind of printed material in a while, and yet it seemed to go with the old-yet-new feel of the place. She had originally assumed they were in a Roman Catholic monastery, but already she was beginning to doubt that. She picked up the brochure to see if it might have answers to some of her questions. It turned out they were guests at the Elemental Retreat Centre, a place for reflection and discussion that drew on both the sciences and the arts. That was intriguing. She cast her eye over the introductory blurb. Owned and run by monks from a larger monastery in the Himalayas called the Temple of the Four Elements, the Centre was 'one of the more popular Western embassies of a natural philosophy of life, where we will help you on your journey to the heart of the universe – and to the heart of your own soul'.

She pursed her lips. Religion for the twenty-first century.

She put the brochure down and walked over to some French windows. They were locked, but as she looked out across a small patio she could see a narrow road winding its way into the forest. She was fairly sure this was where they had arrived the previous evening and met Abbot Leonardo. They really had come in by the back entrance.

Leonardo... now that was an interesting choice for a name. Monks did that, didn't they – received new names? And you'd be hard pressed to find one that better evoked the skills and inspiration of both science and art. She thought about her own choice of surname when she had come of age and wondered whether Leonardo had had a choice.

Her thoughts were interrupted by voices. The door opened, and in came the man himself, followed by Dan, the Stranger and Jack. Suddenly the room seemed to shrink, and Natasha moved back to the patio door as the men arranged themselves around the room.

'Okay, Natasha.' Dan's voice sounded more official than usual. 'I'm going with this, as you know. In fact, I have to get back to Geneva, because Ryan is probably already half way across the Atlantic, bringing that weird crystal with him. So I'm going to have to leave you and Jack to talk to our guest while I'm gone – which I'm happy to do.' And with that his voice softened. 'I've agreed with Jack that you should have what he calls a wee chat with our friend first.'

'There's a bell here on the table,' said Jack before she could respond, and as he shook it a surprisingly pure and loud sound filled the room. 'I'm going to be in the next room. If you need me at any point, Natasha, just ring it. Otherwise I'll come back through in about an hour. Okay?'

'Sounds good,' she said. 'Maybe you can bring some coffee.' The half-serious request seemed to relax them – they were all feeling the effects of a caffeine-free breakfast.

Dan turned to Abbot Leonardo. 'Shall we?'

The two men left, leaving Jack to give whatever instructions seemed best for what was to follow. He scratched his head, trying to think of some last-minute advice.

'It's okay, Jack. We'll be fine – won't we?' She turned to the Stranger.

'We will.' The Stranger's response surprised them both. But it was reassuring if only because it added two more words to his tally.

'Very well,' said Jack. 'I'll leave you to it. Let me just check your eband, Natasha, to make sure you've turned off auto-delete. We need to record everything, naturally.'

'Naturally.' Her eyes flashed, but with that new playfulness Jack had come to enjoy.

'Okay,' he said. 'Now, remember, I'll be just next door.' With this he eyed the Stranger carefully. He could see no change in the benign expression, yet that left him all the more wary. Still, a plan was a plan, and it was time to back his own intuition that this was the best way to start the proceedings. He walked into the adjacent discussion room and closed the connecting door behind him.

'Well,' said Natasha. 'Where shall we begin? How about with your name?'

'Difficult,' he replied, 'when we don't know it.' His voice was like velvet, his tone surprisingly reassured.

'That may be true... so we'll simply have to give you one – for the time being.'

'Okay.'

'Good. As you are clearly English-speaking, with no obvious inflections away from what my friend Jack calls Oxford English, we could go for a British name.'

'Okay.'

'Hmm. Then again, Jack's girlfriend has already called you Icarus.'

'What's that?'

Natasha sat back into the surprisingly comfortable chair. Clearly there was a long road ahead.

8

Hugh Coates was a patient man when it came to business plans, but there were few things he disliked more than inefficiency. And right now he could see no reason for both him and Miranda to remain in the same place. She had checked the latest recordings from the monastery-cum-retreat-centre, and had at last picked up some conversation, indicating that things were about to begin. Some audio tape in the other, smaller courtyard had given them this, as they distinctly heard Abbot Leonardo, whom they had met on their visit, speaking in English to some 'gentlemen' about the suitability of the place he had chosen for the interview. It appeared there were two rooms, connected by an internal door, allowing a measure of flexibility.

Hugh emerged from the bathroom. 'Time to say goodbye, Miranda.'

'But–'

'Things seem to be rolling along quite nicely,' he said, 'and, let's face it, I do have an empire to run!' He ignored her open mouth and continued. 'No need for you to leave. I need you here, monitoring things.'

The mouth closed as disappointment gave way to confusion.

Anticipating the question still forming in her mind, he continued, 'I have someone who can pilot the plane. You can take me to the airport if you like.'

'Yes, of course,' she said, recovering quickly. 'You're sure about this?'

'About what? About leaving the most trustworthy person I have to monitor things and keep me updated? I think so.'

An hour later they were speeding along the autostrada, and Miranda was feeling like she'd just been promoted. Again.

9

Dr Ryan Chase could analyse a molecule down to the sub-atomic level and write a report in copious minutiae, pouring all his attention into the task before him. Everything else remained firmly in the background. Which is why he didn't notice the flags flapping joyously in a feast of colour just a few yards away as his taxi drew up to the *Palais de Nations*. Nor did he register the security checks at the entrance to the foyer. Not, that is, until they asked him to open his sample box. Suddenly the foreground was wrenched into focus. He asked for Ms Bridlington.

'I'm sorry, sir,' the man intoned in some foreign accent, 'but it is not possible for such a busy person to come down here.'

'Busy? Oh, I get it — you mean important. Just call her office and tell them I'm here, will you? Only I'm going to need her say-so before I open this box.'

'Ryan! Are you causing trouble?' It was an unexpected but familiar voice.

'Hey! Dan the man — it's good to see you.'

Dan approached the security barrier, thinking on his marching feet. He had been intending to identify the crystal as a paperweight — which would hardly have been a lie, given its recent tenure on his own desk. But now that Ryan had made such a big deal about opening it, he was going to have to try a different approach.

'Right, let's show the man what we have here, shall we, Dr Chase?' He eyed Ryan directly and gave a small nod. Ryan punched in a code, and then all three men heard a catch slip. Ryan opened the lid and held it up for the guard to see.

'What is it?'

'Well, isn't *that* the question?' Yet again Ryan had spoken before Dan could contain the situation.

'Well, one thing's for sure,' said Dan. 'It's not dangerous.'

Ryan caught on at last. 'No, it's entirely inert.' Once again, not exactly a lie.

'Well, I don't know,' mumbled the security guard.

'Listen... Martin, is it?' said Dan, checking the badge on the befuddled official. 'Ordinarily we'd be happy to leave this here with you, if this was just a souvenir or, er, a paperweight. But we need this for a meeting upstairs with the Head of the WSA.'

It was enough to make the call to Ms Bridlington's office, and soon the crystal and the scientist were allowed through. At the elevator they found Petroc waiting for them.

'Hello, gentlemen. Is everything okay?'

'Sure,' said Dan. 'Why wouldn't it be?'

They ascended in silence. When they reached the third floor Petroc withdrew to his office.

'What is it with this crystal?' said Dan after he had gone. 'If it's not doing strange things on my desk, it's causing mayhem at security. It's enough to make you think the thing is cursed. Or am I overreacting?'

'Ha!' Ryan replied. 'Ordinarily, I'd say you were sounding cranky. But now? I reckon I'm ready to believe anything.'

As they went into Bridlington's office, Petroc's door closed quietly behind them.

10

When Jack heard the unmistakable clear ring of the bell it took him less than three seconds to cross the room and open the communicating door. When he saw Natasha sitting relaxed in one armchair and the Stranger in another, he slowed down fast.

'Ah, Jack. Time for that coffee now?' Natasha beamed. It wasn't often a smile was allowed to break across that solemn face. Jack was fairly sure he hadn't seen Natasha's chipped tooth so clearly since she had fallen during training in a rocky quarry what seemed like half a lifetime ago.

'Aye, right. Coffee. Absolutely. So... how've you two been getting on?'

'We're fine,' said Natasha. 'First off, we've agreed on the name Ariel for our friend here.'

'Cool.'

'Yes, I suppose it is. He didn't seem to like Icarus that much – did you?' He shook his head. 'We couldn't go online, of course, so I started going through the names of the moons in the solar system, starting out at Neptune, but as soon as I got to Ariel he said that would be acceptable.'

'Fair enough. I don't see him as a Triton, do you?'

She stuck her tongue out at him. That was another change. 'I was only trying to be thorough!' she complained, but this time the grin quickly vanished as she continued. 'But, Jack, we have another mystery. It seems that Ariel picked up what Abbot Leonardo was asking Dan when they left the room earlier.'

'Okay,' said Jack nervously. 'So he has good hearing then. What did he hear that was so interesting?' He watched the Stranger, who continued to sit in silence.

Natasha frowned. 'Jack, he was asking about the crystal.'

'Right. Natural enough, I suppose, given that Dan had just mentioned that that was why he had to go back to Geneva.'

'True. But Ariel thought he had... what did you call it?'

'A greedy interest.' The Stranger's words hung in the room.

Jack scratched the back of his head. 'Okay. Vocabulary's coming on, I see. Well, I'm sure there's a simple explanation. Probably something to do with this place and whatever it stands for.'

'Maybe,' said Natasha. 'But there's more. Since we arrived Ariel has heard Leonardo speak in three different tongues. He only understood the English, and it's pretty clear another was Italian—'

'Obviously, since the guy's Italian.'

She ignored him. 'But the third one sounded very different. He couldn't tell me what it was, but he's quite sure he was speaking a third language.'

Jack turned to the newly named Ariel. 'So tell me, my friend, now you've clearly found your own tongue! Exactly when did you hear this other language?'

'Before breakfast. He was talking on a hand-held device. *Tashi delek* is what I heard first, which made me think it was a different language from the two he had spoken before. I didn't recognise it, but more than once I heard a word that sounded like "shell"– except of course it wasn't what we would mean by the sound in English. He was excited.'

'Well, that is interesting,' said Jack. 'Here we are with our high-tech ebands and none of us can get a signal, yet our friendly host is using a communications device.'

'True,' said Natasha, 'though we don't know what the device was. He could have been recording for a journal or something equally innocent. Or perhaps it was an internal call.'

'Maybe,' said Jack, 'although if he was using another language, that could mean he's in touch with foreign powers unknown. We'll need to keep our eyes and ears open.'

He looked at the suddenly eloquent Stranger, relieved that they had finally started engaging with him as a human being rather than an object of examination. He opened the door. 'Come on, guys. It's time we went and found that coffee – if they have such delights in this place.'

11

Constance Bridlington pressed her finger on the slat of her office window blind as she stared out across the city. Behind her Dan and Ryan sat at the table, gazing at the crystal. She did not turn as she spoke.

'So what you're telling me, Ryan, is that this crystal is not only extra-terrestrial, which we knew, but extra-Venusian.'

'Absolutely. It could be an invaluable aid to understanding the origins of the solar system.'

'Yes, yes. And that's good. But... indestructible?' She kept her face towards the window.

'So far, I've not been able to split it, crack it, or even chip a piece off it. Not so much as a mark, in fact. And that's curious. The equipment in my laboratory doesn't pack a great punch, but I've hit it with pretty high levels of amplified light and ultra-sound. Nothing. It remains inert and intact.'

'Which,' put in Dan, 'makes no sense at all when you consider how it was behaving in my office on Alpha.'

'Tell me again.'

'Well, when I looked into it – I mean, really looked – it seemed to catch the light in all kinds of ways. At least, sometimes it did. Then, just before Jack called to say the Stranger was awake, it began to glow and hum. Well, actually, I was outside my office at that point, and it stopped as Sam and I rushed back in. It looked like it had burst into life with a flash, but in the few seconds it took for us to check it out it had calmed down again.'

'Hmm. I'm missing something,' said Constance, still facing the window. 'What is it? What am I missing?'

The two men weren't sure just how rhetorical this question was intended to be, but before they could make a stab at an answer the Director turned round and sat down opposite them with the light of decision in her eyes. 'I think we should up the "punch", as you call it, Ryan. The fact is, I can't keep the military off this much longer.' Dan made as if to speak. 'I know, Dan. We need time at the monastery. But they need to know just how little time they have. Meanwhile, I'm hoping this crystal will keep our security-minded people happy. For a while.'

Ryan leapt from his chair, ready to protest, but just then a call came through.

'What is it, Petroc?'

'A call from a Ms Grantley James, Ma'am.'

'I can't take it right now.'

'The thing is, Ma'am, she's here.'

'In Geneva?'

'Yes. Downstairs, in fact.'

Constance wasn't sure she liked Petroc's dry tone any more than his super-zealous one. 'Very well. Tell her I'll be down in a few minutes. No – you can send her up.'

In the adjacent office Petroc called through to the main entrance. But before going to the lift to meet their visitor, he readied a message for Bruges on his eband. Ms Bridlington may be unsure, but he for one had not missed the fascinating coincidence in Dan Marshall's report.

Life

A rush of air, mossy and moist.
Grass. Dirt. Stone. Leaves rustling, shadows dancing.
Life.
Upward thrust, root to shoot, sap in the stem, trunk of the tree, bark through to branches, brimming to twigs, filling the leaves.
A leaf.
Veins flood with food, humming with light.
Life.
The leaf is green, throbbing translucence.
It fills all things. All things are the leaf. The light.
Where does it end? Look askance for the spaces between. Averted vision. Interstices.
Brain on fire. Eyes water. A rush of air. The earth swoops up.
Darkness.

Chapter 8

Connections

1

The Temple of the Four Elements had opened its Swiss retreat centre some five years before the surprise voyage to Venus. Situated high in the woods overlooking Lake Lugano, the Elemental Retreat Centre had turned the shell of a short-lived Roman Catholic school into an intoxicating blend of traditional and contemporary. The stone walls and courtyards were not ancient but old enough to carry that sense of spiritual history, while the facilities indoors were all that today's traveller could hope for, suitably equipped for convenience and rest. The one sacrifice guests were asked to make – apart from significantly shrinking some of the numbers in their bank accounts – was to break contact with the outside world. To that end signals could not ordinarily find a way out of the facility, or even the grounds, and only the Abbot himself had the means to make emergency calls. Electronically, the place was shut tight.

Jack and Natasha were sitting in the refectory off the corner of the cloistered courtyard, locked in conversation. It had turned out that their first breakfast had coincided with a fast of some kind, but now the delights of egg and bacon, coffee and tea, were restored. They had left Ariel in the meditation room before coming out to talk, and when they reached the cloister in the main building the aroma of fresh coffee had quickly decided their destination. Jack was making it clear to Natasha that the interview needed to get to the events on Venus, in the hope of finding out why Jim and Ryan had lost consciousness. He stopped talking when he noticed the Abbot approaching them.

'Your colleague is on his way to Geneva. Is everything satisfactory for you?'

Jack noted that he didn't ask about the interview itself, and admired the discretion. 'Yes, we're fine, thank you. This is splendid coffee, may I say? In fact, everything here is pretty much top quality.'

'Thank you. Though, honestly, you take us as you find us. Ms Bridlington is a friend to us, but we're really not going out of our way for you.'

'Well, we appreciate the hospitality anyway,' said Jack. When Leonardo showed no sign of leaving, Jack took the hint and asked him to join them. He accepted immediately.

'I wonder, Commander Forrester – '

'Please, call me Jack.'

'Jack, I fully appreciate the nature of our role here, that we are facilitating a private and secure interview with our mysterious friend. However, I wanted you to know that, if I personally can be of any help, you only need to ask. I happen to have experience in helping people recover memories they have buried deep – yes, I know that's classified, but then, as you see, I have Ms Bridlington's utmost confidence.'

Jack leant back in his chair and nodded ever so slightly. 'Well, I can't say I'm surprised. But even so, I would need to talk to Geneva before I allowed you on the interview team.'

'Yes, of course. You may make the call from my office at any time. Meanwhile the offer remains.' With that he rose and glided out of the refectory.

Jack and Natasha looked at each other. She spoke first. 'Would Bridlington really...?'

'I have no idea. But it's probably time we made a call anyway, so we can check it out. I don't want the Abbot's input till I know Ariel has told us all he can recall without any extra "help".'

'Understood,' said Natasha, 'though maybe we should get back to Ariel first.'

'And rush this superlative brew?'

She knocked back her water as if it were vodka, leaving him to savour his last mouthful.

2

Jack followed Natasha along the cloister as they headed back to the meditation room, until suddenly she stopped.

'Actually, Jack,' she said, 'I need to check something out, if that's all right.'

'What is it?'

'It's that statue in the centre of the courtyard. I'd like to take a closer look at it.'

Jack hesitated, wondering how long they should leave Ariel alone, but he couldn't deny his own interest and decided to join her. There on the dais stood a grey stone statue of someone – whether male or female it was hard to tell – with a flaming torch in one hand and a bucket in the other. The bucket was slopping water as it tilted slightly, all exquisitely carved. Hanging from the figure's neck were some panpipes, and plants grew at its feet, also carved in stone. The figure wore a cloak, which when viewed from behind sported several stars. Like everything else they were unpainted.

Having made the circuit she returned to Jack. 'Sorry, just wanted to take a proper look.' As they turned to go, she instinctively put out her hand to caress the stone one last time. 'Oh, I've just remembered!'

'What?'

'Well, this morning...'

Jack sensed a story was coming, but he could feel the clock ticking. 'Tell me later,' he said. 'We need to get back to our boy.'

While Natasha followed she asked her eband to display the photograph she had taken earlier under the statue. They were now crossing the smaller courtyard, and she was about to show it to Jack when he suddenly quickened his pace and dived through the half-open door of the meditation room. Sensing the urgency she followed on and immediately noticed a strong breeze blowing through the room. Ariel was nowhere to be seen. Jack was outside the French windows, now open, leaning over a prostrate figure. It was Ariel.

'There's no visible sign of injury,' said Jack, 'and he's breathing okay. Actually, he's breathing really rapidly. Can you help me get him inside?'

Together they carried him and settled him in one of the armchairs. As Natasha made him comfortable, Jack examined the doors. He had previously ascertained that they were equipped with a high-security electronic lock that needed a code. There was no sign of forced entry. Or exit – he had to entertain the possibility that Ariel had at last tried to escape.

Natasha stepped back to take a proper look at the figure once again slumped in a chair. He opened his eyes, and she caught a look of recognition on his face. He offered a smile. Was that the first?

'Hello, my friend,' she said. 'This is a bit like old times, no?'

He groaned.

Jack returned from a quick sortie in the grounds. 'Natasha, I'm sorry, but I think I'm going to have to leave you with him again. This wretched signal screen means I can't even call Leonardo – that's if he even has an eband.'

'That's fine, Jack. We'll be okay, won't we?' Ariel's eyes said yes, and she turned to Jack. 'At least you're not going out into a Venusian storm this time.'

'Right, there is that. Look, I'm going to leave these doors open for now, but if you see anything suspicious you're to close them immediately, okay?'

'Okay.' She tried to throw him one of those whimsical looks she had recently found inside herself, but it wouldn't come. 'Honestly,' she said, her Russian accent stronger than usual, 'we shall be fine.'

When Jack had gone, she sat down in the other armchair and looked hard at Ariel. 'What happened?'

'I am sorry. Once more I have to say I don't know.'

'Well, I guess you're not up to full strength yet.'

'It's true that I've felt for some time that I've been losing my strength, as if the life was draining out of me. But now... I don't know. It was overwhelming.'

'What? What was overwhelming?'

'The trees, and the leaves, and the sunlight, and the air. Just overflowing with... with life and energy and... I don't have the words.'

She looked at him. 'Well, you're still getting your language back, I think.'

'No, I don't have the words in any language. At least, not in any of the languages I've heard while I've been here.'

'Well, we've been here less than a day.'

'No. I think I mean before that.'

'Ah.'

'I don't know how I got here.'

She took this as her cue to tell him about the trip back from Venus. 'You were in and out of consciousness when we moved you to the Resolution, the ship that brought us back to Earth. At first I tried to give you one of our lovely liquid meals,' and at this she pulled a face to confirm the irony, 'and Jack tried to take you to the toilet, but that didn't go well. Nor could we get you to engage with the gym. You never really regained consciousness. So most of the time – all of the time, really, after the first few hours – you were in a medbed.'

His eyes still looked glazed, but she pressed on. 'A medbed... that's a special kind of medical bed where you could sleep as long as you needed and we didn't have to worry about your bodily needs or functions. When we got back to Earth orbit and moved you again, on the space station, you started to wake up. Don't you remember?'

He sat motionless. The moments passed in silence.

'I remember you,' he said at last. 'And voices. But before that...'

'Yes?'

'It is not clear.'

This seemed to be the moment to take him back to the events on Venus. 'What *do* you recall about the time before you came on board the Endeavour?'

'Voices. Victory, I think. We were in a battle.'

Natasha shivered. 'Ariel, that's the first time you have said "we". Who were you with?'

His blank look said it all, and before she could think where to take the conversation next, Jack returned with Abbot Leonardo in tow. Leonardo made straight for the patient, but Jack called him over to the door and quizzed him on how it could have been opened.

'I really don't know,' he said. 'As I say, I am the only one with the key code, and I have not given it to anyone since I reprogrammed it for your arrival. Not even the maintenance company would be able to open it without that code.'

'What about hacking it?'

'Doubtful. There are six numbers, and there is no wireless component. You would have to know which number keys to press, and an alarm sounds if you fail three times.'

'Okay,' said Jack. 'Let's close it back up for now. Natasha, can Ariel throw any light on the proceedings for us?'

She shook her head.

'As I thought. Well, Sir Abbot, I think it's time to make that call to Geneva.'

3

Jack replaced the rather ornate receiver onto its base on Leonardo's desk. Natasha and Ariel sat in the corner of the small office. Leonardo had made himself scarce. Jack looked troubled.

'What is it?' said Natasha.

'Well, as you may have surmised from my side of the conversation, we're running out of time. Bridlington doesn't think she can hold the wolves at bay any more. Basically, the military are closing in. Most of the space agencies have kept their boys at bay, including NASA, but it seems Washington has been leaning on Dan to let them have access.'

'Can they do that?'

'Well, yes and no. They can't officially step out of line with the others... but, to be honest, I think Dan and our Ms Bridlington are going out on a limb with the whole softly-softly approach.'

She shuddered. 'What do you think they'll do to him?'

Jack turned a smooth stone paperweight over in his hand, clearly playing out various scenarios in his mind.

'Well, if I thought Ariel was my enemy, I'd take the chemical route first. Truth drugs, some form of intoxicant maybe, possibly hallucinogens... and, if those didn't work, maybe hypnosis.'

Natasha reminded him that Leonardo had offered help with memory recovery.

'Aye, you're right. It might be for the best... while we still have the chance to do something humane. And Bridlington has just cleared him.'

Natasha instinctively took Ariel by the hand and led him to the door. Jack hesitated. 'You go on back to the meditation room. I, er need to talk to the Abbot. I'll catch up with you.'

Quietly she led Ariel out of the office.

After a few moments Jack closed the door, went back to the desk and picked up the phone. This was too good an opportunity to miss. Constance had told him she had allowed Melody to join them. Checking her number on his eband, he used the desk phone to call her.

It went to voicemail.

4

Miranda sat back and stretched both her arms high over her head. Her listening devices had been keeping her busy with data, but there was little of interest. She stood up, looked at the clock and decided it was time for some fresh air. Putting her tablet to sleep, she locked the balcony doors and went out into the hall.

The elevator was busy, so she decided to hop down the stairway. As she came out into the foyer she noticed a woman checking in. Well dressed, confident and decidedly English, she seemed familiar. Someone in the media?

She filed the thought away and pressed on for the walk she had promised herself. Later, back in her room, it would be simple enough to access the hotel's records and see who had checked in that afternoon. Just in case it was important.

5

A stream of dappled sunlight found its way in through the west-facing window of the meditation room as Leonardo, Natasha and Ariel waited for Jack to join them. Lunch was well behind them, and the day was proceeding more peacefully at last. Now that it was clear Leonardo was familiar with at least some of the events on Venus, and given that he was about to help Ariel try to retrieve his memories, Natasha felt free to talk more openly about their time on Venus. Laying things out from start to finish might in itself stimulate Ariel's own memory. He was keeping quiet as usual, but she could see that he was listening.

'Well,' said Leonardo at last, 'I gather we are calling our friend Ariel. Good name. I assume you know what it means.'

'Actually no,' Natasha admitted. She told him how they came up with it.

'Oh, very good,' said Leonardo. 'Of course, one of the moons of Uranus. But, as you know, these moons are named after ancient, mythical figures.'

'Like Icarus, I know,' said Natasha. 'But he wasn't keen. So what does Ariel mean?'

'It means God's altar. Or possibly God's lion.'

'Wow,' Natasha breathed. 'Unintentional on my part, you understand.'

'Of course,' said Leonardo with a reassuring smile. 'And I think it is highly fitting that you choose the name of a planet for a man who was found on a different one from ours.' He smiled. 'Of course, in the world of Shakespeare it is the name of a spirit of the ether, no?'

'If you say so,' said Natasha. 'I can't say that foreign literature is my strong point.'

'Ah, si. But "lion" is also good. I think you all showed remarkable courage in visiting such a hostile environment. This Window people talk about – it wasn't open very wide, was it? The elements of that storm must have been terrifying.'

'I admit I was afraid,' she said, and a wide frown creased her brow. 'But that's because I was inside when the rest of the crew were out there in the middle of it all. I feared for them.'

He nodded. 'You must all be very close to one another, what with the training and then living, how do you say in English, on top of one another.'

Natasha turned to look out through the French windows. Although she had told Leonardo about their expeditions outside the craft, she had carefully omitted any mention of the emotions that had run so high. She was wondering how to react when Leonardo surprised her with a question.

'And this crystal...?'

'Yes?' she said, turning back to face him. 'You know about the crystal?'

'Er yes, Colonel Marshall mentioned it. It's nothing really... just that we have a fair degree of interest in the works of nature here at the Centre, and we find crystals one of the earth's more, shall we say, attractive expressions?'

'I see,' said Natasha. 'Though this one, you will appreciate, is not from Earth.'

'Indeed,' he grinned. 'And that just makes it all the more interesting.'

Jack entered the room. 'Sorry, folks. Thanks for waiting. Are you ready to begin?'

'We are,' replied Leonardo, 'but if I may, can I suggest that we go into the chapel? I am used to doing this sort of thing there. I find it conducive – certainly for me and quite often for the patient.'

Jack quickly weighed the pros and cons. He for one would not find it helpful to go into a more obviously religious space, but then again it might help Ariel. It couldn't hurt.

They gained the chapel via the cloister in the main courtyard, entering through a side entrance. They stepped into a long, tall, rectangular space with windows on all four walls, though the ones on the cloister side were high up. Everything was bathed in a warm light at this end of the day. Simply carved wooden chairs with a modern design filled much of the space. Some of the windows were clear, revealing the greens and yellows of the trees outside, while others appeared to be made of frosted glass. Several diffused the light through stained glass that sported a mixture of abstract designs and rudimentary pictures of natural phenomena. Natasha just had time to notice lightning, clouds, waves, mountains and trees, before Leonardo led them off to the right.

Together they climbed three shallow stone steps into an area that Natasha had been told long ago was known in English as the chancel, which included the place where the clergy and choir would normally sit. Now that she knew this was not a church-owned establishment, the lack of an altar was no surprise, nor of a cross, though she did spot an enigmatic version of one on a side wall. It was more like a plus sign, with two equal lengths intersecting exactly half-way. At each of the four points was a symbol of some kind, with a fifth in the centre. Something to investigate at a later date, should the opportunity arise.

'So now,' said Leonardo, 'may I ask you, Ariel, to sit here?' He indicated a plain wooden chair near the wall, not far from where a few narrow stone steps led up to a vacant pulpit. 'I want you to use this space both to relax and to receive. You may want to look at the shapes and images in the windows or on the walls. But I am thinking that you will want to close your eyes at some point, to make the journey back to Venus, if I may put it that way.'

The three of them sat in a wide semi-circle about two metres in front of Ariel. Jack shuffled in his chair, hoping that this was the sum total of the religious – or was that quirky? – element of the proceedings. He was about to ask Ariel a question when Leonardo spoke again.

'Now then, my friend. We know how Natasha and Jack and the others found their way to Venus. Do you recall how you came to be there?'

In the almost tangible silence that followed Jack had to admit that this was a great question, both strategically (for its answer might clear up a lot) and also psychologically, as it could help Ariel go back beyond the apparent trauma of Venus itself.

The answer, when it came, shocked him no less than the others. 'I think I fell.'

Again Leonardo spoke before Jack could frame a question. His words came calmy and evenly. 'And did you fall from a cliff, or from a ship?'

'No. I don't think so.'

Jack watched Natasha as she eyed Ariel carefully, like a mother watching her child perform in public for the first time.

'Right,' intoned Leonardo, and his Italian accent seemed more pronounced. 'You did not fall from your ship, nor from a cliff. Perhaps you stumbled? As you know, we found no evidence of bruising on you, so maybe you did not fall far.'

The 'we' in Leonardo's last sentence impacted Jack like a meteor, and he stood up so fast that the soft blanket of calm that had descended was blown completely away. 'Er, sorry Leonardo, but can I have a wee word?'

They stepped out into the courtyard.

'Leonardo, let's be frank. You know a lot more than any "adequately briefed" host would be expected to know. Just what is going on here?'

'Jack, I apologise. But you must not be surprised that I said nothing to you. I could not be sure how much Constance had told you about me.'

'Aye, well, she probably briefed me as much as she thought necessary. And, to be fair, she probably thought I'd work it out.'

They strolled out into the sunshine and stood close by the statue.

'Tell me,' said Jack. 'How come you two are so close?'

Leonardo looked up at the embossed stars on the cloak of the stone figure. Bedecked in his grey and brown cowl, with the last stray rays of sunlight reflected in his silver hair, it seemed to Jack as though he had been chiselled out of stone as well, a cross between a Moses and St Francis. 'Constance first came here, as a client, a few years ago. She now comes every year for a retreat. When she told me that she would like to use the place in a professional capacity, I naturally needed some assurances. Information.'

Leonardo's use of Bridlington's first name told Jack plenty. 'Okay, that makes sense. So, just how much did she tell you?'

'That you had found the one we are now calling Ariel on Venus – in your ship, in fact. That he was not conscious. That he had since come round but was displaying classic signs of post-traumatic amnesia. And that she needed a safe place before other, shall we say more hardline people got hold of him.'

'Pretty much everything, then.' Jack shrugged. 'Okay,' he said after a moment's reflection. 'At least we now know where we both stand. Let's get back to the chapel.'

Back in Montagnola, sitting quietly in her hotel room, Miranda put down her earpiece and breathed out slowly. At last, a conversation where she had actually placed a bug, and rich with information. So, they found the Stranger on board the Endeavour! And as if that wasn't enough for a day's work, she also now knew where they were interviewing him. She pressed her eband for an encrypted connection with Hugh. She had to find a way into that chapel.

6

Switzerland is home to three major languages, and it seemed to Melody that there were as many forms of sunlight. She was enjoying the Italian kind in the early evening as she sipped her second cocktail, sitting alone at an outside table for two at her hotel restaurant and pondering the unexpected ease with which she had persuaded Constance Bridlington to let her in on the first interviews with the Stranger. But she didn't ponder for long. She was in that familiar mood where she felt the urgent need to relax at any cost. She was desperately tired, and her limbs were still the heaviest part of a body that had not yet adapted to full earth gravity. What with that and the heat of the day, a small slip of a dress seemed sensible as well as making her feel good. She hadn't eaten for several hours, not since she had left Geneva, and her head was buzzing with the alcohol and the heavy scent of flowers as she pored over the menu without seeing a word. After a while she gave up and sat back in a chair that she was sure would have cut into her back if she were sober. Pushing back her hair and widening her eyes, she drank in the vibrant reds and vivid blues of what she guessed were begonias and trailing lobelia as they paraded themselves unapologetically about the place.

A woman approached, looking a little lost. She was a similar age to Melody, in her mid-thirties, though shorter and a bit thick around the midriff. She too was reflecting a range of colours. Her shorts were denim blue, her top olive green, while her skin was a delicate shade of light brown, a bit like one of the smooth Swiss chocolates in Melody's room, though as the woman came closer she could see a light dusting of freckles across her nose and cheeks. She had a full set of dark brown, not-quite-frizzy hair that glowed with a red tinge in the evening sunlight. There was something quirky about her, though Melody couldn't decide if that was a purely physical thing caused by having a round face with asymmetrical features, or whether it was in the way she held herself.

'Oh, hi, I'm sorry... would you mind if I joined you? Only they're saying that the rest of the tables out here have been reserved.'

Her accent was a curious blend of Australian and American, which piqued Melody's interest. 'Well yes, I'd be glad of the company.'

'Thanks. I was kinda guessing you weren't from around these parts. My name's Miranda.'

'Hello, Miranda. I'm usually called Mel.' And I'm so chilled right now, she thought, that I've just given you the name my friends and colleagues use. Hey-ho.

'Nice to meet you, Mel. You here on holiday – or working, like me?'

Melody appreciated the gesture of information-sharing up front. 'Holiday,' she said after only a moment's thought. 'I'm hoping to look around tomorrow.' She racked her brains to think of a reason why she might have chosen this spot. Water sports on the lake? Not a lie she wanted to risk being tested. She went for the literary connection. 'Actually, I'm here to visit the Hermann Hesse Museum.'

'Wow, they have a museum, do they?' Miranda pulled her chair closer to the table. 'When I was a student on my travels I remember backpacking up this way from the lake, trying to find his house. But I guess I was with the wrong crowd, because we never did find the village.'

Melody was not sure whether to believe that, until she recalled how so many ventures were tilted off course by alcohol back in her own student days. Maybe that was it. 'Very well,' she said. 'Why don't you come with me in the morning?'

'Really? That would be fabulous!'

The waiter arrived. They ordered, Melody simply following every choice Miranda made, and by the fifth cocktail it felt like she had known this woman a very long time.

7

As they stepped back into the chapel, Jack and Leonardo could hear Natasha and Ariel engaged in deep conversation. Instinctively Jack pulled Leonardo back and nodded towards some chairs near the entrance. Leonardo took the hint and sat down. In the silence the low voices were remarkably clear.

'I remember falling.' Ariel hesitated. 'But not landing.'

'That's really good, Ariel.' Natasha had broken with Leonardo's two-metre rule and had one of his hands between hers. 'Do you know where you were falling from?'

Silence.

'I'm sorry. It really is a blank.'

'That's okay.' She got up and called the two men to join them. 'Jack, we've made some progress, even in the short time you were gone. It seems Ariel fell from a great height. From where to where... he can't say. Not yet.'

'Okay,' said Jack. 'That would certainly fit with our finding him down in the lowest deck of the Endeavour.' He turned to Ariel. 'But, my friend, we didn't find any bruises on you. Not that we should expect to, I suppose, given what we found out later on.'

At this point Jack eyed Leonardo askance, as discreetly as he could, to see if there was any reaction to this last remark. Nothing showed.

'Well,' said Jack, sensing they had got as far as they were likely to in their first session, 'I don't know about you guys, but I'm in need of a break.'

They made their way back out of the chapel towards the refectory. As they crossed the courtyard, Leonardo drew Jack to one side. 'Jack, it usually helps in these cases to find something to reconnect the person to their past – something tangible, if possible. To that end, is there any chance we might get hold of the crystal Colonel Marshall mentioned?'

'Interesting idea,' said Jack. 'I would think that might be possible.'

The two men caught up with the others. As they crossed the courtyard, the statue guarded its latest secret in silence.

8

The chapel still retained something of the soft light of evening. They had passed their time in the refectory in silence, even though this was not the order of the day and the other monks all chatted away quite freely. Ariel had been reading avidly on a tablet he had brought from his room. As they resumed their positions in the chapel, everyone seemed eager to get going again. Ariel surprised them by speaking first.

'I think I'd like to talk about the trees, if I may.'

'Sorry?' said Jack, totally bemused.

'The trees, outside. They are so full of life.'

Natasha stepped in. 'I think he may be talking about what happened earlier, when we found him on the ground outside the meditation room.'

'Ah, right,' said Jack. 'We may as well go there as anywhere. So, Ariel, what do you think happened?'

'Happened? Oh, I really couldn't say.' And at this his accent appeared almost to fall into Scottish, as if he were mimicking Jack, though that seemed unthinkable to all of them. 'No, I really would like to talk about the trees. Have you any idea how much life is throbbing through them?'

'Tell us more,' Natasha said softly.

'Very well. There is an upsurge. They radiate. They draw down deep, they reach up high, they–'

Jack stood up and began to pace, which seemed to throw Ariel off track. 'I'm sorry,' he said, 'but is this really helping?'

'Help often comes unlooked for,' said Ariel.

'And you would know that how?' Jack returned, raising his voice for the first time as his annoyance levels began to rise. 'And you learnt to philosophise precisely where? Come on, man, I'm beginning to think you're playing us.' Natasha tried to speak, but Jack was in full flow. 'You need to understand, my friend, that the clock is ticking. It's lovely chatting with you about the delights of nature and all, but honestly, we don't have time for this! The wolf is almost at the door, and if this sheep doesn't start bleating soon, not one of us in this place will be able to save you.'

In the silence that followed Natasha walked across to the end of the chapel where she presumed the altar would have been if this place had been normal. The altar of God.

Ariel sat motionless, an expression of wonder still in his eyes.

Leonardo turned to Jack. 'Jack, I appreciate your frustration – we all do. But I really think we must let Ariel say what is on his heart, if we are to make any progress – the progress we all want to see. You have probably noticed how his way of speaking is changing, and I can only think that this is part of his recovery.'

'Aye, you're probably right.' Jack's eyes were on Natasha. Her quiet act of self-removal had done far more to pull him up short than Leonardo's words, wise though they probably were. 'Very well. Let's continue. Natasha, please come back.'

As she turned, her moist eyes caught the light. Leonardo put a hand on Jack's arm, and they both held their peace.

Ariel spoke again. 'I'm picking up a lot of... emotions.'

Natasha resumed her place on the chair and looked Ariel in the eye. If only she could look deeper, somehow fathom this strange man's depths. 'I want to hear more about the trees,' she said. 'Tell us what you saw. What you felt.'

Jack got to his feet. 'Sorry, guys.' He was whispering now. 'Why don't you three carry on? It's been a long day. I think I'll turn in for the night.'

Leonardo nodded, and they let him go.

Chapter 9

Rumours and Reports

1

Melody's head buzzed in all the wrong ways as she sat back in the passenger seat of Miranda's newly hired car, closing her eyes behind her sunglasses against the unfriendly light of late morning. 'I'm so sorry, Miranda. I really did want to go to Hesse's house.'

'Don't you worry about it,' she replied, as she steered the car as carefully as she could around the all-too-frequent bends in the road. 'I took the opportunity to do some work in my room. We can go another time.'

'Oh, thank you. It's not like me to get hung over. But we did have a good time, didn't we?'

'Mm-hmm, we did.'

Melody tried to recall the events of the previous evening. Dinner had arrived, eventually, but then so had the noisy party of guests who had reserved the other tables. Had they retired to the bar? She remembered Miranda guiding her back to her room. How did they get in? She must have used her eband to do that. Did Miranda help her? They had talked on the balcony, seemingly immune to the chill night air. In the fading light they had talked a lot... or rather, Mel had talked. She was fairly sure it had been more personal than professional. That was no bad thing, given the classified nature of the Aphrodite mission, but it was not normal.

She had to trust herself. She was, after all, familiar with so many of the ways one can use to get people to relax and tell their story. As a feature-writer she had learnt to be something of an investigative journalist as well, so the art of steering conversations oh-so-casually was her stock-in-trade.

So why was she worried now?

She had been caught off guard. Her self-imposed ban on drinking in space meant that she had been making up for lost time. But had she really drunk herself paralytic with a perfect stranger? And here she was now, in that stranger's car, allowing her to drive her to a sensitive destination. This monastery was hardly likely to be all it seemed, despite the assurances she had recently been given by Constance Bridlington, and the fact that Jack was still involved only made it more likely that there were other forces at work. Security agencies were bound to be in the frame. All of which needed the most sensitive handling, and up to now she had been the epitome of carelessness.

Still, better late than never. 'I do appreciate this too, you know. I could have taken a taxi.'

'Honestly, it's fine,' Miranda replied. 'Since my boss left me to clear a few things up here, it's been kinda lonely. And it's just great to get out of those four walls and see a bit more of this beautiful part of the world.'

They turned off and made their way along the private road that served to take normal daytime visitors up through thick woodland to the Elemental Retreat Centre. They drove through a row of cypress that acted like a natural barrier, before approaching a high stone wall with a large gate that opened before them and closed behind them. Now they could see their destination – a large building made of grey and brown stone that must have been some seventy metres from end to end. They couldn't see how far back it stretched. On the left side stood what looked like a chapel with a bell tower and stained-glass windows, while the rest was a two-storey mansion with attic windows in a large tiled roof. It looked old, yet within minutes they were standing before a front door that sported a sophisticated degree of security. A sign told them to look up.

As they peered at a camera lens they said who they were and waited. Melody gathered her thoughts. She did not want Miranda to know the real reason why she might be expected, so, ignoring the thrumming in her head, she called up deep reserves of verve and nerve. When a young monk came to the door, she did not hesitate.

'Hello. My name is Melody Grantley James. I booked a couple of days ago to come and look around.'

'Er, yes.' He spoke perfect English. 'I have you on my list.' Was that a northern accent? 'But...'

Miranda took her cue. 'Oh, no, don't worry. I'm not with her. At least, I am, but I haven't booked or anything. If you can't show me around as well, that's not a problem.'

'Miss Miranda! Is that you?' Leonardo came striding out of the dark corridor behind the confused monk. 'How lovely to see you again! Is Mr Greerson with you?'

Miranda was relieved that she had used her real name when she and Hugh had visited before. A query right now could look suspicious. But fortunately only Hugh had given a surname, one that he used at times like this when he was just some visiting businessman. She beamed a sudden smile: 'Abbot Leonardo, great to see you too! Actually I'm just playing taxi-driver for my new pal here.'

Leonardo's apparent confusion lasted only a moment. He caught Melody's uneasy smile and adjusted his face with a smoothness born of years of negotiating ambiguity. He turned to the young monk. 'Brother Leroy, why don't you take our visitor to her room, while I catch up with Miss Miranda here. Miranda, would you like to come through to my office?'

She duly followed, excited to be right in the thick of the espionage again, even though she realised that turning up with Mel had probably raised suspicions. But the potential rewards were high, if only she could get into that chapel.

2

Melody sat on the bed and looked around. Another guest room. In addition to the inevitable ensuite there was a wardrobe, bedside cabinet, a chair and a table. Her eye was drawn to a traditional bookcase which incorporated a small screen that turned out to be detachable, though she couldn't tell what it was for. She opened her case and stood before the mirror on the wall to try out the alarmingly small range of frocks, jeans, shorts, skirts and blouses she had brought with her. 'That's funny,' she said out loud to herself, 'you look different.' Then she realised her image was the right way round. It was a digital mirror, though she couldn't see where the camera was.

She decided to investigate the books on the shelves. There was one about the Temple of the Four Elements. 'Well,' she spoke out loud again, 'I know what they are – earth, air, fire and water.' There were a few titles that seemed self-explanatory, about the human psyche, the search for meaning and mystery, and several titles in German, French and Italian, plus a few more in something which she guessed to be Chinese. But when she reached the bottom shelf, they were like nothing she'd ever seen. The first was called *Number, Word, Note*. Next to it came *Goodness, Truth, Beauty*. For fun she tried *Infinitesimals and Continuity* but it contained too many equations to make much sense to her. *Moments in Time and Eternity* looked more like her cup of tea, and she put it on her bedside cabinet, just in case her stay turned out to be long enough for some serious reading.

She crossed over to the table by the window and studied a plan of the retreat centre. It was a small complex of two main buildings connected by a covered way. In the rear section, a single-storey building, there was a library and reading room, and it seemed the screen in her bookcase was a terminal that granted her access to its treasures. Doubtless even more esoteric volumes awaited her, but maybe also some clues to what this place was about. Right now it seemed a bit of a puzzle.

It wasn't clear whether any part of the building was off limits, but then she couldn't remember when that had last stopped her. And anyway, the library was clearly one of the facilities available to guests, and she was a guest. Bridlington herself had sent her here. That had been a surprise. Clearly she was still proving useful, at the very least allowing them to tick the 'press kept informed' box. And perhaps Ms Bridlington thought her trusted guard dog, Commander Forrester, could keep a tight rein on the troublesome journalist, using their relationship to keep things under control. To keep Melody under control.

She looked back into the mirror. 'We'll see about that.'

She chose a medium-length summer dress and went downstairs, shooting a radiant smile at one of the Brothers as he passed. She was gone before he could even duck. She slowed down in the cloister, stopping briefly at a fountain in a small alcove to taste the cool water. The map was still in her head, so she walked on and turned into a narrow corridor which brought her out into the covered way that would take her straight to the library. As she stepped out of the corridor she saw someone coming towards her.

'Jack!'

He stopped. 'Melody? You're here!'

'I believe I am!' She walked up to him where he stood apparently in something of a daze. 'Shall I kiss you hello, or are we somewhere else today?'

'No, sorry, of course.' They embraced, but she felt the distraction. 'What is it?' she whispered as her lips passed his ear.

'Ah well, it might be best if I begin at the beginning, or at least where you and I left off. Follow me – there's a nice wee room where we can talk more discreetly.'

He led her to the meditation room, but it was occupied, as was the discussion room next door and its neighbouring study area. And the library certainly wouldn't do.

'I know,' said Melody. 'Why don't we take a walk and you can show me around?'

The day was warm and fresh air seemed like a good idea, so they went back out and strayed off across mown grass in the general direction of some outhouses. The car they had arrived in was parked outside a garage. One of the monks, or whatever they were, was working in a shed nearby, so they pressed on, limiting their conversation to the lovely setting and the weather.

They came to a wooded area and a sign that pointed to an observatory. That seemed an interesting place to go, and Jack was keen to find out whether it was as well equipped as everything else there. They followed a path through a mix of deciduous and pine, enjoying the scents of leaf mould and needles beneath their feet. After a few minutes they came to a wide clearing. In the middle was a small hill, with steps to a dome on top.

When they got to the door Melody was surprised to find it was not locked.

'Why lock anything,' Jack observed, 'when the whole place is so secure?'

They went in. After their eyes had adjusted to the low light coming in from a few frosted windows high up in the walls, they took a proper look at the telescope.

'Looks like it's only a five-hundred mill, or twenty-inch as Dad would say,' said Jack, only half-interested.

'Jack, what's wrong?'

'Ah, let's go back outside.'

'What?' she laughed. 'Do these walls have ears?'

'Well, now there's a question.'

She followed him back outside, and they sat on the top of the steps. 'It's peaceful here.'

'Aye, better than that chapel. What do you make of the trees?'

Another surprise. 'What do you mean? They're very nice.' She affected a pop-poetic voice: 'They're whispering softly in the breeze.

Adding to the peace and ease!'

Jack sighed. He decided to tell her everything, both the parts of the story that he had kept from her and more recent events. Of course she would love being in the know at last, but he needed to do it for his own benefit as well. Maybe the two of them together could make sense of things.

'Since we talked on Space Station Alpha,' he began, 'the puzzles have only become more complicated. Ariel – sorry, we're calling him that now, by the way – Ariel has not regained his memory, or says he hasn't, so we still have no clue how he came to be on Venus, never mind in our ship. He was dressed in clothing like nothing we've ever seen. The crystal we brought back from Venus is also like nothing we've ever seen. Did I tell you about that? No? Well, we have a crystal that Dan swore glowed or hummed or something, in his office, yet since then it's failed to show any intrinsic energy, though Ryan says it's so far proved indestructible. And the military are practically at the door, and will be as soon as they force Bridlington to tell them where we are. Oh, and Ariel appears to be a tad indestructible too.'

'What? What did you just say?'

'Ach, I don't know. Schlesinger seemed to think he'd accidentally let a saw slip onto Ariel's hand, and yet nothing happened. Before we could test to see whether our beloved doctor was losing it, Ariel woke up good and proper, and then we had to move him pronto. I have to say, I thought Bridlington would be moving him to a medical facility for proper testing, not a monastery!'

Mel breathed out a long sigh. The long wait since Alpha had just come to an end more sudden and dramatic than she could ever have anticipated. Far from being excluded – not unreasonable, given her previous actions – she now found herself yanked into the inner circle. At last all was revealed – at least, all that Jack himself knew. And that was all she wanted from him.

'I don't know what to say. I mean, thank you for telling me this. You know how much it means to me.'

'Aye, well, it certainly gives you the edge again.'

'Jack, you know I don't mean professionally. Well, not just professionally. I need us to be open with each other.' She paused. 'I need you to be open with me.'

Jack stood up and wandered over to the observatory door. 'Well, I'd love to talk about us, of course, but as you can see—'

'Yes, I know. You have work to do, and a mystery to solve, and a crisis to avoid. And you're right of course. It is all a bit urgent.' She got up. 'Come on. Let's get you back to that chapel.'

'Hang on. Wait! I can't have you just turning up and joining the party!'

'Why ever not? Why else do you think Geneva sent me?'

3

Brother Leroy loved being a monk, especially when he was on garden duty. He particularly liked sweeping up dead leaves, as it was less hard on his knees than weeding. Although he was only 26, he'd never been in very good shape, his physical shortcomings propelling him into more intellectual pursuits from an early age.

Weaknesses, strengths... what were these but sloppy interpretations of a person's innate characteristics? Leroy had never really felt the need to prove himself. He had grown up with a knack for being socially invisible. People simply didn't notice him. Even here at the retreat centre some of the Brothers would joke about him 'decloaking' when they eventually managed to spot him in their midst, as if he'd just turned off some kind of invisibility device.

Today he hadn't actually been in plain view, but no one had heard him. Although the monastery provided him with all the latest garden gadgets, he had quickly renounced the leaf blowers and shredders, so cumbersome and noisy, for the peace and simplicity of a rake and an axe. They were easy to carry, and the act of raking was one of the most peaceful and calming he knew.

He had been wheeling a barrow-load of leaves through the wooded area near the observatory, on his way to the bonfire, when he heard voices. Without knowing why, he stopped. It was that Scottish man who had come in the night with the mysterious man everyone was trying not to talk about. He stopped to listen, drawn perhaps by the fact that they were speaking his native English, which didn't happen every day. Or perhaps it was the subject of their conversation. Yes, that was it, he was eavesdropping. Or leaves-dropping, he thought with a chuckle. He was just a few yards away from them, close by the observatory, hidden by a large clump of tall nettles. And he heard it all, the whole story.

They had found a man in outer space, an invincible man, and had brought him back because he had amnesia. Apparently he was quite passive, and philosophical too. That was interesting. Leroy made up his mind to keep an ear and an eye on the refectory when he was back inside.

4

Miranda closed the door behind her, actually relieved to be back in the hotel for a while, having made a successful foray into the acoustically very compliant chapel. She turned on the tablet Hugh had left for her and checked the reception. The conversation was coming through loud and clear, even though it was likely they were at the opposite end. She would replay it later. First, knowing Hugh would be wondering why she hadn't checked in today, she called him on her eband.

'Hello Miranda. One moment please.'

It sounded like he was leaving a room.

'Okay. Having a lovely time, are we?'

'Sorry for the silence. But yes, things are going well.'

'Do tell.'

'We have new ears – right where the action is.'

'Good girl. I should leave you to it more often. Intel?'

'Early days. But it seems there's a crystal. The Abbot asked Forrester about it when they came out of the chapel.'

'The chapel?'

'Yes, that's where they seem to have made their base. Luckily they left me in the Abbot's office, where I found a more discreet way in.'

'I doubt luck had much of a part to play,' he said softly. His intuition about Miranda was surely being vindicated.

'Though I got the info on the crystal earlier, when they came outside,' she confessed.

'A good sign,' said Hugh. 'The more places they talk, the more chances we have of picking things up.'

'Have you seen anything from the satellites?' she ventured. He was bound to be checking all available avenues.

'Oh yes,' he said drily. 'Lots of tree tops, some rooftops and two courtyards. Nothing beyond the visible. It seems their radio bubble is military strength. Or better.'

'Ah.'

'So, carry on the good work. Gotta go. Keep me informed.'

'As always,' she said, though the call was already ended. She went over to the tablet, but hesitated. 'I need a shower.' This was getting to be real fun now, and she was already planning her story for her next meeting with Mel.

5

'Hold on! Who's Miranda?'

Jack and Melody had been on their way to the chapel when the aroma of fresh coffee had once again drawn Jack off course. Melody was going over the stages of her short but eventful journey since the space station. She could see Jack tense up at the mention of Alice in Canterbury, though that was probably down to her omission of David's name, which had to be suspect. Right now, mercifully, time was against raking over those particular coals, and she so she moved on quickly to talk about Geneva, and how Bridlington clearly didn't want her here, but simultaneously didn't want to exclude her either, so had summarily sent her to Jack. And then Miranda had given her a lift.

'Miranda? Oh, she's just someone I met at the hotel in the village. We seemed to be the only English-speaking people around that night and, well, we got talking and decided to explore the area together. I thought I'd best play it cool and say I'd come for the Hesse museum.'

'The what?'

'It's the house of the writer Hermann Hesse.'

'Ah.'

She laughed. 'Don't worry, Jack. You don't have to bluff. I'm sure they've got some of his books in the library if you're really interested.'

'Aye, like I've got time for that right now. But seriously, didn't Bridlington tell you to come in by the back door?'

'The back door? No.' She fidgeted a little and took a sip of her mocha. 'Actually, she told me you'd contact me.'

'Well, that message hasn't come through yet. But then communication with the outside world is not exactly straightforward around here. You have to go through the Abbot's office.' He recalled his last visit there. 'Actually, I did call you once, but it went to voicemail.'

'You could have left a message.'

'It wasn't that kind of call. I just wanted a chat... you know, to hear your voice.'

'I'm touched,' she said and leaned forward to peck him on the lips. She didn't dare ask him if he'd called during the previous evening. Time to change the subject.

'The Abbot,' she said. 'He's a smooth one, isn't he? Actually, it's odd, only he already knew Miranda. Obviously something to do with her job – she said she was here for work. But it explains why she knew her way to the monastery. To the *front* door, at least,' she added with a grin.

Jack put his hand to his chin. 'I don't know.'

'Smelling a rat already, are we, Mr Security Man? It's not as if this place is private. Anyone can book, you know. And I got the impression she was a friend to the monastery.'

'Maybe,' said Jack. 'Though I don't begin to understand this place, or its abbot. I think I'd better get on the blower to Geneva.'

'Sure – right after you take me over to that chapel,' she said with a smile calculated to melt any lingering frost.

As they neared the door to the chapel they met Leonardo coming across the courtyard. He was hotly engaged in conversation with one of the Brothers and when he saw them he seemed to welcome the chance of escape. They were speaking in German, so Melody couldn't follow everything she heard, but Leonardo was clearly not happy. As they approached they switched to English, perhaps as a courtesy but already she was thinking it was just as likely a cover. 'Very well, Brother Josef,' he said, 'we'll leave it there. You can give me the details later.'

The monk gave a curt nod and disappeared back into the cloister. Leonardo sighed. 'We are actually taking a break right now,' he said. 'It was not Ariel who needed the rest,' he explained. 'He seems to be waking up! But the rest of us needed, er, a breather?'

'Just as well,' Jack said. 'I'd really love to make a call to Geneva, if that's okay with you.'

'But of course. Come with me. It might be as well if I bring you and, er, Miss Grantley James up to date anyway.'

'Aye, and that's another thing,' said Jack. 'How come you knew about Melody's arrival and I didn't?'

'Ah yes.' Leonardo entered smooth mode, with just a tinge of humility added in. 'That would be me. I did get a message from Ms Bridlington, and I was of course going to tell you, but I had not yet had the opportunity. I spoke to her only this morning.'

'Well, not to worry. It was a nice surprise.' He shot his own quiet smile in Mel's direction, which she absorbed in contented silence. 'I daresay our Ms Bridlington has a lot on her plate just now.'

They went into the office, and Leonardo left them to make the call in private. Jack was surprised when the response offered video. He chose it, and the top half of a young man came into view. 'I recognise him,' Mel whispered from a chair by the desk. A voice then came through loud and clear.

'Commander Forrester? A pleasure to meet you, sir. My name is

Petroc Naismith, and I work here with Ms Bridlington. She told me to take your call and to let you know that she is tied up at the moment.' He paused. 'With the military.'

Jack dismissed the picture that came to his mind and simply said, 'I see. Did she ask you to tell me anything else?' He hated this second-hand mode of communication, but right now anything was welcome.

'Yes. She says you have two days.'

Jack ended the call without further conversation. Two days. Was that even a certainty? Maybe one day. Then what? Were the military going to turn up at the retreat centre? How would that play out?

Mel took his hand. 'Come on. It sounds like we've got some planning to do.'

Jack wasn't sure about the 'we', but so far his feeling had proved right, that Mel was going to be the one to help him think things through in clear steps. And even now he could see the big decision facing him: to go off grid and leave the monastery, or to accept the inevitable and hand Ariel over to the interrogation squad.

Chapter 10

Watching and Waiting

1

William Petersen had never shied away from a challenge. He knew this had been one of the character traits that had lifted him through the ranks of the United Nations Special Task Force – that and the fact that the UN was not a popular career choice for anyone in the military. Gone were the heady days of the twentieth century, when the UN had carried at least some clout, and with a sense of purpose. Now all that was lost in the power grabs and games of the nations of the post-post-modern world. Or so it seemed to him at any rate.

He had come from a long line of military men and women from his native South Africa, and so his appointment as one of the youngest generals in the army at the tender age of 34 years was not a great surprise to his family. But his move to the UN Special Task Force was unexpected. To earn their name, the 'Specials' had to deal with anything international or global that was pressing on the day, especially challenges beyond the general UN remit of peace-keeping and counter-terrorism. After five years as head of the US regiment, this was only his third major project since his elevation to the rank of Commander-in-Chief. Neither his family nor his mentors had seen this coming. Bill had become a man of no state allegiance, and that made him an outsider. An alien.

That was the very word that had slipped out of Constance Bridlington's mouth back in Geneva, when she had been talking about the Endeavour's stowaway. When he jumped on it she had made an immediate withdrawal, back-pedalling her way into some guff about the guy's nationality being unknown. But he knew what she meant. What she feared. What she hoped for.

Right now he was on a plane to Lugano examining the security report that had been made on Alpha by the Brits' man Forrester. It had been signed off by Dan Marshall, the Aphrodite mission chief, who had apparently persuaded Bridlington to bring in the Specials as a way of keeping Washington, Moscow and Beijing at bay. For a while.

As the plane continued its hop over the Alps, Petersen instructed his military-issue eband to project the report onto the seat in front of him. It looked like everything was there, but you couldn't really tell, could you? There were accounts of the original find on Venus, the storm, the journey back to Earth, the intermittent coma of the Stranger (really?), and the deficient medical tests. Make that delinquent medical tests. It seemed that Dr Schlesinger had had insufficient equipment to do a full-body scan and insufficient time to run blood tests. That could mean only one of two things: either there was no sense of urgency at the time, or there was a cover-up. But if the man was clearly human, why the cloak-and-dagger approach in Geneva?

If time and money allowed, the best course of action might have been to go back to Venus to search for answers, because right now there seemed to be no evidence of where this Stranger came from or who he was working for. But time and money did not allow. The planet was returning to its normal hell-like conditions. And the budget for the Aphrodite mission had made a hole in everyone's pockets, both government and private enterprise, which meant the window of political will was also closing. No, the only answers available right now must lie in the stowaway's head.

As he looked out of the small oval window at Lake Lugano glittering in the afternoon sun below, his grandfather's voice began to fill his head. 'William, don't you ever turn your back on a problem just because people say it's too difficult, or too complex, or too whatever. I told your father the same. You've got to square up and face up!'

The plane was done circling and already coming in to land. He had decided to surprise Forrester by turning up unannounced early the next morning. Bridlington had assured him that the Abbot would be the soul of discretion, but he insisted on no warnings.

He shook his head as he turned off his eband. Abbots and amateurs... what was it with this operation? It was time someone took control.

2

Jack lowered the blind in the small chamber that was to be his home for whatever time they had at the monastery. Home. Now, where was that? If home was where your heart was, was that back in Scotland, where he hadn't lingered for more years than he could count? Or in London, at the flat? Or was it here, because Melody was here?

He turned on a lamp near a shelf of books, idly scanned the titles on the spines and then slumped into the room's sole chair. What was it that was needling him? If things were different, and he were a normal guest here, a client, then perhaps Abbot Leonardo could unlock it for him. Certainly he presented a more winsome option than David Carter, the free church pastor that had somehow insinuated his way into Mel's life.

But he was not a client, and there was no time.

He looked across the room towards a mirror that hung on the wall, shaking his head when he realised it was digital. This place was full of surprises – not that he had ever really understood the craze for digital mirrors that flared up briefly mid-century once everyone had adjusted to their own selfie image. In his opinion no mirror really showed you the right way round. Surely the only way to see the true person was from the inside looking out. And no mirror did that, silver screen or silvered glass.

He dozed in the chair. When the bell rang that sent the Brothers to their beds, he shook himself awake. It was just after ten. And in a moment his mind cleared. He knew what it was that had been burrowing away just below the surface of his mind.

It was Venus. With all that had been going on, he simply hadn't had the chance to process it properly. The debriefs had been rushed and only partly helpful. But now, as he sat motionless in the quiet, he was able to go back and stand on the Venusian surface once again. Further back, before the storm. He had walked on another world, Earth's twin sister, though definitely not an identical twin. Unless, perish the thought, she represented our own future. When they set out on the mission, Mel had run a piece calling Venus a beautiful sister when viewed from afar, who would turn out to be the ultimate ugly sister when seen up close.

Yet it had not been so.

There it went again, fading from his mind. What was it? The sense of wonder as he stood on Venus and watched his colleagues at work. It was more than the obvious, the amazing environment they'd pitched into. It was a sense of awe at their common humanity, these tiny bipeds who had crossed a slim sound of the ocean of space to reach the nearest island. Further than the Moon, not so far as Mars, but altogether more interesting than either of them, filled with drama and disorientation.

His job had been to get them down in the lander, to park safely and to get them away again. All that would have been excitement enough. He'd have been the second man on the second rock from the sun! But then Ariel turned up. The Stranger. The 'mystery man' who cast doubt on their being the first people on Venus.

But was Ariel a man, a human being? Jack had got the measure of Dr Schlesinger sufficiently well to know that something genuinely terrifying and amazing had happened when that bone-saw slipped.

Yes, you could have it down as a near miss, but the Doctor had been convinced that the blade had made contact with Ariel's flesh, only to bounce off as if it had come up against tempered steel.

Add 'man of steel' to 'mystery man'.

Had Bridlington told the military any of this? There certainly hadn't been any intelligence direct from Jack's people in London. And he'd loved the way Bridlington had contained the whole thing, giving them time to try to coax their amnesiac back to reality.

Reality. What had really been happening on Venus? Why was everyone so disoriented? Was it simply the conditions – tempting enough to draw them there, but too extreme for normal behaviour? How had Ariel got there? Where were his colleagues? Was it all down to one of the less communicative governments? A moment's thought showed this to be unlikely. Not even the Chinese were that clandestine these days, at least not when it came to engaging in the very public business of trans-orbital flight. The only other parties who had the money and resources to mobilise a manned mission to Venus were the privately owned mega-companies.

Or maybe their owners? Maybe it was an even more private affair than private enterprise? But who had the readies for something on this scale?

One thing seemed clear: whoever put Ariel on Venus must surely come looking for their lost boy sooner or later.

3

Melody looked around the breakfast room. How fascinating, she thought, that even when the Brothers weren't officially eating in silence, the most they could manage was a low hum of occasional conversation. She wondered whether things would be different if she weren't there. Jack had advised her to wear something a little more substantial than on her first day, though she had not detected any obvious ogling. Most of them seemed to be older than her, which meant nothing of course, but whenever you met one of them he seemed preoccupied if not plain busy. As she watched them askance she saw an array of beards and hair lengths that defied any sense of regulation beyond the common dress code of the grey-brown cowl. Up to now she had been so focused on the reason they were here that she had given little thought to what kept the Brothers busy.

She was considering what Jack had just been saying to her as she sat with him and munched her way through a bowl of particularly fruity muesli. It made sense. Whoever put Ariel on Venus would be keen to retrieve him. Her own earth-shattering article must have alerted them, whoever they were, to his presence on Alpha, though since the initial press conference there had been a virtual news blackout. That, of course, could not last long.

Leonardo joined them at the table. 'Good morning. Ariel and Natasha are not down yet?'

'No,' said Jack. 'I believe Natasha usually goes for an early-morning run, and as far as I know our mystery man is still sleeping. Or reading.'

'Well, I must say, I do admire the way you are giving him so much space. I don't doubt that there would be others who might apply a little more... pressure?' He looked over his shoulder. 'Speaking of which, we have a surprise guest.'

Jack's spine went cold. 'Already?' he breathed. 'Who is it?'

'He announced himself as General Petersen from the United Nations. South African accent, but talks in the manner of some American gentlemen I have known. I have shown him to the visitors' reception room for the time being. Although... I gather he has not had breakfast yet.'

Melody smiled at the shrewdness of the Abbot.

'Oh sure, why not?' said Jack. His own accent seemed more pronounced, always a sign of stress when he was stone-cold sober. Melody placed her hand on his. 'Well, Jack,' she whispered, 'who knows? This general may know more about Ariel than any of us.'

Jack thought about it. Perhaps the military man was here to give answers rather than ask questions. Yet somehow he doubted it.

Leonardo cleared his throat. 'I took the liberty of calling Constance,' he said, 'and she confirmed the gentleman's identity, and that he had specifically asked that she say nothing before his arrival. I rather think he is using surprise tactics.'

'Oh, Leonardo,' said Melody with a glint in her eye. 'I'm so pleased you're on our side!'

Jack sighed. He wasn't even sure what the sides were, let alone who was on which. 'Right, well, let's give the man some breakfast then. But Mel, I'd appreciate it if you could go upstairs and make sure Ariel and Natasha don't appear just yet. I think Ariel's in his room.'

She knew she was being dismissed but did not argue. This had to start with Jack alone. She left the refectory and darted up the adjacent staircase, hoping to remain unseen by anyone in reception.

'I will fetch the General,' said Leonardo, 'and then leave you two in peace.'

'Peace? Och, I don't think there'll be much of that.'

4

Melody approached Ariel's door with a mixture of trepidation and excitement. She was suddenly on the point of spending some time alone with this enigma of a man. She knocked quietly and waited.

After a few moments Ariel put his face around a half-opened door. He looked surprised.

'Hello, Ariel. Sorry if you were expecting Natasha. I believe she may be out for a run. May I come in?'

He opened the door wide and Melody stepped past him. She smelt different. He closed the door and turned to face her, his hands pressed to the heavy wooden frame behind him.

Melody sensed what she took to be his awkwardness and set about putting him at ease. 'These rooms are fascinating, aren't they?' she sputtered with inane enthusiasm. 'They all seem to have a bed and a chair, a table and a mirror, a drinks machine and bookshelves.'

'And a window.'

'True, true. So they do. What can you see from your window, Ariel?'

He crossed the small room and sat on the bed. 'Trees, of course.'

'Of course.'

'And sky, and earth, and the wind in the trees, and birds, and the Brothers.'

'Ah yes, the Brothers. It's a curious place, isn't it? But then, I guess everything seems pretty curious to you. Would I be right?'

'It is strange, yes.'

She sat down on the chair close to the window. 'What's strange... if you don't mind me asking?'

'It is strange knowing where I am, but not knowing who I am.'

Melody could think of no instant response to this, or follow-up question, but for once it didn't seem to matter. She found it surprisingly easy not to speak into the silence that followed. She checked out the ceiling as it was the one thing she hadn't really studied in her own room. Its plain whiteness did not repay more than a momentary glance.

After a while Ariel spoke again. 'I think I'm changing.'

'In what way?' she asked as casually as she could, suppressing her delight at the confidence he was showing her.

'It's as though things are falling into place. I think I've been here before.'

It seemed unlikely he had ever been to the monastery, but before Melody could respond there was a knock at the door. She noticed it was a distinctive, rhythmical tapping, almost like a code, and Ariel simply raised his voice a little and said to come in.

It was Natasha. Melody noticed that she had cast off the tracksuit for a white tee shirt, grey jeans and khaki jacket. 'Oh, hi. Sorry, I didn't realise–' She made as if to withdraw.

'Oh no, that's fine. Please don't go,' Melody said quickly. 'In fact, I need you to stay a while, if that's okay. Only there's something going on downstairs.' She told them both of the arrival of the General.

Natasha went to sit on the other side of the bed, but then seemed to think better of it and stood in front of the bookshelves. She pressed her fingers together, almost as though she were about to pray. 'What are we going to do?'

'Well,' said Melody, 'I guess that's up to Jack. He's getting the lie of the land right now. Meanwhile we'd best wait till we're called.'

'Yes,' said Natasha, 'but what then?'

Melody sensed her anxiety, if not yet panic. What was the long-term plan? Was there even one? 'I really don't know,' she answered as she looked down on the floor. Same mottled beige carpet.

'You mustn't worry.' Ariel's words surprised them both. 'I'm sure things will become clear.'

Melody glanced at Natasha, as if to plead with her not to contradict him. Better, surely, to let him think he is safe. They could do the worrying for him. She stood up and looked out of the window. Why was she so concerned about this man, her Icarus-turned-Ariel? This attachment that Natasha evidently had – was it now happening to her as well?

She surprised herself by her next question. 'Why do you think things will become clear, Ariel? Is it because things are falling into place, as you were telling me just now?'

'Yes, I think it is.' He turned to face Natasha. 'I know you said the military would be here before long. And I know you said we should move on before that happens.' Melody wondered how many people were meant to be involved in that particular stratagem. Just how close were these two? 'But I have this feeling,' Ariel continued, 'that we should not run. I should not run.'

They heard footsteps sprinting up the stairs. Before Melody had moved an inch Natasha was at the door. She opened it just a little, and immediately her shoulders dropped. 'It's Jack,' she breathed.

'Hello ladies, Ariel. Everybody okay? Seems a little tense in here.'

Melody glared at him. 'Jack! What's going on? What did he say?'

'Why don't you all come on down and have some breakfast,' he said cheerily, 'where there's a bit more room?'

He asked them to give him five more minutes before they joined him, but now the silence had become agitated and the looks strained, so they filed out after three. As Natasha and Ariel left the room Melody took one last glance out of the window. The trees were still there of course, but they seemed less friendly. They could already be hiding the enemy. But, then again, they would provide excellent cover from the enemy. 'Come on, girl,' she said to herself. 'You're getting paranoid.'

As she closed the door behind her she tried to reassure herself. The whole situation had already grown too fuzzy about the edges, so maybe the arrival of General Petersen would bring some of the clarity Ariel had been talking about. As she followed the others down the stone stairs, she wondered just what was going to be on this particular breakfast menu.

5

Jack had returned to the breakfast table satisfied that he'd got the measure of General William ('Please, call me Bill') Petersen. It was clear that this man had to be in charge, and be seen to be in charge. He liked to knock you off balance, only to reassure you as he took control. Right now he was using Jack's first name, unbidden, and leaning across the table, finger outstretched like a gun towards Jack's chest.

'Jack, I'm sure Ms Bridlington had her reasons, but you must see that the finding of a package like this is far too big for...' He looked for a word.

'For a small group of small-time operatives?' Jack put in, not even asking why Petersen was calling Ariel a package. He knew only too well that this man's whole world was populated with 'assets' and 'packages'.

The General was talking again. 'I absolutely don't doubt your credentials, or your abilities, as far as these go. But this is potentially a matter of world security.'

'Aye, well, that's just it, isn't it? Potentially. That's what we're trying to find out.'

'Look,' and with this Petersen moved even closer, 'you are simply not trained for this kind of thing.'

'I wasn't aware this *was* a kind of thing,' said Jack. 'Tell me, where's the precedent?'

The General leaned back, a look of admiration flickering across his face, as he considered Jack's series of calm but firm ripostes. 'Well, of course the situation as a whole is unique. We don't travel to other planets routinely, and you know as well as I do that we never expected to land people on Venus any time soon. But, when you boil it down, what we have here is an individual who has turned up on high-security property and claimed amnesia. That puts him in my jurisdiction.'

Jack was still framing his response when he saw Natasha and Ariel enter the breakfast room, closely followed by Melody. He changed tack. 'Well, here he comes now, your package.'

Petersen stood up suddenly and turned to greet them, though it looked to Jack for all the world like a defensive manoeuvre. The Brothers had long left the room, so they pulled a couple of tables together while Melody offered to go and get some more croissants and coffee. Natasha sat the other side of the General from Jack, pointing Ariel to the adjoining table where he could sit with Melody. Jack spotted the protective move and winked almost imperceptibly in her direction.

As Melody returned with a tray loaded with cups and coffee and croissants, Jack used the moment to pour himself some of the fresh brew while he tried to shake off the flurry of emotions that still dogged him. If ever he needed clarity, it was now, and rising impatience would only make things worse. General Petersen represented the single biggest threat so far to their softly-softly strategy.

'Well,' said Petersen, seizing his opportunity, 'I must say this is all very cosy. I trust you're all having a lovely time in this delightful country, in such a peaceful place.' Natasha shuddered, unsure that she had ever heard the word 'peaceful' said with such venom.

'More croissants?' said Melody. Jack almost choked with delight at her impeccable sense of timing as she burst the growing balloon of tension.

'Ah, the journalist.' Petersen's tone had not changed. 'Why are you even here, Ms Grantley James?'

'Well,' she shot back, 'I thank you for remembering the Grantley, but please, call me Miss James. And, as you mention my profession, let me ask you: why are *you* here, General Petersen?'

'Okay, okay!' Jack intervened. 'Come on, people. We all have a job to do, and right now, so far as I know, I am conducting this operation.' He raised his hand. 'No, General, don't quote me your orders. This is all too big – as you rightly say – to be handled without the utmost care, and until I get a change of direction from Constance Bridlington herself, or from London, that's how it's going to stay. Now, I'm glad that you're here, I really am, because we need to have some joined-up thinking right across the board – medical, political and military. Ariel here... this is Ariel, by the way...'

'How do you do?' Ariel held his hand out to Petersen, who shook it with a good deal more reserve than might normally be expected of a six-foot, square-jawed military official.

'Lovely,' Jack continued. 'Ariel here has already had some time with the medical community, of course, and I fully understand why the military want in before things go any further. So let's all calm down and make the best of this, shall we?'

Petersen had not taken his eyes off Ariel the whole time Jack had been talking, and he spoke now as if everyone else had already left the breakfast table. 'So, we're calling you Ariel. I'm looking forward to having a proper chat with you, Ariel. You will need to marshal your thoughts and get your facts straight before that. But then, I guess this place is very conducive to that end.'

'Yes,' said Ariel. 'And my friends here have been very patient, helping me to piece things together.'

'I'm sure they have.'

'All right,' said Jack, seeing the conversation was cooling faster than his coffee. 'Let's postpone for an hour, and then you can have your "proper chat". What shall we say? Eleven o'clock in the discussion room? Just the four of us?'

'Four?' shot the General.

'Yes. Melody here is not really part of our company,' said Jack, deliberately misreading the objection.

'You think! The thing is, Jack, I'm going to need to talk to the prisoner alone.'

'Well that could be tricky, General,' said Jack drily, 'as there is no prisoner here. And as for Ariel, you'll have no access without me.'

Petersen said nothing, which told Jack what he had already suspected: the General had been trying it on. Ariel remained under the care of the Aphrodite mission team, whose security officer was unchanged.

As they made their way out of the refectory, they ran into a young monk named Leroy who had been detailed to show the General to his room.

'Till eleven, then,' said Petersen.

'Can't wait,' Jack called back as he walked across the courtyard. He wondered just how much Constance Bridlington had told the General. He was fairly sure that the military hadn't brought more intelligence to the table, which meant that our 'Bill' was testing the waters. Jack might know more about those waters than most, but he was definitely beginning to feel out of his depth.

It was Ariel, using Jack's name for the first time, that brought him out of his thoughts as they walked along the covered way to the other building. 'Jack? I was wondering... what happened to my suit?'

'Oh, not to worry, I have it with me, safe enough.'

Five miles to the west, across the trees and up the hillside, sitting quietly in her hotel room, Miranda smiled. 'Have you now, Commander? Well, that is interesting.'

Chapter 11

Suspicions

1

Hugh loved Bruges. Early on in his career he had made it his goal to have a European base there – not his official headquarters, but a true base camp, where he could run his more hidden nexus of communications. Now, as he walked the rain-polished cobbles of the Old Town, he smiled at the thought of all these tourists immersed in the bliss of ignorance. There they were, holding their tablets and ebands up towards the spires and gables of grey stone and red brick all around them, listening to the bells of town hall and church, unaware of the global watching and listening going on in the very heart of this most innocuous of cities.

He stopped on a corner to watch a fine old gentleman play his barrel organ. Just under the top he could make out the words *De Tureluur* engraved in the wood. Checking his eband he was intrigued to discover it was an old Frisian word, meaning 'the hour'. That seemed fitting. Maybe an hour had come, a turning point, a time of revelation.

He turned down Mariastraat just as the rain started up again. Dodging a rickshaw, he slipped into a favourite café to check his messages. There it was: Miranda had called. Tuning in his earpiece he listened to her brief voicemail. Her Aussie accent was a little more pronounced than usual, telling him she was excited. She said she needed to talk. He would have to go back to the office for that. She could have left a message quite safely, given the level of encryption they used, so she must be wanting a two-way conversation.

As he sipped his coffee he trawled down a few more messages. What did young Petroc have to say? A promising field agent, that one, if still a trifle over-zealous. But he had been quick to notice a link between the crystal and the stowaway, spotting that they had both 'awakened' at the same time. And that just felt important. He listened to Petroc's latest message. So the military had turned up. About time.

Back outside the rain had eased. He made his way under a brick arch, moving quickly along the familiar streets and alleyways, before disappearing into a fairly run-down clock shop. It had been his own choice, of course – off the beaten track, with nothing to draw the crowds. No chocolate, no beer, no postcards. But for anyone who did wander in, there were plenty of timepieces to keep them interested.

Today there were no customers. Without so much as a word to the shop assistant Hugh slipped through a door at the back, past an old kitchen, and into a cubicle looking like an empty cupboard. He closed the door behind him. Once he had transmitted a code from his eband the lift noiselessly ascended. Upstairs he waved a quick hello to the half-dozen workers plugged into an array of desks and screens, before disappearing into his office. As he locked the door a red light on the lintel outside came on, showing a black spider in the centre of its web. One or two workers looked up at the familiar sign: the Chief was back at the centre of things, and was not to be disturbed.

Hugh checked the time as he took off his coat and called Miranda on a screen that had been angled up from his desk. He was just about to give up on the facemail when she suddenly appeared, munching on room service. 'Hi. Thanks for calling back.'

'For you, Miranda, anything. Well, almost. What have you got for me?'

'The suit.'

'Ah. They have it in the monastery then?'

'Yes. My guess is, it's in Forrester's quarters.'

'Very good,' said Hugh. 'Another piece of the puzzle. You know our friend Mr Box still disclaims all knowledge?'

'Do you believe him?'

'Funnily enough, I think I do. But we're running checks, of course. So far, no sign of anything quite so... interesting in his project work. Nothing we can detect anyway. And he's still waiting for the space suits to be sent to him.'

'What about the crystal?' She wiped some crumbs from her mouth with the back of her hand.

'Well,' said Hugh. 'I think, as pieces of the puzzle go, it fits into the picture quite close to our friend. As does his coat of many colours too, no doubt. Geneva believes the rock is not original to Venus, and we now know that it lit up, or showed some kind of activity, at the same time as the mystery man awoke.'

'Wow. Okay. What do you want to do?'

'Ha! Yes. Do. I think it may be time to do something, if by that you mean more than monitor.'

'I'm ready.' Her voice was level, but it seemed to Hugh that it was being contained somehow, even restrained. How desperately the poor girl wanted to show she was in control. But then, maybe her zeal for action was no bad thing. He turned to a bank of monitors on the wall behind him. 'Well now, it seems there's a storm coming your way.'

'The military, you mean?'

'That too. But no, I mean thunder and lightning, wind and rain, that sort of thing.'

Miranda thought fast. She knew Hugh would not be wasting

words on a weather forecast. 'I get it,' she said. 'You want me to go take a look.'

'That would be splendid. If you don't mind.'

Her face lit up. 'Under cover of darkness?'

'Perfect. The storm should be over Lugano late this evening. I'll leave the details to you, of course. Oh, and Miranda...'

'Yes?'

'Do take care, won't you?'

2

Dark clouds lowered in the small sky afforded by the rear courtyard. Natasha paced around it, lapping it in moments. This one had no cloister, no strange shrines, and nothing more than a stone bird bath in the centre. On one wall she could see through clear arched windows into the library. She passed a doorway, then the doors into the rooms they had been using, before coming back to the corridor that led from the covered way. She felt hemmed in under the approach of a storm that seemed as menacing as it was inevitable.

As she leant back against the bird bath Jack and the General emerged from the corridor. 'All right, Natasha?'

'Yes, Jack,' she replied. 'We are, as you say, good to go. Ariel is waiting inside.'

They filed off towards the discussion room, away from the electric atmosphere of the storm and, though they knew nothing of it, beyond the range of prying ears.

At the door Jack took Natasha aside. 'Now, don't worry that our General here is going to go over ground we've already covered. He'll doubtless come at things from a different angle, and that could be useful.'

Natasha gave the briefest of nods and they went in. As soon as Jack closed the door behind them, Petersen took control.

'Hello again, Ariel.' He spoke loudly, slowly, as if perhaps Ariel couldn't hear or understand properly. 'I am General William Petersen of the UN Special Task Force. But you can call me Bill. Now, I'm going to ask you some questions. Some of them you may have been asked before, but I want you to answer them as straightforwardly as you can. Is that okay?'

'Yes, I understand.'

'Good. So, first off, tell me how you came to be on Venus in the first place.'

Already Natasha could not hold back. 'General, if we knew that we wouldn't be here now, would we?'

Petersen kept his gaze on Ariel and said nothing. Jack shook his head ever so slightly.

'Bill,' said Ariel. 'I quite thought my friends here would have told you. I don't know how I came to be on Venus.' Ariel held eye contact after he had finished speaking, and Jack was surprised to see Bill look away. Jack couldn't believe Ariel was staring his questioner out. Or maybe it was that Ariel presented no threat to a tough nut like the General who therefore felt no need to compete.

'Okay,' said Bill, and he sat back a little in his chair. 'So what *do* you remember?'

'I remember very little, Bill.' Jack noticed that Ariel's accent was changing. Was that a touch of South African now? 'Just broken images, though I think they were dreams. The first clear one is Natasha here.'

'Okay, we'll get to her in a minute. But tell me about *before*. Go back as far as you like. Where did you grow up? Which school did you go to?'

'Bill, I know you are going to be disappointed by my answer, but honestly, I don't recall.'

'Hmm. Total amnesia, eh?' He turned to Jack. 'Has anyone given him a cognition test?'

'Not as such,' Jack replied. 'But then, as you probably know, we couldn't get very far on Alpha. Mind you, we do know he can speak English and understand Italian.' He decided to leave out the bit about Tibetan. Surely one complication too many at this stage.

180

'And you discovered this how, exactly? Has he been out among the locals?'

'No, no,' said Jack. 'He overheard the Abbot speaking in his native language.'

'Have you tried any other languages – no, don't tell me, you've not had chance.' He stood up, strode over to the window, and looked out towards the chapel next to the main building. 'Weird place this, don't you think?'

The question didn't seem to be aimed at anyone in particular, so Jack took it. 'Aye, it surely is. Natasha here has been reading some of their blurb, which doesn't explain a lot, but whatever it is, this is where we were sent.'

'Sure, sure,' said Bill, still looking outside. 'I gather Bridlington has some connection to the place, and I'll admit it's out of the way. Very discreet.' He returned to the chair. Natasha threw Jack a questioning glance.

'Er, Bill,' Jack asked. 'Would you like to hear from Dr Koroleva?'

'All in good time.' He still didn't look in her direction. 'Ariel, you mentioned some dreams. Let's hear about those, shall we?'

'Very well. Recently I've been dreaming about trees. But before that, before we came here, they were not such peaceful dreams. Flashing lights, war cries...'

Jack winced at the new word.

Bill was on it in a heartbeat. 'How do you know they were war cries, Ariel?'

'It's a feeling. I really don't have any context, but we seem to be fighting, pushing back the enemy, but then I'm falling. Always falling.'

'Who's "we"?' asked Bill. Natasha pressed her hands together but kept her eyes on Ariel.

'Colleagues, I think,' said Ariel, maintaining a level tone. 'Comrades-at-arms.'

Bill's next question came in a flash. 'And who were you fighting for?'

Before Ariel could answer, Natasha modified the question. 'Or what were you fighting for?'

Bill threw up his arms and turned on Jack. 'You see why I said I needed to talk to him alone!'

'Whoa there,' said Jack, not rising to it. 'I'm sure Ariel can answer both your questions.'

'Come on, Jack. Surely you can see she's leading the witness!'

Jack turned to Ariel and Natasha. 'Guys, sorry, can you just give us a few minutes? No, actually don't get up. Bill and I will step outside.'

The two men went into the small courtyard. Bill went first. 'Jack, d'you mind telling me what's really going on here?'

'Hey, Bill, what you see is what you get.'

'But the Russian?'

Jack cleared his throat. 'Dr Koroleva is, as you well know, a highly trained and prized member of the team that crewed the Endeavour. Now, I admit that we have given her more access than you might expect—'

'Like, more than the ship's captain!'

'Aye, right, but that was because, in my judgement, the bond that seemed to have formed between them could be useful to us.'

'In your judgement! Jack, has it occurred to you that this bond might be there for another reason?'

'Go on,' said Jack, slowly filling with embarrassment as he recalled the new closeness he himself had felt to Natasha on board the Endeavour. Could it have clouded his judgement? He shrugged.

Bill sighed impatiently. 'Why, man, I'd have thought it was obvious. The two already knew each other!'

Jack felt a chill run through him: the idea had not once entered his head. No wonder Bill had given Natasha the cold shoulder. He looked up at the sky, even darker now, and tried to gather his thoughts. 'So, what are you saying? Natasha was a Russian spy, and was meant to rendezvous with this guy we're calling Ariel? And maybe something went wrong?' He paused. 'Maybe it had already gone wrong, and she was there to rescue him?'

Bill clapped him on the back. 'That's more like it, Jack. I'm so glad we're on the same page at last.'

3

Leonardo got up from the desk in his office and opened the door to what looked like a walk-in cupboard but led through a second door straight into the chapel. He closed both doors behind him and walked up the long aisle to the place where, just two days before, they had begun to draw from Ariel some of the feelings, if not yet the facts, about his presence on Venus. He took hold of a smooth stone that rested along with three others on a window sill, ready for use in meditation exercises. He sat down and felt the stone's weight in his hand, letting it anchor his thoughts and feelings. So many feelings.

He gazed at the stone, wishing it was the mysterious crystal. Ever since his novitiate in Tibet, when he had received the given name of Leonardo, he had dreamed of finding another crystal from the heavens. All crystal was, of course, an exquisite coming together of fire and earth, air and water... the four elements in harmony, after a process of thesis, antithesis and synthesis (or heating and cooling and hardening, as the geologists in the Order preferred to say). But could this one from Venus be like the ancient crystal at the Temple? Might its extra-terrestrial origin place it in the domain of what some distinguished as a fifth element, the ether, the home of the heavenly bodies and the fire from heaven? His own Order of the Four Elements subsumed this under 'air'. No matter. What excited him was the possibility that this particular crystal might actually explain some of the unique properties of the Temple one, its unusual molecular make-up. And its legendary ability to radiate.

He licked his lips. Dare he hope for even more? Might this crystal turn out to be even more sacred? More potent?

He sighed at his own premature excitement. Even if the Venusian crystal were to come here, there was no way Constance could allow him to keep it. Maybe if he could keep Jack on side the two of them could convince Constance it would be safe here, away from those prying instruments of analysis that could prove so destructive. The one in Tibet had revealed itself to be incredibly tough. That was something they had discovered by accident, whereas the new crystal was almost certain to be subjected to invasive, even destructive processes.

He replaced the stone and walked around the chancel. It occurred to him that Ariel was much like the crystal, a precious treasure vulnerable to the devices and desires of men. And how often it had been *men* in the twenty-first century sense who had taken liberties with nature, *viri* not *homines*, the male of the species not the species as a whole, even though as the century grew older the distance between men and women was shrinking ever further. This was part of the reason Leonardo had decided to come to Montagnola – not just to be close to his homeland, but to lead a community of men. While women had by and large remained true to their innate qualities, even in the turmoil of emancipation and the struggle for equality, men had somehow lost their way, unsure how to relate to women as equal sisters, and even less sure how to relate to one another as brothers. And didn't the rise of binaries and neuters simply underline the fact that men – and women – had lost their way? The community here at the Elemental Retreat Centre brought men, at least, back to themselves by re-immersing them in the sacredness of nature, experienced in community. Male community.

It was Constance who had begun to make him think it was time to consider admitting women to the community, though he'd not got far with the idea and hadn't even broached it with Tibet. She was of course not the only woman to have stayed as a guest in the monastery on retreat. He had always insisted that their advertising should encourage women to come, as this gave the Brothers opportunities to interact with women without having to live in community with them. And interacting with guests was critical to much of their work, apart from now, of course, with their current cache of special visitors. A typical retreat was between three and seven days – long enough for some chemistry between the sexes, short enough to keep the Brothers focused on the reason they were here: to rediscover their link to both nature and humanity specifically as men.

And if that 'chemistry' became sexual, what of it? He knew, courtesy of Brother Josef's ever watchful eye, what sometimes went on. But then these men were not Catholic priests, and he was not here to micro-manage their behaviour. They knew that any special bond between them and the guests, female or male, was a potential threat to their fellowship in the community, where their relationship to nature and humanity was to be carefully monitored and maintained. Each member was here for a minimum term of seven years, and so far Leonardo had not released anyone from their covenant. Those who had decided to leave had done so unilaterally.

And what was he looking for in the men who came to be Brothers? Clearly they would all have a reverence for the sacredness of nature. That much was a given. They could be artists, they could be scientists, they could be businessmen or civil servants or labourers – it didn't matter. While he left Brother Josef to oversee the experimental side of their work, always for Leonardo the goal was a renewal of the Brothers' specifically male qualities of conceiving, creating, initiating, developing and defending. Each of these traits had suffered from the corruption of masculinity over previous centuries, and none had been properly restored through the gender wars of the present one. What was needed was a New Man. And that thought brought him back to Ariel.

What was it about this man? He was vulnerable, obviously, yet strong. He was unsure of so much, yet solid. He was sharp – sharper than any of his companions seemed to realise – yet tranquil. And yes, he was a man of mystery, and Leonardo was no more immune to that particular allure than the rest. There could be no doubt about the amnesia: he was simply too balanced, too spiritually strong, to be lying. Yet even if he had forgotten incidentals, his values seemed secure. Whatever had caused it, it surely had to be the result of profound trauma. Like the crystal, he had come to Venus from somewhere else, forged through the fire. Could it be that his origins lay beyond the Earth?

The thought thrilled him. The four classic elements – earth, air, fire and water – brought together in a man from the ether. The elements incarnate? That the crystal came from the heavens was marvel enough. That this man too might be from another part of the cosmos... well, that opened up all kinds of possibilities for their work.

He reprimanded himself for entertaining thoughts that were clearly running ahead of present reality. Opening the heavy wooden door that led out into the cloister, he left the chapel.

4

Jack needed to talk to Ariel alone. As he approached the refectory door, he hesitated. There was a room on the left that they had never been in. What was it? He pushed its old wooden door open and peered in. It was a lounge, no doubt normally full when the Centre was open for business, but quite empty now. Hoping none of the Brothers would be making use of it, he decided it was the perfect place for a quiet chat.

The next challenge: how to get Ariel away from everyone else. How to get him away from Natasha. Even as he pondered this the answer came skipping along the cloister towards him, her hair bouncing with every step. 'Hey Jack!' she called. 'How did it go?'

'Don't ask!'

'That good, eh?'

'Listen, Mel, I wonder, could you do me a wee favour? Can you and Natasha go for a walk or something? Only I'd like to have a chat with our boy on his own.'

She frowned. 'Trying to get rid of me again?' But she was quick to light up a smile – Jack may have been the man who knew her best, but he could still take her too seriously sometimes. 'Of course,' she said. 'Actually I could do with some girl time with Natasha. I don't feel I've really got to know her.'

Who does? Jack kept his thoughts to himself.

While he waited for Melody to come back down with Natasha, he sat down by the statue in the middle of the courtyard. Even as they emerged from the staircase it occurred to Jack that Natasha would probably guess something was afoot. But maybe that didn't matter. She was not really one to interfere with his stratagems. He was startled, therefore, when she suddenly gasped and trotted over to him. He looked past her at Melody for some kid of explanation, but she simply raised her shoulders in professed ignorance.

'Everything okay?' said Jack.

'Yes. Well maybe,' said Natasha. 'Only I've just remembered – again – that I haven't shown you the photo I took under this very statue the other morning. But as you're here we can take a look at the real thing.'

'Okay,' he said, and she quickly located the mysterious object under the sill. He knelt down and peered up at it. He was about to say something but thought better of it. Turning to both women he put a finger to his lips before talking randomly about the type of masonry that had been used to build the plinth. Melody tilted her head quizzically, but followed Jack and Natasha out through the entrance hall, past Leonardo's office and into the grounds at the front of the monastery. After they'd walked a fair way into the open, Jack began to whisper.

'Well, I've not seen anything quite like that, but I think it isn't good. Almost certainly some kind of listening device.'

'What?' said Natasha, louder than she had intended. 'How can that be a device?'

'I know... hard to believe, eh? But just think about it. You know the kinds of things miniaturisation has led to these days – micro- and nano-technology all over the place. If it is what I think it is, all we can hope is that the listener on the other end is the Abbot. I can't think that it would be transmitting anything through the radio screen over this place. We've all seen how impregnable that is.'

'Wow,' said Melody. 'This place just continues to surprise.' She smoothed back her hair. 'Anyway, Natasha and I were just going for a walk, and as we're out here I think we'll explore the grounds a little. As far as I know nothing's off limits.'

'Aye, you do that,' said Jack. 'But maybe keep your voices down, especially if you start talking about our friend.'

The two women strolled past the front of the chapel with its large double doors. They realised that they had never seen anyone enter that way, and a twist of the heavy iron ring that served as handle confirmed it was locked. Pressing on, they turned the corner intending to walk down the side of the building, but the way was narrow and uninviting, presenting a slim margin between the chapel and what looked like a boundary wall. The brooding darkness of the day was thicker here, as the afternoon sun was unable to penetrate the thick forest that stretched its fingers right up to the wall. Melody shivered, and they quickly decided to walk back to the other side of the main building, where they briefly followed a road for delivery vehicles that led to the rear of the kitchen and infirmary, before they swung right and disappeared in the direction of the observatory.

Jack walked back through the entrance hall, looped around past an alcove with an oil lamp and ducked in through a doorway past a lift before trotting up a set of stone stairs. He had not been up these before, so when he made the landing he stopped to work out just where he was. On the right the corridor did not get far before it came to a closed door. As far as Jack could tell, that would lead above the chapel, presumably for access to the roof. He crossed to a window. There was the front drive, where he had just left Melody and Natasha. Below him must be the entrance hall and the Abbot's office.

Once he had got his bearings he walked along the hallway in the other direction. There were rooms on both sides. The ones on his left must look out to the cloisters, while those on his right would give onto the woods. At the end he followed the hall round to the left, and marched down towards the rooms nearer the other staircase, where he and the others were staying. He didn't know where they had put Petersen. Passing Mel's room and his own, he came to Ariel's and knocked on the door.

As he waited it occurred to him that this might actually be a better place to talk, though he resigned himself to the possibility that the whole place was bugged. After a moment the handle turned with a clunk and Ariel opened the door. He look relaxed.

'Hi Ariel, how are you doing?'

'Very well, thank you Jack. Would you like to come in?'

Jack followed him into the small room with its familiar layout. One of the chairs was by the window and a book was on the sill. Jack picked it up. The title was *Man's Search for Meaning*. 'Interesting reading,' he said. 'I guess you have the same kind of books we have in our rooms.'

'Yes,' said Jack. 'At least, Natasha has a similar range in hers, though not exactly the same titles.'

Jack noted the give-away about visiting Natasha's room. Did that reassure him that she was getting somewhere, or worry him that she was being manipulated? Somehow he doubted that. He read the blurb on the back of the book. 'Auschwitz. Where do you find meaning in that?'

'I don't know, Jack. I wasn't there. But Mr Frankl has some thought-provoking things to say. He was a psychiatrist, you know.'

'Aye, well, I'd love to discuss the meaning of life with you, Ariel, but I really need to concentrate on helping you remember.' He put the book back down, but as he did so he thought better of leaving the subject altogether. 'Although... may I ask why you chose this particular book to read?'

'Well, it's not the only one I've read since I've been here, but I admit it has intrigued me more than most.' Jack wondered just how many of the books he had read in the small amount of time he had been on his own. Ariel continued: 'It strikes me that people look for meaning in all kinds of places.'

'What, like human relationships, you mean?'

'Yes, and in human stories. But also in nature.'

'Aye, well, I've known some folk look for meaning at the bottom of a tea cup.' He paused. 'Or a bottle, of course.'

'Yes,' said Ariel. 'People find patterns in tea leaves, don't they?'

Jack wasn't sure whether or not Ariel deliberately ignored the mention of the bottle, but as he was here to talk about Ariel, not himself, he pressed on.

'And you, Ariel? Where do you look for meaning?'

'Me? You said it yourself, Jack – it's memory I need right now, not meaning. Although...'

'Yes?'

'I don't think I had to actually look for meaning anywhere... you know, before.'

'How so?' Jack probed gently, delighted that he had apparently struck upon a fertile area of enquiry. It wasn't often Ariel spoke about 'before'.

'It's hard to say. I was fulfilled, I suppose.'

'And earlier on, with Bill, you mentioned that you were with others. Do you think you were working together?'

Ariel sat on the other side of the bed, close to the bookshelves. He took a deep breath.

'Okay, not to worry,' said Jack. 'I can see it's difficult. Let's go back to what you do recall, shall we?'

'I can see faces,' Ariel whispered.

Jack sat on the chair. 'That's good, that's got to be good.'

'I recall Natasha's face. She's quite close, looking down on me. Yes, we definitely looked at each other.' Jack recalled his conversation with Natasha on Alpha. 'And the song was so peaceful.'

'The song?'

'Yes. It was soothing.'

Jack recalled Natasha's revelation that she had sung to Ariel, although he was beginning to wonder if there were still things she had not told him. 'Do you remember anything else?'

'Well, yes,' said Ariel. 'There's the other face. The greedy one. He's looking down at me too, but he's not singing. There's a whirring sound, and then I defend myself, and then suddenly he's gone.'

Jack frowned, glad of the new information yet unsure just what it meant. 'How did you defend yourself? Do you recall?'

'It's hard to explain. What I did was instinctive, but I'm fairly sure I neutralised the attack.'

'Do you mean you got into a fight? I'm guessing we're talking about Dr Schlesinger here.'

'Yes, that's it,' said Ariel, 'the good doctor. He really was delighted to have me as his... patient.'

'Well, I'm sorry if he got a bit carried away, and I've little doubt that he was out of his depth, but you'll understand he's all we had at that point. All we've had at any point, come to that.'

They sat in silence for a few moments.

'And what about now, Jack? What's next for me?'

Jack felt the force of the question. There seemed little point now in confronting him with Bill's idea that he and Natasha were somehow in league. Yes, there was a bond between them, but it still looked innocent enough. As they sat in silence, with just the sound of a mower floating in through the window, once more he thought about his time on the Venusian surface. He decided to try to give Ariel a different perspective.

'You know, you're not the only one who has holes in his memory. The Captain and his research engineer — that's Jim and Ryan — they were both overcome by the storm, or by something, when they went out onto the planet's surface. Jim says he saw Ryan lying on the ground. Or what he took to be him anyway. You don't suppose...'

'What, Jack?'

'Well, you don't suppose it was one of your friends he saw, do you?'

'I couldn't say. I wasn't there.'

The precise repetition of the matter-of-fact way he had spoken about Auschwitz struck oddly, as if he had been implying it was perfectly possible he might have been in Germany in the last century, but it just so happened he wasn't. Jack studied Ariel's face. While he could read nothing there, the longer he looked the more of his own memories started to come back to him – memories of that last, eventful EVA. Even the dream he had had before he went out looking for Jim and Ryan. Those voices on the wind.

Jim had said he'd stumbled and fallen before he could check on Ryan who, it was presumed, was the person lying on the ground. Yet when Jack himself had gone outside, they had both managed to return with no clear account of themselves. All they seemed to be sure of were the noises, some of which Jim later said sounded like voices.

Jack drummed his knuckles on the windowsill and stood up. The conversation had certainly been useful, and yet in the end it seemed to have widened rather than closed holes in his understanding. And all the while they were running out of time.

5

Melody and Natasha followed a path through the woods away from the main building. There were more spaces between the trees here, but they spoke in hushed tones, both still wondering whether Jack could be right about the high-tech device under the statue. After a few minutes they came to a fork in the path. There was a signpost with the word Observatory on it, pointing off to the left.

'Ah,' said Melody. 'Jack and I went up there yesterday, only we came at it from another direction, I think. Let's go take a look.'

They passed a narrower path that led off to a high-walled enclosure with danger signs about electricity all over it, but not being in the mood for adventure they pressed on and soon came to the clearing with the hill in the middle. As Melody had hoped, once they got inside the observatory Natasha began to relax and do more of the talking. She was identifying various pieces of equipment, clearly impressed with the quality. 'This is most unusual for an amateur facility.'

'Well, I don't know,' said Melody. 'It strikes me everything's pretty tip-top around here. Even the bugs!'

Natasha gave her a puzzled look. 'The insects? Oh no, I see – the listening device.'

'Or devices,' said Melody. She peered up at the large dome over their heads, recalling Jack's nervousness about being overheard long before the statue's secret had come to light. The wind moaned. 'Let's go outside, shall we? It's chilly in here.'

Melody led the way back into the sunshine. Leaning back on a handrail that ran from the steps round to the observatory, she took up the conversation again. 'I'm intrigued, Natasha. How did you find the thing in the first place? It was pretty well hidden.'

Natasha told her about her early morning walk around the cloisters. 'I think I have worked it out now,' she said. 'Each of the inlets in the wall–'

'The alcoves?'

'The alcoves, yes, each one has one of the four classical elements in it – earth, air, fire and water. It was all a bit bemusing in the dark, but the more I've thought about it, and read up about this place, the more sense it makes.'

'Well,' said Melody, 'you're a geologist and my background is literature, but I suspect we can both point to some meaning in it all. Mind you, it seems odd that they have such symbolic things, given all the high tech.'

'I don't know,' said Natasha. 'I think it is an acknowledgement of the past. They seem comfortable here with both the old and the new, the simple and the sophisticated.'

Melody smiled, her intrigue growing as she looked at the complex woman before her. 'Natasha, you really are a remarkable person. No wonder Ariel's smitten with you.'

Natasha looked down across the clearing below them. 'What do you mean?'

'I think you know what I mean.'

They stood a while in silence, the wind blowing Melody's hair in all directions. The sun disappeared, which prompted Natasha to look up at the sky. 'I think there is a storm coming,' she said. 'Perhaps we should get back.'

Melody complied by hopping down the steps. 'If we head off to the right, we can get back to the covered way. We could pop into the library – I'd like to see what else they've got here – maybe something to explain this place a bit more.' She was not sure Jack would be done with Ariel yet.

'Okay,' said Natasha. Melody led the way, by now fairly sure that Natasha was aware of the rather artificial nature of their little jaunt, though clearly happy enough to go along with it. As they walked she restarted the conversation.

'So, what do you make of Jack?' She tried to sound casual, though she knew in an instant she had failed, so she was relieved by the way Natasha decided to interpret the question.

'I think he's coping very well.'

'Yes, the poor dear. He does have a lot on his plate right now.'

They walked on and soon came to the library. It appeared to be empty. They browsed in one of the aisles for a few minutes before sitting down empty-handed on opposite sides of a reading table. Melody was surprised when Natasha spoke as if their conversation had not stopped. 'I'm sure he's glad you are here with him.'

'What, Jack, you mean? Oh, I don't know about that. I sometimes think I'm more of an embarrassment.'

'You!' exclaimed Natasha. 'How could you be an embarrassment? You're so... savvy, so polished.'

'Ah well, thank you, Natasha, I appreciate the compliment. But no, what I meant was, my profession isn't proving quite so helpful just now.'

'Yes, I see.'

'I mean, it hasn't been a problem before, you understand,' Melody continued. 'But no one was expecting any kind of hush-hush after they got back from Venus. Quite the opposite, in fact.'

'Of course.'

'But Ariel, well, he's changed everything.' She watched Natasha closely, looking for any kind of reaction, some tell-tale clue to her feelings for their mysterious guest. But all she got was the Slavic stone face. Idly she let her slender fingers smooth back her tousled hair while she pressed on. 'I suppose you're worried about him... you know, about what's going to happen to him next.'

'Yes I am, and I don't mind admitting it,' said Natasha, her voice rising and her eyes flashing. 'I don't mind admitting it to anyone who's listening in, and I won't hold back from the General if I get the chance. I know what happens in this kind of case.'

'This kind of case?' said Melody. 'I'd call this pretty unique.'

'Oh for sure, it's a first in many ways. But the process, Melody, the process... it's as old as the human race. Those who are frightened by what they don't understand seek to destroy it.'

At this point, two of the Brothers came in, clearly exercised about some imminent event, though they stopped talking when they saw the two women.

'Well,' said Melody, 'I don't know about you, but I need a cup of tea.' She stood up and smiled sweetly at the new arrivals, before she and Natasha both headed off towards the refectory.

As the two monks went further in they met a third emerging from the book-lined depths. 'Brother Leroy!' said one of them. 'Are you still cleaning?'

'No, no,' said the young monk. 'I got a bit held up back there, but I'm all done now.'

CHAPTER 12

Elements of Surprise

1

In the upper reaches of Earth's atmosphere a storm was building. Elemental surges of power were released as cold clashed with heat. A deluge ensued.

Far below, in the cloister of the Elemental Retreat Centre, it was action stations. Leonardo was barking out orders in a way Jack had never seen before. 'Anselm – water! Francis – wind! Ricardo – earth! Josef – the fire of heaven!' The four Brothers came racing out of the chapel and into the main courtyard. Jack quickly donned one of the bright yellow raincoats that were left nearby for visitors and, leaving Melody and Natasha in the entrance hall, edged out as far as the cloisters. The wind was picking up, the sky lowering, the light dropping, although with a shock that took him straight back to Venus he noticed that the temperature had not dropped with it – if anything it felt warmer in the sultry conditions. He watched the four men take up their positions, each now standing at the half-way point of his side of the square.

Melody joined him, similarly decked in waterproof coat, her hair now tied back in a single pony tail. She was followed by Natasha, for whom a tracksuit seemed always to be enough, who raised her voice over the wind that wailed under the arches. 'They're standing by the shrines of air, water, earth and fire!' Jack nodded, intrigued at what was surely the first obviously religious act he had witnessed in the three days they had been here.

They stood aside as Leonardo came past and watched him make his way towards the statue in the centre of the courtyard. Halfway across he stopped, turned and called to Jack, 'Is Ariel not with you?' Jack told him he had last seen him in his room. The Abbot looked a little crestfallen, but the elements would not wait. After a moment's stillness at the centre he began to circle round the statue, pausing on every side to turn and bow to each of the four Brothers. Or was it to the shrines behind them?

Jack watched as each of the Brothers held up one of his arms. As their large sleeves slipped down he was surprised to see they had ebands round their forearms, and even more surprised to see these were glowing. He nodded to Melody: 'I wonder what that's about.'

'Hmm,' she mumbled, too quiet for Jack to hear. 'The new and the old.'

The three of them fell silent as they watched the ceremony unfold. Eventually they realised that, every time Leonardo stopped and bowed to one of the Brothers, his eband glowed in sync with theirs.

After several more minutes the wind dropped and the rain picked up. Leonardo stopped, turned to the statue, spoke some words they couldn't hear and then made one last circuit, head bowing and arm glowing at the appropriate points, before leaving the courtyard on the opposite side. Moments later the four Brothers filed out the same way.

The three spectators looked at each other and quickly agreed on a hot drink in the refectory. Making their way past fire and earth, they walked round the cloisters to the welcome warmth inside.

'Well, what was all that about?' said Jack as they sat down together. 'I mean, I get that we're in a monastery dedicated to the four elements, but why all the excitement now? Some kind of nature worship?'

Melody wrapped her cold fingers around her mug of tea and took a sip.

It was Natasha who took the question. 'You could say that, though they might argue about the word "worship".'

'Aye, well, it looked like a ceremony.'

'Yes,' she continued, 'unless... unless they were taking readings.'

'Could be both,' put in Melody. 'This whole place seems to be a fascinating mixture of science and–'

'Religion.' Jack finished her sentence, and Natasha noticed that in the same breath he took a swig of coffee, almost as if he were washing his mouth out. Melody threw him a disapproving look, the like of which Natasha had not seen before. She said nothing and sipped her hot lemon.

The uneasy peace was demolished by a crack of thunder. Then all the lights went out.

2

Jack turned on his eband light, immediately noticing a ton of messages registering. Clearly more than the lights had gone out. He headed out of the refectory around the cloisters towards Leonardo's office, but met the Abbot on the way.

'Ah, Jack!' the abbot called over the howling wind that had returned with a vengeance. 'Good to run into you. We have a problem.'

'So I see. The power's down. What can we do?'

Before Leonardo could answer, Bill Petersen emerged from the stairway behind them, hastily donning a yellow raincoat. 'Who turned the lights out?'

'It's the storm,' Leonardo responded. 'I can only think that the generator room has been hit by lightning.'

'Okay,' said the General. 'I guess that's something you can fix.'

'Yes,' said Leonardo. 'I am hoping it needs only to be reset.' He looked across the cloister at the shape of a monk moving slowly in the shadows. 'Brother Leroy! Can you come?'

The young monk suddenly accelerated to join them. 'Brother Leroy, can you go to the generator room and see what's happened to the power?'

As the monk turned to comply, Bill put a hand on his shoulder. 'One moment, Brother. Abbot, would it help if Jack and I went with him? It's getting pretty rough out there.'

'But of course.'

Jack suspected Petersen's sudden urge to help was governed by a desire to see more of what made the place tick, but he could see it made sense. 'Lead on, Brother Leroy!'

The three men made their way round the cloister and through the rear corridor, where Leroy fetched a torch and a waterproof covering for himself from a small cupboard on the wall. Then they stepped out into the darkness.

The rain hit them like a wall of water. Whipped up by the wind, it drove into every crevice it could find. The two men's trousers were soaked in seconds. Bill fumbled with his eband to get some light, but Jack preferred to let his eyes become attuned to the dark. In single file they strove against the lashing rain. Leroy led the way, his powerful torch beam piercing the darkness of the forest that loomed ahead of them. Jack followed, and Bill came a few steps behind, glancing over his shoulder every so often. He didn't expect to see anything, but it was more than he could do to curb the habit of a lifetime.

Jack was just beginning to make out a few outbuildings in the gloom when a shaft of lightning lit up the forest with a brilliant flash. They stopped, waiting for their sight to return, suddenly aware of their vulnerability before such an elemental surge of power.

'That was close!' Bill shouted.

'I think there's quite a bit of metal in some of these sheds,' said Jack.

'The generator is this way!' shouted Brother Leroy. 'I think maybe we should hurry.'

'Well,' said Bill, 'I'll give the fella credit. He's got guts.'

The two men followed the diminutive Brother as he picked up the pace. Wet leaves stung their faces as they soldiered on. Jack noticed the fingerpost showing the way to the observatory off to their left, but they kept on going and soon approached the typically high brick walls that enclosed a power installation, complete with vivid danger signs. Almost at once their attention was struck by a glow that came from the other side of the small enclosure.

'You two go in and sort out the power!' shouted Bill. 'I'll go check out that light.'

'Wait!' Jack shouted. 'What if we need to call each other?' Bill nodded and the two men raised their forearms, holding their ebands close together. Each of them called out 'Accept' and their chosen contact details were duly exchanged.

Leroy unlocked a tall wooden gate in the wall. While he and Jack disappeared inside, Bill headed off along the path. The retreat centre was a block of darkness some fifty metres on his right. The trees on his left were a cacophony of creaking branches. The wind howled.

He became aware of a smell of smoke, or scorched wood, and at last he saw the cause of the glow. A tree had caught fire, struck right down the middle, with the top half split in two. As far as he could see, the rain was winning the day and the fire was burning itself out. As he stepped closer he failed to see a blackened branch lying across the path and his shin collided with it painfully, causing him to lose his balance and land on his hands and knees. He groaned, as much with annoyance as in pain. But what he saw next stifled both.

It was the face of a woman. Her hair was matted, and a large black mark stretched out across her forehead. Holding up his eband light he could see it was soot mixed with blood. 'Jack!' he called into his forearm. 'You'd better get over here quick!'

He got up and shone his eband across the offending branch which he could now see lay across the woman's legs. The feeble light didn't give him much, so when more detail suddenly sprang into view he turned round to see why. The lights had gone on in the building behind him. Moments later the steady beam of some kind of spotlight reached out towards the generator room.

Bill doused his eband and turned to the jumble of twigs and hair at his feet. The branch was solid, but he managed to heave it away. The woman, possibly still in her thirties, was dressed in something dark like a tracksuit or combat gear. Her hair, which also appeared to be dark, didn't quite reach her shoulders. He tried to get the leaves and twigs out of it, and as he looked at her face, the large eyes and full lips, he recalled a training exercise in the Australian bush. Yes, it looked like there was some Aborigine blood there.

'Well, well,' he said, 'now you definitely don't belong here, do you, missy?' After feeling for her pulse he gently moved her into the recovery position, checking her arms, legs and sides until he was satisfied there were no broken bones. Then he heard Jack's voice coming over the wind, and the two men were soon trying to get the surprise visitor to her feet.

'It's no good,' said Jack. 'She's out cold.'

'Right. That branch obviously gave her quite a whack.'

'Hold on, gentlemen!' It was Leroy, making his way towards them as fast as his legs would allow. 'I have just the thing.' And with that he dived back into the trees. The two men looked at each other and shrugged. Seconds later the young monk emerged with a large wheelbarrow.

'Well,' said Jack, 'it's not a bad idea.' They eased the woman down into the barrow, turning her sideways and folding her legs into the makeshift gurney as best they could.

Jack grabbed the handles and squared up against the elements. They had not gone far when a deputation approached them. The

Abbot was accompanied on either hand by more torch-bearing monks. Leonardo was on the point of praising them for restoring the power when he saw the wheelbarrow, and what was in it. His head seemed to jar as he took a closer look.

'Don't ask me!' said Jack. 'All I know is, she's hurt. Looks like she was too near the trees when one of them got struck.'

Leonardo raised a hand to the back of his head, unusually perplexed. Alarmed, even.

'Okay,' said Jack. 'I'm guessing you don't know who she is either, or what she's doing here. Come on, then, let's get her inside.'

Leonardo nodded, and they made their way back to the main building as fast as they could, even though the wind seemed to oppose them in all directions. The Abbot led them to a small sick bay next to the kitchen, which served as the infirmary.

Ten paces behind Bill followed, cursing his eband for having already lost contact with the outside world again.

3

Brother Leroy was excited. So excited that he went straight back out into the storm, using the excuse of needing to remove the wheelbarrow from the infirmary. It seemed to him the elements matched the whirlwind in his soul. These visitors were just off the scale! It was momentous enough that there was talk of aliens; after that he had got wind of some kind of cover-up, maybe even a sinister plot to kill the one they called Ariel; and now yet another woman had joined them, a fascinating woman... a vulnerable woman... struck down by a struck tree. What did it all mean?

Suddenly he realised his legs had brought him back to the generator room. He left the barrow on the lee side of the small brick building and went round to the entrance. The door was still unlocked, what with all the commotion, so he went inside and checked the circuit-breakers one by one. Everything seemed as it should be.

The physical exertion of the evening started to register with his brain, so he sat down on a stool in the corner of the dim little room, lit only by red, green and blue lights from the instrument panel. His legs hurt, but that wasn't unusual. More troubling was the maelstrom in his head and the pounding in his chest. Who was this woman? What was she doing here? And how did she get in?

He decided to settle on the last question, as he might well be the only person who could uncover the answer. It would be best to go out soon, before the storm destroyed any evidence. But then again, maybe he should at least wait till both the wind and his heartbeat dropped a bit. And with that he took a small book from one of the deep pockets in his habit, settled back against the still-warm casing of the emergency generator, and began to read by the light of the circuit board. Agatha Christie would be his companion for the next hour or so.

The next thing he remembered was catching himself almost falling off the stool. That was the trouble with mysteries you'd read before – they weren't mysteries any more. And however satisfying it was to see events unfold when you knew the end from the beginning, it had not been enough to prevent his dropping heartbeat from closing his drooping eyes. He looked at his eband. Almost an hour had passed. The wind was no longer howling, though there were still gusts rattling the door from time to time.

He rose painfully to his feet, stumbled out and locked the door behind him. Torch in hand, he turned left and made for the place that his awakening mind had alighted on as the most likely entrance of the trespasser. This took him along the path away from the main building. As he walked he counted the rough piles of leaves the rain had brought down, presumably arranged by the swirling wind, and began to plan his next morning's work. After a few minutes he saw the perimeter wall rise before him. The path led straight to a small gate.

It was locked, just as it should be. No sign of forced entry. He retraced his steps a little way but then turned left and trudged round to the front of the building. The main front gate was also locked.

What more could he do? He went inside through the front door, carefully entering the key code, before making his way down the corridor. No one else was about. He stopped for a moment, listening to the occasional gust as it whistled around the empty cloister. Something was wrong. Unusual. Uncanny. Then he realised the cloister was pitch black where it was never dark. Sure enough, the ever-burning oil lamp had gone out. He had never witnessed that before. What with all the torch beams and confusion, it seemed no one else had noticed. Surely this was an opportunity to play a small part, unnoticed, in the elemental rite. Casting off his waterproof, he dug out a lighter from his habit and carefully restored the eternal flame, before trotting up the stairs towards his room.

4

'Brother Ambrose! We need warm water, a towel and some dressings for a small wound!' Leonardo's command, given in English, was as clear as it was swift, and the monk turned immediately to his task. Meanwhile Jack and Bill hovered over the prostrate form of the unknown woman now lying on one of three single beds.

'Press?' said Bill. 'But then, how would they know, unless...'

'Now wait a minute,' said Jack, seeing where Bill's thought was going. They both knew Melody was the only member of the press who knew where they were.

'Gentlemen,' said Leonardo, 'I think I may be able to shed some light on who this is.'

Jack waited to see if his hunch was right, sensing that Leonardo knew more than he had been saying. Leonardo invited them into the refectory, but as they turned to go Melody swept in.

'Hi, everyone, what are you all doing in here? Whoa, who's that? Wait... Miranda? What's she doing here?'

Jack was lost for words. Leonardo was starting to say something, but Jack went back to look at the patient on the bed. 'This is Miranda?' he said. 'The one you told me about? Your new friend?'

Bill pounced. 'There! What did I say?'

'Okay, not so fast, Bill!' Jack put up his hand. 'Melody has only just met this woman. Haven't you, Melody?' He glared at her.

'Well yes, I told you, Jack. She gave me a lift here. But, as I recall, Father Leonardo already knew her.'

'That's what I've been trying to tell you,' put in the Abbot.

'Well, try a bit harder,' Bill scowled.

'Excuse me, sirs,' said Brother Ambrose in a soft Irish accent. 'Would you mind carrying on your lovely conversation some place else? I have a patient to attend to.'

'Gentlemen, shall we?' Leonardo led them out and opened up the refectory. Bill was just launching into what promised to be an interrogation when Natasha walked in.

'Come on in,' called Jack. 'Join the party!'

They spent the next ten minutes in dizzying circles of theory and argument, trying to find out just who this woman was, what she was doing here at dead of night, and how she got in. And when she got in. And who the man was who had accompanied her when she first visited.

'What I want to know,' said Bill loudly, turning to Melody, 'is what your part in all this is.'

Melody smiled at her questioner, though it fell on rocky ground. 'My part, as you put it, General, is that I came here with the express permission of Geneva, as I believe you did. I met up with Miranda – if that's her real name – in the hotel. I told her I wanted to visit the retreat house, and she said she'd take me as she had a car. I hadn't seen her since.'

'And you're in the habit of taking lifts from strange women?' fired Bill.

Melody hesitated, reluctant to share more about that evening. Sensing some kind of predicament, Jack came to the rescue. 'Bill,' he said, 'I can't see the point in pursuing this line of enquiry, when Melody's really no wiser than the rest of us. The fact is, the Abbot here had already met her, here in the monastery, so we know that Melody did not lead her here.'

Natasha walked towards the door and turned, her eyes flashing. 'What's the point of being in a café without coffee? And what's the point of putting all the right questions to the wrong persons?'

Jack shook his head and smiled. 'Natasha, you have a wonderful way with words! Let's go look in on our patient – though, if you don't mind, Bill, I don't think we should all go in until she's ready to talk. That goes for you too, Melody, and yes you, Natasha. Let the Abbot and me see how she's doing, and then let's regroup in the morning. After a late breakfast, I suggest.'

'All right,' said Bill, 'but you be sure to let me know the moment she wakes up. I know you've been tasked with security on this mission, Jack, but it strikes me it's getting a little out of control.' With that he marched out of the refectory and disappeared into the cloister. Natasha and Melody made some tutting noises laced with smirks, with much finger-wagging in Jack's direction, before making a quick exit.

'Right. Leonardo, let's you and me have a wee talk, once we've seen to it that our patient is safely tucked in. Perhaps you could ask one of the Brothers to sit with her.'

'Of course,' said Leonardo. 'I don't doubt that Ambrose himself will want to keep an eye on her. He is the most willing and able among our medically trained Brothers.'

As they approached the door to the small sick bay, Jack was surprised to hear a man's voice coming from inside. The accent was not Irish so it couldn't be Brother Ambrose. He pushed open the door, to see Miranda already sitting up. Next to the bed, with one hand on her forehead, was Ariel.

5

Brother Leroy could not sleep. Whether it was because of the doze he had already had in the generator room, or the lateness of the hour, or his racing imagination, he could not tell. He decided he had reached the point where walking was the best remedy, so he got out of bed, donned habit and trainers and left the room.

As soon as he had closed the door behind him, he stopped. Someone was talking in the room opposite. He crept across the hall and waited in silence. It was the General. As far as he could tell there was only one voice, which was strange, since electronic communication with the outside world was not possible now that the power was fully restored. After a few moments he decided that the General was making a recorded note, doubtless ready for transmitting at the first opportunity.

He moved closer to the door but resisted the temptation to press his ear against it. He couldn't hear every word, but the man's frustration was hard to miss. Sometimes his voice was quite loud, sometimes muffled, and Leroy imagined the General pacing up and down as he spoke.

'Something's not right. What I don't understand is why Bridlington would let that journalist anywhere near the place. Makes you wonder if Forrester's got some kind of hold on her. And as for Ms Grantley James — what kind of a name is Melody anyway? — she's definitely got our man singing her tune!' His voice faded for a moment, but then Leroy heard Abbot Leonardo's name, who was summarily dubbed 'another strange bedfellow for our oh-so prim and proper Director'. This last phrase was so clear, sounded so close, that Leroy felt it best to dive round the corner and down the nearest stairs. Experience had taught him that remaining undiscovered was far more important than knowing everything.

The staircase came out between the refectory and the kitchen, but even before he had reached the bottom he heard voices. It was the Abbot and the Scotsman. He waited on the last step until he was sure they had moved on, before peering into the cloister. The voices were coming from the direction of the infirmary, just the other side of the kitchen. The two men were standing outside the door and talking quite softly. Even so, with the storm now largely spent, the night amplified their voices.

'I understand, Jack, that this must be troubling to you. And please understand, it is to me too. I have only met Miranda twice – first with a certain Mr Greerson, who was really interested in our work here and implying, rather heavily I thought, that he might become a benefactor... and then, when she arrived unexpectedly with Miss Melody.'

A strong breeze carried away what was said next, but soon Leroy heard Jack asking whether the first visit had been expected.

'Well now,' said Leonardo, and then there was silence for a while – not even a breeze. 'You know, now that you ask, I have to say that both times Miranda came it was, as you say, out of the blue.'

'Aye well,' said Jack, 'tonight was certainly no exception!'

Again their voices dropped away, before Leroy heard the Scotsman saying that their questions would have to wait until tomorrow. Then he bade the Abbot good night. Leroy stood still until he was satisfied that the Abbot had taken the other staircase to his room. He was about to turn around when he heard the Scotsman's voice again. 'Come on, my friend, let's get you to bed. I think we've had enough adventures for one night.'

Leroy hesitated. Who was the 'friend'? It surely had to be the one they called Ariel. A wave of excitement passed though him at the thought of how close he was to the mystery man, but they were coming his way and now was not the time for meetings.

Noiselessly he turned and ran back up the stairs.

CHAPTER 13

Lies and Accusations

1

The first strands of morning light were tickling at Jack's consciousness as he lay on his bed mulling over the night's turn of events. When he had found Ariel talking to Miranda he had instantly wanted to separate them. She was obviously still shaken but calm enough, so he had followed his security instincts and escorted Ariel to his room before retiring to his own.

He had been sleeping on and off for four hours, a fitful time full of dreams. In the latest and most lucid he was in a large and ancient church, waiting. He looked back over his shoulder, only to see his late mother wearing a smile as broad as her hat. Music played. Was it Sibelius' *Finlandia*? The congregation stood. The bride was coming up the aisle. Such a long aisle, more like a cathedral. When had he agreed to this? He turned back, only to see David Carter standing in front of him, Bible in hand.

Jack was aware of turning in his bed only for a moment before the dream sucked him back in. He was standing outside in the sun, champagne glass in hand, looking down over a lake. Was it a loch? He didn't recognise it. People were smiling. 'Jack, they're ready! Come and face the camera!'

He trotted down seven stone steps to a lawn in front of a marquee that had somehow appeared on the lakeside. There was no sign of a photographer, but now it was time for the first dance. His mother was seated at a large round table, crying. She looked up as he passed. 'Oh Jack, I'm so happy. Double happiness for a double wedding!'

People were calling. Suddenly a voice came from a stage where musicians were waiting. 'Here they come, ladies and gentlemen! Would our brides and grooms please take to the floor.'

He stepped out only to fall. Slowly. Everything and everyone seemed to be moving in slow motion. As he went down he saw a couple in traditional dark suit and white dress turn and look across the dance floor. It was David, minister-turned-groom, and Mel. He tried to put out his hands to break his fall, but his arms wouldn't move quickly enough.

Then a woman called. 'Jack, Jack – come on! They're waiting for us.' He knew that voice so well, those Slavic tones... so comforting. So confusing.

He woke to the sound of knocking on his door. 'Jack. Jack!'

It was Natasha.

Jack fell out of bed and staggered towards the door, where the voice persisted. 'Jack, you need to hurry. Petersen's already downstairs, and he's insisting on talking with Miranda, with or without you.'

'Er, okay. Hold on.' No time to shower. He stumbled back to the hand basin and sloshed water over his face, shaking his head in an effort to dislodge the dream.

Five minutes later he was downstairs in the refectory, grabbing a coffee and following Natasha uneasily through the cloister.

'Jack, are you okay?'

'Oh aye, you know what it's like. You finally get to sleep and then you have to wake up again. I'll be fine in a moment.'

They crossed to the other building and into the meditation room where, just three long days before, Natasha and Ariel had finally begun to talk. Everything had seemed more straightforward then, only a matter of time, although he had always known there would be precious little of that to spare.

One more gulp of coffee and he followed Natasha into the room. His head had cleared enough to make his customary sweep of the place. Bill was standing by the patio doors which were closed and now, presumably, locked once more. Miranda was sitting in the opposite corner, dressed in some kind of heavy-duty tracksuit. She looked restless. There was no sign of Melody or the Abbot or, of course, Ariel whom the General was keeping well out of the way of the newcomer.

'Where's Leonardo?' Jack simply asked.

'I asked him not to join us,' said Bill. 'I'm sure you'll agree, Jack, that we have to have this situation contained.'

'Aye, right, this situation.' Jack buried his annoyance at being late. He was fairly confident Bill would not have asked the new arrival any questions that might divulge their reason for being there, but equally he assumed that she herself must be wondering just who these people were. He turned to her. 'Well, Ms...'

'Miranda.'

'Right, Ms Miranda, how are you feeling this morning?'

'A bit shaken, but I think I'm okay.'

Jack noted the trace of an Australian accent. The girl had an interesting face. Her eyes were not quite level, and her mouth seemed to curl upwards on one side. Not pretty, though some might call her cute. The black mark across her forehead was gone, suggesting that this particular part of the damage had been superficial. 'So,' he said, 'would you mind telling us how you came to be out in that storm last night, in the woodland?'

'Private woodland,' Bill added.

'I'm so sorry,' Miranda said sheepishly. 'But I don't honestly remember.'

Bill let out a loud sigh before turning to face the window and slamming both his hands on the glass.

'Okay,' said Jack, ignoring him. 'So tell me what you do remember.'

'Well, I was staying in Montagnola, after me and my boss had visited a few days ago. I came back unexpectedly when I ran into someone who turned out to be good company.' She hesitated. 'Look, d'you mind telling me just who you guys are? And where's the Abbot? He'll tell you who I am.'

Bill turned to face them. 'No, young lady,' he said. 'He'll tell us who he *thinks* you are. But he hasn't got a clue why you were in the grounds last night, or how you got there.'

Jack sighed. They didn't have time for a game of wits. 'Look, Miranda,' he said, 'I'm a friend of the Abbot. He'll be here to see you as soon as he can. I know he's concerned about your welfare. But, well, he's probably a little too kind to ask what you were doing here, long after dark, wandering around private property.'

'Well, I know it's private,' Miranda answered, choosing her words carefully. 'But it is open to the public. And I'm not exactly sure when I got here.'

'Oh, I see,' growled Bill. 'So we're to believe that you came back here earlier in the day, failed to report in, and then got knocked down by a tree when you couldn't get out. I'm sorry, miss, but you must think we're stupid. You haven't offered any kind of explanation as to why you were in the grounds, unannounced and unauthorised – whenever you arrived!' He was shouting now. 'And don't blame it on your convenient loss of memory! It's obvious you were not injured before the storm. You came here deliberately under cover. So, I'll ask you again, why were you here? Just what is your connection with the press? And who are you working for?'

'That would be Mr Greerson.' The voice was Leonardo's, and every eye turned to see him make his customary silent entrance. 'I'm sorry, gentlemen, but would you mind telling me what is going on here? Why is Miranda out of sick bay? And why are you shouting at her?'

Bill grunted, but before he could speak Jack jumped in. 'Very good questions, Abbot, which deserve answers before we go any further, though not before we offer you an apology, Miranda. May I suggest we adjourn to the refectory, where I for one need a hearty breakfast, and then regroup with both Melody and your good self, Abbot, and see if we can't help Miranda here to... clarify her thoughts.'

2

Jack had a problem, one to add to all the others, and it was called Miranda. He knew that they needed to press on with Ariel, but there was no way he wanted Bill to take over the process. He had to come up with a workable distribution of labour.

He was pacing up and down the chapel, waiting for the others to arrive. His dream had cleared away now, replaced by the memory of Ariel apparently coaxing Miranda out of her sleep. A plan began to form in his mind.

Bill came in, escorted by Leonardo. Natasha and Ariel arrived soon after, followed by Melody, and the three of them made their way up to the chancel.

'I've spoken with Brother Ambrose,' said Leonardo, 'and he is satisfied that Miss Miranda is suffering from only a slight concussion. He is keeping an eye on her, but he is happy for her to have visitors – for short periods at a time.'

'What about her family?' said Melody.

'Or her colleagues?' put in Bill, who was lingering near the door.

'I've asked her about that,' replied Leonardo, apparently to both questions. 'She says that all her family is in Australia, but that she will get in touch with Mr Greerson later today. Apparently he is no longer in the country.'

'Hmph!' sounded Bill. 'How very convenient. I'm sorry, Abbot, but I think she's holding back on us, and I'll bet whoever she's working for is not that far away.'

'Well, whoever that is, I guess we needn't worry right now,' said Jack. 'She's not going anywhere, and we have a job to do.'

'That's true, Jack,' said Bill. 'At least, the last part is. As to whether she's going anywhere, what exactly is stopping her? A part-time doctor in an unsecured sick bay?'

Leonardo put his hand on Bill's shoulder, a move that prompted the tiniest quiver. 'Bill, if Miss Miranda wants to leave, there is nothing we can do to stop her. She has damaged no property of ours, and for her part she is not intending to sue us for the injury she has suffered.' He put up his hand when Bill began to protest. 'General, I think we must leave things be, and press on with the business at hand.'

Once again Jack felt uneasy at Leonardo's inclusion of himself in all this, and could only imagine what Bill thought of that. But it was time to seize the moment. 'Okay, then, that's settled. I suggest we all sit down here in the front row, while Ariel sits facing us in that chair. Don't worry, Natasha, we're here to listen, and to probe as gently as we can. What we need is a coherent summary of the events on Venus. And don't forget, everybody, Natasha and I were there and even we don't understand everything we saw or heard, let alone what we missed.'

They settled down, agreeing to go on no longer than an hour, unless there was a significant breakthrough. None came.

3

The refectory was filled with the aroma of rich dark Italian coffee. Melody and Natasha were sitting together, trying to make sense of the plan Jack had just hastily revealed to them. Bill had gone into the village, doubtless to get an eband signal and communicate with whatever powers he reported to. Meanwhile Jack was going to take a walk with Miranda and take Ariel along with him.

'I suppose Miranda is her real name,' said Natasha.

Melody gave a nervous grin as her embarrassment returned over her own careless introduction to this mystery woman. 'Who knows?' she said.

Natasha smiled at some thought in her head.

'What?' said Melody, her discomfort growing even though she was quite sure Natasha couldn't know any details about an encounter that Melody herself could scarcely recall.

'Well, it's coincidence of course,' said Natasha. 'But Miranda is the name of one of the moons of Uranus. You know, like Ariel.'

'Really?' said Melody, her face visibly relaxing. 'Well, well.'

They sipped their drinks, the vibrant orange of Melody's tropical juice reflected in Natasha's plain water.

'It's not such a silly idea, putting these two "moons" together,' said Melody. 'I've often told Jack he needs to trust his hunches more. He knows letting them talk openly to each other is a risk, but it may just be that they can help each other.'

'Two amnesiacs together,' said Natasha. 'The idea is what you call left-field, I think.'

'Yes, that's exactly what it is.'

'Your influence?'

'Well,' grinned Melody, 'I suppose five years together must have done some good.'

4

A light mist hung in the air as three figures passed the silent outhouses on their way into the wood. Miranda and Ariel walked together a few steps behind Jack. He was making for the place where they had found Miranda during the night.

'I haven't thanked you for what you did last night.' Miranda spoke softly, such that Jack couldn't catch every word, yet he fought the temptation to fall back nearer to them. It was time to leave Ariel's curious magic to do its work.

'What did I do?'

'You brought me back to life.'

'I think, Miranda, that you were only unconscious.'

'Yes, I realise that. But there seemed to be more to it than that when you called me back up. It's hard to explain.'

'Well, I know that feeling. What do you remember?'

Jack could not suppress a smile as he listened to Ariel trying to help a fellow sufferer. The mist seemed heavier here, and sounds were absorbed rather than reflected by the trees, but the sheer quietness of it all allowed him to make out most of their conversation. At last he saw the sign to the generator room.

'Miranda, come take a look at this,' he called. 'This is the tree that did the deed.'

She gazed at the burnt wreck. Jack broke a piece off a heavy, blackened branch and began waving it at her. He was saying something about how a man called Bill had found her more or less under this very branch. Yet as he spoke she heard another voice.

'It's okay, Miranda. I think you can trust this man. Tell him.'

That's all it was. She turned to Ariel. Had he just whispered that to her? He wasn't standing very close, and it had sounded more like a gentle voice inside her head.

She caved. 'Jack!' she called. 'I think I need to sit down.'

'Of course.' He and Ariel each took an arm and gently led her to a nearby bench. She sat down between them.

'Okay, guys. I think it's coming back to me.' She decided to continue with the lie about her amnesia, if only for the sake of her own embarrassment. And perhaps also for Hugh's sake. But, for some subconscious reason she couldn't as yet discern, she had made up her mind to set a course for the truth. 'I came in last night, through a side gate – I guess it's further up the path here. You'll probably find my car parked outside somewhere close by.'

'Isn't that gate locked at night?' said Jack.

'Sure – not difficult to climb though,' she grinned weakly.

'Go on,' said Jack, not at all convinced by the apparent sudden return of memory, but only too pleased to hear what had the clear ring of truth, whatever the reason.

'Well, the weather was pretty rough, as you know. So I thought that was the best cover – you know? There was no one hanging around outdoors, and plenty of noise, so I thought I'd come take a look.'

'Look for what?' said Jack, trying hard not to sound like Bill. 'I mean, we know you'd already been here before, presumably doing a recce. What's your interest in this place?'

Miranda took a deep breath, suppressing the urge to ask Jack the same question. Following a new instinct, she turned to Ariel and gave him a pleading look.

'Miranda,' said Ariel. 'I know how hard this can be. But anything you do recall – anything – will help unblock the parts you don't.'

Well, that's the theory, thought Jack. Not working with you, though, is it? But he likewise kept his thoughts to himself.

They sat a while in silence, until Jack felt the dampness seeping into his clothes. 'Okay,' he said, deciding to go for broke, 'why don't I go take a look outside that gate, while you two here carry on talking?'

When he was gone Ariel stood up and began to walk back and forth in front of the bench. It seemed time to enter new territory and take the initiative. He stopped and looked at Miranda. What did he see? A nervous woman out of her depth. A hard-working girl, determined to succeed.

A riddle.

He stopped right in front of her. 'Miranda, if I may take you back to Jack's question, would you like to tell me why you are here?'

Oh boy, thought Miranda, wouldn't I just? As she looked up into Ariel's eyes she felt a strong desire to bare her heart, not just share information. Her latest intelligence had come via the device in the small courtyard, when the South African had suggested that Ariel and Natasha already knew each other. But then, was that information, or just rumour? No use right now.

'It's difficult,' she said out loud. 'I have certain duties to my boss, you know? To my company.'

Ariel sat back down next to her and waited, enjoying the gentle patter of the dripping leaves all around them.

'Right,' she began at last. 'The thing is, we work in advanced textile technology.' She was thinking fast, following the principle her mentor had instilled in her, to cover a lie in as much truth as possible. 'We lost the contract for the Venus mission. And then that report appeared in The Times after they got back, which everyone knew was the work of Melody Grantley James. Well, it looked like someone had got to Venus before the mission, so we naturally wanted to follow up on that.'

'How is that?'

'Well,' she stumbled, 'we knew they could only have made it out onto the surface with the same kind of suit technology, and we knew it wasn't ours. So it was worth looking into. Developments in molecular models are as important to us as new drug formulas in the pharmaceutical world. We got a tip-off that you were using the monastery for debrief, so...' She hesitated. Yes, go for it. Join as many dots as possible, and confuse the enemy with scattered information. Although this man felt nothing like an enemy. 'So we visited, and then...'

'Yes?'

'I met Melody quite by accident, after my boss left and I stayed on for a break.' Which was sort of true. 'So I decided to come along with her and see what she was digging up, hoping she was being given her usual privileged access.'

'Ah yes. Jack.'

They both paused. While Miranda's mind was racing with ideas on where to take her story next, Ariel was back on the surface of Venus, inserting himself into her narrative, trying to imagine – to remember? – what kind of mission he must have been a part of.

They heard footsteps approaching and looked up, expecting to see Jack. It was Bill.

'Well, well, what *do* we have here?'

'Oh, we're just chatting, you know?' said Miranda, feeling suddenly protective towards Ariel. If there were enemies to fool, this man fitted the profile far better.

'Well, that's lovely.' His tone was as cold as the clinging mist.

Miranda looked down, unsure what to say, and was flooded with relief when she heard Jack's voice. 'Bill! Hey, you're back.' He had clearly been running.

'Well deduced, my friend,' he said drily. 'All buddies here then?'

'Aye, well, why don't you and I have a wee chat a moment?' He took Bill by the arm with as little force as he could muster and gently but firmly steered him in the direction of the perimeter gate. 'I'd like to show you something.'

Bill decided to go along with it, and within a few minutes they came to a small gate, now unlocked. Jack began to share with Bill just how much Ariel had already managed to extract from Miranda, a process he was sure was continuing still. 'She climbed over this gate. And look, here's the car, just where she said it would be. It's locked, but I've been able to run a check, now we're just outside the signal screen. It's hired to a Miss Miranda Freeman.'

'Okay, you have my attention, Jack. So, what do we know about Miss Miranda Freeman?'

'Well, that's where it gets interesting. As far as I can discover, she's not got any social media presence, and so I can't get anything public on her current employment. From a general search I've found a Miranda Freeman who was born in Perth, Australia, who'd be in her mid-thirties now, and I'm guessing that's our gal.'

'Right,' said Bill. 'While we're sharing... I've been in touch with Bridlington, and I daresay you have too.' Jack nodded. 'And I had the riot act read to me, leaving me in no doubt you were in charge. Which is fair enough.'

'Why do I feel there's a but?'

'Because, my friend, I have my own people at the UN to report to, and between you, me and that iron gatepost there... they're not happy with the way Bridlington is handling this.'

'I know,' said Jack, as much to slow Bill down as anything. He began to circle Miranda's car. 'You'll not be surprised that I was expecting some kind of military intervention by now. But you must admit, our friend from outer space is proving useful right now.'

Bill shook his head. 'Jack, I really wonder whether that guy hasn't gotten to you, just like he seems to have duped everyone else on this case. Come on, man! We don't know anything about him. Hell, we don't even know what nationality he is. Or even if he's actually from outer space – for real! But my money is on foreign agent, and Miss Freeman here pretty much qualifies for the same thing. So, as far as *I'm* concerned, Captain Jack...'

'Er, that's Commander actually.'

'As far as I'm concerned, you've just given two hostiles the time and space they need to concoct whatever story is going to work for them and God-knows-what other plans they have. I'm sorry, Jack, but I think it's time I took over.'

5

Jack ran his finger along the spines of the books lined up in his room. Casually he opened one with the name Zarathustra in the title, but when he saw it was in German he promptly put it back. Plans formed and vanished in his head almost as quickly as the titles that passed his gaze. He turned, only to see himself in the mirror, standing there, alone.

But he was not alone. He had allies. Chief among those right now was the Abbot. He was clearly Bridlington's man, her chosen instrument before the tanks rolled in. Natasha and Melody were solid, and even Ariel himself seemed almost up to speed, awake at last to his risky position.

There was a knock on the door. 'Jack?' It was Melody.

When he opened up, he was all but knocked over as she threw herself into his arms, hugging him tight and long. And as they stood there in the doorway, pressed close, it was as if her weakness was turning into his strength. That was so like her. The more she looked to him, supported him, held him, the more able he became.

'I'm sorry,' she said, finally easing herself away. 'I just needed that.' She closed the door and sat down on the bed.

'You and me both.' He closed the blind and sat on the chair.

'Jack, what are we going to do?' There it was... 'we' not 'you'. Early on in this business that had annoyed him, but now it was something he loved about her once more.

'Well, it won't surprise you, my darling, that I've been considering our options.'

'Have you talked to Constance?'

'Aye, I have. And she's talking to her friends in the military at the UN. But I'm not holding out much hope. Once they referred things to the Task Force, to Petersen, it was only ever a matter of time. I had hoped he could see what we're trying to do here, but everything I've done seems to have backfired.'

'But Jack, can he do what he's threatening? Can he take over?'

'Well, I don't really know the answer to that. There's no protocol for this case, as far as I can see, but that makes it just as likely he will. There are so many unknowns about Ariel that our General's bound to play the security-threat card, and you and I both know what that will mean. And as for Miranda, let's face it, she's almost certainly some kind of security risk. I'm thinking she may even be behind that high-tech device Natasha found under the statue. It seems a bit over the top for industrial espionage, but then these days nothing would surprise me.'

Melody stood up and walked over to the bookshelf. She let her gaze wander over the titles, stopping only with *L'Étranger* by Albert Camus, which raised a smile. 'So you think I was her way in?'

'Well no, at least not first off. She'd already visited the monastery, remember, which could be when they planted the device. That's assuming it was them, and there isn't someone else snooping around. Miranda told Ariel something about getting a tip-off that we were here. Well, I can count on two hands how many people knew about this, though I can't really believe any of them would put us at risk. Unless…'

'Unless what?'

'No, surely not,' Jack mused, as much to himself as to Mel.

'Go on.'

'Well, Jim and Ryan took a different view about Ariel, to put it mildly. They could be behind the listening device.'

She turned back from the books to face him. 'Well, I don't know about them, but when it comes to the General, why not play him at his own game?'

'How so?'

'He's got to discover some protocol that will govern the next step, right?'

'Right.'

'Then you can do the same. Maybe the presence of Miranda and the listening device is enough to complicate the issue.'

'Give them something else to talk about in Geneva, you mean?'

'Exactly.'

'Aye, it could buy us some more time, even if we have to change location.' He stood up, but then sat straight back down. 'Or it could make them even more jumpy.'

'You'll think of something,' she said as she leaned forward and pulled him onto the bed. They resumed their embrace under the unseeing eyes of *L'Étranger*, placed between *The Many Paths to Enlightenment* and *Infinite Possibilities*.

6

Natasha's morning ended with a lunchtime concert in the chapel. It was one thing Leonardo had decided not to cancel when he had cleared the Centre of public bookings, guessing it may serve a purpose. As it turned out, only Natasha and Ariel joined the Brothers in the depleted audience. They had talked about dressing up for the event, but not surprisingly Jack, or Dan, had not been particularly creative about Ariel's wardrobe, so Natasha decided to match his shirt and jeans with something similar from her minimal wardrobe.

As they waited for the music to begin, Ariel seemed uncharacteristically nervous. 'What will it be like?' he said, as he watched the small orchestra take their seats in the chancel. All they had been told was that the music would be a taste of Handel and Mendelssohn, plus a Chinese composer whose name Natasha did not recognise.

As soon as the music began Ariel visibly relaxed. Within two movements of the concerto grosso his eyes were closed. Natasha smiled, before closing her own and allowing her mind to follow the intricate patterns of the music. No counting, no analysing, just riding the waves of sound until she was fully immersed.

Afterwards they walked across to the refectory in silence, letting the Brothers overtake them in their rush for a late lunch. Once they were installed with soup and rolls, Natasha shared something of her reaction to the music and how it had engaged a part of her brain she hardly seemed to use these days.

'It is a wonder,' Ariel said. 'Simply a wonder. The concerto took me to the trees, winding up through branches and twigs and leaves, before spiralling down a broad, slow trunk to an intricate network of roots.'

She smiled. 'What about the Mendelssohn?'

'Oh!'

She sipped her soup and waited.

'I honestly don't know where I was,' he said at last. 'It was grand, full of space and air and wave upon wave of...' He paused. 'It was beautiful.'

'I was on the sea,' she said, 'with the wind and the waves.'

'Yes,' he said quietly. 'A sea of liquid and mist, with eruptions of earth and fire.'

'Wow,' said Natasha. 'That's unexpected. Hardly a common reaction to the Hebrides overture, I would think.'

'If you say so,' said Ariel. 'But these were the images in my mind, though I felt them more than saw them.'

Natasha wondered whether he was simply interpreting the music through the four classical elements, or whether he was actually talking about Venus. It struck her that they had no idea what his own experience of the planet was. She took his hand, as if checking he was still solid, gripped afresh by the thought that this man might truly be from another world.

.

CHAPTER 14

Disappointments

1

Petroc was in a quandary. It seemed to him that he had crossed that blurred line between surveillance and involvement. Having eavesdropped on a recent conversation between Bridlington and Forrester, he had learned of Miranda's detention in the monastery, information which he had duly passed on to Hugh Coates at the earliest opportunity. Expecting some kind of rescue mission to be launched, possibly involving himself, he was disappointed and disturbed to be told by his secret boss that 'Miranda will be fine' and he should do no more than look out for a message from her.

Petroc had met Miranda on several occasions, and with each one she grew more magnificent. Talented and confident, she had found her way to the heady atmosphere at the summit of the organisation in scarcely more than a dozen years. She was everything he wanted to be, yet so different. He both envied her and admired her. Yet here she was, abandoned in the lions' den, and he could do nothing because, officially, he knew nothing.

Another call came through from Montagnola, this time from Abbot Leonardo. That was unusual. He assured the Abbot that he'd get the Director to call back, and then trundled off to the small meeting room where she was going head to head with some top brass from UN High Command.

He knocked and went straight in. Bridlington sat at the far end of a table, light pouring in through a window behind her, while the two officials – a man and a woman – sat at the near end, their backs to the door. They turned as he came in. He didn't need a surveillance device to tell him this was not going his boss's way.

'What is it, Petroc?'

'I thought you should know that there's been a call from the retreat centre. Given the circumstances.'

'Thank you.' She continued to waver between annoyed and impressed by her aide's grasp of what was going on at any given time.

After he had left the room she decided to wrap things up. 'Well, it's clear that you've let your dog off the leash and we're all going to have to live with the results.' The woman began to protest but she continued. 'Don't worry, Beth, there is more we can do right now, here in Geneva. I've got Jack's contacts in British Intelligence looking into this couple who came visiting – and probably leaving behind more than they should – a Ms Freeman and a Mr Greerson, and doubtless you'll be following them up as well. Meanwhile I'd be grateful if you could turn your attention to the crystal. It clearly has some peculiar properties, and while one of the scientists on the Aphrodite mission has made good progress, I think we need more minds – and more tools – on this.'

The woman called Beth replied. She was African, though her accent was Welsh. 'Constance, you don't offer something for nothing. If this thing really does present a security risk, or has some kind of military angle, why–?'

'Why am I being so uncharacteristically co-operative? Don't

worry, Beth, I haven't gone soft. I will give you exclusive access to this crystal – exclusive because it has to be, as we can't actually cut the wretched thing into pieces – on the condition that you instruct the Task Force to hold their horses.'

'Leave Petersen out in the cold, you mean?'

'No. He can stay on the field, if that's what he wants to do. But he may not remove the Stranger until our man says so.'

Beth turned to her colleague. 'Nathan, I'm happy with that. What do you think?'

'I think it's a start,' he nodded. He was American, about fifty, and corporate from head to toe. 'Though we should of course be kept in the loop from now on.'

'You have a deal, Constance,' Beth affirmed. 'But I'll need reports every day, and we review the situation in a week. And if we're not satisfied that we know enough about who this man is, or what he is, then we bring him into our facility and find a way to get into his brain.'

'Thank you.' Constance picked up her tablet. 'Now, I have a telephone call to make.'

2

Miranda looked out of the small window in her latest place of rest. Or was that prison cell? The afternoon sun had already set behind the trees. Down below she could see in the centre of the courtyard the statue that secretly housed one of their more advanced listening devices. That was a week ago. No time at all in the type of game she and Hugh played.

She had brought nothing with her to the monastery bar the clothes she wore, some hastily purchased mountain wear she deemed suitable for her nocturnal escapade, plus her eband and a sample bag for the Stranger's suit, should she be fortunate enough to find it. The bag was still there in her pocket, vacuum-packed flat. Finding the suit had always been a long shot of course, but she hadn't expected to be caught. But then again, who could control the weather?

Still, here she was, more or less where she wanted to be.

People were still about, but everything up here on the first floor seemed quiet enough, so she decided to break her confinement and take a look around.

She stepped outside into the hall and closed the door quietly, aware that her nemesis, who the Abbot had informed her was one General William Petersen of the UN Special Task Force, was just two doors down. She knew her priority must be to get a message out, and right now the best way seemed to be by linking with one of the devices she and Hugh had secreted at various points, which could then send something on a secure link to her tablet. She was relying on Hugh to have the presence of mind to access her device remotely. She briefly entertained the thought that he might even come back to Montagnola to get her, but quickly suppressed it.

So much for the plan. The flaw was that she didn't actually know how to establish such a link. She would simply have to get to one of the devices and try to work something out.

Next challenge: there were no devices up here on the top floor.

Which brought her back to the reason she was here. She now knew where Forrester's room was, conveniently not far from the stairs, so she set off along the corridor. She chose to go without shoes so that it would appear to anyone she chanced to meet that she wasn't really going anywhere. And bare feet were quiet feet.

The stone floor was smooth and cold. She was surprised there was no carpet, but then she guessed it would be easier for the Brothers to keep clean. She had already picked up that there were no ancillary staff. Once she had rounded the corner nearly all the rooms were on her left, their windows doubtless facing the grounds outside. Earlier on she had carefully noted who went into which room. First came the cosmonaut's, Natasha Koroleva. She had turned out to be nothing like her reputation. The icy Slav had definitely thawed out for some reason or other.

She wasn't sure whose room was next, but thought it most likely Ariel's, as Jack's came after that. It was here that he had left Petersen to escort her to her room, who doubtless would have locked her in if he had had his way. Happily for her, all the doors were key-coded to residents' ebands.

She approached Jack's door and gently pressed her ear to it. Someone was moaning... a woman. It took her two seconds to recognise the sound of intimacy. It took another three seconds for her to step back from the door.

'Hello.'

The voice came from along the corridor. She gasped, lost her balance and sat down hard on the stone floor. When she looked up she saw Ariel emerging from the room next door.

'I'm sorry, I didn't mean to startle you. Are you all right?'

'Sure, yes, I'm fine,' she mumbled, her thoughts still caught in a whirlpool of envy and embarrassment.

Ariel helped her to her feet and invited her into his room. 'I think I'd best close the door,' he said quietly, 'as General Petersen might not be pleased to see you wandering about.'

'Got that right,' said Miranda, pulling herself together as she realised this could be a serendipitous meeting. As she followed him in, she looked around for any sign of the treasure she was hunting.

She knew that the suit had undergone a change in appearance since it was first seen on Venus. Why Hugh was happy for her to try to acquire it wasn't so clear. His game was normally information, not theft. Ordinarily he would have waited to find out, through the usual clandestine means, just what the intelligence on the suit was. Her best guess was that he wanted to take a look at it, maybe remove a small specimen, and then replace it before anyone even knew it had gone missing.

She sighed, thinking she must have been mad even to suggest infiltrating the scene like this.

'What's that?' Ariel asked.

'What? I didn't say anything. Did I?' She still couldn't be completely sure when she was thinking and when she was speaking out loud.

'I think you were wondering whether you were mad.'

'Right. Well, I mean, it was pretty daft wandering around like that.'

They eyed each other in silence for several seconds.

'Okay,' said Miranda, 'I admit it. I was actually hoping I might get a look at that suit of yours.'

'Well, I can't see why you shouldn't take a look at it,' he said. 'I mean, if you think that with your, er, knowledge of textiles, you could help us.'

Her heart skipped a beat. Was he really going to hand it to her on a plate?

'However,' he went on, 'I don't have it any more.'

'No, of course you don't.' She walked to the window and leant back on the sill. 'Ariel, can I ask you, who are these guys?'

'Well, I expect you're already aware of the members of the Endeavour crew.'

She nodded, thinking it futile to continue with any pretence of complete amnesia.

'They have been with me since they found me, more or less, apart from a rather strange encounter with a man in a white coat. Though that's all a bit muddled.'

'Memory problems, eh?'

'Yes. Anyway, in more recent times we have been joined by the General, whom you know.'

'What is he a general of? Do we know?'

'I'm afraid I haven't discovered that as yet. But it's clear that the others don't like him. I sense that he wants to take me somewhere else, somewhere they can...'

'Oh right, of course. I guess if you're Person Unknown they're going to have their guard up.'

'Which they do. Except Natasha.'

Miranda sat on the chair. Hugh was going to love this. Although, as she thought about it, she was no longer quite so happy about that. Why did he have to know everything, or as close to everything as he could get? She looked at Ariel and found his eyes were already on her.

'What are you looking at?' she asked simply.

'You, of course.' He sat down on the bed.

'What do you see?'

'Something of an enigma. I sense you are telling me the truth. Some of the time.'

She held his gaze. She wanted to tell him the truth. Tell him everything. Tell him about an Australian backwater where they didn't play nice with girls who liked girls. Tell him about a man called Hugh Coates who saw in twelve months what her teachers failed to see in twelve years, and who was like a father to her. Only kinder.

'I see.'

'What do you see?' She repeated the question because this time she was quite certain she hadn't uttered a word.

'I'm sorry, I didn't mean to pry. I thought you were letting me in.'

'This is weird.' She stood up and looked out of the window. It was getting dark, though she thought she recognised the path into the forest where they had found her. And it was only now she realised that there were things she really couldn't recall. She had remembered clambering over the iron gate set into the wall, but only now did she feel again the rain on her face as it suddenly began to lash down, as if someone had turned on a giant shower in the heavens. Then the flash. She couldn't see a thing now, and her head was full of thunder. There was a loud crack, searing pain, then darkness.

She gripped the edge of the windowsill.

'Miranda.'

'Yes?'

'Will you let me help you?'

'And how are you going to do that, my friend?' She turned to face him. 'Wait, did you just... do that?'

'Do what?'

'Did you just get in my head? Give me those memories?'

'I certainly didn't give you anything. I, er... how to put this... I did read you while you were sitting down a moment ago. But I don't know what just happened to you at the window.'

'You *read* me? What the f–'

Her last word was drowned out by a loud knock on the door. Instantly she dropped to the floor and flattened herself half under the bed, out of sight.

'Come in,' said Ariel, calm as the deepest lake.

Natasha opened the door and, before Miranda could move a muscle, flopped down on the bed, clearly very much at home. With no introduction she started talking excitedly about some kind of concert they had clearly both attended. Evidently she was still transported by the music.

What to do? She would have to reveal herself and try to explain. But before she moved a muscle Ariel was speaking.

'Natasha, I'm sorry to interrupt, but do take care not to roll off the bed. Only you might squash Miranda.'

Natasha leapt to her feet as if she had just discovered a snake on the pillow. At the same time Miranda stood up. 'Hi!' was all she could muster.

Ariel continued in the same even tone, as if this sort of thing happened every day. 'I was having a talk with Miranda here,' he said. 'She dropped to the floor as soon as you knocked, fearful no doubt that the General was on the prowl.'

'That's right,' Miranda spluttered, following Ariel's welcome lead. She couldn't tell which bothered her more, what Natasha must be thinking or how Ariel could remain so calm.

'Right,' said Natasha as she backed up against the bookcase. 'I, I didn't mean to interrupt.'

'That's quite all right,' said Ariel. 'I think we had reached an interesting moment.' Natasha responded only by eyebrow. 'Miranda here had let me read her – at least, I thought that she had let me – but then she became uncomfortable.'

'Read her?' said Natasha. 'What, like her palms or something?'

'No, no. We were looking intently at each other, and so I read her mood... and her thoughts.'

Natasha looked across to Miranda who was now back at the safety of the windowsill. 'Did Ariel read your thoughts? How is that possible?'

'I don't know. I had a lot going on in my head, and the way he spoke it seemed like he knew what I was thinking. So I broke off. But when I looked out the window... I remembered the accident in the storm.'

'Okay,' said Natasha. 'That's good, isn't it?'

'I don't know,' said Miranda. 'Not if he's messing with my head.'

Ariel walked round the bed to Miranda. With each step he took Natasha pressed her back harder into the books behind her. He proceeded to take Miranda's hands in his. 'Miranda, I did not intend to... to violate you in any way. I honestly thought we were together in that moment.'

The books pressed harder.

'Together?' said Miranda quietly, finding it even harder to turn away from those eyes which, this close to the window, were reflecting a deep grey-blue. She only pulled away when the door slammed.

Natasha was gone.

3

Leonardo put the phone down. It was a rather decorative affair, a throwback to earlier times, before landlines became a rare species and mobile phones went out of fashion, eclipsed by the almost universal eband. Even its receiver was connected in full twentieth-century style by a cable. Maybe this was why it looked like a landline phone, even though the wire only ran as far as the satellite link in a lowly-looking shed that stood deep in the monastery grounds.

He crossed to the inner door and went into the chapel. So Constance was going to hand the crystal over to the UN Special Task Force. It made him sad. It made him angry. He knew he needed to process these emotions before he could pass on the news to Jack. Not that the commander would be particularly worried about the crystal, especially when he heard the good news that Constance had bought them at least another week.

But there was something else niggling at the back of his mind. Constance had been happy to speak with him direct, even now when Jack was running things at this end. Such a show of trust might only serve to feed Jack's angst. And while Leonardo had basked in the privileged access he had been granted, right now he knew he needed Jack's trust. Because, while the crystal might remain out of reach, the mystery man himself was staying a little longer. Ariel from the kingdom of the Air. And Jack Forrester was still the key to maintaining access to him. At least for now.

4

The refectory was quiet, as Jack, Melody and Ariel sipped their bedtime drinks – a single malt and two hot chocolates. The whisky came courtesy of Ambrose's private supply.

'Natasha's gone to bed already then?' Jack asked innocently.

'It would appear so,' said Ariel from the depths of his mug.

'Right. Well, Petersen's gone.'

'Gone?' said Melody. 'As in, gone to bed, or gone to hell?' She suppressed a pang of guilt over the jest.

'Ah well, that I couldn't say. Bed most likely, but not here. Doubtless off conniving somewhere.'

'I wouldn't be too worried about that.' They looked up to see Leonardo silently cross the room towards them. 'I've been speaking with Geneva.'

'Bridlington?' Jack looked surprised.

'Yes. We do, er, go back quite a long way, as I think you say in English.'

Jack shrugged. 'Maybe that's just as well right now. So tell me, then, why shouldn't I be worried about our General?'

'I did not mean you should cease from worry altogether. But it seems Constance has managed to delay military involvement for another week, maybe more.'

'And how did she manage that, I wonder?' Jack said as he studied the contents of his glass.

At this Leonardo became noticeably crestfallen. 'She has handed over to them the crystal you brought back from Venus.'

Melody drained her hot chocolate. 'I can't help noticing, Father Leonardo, that you are very interested in this crystal.'

Jack shivered at Mel's choice of title for the abbot, which she had used more than once, but he was eager to see where this went.

'Well, yes, that is true,' said the Abbot cautiously.

'Oh, it's okay,' said Melody. 'I understand, or at least I think I do. I've read your publicity – earth, air, fire, water. The four basic elements of classical thinking.'

'You are very astute, young lady.'

'Thanks for the "young", but yes, I can see why you might be interested in such an usual piece of "earth".'

'Well, that's just it,' said Leonardo, and suddenly the light returned to his eyes. 'We like to extend the four elements in our thinking, adapting to our scientific understanding, and that's why we're always interested in things that do not originate from *the* earth, our planet.'

'You mean, you have other specimens?' she asked.

'But of course.'

'Ah, I get you,' put in Jack. 'Meteorites.'

'Exactly so.'

'I suppose,' said Melody, 'the ancients thought that coming from the sky made them like a piece of the earth that came out of the air!'

'Now you, er, get the hang of it!' said Leonardo with a grin. 'The old classifications are a useful alternative to the modern ones. As you may know, it was generally believed that the air became purer the higher you went. The realm of the gods, or spirit, was called the ether. Today we would associate that with outer space.'

'Oo,' said Melody, 'I feel all ethereal... you know, having recently returned from a space station!'

Leonardo laughed, but Jack had not moved his gaze from the whisky. 'But why stick with the ancient classifications at all? Surely the modern ones are much more accurate?'

'That is a good question,' said the Abbot, warming to an audience. 'And the answer probably has as much to do with history as anything else, specifically our history. The Order of the Four Elements goes back to medieval times, before the period we usually refer to as the Enlightenment, when so many ancient ideas were rediscovered and celebrated.'

'The Renaissance,' said Melody. 'The rebirth of ancient ideas for more modern times.'

Leonardo's grin achieved a new breadth. '*Esattamente!* And really, these ideas are not so bad as you may think. As general categories they fit. After all, everything is either matter or energy.'

'So where do you put crystal in your basic classifications?' Jack asked.

'Well, that is the joy of it. The crystallising process behaves like water, but of course the heat needed to make it happen means fire, while its solidity qualifies it as earth.'

'And this one came from the ether – through the air!' said Melody with a triumphant flourish.

'Ha!' exclaimed Leonardo. 'Right again! And there is more, for the shape of the crystal is significant.'

Jack frowned. 'How's that?'

'I have learnt that it is not so much a perfect sphere as a ball with flattened faces, each face being a pentagon. You are familiar with Plato's archetypal shapes?'

'Er, familiar? No, not really,' said Jack. He drained the glass.

'Well, he matched certain three-dimensional shapes with each of the four elements, but the dodecahedron – a twelve-faced spheroid where each face has five sides – he connected with the fifth element, the ether.'

Jack's face glazed. Melody smiled, but Leonardo sensed the courtesy and got to his feet. He took a long look at Ariel, but thought better of saying any more and bade them goodnight.

The others soon followed. 'Well,' said Jack as they left the refectory, 'I don't know if I should be reassured or worried by that conversation.'

'How so?' said Melody.

'I mean, do I consign our abbot here to the fringes of loony, harmless at least? Or do I reckon on his interest as a potential conflict with our own?'

'What is our interest in the crystal?' said Melody as they began their walk round the dimly lit cloister.

'I wish I knew,' said Jack. 'Ryan didn't seem to get far with it. But what bothers me is that the military were happy to take it as reasonable recompense for the delay in getting their hands on Ariel. Now why would that be?'

She shrugged, before turning round to check that Ariel was still with them. She at least had not failed to notice that he had been silent throughout the conversation.

5

The shining teardrop that was the river-bordered centre of Bruges receded into the clouds below as Hugh settled into his thinking seat. His current pilot was busy in the cockpit, and there he could stay. It wouldn't take long to get back to Montagnola, and he needed to crystallise the rather fluid plan in his mind.

Of course he was mad to be doing this, whatever 'this' was. His place was in the background while he fielded others, shielded from any situation where he was anything other than the public but private Hugh Coates, builder of lofty empires, doubtless eccentric but ultimately boring.

But this was different. He had enjoyed his outing as Hugh Greerson, entrepreneur, businessman and humanitarian. Enjoyed it too much. 'Gotten sloppy,' as his colleagues west of the Atlantic would say. And yes, it had clearly been unwise, for now Miranda was off grid and he didn't know why. He had no other available agents in her vicinity, barring young Naismith, and he wouldn't be suitable.

Clearly too hungry for it. Attachment issues maybe?

He tapped his fingers on the arm of his seat. What about himself? Had he got too close? Really, what did he think he was going to do? Turn up at the monastery in Montagnola and play the worried boss? It was out of the question, and a cool mind knew that. This time he would have far more than the Abbot to deal with. It was too risky. And what would it accomplish? Did he even have a single reason to believe she was in danger? Out of her depth, maybe, but then, isn't that how you learned to swim, as long as you knew the basics? And Miranda certainly knew the basics.

He gave a voice command to the seat arm panel. 'Flight deck.'

'Yes, Mr Coates?'

'Change of plan. We're going to Geneva.'

6

After the best night's sleep since he had returned to Earth, Jack was not too concerned when Natasha failed to appear at breakfast. But when he broached the subject of what to do about Miranda, the room went as cold as the toast. Ariel seemed to have something to say about her but wouldn't come clean, insisting that Jack needed to find Natasha first. Melody shrugged, but her eyes told Jack he should probably comply.

He had not put Miranda and Natasha in the same mental compartment before, so as he walked around the buildings he racked his brain over what on earth could have happened. How had Miranda upset the balance?

And had she upset Natasha?

He found her in the chapel. She was seated in the second row, not far from where they had started to talk to Ariel just four days before. Jack approached slowly, his shoes sounding on the stone floor, but she didn't look round. He drew level, then sat on the opposite side of the aisle. He could see her eyes were open, but he couldn't tell if she was praying or thinking, or simply staring.

After two long minutes he spoke. 'We've been wondering where you were.'

She turned to face him, eyes glistening. 'Sorry, I needed time to think. It's peaceful in here.'

'Aye, I reckon we've brought a good deal of unrest into this place.' He crossed the aisle and sat astride the chair in front of her. 'Still, we can't stay here much longer.'

'I certainly can't, Jack. I mean, I can't stay here any longer.'

'Now why would that be?'

'I'm emotionally compromised.'

Jack let out a long breath. He was pretty sure Melody would know why on earth Natasha would say something like that. But Melody wasn't here. He decided to play dumb, except of course he wasn't playing. 'In what way? I mean, why? How? Since when?'

'Oh Jack, isn't this whole thing weird? And doesn't it just mess with your head? And your heart? I've become too involved, too close to...' She saw his face go pale. 'No, don't worry, I'm not talking about you! Though, now I think about it, it did all start on Venus, didn't it? It was like a fever.'

He recalled the Endeavour's airlock and their closeness, bordering on intimacy, as she had kitted him out for his search for Jim and Ryan on the surface of Venus. But until now he had not been sure it had meant anything to her as well.

'Right,' he said. 'Good. Not the time to talk about that, then. So what is it?'

She sighed. 'Oh, it's stupid, I know it is. But it's like he's got inside my head. Though it took getting inside *hers* to see that. Oh, I don't know...' Her words trailed off.

'Okay,' he said slowly. 'So let's assume we're talking about Ariel here. Tell me what's happened.'

Still the words wouldn't come.

'I blame myself,' Jack continued. 'I've put too much on you. We don't know anything about this guy. I'm sorry, Natasha. Please believe me that I only did what I did because I had confidence in you.'

She smiled at that.

'There you go,' he said. 'That's more like it. Now, come on, Cosmonaut Koroleva, tell me all I need to know in order to grant you leave of absence.'

Her shoulders dropped and she leaned back, drawing strength from the air of formality Jack had assumed. It would make things easier. 'Right. Okay. Where do I begin? I've been going over and over it in my head. I have to begin on Venus, of course. On the Endeavour, when I was left alone with Ariel the very first time. There was a... a connection. You remember I told you I'd looked into his eyes?'

'Yes you did. Eventually.'

'Yes. Sorry.'

'And it told me enough to make sure we brought you along for all this. Was I wrong? Have I exploited something I shouldn't have? Have I exploited you?'

'No, you haven't. Of course you haven't. I wanted this, right from the start, to be there for him. But, well, I think it was a kind of motherly thing at first – no, really – but then it became... I don't know... sisterly? I know I have to let him go.'

Jack stood up and crossed over to a stained-glass window that featured a rainbow. 'Natasha, are you being entirely honest with me? With yourself?'

She clasped her hands together. 'As I say, that's how it began. I felt this urge to protect him. But now...'

'Now?'

'Now, thanks to Miranda, I realise it's more than that, and I need to sort out my feelings, and I don't want to compromise the mission.'

Jack decided to hold his peace for a moment, before changing direction. 'It was a crazy time on Venus, wasn't it?' he said. 'I think that's when Jim began to lose it with me, like he was jealous or something.'

'Jealous? What do you mean?'

'Well, I suppose I mean envious really. He resented my being put in charge of Ariel. But, Natasha, I have to say I don't really know why

DISAPPOINTMENTS

he reacted so strongly.'

She nodded. 'No, it was strange. And then, what about Ryan? He had it in for Ariel from the start.'

Jack sat down again. 'You know, I'm not going to grant you leave of absence, not right now anyway, and I'll hear about Miranda's... interaction with Ariel all in good time. It seems to me that the emotions of every one of us have been played with since... well, since then. And we need to get to the bottom of it. As for your connection with Ariel, I may have to ask you to push it back and be the professional I know you are.'

'But–'

'I know, and I'm not going to involve you in the meetings with Ariel any more, not if I don't have to. But things are set to move on apace any time soon, and I need you here, Natasha, I really do. So why don't you take a back seat for a day or two? Get reading some of those unusual books they have. Walk around the grounds, a bit further afield. You'll be getting a bit of a rest, but at the same time you'll be working for the cause. I need to understand this place, and Ms Bridlington's strategy, and I need everyone's mind to be clear. Okay?'

She stood up. What had seemed impossible only minutes before now presented itself as her duty. And that was something no one could accuse her of neglecting.

7

A few rays of sunlight streamed on to Miranda's face, calling out delicate shades of red in her dark brown hair. She was sitting in the meditation room next to a small window. Ariel was standing by the patio doors, looking intently at them, as if he was trying to make them talk. Jack sat opposite Miranda. Bill had not returned.

'So, Miranda,' Jack began. 'We're going to need to make contact with your company, whatever else our friend the General decides to do.'

'Do?' she said, one hand pulling idly on a strand of hair.

'In terms of deciding what action to take against you, or your company, for the way you, er, entered the proceedings here – proceedings you need know nothing about. In fact the less you know, the better.'

'Well, that's kind of you, Commander.'

Ariel looked up. 'But Jack, Miranda clearly knows a lot, given that she came here with the express intent of finding and... studying my suit.'

'Quite so. And that's what I need to talk to you about now, Miranda. You came here with your boss originally, didn't you?'

'Mr Greerson, that's right.'

'And the thing is, now that we've established your intentions were undeniably clandestine, we're going to have to speak to him. We need to know what brought him here, to a place even I didn't know about a day before we arrived.' He decided to call a halt there, not wanting to share his misgivings about absent members of the Endeavour crew.

'So, you want me to give him a call?'

'Aye, that would be helpful.'

'Jack, Jack, I think I have it!' Ariel's voice cut through their conversation like a car swerving in from the fast lane. Jack and Miranda looked equally mystified. 'The French windows,' he continued. 'I remember what happened.'

'Okay, that's great,' said Jack. 'You and I need to talk about that. Miranda, can I ask you to go on ahead to the refectory? You just cross the small courtyard here, through the narrow corridor, over to the main building, and turn left as you enter the other courtyard. Okay? We'll join you in a moment.'

Miranda left, barely suppressing the smile that tried to surface. Jack had no idea she had been carrying a mental map of the place for over a week.

Once she had left, Jack turned back to Ariel. 'Well? What have you recalled?'

'I opened them. The doors, I opened them.'

'But they were locked.'

'Indeed – as Leonardo said. But I can see it now. I reached out for the handle, felt some resistance, pushed on with...'

'Pushed on with what?' said Jack, becoming suddenly more engaged. 'Hardly with force. The frames and locks are made of tempered steel!'

'No, not force exactly, more... expression. I expressed myself, my desire to open the door.'

'Well, we're going to have to get to the bottom of that, whatever it is,' said Jack, scratching his head. 'But why did you end up on the ground?'

'It was the trees mainly, I think.'

'Ah yes, right. The trees.'

'I did try to tell you something about that in the chapel. The surge of life was intense, Jack. I've not experienced anything like it since... well, I can't remember since when. But it did seem familiar.'

'Well,' said Jack, 'I suppose we should be pleased that you're finding anything familiar. Let's pick up on this later. I'd rather not keep Miranda waiting.'

8

Natasha decided to skip lunch and explore the grounds further afield now that she had more time. It was a warm day and dry as she set off in her beloved tracksuit and trainers past a shed and some garages (which proved to be locked) along a path that led deeper into the wood. She was surprised to find the way so easy, doubtless kept clear by the Brothers as they combined manual work with study and prayer – or whatever it was they did on the spiritual side of things. That was something she needed to look into when she got back. But right now the forest beckoned.

The first thing she noticed was the change from leaves to pine needles under her feet. The smell became keener, less dank and more invigorating. There were not so many deciduous trees here, nor even much in the way of cypress. The pines were quite old, judging by their height, although she wasn't sure how long these particular trees took to grow. The forest might be centuries old, but so much here was tinged with the twenty-first century that she would not be surprised if that was true of the forest also.

She saw a clearing on her left and turned into it, only to find an old shed with a cluster of satellite dishes on its roof, standing there quietly, confirming her thoughts about the unapologetic mix of old and new that permeated the whole place. Instinctively she looked back the way she came, before walking the perimeter of the clearing. No one. Just birdsong, and the rustling of some woodland creature too small or too quick to see.

She walked over to the wooden door. It was padlocked. No surprise there. Something was odd about the timbers of the door frame. They were warped, almost as if they were losing their grip and coming away from something. She shone her eband into the crack between the door and the frame and peered in. Something was reflecting the light. It looked like solid steel. She stepped back. Here it seemed the old not only contained the new but concealed it.

She circled the shed. There was no sign of any pipes or cables going in or out, though they had to be there, equally hidden, feeding the satellite dishes. Jack had told them about the generator room, and it hadn't sounded like there was anything there to explain the electronic shielding that engulfed the place. Perhaps this was the source. She checked her eband for a signal, but it was dead as usual.

She walked on past the place where the woodland creature had made a sudden sound. Finding another path, she followed her wanderlust. It was not many minutes before she was startled by a voice.

'Hello!' The young monk spoke in an English accent she couldn't quite place. 'I'm Brother Leroy. Out for a walk?'

'Yes,' said Natasha. 'You too?'

'Ah, that would be nice,' said Leroy. 'No, I'm working.' He lifted

DISAPPOINTMENTS

the rake she had not seen under his hand, positioned like a walking stick. 'Are you working too?'

Natasha was thrown by the question, and wondered whether he had seen her snooping around, but she decided to make no assumptions. 'Actually I'm taking a break. I needed some air.'

'I love it out here,' said Leroy. 'I can be myself, here under the trees.'

'Ah, you're mad on trees too!' It was out before she knew.

'Oh, you like them as well, do you?' He hesitated. 'Sorry, they tell me I'm not good at picking up what people are trying to say to me. You know, between the lines.'

Natasha looked at him with a mixture of curiosity and compassion. Something about him was not quite right, yet his heart seemed to be in the right place. On an impulse she decided to explain. 'Actually, it's not me I was thinking about – although, yes, the trees are very fine. It's one of our friends. We're here to help him.' She knew she didn't owe any kind of explanation to this young man, yet something about him, an air of being overlooked, made her want to. Anyway, she reasoned, this was as good a cover story as anything else. It was true, so far as it went.

Leroy leant his rake against a tree. 'Are you hungry? I have a few bits and pieces from the kitchen just over there. I mean, only if you'd like.'

'Actually I've not had anything to eat today, so I'd be honoured, thank you.'

She followed him for quite a way and at quite a pace, and was just beginning to wonder how much further it could be when she saw a bench. To her surprise it was beside a road. 'Oh,' she said, 'where does this go?'

'Well,' said Leroy, as he sat down and opened his lunchbox, 'I suppose that depends on what direction you're going in. It goes to the monastery if you look that way.' He turned round. 'But that way takes you to the back gate.'

'Right,' she smiled. She walked up to a bend in the road, and there about a hundred metres further on was a pair of large wooden gates. It had to be the way they had first entered the complex a week earlier.

When she returned Brother Leroy was pouring some steaming water from a flask into a small cup. He looked up. 'I'm sorry, I don't have any tea or coffee or anything.'

'Water is good,' she said, and sat down beside him. 'It's my favourite.'

He handed her a piece of fresh bread and a hunk of cheese, looking at her as if he were checking she was really there, sitting down on the bench with him. 'Well,' he said. 'This is nice. I don't usually have lunch with anyone.' She wasn't sure whether he meant it was unusual to eat alone out here in the forest, or whether it was a more general observation. She decided not to pry. At least, not yet. For several minutes they ate in silence, interrupted only by the repeating chorus of a pair of wood pigeons.

'Do you mind if I ask you something, Miss... Oh, I don't actually know your name.'

'It's Natasha.'

'Natasha. I like that name. Are you Russian?'

She nodded.

'Can I ask, Natasha... the friend you're helping, is he the man who has meals with you and the other visitors, the ones who've been here for the past week? Sorry, do you mind me asking?'

'No, that's fine, though I am not at liberty to talk about it. But yes, he is that man.'

'Hmm. And then you had the army man come and join you.' When she made no response he took another bite from his bread and cheese. He stole a glance at her from the corner of his eye, and then another, trying to imprint an image in his mind of the extraordinary face before him, its features somehow soft even though they looked like they had been carved out of stone. 'I was there, you know, when they found the lady out in the storm.'

Only now did it occur to Natasha that, even if Leroy had picked up more than most, he was probably not the only one of the Brothers with questions about what they'd seen. And even heard? For the first time she realised how little she had thought about that. All their sessions with Ariel had been behind closed doors, but they had often gone on talking in the refectory, and it seemed obvious now that this had been a little lax on their part. That was not like Jack. Or was it? She realised that, however much she knew Jack the astronaut, she knew next to nothing at all about Jack the secret agent. Still, he seemed to have the utmost confidence in Constance Bridlington who had chosen the venue for their delicate operation.

She was here to find out more about the place, so best make the most of their conversation. 'Leroy, may I ask you something?'

He looked at her like a dog waiting for its mistress to throw a stick. 'Of course. We're here to help.'

'Just before that storm you mentioned, something was going on in the courtyard. Can you explain it for me?'

'Oh yes,' he said eagerly. 'We were taking readings and pooling them together in an elemental analyser. Well, when I say "we", I mean four of the Brothers and the Abbot, you understand.'

'Readings? Of what? If you don't mind me asking.'

'Air pressure, electrical activity, humidity... that sort of thing.'

'Hmm, well, that's air, fire, and water, I guess. What about earth?'

'I see you already understand quite a bit,' Leroy said, ever so slightly crestfallen.

'No, not really,' she said. 'I mean, the whole thing looked so religious, if you know what I mean. Ceremonial. So my question is, what were they actually doing? How would they characterise the act itself?'

'Wow,' said Leroy, taking his time over the word. More bread and cheese. 'The thing is, I've been trying to work out that very thing – what you just said. When you apply to come here, they send you all kinds of stuff on the four elements, obviously. But with it comes a load of scientific data – on the environment, mainly. Water leads them to try to understand the reasons for flooding, as well as the pollution of our waters. Air too – that's polluted. The earth is racked by quakes as well as exploitation for resources – you know, mining and farming. And each year fire ravages more of our forests.'

He paused, but she could see his brain was still firing and waited for him to continue. 'It all made sense as a way of tackling our planet's chronic maladies. And that's what got me interested. I'd been looking at the new-earthers, of course, but it seemed to me we should be trying harder to mend our own planet rather than try to find a new one. And I'd been thinking about doing a sabbatical or some kind of retreat anyway. You know, something a bit longer than the norm. I wasn't sure till I learned about the Centre here in Switzerland, which seemed just right for me and I applied to become a Novice.'

'What made it just right?' asked Natasha, looking at him intently. He dropped his gaze.

'Well, I don't mean to boast, but...'

'Go on. It's not like we have an audience.'

'No, right. Well, for most of my life, in school and college, I'd got used to being at the top of the class in most things – not sport or music, but the humanities and the sciences. My parents sent me to various extra classes, just to stretch me a bit, and I entered university a year early. But I didn't find it easy to get a job after that.'

'What did you want to do?'

'Well, that's just it, I didn't really know. I had done some thinking on how a new philosophy of science could be developed, but no one was really interested. Commercial companies couldn't see any value in it, and the research institutes I tried said it wasn't really their field. And that's when I first read about the Temple of the Four Elements and applied to Xizang – you know, the region that's still called Tibet by a lot of people – and they advised me to come here first. You have to commit for seven years, during which time you move from Novice to Brother, which I did last year... but they help with academic studies. So I came here for a visit, met Leonardo who is amazing, and it was a no-brainer after that.'

'He is interesting, isn't he?' Natasha remarked.

'Absolutely,' said Leroy. 'Sometimes he looks like a man out of his own time, like he's been wrenched out of the Middle Ages, but then you see him so at home with the latest technology – and I mean the latest – and you realise how complex he is.'

'Hmm,' Natasha mused under her breath, 'aren't we all?' Louder she said, 'You say they help with academic studies. Is that true for everyone here?'

'I think so,' Leroy replied. 'Brother Josef, for instance, the keeper of the attic – he's involved in research into dark energy fields.' He gobbled down his last piece of cheese. 'Did you know that they're a kind of fifth element to many scientists?' he asked cautiously.

'No, I'm not sure I'd heard that,' said Natasha, though she had a suspicion it was something she had learnt on a foundation course. 'My focus has been planetary formation.'

'Ah well,' said Leroy exultantly, 'if you take matter, light, sub-atomic particles and dark matter as the four basic categories of the universe, then dark energy becomes a fifth element.' He smacked his lips as he finished. 'That's "quintessence" in the Latin.'

'I suppose it is,' said Natasha, whose impression of this young man seemed to change with each verse of the pigeon chorus. 'And the Centre helps him with this, you say?'

'Yes,' said Leroy. 'In fact, I think Brother Josef is even allowed to deal direct with Xizang. They must consider it pretty important research.'

A breeze rustled through the beech leaves and seemed to break Leroy's concentration. 'Oh dear,' he said. 'I've done it again.'

'What have you done?'

'I've been talking too much. The Brothers tell me I do this a lot. I don't think they like it.'

'Do they listen when you talk?'

'Not really. Not any more. I can't blame them, I suppose. It's not surprising they put me to work out here, even though I've got weak legs. Not that I mind, though. It gives me time to think.'

'About a new philosophy of science.'

'Yes, exactly!' He closed the lunch box. 'Thank you, Natasha.'

'For what?'

'For not pitying me.'

She smiled, and he noticed a small chip on one of her front teeth. Somehow it made her more real. They walked slowly now through the trees back to the monastery, both feeling the need to process the conversation they had just enjoyed. Leroy cherished the new information about the man from the ether and his love of trees, delighted that he had gained this openly, direct from one of the inner circle. Natasha still had questions, unsure whether Brother Leroy had inadvertently confirmed her suspicion that this was a place of pseudo-science, or whether he was right to believe they were doing valuable work for the salvation of the environment.

But that was the nature of the really interesting questions of life. Answer one, and two more rise up to take its place.

9

Less than 150 miles away another young man was in for a surprise lunchtime encounter. Petroc Naismith answered his intercom to be told that Hugh Coates was downstairs asking to see Ms Bridlington.

'Okay, thanks,' he answered as coolly as he could. 'I'll let Ms B know.' A sudden mix of shock and anticipation left him shaking. What was the Chief doing here? And how could he not have warned Petroc, his secret agent?

Bridlington was not surprised by the news. 'Bring him up, please, Petroc.'

'But he's not on the schedule, Ma'am.'

'I'm aware of that, Petroc.'

'Very good, Ma'am.'

Duly collected, Hugh went into the Director's office. At no point did he show the slightest recognition of Petroc, which simply raised the excitement level. This had to be connected with Miranda's disappearance. But then, how could it be? Unless. Unless Bridlington was also an Infostructure agent! A higher level, perhaps, so secret that someone on Petroc's pay grade wouldn't know about it.

He sat back in his chair and promptly slapped himself on the forehead for forgetting to listen in. This was one conversation to hear live. Quickly he closed his door, fumbled with his eband and sat back to listen.

'Thanks for agreeing to see me at such short notice, Madam Director.'

'Constance, please. Call me Constance.'

'As you know, Constance, I have a good deal of interest in the Aphrodite Mission.'

'Of course. Your company's work on nuclear drives got us there. And in fact, Hugh – may I call you Hugh? – I am in a position to tell you that the climatic Window on Venus has continued to close and is now almost back to normal. If we had tried to get there by the old methods, we would never have made it.'

Hugh smiled (though Petroc could not see it). This was not news to him, of course, but the question now was whether to come clean or whether to fake the usual surprise. He went for the former, realising she would probably expect him to be well informed.

'Actually, I was aware of that, yes. But I thought I'd call in and see you while I was here on other business. I wondered when you might have a report on the functioning of the hardware.'

Constance studied the face of the man before her. He maintained a serious demeanour yet there was a sparkle in his grey eyes. Maybe it was contact lenses, but she fancied there was more to it than that. One of the richest men in the world, he was seldom seen in public, any photos of him quickly lost in a sea of boredom. For Hugh Coates was no celebrity – just a man in the background people quickly forgot.

'Yes, of course,' she said. 'We should have something soon.' She leaned back in her chair. 'Actually Hugh, if you don't mind me asking, I've often wondered why you invested in nuclear drive technology, given your expertise – passion, one might guess – for telecommunications.'

Hugh gave an easy smile. 'No, Constance, I certainly don't mind you asking. The thing is, I've always considered myself a "both-and" kind of person, and the way I see it, wires and wireless are one way of bringing people together, and vehicle engines are another.'

'Yes, I see.'

'So, once I became convinced that nuclear fusion would deliver the most efficient way of getting us to where we want to go, right across the solar system, I decided that was where half of my energies should go.'

'Half of your "both-and", so to speak.'

'Precisely so. Needless to say, I'm eager to have the details on how our latest model performed in the somewhat unexpected rush to Venus.' He gave a slight cough. 'Do we know yet if the latest modifications to the hydrogen propellant proved themselves?'

'I'm sure they did,' said Constance. 'Certainly we know that there were no problems with the nuclear drive. It got the crew to Venus orbit and back in record time, and even managed a low-cost stop-off for a telescope repair. I believe there were some braking issues there, subjecting the crew to more G-force than we had intended, but they seem fit and well – and we can't exactly blame you for the laws of physics! But I'll let you have the detailed analysis on engine performance as soon as it comes my way. You'll understand that we've been somewhat exercised by other considerations.' She got up from her desk and went and sat down at the far end of the conference table. 'Do you have time for a coffee?'

'That would be splendid, thank you.' His transatlantic accent was leaning eastward.

Petroc switched off his eband and attended to the call for refreshments. This would take him out of the conversation for several minutes, so he would just have to wait for the recording. Not that he'd miss anything the Chief needed to know, of course... so why did it matter? But it did. It seemed eavesdropping was addictive.

When he returned from delivering the coffee they were well into a discussion about the stowaway and the interest of the military. 'It's to be expected,' said Hugh. 'Have you heard from Conway Box?'

'Should I have?'

'No. I just thought, given his contribution to the mission, engineering those space suits, he may have been in touch.'

Her eyes flashed. 'Well, perhaps he didn't just happen to be in Geneva like you.'

'Indeed.' He didn't flinch. 'Still, I imagine you have everything under control.'

'Then you have an overactive imagination! But I can't complain. They've given me enough room to debrief the crew and examine the stowaway. For the moment.'

'Well, I'm sure you're managing admirably.' He got up. 'Thanks for the coffee. Must dash. People to see. But it's been a pleasure.'

She summoned Petroc and said goodbye. When he was gone, she stood at the window and wondered why on earth a man who assiduously avoided meetings outside his own domain would come and see her in person.

10

When he could get away Petroc liked to take lunch in a small café a few streets from the office, and today was one of those days. The Chief had left as he had arrived, without a word, and the office was relatively quiet. Sitting at a table in the corner of the small restaurant, with his eyes on his panini, he replayed the conversation between his secret boss and his public one.

It took a moment to realise that Hugh's real-time voice was cutting in over the recording. He looked up.

'May I join you?'

'Mr Coates! Why yes, of course. I don't think anyone here will recognise you.'

'Ah, come now, Petroc, you know that isn't true. But what does it matter if someone does see me drop in for a quick bite and bump into a fellow I've only just met at the UN?'

Petroc's admiration swelled, and he recalled his training at

Infostructure: whenever possible hide in plain sight and let nothing need more than the simplest explanation.

They ordered lunch. 'What have you got for me, Petroc?'

'Sure thing. You already know about the military. But what she didn't tell you was that General Petersen arrived this morning. I've not had chance to review their conversation.'

'Well, we know that he wants to get his hands on the mystery man,' said Hugh. 'But maybe he's back because of the crystal.'

'Could be,' said Petroc. 'Do we know what they're doing with it? If I may ask?'

'You may. But you do understand, Petroc, why I don't like to tell you too much? You have enough to juggle in that devious head of yours, without worrying over yet more information you're not supposed to know.' Hugh's food arrived just as the level of general conversation in the café dropped, so he took the opportunity to bite into his freshly baked baguette before continuing. 'They seem to be thinking the crystal is man-made. It appears to have been polished by artificial forces.'

'Wow.' Petroc took a sip from his blueberry crush. 'Er, Mr Coates?'

'Yes?'

'Do we have word from Miranda?'

'Word? No. But I take her silence to be progress.'

'But how can you be sure? Who knows what's happened to her?'

'Petroc, I have my sources, as you know, and my devices. And while I've not got a complete picture, I have enough to tell me that things are playing out quite nicely in the monastery. So please don't worry. Now, I really must get back.'

Petroc dutifully said a loud and clear 'Goodbye, Mr Coates, lovely to meet you' and watched the Chief leave the café. And now he began to join the dots as best he could, though the picture he imagined was nothing like the one belonging to the young man in the monastery. There was a mysterious stowaway who had somehow got to Venus first. There was a crystal that had been polished if not cut by natural forces. Or possibly even artificial ones, though what would that mean? It was so hard to make anything of it. And right now Miranda was at the centre of it all.

What he wouldn't give to be with her.

CHAPTER 15

Emotions

1

Ever since The Times had broken the story ahead of the press conference on Space Station Alpha the wheels of social and mass media had been turning relentlessly. No one was surprised at the 'I-told-you-so' announcements of an alien invasion, and they didn't bat an eyelid at the avalanche of inevitable conspiracy theories, many of which were given extra fuel by the 'obvious cover-up' when that press conference was subject to an online blackout due to 'technical difficulties'. This was all manageable, and the whole business might well have been contained, if the more serious players had not been involved from Day 1.

For that had always been the odd thing about the Icarus story, as it soon became known: it had been a more than half-credible institution, The Times in London, that had fired the gun that started the avalanche. Social influencers were the first to latch onto the journalist girlfriend of one of the crew, knowing that she had a track record in stories on space exploration. That was simple enough arithmetic for anyone. The story had a solid core of credibility that even the most sensationalist claptrap could not bury.

There were no pictures of the alien, and practically no information. As the days became weeks international news turned to more pressing issues of global warming and economic injustice. But that didn't stop a long line of pretenders appearing, each one the 'real' man from Venus, or his associate. Even his wife.

Even the New Earth movement wasn't about to miss the bandwagon. A mixture of scientists, politicians and die-hard climate activists committed to finding a new home for the human race, starting with the Moon and Mars but ultimately travelling to the stars, they were not slow in wondering out loud whether Icarus might be a messenger sent to help us on our way.

All this was too much for Jim Adamson and Ryan Chase. Duty-bound to decline all interviews, they decided to go to ground and wait for the next stage. After all, there was no way Jack would be able to hold onto the Stranger or the crystal for much longer.

2

Miranda was leaving. With Petersen gone, and time running out, Jack had asked Melody to escort her back to the hotel in the hope this might free him of the whole complication.

She picked up her jacket, sample bag still empty, and left her room for the last time. As she turned the corner past Ariel's door, she felt a pang of regret. Maybe even remorse. She knocked softly.

For a moment she thought she had missed him, but then suddenly there he was, standing still and looking right at her.

'Can I come in?'

'Of course.'

She went over to the window, taking a last look out across the trees, and then perched on the chair. 'Ariel, they're letting me go now, and I feel we should leave on better terms. Yesterday things got a little intense, didn't they?'

'They did.'

She swallowed. An unsettling idea had been forming in her mind. Did she dare do it? Well, she was here now, so why waste the opportunity?

'So, the thing is, I think I may know something about what happened to you on the Space Station.'

'Really? How is that possible?'

'I, er, I don't really want to tell you how, and I'd appreciate it if you didn't scan my mind, or whatever it is you do.'

'Miranda, I wouldn't "scan" you, as you put it, unless I felt you were letting me in.'

'Right. Been there before. Anyway, I have had sight of some footage which shows you, lying on a table, being examined by some guy in a white coat. Would that be connected to that jumbled memory you mentioned?'

'Well, I suppose it would.' He sat down on the bed. 'Please continue.'

'In one piece of footage there are some men watching the white coat examine you. You can't make out their faces, and there's no sound, so I don't know who they are. You're still in your suit, and that seems to be the main area of interest. In the second clip I saw, the guy seemed to be on his own, and he was...'

'Yes?' His eyes widened, and she decided to engage them once more, suddenly hoping against hope this would not be the last time.

'He was trying to set light to you! At least, that's what it looked like.'

'Well!'

They sat quietly for a moment.

'Listen,' she said at last, 'I have to go. But there is one more thing. I've also overheard a conversation implying it's not only your suit that's super-resilient, but that you yourself...'

'Me myself?'

She leaned forward and dropped her voice. 'They suggested that you were also showing signs of, well, enhancement I think they called it.

She let him look at her, into her, and now that she knew how much she wanted this, she opened like a flower to the sun. She couldn't tell him about Hugh, not in so many words, but she let the memory of him showing her all this on the plane linger in her mind.

'Thank you,' he said, and looked away.

'Are you going to be all right? Is this going to help?'

'I'm sure it will. I need to think about it all. Now, you must go.'

'Will we meet again?' Her voice faltered.

'I don't know, Miranda.'

3

Miranda and Melody felt their ebands burst into life as they walked through the small gate to the hire car that still waited in the layby where Miranda had left it less than two days before. As she steered away from the monastery grounds she pushed the excitement and drama of the last couple of days towards the back of her mind. There was no chance it would stay there. She concentrated hard on the bends in the road, glad to be avoiding eye contact with her passenger who was busy scrolling through her messages.

The journey was not long, and soon they were walking across the piazza in the centre of Montagnola where the early evening sun was already painting the stones and shutters in the soft golden hues of the hour.

They stopped in the foyer as Miranda brought up her electronic room key on her eband. 'It's good to be back,' she said. 'I've been in these clothes way too long! Do you want to come up for a drink, or whatever, before you go back? You know, make sure I stay out of trouble?' She gave an awkward grin.

Melody tilted her head in response and took a proper look at her charge. No, she thought, Ariel may be able to read this one, but I sure as heaven can't. 'No, I'd better not,' she said out loud. 'You know, things to do. Thanks all the same.'

'Sure thing. Well, I'll say goodbye then.' Not waiting for an answer, or even the elevator, she fled up the stairs.

Melody shrugged, but her thoughts were already elsewhere. The phrase 'sure as heaven' was one of David's, and she was eager to check a message from him buried in the middle of the hundred others that had recently surfaced.

She marched into the bar, ordered an orange juice and took it with her to a quiet corner. Her heart raced as she opened the message. It was surprisingly brief, and amounted to little more than an apology for being 'on edge' during her last visit. He hoped she was well, wherever she was.

That was it. Her excitement turned to frustration. The message was polite enough, but then that was the problem. She and David were way beyond polite. There didn't seem to be a shred of emotional honesty in the message. Still, she had to answer it. Who knew when she would be able to get a signal again?

She sent an equally anaemic response, downed the rest of her drink and called a taxi, attending to other messages while she waited. Of Miranda she gave no further thought.

4

General William Petersen breathed in deeply as he entered the headquarters of UN High Command, the executive division that had come out of the old Security Council. It was good to be away from the dithering discussions that characterised so much of Constance Bridlington's world down on the third floor. Here the air was clean and the decisions were sharp. As head of the UN Special Task Force he was answerable only to the three people he was about to visit. They in turn were answerable to all the heads of state of the member nations – in theory, at least, though he was banking now on some latitude in that regard.

He made his presence known and was quickly escorted to a meeting room without windows. The aide left, promptly closing the door behind him. Already seated on either side of a large, highly polished oval table were Nathan Dexter, a clean-cut suited American around fifty years old whom he knew, and a man he took to be Mr Takahashi. He was also wearing a suit, yet there was not a whiff of the corporate about him. These were the two men in the triumvirate who ran the show. The third was Beth Griffiths, who only now appeared through a door at the other end of the room. She too was about fifty, with shoulder-length frizzy hair which was tied back in a thick pony tail. Her suit ended just above the knee. Bill had never found it easy having a female boss, although he had managed to convince himself he had no issue with her being Black. He knew she had been brought up in Britain by her Welsh father, though he hadn't heard the full story, and little from Beth herself.

'Bill,' she said. 'This is unexpected. What brings you here? Something too delicate for the usual channels?'

'Ah, Beth, astute as ever. Gentlemen, good morning.'

Nathan said hi, and the other gave a short, sharp nod.

'Ah, don't mind Takeshi,' said Beth. 'He's a man of few words.'

'Suits me,' said Bill.

As Nathan began to pour himself some coffee from a silver pot on the table, Bill launched in. 'You're all busy people, so I'll keep this brief. You are aware, of course, of my current project. I've just come from the weirdest detention centre I've ever seen.'

'Bill,' said Beth, 'I believe the term is debriefing.'

'Well, there's the rub. The astronauts needed debriefing, but the stowaway—'

'As I understand it,' said Nathan, breaking in while vigorously stirring his coffee into a miniature whirlpool, 'the guy was found unconscious.'

'True,' said Bill, 'but that makes him all the more a stowaway. He clearly needed somewhere to crash.'

'Either that, or someone stowed him against his will,' said Beth.

'What did you make of him, this Ariel?'

'I won't deny he seems genuinely confused. As I said in my message, he's out of his depth somehow.'

Nathan stopped stirring and ventured a quick slurp. 'So, what do you think, Bill? Someone dumped him there?'

'Maybe. Or maybe he's the sole survivor of something that went wrong.'

'Or was about to go wrong,' said Beth. 'For all we know, the rest of his crew were left on the planet, and God knows what's happened to them now.'

Bill looked puzzled.

'The thing is,' Nathan explained, 'conditions on that part of Venus are back to their lethal normal. So we can't see how anyone else could have survived.'

'Maybe they left before the Window closed,' said Bill.

'Not likely,' said Beth. 'There were six radio telescopes and a dozen other devices trained on Venus at that time. Nothing. The Resolution was the only spacecraft that left orbit.'

Bill pushed back against the table in his chair. 'Okay,' he said. 'What about before? I take it we were looking before the landing as well? Could somebody still be circling the planet?'

'Also unlikely,' said Beth. 'I'll admit we weren't looking so closely before the mission.' She poured herself a coffee. 'But then, why would we be?'

Seeing it was clearly self-service today, Bill took the silver coffee pot, stealing a glance at the silent Japanese guy as he poured. His face was stone, his thoughts unreadable. Bill sat back down. 'I said I'd keep this short, so here goes. I think it's time we stopped pussyfooting around with this guy, whoever or whatever he is. We need answers!'

'Well, Bill,' said Beth, 'I think that's precisely why we're "pussyfooting", as you so nicely put it. Constance sees the softly-softly approach as the most likely to stimulate the man's memory.'

Bill snorted at that, and he noticed Mr Takahashi actually move his head ever so slightly at the same time. Did he feel the same? Time to press the point. 'Beth, gentlemen,' and at that he looked directly at Takahashi, 'I propose we speed things up a little and go get him.'

Nathan was just reaching for the coffee pot, but stopped half way. 'Whoa! You mean, kidnap the guy?'

'That's exactly what I mean. And now is a good time, what with that woman breaking security anyway. Any number of people would fall under suspicion.'

'Yes, what was her name again? Melissa?' asked Beth.

'Miranda. I can't believe how Forrester has let her roam around with access to the prisoner.'

'Sorry, Bill,' said Beth, 'but I remind you, it's not a detention centre and he's not a prisoner.'

'Well, he damn well ought to be!'

'Okay, okay,' said Nathan. 'And bear with me, Beth. We're struggling as it is with the media interest, never mind the potential security risk. So let's say we did snatch the guy. My guess is, that wouldn't be a difficult operation. But my question is, where does it go from there?'

'I've thought about that a lot,' said Bill. 'I need just two guys with me—'

'You?' said Beth. 'You want to do this personally?'

'Why not? For a start I know the place. I can get to his room at night, no problem, and we'll have him out of there before any of those monks get up for their early morning dose of self-mutilation, or whatever it is they do before the sun rises.'

'And then?' repeated Nathan.

'We take him to a secure facility — your choice — and we use the chemical and scanning techniques we have to get to the truth.'

'Sure, sure,' said Nathan. 'But what then, Bill? What about when we've finished with him?'

'That depends on how we carry out the interrogation. We can either quiz him openly, in which case I'd like to do it. At the end we have what we want and no one cares how we did it. Or, I don't show my face, we don't let on who we are, and we dump him somewhere near the monastery after we're done with him. The trouble with that option, of course, is that we wouldn't be able to say how we got our intel.'

'Okay,' said Nathan, 'let's say we go with this. I guess we don't actually need to decide which of your options we take straight away. We can start incognito, and if it works and we get what we want we can come out in the open, when the time is right.'

Bill smiled. Takeshi remained ominously silent, but if the American was coming round, he knew he must be making headway. Time to settle it. He looked to Beth.

'I don't know, Bill. What if it doesn't go well? What if we don't get what we want?'

'Then I guess no one need ever know.'

5

'Time is not a fourth dimension, it is an aspect of the three dimensions.'

Ariel was holding forth in the chapel before his captive audience of two, Jack and Leonardo. Jack didn't know whether to be happy that Ariel had found his stride, or worried that his conversation was becoming ever more abstruse. What was clear was that Leonardo was in his element.

'But Ariel, if I may,' said the Abbot. 'How can you be so sure? I mean, how does it help to see it that way?'

Ariel walked around the chancel, where choirs must once have sung and where the orchestra had so recently transported him. He looked up at the stained-glass window, a shadow of its normal self before the deepening darkness outside. 'Perhaps a thought experiment will help,' he said. 'Imagine everything stopped. I mean everything.'

'Not possible,' put in Jack. 'There has to be movement at the sub-atomic level, just for things to exist. Doesn't there?'

'That may be true,' said Ariel. 'But remember this is a thought experiment, a picture to help bring one particular thing to light. If there were no movement anywhere in the whole universe, absolutely no movement, there would be no change. You would not be able to mark off any time, because time requires movement, however you demarcate it – aeons, minutes, milliseconds, doesn't matter. These are all marker points – stretched and compressed by movement, interestingly enough.'

'Ariel,' said Jack as he got out of his seat, 'I think you must have been an astrophysicist – must *be* an astrophysicist.'

'Ah, I don't know,' said Leonardo. 'Perhaps a cosmologist. Or more likely, it seems to me, a philosopher.'

'Any of those ring a bell, Ariel? No? Come on, then, let's call it a day.'

They made their way back towards the refectory, where Jack bid them good night and carried on up the stairs. First he went to Melody's room, but there was no reply. Not back yet perhaps. He walked back down the hall to Natasha's door. She called him in.

She was sitting on the chair by the bed, reading a large tome that had apparently come from the library. 'Are you allowed to take books out?' asked Jack.

'*I* am, yes, though that doesn't mean you could!' Before he could ask she told him about her new friend Brother Leroy and their conversation, and his knowledge of the place. Including the library.

'Well, I'm glad you've been making progress,' he said. 'I'm not sure whether I have. Ariel is talking a lot more now – in fact, it's hard to stop him.'

She went to the window and looked out into the gloom of the forest. 'Anything useful?'

'Ah, I wish I knew. I guess his psyche is adjusting. He seems to be showing what kind of person he was, or perhaps what he did for a living. In fact, his knowledge is voluminous.'

She turned and gave him a questioning look.

'Oh, sorry, very large. Like he'd know what's in that volume you've got there, and many more besides.'

She nodded. 'I see. Do we know how Melody got on?'

'No, nothing yet. She's not called Leonardo's office. I expect she's on her way back by now.'

She frowned.

'What?' said Jack.

'Nothing, I'm sure. I just got the impression that Miranda... that she was quite keen on Melody.'

'Aye, I guess I'm banking on that, hoping Mel's powers of investigation might unearth some more.'

Natasha smiled. 'Ah well, I think I need an early night.'

They bid each other good night. When he had gone, she sighed. He clearly had no idea.

6

When she got back to her room Miranda went straight to the drinks cabinet, resisting the pull of both tablet and shower. She poured herself a very large whisky, downed half of it and then put her head in her hands. She sat motionless for a while, until her eband vibrated. It was a reminder to call Hugh.

It had been part of the deal. She had tried to call 'Mr Greerson' on Leonardo's phone but had been told he was away. She had used a number Hugh had given her for just this eventuality, so that if they did try to trace it they wouldn't get very far. But Forrester seemed eager to see the back of her. So here she was, alone in her hotel once more. She had wondered whether Mel would stay to make sure she called Hugh. She had wondered many things. But these were fantasies. Miss James clearly had other things on her mind.

'Come on, you silly female,' she said out loud. 'Pull yourself together.' She downed the other half before sending an encrypted message from her tablet to Hugh's eband. To her surprise he answered in person, audio only.

'Not asleep?' she said.

'Not in America. Back in Bruges, in fact.'

'Back? Where did you go then?'

'I decided to go into the lions' den. Absolutely stupid, I know. Well, no, actually you have been in the lions' den. I went to the ringmaster's quarters.'

She shook her head to blow the cobwebs from her mind and grasp his metaphor. 'You went to Geneva?'

'Yes. As I say, stupid. I was there "by chance", for another meeting, and called in to see if there was anything they could give me on the nuclear drive's performance. But...'

'But?'

'Ms Bridlington may be a tad naïve when it comes to technology, but she's no fool. I could tell she was sniffing for something else.'

'You weren't worried about me, were you?'

'Of course not.'

'But do you think she'll put you together with me?' said Miranda, feeling the first nag of a worry.

'Yes, she may do. Anyway, enough about me. How are you?'

She told him about the accident in the storm and the subsequent interrogations, not holding back on General William Petersen. He was particularly delighted with her improvised story about textile espionage.

'Are you sure that was okay?' she said. 'I mean, I could have just said I was a tourist.'

'No, it wouldn't have washed. You'd been there before. There had to be something behind that. And you gave them something.' He paused. 'Mind you...'

'What?'

'It does raise the risk level of my visit to Bridlington. If they use Forrester's people at British Intelligence to look into you, they may connect you with me.'

'But we have that covered, don't we? There's nothing about me on social media, no public links to Infostructure.'

'No, but these are not amateurs.'

'So what do we do?'

'Ah, there you go again, Miranda. I think we've *done* enough – you and me both. We'll continue to monitor the situation. In the end, we've done very little to draw fire. They don't know we've bugged the place, as far as we know, and we've not stolen anything.'

'Okay. But you've got to make contact with them – as Mr Greerson.'

'Hmm. That could be awkward, as the Abbot may see through my appallingly thin disguise. I think our friend may have to die.'

Miranda gasped. 'What? We can't kill the Abbot!'

He laughed. 'No, no, my dear. My, that general has spooked you, hasn't he? I'm talking about Mr Greerson. He may have to come to an untimely end. Then all they'll have is Leonardo's memory of my one visit. And anyway, they have bigger fish to fry. Like, who on earth is the mystery spaceman?'

'I guess.'

'Oh, for sure,' he said. 'Now, tell me the part you've left out.'

'What do you mean?' Thoughts of her evening with Melody flashed across her mind. She was glad this conversation was audio only.

'The spaceman! What's he like? Did you get to talk to him?'

She coughed. 'No, 'fraid not. They didn't let me anywhere near him.'

'Ah well. That's not really surprising, I suppose. Okay, you get some well-earned sleep, and we'll talk again tomorrow.'

He signed off, and she crashed onto the bed. It was the first time she had ever lied to him, and she didn't even know why.

7

Melody slammed the taxi door and made straight for her room. David's message had put her out of sorts, and she didn't want to see anyone else. Correction, she didn't want to see Jack.

She took the stairs by the entrance and headed along the hall. As she approached the corner to take her round to her room, she heard voices. Instinctively she stopped while she was still out of sight. It was Leonardo and Ariel. Leonardo was saying how much he had enjoyed their conversation, and especially Ariel's growing confidence. He then said goodbye, so she thought she'd better get moving again, ready to bump into Leonardo with innocent surprise. But he had taken the other stairs and was already gone. She saw Ariel standing in his doorway and looking her way. He must have heard her heels on the floor. He was about to call out when she put her finger to her lips. She slipped off her shoes and tiptoed past Jack's room. Ariel watched, fascinated, and then ushered her inside.

'Sorry for the cloak and dagger,' she said as he closed the door, 'but I really don't want to... to see Jack just at the moment.'

'Oh dear. Was it something he said?'

'No, no, I just...'

'Melody.' He spoke her name with such tenderness she had to look at him, right into his eyes. He asked if she wanted to talk about it. She did.

'Would you like a cup of...?' He examined the various buttons on his drinks machine. 'Er, a cup of just about any hot or milky drink you can think of?'

'Does it do a chilled dry white?'

'Ah, I'm afraid not.'

'No matter.' She sat down on the bed, then thought better of it and moved to the chair, leaving the bed to Ariel. The Centre clearly didn't reckon on people entertaining in their rooms, at least not socially. 'I received a message while I was out,' she said.

'Yes, I believe you don't get them because of the shielding here.'

She smiled. 'Yes. The thing is, it was an upsetting message.'

'Bad news?'

'No, it's more complicated.'

He looked at her intently. 'I see.'

'What do you see?'

'I see you want to tell me about the two men in your life.'

'Lumme, Ariel, you really can read minds! Jack said something this morning about you and Miranda.'

'Yes, I'm sorry to say I misread the situation.'

'But you didn't misread her, I gather.' She took a deep breath. 'Well, no point mincing words if you want a gourmet conversation, as my mother used to say. The thing is, Jack loves me.'

'Of course.'

'And I think David loves me.' She gave a quick shake of her head before he could say anything. 'No, not like he loves his wife – not in that way. Not exactly. It's just that they've been really kind to me over the last few years, so helpful. Alice is like a fountain of positive energy, brimming over with life and love. David is really thoughtful, and he's helped me come a long way on my spiritual journey.'

'What's that?'

'Oo, you ask all the easy questions, don't you?' She stood up and walked over to the bookshelves. 'My spiritual journey is a nonsense. If you ask Jack.'

She turned to see Ariel frowning.

'No, okay, that's not fair. My spiritual journey is a development of... of understanding that Jack and I don't share. You see, David is a Christian. Worse than that, he's the pastor of a church.'

Ariel shivered.

'Someone just walk over your grave?' she asked.

'No, not sure what it was. This can be a draughty place.'

She wasn't convinced. 'What?'

'I don't know. Never mind. Please go on with your spiritual journey.'

She returned to the chair. 'I met David quite by chance in a large, cold cathedral. Except by the time I came out it was a warm place of intimacy. We talked about some of the statues there and the history behind them. That took us into politics, and while we didn't agree on everything we found we could get straight to the point – you know? – and then go even deeper.

'It might have stopped there, but then a while later, several months in fact, I got in touch with him. It's like he'd planted a virus somewhere deep inside my head. I'd not known Jack very long at that time, and what with his schedule and mine, it was a fairly bumpy relationship. No, more jerky than bumpy, with stops and starts as we tried to get things going again every time our paths crossed. Sometimes it went well; sometimes, if I'm honest, it felt a little awkward.'

'You are honest.'

'Thank you. Anyway, after a while we – that's Jack and I – had more ons than offs and we seemed to settle into a routine. We'd go out together, live together for a while, and generally enjoy the nice things in life that both our salaries provided. Now, I know this is going to sound cheesy but, despite all that, I was starting to feel like something in my life was missing. I wanted more out of life, but every time I tried to express that to Jack he just suggested we take a holiday somewhere exotic, as if that would satisfy my need.'

'More likely plant it deeper.'

'Precisely! And it was about this time that I met David, and, oh Ariel, it was so different. We connected on a level that I hadn't ever known before. Ever since school I'd either had physical relationships with men or stormy ones with women! Now this guy comes along, and then his wife, and I fall in love with both of them.'

She went over to the drinks machine and selected chocolate. When the buzzing and pouring had stopped, she took the steaming drink back to the table and chair.

'Do you think it's an intellectual mismatch, you and Jack?' said Ariel.

'Hmm, I don't know. He's a pretty smart guy. Maybe David's a better psychological match.' She sipped her drink.

'But that's not it.'

'No, it's not,' she assented, 'and I'm sure you don't need to be a mind-reader to work it out. One thing led to another, as they say, and we started to send each other messages, David and I, and that's when I realised it was getting a bit too intense. But you know the amazing part? It wasn't just Jack I was worried about, it was Alice. I'd never had a friend like her, not since primary school anyway. Not ever, really.'

She closed the blind and turned from the window. Ariel was sitting, looking straight at her, but somehow this left her more unfettered than unnerved.

'So I decided to call it off – well, not that there was anything to call off, but at least try to cool things down a bit. I made excuses when he suggested we meet to go over some theological issue I'd raised. I don't know... I think he began to think that I was going off Jesus! But, truth is, I hadn't really got that close to Jesus – I'd just got too close to *him*! I felt lousy. And the worst thing? I couldn't talk it over with anyone, because the three people that meant the most to me were the problem.' She noticed Ariel was now lying on the bed with his eyes closed. 'Are you okay?'

'Yes, I'm fine.' He kept his eyes closed. 'What about your family?'

'To be honest, they weren't a great help. Ever since Daddy became the second Earl of Oswestry he's fallen a bit too much in love with the limelight. And he's never been a huge fan of my journalism. My mother tried, but she didn't get the religion, and didn't really understand the human triangle either. Sorry, am I keeping you from sleep?'

He answered by opening his eyes. They were filled with tears.

CHAPTER 16

Questions

1

Box Industries was incontestably one of the most efficient multi-national corporations in the world. The mainstay of their success was the placement of laboratories, factories, distribution hubs and offices on all continents. While they had pioneered hundreds of fibres and fabrics for specialised uses and extreme environments, the power in the engine room was fibrogenotex, a textile with a molecular structure that yielded the holy grail of suit-makers: a stable mix of strength and dexterity. From there the flexisuit was a small step.

In common with traditional space suits there were two parts, not counting anything else the astronaut chose to wear next to the skin. Fibrogenotex formed the basis of the inner garment, but due to its unique stiffening and moulding properties it also played a key role in the outer suit. And it was here that Conway Box himself could honestly claim some personal credit. Although he had not developed the polymer itself, it was his creative thinking that had incorporated it into a metallic shell strong enough to survive several hours on Venus. Working with experts who were forging tough new metals, he had come up with a design whereby his polymer individually covered dozens of small metal plates and held them together in an inferno-resistant seal. The result was a truly flexible, phenomenally tough suit, something that could resist the pressure, heat and acidity that was waiting for them.

His final tour de force had been to offer the suits at no charge, in the noble cause of global cooling. It had paid off. The minute the word was out that the astronauts had made a successful EVA, the orders came rolling in. From explorers of the ocean depths to volcanologists playing with fire, everyone wanted the suit that would take human beings into the very guts of our own sick planet.

He had been reading an interim report on the astronauts' suits, although right now he was looking out across a vast tea plantation, an undulating array of green hills crossed by dark lines and peppered by upright trees. He had chosen the region of Assam in the northeast of India early on in the company's growth, a vision made possible by the convenient fact that his wife's family already owned half the state, or so it seemed. They were, as she had told him early on in their relationship, 'big in tea'.

He reached for the intercom. 'Selena, do you have a moment?'

As head of research and development Selena Chandra was leading the review of the space suits' performance on the Aphrodite mission. As soon as he called she made her way into the kingdom of light and glass that was Conway's work complex. With her head slightly bowed she walked into his office and came to rest on the corner of his desk.

Her slender figure was as elegant as always, dressed all in white, the loose blouse and flowing dress evocative of a traditional sari. Drawn by her large brown eyes and long jet-black hair, he gazed at her for a few moments, probably one too many, before catching himself. 'So let's cut to it,' he said suddenly. 'I need to know what your expert eye has found, because I'm danged if I can see anything here that would have caused Adamson or Chase to black out. Am I right? Or am I...?'

'Right, sir – you are right. At least, I agree with you. The suit belonging to Commander Forrester was tested severely, but it did the job we designed it to do. The lead-infused filaments performed admirably in warning him of imminent danger.'

'Okay, good. Keep on going, obviously, but in the meantime I'm going to put it out there that preliminary findings indicate no leaks or bungling on our part, blah-blah-blah.'

'Very good, sir.'

He watched her go. How he loved Indian women. Such grace, charm and beauty. And Selena had them all, with a brain twice the size of his own.

He told his secretary to announce the interim findings. 'No evidence of faults in design or performance to explain the astronauts' blackouts on Venus.' Then he called Hugh Coates.

'Hugh, hello. I feel I owe you one, after the tip-off about the stowaway's gear. We have the space suits at last, and it's looking pretty certain that they had nothing to do with those guys blacking out.'

'Interesting. Thank you, Conway.'

'So, what do you think?'

'What do I think about what?'

'Aw, come on,' said Conway. 'On Venus! What do you think happened?'

'Well, I really couldn't say. But if I were to speculate...'

'Yes?'

'I would have to say it had something to do with the stowaway. Wouldn't you?'

'My thinking exactly,' he bluffed. 'He obviously took them out so he could steal aboard the ship.'

'Well, my friend, I'm not sure there's anything obvious about any of this. But that would be my guess. We need to find out just what the sequence of events was, when they were on the surface.'

They ended the conversation, Conway brimming with pride over the way Hugh had implicitly included him by using the word 'we'. He chuckled as he thought what a humourless bore Coates was. Still, he had to admit it was a good idea. The question now: how to get to the astronauts' reports when they were almost certainly still classified.

He hit the intercom. 'Selena. Sorry, angel, but I need you again.'

2

Ryan Chase was still adapting to being in new territory, in more ways than one. His first ever visit to Switzerland had cut him out of his own research, and that he couldn't stand. After he and Jim had left Bridlington's office almost a week earlier, he had decided to stay in Geneva and book into a hotel. He told the lab in California that he was taking the break he was due, but in reality it seemed madness to abandon the place where the crystal now resided. Once Jim had returned home to Wyoming for his own down time, Ryan set about the task of analysing and sharing the masses of data he had gathered on Venus, all of which could initially be done from his hotel room a few blocks away from the UN building.

On his second day in town he contacted Dan Marshall who called back in between debriefing sessions in Florida. Maybe his old mentor could wrest the crystal back from the military. But though Dan's heart was in the right place, it turned out his hands were tied. It had been Bridlington's decision and there was nothing he could do, although he was able to say that the crystal had gone into the care of the UN High Command, under the protection of a certain Mr Takahashi. 'Hang in there, Ryan. I'm sure you'll get your shot at it before too long.'

But it was already too long. Whether it was the impatience of not knowing what Forrester and Koroleva were doing with the Stranger, and where they were doing it; or whether it was simply the bracing Swiss air and the excitement of roaming free far from home; whatever it was, a dogged determination now gripped him. He was going to get the crystal back, even if he had to steal it.

Where would they be hiding it? The UN building didn't contain any laboratories, so they couldn't work on it there. He sat in his hotel room and started an online search, working into the night, trawling through associated laboratories. All the connections were vague at best. What about Takahashi? A search on him didn't reveal much, but when he cross-checked it with recent purchases of the kind of equipment he had in his own lab, a number of orders came up. In the few cases where he could access the delivery address, it was always the same, a secure facility owned by the UN on the outskirts of the city.

He had found the map that would lead him to his treasure.

3

The air was crisp with the tang of cut grass and leaf mould as Jack ran along the path towards the observatory. A keep-fit run before breakfast seemed sensible, not knowing when this mission might end or what direction it might take. But he also needed to clear his head and think about the next stage. Sleeping in this place did not seem to clarify his thoughts in the normal way. By contrast, Ariel was really 'waking up' now, even becoming animated at times. They needed to capitalise on that if they were ever going to break through the amnesia.

Taking Natasha out of the process had seemed a significant loss at first, yet the last major conversation had definitely broken new ground. It seemed that the more philosophical approach taken by Leonardo was getting somewhere. Surely something had to come of that.

He emerged into a familiar clearing and stopped a while at the foot of the small observatory hill to catch his breath. Time had always been against them, he knew that. Weeks had dissolved into days, but now it felt like a matter of hours before he would lose control of the process. Bill's disappearance unnerved him. And how much time Constance had really bought them by handing over the crystal no one really knew. If you gave these people anything, they generally wanted more.

He set off again, past the observatory, and followed a rough track that must be taking him towards the eastern perimeter. After a while he slowed down, looking for some kind of right turn that might take him round to the front of the grounds.

Thinking of the crystal had brought Ryan to mind, and that led to thoughts of Jim. He'd tried to contact him, but it seemed they had entered unanswered voicemail territory. According to Constance he was taking time out. No interest in the debrief, no interest in Ariel. It didn't feel right.

As he ran he smelt the remains of a bonfire before he saw it. A pile of leaves and twigs lay gently smouldering in the middle of a small clearing. There was a rake leaning on a tree on the far side. He dropped to walking pace and looked around. Natasha's conversation with Brother Leroy sprang to mind, but there was no sign of the young monk.

He picked up the rake and pushed some leaves further into the smouldering mass. A few of the drier leaves ignited briefly, and he watched their filaments curl as he stoked the fire. He thought of Ariel. Well, my enigmatic friend, if it's philosophy that will fire up the neurons in your brain, then philosophy is what we shall have.

His mind clear at last, he returned the rake to its perch and pressed on into the woods.

4

Several Brothers were scurrying in various directions as Melody and Natasha finished their breakfast and left the refectory together. The two women had been swapping accounts of unusual dreams, but now they wondered out loud just what the Brothers did when they weren't cooking, cleaning, studying, or gardening.

On a separate table Jack drained his second mug of coffee. Standing up with a little less speed than usual, he addressed Leonardo and Ariel. 'Ah, I am definitely out of form. That was a lovely run earlier on, but I think I'm paying for it already. Anyway, time we got ourselves to the chapel.' He winced again. 'Now there's a sentence I

QUESTIONS

didn't expect to be saying any time soon.'

He led them out of the refectory past the lounge. This had been taken over by the Brothers for what looked like an art class, and it occurred to him only now that being given the free run of so many rooms, including the chapel, must have caused the residents significant inconvenience. He sighed at his slowness to embrace the place and then dived into the chapel with a new resolve. 'Come on, chaps. Let's get to it!'

'Well,' said Leonardo to Ariel as they followed him in, 'his limbs may be suffering a little, but our Jack seems quite buoyant this morning.'

They took up their customary position in the chancel, though not before Jack looked around with a little more interest than before. His eyes scanned the windows before coming to rest at the other end of the chapel. 'Leonardo,' he said. 'What's that up there?' He pointed to a large boxed-in area, high up in the corner. 'I've not noticed that before.'

'Oh, that's just the old stairs to the attic.'

Jack was on the point of asking about this attic he had not heard mentioned before, only Leonardo was already addressing Ariel.

'Ariel, may I say, you seem a little distracted this morning? What is it?'

Jack joined them and they both waited for Ariel to gather his thoughts.

'Well, I've been thinking.'

'Aye, it's been getting a tad too philosophical for me,' said Jack, but quickly added, 'But that's okay, if you're finding it helpful.'

'Well yes, I am,' said Ariel, 'although that is not the only reason I am feeling so much better. You see, I have had two very important conversations recently, on top of our time together yesterday. They were both... emotionally charged, and it's taken me a while to process it all.'

Jack was suddenly all ears. Both men studied him intently.

'Yesterday afternoon I had a brief yet extremely important

conversation with Miranda. Then, last night, a very moving time with Melody.' Jack shifted in his chair. He wasn't sure which one of these scenarios worried him more. 'As she was leaving,' Ariel continued, 'Miranda called in to see me. She told me something that didn't make a lot of sense at first, but I think I'm beginning to put it all together now.' He related the two scenes Miranda had described, in which some people were watching a man in a white coat as he examined Ariel's suit, and then, perhaps later, the same man trying to set light to it.'

Leonardo let the silence fall as he watched Jack drop his shoulders, open his mouth, close it again, and then sit back. 'Jack,' he said, 'would you like me to leave?'

Jack let out a long sigh. 'Well, I should ask you to leave... but, you know what? I'm not going to. I reckon we're in this together. Basically what Ariel has just described is the Space Station's doctor carrying out various tests on his suit. This was before Ariel woke up. But what I don't understand is how on earth Miranda knows about it. You say she saw it, saw footage?'

Ariel nodded.

'Then I can only think she's gained access to the station's internal CCTV.' He blew out another sigh. 'Well, this changes things. Looks like Bill was right all along. Our friendly Aussie is on a whole different level from your average industrial spy.'

'But that isn't everything.' Ariel spoke so softly Jack almost missed it.

'What? More?'

'She said she had reason to believe that you all... that some of you, perhaps... believe I have been enhanced.'

'Enhanced?' Leonardo blurted.

'Hold on, hold on,' said Jack. 'What do you mean, she had reason to believe?'

'Jack, this is difficult,' said Ariel. 'I should probably distinguish between what Miranda told me and what she showed me.'

'Showed you?' Jack fought to steady his voice as he leant forward.

'Yes. She allowed me to look inside. I think she wanted us to do it again, only this time with her full knowledge.'

'I don't know what to say,' said Jack. 'I mean, I don't really understand what I'm hearing.' He looked at Leonardo, but all he saw there was avid interest. Small wonder.

'I am able to read people,' Ariel explained. 'If they allow me to. Well, probably if they don't, but that is not my way.'

Jack was on his feet now and pacing up and down. 'Well, did she say how she had come by this knowledge?'

'That's just it – she didn't so much say as allow me to read.'

'Okay, okay,' said Jack. 'And what did you read?'

'That her source was a man called Hugh. He showed her the footage on a plane, I think. I believe he is very important to her – her father, perhaps, or uncle, or possibly her employer.'

'Well, I'll be...' Jack returned to his chair. 'Right. We need to get her back. Double quick. I'll ask Melody to go and pick her up from the hotel. No, better still, I'll do it myself.' He turned to Leonardo. 'I take it our car is in one of your garages.'

'*Si*, yes, of course.' Leonardo still seemed to be lost in thought.

'Talking of Melody,' said Jack as he turned to go, 'what about your conversation with her?'

'Ah,' said Ariel as he looked first at the floor and then at Jack, 'I think that maybe now is not the time.'

5

'Well, here we are again,' said Melody, as for a second time she and Natasha brought their walk to an end in the library. There was no one around, so they carried on talking while they ambled up and down the aisles. Leaving Natasha in Classics, where Plato's *Timaeus* and *De Natura Deorum* rubbed shoulders with Cicero's *De Rerum Natura*, Melody went off in search of Literature, breaking off every now and then to record something about a book and noting it for further research. She was intrigued to see *Das Heilige* by Rudolf Otto, recognising the German word for holy, and particularly interested in a slim volume she thought was called *Wandering* by Hermann Hesse, and she leafed through its pencil sketches of various trees with surprising satisfaction, though she couldn't penetrate the German text. But still the bad taste left by David's message wouldn't go away, even if it had been sweetened a touch by her conversation with Ariel. Eventually, just after she'd noted *Time and Relative Dimensions in Space* which she was sure rang a bell, she decided to try once more to probe Natasha on the relationships between the Endeavour crew.

'Natasha,' she said as nonchalantly as possible, speaking over the uneven tomes from the next aisle, 'when you were on Venus...'

'Yes?'

'Well, the thing is, I have the impression things got a bit weird. I mean, I know finding Ariel was weird, but how did you all handle it? As I understand it, the mission was dangerous enough, without having the extra mystery.'

Natasha stared at the books in front of her. 'Well, we were trained for extreme conditions.'

'Sure,' said Melody, 'but how did you cope as a crew with something no one could have anticipated? Did relations between you become tricky in any way?'

Natasha walked round to Melody's aisle. 'Are you researching for your next article?'

Melody looked down. 'I'm sorry,' she whispered. She was surprised to find Natasha's hand taking her own.

'Melody, why don't you just come out and ask me?'

They walked back to the reading tables and sat down. 'Okay,' said Melody. 'Here goes. But please, please don't think I'm having a go at anyone. I just want to know what happened between you all. And maybe... you know... between you and Jack.' She flicked her hair back. 'There, I've said it.'

Natasha studied the table in front of her. Idly she picked up a cheap-looking pen, wondering when she'd last used one of those. To Melody's alarm she snapped it in her fingers. 'Ah, no wires, no circuitry,' she said, smiling. 'No bugs!'

Melody relaxed.

'Yesterday I asked Jack if I could leave.'

Melody's eyes widened.

'I don't know what you are thinking,' Natasha continued, 'but it was not because of anything between me and any members of the crew.'

Melody picked up a piece of the broken pen and started rolling it between her fingers. 'No,' she whispered. 'It's because of Ariel, isn't it?'

'Yes,' said Natasha. 'From the start I had this crazy connection with him. I was the one who found him, of course, and I was left alone with him, and I think a bond formed between us right from the start.'

'A bond? Sounds like a two-way street then?'

'I, I don't know,' said Natasha. Her voice was monotone, as though the energy had been sucked out of it. 'I was beginning to think so. But now he has this deep thing going on with that girl, Miranda, and... well, I can see how foolish I have been.' She looked out of the window. 'We know nothing about him, who he is or what he can do.'

In equally flat tones she told Melody what had transpired in Ariel's room two days before, when she had disturbed them both, only to be told they had experienced some kind of 'togetherness'.

When she had finished Melody stood up and walked over to the window. She could see one of the Brothers over in the refectory. Did they have any idea what was going on in their midst? 'Okay,' she said. 'You've been honest with me, as a friend, and I want to return the favour. Or should I say, the honour? I'm going to tell you about my conversation with Ariel last night. It may help you understand him a little better – maybe in a good way, I don't know. But I also want you to understand why I'm feeling a touch vulnerable in my relationship with Jack.' She came back to the table and sat down.

'Some years ago I got to know a man called David. Long story short, his wife soon became my friend – probably my best friend ever

– and he became a kind of spiritual helper. Now, I don't know where you stand on things like faith and the church–'

'Part of my childhood was in a Russian Orthodox orphanage,' said Natasha. 'I wouldn't say it was all bad.' Was that a smile? 'But please, go on.'

'Well, the thing is, David was, I mean he is, a church pastor – like a priest, only he's not into, well, you know, candles and icons and all that kind of stuff.'

Natasha nodded.

'So, as I say, keeping it short... David and I became close.'

Natasha said nothing.

'Not that we...!' She flicked her hair again. 'But the trouble was, he got to the heart of me. Not my heart, in a romantic sense... at least, I don't think so... but he understood me, and my yearning for a different kind of satisfaction... fulfilment, I suppose. Golly, this is difficult.'

'I understand. Please, go on.' The steely Natasha was returning, which somehow strengthened Melody's desire to talk this out.

'It's complicated,' she said, 'because David was starting to give me what I suppose I had hoped Jack would. And Jack's not stupid. He soon realised that the distance opening up between us was somehow tied up with David.'

'Ah,' said Natasha. 'I think I see. That is, I think I see why Jack is so negative towards religion.'

'Huh! He's always been like that. Of course, it wasn't an issue at the start of our relationship. But once David and Alice began to open things up for me, well...'

'And you told all this to Ariel?'

'Yes, I did,' said Melody. 'And d'you know how he reacted?'

'With annoying curiosity, I expect,' said Natasha, with more force than she intended.

'No, not at all,' said Melody. 'Natasha, he was crying! I really didn't know what to say, so I left.' She gave a weak smile. 'It was getting late anyway.'

A faint frown creased Natasha's brow. She still didn't know what to make of her starman, except she knew now beyond all doubt that he was not *her* anything. She had been foolish, for sure, but maybe not in the way she had thought. Far from trashing her own connection with Ariel, the business with Miranda simply called for her to reinterpret it.

'Thank you, Melody. Actually it does help. And I want to tell you what I think you, you so incredible, smart lady...' and here she flashed her eyes at Melody with a mix of admiration and unveiled envy, '...what I think you really want to know about what happened on the surface of Venus. Between the members of the crew, including me and Jack.'

It was Melody's turn to take Natasha's hand. She braced herself, simultaneously excited about the growing trust between her and Natasha and fearful of what was coming next.

'However,' said Natasha, looking over Melody's shoulder. 'Now is not the time.'

'What?'

'Turn around.'

Melody turned to see a line of monks emerging from the main building and coming towards them.

'I think something has just finished,' said Natasha. And with that several of the monks spilled into the room. It had become a public library once more.

6

Selena Chandra had not been to Europe before. She was eager to take in the colours and sounds and smells of Geneva, maybe take a trip on the lake, and try to taste what she could before returning home. She woke early in a very smart hotel room and quickly showered and dressed before her breakfast meeting with Conway. She was feeling pleased with herself, though drained, having fought off his advances the previous evening and guided him into his own room sufficiently intoxicated to present no further problem. For now at least.

Today was the day they were due to meet Constance Bridlington, formidable by reputation but really quite fascinating, a woman who had made it to the top and who, unlike most women in Selena's world, didn't suffer fools. She knew the meeting would be guided by Conway, at least on their side, but she was hopeful that the Director would at least notice her, maybe even encourage her in some way.

Conway was uncharacteristically quiet at breakfast, which was no bad thing. She got the impression he remembered less of the previous evening than she did, and that what he did recall looked altogether more ridiculous in the cold light of coffee and muesli.

They took a taxi to the *Palais de Nations*, passing the vast Ariana Park as they drove along the hopefully named Avenue of Peace. When they arrived Conway strode immediately into the reception area, leaving Selena to pause alone outside and look up at the flags, eager to spot her own flapping there in the midst, its saffron, white and green mirrored in her jacket, belt and trousers.

She entered through security, who decided she was to be the next person to be randomly searched, which meant that when she caught up with Conway he was already by the elevators being greeted by Petroc. The two men watched as she made her way towards them across the highly polished concourse. She was a slight figure in a world of much taller people, but with her back uncommonly straight she held her head high. Petroc shook her hand warmly.

Fifteen minutes later, with catch-ups and introductions complete and coffee flowing, Conway asked Selena to begin her presentation. She linked her tablet to a large screen on Constance's office wall and proceeded to take them through the findings. Conway sipped his coffee and nodded occasionally.

As she began to wrap up, Conway made a show of leaning across the table towards Constance and said, 'I wanted you to see the findings in some detail, even though it had to be summarised, for two reasons. The first will not surprise you: to exonerate Box Industries.'

'I hardly think that's necessary,' Constance retorted. 'No one's

QUESTIONS

blaming you for anything.'

'Ah well,' he said, 'that brings us to my second reason for requesting this meeting. If we're ever going to be sure that suit failure was not the cause of the trouble, we really need to know more about the mission itself. What happened when.' He leaned back in his chair. 'In some detail.'

Constance removed her glasses and left them dangling round her neck. 'Well, I'm sure you will understand, Conway – and you too, Dr Chandra – that there are several dimensions to the Aphrodite Mission, and some of these have proved somewhat delicate. Quite frankly, the security levels have gone through the roof, as I'm sure you will appreciate.'

'I do, I do,' Conway purred, 'but I trust you appreciate my situation. Now I don't need to know all about the stowaway. But I do need to talk about the suit – that is, our suits of course – and any factors that may have a bearing on how they performed.'

Selena watched her boss, impressed with the obvious clout he had here in the heart of the World Space Agency, and yet at the same time embarrassed at his handling of the discussion. He had told her beforehand about the interest in the spaceman's suit, but he was becoming way too obvious and losing any air of objectivity he might have had. She decided to step in.

'Sir, if I may.'

Conway nodded.

'I think some technical information may help to clarify the situation.'

'Go on,' said Constance, wondering for the second time in two days what the real agenda of the meeting was.

'As you know, we provide protective clothing for people working in extreme environments. We provided the astronauts on the Aphrodite mission with a two-tiered system – the inner flexisuit, which covers the whole body from the neck down, and the EVA suit, comprising solid boots at the ends of the leggings, gloves at the ends of the sleeves, and a helmet with radio, intellivisor and neck seal. Both the inner suit and the outer shell provide unprecedented resistance to outside pressure.'

'Yes, I do know that, though thank you for the commercial,' said Constance with more tartness than she intended.

Selena was not thrown. 'But the reason I mention it, Ma'am, is that the neck seal is... though we would never put it this way in any advertising... what we might call a weak link in the environment suit. The boots and gloves are all of a piece with the suit, whereas the helmet has to be detachable. As of course does the life-support system, which as you know takes the form of a backpack that plugs into the torso. Again, the seals were not made by us.'

Conway had nearly choked on his cookie when he heard Selena talking about a potential weakness in their product, but he very quickly saw where his clever assistant was going with it, and was only too glad the crumbs had stopped him jumping in. He knew there had to be another reason he had brought her along.

'Well, that's fair enough,' said Constance, eager to meet this conscientious young woman half way. 'I have no trouble in telling you more about the events on Venus, as far as we know them from the crew. But I appreciate you giving me reasons to tell you, should there be any questions in other quarters.'

Conway grinned, and risked a wink in Selena's direction. She looked away. 'Presumably you have CCTV as well,' he said to Constance.

'Actually no,' she answered before quickly regretting it. 'The system went down.' That was one piece of information too many. But on second thoughts... they needed more minds on this, and the young woman before her might have exactly the right kind of mind. No way was she going to talk about Ariel's suit, not if she didn't have to, but a longer discussion now might throw light on the crew's unpredictable behaviour. She continued. 'And no, we don't know why the cameras failed. For now we've put it down to the storm.'

'Right,' said Conway. 'Er, there is evidence of abrasion on the suits, isn't there, Selena? But that was to be expected.'

'Yes,' she said, 'especially Commander Forrester's. Our difficulty, Ma'am, lies in a lack of a control. Naturally we tested the suits in the type of conditions we knew they would encounter, but this is the first time anything like this has been attempted.'

'Constance, my dear. Call me Constance.'

Selena lowered her eyes and offered up a smile so demure that Conway could barely contain himself. He poured more coffee.

'And the body cams?' Selena ventured.

'Inconclusive,' said Constance. She made her customary walk to the window as she considered whether to ask for a separate meeting with Selena. She knew it wouldn't fly, so she turned to them both and pressed on. 'When the crew found the stowaway – we call him Ariel now, by the way – it was not initially the whole crew. Dr Chase was still outside. And this was precisely the time when the storm surged – a drop in light levels and a rise in atmospheric activity. When they couldn't get Dr Chase to respond on the commlink, the Captain went out looking for him. From the brief discussion I've had so far with Captain Adamson and the debriefing reports I've seen, it appears that he saw his colleague lying on the ground. That's when he himself passed out.'

No one spoke for several seconds, until Selena said, 'So, thinking out loud for a moment... might it be possible that some kind of localised atmospheric condition, a vortex maybe, occurred?'

'Possibly, yes,' said Constance, returning to the table. 'Go on.'

'Well, I can't see how a sudden climatic change would affect the systems as such. But if they lost their footing...'

'Blown over, you mean?' Conway had begun to listen again.

'Perhaps, yes. Or they could have been disoriented in some way. Maybe the changing light levels, or aberrations in the intellivisor display, or even the air flow from life support.'

Conway liked the sound of that. These were all specialised equipment made by other parties. 'Right,' he said. 'Though one of the functions of the intellivisor, as I understand it, is to manage changing light levels.' Ouch. He hated thinking out loud.

'That's true,' said Selena firmly, as if Constance were somehow feeding her confidence, 'but very sudden flashes, coupled with whatever data the crew members chose to have on display at the time, could look like a firework show right in their face. And if they had microphones on, the noise itself could be a contributing factor.'

Before Constance could respond Conway cut in. 'Well, what can I say? As you know, Constance, the helmet and the life support contain a lot of other people's work. Textiles is our line, not electronics. Or even air seals, if it comes to that.'

'Conway,' said Constance, 'if you can just climb off your high horse for one minute, and take out the politics and the blame, we might actually make this meeting count for something. I do think we are getting somewhere.' Selena looked at the wall to conceal her smile, while Constance tapped her desk and summoned Petroc. 'Now, what I propose to do, without a moment's delay, is bring together all the data on the climatic conditions, the intellivisor logs and the ship's systems, and see if we can't build a workable hypothesis.'

The young assistant appeared. 'Ah, Petroc, could you show our visitors out, please.' She turned to them. 'Thank you both for a very useful meeting. And, Conway...'

'Yes?'

'Would you mind ever so much if I stayed in touch with Selena, until we've got this thing sorted?'

Putting on his warmest smile he gushed his reply. 'Why of course not. We're only happy to help. Keep us informed, won't you? We have a lot riding on this.'

By the time he was descending in the elevator with Selena and Petroc, Conway had already buried the feeling of being thoroughly eclipsed and was praising himself for bringing her along. He had been allowed a glimpse of the unreported facts regarding the Aphrodite mission. But what to do with that information? He was no longer so sure that sharing it with Hugh Coates was a priority.

But then he didn't know that the young man in the elevator with him already had that in hand.

7

Jack wasn't sure if he'd ever been played so completely. Miranda had seemed so genuine. Taking the car they had brought from the airport, he drove slowly round the monastery to head into the village, hoping against hope the villain was still there. When he got to the front gate it occurred to him he should call his people in London and get them to dig a little deeper. He hesitated as he nosed out of the entrance, earning a loud blast on the horn from an approaching delivery van. He turned out of the way as fast as he could, veering left and heading up the road in the wrong direction. When he saw the layby where Miranda's car had been parked, he pulled in to stop and turn round.

He got out of the car and checked his eband for a signal, which came through only when he crossed to the other side of the road. His usual contact was not in the office. 'No matter,' he said to the analyst on the other end of the line, 'I need you to run a check for me.' He gave them the details, such as he had, on Miranda Freeman from Perth, Australia, and asked for them to cross-match with middle-aged business executives called Hugh, probably in the textile industry.

He disconnected and crossed back over to his car. Without thinking he opened the door on the passenger side. 'Jack,' he said out loud, 'you're in Italy!' He closed the door, and as he turned he saw next to him a loose stone in the otherwise perfect wall of the monastery grounds. Possessed by a sudden impulse to tidy it up he pushed on it. It resisted. He pulled it out, felt inside and brought out a small rectangular box. It was largely made of metal, but with something translucent as well, behind which he could see what looked for all the world like micro-circuity. 'Well, well,' he said. 'I wonder what you are.' It was clearly not meant to be there. A relay, perhaps? In which case, it was almost certainly there to receive from the piece of trickery in the courtyard... which meant that someone had been able to get a signal out. He photographed it, replaced it behind the stone and drove off.

He approached the village with mounting ire. It was only as he pulled up to the hotel that he began to have misgivings. How was he going to persuade Miranda to come quietly – that was assuming she hadn't left already? He could hardly force her into the car. Perhaps he should have asked Mel after all. He went to the desk and got them to call her room. While he waited a message came through from London, linking the Freeman woman not with a textile company but the giant communications multi-national called Infostructure. His heart sank. Which was why he could hardly believe it when the receptionist gave him the room number and said he could go up.

Her door was open. He closed it behind him and crossed the room. There was a tablet on the bed, but no sign of a suitcase. He found Miranda on the balcony, sitting back, her eyes hidden behind sunglasses. There was a bottle of white wine that looked as chilled as she did and two glasses on a small table between her chair and another. He accepted the unspoken invitation and sat down.

'So,' he said, but then dried up. He wasn't sure how to do this. She was acting as though there were no problem, no new problem at least, so he decided to play along. 'May I?' She nodded and he poured. 'Cheers.'

They sat for a while, watching the world go by. There was not much traffic – just a few people walking or cycling. He felt his body relax. At length he spoke. 'I gather you and Ariel had a wee chat last night.'

'He told you, did he? How is he?'

He'd not expected that question. Where was this woman coming from? If she was a spy, she was one of the coolest he'd ever met. But perhaps she was just someone caught up in something she herself didn't understand. He was beginning to sense that the truth was somewhere in the middle. 'Ariel is okay. Actually, I think he's starting to put some things together. The thing is, Miranda–'

'May I ask what he told you?'

'Er, he told me about the footage, and the idea that he might have been enhanced in some way – messing with his cellular structure maybe, though I'm wondering now whether it wouldn't more likely be a brain thing.'

'And that's why he's lost his memory?' She put her glass down and sat up in her chair like someone who had just woken up. 'Jack, you could be right! But who? Who would do that? And why? And what was he doing on Venus?'

'All good questions, Miranda, but what I want to know is, why are you asking them? What's it to you? Why are you really here? And who is Hugh?'

The shock on her face was plain to see. She was quite sure she hadn't mentioned Hugh's name to Ariel, as either Coates or Greerson; in fact she had not realised it was in her mind at all. 'Sorry?' she said. 'I don't understand.'

'You are aware, I believe, of Ariel's ability? In fact, I believe you were the first to experience it. As far as we know.'

She slumped back. Jack watched her in silence. Had the fight gone out of her, or was this yet another ploy?

'Jack,' she finally said in a half-whisper, 'Hugh is dead.'

'What? Your boss? When? How?'

She had to think fast, since Hugh hadn't said anything about how he might kill off his alter ego. Her hesitation was enough for Jack to press his advantage.

'Miranda, how about you tell me the truth? You know, the whole truth?'

'I don't know what you mean. I'm still coming to terms with it, Jack. I know he was only my boss, but I did admire him.'

He shook his head. 'Okay, you can stop now. You see, we've done some checking up on you.'

'More invasion of privacy!' She was surprising even herself now.

'Oh Miranda, come on. You could never have hidden the truth – not enough of it anyway. Once we found out you moved straight from university in Perth to Infostructure, it wasn't that hard to track you. You rose pretty quickly, I have to say.'

She poured more wine and drank deep, her mind still racing. Hitching her sunglasses over her hair, she turned her large grey-brown eyes in Jack's direction. 'So, who's *we*?'

'Well now,' he said, 'you can hardly be surprised about the level of security this whole mission has attracted. And then there are the devices we've found in the monastery.'

'Devices?' She played dumb, but even as she did so she could feel the edifice of lies and half-truths crumbling around her. She looked at Jack. His eyes were grey, kind enough but... how she missed the deep blue of Ariel's. He would give her the strength she needed right now. If only she could see him again. Maybe only the truth could lead her back to him now.

'Aye,' Jack continued, 'tricky little listening devices. Very high tech. Are you going to tell me you know nothing about them?' He looked back into the room. 'That tablet on your bed. What would I find if I turned it on?'

'You'd find you had a very sore arm half way up your back!'

He stood up and started to walk back inside.

'Okay, okay!' she called out, surprised at the relief his heedless action provided. The game was up. 'Come back. You're right. I am an assistant to Mr Coates. One of his pilots, in fact.'

'Ah, that makes sense,' said Jack as he sat back down. 'Ariel mentioned an aircraft.'

'Wow,' she breathed. 'I don't think I did. But...'

'Yes?'

'I was thinking about the time when, you know, when I told him about the footage. I would have had a mental picture of where Hugh showed it to me. But that's all.'

'Aye, right,' said Jack, 'and it was clearly enough.' He felt a twinge of fear as he considered how little they understood the extent of Ariel's ability. He decided to switch to that for a moment. 'So, tell me, you let him in, right? He said something about reading you.'

'Yes,' she said. 'And it sounds like he got a lot more than I thought – though he got exactly what I was thinking! Even subconsciously.' She downed the rest of her glass and stood at the edge of the balcony between the flower baskets. A few people were still coming and going, oblivious to the mystery in their midst. 'But you see, I wanted him to know. I thought it would help him.' Only honesty could honour that continuing mystery now.

Jack joined her, picking up the shift in her mood. 'But surely you knew he might not keep it to himself. He doesn't tend to hold back, you know, not when he actually finds something out or thinks something through.' Idly he pulled a dead leaf from under the flowers and let it float down to the square below. 'You and your boss have been so careful to stay in the shadows up to now, and yet you told Ariel anyway. That was quite a risk you were taking for him.'

She looked at him once more, but this time there was a smile on her face. 'Yes, I suppose it was.'

8

Melody and Natasha sat on the steps of the observatory, squinting in the strong autumn sunlight. A steady breeze was getting up, sweeping through the trees, its ebb and flow bringing to Melody's mind the sound of sea on shingle. They waited for Brother Leroy to pass, who had seemed eager to stop and chat until Melody had said they were hoping for some girlie time together. He quickly disappeared into the trees.

'So,' she said, turning to Natasha, 'where were we? The crew on Venus...'

'We'd had a tricky descent onto the surface,' Natasha began, deciding a more complete picture would be needed if she was going to talk about the emotional exchanges between the crew. 'Jack was watching the radar like a hawk, while I kept an eye on the atmospheric readings. Ryan couldn't stop talking – I can't even remember what about now – and Jim was checking on the engines. He was still running scenarios and checks on the nuclear drive.'

'I thought you didn't use that for landing and take-off.'

'We didn't. The Endeavour had more or less conventional engines. He was checking remotely, making sure the Resolution's nuclear drive remained online and operational so we could get home in weeks rather than months.'

'Wow!' said Melody. 'Jack didn't mention that. Probably didn't want to worry me.'

'Oh, there was a Plan B if the drive did fail,' said Natasha. 'Extra supplies would be sent out from Alpha on a course that would intersect with our trajectory.'

The breeze fell silent for a few moments. 'While I'm interrupting you,' said Melody, 'I thought there was room for only two in the Endeavour's cockpit, yet it sounds like all four of you were busy. Sorry, just trying to get a picture. Occupational hazard!'

'There was an extra pull-out seat for take-off and landing, which I used. And Ryan was in his quarters, not far away, talking via the intercom. Bear in mind we were all suited up at this point, just in case we lost hull integrity.'

Melody shivered. She wasn't used to hearing such details, and she found they both fascinated and appalled her. The breeze picked up and the rustling of the leaves grew louder. Natasha raised her voice a little. 'Anyway, the landing was fairly stressful. And then there was the big unknown. Even with the relatively benign conditions – ha! – would the hull survive the pressure long enough for us to do anything worthwhile?'

'Gosh,' said Melody. 'It must have been awfully dramatic.'

Natasha smiled. 'The landing went fine. Then... I don't know if it was the pressure of time, or just the desire to let off steam, but we made our landing checks in record time and went outside as soon as we were able. I can't tell you what it did to me when I stepped out and saw the landscape. Everything was bathed in a deep orange light. It was...'

'Beautiful.'

'Yes. It really was. Like nothing we'll ever see again, I think.'

The wind dropped for a moment, though Melody thought some of the leaves were still rustling. She was tempted to investigate, but Natasha was in full flow now and she didn't want to stop her.

QUESTIONS

'So we got to work. The first EVA went well, and it included my discovery of the crystal.'

'Ah yes, the crystal.' She smiled. 'So you found that as well as Ariel!'

'Yes, but then digging into the surface was my main job. Ryan was taking atmospheric readings at that point, and I was concentrating on the lithosphere.'

'Er, that would be the ground then?'

'Yes, that's right. There's still a lot we don't know about the crust of Venus, even with the data we've amassed from unmanned landings. I found the crystal buried in softer material – solidified lava flow, basically.'

'Right. Go on.'

'It was the second excursion when things started to change between us.'

'You and Jack?' She spoke evenly, summoning her best neutral journalistic voice.

'All of us, actually. Jack had become a bit, how do you say it, dreamy.'

'Possibly,' said Melody, a slight frown now running between the curtains of her hair. 'Though it's hard to imagine.'

'Ryan was even more obsessive than ever. I think he went back out that last time because he felt he just had to get better readings than mine.' She sighed. 'Oh, I don't know. It seems silly now.'

'No, please, go on. Stick with it. It's good to think about how you were all feeling back then.' She tried a reassuring smile. 'And any effects it had on people's behaviour.'

'Okay. When I found Ariel things really started to kick off. Jim got all uptight about Jack being put in charge, as if that meant anything at all really. And Ryan started accusing me of being a spy—'

'What? You can't be serious!'

'Deadly serious. Honestly, Melody, the emotional storms in the ship seemed to match the weather outside!'

Melody turned her head into the strengthening wind and let it clear the hair from her face. As this meant she was effectively talking to the trees, she raised her voice. 'Natasha, I had no idea. This really has to be investigated, surely?'

'I think so,' said Natasha, 'and Jack says that Director Bridlington means to organise some kind of psychological assessment. When we are finished here.'

They sat a while in silence until the breeze died down again and they could talk more easily.

'So,' said Melody. 'Ryan really had it in for you.'

'Yes,' said Natasha. She dropped her voice further still. 'Whereas Jack was very supportive.'

'That's good, that's good. Isn't it?'

Natasha looked directly at Melody. She was clearly desperate to find out what if anything had passed between Natasha and her boyfriend. Why was she suspicious? Natasha was quite sure she had given her no grounds, so it must have come from Jack. Was this a kind of jealous possessiveness showing itself? That didn't seem to be Melody's style. Or maybe some kind of confidence crisis? It was true that Melody had proved less sure of herself when viewed up close, but that didn't strike true either. Perhaps it was simply a case of imagining the worst and hoping to find the truth was really not so bad.

Natasha stood up and stretched her arms up to the bright sky. She replayed in her mind the moment of unexpected intimacy between herself and Jack, when he was preparing to go out and look for Jim and Ryan and she helped him with the intellivisor. But really, now it came to it, what could she say about it? That they had become close for a moment? Did she even understand what 'close' meant here? Was it even a thing? Yet she had discovered that Jack had felt it too.

She looked down at Melody. No, perhaps some things were best left unsaid. 'Yes,' she said, 'it is a good thing. Jack has been a model of professionalism all through – both as a pilot and as... whatever he is in the world of international security.'

Melody now stood and looked round at the trees behind them.

Were they laughing at her rather pathetic attempts at teasing out what had gone on with Jack? Had she got it all wrong? And yet, as she looked at Natasha again now, standing so tall, so strong, so magnificent, she couldn't see how Jack could fail to be attracted. Okay, but that had never been an issue before. Their relationship wasn't like that. And anyway, it was common knowledge that this particular cosmonaut was impervious to romance and sentiment.

But that was before the emotional storms on board the Endeavour. What if the stony Slav had softened? What might have happened then? No, she thought, let's not even go there. Not now, at any rate.

'Come on,' she said out loud. 'Let's go back. I've already strayed into territory best left for the professionals. But, Natasha...'

'Yes?'

'Thank you. For telling me about this, I mean.'

'Has Jack said nothing then?' Natasha asked, immediately wishing she hadn't. It felt like raising a lid that had just been firmly shut.

'Not in so many words,' said Melody. 'Though his body language has been quite eloquent. I knew there was more going on, if you get my meaning, and that it wasn't just security protocols that kept him from telling all.'

'Looks like you can read people as well, doesn't it?' said Natasha with a forced grin, still unsure what Melody was reading between the lines of their conversation.

'Well, yes, I suppose we all can – at least, when we know someone really well.'

They began to amble back to the Centre.

'Still,' said Melody, 'it's good you're all going to be assessed for the psychological stress you've all undergone.'

The conversation was over, and they gathered pace along the path towards the monastery.

Brother Leroy decided to return by another way.

9

'So, tell me about your wee talk with Melody.'

Jack was sitting with Ariel in the empty lounge next to the refectory, having left Miranda with Leonardo in the chapel, unsure as yet what to do with her. Her tablet would go to Geneva, or perhaps even London, for examination. Right now, however, he had a conversation with Ariel to conclude. 'What was it you wanted to tell me?'

Ariel looked into his eyes. Immediately Jack looked away. 'Just tell me straight, my friend.'

'Of course,' said Ariel. 'As you know, she got back quite late last night. You had retired for the night, and she was sort of passing my room—'

'A lot of people seem to do that,' Jack interrupted.

'Yes. Well. We got talking, and she told me about David and Alice.'

'What!'

'And Jesus.'

'Whoa! Whoa there, boy! Slow down at least. Just what did she tell you?'

'That she had found in David a man who understood her spiritual longings, and in Alice a rare friend.'

Jack looked at Ariel, sitting so calmly, as if this wasn't just about the most annoying thing they could possibly be talking about right now. He had decided in his own mind that Melody's fling with Jesus was over – and all that went with it.

'I'm sorry, Jack. I thought you should know.'

'Oh you did, did you?' He leapt to his feet. An old familiar feeling began to rise, like a friend you thought you'd lost touch with. He had forgotten how comforting anger could be. 'You thought I should know? You thought I should know that you can read people's dirty secrets, so you can go and share them and to hell with the damage!' He walked towards the door.

'Jack.'

He turned back towards Ariel. 'What?' He almost spat the word out.

'Melody told me this. I did not read it.'

'Oh, and why did she tell you?'

'I don't know. Why do you think she told me?'

Jack hit the door post with the palm of his hand. 'Oh man, I could really do without this. What the heck is going on here? Who the blazes are you, Ariel? Damn it, man, if you're so good at seeing into people's heads, maybe you should go look in a mirror and tell us what you see in there!'

He swept out into the courtyard, leaving Ariel alone with more tears he didn't understand.

CHAPTER 17

Closing In

1

To the untrained eye the UN facility on the outskirts of Geneva was dull and uninteresting. In sharp contrast to Ryan's steel-and-glass lab back home in California, this was a grey hulk with few windows and even fewer doors. He paid for the taxi and waited for it to disappear before starting to circle the perimeter.

He didn't get far. An ugly brick wall stretched up before him, topped with barbed wire. He turned back and, giving the front of the building a wide berth, checked out the other side. The same.

He contemplated walking in through the front door and announcing his arrival, but couldn't decide what he would say next. While he might be able to bluff his way past reception, if there was a reception, ultimately he had no authority for visiting, and no ostensible reason apart from the crystal.

He walked back to the main road and sat on a bench. It should only be another hour before the workers came out, assuming they didn't keep his hours. He shivered in the autumn air and pulled his light jacket around him. For the first time since Venus he missed his space suit. As he sat there he thought back to the telescope repair entrusted to him on the journey back.

The Resolution had matched the scope's orbit around the sun and Jim had flown them alongside. Then, donning a standard space suit and securing a tether, Ryan had gone through the Endeavour's airlock and used the suit's jet pack to cross the short distance to the scope – though this was far more than a telescope, equipped as it was with a comet-tracker and asteroid-warning system. It was the sort of exercise he loved: assessing the damage, applying the patch, testing the results. Other minds more specialised than his had developed the necessary enhancements so that they could continue to probe the secrets of the stars and track down the wayward wanderers, but he loved being a part of the fix, taking things a step at a time, carefully, methodically, relishing the fact that he was doing something others could only dream of.

Of course, there was that moment when he nearly fainted as he was finishing up, but he wasn't being monitored at the time and it hadn't happened since, so there didn't seem to be a reason to tell anyone about it. He had put it down to being an inexperienced spacewalker, though he wondered now whether it was some kind of echo of the black-out on Venus. Anyway, if he had had some kind of brain seizure, his medbed data would reveal it. What did it matter? He was perfectly all right now.

He shivered. The bench was cold, and the hour came and went. Then another. By the time it became dark no one had emerged from the building. He thought about calling another taxi and giving up on the whole enterprise. But that was never going to be an option.

He strode up to the door, lit only by a faint security lamp overhead. It was locked. That turned out to be a relief, as the challenge to break in gave him the nudge he needed. Pulling a small device from his pocket, he clamped it onto the conveniently magnetic case of the number pad by the door. He had found it in a high-end electronics store in the city and had lost no time in making a few modifications.

He turned it on and then went for a short walk while it worked. Round the side of the building he now saw a window, fairly low and quite large, but short of trying to break the plate glass there seemed no hope of a way in there.

He returned to the door just as his gizmo gave a little chirp and the front door clicked open. He retrieved his device and stepped into the darkness.

2

Less than two miles away Jack was sitting in the Geneva office of the WSA Director, relieved that her unexpected call had postponed his appointment with a whisky bottle, and hoping that it had cancelled it altogether. Certainly his outburst against Ariel had retreated from the front of his mind with every mile he had travelled across the alpine landscape.

Constance was standing by the window, her place of choice when she needed to think more creatively. She had called him in to deliver Ariel's suit and to review the data she had begun to put together after the meeting with Selena Chandra. 'You really should meet her, Jack,' she said to the window. 'She has a sharp mind – just what we need right now.'

'Aye, well, I don't doubt mine's become a wee bit cloudy. Honestly, Constance, you wouldn't believe how tricky this whole thing has been. I don't know how you found that place near Montagnola, but it's certainly different. And while we're talking about meeting people... when are you going to meet Ariel?'

She turned and looked at Jack. 'You must be shattered,' she said. 'I appreciate this has been quite a strain.'

'Well, we always knew the fun might really begin after we got to Venus. Let's face it, I probably wouldn't have made the mission if it wasn't for my security connections.'

'But you are an excellent pilot. And astronaut.'

'That's true, of course,' he grinned. 'But you and I both know that the anomaly was always going to attract security concerns.'

'Speaking personally,' she said, 'I've always been comfortable with the idea that the so-called friendly Window at Nightingale was a natural phenomenon. There's never been a shred of evidence – so far as we're aware – that anyone had sent anything to mess with the conditions on such a large scale.'

'So far as we're aware,' Jack echoed. 'Then again, while it may be large-scale for something artificial, for something natural it's incredibly localised, and that in itself is bizarre. Or was. I gather our Window's closed again.'

She nodded. 'But whatever the reason for the Window,' she said, 'we need to know who put Ariel there, how they did it and why.'

'You have theories?' said Jack.

'Oh, I have as many theories as there are members of the WSA, including this idea of physical and mental enhancement, though quite why anyone would send him to Venus when there are perfectly extreme locations on Earth I don't know.'

'Maybe the two ideas are connected,' said Jack. 'Maybe someone who has a vested interest in global cooling really did cause the anomaly, and Ariel is a part of that.'

'Possibly. In which case I think private enterprise has to be the prime candidate. Someone who wants a lead on solving the single largest threat to the existence of humanity.'

'That would make sense,' Jack mused, 'but then, why the secrecy? Who do we think would want to work in isolation when the whole world is under threat? Any candidates?'

'Not many.'

'Hugh Coates has to be up there,' said Jack. 'He has the money, and the stake in the nuclear drive. And now we know he's hacked into our security as well. Mind you, I didn't have him down as a philanthropist trying to save the world.'

'Ah, Jack, how sweet. Didn't you know global cooling is big business? Ever since forest fires and urban floods struck at the rich, in fact.'

'Aye well, I guess I'll leave that to you and my associates in London. I've got enough on my plate. And things are moving frustratingly slowly with Ariel.'

'Nothing you can't handle, I hope.'

'No, no,' said Jack, conveniently putting his angry outburst with Ariel down to tiredness.

'Well, we are where we are,' she said and sat down on the opposite side of the table. 'Let's set to it. When we put it all together, what have we got?'

'Okay. There's the anomaly to begin with: about two-and-a-half thousand square miles – that's the whole of Corona Nightingale and a bit more – all showing low levels of carbon dioxide and sulphuric acid, as well as those drops in temperature and pressure. Then, when we got there, the crystal. And Ariel and the weirdness. And now Miranda – in fact, the whole security breach after our return.'

'Sorry? What weirdness?'

'Ah. Didn't I mention that?'

'Jack...?' The sense of mild annoyance was impossible to miss.

'No, okay, I didn't mention it. Ariel's pretty much eclipsed everything.'

'So what have you not been telling us?'

'I've not been telling you what I hadn't really noticed myself, not till we had time to slow down at the monastery. What with all the experiments on Venus, not to mention the zero-G experiments on the flights there and back. Mind you,' he smiled, 'when we first landed we could hardly hold Natasha and Ryan back. They were both like the proverbial kids in the sweetshop.'

'Hardly surprising, I would have thought.'

'No, you're right. The first EVA's weirdness was all quite explainable – the strange conditions, the new findings. The wonder of it all.'

'And your second excursion?'

He paused for a moment. 'As I look back, that's when things started to change. *We* started to change. Natasha had brought in the crystal on the first outing, and we'd all been pretty delighted with it. But the next time we went out I sensed a change in Ryan. He'd become quite negative towards Natasha.'

'Jealousy? She made the find, after all.'

'Maybe. But whatever it was, it got a lot worse after we'd found Ariel. Ryan's negativity seemed to settle on both him and Natasha. But then, Natasha herself was showing another kind of weirdness.' He paused.

'How so?'

'She was... well, softening.'

'Yes,' said Constance, 'I gather she became attached to Ariel quite early on.'

'Sure,' said Jack, swallowing hard, 'but it wasn't just with Ariel. I noticed it with me too.'

She stared at him. 'Come on, Jack, out with it. You know you're going to have to come clean sooner or later.'

His fingers drummed the table. 'Och, I don't know. Little things. She was more attentive than usual, more helpful.' He pressed his hand to the back of his head. She had never seen him look this awkward.

'Okay, I don't think you need to say more at this point. You can leave the details for the psychologist. As you say, Ariel has rather eclipsed everything else, but once we're done with him – whatever form that takes – we should get all four of you properly debriefed. I'll get in touch with Jim and Ryan.'

She leant across to her desk, called Petroc and asked him to contact the two men.

'Okay,' Jack continued. 'So we've got weird atmospheric conditions on Venus, weird emotions flying about, a weird rock and Ariel.'

'Right,' said Constance, getting to her feet. 'It's time we put all the data together. I may have been hasty in letting you take Natasha to Montagnola. I think it's time all four of you came together again, with me, Ariel and Selena Chandra. If you don't mind.'

He shrugged. 'I'd be okay with that. But you're going to need to widen the net, surely. What about all the other stakeholders – the space agencies?'

'You can leave them to me. I've promised to share all data with them.'

'Okay, that may satisfy the scientists, but the military...'

'Again, my problem.'

Petroc came through on the intercom. 'I've informed Colonel Adamson, Ma'am, but I've been unable to contact Dr Chase.'

'No trouble, I hope,' Jack called out.

'I don't know, sir,' said Petroc. 'According to his lab in California, he stayed on in Geneva. But they've not heard from him for several days. Apparently he's on vacation.'

'Thank you, Petroc.' She clicked off.

'Hmm,' said Jack. 'Ryan on holiday. I don't think so, do you?'

3

A pale morning glow seeped into the chapel as Leonardo led Natasha to a small circle of chairs in the chancel. Ariel was already seated next to Melody. Miranda, it seemed, might join them later. Not for the first time Natasha felt there was something odd about the chapel, but only now did she realise that the traditionally eastern end was in fact facing north. But then, that wasn't really so unusual... there was something else. She bookmarked the thought and followed Leonardo to join the group. She had agreed to come because it seemed churlish to refuse, but now, being together like this without Jack, she felt less sure. The whole arrangement felt like a recovery session. What was Leonardo up to?

'Thank you all for coming,' he said. 'Let me start by saying that this meeting is purely my idea, not Jack's, though he did ask me to make sure that you were all okay while he is away. So I thought it would be good for us to talk – not just individually but together. I think your presence here shows that you agree this could be a valuable exercise.'

That sounds reasonable, thought Natasha, but I wonder how long before you start asking about the crystal.

Leonardo continued. 'Constance told me that while Jack is in Geneva they will be trying to join up some dots, and I thought it might be good if we tried to do the same. We know each other better now, and I should emphasise that we are not here to judge one another. Our purpose is to clarify.'

'What are we clarifying?' asked Natasha.

'Where we are, where we have come from, what we are trying to do... anything that may help our friend Ariel here to reconnect with his humanity and, of course, his memory. With such a group I think we could bring more clarity to the situation. You, Melody, with your journalistic expertise, and you, Natasha, our resident scientist, should both be able to, er, stimulate Ariel's thinking... and this in turn may well bring his memory back online, so to speak.'

Leonardo rubbed his hands with evident satisfaction and handed over to Melody who went on to enumerate some of the things they had learned about each other. Natasha was surprised that she could talk so easily about her relationship with Jack. Then she began to talk about Ariel, and even David and Alice, as she related something of her conversation with Ariel about Jack and David. Natasha didn't know whether to envy such easily won trust in Leonardo, or whether to think less of her for sharing her heart so easily.

The sunlight had now grown in strength, and Natasha's attention was suddenly caught by the stylised depiction of trees in one of the richly coloured stained-glass windows. She was just about to connect this with her unease about the place when she realised Leonardo was asking her to comment.

'Sorry, what?'

'Melody was asking if it was all right for her to talk about Jack on Venus,' he said.

Natasha's eyes widened as she quickly weighed up which would be more problematic – to shut the subject down as a no-go area, and thereby feed suspicion, or to let things come out in the open. But then did she even have the right to talk about the emotions on Venus when Jack was not here? Then again, surely Melody would not break any confidences. 'Yes, why not?' she found herself saying at last. If Leonardo wanted to play the professional, so be it. She was among friends.

'Okay, if you're sure,' said Melody, who then proceeded to describe how relieved she was when Natasha had told her about the heightened emotions of all the crew on board the Endeavour. Natasha soon joined in and provided a few details, describing the change in Jim and Ryan but mischievously omitting any mention of the crystal. Leonardo would have to ask.

He did not disappoint. In response she explained a little about her role as a planetary geologist, and that after she had found the crystal they gave it pride of place in the cockpit. It had been soon after this that emotions seemed to heat up, if not boil over. She kept it succinct, and Leonardo sensed that this was the ration for the day. Scooping out a small tablet from a pocket inside his habit, he spoke quickly in Italian. Natasha picked up the names Anselm and Miranda. Within seconds the door opened and in they walked.

'Thank you, Brother Anselm,' said Leonardo, who promptly disappeared. 'And thank you, Miranda my dear, for waiting. I know you understand that some of our discussions have been a little sensitive, from a security point of view.'

How you are loving this, thought Natasha, being in the know when you really have no authority. But then, authority was a slippery thing – just when you thought that someone had given it to you, or even taken it away, you found that someone else had imbued you with a fresh dose, simply by virtue of looking up to you and trusting you.

Miranda took the empty chair and, clearly already briefed, dived straight in. 'Hi everyone,' she said. 'I think you all know that I'm not what I seemed. I'm really sorry, Mel, that I couldn't tell you what I was doing when we met. I want you to know that I really enjoyed your company. I wasn't using you.'

'I think you were,' said Melody, then quickly added, 'but that's okay. In my line of work you have to make the best of the opportunities that come your way. I can't say I would have done anything different if it was me.'

'Sure...' choked Miranda, but then trailed off. This was not the place to say what that first evening together meant to her.

Leonardo watched and waited, till Natasha broke the awkward silence. 'But then Miranda had already done her dirty work. Sorry, no judgement intended, just a figure of speech. She had already bugged the place. Are there any in here?'

Miranda was glad of the directness which threw a blanket over the emotional fire that had begun to burn, and she knew the time had come to give them the explanation they were owed. She followed her training and lied accordingly. 'Er, no, no bugs in here.' She consoled herself with the thought that she had told Jack about every listening device, even the one in the chapel, on their return from Montagnola. That was enough.

'May I ask a question?' It was Ariel.

'Of course,' said Leonardo, eyes flashing in the chapel's soft light.

'It's for Melody and Natasha,' said Ariel. 'Why do you think Miranda told me about the espionage she saw – you know, the footage from the space station?'

'Fair point,' said Melody. 'Miranda, we really do appreciate you caring about Ariel that much – enough to torpedo your own plans.'

Natasha felt less forgiving. 'But what were those plans?' she asked, a little more forcefully than she intended. 'What was your game? And who were you working with? Who *are* you working with?'

'Those are fair questions,' said Leonardo, 'and I think we must allow them in the spirit of the clarification we are all trying to realise.'

'Sure,' said Miranda. 'It's out there now anyway, thanks to Jack. I work for Hugh Coates.'

'What?' said Melody. 'The trillionaire who owns half the internet, not to mention a fair chunk of space travel?'

'The same,' said Miranda.

'I'm sorry, I don't understand,' said Natasha.

'Let me see if I can help,' said Leonardo. 'Miss Miranda first visited us here at the Centre with her boss, a Mr Hugh Greerson, who it seems was in fact the very same Hugh Coates.'

'But I thought he kept out of the limelight,' said Melody. 'I've tried to get an interview with him on several occasions. And no joy.'

'*Si*, he does, as you say, keep his head down. But I suppose he was driven by knowing he was onto the world's biggest mystery. As soon as he found out about us here, he decided to come see.'

'And place the bugs?' said Natasha.

'That's right,' said Miranda. 'You have to bear in mind, it was just the most sensitive operation, and he didn't want anyone else to know about it.'

'Except you,' said Natasha. Miranda said nothing.

'Very well,' said Leonardo to the stone floor at his feet. 'I think we have brought things into the light.' He looked up at Ariel. 'Now, my friend, in so many ways you are the glue that holds these three ladies together. We know so little about you, yet what do we know? You are a thinker, a lover of life, sympathetic to your fellow man and woman – a man of the spirit, I think.'

'I thank you, dear abbot,' said Ariel, 'for letting the light shine more widely. Truly I have felt too often that all the lights have been turned on me. And I can't say that that has been of any great help. So your wisdom is much appreciated here today.'

Leonardo raised his hand in modest denial. Natasha felt a heel. Miranda looked down. And Melody smiled. The glue was still very potent.

'You have all shared your thoughts so openly,' Ariel continued, 'and I wish to do the same. Though I may speak for all of us when I say we would appreciate a personal contribution from yourself, dear Abbot. However, I also appreciate that you are in something of a facilitator's role today, so we won't press you on that.'

'It is appreciated,' said Leonardo, matching the rather formal style that seemed to be emerging from Ariel. 'Pray, continue.'

'As I have listened to the three of you, and of course to Jack in recent days, I have been able to know myself a little better. My absent memory is as frustrating to me as to you—'

'More, surely,' said Miranda, causing Natasha to believe that she had definitely lost the mantle of Ariel's champion.

'Yes, well, it is frustrating,' Ariel continued. 'And yet, as I have listened, and walked, and talked, and enjoyed the superlative surroundings in which we are placed, I have come to see that I am very at home here – here in the English language, here in present company, and here in a place like this, with the space that is made for philosophical reflection. I have not met Ms Bridlington, but it seems she chose very wisely.'

They all sat back in their chairs as he settled into his stride.

'It has been particularly helpful to hear you go over the events on Venus. I've started to match some of the things you've described with images and recollections in my head. As for further back, and how I came to be there – where you found me, Natasha – I can't honestly say that it is clear. But some things feel more solid. I know I served with others. In battle. I think a fall caused my amnesia and disorientation. I seem to be able to do things that people find unusual, like reading people's thoughts and feelings and influencing objects that hinder or threaten me. They say my suit is strange. And the crystal seems to fascinate a number of people, though it means nothing to me.'

At this last remark Leonardo sat up, a frown forming rapidly across his heavy brow. 'Are you sure?' he said. 'I mean, how can you be so sure? Perhaps it will come back to you.'

'Perhaps,' said Ariel. He shrugged. 'I know I am a part of something – I feel I can say in present company that it was an army, without anyone trying to arrest me! All in all, I am very grateful for the friends I have made here. And I am hopeful that old friends will eventually find me.'

They sat in silence for a few minutes. Finally Leonardo spoke. 'Does anyone wish to say anything more? Or shall we adjourn for the rest of the day?'

No one felt the need for more words.

'In that case, may I just ask one question, and then we'll leave it for the day, and let our surroundings continue to do their work. Miranda, you are now an honorary member of this little group, so may I extend to you the library, refectory and grounds, as well as the room you already have?'

'That's really kind,' said Miranda.

'Good. So, to my question. Natasha – you are aware of our interest here in the crystal, given its unique properties and associations. Would you be so kind as to give us a fuller account of how you came to find it and extract it?'

Natasha gave a thin smile, deciding it was useless trying to resist the man's ardent interest, and even feeling a new level of respect for his persistence. At least he wasn't making a secret of it. And, given what Ariel had said about how helpful all this was, she thought it best to go over it for his sake.

'Very well,' she said, and with that she stood up and began to walk around the chancel, enjoying its growing familiarity. 'It was our first day on the surface – though, you must appreciate, the days we were marking were artificial, as an actual day on Venus is several months long. It was our first proper excursion at any real distance, and I was the one working furthest out. I could see Jack a little way off, but the others were hidden over a ridge nearer the Endeavour. I was gradually making my way up a scarp, moving slowly through the dense atmosphere, when I noticed some different-coloured rock.'

'The purple patch, I believe some fly journalist called it,' said Melody.

'Sorry, what's a scarp?' said Miranda.

'Oh, basically an escarpment – a steep slope. There are quite a few in the coronas on Venus.'

Miranda wanted to ask what coronas were but thought better of it.

Natasha continued to circle the chancel as she spoke. 'I could not understand what might cause the colour of the rock to be so different, so I started to take samples. I won't bore you with the details, but the rock was fairly soft, which is not uncommon on Venus where there's so much volcanism. That's actually how I discovered the crystal – my trowel hit something far more solid. So I felt it before I saw it.'

'Fascinating, fascinating,' said Leonardo, whose face appeared to Melody as transfixed as any painted saint's. She had to agree that this level of detail in the account was really quite refreshing, and she discreetly turned on her eband recorder, assuring herself that it would be unnecessarily interruptive to ask permission.

Natasha continued, at times miming her actions as she spoke. 'I switched to a small power tool, and it didn't take long to dig around the object. It was only about the size of a tennis ball – maybe a bit larger – and although it was basically round it seemed to have a lot of straight edges. That seemed strange, and in fact I found it quite hard to focus my eyes on it, which I initially put down to my helmet's visor.'

'What were you thinking when you looked at it?' asked Leonardo. 'Did you take it straight back to the ship?'

'No, no, I bagged it and carried on to the top of the scarp, where I took some more samples.'

'What was the view like up there?' said Melody.

'Stunning, naturally, in the weird way that everything was. Ridges and scarps, with troughs in between that looked like lakes of fire in some kind of sulphurous inferno. Lots of yellowish cloud and orange rock and red and green lightning.'

'Green lightning?' exclaimed Miranda. 'That *is* weird.'

'Totally alien, the whole environment,' confirmed Natasha with a nod, clearly so much happier now she could talk about a time when she was in her element, doing what she had been trained to do.

'It must have been amazing,' Leonardo sighed.

'How high were you?' asked Melody.

'Oh, I don't know. I hadn't climbed very far. I was really only on one of the ridges of the whole corona. I could see Jack, quite a bit smaller now, and what turned out to be the ship when I looked at it long enough. It looked so different, reflecting the colours around it – quite dazzling, really.'

She sat down again. It had all come back to her so vividly. She looked at Ariel, probing him for some kind of reaction. Maybe this had helped. He certainly looked engaged. But then, to her horror, his face began to contort.

'Ariel!' she called out. 'What is it?'

'Look out!' he shouted, before lurching forward and collapsing onto the floor.

4

Ryan closed the front door behind him and quickly passed through the building's reception area, a simple affair amounting to no more than a desk and a chair in an anteroom with bald walls and a white ceiling. The desk was surprisingly low-tech, with the a standard-grade screen built into it. Not at all what he had expected.

The inner door led to an equally plain corridor with a series of rooms off it. He tried each door. They were all locked. Until the last.

He went in and, even before he ordered the lights he recognised the familiar smell of chemicals used for cleaning and dissolving. He switched on, and as the ceiling burst into light he took a breath and let it out slowly. It was a lab much like his own in size and layout, but the equipment was state of the art. As he had hoped, the reception desk had been a front. He approached a corner where a mobile chair had come to rest. And there it was. The crystal sat, still obstinately intact, in a small clear box next to a quantum microscope. For a moment the equipment seduced him, and he allowed himself to caress the controls of a machine more sophisticated than anything he had seen before. It was certainly beyond his budget, and surely beyond the usual funds of the UN. But nothing was usual here.

He turned his attention back to the crystal, gazing at it for several minutes. Was it glowing? Pulsating? The lighting was too strong to see for sure, so he called for them to be turned off, leaving the door open so that the corridor threw enough light for him to see where he was going. Sure enough, the crystal was faintly glowing, fading every few seconds, then glowing brighter again. He decided to video it on his eband and timed the periods of change, fascinated to see that they were irregular.

Transfixed, he let the crystal fill his mind. The rest of his surroundings were nothing now. He didn't hear the quiet footsteps behind him, and when the cry 'Look out!' came into his mind it was already too late. His ears rang as something hard hit his head, and he collapsed to the floor.

5

Jack was speeding south down the autostrada towards Montagnola. A few miles from the retreat centre he pulled off into a local lane at the edge of a small lake that stood apart from Lake Lugano. He needed to make a call to London before he lost signal once again.

He got out to stretch his legs, picked his way through the branches between two trees and stood at the water's edge, looking out across the bright blue lake. Once his head was clear, he returned to the car and made the call, using the bespoke encryption installed in his eband. This time his handler, Darlene Piper, was available.

'Jack, monastic life suiting you?' Her gravelly voice came through clearly on the car's speakers. Jack presumed this was how inveterate smokers used to sound. Why Darlene's voice was like this he didn't know, but it certainly suited the hard-bitten individual he had come to know in recent years. Her accent was educated British English but not posh. She had once revealed to Jack that she was from Surrey, from a not so well-to-do part of a well-heeled neighbourhood.

'Darlene, hello. I presume you've heard about the listening devices we found?'

'Yes. Let's leave them be, shall we?'

Darlene often turned her orders into something like questions, but Jack had long since learned that these were of the rhetorical variety.

'Sure,' he said. 'May as well, now we know who put them there. Any intel yet on why?'

There was silence at the other end.

'Darlene? Are you there?'

The silence continued a few seconds more. 'Jack, I need to tell you something. Something about Hugh Coates. The thing is, he may not be working against us.'

'Sorry, Ma'am, what are you telling me? Does he work for us?'

'It's not that simple, Jack, but yes, he has done us some favours in the past.'

Jack waited as some children wandered past on bicycles. 'Now why would Hugh Coates do us any favours?'

'Long story short, we found that his communications infrastructure was not entirely neutral.'

'You mean, he was spying?'

'Yes. Not to sell on to anybody, as far as we could tell, but obviously it would have embarrassed him if his secret got out.'

'Ah, right. So, in exchange for our discretion...'

'He helps us out from time to time. That's right. It's called a mutually beneficial arrangement.'

Jack watched a couple of birds squabbling in the trees nearby. The smaller one appeared to be getting the upper hand. 'How do we know it's only us he helps?'

'Well, we don't,' she said. 'But better to have his intel sometimes rather than never. He really is one of the best when it comes to surveillance. As far as I can tell, there isn't a country in the world where he doesn't have ears.'

'Okay. So, what then... is he helping us now?'

'We're not currently aware of his intentions,' she said carefully. 'At least, not as yet.'

The larger bird flew off.

They closed the call by arranging for a pick-up of Miranda's tablet which Jack had left in Geneva. He got out of the car again and returned to the lake. It seemed darker now, an inky blue, and the sky had turned sombre. Time to go.

As he began the last few miles of his journey back to the monastery, he felt more than ever before that he was descending into a web of enigmas, all somehow connected through the biggest one of all. Ariel.

6

As he stood in the gloom of the autumn dusk and looked at the wall and trees surrounding the Elemental Retreat Centre, Bill Petersen felt much happier. He was dressed in combat stealth gear, as were the two soldiers either side of him. Thanks to his meeting with High Command in Geneva, the rules had changed and at last the gloves were off. Beth Griffiths had authorised the forcible detention of the Stranger, currently dubbed Ariel. The mission was to remain clandestine until such time as they had something to share with the rest of the world. The whole meeting had gone surprisingly well, and if it hadn't been for Takahashi's ominous silence Bill would have felt totally at ease. Never mind. Right now he was exactly where he wanted to be.

The three men checked that the safety mechanisms on their weapons were enabled, with orders to threaten but not actually shoot. The acolytes had semi-automatic rifles, while in addition to a small pistol Bill carried an electric pulse gun, fully charged and enabled. They had parked their vehicle outside the grounds in the layby where Bill had first challenged the WSA's strategy in general and Jack's tactics in particular. He smiled now at the thought that the Australian interloper had given him his way in. They prepared to climb over the gate and make their way through the woods towards the main building. There was no camera in sight.

Even as their feet hit the ground Jack was emerging from a tunnel and swinging the car off the autostrada for the last few miles to the monastery. There was no straight road into the village, but he was glad of the twists and turns that kept sleep at bay. He decided to take an earlier turning off the main road to bring him to the monastery without going through the village centre. With the lateness of the hour he could think of nothing better than going straight to bed. Now was not the time to talk with people, especially not Ariel. Their sorry parting was back at the front of his mind, and he would need a good night's sleep before he could face the cool-headedness of his increasingly aggravating charge.

The perimeter wall of the monastery grounds was on his right now. Nearly there. He passed the small gate, though he slowed down when he saw a black car he didn't recognise parked in the layby. That woke him up a bit.

A minute later he drove through the main gate and pulled into the front drive. Much as he wanted a closer look at that car, it was too dark to go walking through the woods. It was probably nothing anyway, and sleep beckoned. He went inside.

There was no one about. He walked sluggishly up the front staircase and made his way towards his room as quietly as the stone floor would allow. He stopped at Melody's door, thought about knocking, decided against. He unlocked his door and went in, crashing on to the bed.

He dozed. When he checked his eband almost half an hour had passed. Why was it so quiet half way through the evening? He sloshed water over his face and made his way down the other stairs, emerging into the main courtyard just as Natasha came running through from the rear corridor.

'Hey, Natasha!' he called. 'Where is everyone?'

'Oh, Jack, Jack. They're gone!'

'Who's gone, Natasha?'

She ran up to him and all but collapsed into his arms before quickly pulling back. 'Ariel and Miranda. And, Jack, they've got Melody too!' She sounded close to tears.

'Okay, slow down, Natasha. Who's taken them? What's happened?'

'It was Petersen, I'm sure of it. I'd know that voice anywhere.'

They sat down under the statue, ignoring the growing chill of night, and Jack let the words come tumbling out of her. 'They were wearing suits with head coverings – you know, like balaclavas. There were three of them. We were just taking Ariel to the infirmary to lie down–'

'What? Why did he need the infirmary?'

'Oh, that's another story. We'd just left Ariel in there – that's me, Miranda, Melody and Leonardo – and when we came out, there they were, running across the courtyard towards us. I heard them before I saw them, as they were dressed in black. I'm sure it was that odious man giving military orders, so I ran towards them–'

'Natasha!'

'Sorry – natural reaction.'

'Aye,' Jack sighed. 'For you, at any rate.'

'But Jack, it was like running into an electrified fence. And yes, I know what that's like because I have done it! When I got my movement back, I realised I'd been hit with some kind of stun gun. As soon as I got up I ran out the back, to see if they'd gone that way. But nothing.'

The image of the black car in the layby instantly formed in Jack's mind and he sprang to his feet. 'That's because their car is out front! Come on, Natasha. I've been asleep – literally! Follow me. I think I know where they parked. If they've got all three of them, as you say, they won't be able to move very quickly. How long do you think you were out of action?'

'I don't know. A few minutes maybe.'

They ran now, out through the front entrance towards Jack's car. He shouted at his eband to unlock it, and as soon as they were in he slammed the car in reverse, span round and shot out through the front gate, cornering hard into the road past the monastery wall. Within seconds they saw the black car. He slowed down and came to a stop a few metres short. He turned to Natasha. 'I don't suppose you saw whether they were armed with anything else?'

'No. It was dark, and it all happened so fast.'

'Okay. Follow me.'

She was out of the car before him. Together they walked up to the vehicle and shone their ebands inside. It was empty. They looked at each other, then at the gate, and within seconds both were over it and back inside the grounds.

They walked a few steps before the silence was shattered. 'Get off me, you bastard!' The unmistakable tones of Miranda. Instinctively using signals they had learnt in case of radio failure on Venus, Jack now motioned to Natasha to go into the bushes on one side of the path, while he disappeared on the other. For all the darkness, Natasha's light-coloured tracksuit was still managing to reflect the tiny amount of ambient light in the woods.

A few moments later two figures emerged from the gloom. The one on the right was fidgeting, hands behind its back, clearly being pushed along by someone behind. The other person kept pace, but there was no agitation. Jack panicked. If the one on the right was Miranda, and the calm one Ariel, where was Melody? But then he saw movement on the other side of the path and dimly made out Natasha holding up her hand with what looked like three fingers outstretched. He looked again, and in the gloom he could now see a third form trailing behind the others which soon resolved itself into two figures, the one helping the other to walk.

Jack bit his lip and pushed down the urge to jump out. What could he do anyway? He wasn't armed, and he didn't even have clear sight of the enemy. How many were there? Were they all here? He knew he had to wait. And he had to trust that Natasha would do the same.

The ramshackle group stumbled past. With no moon, and trees overhead, it was impossible to be sure, but by the time they had gone by Jack was fairly sure he had worked out who was who. On Natasha's side of the path there was Miranda – no doubt about that. On his side, he decided it had to be Melody, who he knew was good at saying nothing when nothing was the best thing to say. And in the middle, a few steps behind, came Ariel, stumbling and every so often moaning. Each one was accompanied by a guard, and Jack hazarded a guess that the one with Ariel would be Bill. He stepped out behind them.

'Hey, Bill! Nice night for a walk!'

Natasha did not hesitate. Even as Bill turned she struck the man next to Miranda with a branch and he fell to the ground. Miranda swore with relief. As soon as Melody heard Jack's voice, she dropped to the ground. Her guard's grip had been slack anyway, so for a moment he was confused. But when he saw Bill let go of Ariel and turn to face Jack, he went to secure their prime target. Ariel had fallen to the ground in a sitting position, so the guard lifted up his gun and brought the butt down on his head. As soon as the gun made contact, the sharpest pain he had ever felt ran all the way up to his shoulder. He yelled, fell back over Melody and lay on the ground in agony, clutching his shattered arm.

At the same time Jack turned on his eband light and shone it into Bill's face. As he had hoped, the night glasses he was wearing were tuned to high sensitivity, and Bill turned away, momentarily blinded, before shouting, 'Abort! Abort!' With that, both Natasha's and Melody's guards scampered away as best they could, following their commander to the gate.

Miranda called after the men, but she thought better of pursuing them and turned to see what state Melody was in. Jack and Natasha converged on Ariel, still slumped on the path. 'It's okay, I've got this,' said Natasha, and instantly Jack went over to Melody who even now was getting to her feet, Miranda's arm firmly around her waist. 'Mel! Are you hurt?' Miranda quickly handed her over, who surprised him with a full-on kiss. 'I'm all right, honestly, Jack. Just a bit shaky, that's all.'

Jack turned to Miranda, and she put up her hands to show she was unhurt. 'I'm okay,' she said, visibly calmer.

'Jack, can you give me a hand?' Natasha was trying to lift Ariel to his feet.

'Is everyone all right?' said Ariel. 'I think I've been out of it for a while. Did they take the crystal?'

'I think you must be confused, my friend,' said Jack as he took hold of him. 'We don't have the crystal here. It was you they were after.'

Once Jack was sure there was no one else in the vicinity, they made their way back to the monastery, Ariel between the steadying arms of Natasha and Miranda, with Jack and Melody following on in what had now become the complete darkness of night.

Back at the perimeter wall it took five agonising minutes for Bill to heave his wounded men over the locked gate and into the car.

7

Leonardo welcomed the small party off the battle field and into the refectory, ordering hot drinks for them all. As they sat themselves down around a large table, Natasha asked him if he was hurt.

'No, no. They let me be. One of them pointed a gun at me while the other two took Ariel.'

'What was wrong with Ariel?' said Jack.

'He had another episode earlier on today,' said Leonardo. 'He has only been half-conscious.'

Jack decided to probe. 'What brought that on?'

'We decided... well, I decided, but the others were happy to agree... we had a review session. I thought it might be helpful to you, while you were away, for us to go over the events on Venus and see if it helped Ariel to remember.'

'Probably a good idea,' said Jack.

Leonardo relaxed visibly. The drinks arrived, and everyone submitted to the camomile tea the Abbot had chosen for them.

Ariel looked up from his steaming mug. 'It was a good idea, Jack. Natasha took me right back there, and although I haven't remembered anything new as such, I have put various bits and pieces in place.'

'And... you were all happy to meet together on this?'

They all nodded their agreement. Whatever they had thought of it at the time, it was plain to see that events since then had brought them closer together.

Miranda set her mug down on the table. 'What I want to know is, why did three armed guys just run a mile when you jumped them?'

'Aye, it's a fair question,' said Jack, 'and I have an idea I know why. They were probably banking on doing this with total anonymity. I agree with you that one of them was Bill, although,' and with this he chuckled, 'I only had the word "abort" to go on!'

They laughed for several seconds at this, succumbing to the relief and exultation of defeating their enemies so roundly.

Jack continued. 'My question is this – why did they take you two, Miranda and Melody? Why not just Ariel? Or, if they were cleaning up, then why stun Natasha and leave Leonardo?'

'Well,' said Leonardo, 'given what I have already heard about tonight's events, stunning Natasha clearly proved to be a necessity, whereas I presented no threat. However, I agree it is odd that they took Melody and Miranda with them.'

'Well,' said Jack, trying not to grimace as he drank the unfamiliar brew, 'let's think about it. Petersen has been here. He has Natasha down as a threat to security – sorry, Natasha, but he made that pretty plain – but maybe he sees a different kind of threat in you two.'

'Mmm,' said Melody. 'I can see how he might. Miranda broke in, and it might be said that I pushed my way in. Both of us are from outside the original mission.'

'But what was he planning to do?' said Miranda.

'I don't know,' said Jack. 'With Ariel, almost certainly try drugs or some other form of neurological technique to loosen his memory. But whatever he intended, one thing is clear to me now. He didn't mean to be identified. It's the only reason I can think he ran off.'

'Well,' said Leonardo, 'that makes sense. Whoever authorised this kidnap attempt is not going to come out in the open.'

Ariel stood up, knocking his chair to the floor. 'Ladies, gentlemen, I see it is now beyond doubt that I am putting you all in danger.'

Jack looked up at him, the last dregs of his anger now fully drained.

'Ariel, my friend, I think we've always known something like this could happen. And if anyone's to blame, it's me. I should have been ready.' He raised his hand against the loud protestations that followed. 'However! However, I do agree that we may need to move you somewhere else.'

'But Jack,' said Melody, 'can you make that decision?'

'Officially, no,' said Jack. 'But I think we're way past official now, don't you?'

'Jack,' said Ariel, 'you know that we will do whatever you decide. We all have the utmost confidence in you. Before we retire for the night, however, I think I should tell you about a new piece in my own personal jigsaw puzzle.'

'Go on,' said Jack. 'Would this have anything to do with your latest episode?'

'Yes,' he answered, sitting back down on his chair a split second after Miranda righted it. 'When Natasha was telling us how she found the crystal, and mentioned the red and green lightning, and the Endeavour reflecting the rainbow of colours around it, I felt a new connection with it all. And then I looked, as it were, and saw in my mind's eye Natasha holding the crystal. I imagined it – I'm pretty sure it wasn't a memory, though it's so hard to tell the difference! But I looked, and I gazed into the crystal in my mind, and I saw a young man looking back.'

'A young man?' Miranda blurted.

'What did he look like?' asked Melody.

'It was hard to see. His face was in darkness, though there was a light thrown across it, going on and off. I am fairly sure it was Dr Chase.'

'Ryan?' Natasha gasped.

'Yes, but I wasn't so much looking at him as the man standing behind him.'

They all started talking at once. 'Where was this?' said Jack over the rest.

'I have no idea, but the man raised his arm with some object in his hand, and for a brief moment I caught a view of his face, before he struck Dr Chase on the head. And I remember no more.'

They were silent now.

'And did you recognise the second man?' said Jack.

'No. I can say that he was oriental in features.'

'Well, this is getting very interesting,' said Jack. 'And it makes me all the more determined to get you and Constance Bridlington together – maybe here or in Geneva, but maybe better somewhere else.'

'You are most welcome to stay here,' said Leonardo, whose face had become increasingly restless as the discussion had gone on. 'And,' he added, 'I can't help thinking you should also reunite Ariel with the crystal.'

'One thing at a time,' said Jack. 'Right now we don't even know where the crystal is. Which brings me back to the person who let it go. I'll call her in the morning.'

8

Bill Petersen was back inside the windowless room at the top of the UN building in Geneva. Across the table from him sat Beth Griffiths. There was a steely look in her shining brown eyes.

'I'm all ears, Bill. What went wrong? And what in the name of all-that's-not-stupid were you thinking, taking the two women as well?' Exasperation had given wings to her Welsh accent.

'Okay, Beth, I admit it's not what we agreed.'

'Too right!'

'But you don't get where you and I have got to in this game without showing some initiative. I took two of my best men, just to contain the situation, but when we got into the place and did the full recce, I saw the value of questioning the Freeman girl.'

'But Melody Grantley James!'

'Look, I admit it, I couldn't resist the opportunity when it came to it. Only it bugs me that someone like her can be in the core of an operation like this. What clearance does she have?'

'Full WSA, that's what!'

'Okay, okay, I don't want to start a war between you and Bridlington, but you have to admit, it's not right. I mean, she's Forrester's girlfriend for heaven's sake!'

'I think you'll find it's more complicated than that. All you need to know is that it's perfectly legit, agreed at the highest level. As for a war with Constance... you, my friend, have got to make sure it's over before it begins. You're going to have to eat humble pie.'

'I'll eat whatever you want me to eat,' he grinned, 'but in the end I need you to back me up on the manoeuvre. Unless you're going to hang me out to dry.'

She dropped her eyes. 'Well, you know I'll do my best for you. Now, tell me what happened.'

'As I say, we did the recce and saw our chance. Ariel was clearly in some kind of difficulty – probably another reason I thought I could stretch things a bit, bearing in mind there were three of us and it turned out he'd be easy to contain. We neutralised the Russian–'

'How? What on earth did you do to her? I mean, she's only a WSA astronaut!'

'Nothing nasty, don't worry. These new pulse guns don't cause permanent damage – at least, not to someone as fit as her. She would only have been paralysed for a few minutes, half-hour tops. That left the Abbot, who just cowered in the corner and gave us free rein. And the two women.'

'Okay,' said Beth, thinking out loud, 'then maybe we can say you took them along because you didn't want to use excessive force. And... yes, I know! It became clear to you that their presence would help pacify Ariel. And you had no intention of taking them further than your vehicle.'

Bill gave a low whistle. 'I see why you're in this job. Not that I ever doubted you!'

'Right,' said Beth. 'Carry on. You got them away from the building.'

'Correct. Forrester was supposedly here in Geneva—'

'Yes, sorry about that. We'd assumed he would be staying for more than a couple of hours.'

Bill felt like gloating, but settled for the equity it gave him in the blame stakes. 'Sure,' he said. 'We took them out via a path I was already familiar with, heading for a small gate next to the vehicle. That's when they jumped us.'

'Who jumped you?'

'Well, Jack, obviously, plus one other, unknown.'

'And what did you say to him?'

'Nothing. I gave the order to abort and withdrew before we could be identified.'

'Except Bridlington is on my case and mentioning your name.'

'It was always a risk they might recognise my voice, I guess. But most likely Jack was guessing.'

'And you sustained injuries?'

'We did,' and with this Bill stood up and started to pace around the room. 'And that's where we had a bit of a bonus.'

'I hardly think Corporal Maddox would agree with you. I've just seen the medical report. His arm is shot to pieces. If his left hand hadn't slipped when it did, I'm told both might be shattered. As for his weapon, it's a wreck. What are you not telling me? What's this bonus?'

'The bonus, Ma'am, is simply this: all Ed did was bring his gun down on the target – Ariel's head or neck, he thinks.'

She shifted in her chair. 'Just what are you saying, Bill?'

'I'm saying that we had that guy right from the monastery to where Forrester jumped us. At no time did anyone get near him, and he had no protective clothing. Yet when that gun butt hit him the force came back with interest!'

'Which means...?' said Beth, getting to her feet.

'Which means, the guy really has been enhanced. Either that or...' He trailed off, and neither of them dared say any more.

9

Jack picked up the phone in Leonardo's office. 'Hi Petroc,' he said, 'Here I am.'

'Putting you through now, Commander.'

The voice of Constance Bridlington came on the line. 'Jack, how is everybody?'

He gave her reassurances about everyone, particularly Natasha. 'I feel responsible,' said Constance. 'And I feel the injury myself in a way. I tell you, I won't find it easy to be civil when I next see him.'

'And when's that likely to be?' asked Jack.

'I don't know. I hardly think Beth Griffiths will bring him to the review. Talking of which, I need you back here the day after tomorrow for that, as well as Natasha and whomever else you consider should be there.'

'Constance, I really think it's time you met up with Ariel. I'm saying nothing against the way you've given us space so far. It's been invaluable. But I think it's time. And, if you're okay with it, I suggest he be at the meeting too.'

The seconds ticked by.

'Very well. We may have someone representing the military at the meeting – hopefully only Beth. Either way, she will certainly have to give account for the kidnap attempt.'

'If she owns up,' said Jack.

'She already has, to me personally. I think she has some story cooked up. But – and this is with no disrespect to the danger you were all in – I'm more interested in other things. I'll have Selena Chandra there, as you know, and Dan, Jim and Ryan of course.'

Ryan's name brought Ariel's vision to mind. 'So Ryan's back then?'

'Well no, actually, he's still off grid. I'm hoping Jim will track him down in time. Either way, we meet the day after tomorrow. I've booked you an early flight, so you have one more full day at the monastery after today, Jack, one more day. After that, my guess is this will be out of my hands.'

10

Ryan was whistling as he worked away in his lab. The crystal, now the size of a large box, was glowing happily in the corner. He turned to his assistant and was surprised to see his old school flame there. He'd not seen her in years. Then the voice came, calling for him to look out. The laboratory started to spin around the crystal which was now in the centre of the room, while he and his friend were riding carousel horses around it.

He woke up. He was still in a lab, but with the pain in his head came the memory that he wasn't in California. He was seated on a chair with his hands tied behind its back. Immediately he tried to pull his hands free and was surprised to feel the rope fall away.

He stumbled to his feet while the pain rolled around his head like a loose ball bearing. The lights were off and there was no one around. He turned on the torch in his eband.

The crystal had gone.

Chapter 18

Conversations

1

Jack sat at the small table in his room and leafed through one of the books he had pulled off the shelf. He was bathing in the unexpected relief that had flooded in when Constance had told him their time was up. He had the rest of today and all of tomorrow to continue the work of stimulating Ariel's memory, though he knew it was by no means simply down to him. Leonardo had played a key role, as had their surroundings here in the Elemental Retreat Centre. And he had always known Natasha was his best hope, because of the primal bond between her and Ariel. But Melody's input had made a key difference as well, for him personally at least. As for Miranda, she had turned out to be the curveball that triggered the change in the pace of the game.

He had made up his mind how to use these last two days. Each of his new-found crew was to have some quality time alone with Ariel, much as he had allowed with Natasha when they first arrived. Was that really less than two weeks ago? It felt like a whole chapter of his life had passed since then. The journey to Venus had been like nothing else, of course, but that was crammed with things to do, all quite fast and furious. This place allowed you to step back, to think, to try to make sense of it all. And while he still cherished hopes that Ariel's memory might return, he was thinking as much of the others now. This might be their only chance to benefit from whatever latent powers he carried. He had little doubt those powers were positive and life-affirming, and it seemed increasingly obvious that it was in human relationships, in conversation in the fullest sense of the word, that light would be shed on the enigma that was this man. Because, for all the progress Ariel had made with his communication skills, they were no closer to knowing who he was or where he had come from. Who were the comrades he felt he had been fighting with? And who on earth were the people they were fighting against?

There had been some progress, of course. Ariel was opening up discussion on a wide range of issues, and he had started to express how he was feeling. But were his intuitions about his own past correct? He had made it sound like he had been a soldier but presented more as a philosopher. And wasn't it even more likely he had been part of some secret climate experiment? Whichever it was, surely somebody had to be looking for him. And whoever they were, they had to be connected to the crystal. After all, he clearly was.

2

The Brothers filed into the chapel. It was the first time Jack had seen it buzzing. He counted seventeen of them, not including Leonardo. Finally Ambrose came in, accompanied by the young monk who had helped them on the night of the storm. A full score.

Jack decided to sit near the back. Melody had joined Natasha and Miranda further up. He felt a twinge of big-brotherly satisfaction – or was that fatherly? – over the respect and friendship that were growing between the three of them.

Leonardo walked to the centre of the aisle at the front and faced the congregation. The buzz of conversation ceased abruptly, the air heavy with expectation.

'Brothers, friends, I want to welcome you to our gathering which this morning features a visiting speaker. You are all aware that we have had some special guests among us in recent days. The sad truth is, they will be leaving us shortly, and we do not know when or whether they shall return. Consequently I did not want you to miss the opportunity to be addressed by a singular mind. Some of you have met him. All of you, I think, know that I have the highest regard for him. I believe his presence among us is of the utmost significance.'

No one stirred. All eyes were on the Abbot.

'Very well. We shall be using English, as is our custom when all of us are together. But now, enough from me. Brothers, friends... I give you Ariel.'

Jack was about to applaud before realising only just in time that this was not the convention here. As eager as anyone to hear what Ariel would have to say if he were given a larger audience, he had quickly fallen in with Leonardo's suggestion that Ariel address the Brothers. Ariel himself had accepted readily.

Leonardo sat down in the front row and Ariel stood, though very soon he was pacing this way and that as he spoke.

'I am very grateful for the invitation to address you all. You have been magnificent hosts to us during these past days, letting us get in your way while studiously keeping out of ours.' A ripple of laughter. 'With all of thirty minutes to prepare, I have decided to speak to you on the subject I have been thinking about for some days now. And nights. And that is, singularity.'

Jack noticed Leonardo sit up at this. It was clearly not what had been expected. But then, who knew what to expect?

'I appreciate that you who live and work here are very practised at the art of reflection, turning things over in your mind, using your treasure-filled library, enjoying the peace of this place when you need a time of contemplation. I also understand that visitors here are deliberately kept within the same confines. Or should I say, borders. No signal connecting us with the outside world. Just the place, the time and your own thoughts, nudged along by those books, as each of you sees fit.' He paused. 'Or as the Abbot sees fit!'

There was more laughter. Jack was amazed and encouraged by the level of sophistication Ariel had reached, or presumably recovered, since they had arrived.

'It seems to me these conditions are very appropriate for a place dedicated to the four classical elements of earth, air, fire and water. These of course were taken by the ancient world to sum up the entirety of physical matter. And you all clearly dedicate yourselves to the study of... to reflection on... the physical universe. You have said that spirituality *is* physical – it is about our relationship to the physical universe.'

Jack could see Leonardo was nodding ever so slightly in agreement. Ariel pressed on.

'But herein lies the *metaphysical* problem. If metaphysics is about the relationship between the human person – the soul, if you like – and the universe, in what way is it *meta*, "beyond", the remit of the physical sciences? Just as you create a shield around this place from anything beyond, have you in fact done the same in your basic philosophy? Is there nothing of value beyond the shield?'

He stopped pacing as he paused. Leonardo was no longer nodding.

'I am aware – again thanks to your books which have stimulated so much of my memory – that some believe there is a "beyond", an "outside", to this universe. But it always seems to be couched in terms of more of the same. Multiverses really only make the universe bigger. But my question is this. Is it possible to stand *outside* the universe, in a meaningful sense? However you answer that, you would need to be thinking about something that is not part of the universe. Or rather, someone, since we are thinking about perception here.

'Clearly if we define the universe as containing everything, as I hinted a moment ago, then this someone would need to be beyond matter.

'And this appears to be the universal understanding of religions, that nature – things that are born and grow – is also creation – things that owe their existence to one who is not part of them. The belief in a Creator.

'I have been thinking about this, as I say, and I can see that the understanding here in this place is not to look *out* for a beyond, but to look *within*. And let me say right away that I agree with such a commendable quest.'

Did Leonardo's shoulders just drop? Was that relief?

'I believe that as we look inside ourselves we begin to glimpse the infinite. There is no end. And yet, paradoxically, there is. There has to be. There has to be a limit to how far we can see inwards, much as there still is for cosmologists and others who look outwards. We might like to think of that limit as an event horizon.'

Jack was hooked. Instantly he could see the relevance of this. He knew, of course, that an event horizon was not just a barrier but a border. Things may exist either side of it, even if they only pass one way when they cross. Just as no energy, no light, nothing could directly escape a black hole out there in the wider universe, so Ariel was suggesting that the fundamental part of the human person may be similarly off limits to those of us outside, beyond the event horizon.

He tuned back into what Ariel was saying.

'The human person may well be there at the end of an introspection that seems endless. And yet... each one is particular, existing in the here and now, with memories and thoughts unique to the individual. In-divid-ual... that cannot be divided further. We go on analysing our thoughts, our memories – and believe me, I know something about this, struggling as I do with such severe amnesia – yet we sense there is a thing, a point, at the base of it all. And it seems to me that this point may rightly be called infinitesimal.'

He began to pace up and down again.

'Several of your books have taught me, or reminded me, that this has been a century in which people have searched not only for meaning but also for freedom. Now "freedom" is a dynamic word. It suggests a process, a movement from one thing towards another. From a lack of purpose towards meaning, perhaps? And these things have always been at the heart of our deepest, widest concepts, not least those universally recognised realities called good and evil. But how do they fit in with this understanding that we are infinitesimally small at root? What difference might it make if we find we are *a part of* the universe yet also *apart from* it? Surely, at the very least, it means that we have a singular responsibility, that we are answerable somehow, accountable to live according to the truths we have perceived, however they have been revealed to us.

'What point can there be in understanding evil, except to know how I can personally move from evil towards good? Am I free to do what I *want*? Or am I free to be who I am *meant* to be?'

He let the questions linger in the air.

'Let's come down to earth, shall we?' he said, and the room seemed to relax a little. 'Let's think how we might apply what I have been saying to a specific area. Let's talk about discrimination.'

At this point Jack caught sight of Melody's hair being shaken back before she whispered something to Natasha.

'I appreciate that this is a loaded term,' Ariel continued, 'but let's be good thinkers and try to learn from its root meaning. Discrimination is about seeing difference. And in our context this morning that means seeing that each person is unique, separate, individual. This is to say nothing about their connectedness — that is where the idea of relationship comes in. We are separate yet two can become one through joining. So can three. Or, indeed, twenty.'

And with that last remark he looked across his audience. All eyes were on him. Jack wondered if he was thrown by that. He didn't appear to be.

'This leads us to consider another of the paradoxes that are generated by the event horizon of our singularity. We all have something in common, and that is that we are all different! We are each singular. If difference is common to us all, diversity is something to be embraced. So, you see, here the notion of discrimination has led us to embracing diversity, not eschewing it.'

More whispered words between Melody and Natasha. Jack

couldn't help feeling that this kind of teaching method would not go down so well in a university. He himself was beginning to feel he was in something more like a magician's audience than a lecture theatre. After all, wasn't that a sleight of hand he had just witnessed?

'And so I must move to concluding my address,' Ariel said. 'And I will do so, if I may, reverend Abbot, by asking you to consider a practical proposal, in the light of all this. You may find it challenging, but that is for you to deal with – I'm just the speaker!' A little laughter, though perhaps less relaxed now. 'How would having Sisters in your community change your community? At what levels would there be change?'

Okay, thought Jack. Didn't see that coming.

'We have said that every person is different from every other, and that this is therefore something we paradoxically all have in common. All share this universal fact of difference. But I am aware that some *areas of difference* seem to coalesce, though I do not understand why. It seems to me that the human race is inherently tribal. It cannot seem to function otherwise.'

Jack felt a chill, or was it a thrill? Ariel was sounding almost as if he himself were not a member of the human race.

'Now you don't need me to enumerate the benefits of tribal cohesion, the sense of belonging it engenders, and perhaps above all the security it promises to its members. So I repeat my question. In what ways, at what levels, would the cessation of gender discrimination change your community? And would those changes hinder or serve the purpose of the community?'

He left the question hanging and sat down. It seemed to Jack that the silence was of an entirely different order from the quiet before the talk began. It had been filled with unfamiliar concepts and provocative questions. Jack watched as Leonardo stood, cast his eyes over the Brothers, waited a few more moments and then spoke.

'My brothers,' he said, 'I knew that our speaker this morning would give us something to think about, and I have not been disappointed. Let me assure you, Ariel, that we shall treat your, er, proposal very seriously. How refreshing to have it emerge from metaphysical speculation, rather than political machination. I think you have said more to us in ten minutes than some speakers manage in sixty!'

With that the audience began to buzz again, and one by one they returned to whatever duties awaited them.

3

Lunch took a while as Jack, Melody, Natasha and Miranda tried to digest all that Ariel had said. He for his part sat quietly and let them skim the surfaces of metaphysics and gender equality without any more input from him. When the coffee and the conversation had been drained, Jack told them what he had in mind.

'As you know, we fly to Geneva the day after tomorrow, and I've been thinking how best to use the time remaining. We've all been doing our bit to help Ariel remember, but I think I speak for everyone when I say that we're beginning to receive as much as we've been giving, if not more. So, while this morning's address in the chapel was stimulating, I feel each one of you deserves a longer and probably last piece of quality time with our man here. I've drawn up a basic programme for you all. There's no particular reason for the order, so you can change it if you like, but since none of you are going anywhere, I hardly think that matters. I've spoken to Ariel, and he's agreeable.

'So, Melody my love, you're on this afternoon. No-holds-barred interview with the mystery man of the moment!'

His tone stung a little, although she could not deny the favour was as much professional as personal.

'Tomorrow morning, Miranda, your turn. Leaving the afternoon for you, Natasha. Leonardo gets an evening – I feel we owe him that at least.'

'What about you?' said Miranda. 'I mean, I hardly feel I qualify for this.'

'Aye, well, I'm sure we'll get some time together in between.' Melody flicked back her hair. She realised she was going to have to tread carefully if she and Ariel were to talk about Jack again, as she could not rely on tell-it-all Ariel to hold his peace if Jack asked him anything outright.

'Needless to say,' Jack continued, 'we're doing this primarily for Ariel's benefit, but I'm hoping you're all going to get a lot out of this yourselves. With any luck, the more we talk about what's on *our* minds, the closer he'll get to what's hidden somewhere in his. But the agendas are all yours. Enjoy!'

The group dispersed, leaving Melody and Ariel alone in the refectory.

'Shall we?' said Melody.

4

David's message came before they even started. The day had begun warm so, with only a thin sweater over her top and jeans, Melody had suggested they take a walk in the forest. Ariel was wearing one of the sets of baggy shirt and trousers that had become his signature look. They decided to walk out through the front gate first and cross the road to get a proper view of the monastery. Ensuring her eband was in self-righting mode, she held it up to take a photo, and even as she did so it gave a little squeak.

'Well, look at that,' she said to Ariel. 'We must have just strayed outside the signal lockdown area. I've just received a load of mess–'

'Something wrong?' said Ariel.

'Erm, no. Well, yes. I've had a message from my friend David. You know, the one–'

'Yes, I know.'

'It was sent this morning.' She opened it. It was as brief as the last one she'd received, but there the similarity ended. 'I'm in Geneva on sabbatical. Can we meet up?' She stood rooted to the spot.

'Are you going to answer it?' said Ariel.

'Er, yes. Of course, I've got to do that out here, haven't I? I feel a bit guilty, you know, answering messages when we're supposed to be on retreat.'

'But we're not, are we?'

'No. I suppose not.' She flicked back her hair. 'He says he's in Geneva – right now, can you believe? Apparently he's on sabbatical. If I remember rightly, he was planning to do something on Calvin and theocracy... if that means anything to you.'

'As I recall, he was a famous Christian thinker based in Geneva in the sixteenth century. Will you go to see him? David, I mean.'

His directness was strangely welcome. 'Well, it would be rude not to, wouldn't it? After all, it's not as if I'm invited to your special review meeting. I'll have to find something to do. Oh, Ariel, what should I do?'

'What do you want to do? What would be best?'

'Well,' she said, 'I know you know those are two different questions. I want to see him. I feel sure this is his way of making up for the... cool exchanges we've had just recently. But what would be best? That I don't know. I suppose it can't do any harm.'

'Then you suppose wrong.'

'Ouch! All right, I'll tell you what. I'll message him back now, while I can, and say that I'll contact him again in a couple of days. How's that?'

She didn't wait for an answer and sent the message. She took a few more photos, including a secret one of Ariel with the monastery in the background, in case it proved useful should she ever be allowed to write openly about it. Then they strolled back to the grounds and turned into the woods.

For a while they let the trees do their work, surrounding them with what Ariel called upstretched life. Melody noted the phrase on her eband. 'Yes, things feel right here, don't they?' she said. 'When I walk under these trees I feel a bit like I do watching a play or listening to a symphony... you know, like the world is something I can grasp. I don't mean grab, I mean that somehow it's become something I can understand.'

When they reached the observatory Melody sat down on the steps outside. Ariel looked up at the circular roof that imitated the dome of the sky above. He stood there for some while, till he remembered Melody and realised she was now expecting to engage in serious conversation.

'It's funny,' she said, 'what pressure having a schedule puts on you.'

'Is that bad?'

'I suppose not,' she said, 'though I'd love to spend more time here. When I feel under pressure my father just reminds me that our taps wouldn't be much good without water pressure. They need it to work. Knowing this may be the last proper conversation you and I have for a while does help bring the important things to the surface.'

'And what are the important things?' Ariel sat down on the step next to her.

'Right and wrong, good and evil. You know... the usual.'

'Are we talking in the abstract here?' Ariel asked, 'or does this have a personal context?'

'Oh, Ariel, you should be a diplomat! Perhaps that's what you were in your previous life!'

'My previous life... I wonder, is this now going to be a different life?'

'Maybe. That's exciting, though, don't you think?'

They said no more for a while. Melody watched a lone ant, fascinated by the way it crossed one of the steps. It went this way and that, but always in the same general direction. 'You know,' she said at last, 'I think I'm a bit like this ant down here. When you first look at him — and my apologies if you're a she — he's wandering about all over the place. But after a minute or two you realise that he's making his way from one end of the step to the other, probably checking it all out for food or whatever it is he's after, but always going from A to B.'

'And where is B for you?'

'I knew you were going to ask me that!' She smiled broadly, and her eyes caught the sun in a blaze of iridescent aquamarine. 'Well... sitting here with you, and the trees, and the ant, I'd say what I'm looking for boils down to some kind of enlightenment.'

'What kind?'

She paused. 'Oh, I don't know... perhaps I want to see a resolution to the sort of questions I was engaged with in my degree. I did Literature as a major, but I also took an aesthetics course from the philosophy department. I can remember journalling about truth and beauty and justice. I got to the point when I could see... sort of... that they all worked together in harmony, or at least they *could* do, but my tutor shot me down when I said they *should* do.'

Ariel sat in silence. She pressed on, fairly sure he was still listening, though feeling she could lose him to the trees at any moment.

'That's when I got introduced to the *is* versus *ought* dilemma, and discovered how hard it is to derive an ought from an is.'

'But then, you were in a university.'

'True.'

'So did the university of life help later on?'

'My, you really do have a knack at asking key questions, don't you?' she said. 'Maybe a journalist, not a diplomat. And the answer to your question is, yes, I think so. When I met David and Alice, in fact. Thinking about it now, I think David taught me you can cross from an ought to an is by the bridge of religion.'

'How so?'

'Well, basically because, when God tells you something *is* to be done, then we *ought* to do it. So truth and justice – what's right – come together.'

'And beauty?'

'His ways are beautiful... David used to say that a lot.'

'What do you think he meant by that?'

She stared ahead across the trees towards the horizon. 'That the life lived for God – he'd say for Jesus – is a beautiful life.'

They sat in silence again and enjoyed the beginnings of a fresh breeze on their faces. When Ariel spoke, his voice was soft, as if he were almost thinking out loud. 'Are the ways beautiful because they are his ways, or because they just are?'

'Well, that's the point,' she answered. 'They "just are" precisely because they are his ways. He is the basis of true beauty – so David would say. And of reality.'

'And Alice?'

'Oh, she just lived it! She left the philosophising to David. She really was, is, beautiful. You know, as a person. Kind, thoughtful, positive.'

'And do you think you could live like that?'

'Oh, now you're sounding like David! I'll tell you what I told him – that I don't know. Not without help, that's for sure.'

'Help from him?'

'Not exactly. Fundamentally it's got to come from Jesus.'

'The one who died and then rose again?' said Ariel, almost too quietly for Melody to hear.

'Yes, well, so the dogma goes. Jesus came back from the dead and then he went to heaven and sent the Holy Spirit to help us. So they say.'

'I'm guessing there's a lot wrapped up in this dogma,' said Ariel.

'Oh yes, trust me! Books and books of it. Not that you'd find any of those books around here.'

'Why is that, do you think?'

'Well, I suppose it has a lot to do with what you were talking about this morning. You know, not opening themselves up to something outside their event horizon.'

'The inner one, or the outer?'

'Well, definitely the outer, what with Jesus sending the Spirit from heaven and all. But I think the inner one as well. Alice might not have talked like David, but she did often quote the Bible, and I can remember sitting in her kitchen one day going through one of the Gospels – they're the bits about Jesus' time on earth, by the way – and telling me that, if I were to receive the Spirit, it would well up inside me. Except she said "he" not "it", which I seem to remember I took exception to at the time. And before you ask me why, no I wasn't making some kind of feminist point. I just thought it curious that anyone should think of a great spirit as male.'

He smiled. 'I see you can already anticipate my questions.'

'Well, if I can, it's because you're so like a mirror, Ariel, reflecting back to us with your questions. Yes,' she said, pulling back some strands of hair that a growing breeze had blown into her eyes, 'in fact, now I think about it, I reckon we've all been looking at ourselves while we've been looking at you these past few days.'

One ant had now become half a dozen, so she got up and started to walk back towards the monastery.

'Does this mean we've finished?' said Ariel.

'No, not at all,' she said. 'But it's getting a little chilly. Let me ask you a question, if I may, as we walk. It strikes me you're an impartial thinker. What do you make of the fact that religions are often at each other's throats when they all sound like they're saying much the same things? It's been bugging me for ages.'

They could see the monastery now as they came to the edge of the woodland. The breeze was getting stronger and coming from the east.

'Well,' said Ariel, 'it strikes me that to answer your question I will need us to turn right here and go back into the woods. We may not need to go far – perhaps just up to the garages.'

'Well, I'm impressed if you can give me an answer within garage range!'

They set off again.

'I wonder if we should start by thinking about what religious people say is true, rather than looking at whom they follow or what they stand for,' he said.

'Well, that ought to be straightforward enough,' she agreed. 'Though I suspect that who they follow and what they value actually cause most of the friction.'

'I think so too,' said Ariel. 'But it is good to recognise that, isn't it – that religious disagreements are often personal or cultural rather than purely intellectual?'

Yes, it was, she realised. 'You know, you really are quite good at this.'

'So,' he continued as they turned into a more woody area, 'if we just look at what they actually say, they do clearly disagree at times. And when they do, they can't both be right. Not at the point of disagreement.'

'Right,' she said, 'though they could both be wrong.'

'I see you don't need me to help you think clearly, Melody.'

'Oh, but you are helping,' she said. 'When you're not a mirror you're a sounding board, helping me set it all out logically in my head.'

'Happy to help. You are certainly a logical thinker.'

'I'll take that as a compliment,' she smiled. 'It's not most people's first thought when they meet me. They seem to fix on the blonde hair, or my legs or whatever, or my accent. They don't generally seem that interested in what's going on in here.' She tapped on her forehead.

'Might that not be useful in your line of business?'

'Ssh!' she whispered. 'Trade secrets.'

'My lips are sealed.'

'You know,' she said as she clambered over a small branch that had probably come off in the storm, 'you really do seem to have got all your language back. I mean, all the subtle stuff, the art of conversation, the idioms, the light touches.'

'Yes,' he nodded, 'I think perhaps that side of things comes from a different part of my mind. My memories are sealed up tight somewhere else.'

She stopped and looked at him. He was several inches taller than her, but the notion forming in her head would not go away. 'Come here and let me give you a hug.'

He obliged, without lifting her off her feet.

'So,' she said, 'two religions can't both be right at the point where they disagree.'

'Indeed.' They started to amble again. 'It seems to me, from what

I've read here at the monastery—'

'Which is a lot,' she interrupted.

'Yes, well, it seems to me that there are several points where religions disagree with one another.'

'Like what?'

He thought for a moment. 'The pagan says that this world, this universe, is all there is. The Jew and the Christian and the Muslim say there is a Creator.'

'Right,' she said slowly. 'So where does that leave my question about how different religions really are? And how do we know which one is right?'

'Well, I think you just clarified that they could all be wrong, but they can sometimes be right as well. But your second question is new – it could take us beyond the garages.' There was a distinct twinkle in those deep blue eyes.

She laughed. 'To the garages and beyond!' she called out for anyone to hear. 'We shall suffer the cold in the quest for truth!' The truth was, she was enjoying this far too much to turn back yet.

They passed a shed before making their way between the garages. There was ivy growing up one of the walls, and she shuffled and kicked her way through the crisp dead leaves piled up at its foot. 'I haven't done that since I was a child!' she exclaimed. 'You know, my grandmother told me she could just about remember the time when the leaves didn't start dropping before summer was over. Which is why they call the autumn the fall, of course.'

Ariel waited for her to finish with the leaves before taking up the argument again. 'We have established that religions can be wrong or right, but they can't all be right all of the time. Logically speaking.'

'Correct,' she said.

'As to your second question, how do we know which one is right? I think we have to say that most of the ideas coming out of these religions – whether stated or implied – are not to be proved by rational means, even though the statements themselves are for the most part rational.'

'I'm confused.'

They were back in the thick of the trees now, though keeping to the path.

'Let's put it this way,' said Ariel. 'We have established that when religions contradict each other, one being wrong doesn't mean the other isn't wrong as well.'

'Whoa there!' she shouted, and stood still. 'Too many negatives! I'm still confused. Maybe I don't think quite as logically as you.'

'I'm not putting it very well,' he said. 'When things are logically incompatible, if one of them is true the other *must* be false. So, if it is true that you are a White woman, then you *cannot* be a Black woman.'

'Except perhaps emotionally, or symbolically – you know, if I stand with my Black sisters and brothers.'

Ariel's shoulders slumped in a look of aggrievement.

'Sorry,' she said, 'go on. Let's take your statement as one of pure biological fact.' He nodded, but before he could continue she giggled and said, 'Yes, and let's not even think about mixed-race people.'

He raised his hands in mock submission. 'Very well! How about this? If I'm holding a white chess piece, it cannot be a black one.'

'Better, much better!' she taunted.

'Good,' he said, and the twinkle returned. 'But the thing about many religious claims, it seems to me, is that they are not like that. They say things which may or may not be true, and logic won't help us to arrive at the truth. At least, not at first, even if we can deduce new things later on. When some Christians say that the Bible is God's last written word on reality, and Muslims come along and say, "No it isn't, that came later with the Qur'an," all that logic tells us is that they can't both be right. It doesn't tell us if even one of them is actually right.'

'Okay, I get that,' she said, beaming with unabashed glee.

'Now,' he said, warming to his theme, 'we may be able to say something is true *if* certain other things can be shown to be true, but we haven't established whether they are actually true.'

'I'm losing it again!' she laughed. 'Examples please!'

'Very well. Remind me of one of the central tenets of the Christian religion.'

'Well,' she answered, 'obviously that claim that Jesus rose from the dead is up there with the best of them. David used to say everything flowed from it, in fact.'

'Right,' he said. His head was tilted, as if he were listening out for something, desperately trying to catch memories in the whispers of the wind.

She came to another halt and looked at him closely. If only she could see inside his head the way he could with others.

'Right,' he said again, returning to the discussion at hand. 'Okay. Someone says Jesus rose from the dead. Now, I may be able to discover that certain aspects surrounding such a claim are true. Presumably people offer certain facts as evidence?'

'Oh yes,' she said. 'Things like, no one could find a body… or, perfectly normal, rational people claimed to have met him after he was crucified. Oh, and a Roman centurion certified him dead.'

'Interesting.' Once again his attention seemed to float off somewhere under the trees. 'Right then, all of those things may well contribute to a sense of what *may* have happened, but they are hardly enough to bring a real conviction.'

She nodded. 'So how do I get a conviction?' she asked.

'I really couldn't say.'

'Then how does this help us?' She was almost pleading now.

'It helps us by not asking for too much when we talk about the claims of religion – any religion. They are not nonsense – most of them at least make a lot of sense, *if* they are based on reality.'

'Okay. So how do we know if they are? Based on reality, I mean.'

He paused. 'What would David say?'

'Oo, that was tricksy!' she laughed. She dodged behind a tree at the side of the path and then poked her head out. 'I'm sure David would say that the truth had been revealed to him in some way.'

Ariel sighed. It was the first time Melody had heard him do that, and she thought she detected longing there. 'Revealed, you say? Now, wouldn't that be something!'

She came back round the tree. An intense look in his eyes confirmed the sigh. She felt the urge to hug him again, and tell him it would all come back to him, but she didn't know that. 'It's getting quite dark here under the trees,' she said. 'Maybe we should turn back. It's been really great, but I think that's enough cool, logical thinking for one day. For me, at least.'

'Yes,' he said, and they began to walk back, though he was apparently not quite ready to bring things to a close. 'Revelation is a fascinating notion, isn't it? It's not reached by reason alone, yet at some level it has to make rational sense. And it's not always possible to test its claims, yet they are open to testing. In principle, at least.'

She looked up between the trees as a brief space opened above them. The sky was filled with dark clouds, yet shot through by a bright stream of sunlight.

'Look at that sky,' she said. 'Makes me think of another big idea David goes on about.'

'What's that?'

'The idea that Jesus will come back again in a dramatic way that no one can miss – like this sky – and take human history into a whole new era. A new creation.'

'Well now,' he said. 'That's not something we can test right now, is it? And yet it is open to the test of time.'

'Time will tell, you mean?' she whispered.

He nodded, and they walked back to the Centre in silence.

5

Dinner was boisterous. As the wine flowed (Jack's treat) Miranda became fired up about gender identity and the rights of the individual, while Natasha felt it would be quite impossible to build a political platform on anything Ariel had said that morning. Jack was happy to see them in full flow, unworried by any signs of disagreement between them, confident their paths would soon diverge.

Melody sat quietly for the most part, still bathing in the warmth of her walk in the cold, letting the wine seal her contentment, if only for a while.

It was later than usual when they finished, leaving Leonardo and Ariel to talk at the table.

Leonardo smiled. 'You have certainly stimulated your friends,' he said. 'It is very much in keeping with what we stand for here.' He sipped his rapidly cooling coffee. 'Though I think that Miss Melody is perhaps now in the more reflective state that we aim for. But then...' (another sip) 'she has spent time with the teacher. Proper time, as we call it here.'

'Yes,' said Ariel. 'I think it is very astute of Jack to give me time with each of my new-found friends. It is already proving helpful.'

'As I say, it shows in her demeanour.'

'I meant helpful to me,' said Ariel, 'though I won't deny that Melody did seem much... freer, more at ease, by the time we were done.'

'Are you happy to talk some more?' said Leonardo with a hint of hesitation in his voice.

'Proper time, you mean?'

Leonardo laughed. 'Precisely so! And once again, I trust it will be mutually beneficial. But first, let me see if there is some coffee that is still somewhere in the vicinity of hot.' He went behind the counter and brought back an Italian-style coffee pot.

'Where are we going?' said Ariel as Leonardo sat down. 'In terms of conversation, I mean – unless you would like an evening walk?'

'No, no,' said Leonardo, 'it's dark and cold out there. This suits me fine.'

'It's interesting,' observed Ariel, 'how darkness and cold are generally unwelcome, whereas light and warmth are so welcoming.'

Leonardo took his cue. 'Indeed,' he said, 'though we are careful here to honour all of life through the anciently recognised poles.'

'Hot and cold, light and dark,' Ariel mused. 'Manifested in earth, air, fire and water. I noted from one or two of the books here that there is some divergence over how to interpret these in terms of the table of physical elements used by scientists.'

'Sure, sure,' said Leonardo, brushing a crumb off the table, 'that is bound to be the case. But, you know, they still pretty much cover it – solid, liquid, gas and plasma.'

'Yes, I can see that forms of plasma like lightning or the stars could qualify as fire,' said Ariel.

'Yes, and we take modern science very seriously here,' said Leonardo. 'But we do not attempt to harmonise the old ways with the new at any cost.'

'That would indeed be perilous,' Ariel observed, 'if only because scientists do not stand still long enough to hold the note in harmony.'

'True, true,' nodded Leonardo as he poured the steaming liquid from his coffee pot. 'Although we have not had a proper revolution in science for some time now. I know people speak of such things, but we are still using the categories of the previous century.'

'But why use the classical ones?'

'We believe the old way is more in tune with our spiritual views and goals.'

'Goals?'

'Well,' said Leonardo, 'one goal really – to develop a truly all-encompassing view of reality. All of it.'

'A theory of everything?'

'*Si*, but not limited to the horizons of the physical sciences. And so, while I would love to talk to you about the "proposal" you boldly unveiled in public this morning, that we accommodate more than one gender here in the *mon*astery...' He paused to see if an apology might be forthcoming for not talking to him first, but Ariel remained silent, causing him to wonder why he should be so defensive of his own authority. He pressed on. 'As I say, while I would love to discuss your idea, I think it would be remiss not to probe you a little on what you said before that, about the fact that we define spirituality in terms of physicality. Perhaps... even as I think about it now... if fire and plasma are not a precise fit, there is a reason for that. Perhaps fire points the way to spirit.'

He sipped his coffee and watched Ariel closely. What wheels were turning in that opaque head of his?

'May I ask you, Leonardo, in what way fire would "point the way" to anything? To speak in such a way suggests you are pointing *beyond* the elements, does it not, rather than to them?'

'I don't see why,' said Leonardo. He spoke thoughtfully, making an effort to assume an air of humility while holding his own corner. 'It begs the question to say that spirit is not matter. First you must prove it.'

'I guess the burden of proof is fixed firmly in between us,' said Ariel. 'After all, I am not out to prove anything. But tell me, then, what makes you think that spirit is made of matter, or must always be linked to matter?'

Leonardo took a deep swig from his mug, willing the caffeine to help him at this late hour. 'Let's define matter, shall we?' he said. 'Matter is what all things – nature herself – is made of. That is my definition.'

'Who's begging the question now?'

'Touché, my friend!' Leonardo beamed. 'Let us then admit that we do not know, but let us also agree that spirit – whatever it is – is worth pursuing.'

'So what is it?'

Leonardo felt the shift. It was not a burden of proof but of explanation that had fallen into his lap, and he felt its weight. He drained the cup. 'Right,' he said at length, 'what is spirit? It is the ground of our being, the air that brings the breath of life, the fire that ignites us, the water of life that springs up in all living things.'

Ariel saw the practised answer. 'I recognise the four elements in your response,' he said. 'And I do find that it resonates with me. Living here these past days, surrounded by trees, has exposed me to the water you refer to. Every tree seems to be straining for the sky. I know the sap rises, but this water of life is something more.'

'Yes, yes, very good,' Leonardo said, pushing his fingers back through his full head of silver hair. 'And if you could just see the mountains in this part of the world! Like the Himalayas near our mother monastery, the Alps remind us of our grounding in solid earth.'

'Shouldn't that be "father monastery"?' said Ariel with the slightest of grins.

'Ha!' cried the Abbot. 'Perhaps. Although... men have long explored the world and fought their battles in female ships, and served in female institutions. Even the church is a she.'

Ariel nodded. 'So man needs woman.'

'Well, well,' said Leonardo, 'we seem to be touching on so many areas you raised in your rather brief but not at all simple address.'

'Do you want to look into any of them more deeply?'

'I think we should go further in this matter of spirit,' said Leonardo, chuckling at his own play on words. 'Though I warn you, I may struggle outside of my native Italian.'

'My apologies,' said Ariel. 'It seems that English is the language I can use best when discussing such profound concepts.'

'Then I shall do my best,' said Leonardo. 'It will be good for me. Most of our guests use it here, and of course it is our *lingua franca* when we have our own plenary sessions.'

'Thank you,' said Ariel. 'So let us go deeper. You said nature (which is also female, I notice) includes all things – matter and spirit, whether we think they are of the same order or different entities. Is that right?'

'Just so.'

'In nature things are born. Is that not the meaning of the word?'

'Born, reborn, born again, on and on,' said Leonardo.

'And this is a circle? I mean, it had no beginning and will see no end?'

'We believe so. Though if you push me, I will admit that I do not know.'

'Where does that belief come from?' asked Ariel.

'From our elders, those who have meditated for longer than I have been alive.'

'And these live in Tibet?'

'Yes they do,' said Leonardo. 'And some of them are very old. Very old indeed. They have found the wisdom of the East to be closer to an enlightened understanding of reality, though they look to the West for complementary understandings in its scientific categories.'

One of the Brothers came in and fetched something from behind the counter, before scuttling off again.

Ariel continued. 'Can you tell me about the ceremony during the night of the storm? Natasha has told me a little more about it, but I don't think she understood exactly what you were doing.'

'Of course. How could she? But you are right to connect it with the fusion of scientific and spiritual understandings that are at the heart of what we do here. What we are. We were taking readings – static electricity levels, instances of lightning to ground, rainfall, wind strength, temperature, even sound levels – and sending each to its appropriate receptor in the four shrines, before collecting them together in the centre.'

Ariel sat in silence. 'I see,' he said. 'Or rather, I don't. That is to say, I understand the words you just said, though I am less clear on why you did those things.'

'It is a matter of the heart,' said the Abbot. 'It is more about experience than understanding. In a way, it is about encounter.'

'Encountering nature in all her power?' Ariel asked.

'*Esattamente!*' Leonardo's face lit up at his student-teacher's ready grasp of what really mattered. His intuition that Ariel might be a convert in the making was slowly becoming a conviction. But then he looked into Ariel's eyes and read something else there. No, this was a man playing along. Or, seen more kindly, a companion walking along a road with him but with no commitment to a destination. 'I think perhaps you and I are now going round in circles, no?'

'Well, that would be my point,' said Ariel. 'The view of nature you espouse seems to be a closed circle. But what if there were something beyond?'

Leonardo let the question fill the silence of the room. 'Go on,' he said at last.

'What if nature were creation?'

Leonardo frowned. 'I realise,' he said slowly, 'that many use the words interchangeably, talking about creation but meaning nothing by it. But I rather think that you are carefully using the word to imply a being or beings who created what we see.'

'Would that be a problem?' Ariel was looking at him now, and suddenly Leonardo realised that that didn't happen very often. He thought of Miranda's experience of being 'read' and looked away.

They sat in silence for a while.

'No,' said Leonardo, his thoughts now arranged. 'That would not be a problem. How could it be? If nature is creation, if a force or forces unknown caused it to exist... forces that therefore pre-empt – is that the right word? – predate, predominate over, the universe... then yes, I can see how our spiritual quest may take us there. Whether it should or not... whether it even can... I do not know.'

'But wouldn't you like to know?'

'Ah, my friend,' said the Abbot, 'you tempt me.'

'I didn't mean to.'

'No, no, I didn't mean like a devil! I mean, you lay before me something that is not just truly attractive but attractive if it were true... something alluring to a man like me, set in his ways... the possibility of a spirit world that is beyond nature, not part of it. Or are we saying, not *only* part of it?'

'I suppose so,' Ariel mused. 'It could be part of nature while still having its origins apart from it. Just as I feel that *I* am a conscious being – I don't think of my body as a conscious being.' He checked Leonardo was still with him. 'Or think of photons of light passing through water. These look like they are part of the water, but actually they come from elsewhere. Maybe the ether, your fifth element – or is it four-point-fifth? – is a gesture in that direction.'

Leonardo chuckled. If it were anyone else he would think he wasn't being taken seriously. But it didn't feel like Ariel was one to play mindless games, or mind games. 'Okay then,' he said. 'Are we saying there may be some kind of interaction? Does pure spirit interact with nature, and so become something more?'

'More? From what point of view?' said Ariel.

Leonardo laughed. 'Well, I don't know about you, my friend, but I only have my own point of view! And as one who inhabits nature – or yes, call it creation if you wish – I see the infusion of spirit as making something more. I experience the world as something more when I become aware of the spirit latent within it... whether it's coming through it, as you suggest, or simply being generated by it.'

'If spirit were something generated by nature,' said Ariel, 'that is one thing, one kind of more. But if spirit gave rise to nature?'

'I don't know about that,' said Leonardo. 'In both scenarios we have nature – matter, if you will – and spirit.'

Something was gnawing at the fringes of Ariel's mind, and he desperately wanted to uncover it. He closed his eyes. He could see shapes, and the shapes became faces, and the faces became familiar. 'I think I have it,' he said at last. 'We know that nature contains persons, but nature is not personal. Spirit is... can be... personal.'

'Ah, my friend,' said Leonardo, 'there you go begging the question again! How do we know nature is not personal?'

Ariel opened his eyes. The faces faded. 'So, what are you saying, Leonardo? That this amazing texture of trees and mountains, sky and stream, oceans and stars... is personal?'

'I believe I am, yes,' said the Abbot, 'and I thank you for helping me see more clearly what it is I believe. I believe that, while none of these things in themselves are encountered by us personally in the way you and I are interacting now, they do nevertheless have spirit. And I can interact personally with spirit.'

'I'm glad this is helping you,' said Ariel, 'and I think it is helping me. Though I cannot as yet say where it will take me.'

Another Brother appeared at the refectory door. It was Leroy. 'Sorry, sirs, I was just coming to lock up.'

'Do not worry, Brother Leroy,' said the Abbot. 'I will take care of that. I think Ariel and I have a way to go yet before retiring.' Leroy backed out of the door away from his mentor and the visitor, his pride and joy plain to see.

'Let's pursue the notion of personal encounter,' said Ariel. 'This morning I described persons as singularities, trying to evoke something of the infinitesimal about the roots of each person.'

'Yes, yes. Go on.'

'I have been thinking about the way I can read people, and I see it now more as an open and respectful encounter. And so, another way of looking at this, which may give you more clarity, is to talk of persons as subjects and everything else as objects. I encounter you as subject to subject, singularity to singularity. I may encounter you as object, but that will not be spiritual – it will be you as a body, or a name or number, some*thing* that may be useful to me, or of course may be in my way. As part of my world you are an object. In your world you are subject. But in true personal encounter, you are subject even as I am subject.'

Leonardo almost gasped, but nodded wisely instead. Before he could respond Ariel was speaking again, and it felt like a closing thrust. 'Which surely gives persons an advantage over non-persons. It's more than an additional feature to the universe, it's a whole extra dimension of being.'

'Oh, my friend,' whispered Leonardo. 'That is, if I may say so, beautiful.'

'And is it true, do you think?'

Leonardo sighed. 'Even now, ever the gentleman! I don't know if you have just said Checkmate or simply Check, but I sense you have just opened up a whole new world of ideas, and I shall have to sleep on it. But I also know I shan't get any sleep if we don't at least touch on your proposal about women in the Order. Why did you make such a proposal? What led you there? Was it simply this sequence of thought, from individuality to diversity, all persons equally different? All subjects and not just objects?'

'Yes,' said Ariel, 'it all hangs together. But to answer your first question, it was an intuition on my part. Yes I had got there by reasoning in the way I outlined this morning. But I sensed that such a vision, though it may be many arguments and possibly even many years away from reality, would nevertheless arrest you. It would catch your attention in such a way that you had to say why it could not be, or else find a way to make it reality.'

Leonardo smiled. 'Well,' he said, 'as you can imagine, I have been giving it some thought as the day has gone on. The absence of women is a longstanding tradition, both East and West. Some of it was originally practical – men were seen as more able in matters of contemplation, while women brought up children and ran households. But it was also because of sexuality, what is nowadays called heterosexuality, still the most popular way of making babies even now. I think most monastic orders realised that men could not escape sexual desire by joining brotherhoods like ours – be they Hindu, Buddhist, or Christian – but they could at least escape procreation.'

'Why would you do that?'

'Oh, I think it comes down to the avoidance of distraction.'

'And responsibility?'

'Responsibilities, for sure,' answered the Abbot. 'The spiritual quest is all.'

'But if spirit is sought in all life, and in personal encounter, why would you avoid this kind of encounter?'

'It is a choice,' said Leonardo. 'I think I am too tired right now to explain further.' He would not normally have made such an admission, certainly not to any of the Brothers, but here only utter transparency would do. 'I am afraid that the coffee's best endeavours have not been enough!'

'Of course,' said Ariel. 'Perhaps we should leave it there. But I do think that you will be helped in your thinking when you try to answer my question how women would change the community.'

'Yes, I believe I shall. I was actually grateful for the question. And you should know that, although we do not mix, Sisters are perfectly welcome in the Order, since these days they obviously do qualify as those who can meditate and work. Just as indeed women are welcome here as paying guests. Or paid-for guests!'

He got to his feet and stretched before taking the coffee pot over to the counter. 'But I realise that your proposal was that we live together under one roof, and there I see difficulties. Relationships would become complicated. We have had Brothers in relationships with female guests in the past, and indeed with male guests. And these have led either to troublesome break-ups or to the Brothers in question leaving us.'

'Distractions,' said Ariel.

'*Sì*, distractions, taking the Brother away from the journey of learning, the spiritual quest, which he had committed himself to following.'

'And he couldn't do that away from this place, or somewhere like it?' said Ariel.

'No. Not with the intensity, the focus, the singleness of purpose, all of which are enhanced by the rhythms of daily life here.'

'Are there "relationships" between the Brothers themselves, may I ask?'

'Oh for sure,' said the Abbot, 'from time to time. But these we can manage within the traditions and rhythms of our community life.'

'Removing the distracting element?'

'Reducing it, at least. But honestly, Ariel, I will go on thinking about this, and – who knows? – I may even suggest to my superiors in Tibet that we try an experimental community with both sexes. I will tell them the idea came from you!'

'They do not know me,' said Ariel.

'Ah, well now,' whispered Leonardo. 'They know many things, and when I have told them of our time together here with you as guest, I think they will treat the idea with the utmost seriousness.'

And with that he loaded the dishwasher, before together they made their way out into the night.

6

Melody woke early. She couldn't remember when she had last slept so well. She skipped down the stairs and emerged into the courtyard only slightly disappointed that she was too early for the aroma of freshly ground coffee. She carried on past the refectory, slowed down at the water shrine, playfully splashing her face with the water (with only the briefest glance over her shoulder), and then made off towards the annex at the back of the main building. When she saw Ariel wandering in from the woodland, she waved and waited for him.

'Wonderful!' she exclaimed. 'You're exactly the person I wanted to see. I wondered if you wouldn't mind extending our conversation just a teensy bit. Only there was something I wanted your opinion on, but yesterday didn't feel like the right time.'

'Of course,' he said. 'Do you want to go inside?'

'Super – it's a little chilly out here.'

They made their way along the corridor of the smaller building and into the courtyard. There was a study area there which was free. 'It's about David,' she said as they closed the door and sat down. 'And Jack. Do you think it's possible to love two people at the same time? Romantically, I mean? And is it right?'

'Well,' said Ariel, and he drew breath. 'I imagine you can answer the first question better than I can, but we'll have a look at it. What we discover as we think about it may help us with the second question.'

'Fantastic,' she said. 'I knew this was a good idea! Okay. I love Jack. That's an established fact. I don't want to pick it apart so much that I start to doubt it.'

'Sounds very sensible,' said Ariel.

'Well, yes, you know me. So, there it is, I fell in love with Jack, and he with me, and we've made sense together as a couple. We've had our ups and downs, we've never lived together in the same space for more than a few months at a time, courtesy of our jobs, but we have a place we both call home.'

'Sounds like a marriage.'

'Now you're starting to sound like my mother!' She raised her hand. 'No, sorry, you're nothing like my mother. I know that wasn't a loaded comment, not when you said it. But yes, if you like, Jack and I are a bit like a married couple. We fell for each other, we're committed to each other.'

She got up and crossed to the window. The view was not altogether different from the one in the library, where she and Natasha had talked three days before. The covered way was just starting to allow the sun to peek through, its pillars casting shadows across the glistening grass between them and the main building.

'And what about David?' Ariel prompted.

'It's different. I don't just mean he's different – *it* is different. Our relationship hasn't had any physical aspect to it. I don't even find him particularly attractive that way. I mean, he's not ugly or anything, but we became friends before... Gosh, I don't even know what I'm trying to say here.'

'You seem to be saying that you *were* friends, but now you may be more. Why do you think that is?'

'Oh, I don't know!' she whined.

'Have you told Jack that you're going to see David when we go to Geneva?'

'No,' she whispered to the window. She turned to face him. 'Oh Ariel, what am I going to do? If I tell Jack, I know he'll be mad. But if I don't, I'll feel... you know... unfaithful.'

'Why do you think Jack will be angry?'

'Because he thinks David is a bad influence on me. He hates it when I talk about faith and stuff.'

Ariel joined her at the window. 'Melody, do you think Jack thinks you're in love with David?'

She grimaced. 'I don't know,' she said thinly. 'Maybe?'

'So, from his point of view, David is a double-threat. He will influence you to believe in something he doesn't share, and he will take you away from him. Is that right?'

'Possibly,' she said, still grappling with the icy intensity of Ariel's logic. 'I really don't know what he thinks, and I hate that. But I can't get him to talk about it. And I don't know if that's because he thinks David is a romantic threat, and that I'm getting too close to him in that way, or whether he thinks he's a threat to my sanity. And if all that's not bad enough...'

'Yes?'

'There's Alice. She's a great friend. She'd be mortified if she knew I was having this conversation – even in my head, let alone out loud with somebody else!'

They stood by the window for a while. Already the dew was gone from the sunniest parts.

'Let's return to your questions,' said Ariel at last. 'First, is it possible to love two people romantically at the same time? If we define romance as a syndrome with certain feelings and actions, then it would appear the answer is yes. But if the romance leads to the sort of commitment you referred to earlier, one can see why having two such relationships might issue in a high level of inner conflict... a conflict which sooner or later may threaten the integrity of one or both relationships. Even the integrity of the person in love.'

'That's my sanity in question again, is it?' she said.

'Not in the way Jack might suppose, but in the sense of your mental health, then yes, I can see that such a romantic conflict may set up a self-contradiction in such a rational person as you – to say nothing of your intuitiveness. Put simply, you cannot give *exclusive* commitment to more than one person at a time.'

'Right,' she said, thinking out loud. 'Which is why people often leave someone for somebody else. But I don't want to leave Jack. And I'm pretty sure Alice doesn't want to leave David.'

'And David?' said Ariel? 'What do you think he wants?'

'I have no idea.'

'Perhaps you should ask him.'

'How?'

'Perhaps now is the time to be direct.'

She sighed. 'You're probably right. It will probably scare him off, but then maybe that would be for the best.'

Ariel nodded. 'It would certainly force him to face the situation.'

Just then they saw Leonardo emerge from the main building. He waved when he saw them in the window.

Melody went to the door. 'Thank you, Ariel, I just knew you'd help. Oh, I do hope you'll be around and available again after... you know... Geneva.' She had no idea what Ariel's prospects were in that place, or what was likely to happen after that, but she sensed it was going to separate him from her, at least for a while.

As she left the room it dawned on her that both her conversations with Ariel had in fact been about the same thing. Whether it was religious faith or personal relationships, what vexed her was commitment.

She exchanged a hello with Leonardo in the corridor and felt a twinge of guilt as she imagined Ariel sitting down, ready for what looked like his second appointment before breakfast.

7

Leonardo had taken to his bed in great excitement, and had just begun to find sleep when he realised that they had not discussed the crystal. It worried him that Ariel set so little store by it. Could it really be an unconnected coincidence that this strange object and this strange man had both been found on Venus? He still doubted that, and he was anxious to take what might be his last opportunity to probe Ariel on the subject.

They talked for a few moments about the value these fuller conversations were having, but with breakfast approaching Leonardo wasted no time. 'Tell me, my friend, why you are so convinced that there is a personal dimension beyond the world of matter? Or were you just provoking me?'

'I don't know,' said Ariel. 'A hunch maybe.'

'It seems to me,' Leonardo pressed, 'that there is in fact a non-personal factor in this whole business of finding you on Venus, one which many are overlooking – including yourself.'

'The crystal, you mean?'

'*Si*, the crystal. It is a mystery just like you, my friend! Tell me you have no connection with it!'

Ariel returned to the window and looked out past the main building towards the trees that formed the western border of the monastery grounds. 'I will admit, dear Abbot, that at first I was unaware of... uninterested in... this stone that is so precious to you. But Natasha has told me that it first showed signs of activity when I awoke back on the space station, and I have been thinking about it more since I glimpsed Dr Chase the day before yesterday.'

'I too,' said Leonardo quietly.

Ariel continued to gaze at the trees. 'We know that Dr Chase carried out the first tests on the object.' Leonardo noted Ariel's last word and wondered whether, even now, he was making a point. 'But we also know that it was passed to others in Geneva.' He turned to face Leonardo. 'The thing is, Jack has told me that no one actually knows where Dr Chase is right now. And I can't help feeling that in my vision he was looking down, peering at me just the way he would if I were his beloved crystal.'

Leonardo rose from his chair. 'You mean, you were looking through the crystal?'

'It may well be, yes.'

'I knew it! I knew there was a connection! Well, this is extraordinary.' He went over to Ariel and held him by his upper arms. 'You will of course report this to Jack?'

Ariel nodded.

'So now, my dear, dear friend,' he continued, releasing his grip, 'can you not see that there can be a spiritual connection between you and something made of matter?'

'My dear Abbot, have you just put me in Check?'

8

Ariel was silent during breakfast. He was still planning his next move in the debate with Leonardo, feeling that there had been some sleight of hand over the word 'spiritual' in his earlier conversation. But then, it was a slippery word. No matter.

Miranda was next up, and her sense of privilege was beginning to vie with a growing nervousness. She replayed recent events in her head, trying to see how such an opportunity had come about, but it was beyond her. Perhaps the mix of truth and falsehood she had learnt from her mentor had changed – certainly the lies seemed less frequent now – and maybe that had played a part, though she could not work out how.

When breakfast was finally over, she and Ariel left for the venue of her choice, the woods. Yesterday's breeze was gone, and the day was sunny and warm, which had put her in a plain tee shirt and shorts. She was eager to explore an area away from her somewhat inglorious entry on that stormy night a week before.

For the first ten minutes they said very little. They passed the garages and then turned right, veering off from Ariel's walk with Melody the previous day. 'I've not been to this part before,' he said.

'Me neither,' said Miranda, picking up a branch and flinging it into the heart of a thick clump of leafy undergrowth, releasing spores from the fungi that even now were springing up like a miniature forest within the forest, new life out of death and decay.

At length they came to a brave attempt at a clearing, a grassy area populated with tall, straight and quite narrow trees, which Miranda thought might be some kind of birch. They stood like statues in the stillness, granting the sunlight only limited access through the forest roof and letting it filter down to the floor. Miranda remarked on how green the light was and, examining some larger trees on the edge of the clearing, identified a beech leaf. 'I love it here,' she said. 'It's a kind of deciduous haven in all this spruce and cypress.'

'Does nature mean a lot to you?' Ariel asked.

'Uh-oh!' she replied. 'Interview commences at 09-30 hours!'

Ariel stopped. He looked bemused.

'Only joking,' she added quickly. 'And, to answer your question, I guess it does. But no more than the next person. I think we've all got it now – how fragile the environment is.'

'I meant, do you connect with it personally?'

It was Miranda's turn to look unsure.

'Sorry,' he said in response, 'blame Leonardo. We were talking about... but then, I suppose I shouldn't tell you what we were talking about. What would you like to talk about, Miranda?'

Why did the addition of her name on the end of his question place a distance between them? She hated it. She was neither his student nor his employee. But she could hardly expect to be called his friend either. She responded quickly. 'I feel a connection to you actually.'

'In what way?'

How she wished he had been at least a little fazed by what she had said! She didn't want a textbook kind of conversation about their relationship, if they even had a relationship, so she decided to go with what she had been rehearsing half the night. 'When you were speaking to all of us yesterday,' she said, idly picking up another branch, 'you described your subject as singularity. That got to me right away. We are all single in a way, even when we're in a relationship. We are ourselves, individual, that which cannot be divided.'

'I said that, yes, though I do understand that people can feel divided. Conflicted, even.'

'Are you reading me again? Sorry, didn't mean that. I guess you can't help it.' She started to wander round the clearing, gently trailing the branch in her hand against the slim trunks as she went.

'Please,' said Ariel as he followed on behind, 'let me assure you that the kind of reading you are referring to is not something I would do without your full knowledge. And participation.'

She turned to face him. 'Except... I didn't know, did I?'

He pulled up short. 'I, I... I thought we were connecting.'

'No, stupid,' she said without thinking, '*you* were connecting, and you didn't exactly knock on the door before coming in!'

'Then I misread you... in the other sense. I misread the situation.'

'You know what infuriates me?' she growled. 'You're so bloody humble!' She kicked a conveniently placed stone and promptly wished she hadn't. 'Oh, come on, mind-reader, let's face it. I can't keep anything from you!'

'I'm sure you can, if you want to.'

She squeezed out a sigh. 'Ariel! Why d'you think I'm here? I mean, I haven't got a clue why I'm here in this place, and in present company, but why do you think I leapt at the chance of talking to you?'

He looked at her, now just an arm's reach away. 'I don't know,' he stuttered.

'*Because* you can read me, of course! Because I feel like you're only the second person who's ever got me.'

Ariel sat down on a fallen tree trunk, not even bothering to ask who the first person might be. This was not what he had been expecting. The safety switch of yesterday's intellectual conversations was firmly off, and he needed to rethink.

She sat down next to him, and he looked up at the tree canopy overhead. His eye traced the branches, the twigs, the leaves. Where was their thrumming life now, their surging sap? Why couldn't he feel it? It was as though Miranda had set off a tear gas canister, and he couldn't breathe or get the perspective he needed.

But did he need it? Wasn't this still positive, this interaction with someone who touched a different side of his soul?

She was gently prodding him with the branch. 'Hey, Mr Space Man. Where've you gone?'

'I'm sorry,' he said. 'I was looking at the trees. They seem different today.' He turned to her. 'You said you wanted to talk about our singularity as persons.' He continued before she could interrupt. 'And you said that you felt a connection with me. Would you like to talk about that?'

She breathed out, then looked up at the canopy. 'You know I would.'

'Good. So would I.'

She smiled. 'That's great then! Let's walk.'

After about five more minutes they came to what must be the outer wall. It was the same as the one at the front, about seven feet high, made of stone and mortar. 'No gates to climb over this time!' she said.

There was a path in front of the wall, and they decided to turn left and follow it. With every step into unknown territory Ariel's excitement grew. He could no longer say it was the trees invigorating him, nor that it was the conversation with Miranda. The two had become as intertwined as the undergrowth which, he noticed, was far wilder in this part of the grounds.

Suddenly Miranda stopped and used her foot to scrape away some ivy and bramble from a large lump of masonry. It turned out to be an old capstone. Pulling a sleeve over her hand she tugged at the thorny undergrowth, and together they cleared the ivy from an inscription chiselled into the lower rim.

'Any good at Latin?' she asked. 'I can make out some of the letters... though they're probably not all here... IN GLORIFICANDO...? something... can't see, it's full of moss. Then it goes on GLORIA HOMINIS. Any idea what that's about. Glorifying man? I guess that goes with the place.'

'I don't know,' said Ariel. 'The thing has been discarded, so perhaps it comes from the building's first use. Might the disfigured word be "deum", D-E-U-M?'

'Could be,' she said. 'So what would that mean?'

'In glorifying God is the glory of man.'

'Ah,' she said. 'Definitely from earlier days, then.'

They walked on. The path soon veered away from the wall. As they turned back under the trees both felt it was time to go deeper. With one eye on where she was treading, Miranda held out her hand to Ariel, asking him to help her up onto a fallen branch. Carefully placing his hand on her hip, he pushed her upwards. She clambered to the top and then jumped down the other side. As she landed she turned her ankle. Almost before she knew it the ground was rising up to meet her.

It never came. She was in Ariel's arms and he was laying her gently on the mossy forest floor. She lay there for a while, motionless and speechless.

'What just happened?'

'You landed rather awkwardly, and I swept you off your feet. So to speak. Can you stand?'

She looked at him askance, her whole body trembling. He must have been closer behind her than she thought, though she couldn't see how he managed to get over the fallen branch so quickly. 'Sure,' she said. 'D'you want to give me another hand?'

He helped her onto her feet, and she took a few faltering steps but could only manage a hobble. 'This is great!' she said through gritted teeth. 'We're about as far from the Centre as we can be and now I can't walk. Jack's taken my eband, so I can't even try connecting to his. Stupid, stupid ankle!'

Ariel guided her back to the offending bough and sat her upon it. 'Here, let me take a look at it,' he said softly.

She lifted her leg, surprised to see it looking normal. 'I guess it's not swollen up yet,' she said.

'Was it painful when you put your weight on it?'

'A bit.' She relaxed and let him massage it for a while, enjoying the care and attention. She felt the rough bark on her palms as she stretched her head back and looked up at the canopy, basking in the soothing waves that emanated from her ankle, from the trees, from Ariel.

A small bird flitted from branch to branch under the forest canopy and she tracked it for a while. Then she lost it. But now she herself was lost in the twigs and the leaves, criss-crossing, interlocking, a spangled filigree ablaze with sunlight, always moving, gently rustling, dancing in the faint breeze that seemed to be passing over them way up there. The lines of the twigs became less distinct as she gazed on them. Now the light was getting stronger, the trees fuzzier, the breeze louder – more a rush of air.

She was walking in a garden. She looked down now and watched the long, flowing waves of her dress dance around her ankles as she trod barefoot on the soft earth. The dress was as green as the moss at her feet, flecked with lighter and darker hues and crossed by countless thin dark lines.

She stopped. She was safe. This was a walled garden, and her hand was in the hand of the man who tended it. She turned to look at him.

'Miranda, Miranda, wake up!' Ariel was looking down at her, concern creasing his brow. She smiled back, not wanting to move, content to stay in the garden of lights.

Ariel was still speaking. 'I think you fainted,' he said. 'You had your head right back, and I think you must have cut off the blood supply to your brain. I was too busy looking at your feet. I'm sorry.'

'What?' she said, realising she was actually flat out on the ground. 'No, please don't say you're sorry. That was...'

'Well, as long as you're all right.'

'Oh man, I have never, ever felt like this. Can we stay here a while? Come and lie next to me. It's really very comfortable.'

He looked at her as she patted the ground in a welcoming gesture. She was the same Miranda, yet there was something freer about her, easier. He had never seen her so relaxed. It was as though the guile and subterfuge had been sucked out of her. He lay down by her side and they looked up at the forest canopy together.

'Dappled,' he said.

'Sorry?'

'Dappled – it's the word I've been trying to remember as we've been walking under the trees. The forest here is a constantly shifting mix of light and shade.'

'Mmm,' she breathed. 'Sounds like life.'

'Has that been your experience?'

She loved that he didn't say her name this time. She let the question dance around like a feather in the warm air for a while. 'Well,' she said at last, 'there's been good and bad of course. But that's not it. I think I meant that it's never really been clear just how good the so-called good things are, nor how bad the bad things are. We make a judgement call, sometimes because we have to but often because we just can't resist it, and then later on we find we got it wrong. Things turn out better. Or worse.'

'Are there any examples you'd like to talk about,' he said.

'Well, Hugh obviously. For years I've seen him as the best thing that ever happened to me. Now, I'm not so sure. Then there's all this business, getting caught and thinking the whole world's gonna come crashing down, only to find that it's more together than it's ever been.'

'How so?'

'I don't know. Don't you feel it too? Isn't this just the perfect place? I mean, it's like everything in my life so far has kinda washed up on this shore. It's all here. My confusions, my fears...'

'Confusions?' he probed. 'Are things clearer now then?'

She sat up and looked down at him. 'Ariel,' she said, 'I think you're the brother I never had.'

He joined her. 'Do you mean you never had a brother, or just not one like me?'

'Ha! I certainly never had one like you! I had three brothers, a dad who kept total control, and a mother who was... quiet.'

'Not like you then?'

She pushed him playfully. 'What are you saying, Mr Space Man! No, don't answer that. I know I speak my mind. But I can hold confidences too, you know.'

'Yes, I know,' he said quietly. 'And I'm sure Mr Coates would not have employed you in the way he did if that were not the case.'

'You bet,' she said. 'But the thing about Hugh was, it was like he could really see me... who I was. He wasn't one to go for any of that "sell the image" stuff, but cut to the reality. I guess that's what made him so good at the communications business. He let people have whatever content they wanted on it, of course, because he was just the service provider. But people don't get that... that to provide a service you've really got to understand people.'

'Read them, even.'

'Hey, Mister!' She prodded him again. 'Who's getting clever then?'

He stood up, and she knew that she had to try walking again, though it was not the ankle that made her reluctant. 'It's so peaceful here.'

'It seems to me you are very peaceful,' said Ariel as he extended a hand to help her up.

'I just don't want to lose it,' she said, hauling herself up. They took a few steps together, and then she tried some on her own. 'Doesn't seem too bad,' she said, 'though I might just need to lean on you a bit.'

They trudged on, hand in hand, with Miranda leaning into him from time to time. The sun went behind a cloud.

'The light does weird things here, doesn't it?' she remarked.

'Yes, it is an ever changing mix of light and shade,' he said. 'So, tell me more about your confusions. If you'd like to.'

'Nice segue, bro,' she said. 'And if we run with the light and shade theme, then yes, it can get confusing. As I was saying, good and bad aren't always what they seem to be. And nor are people – which should be no surprise. It's that image thing again, people projecting falsely when they can't face the reality inside.'

'Is that how it's been for you?'

She stopped and turned him to face her. A bird fluttered overhead. Somewhere higher an aircraft. A light breeze sent whispers through the leaves.

'Can we do it again please?'

'Do what, Miranda?'

'You know what. I want you to read me. I'm sorry, Ariel, but I can't really talk about it. It's hard enough to give it any space at all in my head.' She looked at him intently.

'Very well.'

She was younger, a teenager. She was examining one of the few freckles on her face. As she stared into the mirror she noticed her brother creep into the room. 'Get lost, Tom!' she was saying. But he didn't. He made some comment about her misshapen face and no one wanting that, and then, before she knew it, his breath was on her neck and his hands around her waist.

Ariel fell to the ground.

'No, no, no,' she mumbled as she lost her balance and landed on top of him. 'Oh, come on, Ariel, don't do this to me! Wake up, fella!' But he didn't stir.

She let the tears fall. The sun came out but the light now seemed a mockery. The minutes went by. What to do? The clear fact that there was nothing she could do lay like a suffocating blanket over everything.

She sat against a tree and dozed. She was back in the garden, safe behind the wall, holding the hand of the gardener. Her neck was stiff, and she couldn't quite see his face. But she felt his warmth, his breath, his love.

A man was calling her name again. No, I don't want to leave. Let me stay here for ever. Please don't banish me beyond the wall. Please don't leave me.

She woke with a stiff neck, but relief flooded her when she recognised Ariel's face looking down at her, just as before. 'You look terrible,' she said.

'You don't look so good yourself.' How different it was when Ariel said those words. How totally friendly and safe. No manipulation. No exploitation.

'Ariel, I'm really, really sorry,' she said as she got to her feet. 'I'm sorry I did that to you.'

'You didn't do anything to me,' he said. 'Nothing I didn't allow to happen.'

'But–'

'No buts. Just know that I now understand.'

'Yes, I believe you do.'

They decided to give more attention to walking than to talking, and very soon they came in sight of the strange little shed that Melody had seen several days before when she had bumped into Leroy. 'Well, well,' said Miranda, 'now that's a lot of satellite dishes.'

They tried the door but got nowhere. There was a bench nearby and they both took the opportunity to sit. 'Are you okay now?' she asked.

He nodded. 'You grew up in Australia?'

'Yeah, the land of promise. The century belongs to us! So they say.'

'And Hugh?'

'My saviour!' she said with a grin. 'He spotted me straight out of college. Gave me an internship but very soon made it clear he wanted me in his entourage. Then the plane. I got my pilot's licence and before I knew it I was his personal confidante.'

'Personal?'

'No, nothing like that! Personal as in assistant, bag-carrier, driver, pilot. We just clicked, I guess. He was everything my father wasn't, able to see where I could fit in the world. And he was a man of the world, for sure! We went to every continent, and pretty soon he let me in on his secret sideline.'

'Spying, you mean.'

'He always said it was surveillance, not spying, because we didn't interfere. Hell, we didn't even do anything with most of what we learnt.'

'Would you say he was an honourable man?'

'Light and shade again, my friend, light and shade. Anyway, as the years went by and I became a citizen of the world, I came to accept myself, my sexuality, my identity.'

He looked at her. 'And is this why you wanted to talk about singularity?'

'I guess so,' she said. 'To me, identity is really important. I know it's wrapped up with gender somehow, and upbringing and all that, but I really liked what you said yesterday. It made me think that, if I dug deep enough, I'd find the real me.'

'Digging can be dangerous,' said Ariel. 'As you go down, you take some of the material with you. You can't just throw it all aside.'

'I get that,' she said. 'But still.'

'Still.'

'It's funny,' she said at length. 'They say that every atom in the human body is constantly being replaced by a new one. So are we even the same person after they've all been changed? Or have I been a new me every few years?'

'I think that is an excellent question.'

'Goodie,' she quipped.

'No, really. It's an excellent question because it shows how absurd it is to say identity is purely physical. When we say we are not who we used to be, we are not referring to this accident of molecular structure.'

'Okay,' she said, scratching her head. This was certainly not the kind of conversation she was used to, but she was determined to stay with it. She hadn't had a friend who wasn't a colleague for several years, nor had she been near academia in a while. She was beginning to think Ariel must have been some kind of professor before his amnesia, presumably the sort that might become involved in experimentation with human enhancement. She looked at him again, trying to work out how old he was, and decided to pursue that particular biological mystery.

'So, where does the aging process fit into this?' she said out loud. 'Obviously I don't stop aging just because my cells keep getting renewed. *I* don't get renewed – not even physically. Maybe that's because the cells and their atoms don't all change at once. When my liver gets damaged, or my bones broken, they don't suddenly become undamaged overnight.'

'That is true,' said Ariel, 'though livers and bones do mend, of course, given the right circumstances. But you are right about aging. It is something of a mystery. As if there's a built-in program that no one can fathom.'

'I saw a report recently from a company in the forefront of genetic research,' she said, unguarded, not caring that Ariel might realise these data had not been obtained by legitimate means. 'It said that we're getting close to understanding aging.'

'Understanding the physical process, perhaps,' he said. 'But there I go again, begging the question.'

''Scuse me?'

'Oh, it's something Leonardo said. The truth is, Miranda, there does seem to be a way of reading life that sees everything as basically physical – not just inanimate objects, but animate ones.'

'Isn't *anima* the Latin for soul? I think I read that somewhere.'

'It is indeed,' he said, almost as if he were remembering something. 'And the materialist view, as it is known, sees all life – all growth, all development, renewal, consciousness, everything – as made up of particles, whether that's in the form of matter or energy. These days you seem to have a lot more particles than the ancients did – sub-atomic ones, quantum ones – but it all boils down to the same thing: we are what we're made of. We ourselves can even be seen in terms of *quanta*, packets... single frames in a movie, with continuity even when not continuous.'

She stared at him.

'Sorry,' he said, 'thinking out loud.'

'That's okay,' she said. 'You're allowed. Do you think the important things in life are just metaphors then?'

'How can they be? When you grow bigger, you really do change. That's physical. When you grow wiser, surely the change is just as real. But no one would say it was physical.'

'They might say it depends on something physical. I mean, I can't get wiser if I don't have any brain cells.'

'That is true, Miranda, that is so definitely true.'

'Spare my blushes, sir, but did I just say something profound?'

'Absolutely,' he said. 'You have just put your finger on what it means to be *animate*. Life seems to need a body, but it cannot be identified with that body. Living things are physical, but life is not.'

'Well, I'm glad we got that cleared up!' She got to her feet.

'Cleared?' said Ariel. 'Yes, but–'

'No, don't ruin the moment,' she said. 'Come on, we need to get you back for your next session. And lunch is calling. I reckon if we follow this path, we'll eventually get back round to the Centre.'

'I bow to your sense of direction.' He stood and bowed with a great flourish, like a court servant before his queen in ancient times.

It took them another half-hour to walk back. Miranda loved every minute, safe with her new brother. She took it all in – the trees, the peace, the company – though she didn't notice she wasn't hobbling any more.

9

Lunch for Melody and Miranda was relaxed and happy. Leonardo was feeling upbeat too, if sad that he faced the end of what had to be the most extraordinary visit he had ever experienced. Jack had given up trying to squeeze information out of Melody and decided simply to enjoy her new-found sense of freedom and purpose.

Natasha came late to the table and ate little. She and Ariel left while the others were still in full flow. She chose the chapel.

They walked quietly to the chancel, and Ariel watched as Natasha moved restlessly from wall to window to wall. 'What is it?' he said.

'So many things.'

'Are you sad to be leaving?' he asked.

'No, I want to leave. This place is... not right somehow. It looks like one thing but feels like another – as if it wants to be all things to all people. Sometimes it makes me think of the convent where I grew up, and then it feels more like a Buddhist monastery.'

'Why does that bother you?'

She plonked herself down on a chair, and he sat a few feet opposite her. 'Or is there something else?' He dropped his gaze.

'There are so many things,' she repeated, almost in a whisper. 'I don't know. I felt, no I knew, that you and I had a connection. Yet now I'm just one of the guys. Was I always?' She could see no sign of an answer, so she leaned back and sighed. 'Oh well, never mind, let's get to it. I have my slot, just like everybody else, and I certainly don't want to waste it.'

'Do you remember our first proper conversation, in the meditation room?' he said, still studying the floor.

She smiled. 'Of course.'

'That was so important. Almost as important as the songs you sang on our flight from Venus – and no, I wasn't really aware at the time, and of course I didn't know you from Adam, or should I say Eve? But I realise now just how much I owe to you for such a soothing welcome back into the world.'

She stumbled through a smile into tears and then back again.

'And then, in that first proper conversation,' he continued, and now he was looking directly at her, 'you opened the door to my speaking.'

She smiled again. 'Not bad for a Russian speaking English then?'

'No,' he said, 'not bad at all. And while we covered several areas that helped me get my bearings on recent events, do you know what was even more important? I do, now. It was your love.'

She walked over to where the altar should have been and looked up at the stained-glass windows. They had that cold darkness that comes when the sun is in the wrong direction. In one window she could still make out a tree with a snake slithering down from a branch, and a man and a woman next to what appeared to be a camp fire. She took it to be a relic of former use, proof that this had been a Christian chapel, although even here something was not quite right. In the other window there was a bright rainbow over dark clouds.

She turned to face him. 'So you do know.'

'Of course.'

'Then that's all that matters,' she said. 'I can't explain it, and in fact I have no desire to. Some things are left best unexplained. Protected.'

'Like me, you mean?'

'Maybe,' she said. 'But certainly what we have, yes... sorry, I mean, what I feel for you. I don't understand it, but I'm glad you're aware of it, and I'm so glad that you–' Her voice broke off. She let out a long sigh as she half-sat on a low sill in the wall under the windows, between the tree of knowledge and the rainbow clouds. 'I'm so glad that you know it is love... that you haven't just read my thoughts and...'

'Ah, is that still bothering you?'

'Of course.' She spoke quietly, with no edge.

'Natasha, I don't know who I am. I don't even know what I am. But our bond was formative in my remaking. It wasn't anything I read in you, or even thought consciously about.'

They sat in silence for several minutes, and then he walked towards the other end of the chapel. 'It's funny how we didn't notice this part of the ceiling,' he called out. 'Even Jack only noticed it the other day. Apparently it's where the stairs go to the attic.'

Natasha welcomed the change of mood. 'Woo!' she cried spookily, 'I wonder what's in the attic!'

They both laughed a little, and he made his way back to her. They stood together now, looking up at the stained-glass windows.

'What do you make of these?' said Natasha.

'I suppose the one on the left is the Garden of Eden, and the one on the right the world after the Great Flood.'

'Yes, I suppose so. Then why leave them there after they... desecrated the place? Er, I think I mean deconsecrated.' But she wasn't sure.

Ariel peered at the one on the left. 'I think they may have adapted them a little,' he said. 'I don't think the camp fire is original in this one. And over here the rainbow looks much brighter, newer, than the rest.'

'Another mystery!' she said.

'Well, maybe not,' he said. 'If we look for the four elements–'

'Of course!' she cried. 'We now have earth and fire in the Garden! Yes, and air and water in the Flood!'

They congratulated themselves on their interpretation as they stared up at the windows.

'The tree interests me,' said Ariel at length.

'Of course it does!' she laughed.

'What? Oh, yes, me and trees. But here the tree is, we assume, the tree of the knowledge of good and evil. The tree with a serpent's bite, you might say.'

Natasha nodded. 'Actually, I've long had a fascination with that story at the beginning of the Bible. When I was young the Sisters used it... well, almost as a form of abuse. We were told it was wrong to look into things too deeply.'

'What things?'

'Anything they didn't approve of! How our bodies worked, how other people's bodies worked – especially boys'! But it didn't stop there. In one of the homes–'

'There was more than one?'

'Three orphanages, a convent and a foster home.'

'Sorry. Do go on.'

'In the convent,' she continued, 'our education consisted of how to prepare to live apart from the modern world. We were told to turn our backs on what we had learned before about the wonders of science and technology. These wonders were not so wonderful. So they said.'

'Remarkable,' said Ariel. 'And here you are, a celebrated planetary geologist and cosmonaut, not to mention mistress of the man from outer space!'

'Am I your mistress?' Her eyes flashed.

'It was a figure of speech. "Master" if you like.'

'No, no, I like mistress,' she teased, though her easy smile soon dissipated. 'I like being a woman, not just a human being. It's taken me thirty-five years to work that out, and to stop trying to be like the men I'm always competing with, but I think I've come to an understanding now. I think I can be myself and not worry about what's supposed to be feminine and what is masculine.'

'You are yourself.'

'Exactly!' she cried. 'A singular person. A singularity, I believe you called it.'

'That word does seem to have made an impact,' he said. He studied her face, the chiselled Slavic features that the press had made so much of. 'So tell me, Dr Koroleva, how did the little nunnery girl become a scientist?'

'Good question!' she said. 'I sometimes wonder. But as I think back – and I guess I'm not the only one who's been doing that just lately – I can see that it was all really a process of self-discovery. Some of that was made when one of the sisters in the convent took the trouble to notice my interests and fanned the flame. But a lot of it, I don't deny, came through rebelling against the things I was being taught.'

'Why did you rebel?'

'Oh, I don't know. I think it may have had something to do with the fact that the teachers in question were either mean or miserable. Or both!' They laughed again. 'But I always had a thirst for knowledge. Which brings us back to this tree,' she said, looking up at the window.

'Ah, but is it not the tree of moral knowledge, rather than scientific knowledge as such?'

His question seemed to hover between her and the picture. She gazed at the tree, at the serpent, and suddenly she realised it was looking at her, as if it were offering her an invitation. 'Do you want to know?' it whispered.

'Do I want to know what?'

She didn't realise she had spoken out loud. Ariel looked across at her, checking that the question had not been directed towards him. He followed her gaze to the window, to the picture, to the tree. Immediately he decided to follow an impulse to break into whatever conversation was going on. 'Tell me, Natasha. Do you see your scientific training as a world apart from your childhood education? I mean, do you see them as different paths? Or is the pursuit of all knowledge made on the same path?'

'What?' She turned and stared at him almost as if she'd forgotten he was there. 'Knowledge is knowledge,' she said, 'unless we say there are separate forms of knowledge. I don't know if that's true – it may be. But what I do know is that I still have what was good and valuable from my childhood in here,' she pointed to her heart, 'and I've never let the atheism in the scientific world totally root that out.'

'Why would you?' he said. 'After all, it's not like you're one to go along with the crowd, is it?'

'No,' she smiled, 'it really isn't.' She turned from the window, the spell broken. 'Come on,' she said suddenly, 'I'm getting a sore neck looking up at this window so close. Let's go sit down.'

They made their way to a row of chairs about half-way down the chapel. 'Okay,' she said as they sat down together, 'you're right of course. It's specifically called the tree of the knowledge of good and evil, not "knowledge" as such. You clearly know your Bible.'

'Apparently so, yes. Although it took a while to find it here. I eventually found one in the library, along with other sacred writings.'

'Ah well,' she mused, 'it's just as well the story of Eden comes at the beginning of the book – though I know you read fast. Amazingly fast.'

'Yes, it does seem to be one of my gifts. Though I had not read very far into it before I had my talk with Melody yesterday.'

'Right. So, if you were teaching at my convent—'

'Unlikely.'

'I know. But if you were, what would you tell a teenager with a hunger for knowledge as well as experience?'

Ariel leaned back a little. 'I think I'd want to talk about innocence.'

'Whoa,' she breathed. 'Good luck with that in a classroom of teenage girls!'

'I thought it was a convent school.'

She looked at him, wondering if she'd just seen proof that he really did come from another planet. She let it pass.

'If I think about the trees where I was walking earlier,' he said, 'they positively surge with life.' He glanced towards the stained-glass window. 'I wonder, why do you think it is a tree?'

'Because it bears a fruit, the infamous apple,' she answered.

'True,' he said. 'And this fruit brings death, we are told. Whereas the tree of life shields us from death, brings life everlasting.'

Natasha shook her head. 'It's always been a mystery to me, why to know good from evil should be the antithesis of life. I still don't get it.'

'Well now,' he said, 'the version I was reading the other day doesn't talk about knowing good *from* evil, but knowing both good *and* evil.'

Natasha thought it unlikely that even Ariel could remember that kind of detail unless the story was already known to him. 'Well, that's true,' she said, 'but surely it comes down to the same thing. If I know them, I know them apart. And surely it's good to know what good is – if you see what I mean.' She wondered if his other conversations had been this complicated. Melody, Leonardo and Miranda had all come out happy. She wasn't sure where this was going to take her.

They tried to study the windows afresh from their greater distance, but with the approaching evening they were growing even darker. 'The sun's going down behind the trees,' she said, 'and the angle's all wrong for seeing the pictures from here.'

'Fascinating,' he said, 'how the trees outside are masking the tree in the window.'

Natasha sprang to her feet. 'Perhaps that's it!' she said. 'Perhaps the tree of life provides an antidote to the tree of knowledge.' She sat down again when Ariel made no immediate reply.

'The thing is,' he said eventually, 'the tree of life is apparently still available to them after they have tasted the fruit of moral knowledge. If you remember, there are fearsome creatures and a flaming sword posted to keep them from getting to it.'

'There's our fire then,' she said. 'Not so much a camp fire, but a flaming sword. A bit different!'

'Yes, and possibly flaming creatures. Where there are cherubim there are often seraphim, those who burn with the celestial flame.'

She gave him a sideways glance. 'It's funny,' she said. 'Cherubs were always such sweet little fellows in the pictures I was shown as a girl. It sounds like most of their power has been drained out of them.'

'A bit like that camp fire, then,' said Ariel. 'In the original story the fire stood as a barrier against humanity, not warming their feet!'

Natasha was already projecting some text from her eband onto the back of the chair in front of her.

'I thought there was no signal here,' said Ariel.

'There isn't,' she said. 'I have the Bible on the memory.' She still managed to surprise him. 'Here it is,' she was saying. 'The man has become like one of us by knowing good and evil.' She paused. 'One of us?'

Ariel's response caught her off guard, as suddenly he grasped the chair in front of him. It seemed to him that the whole chapel was collapsing. The stained-glass window was rushing towards him, the serpent stretching itself out, eyes glinting in the firelight, mouth opening, tongue flicking.

'Ariel? Ariel, are you all right?' Natasha's arm was round his shoulders, and he let himself fall into her. She laid his head on her lap and gently stroked his hair. She was back on the Endeavour, holding him, soothing him. She listened to his breathing till it became calm. Finally he sat up.

'Was it something I said?' she asked.

'Something you read, I think.'

'Have you remembered something?'

'I don't know. Not remembered as such, but... something's tapping on my memory, like a fish under the ice. I just can't quite see what it is.'

'Well, maybe you will. Don't force it. We can change the subject if you like.'

'No,' he said. 'This is good.'

'All right,' she said hesitantly. 'If you're happy, I'm happy.'

They talked more about trees. Natasha was convinced this was the most positive part of their conversation so far. He tried again to express the upward surge of life in them, and how he felt it in himself. He expressed his delight in the way the water of life rose up through the trunks, the branches, the twigs, into the veins of the leaves, shading those fortunate enough to be below them. 'And not just shading them from light and heat,' he said, 'but actively cooling them with the water they hold in their leaves.'

Natasha was about to compare this with the trees of life and knowledge when she stopped herself. She didn't want to risk another seizure, or whatever it was. But then, perhaps it would help him to unlock whatever was eluding him.

'Don't worry,' he said. 'It's all right. We can talk about the trees in paradise. I can see it too. The tree of life brings coolness and shade to those who have acquired the knowledge of good and evil. At least, it could do if it were made accessible.'

She didn't care now if he was reading her mind or if this was just them thinking along the same lines. What did it matter? 'Okay,' she said, 'let's take the text on its own terms. What is it telling us? We need Melody here. She's the one with the degree in literature, not to mention her thing about the Bible. Not that I can work out what she actually believes.'

He made no comment.

'So,' she said, 'humanity tastes the fruit of moral knowledge, as you call it. We get to see good and evil. We become aware, no longer innocent.'

'Those who have done what they were told not to do,' said Ariel. 'And I suppose that is a new kind of knowledge. Evil is known on the inside, not just as some outside threat.'

'Right,' she said. 'And yet that fact doesn't appear to disqualify us from living for ever – not in the story. It's as though there was a danger that Adam and Eve might carry on living as if nothing had happened.'

'But something had happened.'

'Right again,' she said. 'But it seems we need God to make sure we really understand. And to ensure that human disobedience is actually punished.'

'Punished and forgiven,' Ariel whispered. She barely heard it, but it stopped her in her tracks. Maybe she could understand the forgiveness better if she understood why the original disobedience needed to be punished in the first place.

'Leaving Eden,' she mused. 'In a way, going into space is a bit like that. As soon as you leave Earth's atmosphere you say goodbye to all the life and... and the order that there is on this planet... still... even now, with the climate crisis.'

A door opened. One of the Brothers came in, saw them, said '*Scusi*' and turned around and went out again. Natasha laughed. 'I think they'll be glad to get their curious monastery back again, don't you?'

He nodded, and they started to wander some more. Natasha saw again the cross that looked more like a plus sign, realising this time that that was exactly what it was, a fact confirmed by a nearby line that now revealed itself as an embellished minus sign. Yin and yang? She could see no proper crosses anywhere.

They carried on walking down the side of the chapel, looking at the depictions of nature in the windows, till at last they came to the door that linked to Leonardo's office. 'I know!' she said suddenly, looking up at the lower ceiling now directly above them. 'Why don't we go and see what's in that attic?'

He looked at her askance. 'What's this?' he said. 'Is this the naughty girl from the nunnery starting to surface?'

'Maybe!' Her eyes flashed. 'What, are you scared?'

'We don't have permission.'

'Didn't Leonardo say we had the free run of the place?'

'Natasha,' he said in a mock warning tone, 'you're not the first person to take that approach, you know.'

'Oh, and which approach might that be?' She blinked several times.

'You know, "Did he not say...?"'

'Oh,' she said after a moment's thought about the passage in Genesis they had been reading. 'Well, never mind. Last time I looked,

Leonardo wasn't God.' Her face began to implore.

'Very well,' he said. 'After you.'

He couldn't help feeling like someone who was following just when he should be leading.

10

The dinner table was alive with conversation once more. Natasha and Ariel arrived to find Jack, Melody and Miranda in full flow. No one asked them how they had got on, as that would have broken the unspoken protocol that had quickly formed, but Jack was relieved to see the spark back in Natasha's eyes. 'Sorry we're late,' she said as she bounced onto her chair. She looked around the room with mock intrigue, as if looking for spies. But apart from Brother Leroy who seemed to be on counter duty, they were the only ones in the room. 'Actually,' she continued in hushed tones, 'we've just been up to the attic.'

Everyone stopped talking and Jacked turned to her.

'Don't worry,' she said. 'It was locked.'

Jack's relief was matched only by his disappointment. It would have been interesting to know what was up there, and an unauthorised visit by one of the crew might have done the job. He thought about making a comment but noticed Ariel shake his head slightly, and soon they were discussing the relative merits of scientific knowledge and artistic insight. A few minutes later Jack noticed Leonardo emerge through the kitchen door behind the counter and signalled an invitation for him to join them.

'Are you sure?' said Leonardo as he sat down next to Melody. 'I don't want to interrupt your final dinner here.'

'Of course we're sure,' said Melody. 'We're all going to miss you – you've been an amazing host.' She leant towards him and lowered her voice. 'Let's face it, this is your doing. Everyone's so free with each other because of you. It's not just the space you've given us, but your own input too.'

The wine flowed and the food diminished. As Melody and Miranda persuaded Natasha to show them round the bright, starry sky outside 'one last time', and Ariel retired to his room 'for one last read', Leonardo told Leroy to bring a bottle of whisky. 'For you and me, Jack,' he said. 'One for the road, I believe they say.'

They adjourned, Leonardo with bottle and glasses in hand, to the lounge next door. Jack was delighted to see a fire burning in the grate. It was hardly required for the slight evening chill, but just right for a relaxed conversation. Even so, when Leonardo offered him a third glass, Jack declined. 'Gotta rise early tomorrow,' he said. 'And I'll need all my wits about me in Geneva.'

'*Ah si*. About that,' said Leonardo. 'Jack, I realise that my role in this continuing adventure of yours is now almost over. Yet I would consider it an immense favour if you were to update me some time on your progress in Geneva.'

'Well now,' said Jack, holding up his glass to the fire and peering through the last mouthful of amber nectar, 'you have been an "amazing host", as Melody rightly said, and we're certainly grateful to you. I'll see what I can do – though I'd have thought that Constance would keep you apprised.'

'She probably will,' he said, 'but you know how it is.'

Jack knocked back the contents of his glass and got to his feet. He still didn't really understand the relationship between Constance Bridlington and the strange monk. Maybe it didn't matter. Maybe it was just water running under the bridge, soon to be out of sight and forgotten. But he couldn't help feeling that their stay here had come about through forces more powerful than the World Space Agency. He just didn't know who they were. His colleagues in British Intelligence had been late filling him in, and doubtless there was more they were not telling him.

He bade Leonardo good night and pulled himself away from the welcoming hearth. Taking the nearest staircase, he came out onto the landing opposite Ariel's room. He knocked.

'Sorry to disturb you,' he said when Ariel appeared. 'I know you're reading. But I think we should probably go over a few things before we get drawn into meetings and politics and God-knows-what.'

'Yes, I suppose he does,' said Ariel.

'What? Oh. God. Not you as well! What is it with this place?'

'Jack, I hardly think I'd find that kind of belief here now, would I? You know, the type with a personal, all-knowing God.'

'No, I suppose not. But honestly, Ariel, what do you make of this place?'

'It is curious,' said Ariel.

They talked a while about the Abbot and Bridlington, the unusual angle that the Temple of the Four Elements had on global cooling, the military and Petersen, the crystal and Ryan, and what they might be stepping into in Geneva, although Jack had to admit that, even there, he wouldn't really know the rules of the game. Having Ariel prepared was the best he could hope for.

For his part, Ariel was relieved Jack did not ask for details from the conversations he'd had, not even the one with Melody. The rendezvous with David would remain a secret for now.

'So has this been of any use?' Jack asked. 'Has any of it really helped you?'

'Helped me? Why yes, of course. Helped me remember? Not exactly, but even then, I think it's been positive. I feel that things are falling into place. I just can't quite see what they are yet.'

'Aye well, that's got to be something,' said Jack with a sigh, and he went to the door.

'Jack.'

'Yes?'

'There was something else. When Natasha and I went up to the attic earlier on, I sensed something.'

'You *sensed* something?'

'Yes. The thing is, the door was locked, as Natasha said. But I have discovered that this needn't be a problem for me, if you get my meaning. Yet I felt resistance.'

'What? You couldn't open it?'

'I decided not to try.'

'Right...' Jack wasn't sure where this was going.

'I was just wondering... you know... whether perhaps you and I should go and take a look.'

Jack smiled. 'Well, I have to admit that I've been intrigued about the attic ever since Leonardo brushed it aside as of no interest. And when you said it was locked, well, I suppose that just made me more curious. But I don't know... we've got an early start–'

'That's absolutely fine,' said Ariel. 'If it's locked, it must be for a reason.'

'Probably storage.'

'Yes,' said Ariel. 'Storage that made me feel uneasy.'

'Oh, come on then!'

They made their way past other rooms along the front of the building, all the way to the door at the end of the corridor. It led to a set of narrow, winding steps. Jack went first, deciding he had better take responsibility should they encounter one of the Brothers at any point. The stairway rose steeply and turned before they came to an old oak door. It was dimly lit by an emergency exit sign that pointed back down the stairs.

Jack tried the handle. It didn't turn. 'That's funny,' he whispered. 'You'd expect an old door like this to be locked by a key or card, and you'd also expect it to rattle a bit when you tried it. But this door is sealed.'

Ariel recalled the shed with the satellite dishes. 'But that's not so unusual here,' he said. 'There do seem to be some very sophisticated locking mechanisms.'

'Aye, and if that's the case, it's probably alarmed as well.'

'What do you want to do?' said Ariel.

'Oh, blast it,' said Jack. 'We've got this far. And we're out of here in the morning anyway. Go on – do whatever it is you do.' He backed away from the door.

'The thing is,' said Ariel, 'I don't really know how I do what I do! Still, here goes.'

He took hold of the handle and closed his eyes. He brought to mind the trees outside the meditation room when he had somehow opened the patio door and collapsed outside. The trees had been surging with life.

He turned the handle.

'Do you want to know?'

He stepped back. 'What do you mean, Jack?'

'I didn't say anything. Did you hear someone? I think we'd best leave this if there's someone in there. I really don't have the authority to go poking around.'

Ariel approached the door again, deciding not to touch it. Where had the question come from? It reminded him of something. Something recent. What was it? Then in his mind's eye he saw Natasha gazing up at the stained-glass window and its tree. And its serpent.

The door moved. No, it wasn't the door, it was everything. He put his hands out, trying to grab hold of the door, the wall, anything.

'Whoa there, my friend!' Jack steadied him. 'Are you okay?'

'Just a little dizzy. Sorry, Jack.'

'Never you worry,' said Jack. 'I think we'll call it a night. Come on.'

They squeezed their way down the narrow stairs together. This particular mystery would have to wait for another day.

11

Very early in the morning, while it was still dark, Ariel left his room for a last walk among the trees. The clouds were thick and dark, the ground moist, the air chill. How he missed the fourth element now!

And yet there was an electricity in the air. Another storm brewing perhaps. He made his way to the observatory and sat on the top step, letting the cold and damp envelop him. He breathed in deeply. A bonfire was smouldering somewhere nearby.

This place seemed so familiar. Was that simply because he had spent most of his waking life since Venus here, or was it something deeper, something about being on the earth, under the sky and trees? Even the electricity in the air stabbed at his recalcitrant memory.

He stood up and stretched. He seemed to ache more these days. More than when? More than on the space station, for sure, but then he was half asleep most of that time. But there was more to it than that. Ever since they had arrived he had begun to feel more solid, as if weighed down by something more than gravity. And hadn't he felt the cold more this morning? Was that simply the advancing year, or was something happening to him?

A rustling in the distance interrupted his thoughts, all the more curious as there was no wind. He walked round the side of the observatory, guided to a clearing by a pillar of smoke. There in the middle was a pile of smouldering leaves, close to which stood what surely had to be the monastery's unofficial gardener. His back was turned, so Ariel waited quietly and watched.

Leroy was standing very still. Was he feeling a connection between the sky above his head and the earth beneath his feet? Or perhaps he himself was the connection. Every few seconds his head made the slightest of movements as his gaze alighted on various small details in the clearing before him. Here was a leaf, well on in the process of decay. There was a mushroom piercing the leaf mould on the forest floor. And now a beetle scurried away from the fire. Leroy breathed in deeply, letting the sight and the sound, the scent and the taste, of the forest around him evict his busy thoughts, claiming for themselves the territory in his mind that was reserved for reflection. Thus might he gain wisdom.

He felt located, resting and delighting in the single perspective of a single person in a single place. Wasn't that something to do with what Ariel had meant by singularity? Surely he could enjoy the whole world through this one place. Right now he was passive, reflective. As the day wore on he would actively care for this world-within-a-world, defending creaturely habitats and tending to the endangered plant species that had been carefully planted here in this temple among the elements.

He turned back to the pile of leaves. Ariel saw his cue and made an obvious entrance into the clearing. 'Good morning, Brother Leroy!' he called, his voice quickly absorbed by the morning mist.

'Oh – hello, sir. I didn't see you there.'

'Ariel. My name is Ariel. I wondered whether we would meet eventually. Would you care to join me? I thought I might sit on the observatory steps and watch the dawn.'

'It will rise behind you,' said Leroy, 'but I suppose that doesn't matter. The sun's rays extend everywhere, no matter where it is in the sky.'

'So they do,' said Ariel.

They made their way to the front of the observatory and sat down together.

'I, I've hoped for this for quite a while now, you know.'

'Oh?' said Ariel. 'For what, precisely?'

'The chance to talk with you. You know, really talk.'

'Well,' said Ariel cheerily, 'here we are now, and I don't think we're likely to be interrupted.'

For the next hour, as the light grew and the birds began to sing, they talked about the trees, and the Elemental Retreat Centre, and Leroy's hopes which, he said, felt as though they were going to be suffocated by the questions in his head. They walked around the observatory a few times, before coming back to the steps and watching the rosy touch of dawn.

'I know who you are,' said Leroy at last, as if this pronouncement had been eating its way out of him.

'Well!' said Ariel, and he laughed. 'Then why didn't you speak up before? Because, if that is true, then you know something no one else does!'

Leroy looked down at his feet. 'No, sorry, I didn't mean anything like that. But I do know what the others know.'

'Oh?'

'Yes, you've come to us from outer space, and you're made of something indestructible. Or almost... I expect there's something that can harm you, but we certainly can't.' He swallowed quickly. 'Not that we want to, of course! Well, the military do – that man who came here clearly had evil intentions. Still has, presumably.'

'If I'm from outer space,' said Ariel when Leroy has stopped for breath, 'what am I doing here? And why can I speak English as well as an Englishman like you?'

'Well, you've clearly been on this planet before,' said Leroy, as if that were a more reasonable explanation than the idea that Ariel might himself be from England. 'You're here this time because we brought you here, didn't we? From Venus. I expect your friends are looking for you as we speak.'

'Extraordinary,' said Ariel.

'Sorry,' said Leroy, 'I didn't mean to show off. I just see things, and hear things... you know, while I'm working.'

'That's quite all right,' said Ariel. 'Your tasks seem to take you all over the place.'

Leroy held still, but inside he was abuzz with the knowledge that he had been noticed, and by the spaceman of all people. 'That lady who came with you,' he said. 'The one from Russia. She's nice.'

'Yes, she is.'

'She said they were all trying to help you remember. Why do you think you have amnesia?'

Ariel smiled. This might be an unscheduled meeting, but it was the first time someone was asking the questions that were critical to him. He decided to run with it. After all, what harm could it do? And Leroy had the advantage of being totally outside the situation. 'Well,' he said at last, 'I think I was involved in a battle with my company.'

'Where?' said Leroy.

'On Venus, I suppose. Or nearby.' That last idea sent a shiver down his already cold back. Nearby? Had he crash-landed on Venus? He chased the thought as far as he could, but it didn't take him beyond the now familiar memory of falling from a great height.

Leroy left the spaceman to his thoughts for a while, until he thought he ought to say something. 'Have you come here to help us?

I mean, the human race. We're so dreadfully alone on this planet, and we have rather made a mess of it. We've even got weapons pointing at ourselves from space!'

Not for the first time Ariel was unready for the new train of thought set off by the underestimated monk. 'Alone, you say? In what way are you alone?'

'Well,' said Leroy, 'we're the only species in the world that understands what a mess the environment is in. We know we're one of the main causes, yet we can't seem to sort it out. Isn't that why we went to Venus when we had the chance? I mean, everybody's trying to find a way to bring the global temperature down, and when we detected that dramatic drop on Venus, well, we just had to investigate. And so I thought, you know, maybe you came to rendezvous with us. Tell us how to care for our world, how to get on with all the other species we share Earth with.'

'Maybe!' said Ariel, finding Leroy's optimism infectious. 'Tell me, Leroy, have you always been interested in outer space?'

'Oh yes,' he beamed. 'I suppose it helped being born in the middle of the century, when SETI overcame the last of the scoffers and attracted the kind of funding that showed we meant business.'

'SETI...' said Ariel. 'That's the Search for Extra Terrestrial Intelligence, yes?'

'That's right,' said Leroy. 'Finally we have a half-decent system where we can channel our, our longing.' He said this last word with such force that Ariel looked afresh at the young man. And this time Leroy met his gaze.

Ariel saw the yearning. He felt it – the desperate desire to meet another mind at least as rational as his own. To find meaning in relationship. To accept differences – not just human ones, but across all species. To end exploitation. To extend exploration. It all came tumbling out of Leroy's eyes and into Ariel's mind.

After a few minutes they both looked away. 'Thank you, Leroy. Thank you for letting me see something I had not really understood before.'

Leroy extended his hand and gleefully shook the hand of the man who, just possibly, had come to save the planet.

Ariel set off for the monastery. As Leroy walked back to his bonfire, he turned one last time and called out, 'I hope your friends find you!'

12

Breakfast was muted that morning and mostly consisted of coffee and water. Not even the night's dreams stimulated much discussion. Less than an hour later, with packed bags loaded, Natasha, Melody, Miranda and Ariel stood by the car, failing miserably to get any kind of conversation going. Mercifully Jack arrived with Leonardo after just a few minutes.

'Here we are then,' said Jack. 'It's going to be a bit of a squeeze in the back, but we've only got to get to the airport. And we'll be quicker than when we first arrived as we're leaving by the front door this time.'

They all looked in Leonardo's direction, as if he might give them some kind of blessing. 'Let me say *ciao*, my friends, not goodbye. I hope that it will not be long before we meet again.'

Jack asked Ariel to join him in the front, while Melody and Natasha did their best to accommodate Miranda plus bags in between them.

As they drove down the drive and through the front gate, Leonardo waved and turned back towards the building. 'Ah, Brother Leroy,' he said, seeing the young man emerge from the trees. 'Come and help me in my office, will you? We have a lot of bookings to reinstate.'

PART TWO

THROUGH MANY DANGERS

Ein Baum spricht: in mir ist ein Kern, ein Funke, ein Gedanke verborgen, ich bin Leben vom ewigen Leben.

Hermann Hesse, Wanderung

A tree speaks: in me there is hidden a kernel, a spark, a thought – I am life from eternal life.

Chapter 19

Review

1

Geneva was busy. They had been fast-tracked through the airport, but Melody still felt the sheer weight of humanity crowding around her, and she could see the others felt the same. Montagnola had been a deep experience and a shared one, and it lingered still, its tranquillity not going willingly.

Although Jack had been in the city once during their stay, he felt more harassed this time. He had already put Miranda on a flight to London, escorted by Darlene Piper who would doubtless be questioning her before giving her back to Hugh Coates. Necessity made her goodbye a brief affair, which was surely for the best. She knew as well as anyone that the time she had been given with Ariel was a privilege she could not possibly have hoped for. Jack began to ask himself why he had allowed it, self-interrogation being his customary exercise prior to meeting with Constance. He decided it was Petersen's fault. His failed attack had served only to strengthen the bond that had already been forming between them all.

Their route to the World Space Agency building gave Ariel his first clear sight of mountains from the ground. As he sat in the back of the chauffeur-driven car he gazed upon their pin-sharp sturdiness. It was as if they were guarding the city and, when Melody described the alpine flowers that grew at their feet, he smiled at the combination of delicacy and strength this evoked in his mind. Something about that resonated with him. 'Wait till you see the lake,' Melody said, warming to her new role as guide. But this was no time for touring, and all too soon they arrived at the UN building.

Jack could not help thinking how strange it was to see Ariel in these new surroundings, dressed, like the rest of them, in smart-casual wear, no longer the universally acknowledged centre of attention. And while Jack was pleased that things were moving on, he felt uneasy, troubled by the growing realisation that he could no longer protect Ariel. Even Constance was bound to lose her grip as this new stage in the proceedings began.

They cleared security in the foyer, to be met immediately by Petroc, who looked like he'd been waiting in unbroken anxiety since the moment they had called to say they had arrived at the airport. 'Commander Forrester, welcome back. And Miss Grantley James.' Jack missed his cue to introduce Natasha and Ariel, so Melody obliged. Petroc was the first person for a long time to be introduced to Ariel, the man everyone wanted to meet, so Melody was curious that the young man seemed crestfallen. She chatted to him as they walked to the lift and soon discovered that he had been hoping to meet Miranda as well. 'Oh, er, you'd best talk to Jack about that.' Automatically she made an eband note of his curious interest.

As they entered the WSA suite and passed Petroc's office, Ariel slowed down, apparently fascinated by the soft, silent carpet under his feet. They came at last to the Director's office, and Jack led them to the conference table near the window. Constance was seated behind her desk, but once she had dismissed Petroc she went to the far end of the table and addressed them. The floral house jacket had gone, replaced by a wide-lapelled, light brown skirt suit. Lest anyone should think she was not ready for business.

'Ladies, gentlemen, welcome. I want you to know that I have been kept fully apprised of your progress in Montagnola, and that I appreciate the efforts you have all undertaken to bring some clarity to the extraordinary situation we find ourselves in. For our part here in Geneva, you will be glad to know we have been able to keep the shutters down. As far as we know, there was only one journalist who started to look into the Centre at Montagnola, and he was neutralised.'

'Ouch!' said Melody. 'What does that mean? Would I know him?'

'Nothing quite as unpleasant as it sounds, Miss James,' said Constance. 'A few false trails and he was soon looking in far more interesting directions, all ultimately unfruitful. I'm afraid I don't recall his name.'

Melody doubted that last point, but as Constance continued her summary she warmed to this formidable woman, surprised to find in her a silent member of the team. She really did seem to be on Ariel's side. Whether she truly appreciated the bond that had been forged in Montagnola, and especially that it was no longer confined to Aphrodite mission members, Melody could not tell. But she liked her.

A period of general discussion followed. The coffee had less about it than the refectory's brew which had become such a settling constant over the previous eleven days, but it was not long before they were all at ease again. Jack had originally wondered why Constance had chosen to meet Ariel in a group setting, but he soon saw the wisdom in her decision. She didn't want to be just one more face grilling him from the other side of the table.

'Okay, everyone,' said Constance, 'let's break for half an hour. Miss Grantley James, I hope you have something you can do while you're here.'

'Absolutely,' Melody replied. 'I'm looking forward to playing the tourist.'

'Jolly good,' said Constance. 'We've booked you into the same hotel as the others. Petroc will give you the details. Jack, Natasha,

Ariel – we'll be meeting with Jim and Ryan shortly, when I'd also like you to meet Selena Chandra. Then, after a light lunch, we get to it.'

'Ryan?' Jack's surprise was echoed by the others.

'Yes,' said Constance. 'Sorry I didn't tell you, but it was only yesterday he walked in here. You'll hear more later.'

'But is he all right?' Jack pressed.

'Yes. He's shaken, and he's not happy, but physically he's okay. Why? What is it you know and have not told me?'

'Ah, well,' said Jack, 'it looks like we've all got some catching up to do.'

'Very well,' she said with a passing frown. 'That is why we're here, after all.'

2

After an inconsequential conversation about travel and accommodation in Constance's office Jack, Natasha and Ariel moved to a large conference room for their next meeting, where they were greeted by a stunning view of the lake and mountains. The large oval table was set out for ten people, so Jack guessed it must be the venue for the formal review later on. Jim, dressed in his air force uniform, gave him a cool handshake but did at least manage a 'Hi, buddy'. Ryan, dressed in a check shirt and jeans, raised a hand from the corner. He looked worn out, an impression made all the stronger by the bandage around his head. 'Don't worry,' he said. 'It looks worse than it is. It's holding a cool-pack in place.'

An elegantly dressed Indian woman came over to them and held her hand out to Ariel. 'Hello,' she said. 'I'm Selena Chandra.'

'And I am Ariel.'

Jack appreciated the overture of friendliness, especially one aimed so precisely. He sat down, joined by Ariel on one side and Natasha on the other. For several long moments the conversation went in fits and starts, until Selena got up and left the room to find Ms Bridlington.

Jack broke the uneasy silence. 'So, Ryan, what's the story? Did you get mugged?'

'I sure did,' he shot back. 'I had my crystal taken, then I found it, then I got this.' He pointed to his head wound.

'What have I missed?' said Jack. 'I don't remember it being *your* crystal.'

'Well, how are we all getting along?' Constance breezed into the room, followed by a silent Selena. 'You know, don't you my friends, that you are all going to have to meet with a psychologist? I'm not happy about this... this whatever-it-is going on between you. But worse than that, I don't understand it.' She raised her hand before anyone could either protest or explain. 'But that must wait. As you know, we are being joined this afternoon by Beth Griffiths from High Command, possibly plus one of her two senior associates. We need to be ready. Now I'm not suggesting for a moment that we concoct a story for them, even if we could. No, the purpose of the meeting will be to put all our cards on the table and find out just what we know.

'Which brings me to Selena here. She is head of Research and Development at Box Industries. That's right, the very company that gave us the space suits that kept you all alive on Venus.'

'Not all of us.' Jim was looking at Ariel.

Constance responded without missing a beat. She asked Jim to bear in mind that finding out what Ariel's suit was made of, and about the crystal, and who Ariel was working for, were the shared goals of everyone in the room. She went on to explain the roles played thus far by Box Industries and Infostructure. She said nothing of what Selena had just told her outside the room, that Conway was currently talking to some old friends involved in bio-engineering, shamelessly pumping them for information. That could wait. Right now it sounded not unlike one of the dead-ends she had already fed to the unnamed journalist.

As Constance continued to speak and answer specific questions, Ariel turned his gaze to Jack's erstwhile friend and colleague, Jim.

They locked eyes for a while, until Ariel looked away, deciding that was the polite thing to do. He looked around the room. There was a large green plant in the corner, and through the windows he could see across the lake to the tree-clad mountains beyond. He decided to settle his gaze there, only dimly aware of the discussion going on around him. He tuned back in when Ryan spoke about his ordeal in the secret laboratory on the outskirts of the city, though he took his lead from Jack who remained quiet about Ariel's latest episode. For her part Constance upbraided Ryan for going off on his own, thereby losing her the moral high ground in her argument with High Command about their botched kidnap attempt.

'How do we know it was them?' Jim asked. 'It's just the sort of thing the Israelis might do, or the Saudis.'

'Because I was there!' said Jack before Constance could answer. 'It was Petersen. And I'd like to see them deny it!'

'They won't deny it,' said Constance calmly. 'I've already spoken with Beth. She has an explanation.'

'Well, I look forward to that,' said Jack.

'That's what this afternoon is all about,' she answered with customary calm. 'But first, Jack, I would very much appreciate it if you could give us a summary of the time you've had with Ariel these past eleven days. Although it's not been possible to have everyone there, I think it only fair that the rest of the crew come up to speed.'

Natasha wondered how Jack would accomplish anything like a summary without making Jim and Ryan feel they had missed out on something special, but in the event that was not an issue. He glossed over the more in-depth conversations they had enjoyed with Ariel, something she soon realised was wise since two of those involved were the interlopers Melody and Miranda, red rags to these particular bulls. Instead Jack dwelt on the more formal questioning of Ariel, the calming effect of the place and the spats with Petersen. Finally he came to the part they were clearly impatient to hear, which up to now had been little more than hints in the occasional update from Constance.

'Of course, there are the anomalies we've discovered in Ariel, even without knowing who he is. In order these are, if I'm not mistaken, the ability to resist wounding, to open unlocked doors, read minds and return the force of heavy blows. Would that cover it, do you think, Natasha?'

'I think so,' she said with a grin. 'Unless you want to add his ability to understand people and help them understand themselves.'

Ryan grunted. 'Comes from being a mind-reader, I guess. Though I'd really like to see that before I know what I think.'

'That's not what I meant,' said Natasha with a frown. 'He is a sympathetic soul.'

'Well, I'm glad you've found a new buddy at last,' said Ryan.

'Okay, guys,' said Jack. 'Enough. Ryan, it's not just Natasha we're talking about here. Several of us have been, shall we say, enriched by Ariel's manner.'

He hesitated, wondering whether to mention Leonardo. Constance saw her cue and got to her feet. 'Very well,' she said. 'I think that will have to do for now. I thought we could all eat in the canteen today. Meeting starts at two o'clock sharp.'

And with that she marched out, quickly followed by Jim and Ryan.

Selena looked stunned. 'Don't worry,' said Jack. 'We all love each other really.'

'Well,' she said, 'I must admit I was beginning to wonder how on earth you managed to carry out the mission to Venus. I thought astronauts were very close.'

'Oh, we are, we are,' Jack said. 'At least we were... right up to, well, you know.'

'Please don't worry about hurting my feelings,' said Ariel, now standing at the window and gazing out once more. 'I'm just as eager as you are to get to the bottom of this. More so, I suspect.'

'Of course you are,' said Natasha. 'And that's what really gets me in all of this. No one seems to care what you're going through.'

'Please, Natasha, do not worry,' said Ariel as he allowed his gaze to zoom in on what just might be an alpine meadow beyond the lake.

'It seems to me that we are all on the same side – even General Petersen – since we all want the same thing. We want to know why those conditions prevailed at that time on Venus, and we want to know what I was doing there.'

'That may be true,' said Natasha, joining him at the window, 'but you're not the only one with hidden depths here, you know. I mean, what did happen to Ryan and Jim in that storm?'

'Well, we're all going to have to be honest at the table this afternoon,' said Jack. 'Otherwise we may just need you to go digging in their heads, Ariel.'

Ariel turned around, visibly alarmed. Selena looked embarrassed, as if she had just overheard a conspiracy.

'Don't look so worried,' said Jack. 'I'm only joking.'

3

'*Bienvenue à Genève, et à La Cathédrale de St Pierre!*' The guide had spotted Melody as she crossed the square towards him, needing only seconds to take in her golden hair, designer sunglasses, white blouse, almost knee-length skirt and black ankle-strap shoes. He welcomed her as if she were a long-lost soul, and a French one at that, which she found strangely gratifying. She threw him a *merci* as she reached the top of the steps and, donning the fern-green crepe jacket she had thrown across her shoulder, dived in between the imposing pillars of the entrance. His eyes followed her until she was lost to the interior.

She paused as she went through the door and entered the familiar micro-climate of a cathedral – a drop in light and temperature, with more of a hush than a silence, as scores of tourists milled about, holding up devices or forearms to ensure they had the requisite images to take away with them. 'Oh, David!' she said out loud to the vast space around her. 'Another cathedral! Really?'

'It seemed like a good idea at the time!' She jumped as the man in person emerged from the shadows on one side of the entrance. Perhaps emboldened by his surroundings, or simply because they were far from home, he stretched out his arms. And she walked straight into his embrace.

They clasped each other for as long as it took to say sorry, and then a little longer to say hello, till she pulled back, aware that a man seemed to be watching them from the other side of the entrance. David released her, holding her by the arms and taking a good look at her. He was not much taller than her.

'What?' she said.

'You've changed. What is it? Something's different. Something inside, I mean.'

'Oh, David,' she said a second time. 'If you only knew. But I can't talk about that right now.'

'Classified?'

She nodded. 'So why here? Why make me come to one of the busiest parts of the city?'

'Well, I think it really is a good idea,' he said with a smile as he took her by the hand and started walking. 'And not just for old time's sake. Come and see the chair from which John Calvin preached.'

She let him guide her, as she always had done, and together they examined the carved wood of the chair, a much slighter, less heavy affair than she was expecting. David chatted away about some of the ideas he was exploring for his sabbatical project. 'I want to explore an idea that's been brewing in my mind,' he said excitedly as he ran his hands over the chair. 'You see, I believe it's no coincidence that the very place Calvin and others used as a laboratory for civic rule under God eventually became this great city of liberality and human rights.'

'That's fascinating,' said Melody, meaning what she said, but even more pleased to see David so alive with it all. He was even dressed differently, wearing denim jeans and a jacket that looked less than five years old.

After a tour of much wood and stone they spilled out into the bright and busy day and searched for a café. 'Is there somewhere more green?' Melody said. 'And less rectangular! All these buildings, all this traffic!'

They dived into a side street and round a corner and were almost immediately rewarded by the sight of trees straight ahead. They ran towards them like a couple on holiday and soon discovered a cobblestone square complete with café. '*Parfait!*' Melody shouted. David beamed as if heaven were shining down on him. There were parasols out, but Melody went for a table under the trees.

They ordered beers and caught their breath. David kept looking at her, trying to decide what was different. There were the familiar looks you might see on a model – not the sort that might command a catwalk, but the soft, natural features of a face without blemish or, as far as he could tell, even a smidgen of make-up. It was the same fair hair, same blue eyes, same lively symmetry. Yes, her looks were the same, but her look was different. 'You're going to have to tell me what's happened to you,' he said at last. 'Just leave out the classified bits!'

She laughed. 'The thing is,' she said, 'I'm not really sure what's considered classified and what isn't.'

'So... it hasn't actually been classified yet?'

She waved the back of her hand at him in a light swatting motion. 'Nice try!'

The beers arrived. 'Cool and long and blonde,' David mused as he peered into his glass.

'Just like me!' she quipped, eager to say it before he could. Her heart raced. What was she doing here? 'Anyway,' she added quickly, 'I think you've changed as well. You're so... relaxed!'

'Ah well,' he sighed. 'You can put it down to the Swiss air, I suppose. I've got the bit between my teeth with this project. And being here... I don't know, it just makes me feel closer to it all somehow. I remember when I was on holiday in Crete I felt something similar, as though I was back in the book of Acts and the apostle Paul was being blown right past on the waves.'

'Have you ever been to Israel?'

'Yes,' he said. 'And some of it does connect you to the past, especially the shores of Lake Galilee, where you know you're where the Master trod, or probably trod, or maybe just possibly came this way!'

They both laughed.

During the hour that followed Melody felt her barriers lower with every sip from her glass. She was in the moment, and said yes to another when the nice waiter saw her glass was empty. She sat back and allowed the alcohol and the company and the place do their work, revelling in the dappled light under the trees and the gentle breeze that fingered her hair. She smiled and nodded as David talked some more about his project. She was just happy that he was on side again, the man she could trust. And it occurred to her that in him lay the perfect sounding board she needed, someone who knew her really well yet knew next to nothing about what she had been through these last two weeks. Someone who just maybe could give her some perspective. How glad she was to be here and not in the UN building, where the air would be thick with politics and the knives were probably already out.

David sipped his second beer more slowly, savouring the slow ascent into contentment. Or was it a descent? He looked at the woman in front of him, dazzling, daring and disarming in her beauty. It had never been a purely physical attraction, he knew that. But now it was deeper than ever. She was so settled, so at peace with herself. 'I don't think I've ever seen you like this,' he said.

'Like what?'

'Melody, you really seem to have grown spiritually. Am I right?'

'Well, I don't know. You tell me.'

'Well, speaking as your de facto spiritual director–

'Oo!'

'No, really. It's been wonderful seeing your progress towards a knowledge of Christ over the years we've known each other. But now...'

'Yes?' She flicked her hair from her face and he dived for cover in his glass.

'Well,' he said at last, 'it seems to me that you've crossed some kind of Rubicon. You've come into an open space where you can breathe. Would that be right?'

Inwardly she had to admit that it was. Things had fallen into place. But how could she share this with David without telling him too much about Ariel? She didn't know the answer to that question, so she went with her instinct and decided to open her mouth and see what came out.

'The thing is, David, Ariel is a very complex individual.'

'Ariel? Who's he?'

She froze stone cold sober. She could kick herself for not thinking this through. Up to now she had said next to nothing about her time in Switzerland. As far as David knew, she had come to Geneva after leaving his home a couple of weeks ago and had never left the city.

'Er, sorry,' she said. 'Didn't I tell you? We've called the Stranger Ariel. Has that not made the news yet?'

'How could it?' David asked. 'There's been a virtual news blackout since they took him off the space station. Everyone's convinced he's back on Earth somewhere, and I'm guessing that he's been with the crew. With Jack.'

It was the first time his name had been mentioned. She closed her eyes and put her head back a little, breathing deeply.

'Well, it's not rocket science,' David said, 'if you'll pardon the pun. I mean, just when you'd expect loads of in-depth interviews with the crew about humanity's first visit to Venus – probably our only visit in person – all four of them go underground. So I'm thinking they're all still together somewhere, the crew and the mystery man. Some people are calling him Icarus – that was yours, I believe – but no one knows who he is or where he is.'

Melody's mind began to race as she thought of Ariel just a few miles away in another part of the city. 'Have they shown any photographs of... you know, the Stranger?'

David looked mystified. 'Just where have you been?' he asked. 'Of course they haven't. Which has just fuelled the conspiracy theories!

My favourite is the one that says he's escaped and is now roaming our streets somewhere, unknown and unchecked.' He looked over his shoulder in mock alarm.

'David, why did you want to meet me?'

'Well, I'd have thought that was obvious. I'm here in Geneva. I knew you were in Geneva. So here we are!'

'How's Alice?'

He leant back from the table. 'She's fine. I told her I might see you, if that's what you're worried about.'

Melody felt the world begin to spin ever so slowly. She had lost control of the conversation, and she wasn't sure David really knew what he was doing either. This wasn't how she had imagined their reunion. But just as she was on the point of saying she had to leave, a bird flew silently between them and came to rest on a branch over their heads. They both looked up into the tree, and as they did she felt unexpectedly reassured, remembering that she did after all want Ariel and David to meet.

'All right,' she said, sitting up straight and swallowing hard. 'Are you ready? 'Cause here goes. Ariel is with the crew, as you say. He appears to be suffering from acute amnesia. I have been granted access as sole representative of the press. I've been able to meet with him and talk about... well, all kinds of stuff. It's been the most strange, most wonderful time, and...'

'And?' He held his breath.

'And I think it would be wonderful if you could meet Ariel.'

'Okay,' he said slowly and drained his glass, his hand shaking ever so slightly at the second wave of excitement to hit him in just one day. 'And how exactly is that going to happen?'

'Ah,' she said, relaxing once more. 'That I couldn't say.'

4

The restaurant in the UN building was not what Selena had been expecting after Constance had called it a canteen. She herself decided it was a bar. During the meal she had got to know Natasha Koroleva a little, to whom she felt drawn. Although the cosmonaut was clearly wary of talking to strangers, she managed to pick up that the Russian military had sponsored her training as a planetary geologist, and that after cosmonaut training in the 'starry townlet' of Zvyozdny Gorodok (the famous Star City) they had arranged further training in the United States during a period of partly thawed Russo-American relations. Ostensibly this was to position her for future joint space projects, though the rumour machine soon 'confirmed' that she was not just a Russian spy but an American one as well.

After lunch, sensing how important it was that she gel with these people where possible, Selena sought out Beth Griffiths and soon found her utterly fascinating. The product of a Welsh father and Kenyan mother, she was determined, charming when she wanted to be, doubtless ruthless too, and clearly at the top of her game. And even just a few minutes with this surprisingly approachable woman uncovered the simple yet bonding fact that each preferred the other's national tea. Sadly, the plantations in both their homelands had taken a beating from the annual flooding and poor crop yields of recent decades, and both had been assured by their parents that it didn't taste like it used to. Yet another casualty of climate change.

She stayed close to Beth for the rather complicated walk back to the conference room, stopping every now and then to allow her to greet someone or tell them what they should be doing. Gradually they crossed between buildings within the *Palais de Nations* complex, passing signs to the famous Assembly Hall and Council Chamber, as well as something called the Human Rights Room which piqued her interest.

Finally they were back in the conference room where they had met before lunch. Their places had been reduced to nine, now all named. Selena found herself seated near one of the doors, with a clear view across the lake to the mountains beyond. Next to her sat Dan Marshall, the Aphrodite Mission Controller, who introduced himself as a starstruck colonel who had joined the World Space Agency after a brief career in the Canadian Air Force. Also on her side of the table were Colonel Adamson and Dr Chase, with Commander Forrester, Ariel and Natasha on the opposite side. She felt sorry for Ariel, sitting with his back to the landscape outside, now forced to concentrate on those in the room. But maybe it was for the best.

At the two ends of the large oval table sat the most senior personnel present, Constance Bridlington on Selena's immediate right and Beth opposite. She sat unaccompanied.

Constance had them all introduce themselves. 'I'm aware that our friends on my right have already had a long day that started for them on the other side of those mountains, so I don't expect us to cover all the ground we need to cover this afternoon. We have this room for the rest of today and all of tomorrow. I say that now because I don't want to rush this. I want everything out on the table, no matter how insignificant you may feel it to be. For that reason I have not asked anyone to take minutes, though we are all free to make our own notes. As for recordings, I trust every person in this room to be very discrete with anything they may be doing. And yes, I'm happy to declare that my eband is already on. You will appreciate that we have to balance the need for transparency with security issues, and while some of you may be tempted to think that all the transparency is at my end of the table and the security concerns at the other end,' and at this she nodded to Beth who responded with a brief grin, 'nevertheless I want you to know that both concerns are high on my agenda.

'I'm going to outline what I think we know, from before the mission right up to the present time. I'm grateful to each person in this room for providing me with insight and information. I think it's fair to say some of you will know more than others, though none of you knows the sum total of what I have been able to collect.

'Very well. As soon as we come to something you have been involved in, you need to correct any inaccuracies you hear – and of course answer any questions put to you. Are we all agreed on this?' Unanimous nodding in agreement. 'I want to begin by recounting the reasons for this mission. You are all of course aware of the famous Window that the whole world knows about, the window of opportunity afforded us by the mysterious drop in the levels of pressure, temperature and acidity in a certain locale on the planet Venus. But not everyone in this room will know that the mission wasn't called Aphrodite just to use the Greek name of the Roman goddess Venus. The WSA had been planning a manned mission for some time, to land what was effectively a small laboratory in the region called Aphrodite Terra. The crew wouldn't be able to land, of course, and were set to stay well away in orbit. The lab was expected to last up to a month before the conditions finished it off, relaying data on atmosphere and crust back to Earth via the crew. While they were there the crew were to launch a satellite to go on monitoring after they had left.'

Selena held up her hand.

'Yes, Selena?'

'Well, the thing is, we all know that manned expeditions are expensive and usually unnecessary when it comes to exploring the other planets. Probes sent from earth orbit do the job just as well, if not better, and cost far less. So...'

'So why were we ever going to send human beings? A good question, and I think at this point I'd like to ask my colleague at the other end of the table to chip in.'

Beth cleared her throat as she tried to read Constance's signals.

'Utter transparency,' said Constance.

The room waited, wondering what on earth a security organisation like High Command could have to say about an astronomical mission.

'Right then,' said Beth. 'The Aphrodite mission was really a result of three main factors. First, as you all know, the need to do complex work on the planet as part of our efforts to understand and tackle global warming. Despite the wonders of remote control, it was felt we needed people up there to manoeuvre a number of the probes. Second, to try out the new nuclear drive which had already been hailed as the game-changer in taking us to Mars in a commercially realistic time frame. Venus was closer, being currently on the same side of the sun as we are, and the need was greater.' She paused to drink some water.

'Do go on,' said Constance.

'The third factor comes out of the second and involves the, er... well, what we used to call the space race.' Up to now Jim had found Beth's musical voice quite soporific, but at this he suddenly looked up. Were we at last going to get some of the missing back story, something that might explain Jack's presence on the mission?

'As you can imagine,' Beth continued, 'the race to find a way of flying directly to the planets has been quite fierce. Using the gravity of various planets to slingshot our way from place to place has meant taking the long way round in journeys that often amount to several years. The potential mineral dividends from the asteroid belt alone have really upped the stakes in the search for direct flight. Cutting journey times to a fraction of the old days is likely to pay huge dividends. We all know that big businesses have long been panting for this, not to mention certain governments.'

A murmur went round the room.

'The World Space Agency has an arrangement with its member organisations to use their own intelligence services to protect industrial information from those who have elected not to join us.'

'What exactly were you expecting?' It was Jim who asked the question.

'We didn't know what to expect,' said Beth. 'But we had intel that others were working on a similar kind of drive, so we were keen to ensure that, whoever finally made the crew, someone with the right security clearance would be on hand.'

Jack didn't move.

'And you didn't think to tell the rest of us?' said Ryan. 'Not even the Captain of the whole damn mission?'

'May I step in here?' said Dan Marshall, causing Selena to start at the sudden voice right next to her. 'I understand the frustration, Ryan,

Jim, but you need to remember this was a back-up. Jack was there first and foremost because he was the right pilot for the job, and not just because he had a certain level of clearance. In fact, Jack knew very little about why he might be needed in that capacity. We simply wanted someone who could relay messages in the unlikely event you encountered another ship.'

Dan hesitated, but when Jim started to shake his head he continued. 'I would remind everyone that I was actually the head of the mission. Jim was Captain of the ship, responsible for the well-being of both vessels and crew. Jack was a pilot with hundreds of hours of storm and desert experience. We didn't actually brief him before the mission, because there wasn't really any security brief to give him.'

Constance broke in. 'Jack, would you like to give your honest perspective on this aspect of the mission? I think it would be helpful.'

'I hope,' said Jack, 'that both Jim and Ryan will bear me out, and Natasha here, when I say I was as mystified as anyone when Ariel suddenly appeared. None of us could fathom how anyone else could even have got to the planet, never mind on board the Endeavour.'

'And that's to be expected,' Dan said. 'We had only told Jack that issues might arise where his clearance with British Intelligence could be useful, what with all the interest in this mission from so many interested parties. But he knew – as did we all – that there had been absolutely no sign of anyone else shooting off into that region of space. Or any other region, come to that.'

'Um, well...' said Beth, and suddenly all eyes were on her. 'That's not strictly true.'

5

'*Bienvenus, Benvenuti, Willkommen an bord!* Welcome aboard, ladies and gentlemen! We hope you enjoy your trip today.' The disembodied voice came over the quayside from the vintage paddle steamer. 'As we leave the quay you will see on your right the magnificent *Jet d'Eau* shooting up into the sky – in fact, with the wind as it is at the moment, you may well feel it too! Then, when we've turned out into the lake, you will be able to see the United Nations building on your left. And when we get right out onto the lake, look to your right for Mont Blanc in the distance. We will leave you in peace now, to enjoy the calm of the waters and the mountains.'

David took Melody's hand and helped her off the ramp and on to the waiting vessel. They found somewhere to sit on a long seat on the starboard side and turned up their jacket collars, ready to face the waters from the lake below or from the fountain above, or even from the clouds that had quickly rolled in, unannounced, over the mountains.

They talked for a while about the last few months, going over some of the things they had been doing while four human beings had stood on Venus for the first and possibly last time. Or was that more than four?

'You've had an amazing privilege, Mel, being able to report on this mission. Yes, I know you had the connection with Jack, but to be honest that could have worked against you. No, it was your consistent work in astro-journalism that got you there.'

She smiled, inwardly recalling how she and Jack had first met, and still unsure whether her relationship with such a seasoned astronaut was launched by love or career advancement. She decided it didn't matter. The attraction had been instant, and the fondness they had for each other had grown naturally enough.

But now a spotlight seemed to have been turned on that relationship. David had begun the process, filling her mind with the blessings of faith, unsettling her heart with a different kind of attraction. And, as she thought about it now, she could see she had been getting that under control, coming to terms with a level of faith and doubt that might happily coexist. Until Ariel came along. Suddenly all the big questions David had raised jumped up again like so many yapping puppies craving her attention.

But then the peace had come. She tried to tell David about her walk in the woods with Ariel, but she didn't have the words to do it justice. Not yet. She hadn't even written anything about it. It was all just too close, too intimate.

David saw her struggle. 'Tell me about him. Not what you can't say, but what you can.'

'Thank you!' she beamed, as the wind threw back her hair in a long trail. 'He is... remarkable, unusual, open, sensitive. Vulnerable.'

'You think someone wants to hurt him?'

'I think there are some who are afraid of him. Not him in person, since he's not in the least threatening... well, except for – oh, but I suppose I can't talk about that. But I think they fear what he stands for.'

'Which is?'

'The unknown! Who is he, where does he come from? What's his agenda, or what would it be if he could remember?'

'Wow,' said David. 'What nationality is he? Just trying to get a picture here.'

A wave of cheers and screams broke in as they passed near the giant fountain of the *Jet d'Eau*. They enjoyed it for as long as it lasted, and then the steamer turned and started to make its way along the northern edge of the city. As it did so Melody noticed a man further along the deck who was strangely familiar. He was looking towards the fountain, only she felt that he wasn't really looking. Then she remembered where she had seen him. He was the man who had been watching them in the cathedral. She shrugged. Perhaps he was one of Constance's cronies keeping an eye on them.

David was talking again. 'So, do we know his nationality?'

'Actually, we don't,' she said. 'British, we think. Or at least I think. D'you know, we've not discussed that really? How odd, don't you think? He speaks very good English, he's sort of White–'

'Sort of?'

'Yes, well, he's fairly brown. His features are quite chiselled, I suppose.'

'European then?'

'Possibly. It doesn't really matter, does it?'

'Well,' said David, 'I'm guessing it matters to those fearful people you mentioned, the ones asking who he is and where he's from. Not to mention whoever he's working for.'

Melody looked out over the water. All these questions from David... why hadn't she been asking them? Quite simply, she had failed to notice when her interest in Ariel had changed from professional to personal.

Suddenly she realised people were pointing towards the shore. And there it was, the *Palais de Nations*. 'It's funny,' she said, 'Ariel is in that building right now – for all we know looking right at us.'

'He means a lot to you, doesn't he?'

She allowed him a brief smile. 'It's hard to explain. Why don't we wait till you meet him, and let's enjoy the trip.'

They spent the next hour as tourists, talking only about what they saw and sitting still as, one by one, everyone out on the deck fell silent. David watched the strengthening wind lift Mel's hair, her profile against the dark trees as poised and graceful as ever. How kind God was to give him this day, these moments. He was grateful, although even as he launched a prayer of thanksgiving heavenward he felt the guilt creeping in like a mist in the lowlands. Not for the first time he shrugged it off. Especially now. He needed to get to know this new Melody. Maybe she had even overtaken him in some way, become party to a spiritual dimension he hadn't yet experienced for himself.

'Oh, aren't those flowers lovely!' Mel leaned out and zoomed her eband in on some of the flora between the edge of the lake and the forest beyond. 'He'd love this,' was all she could say.

6

Almost immediately after Beth's bombshell about an unscheduled space flight Petroc had entered the room, as if on cue, to ask if anyone wanted fresh coffee. Selena had wondered why the standard coffee jugs were not out on the table, but she later discovered this was yet another of those carefully planned details that Constance Bridlington was so good at. She had asked Petroc to come in after half an hour, and then every hour, in the belief that interruptions usually benefited long meetings where people sat for hours on end.

Coffee was poured, water replenished and folk began to talk quietly for a few moments.

'Now then, Beth,' Constance began, 'would you like to tell our good people here what up to now only you, I and Colonel Marshall have known?'

'Of course,' said Beth. 'What all of you do know is that the State of Israel has been very cagey about their exploration of space, and for that reason we have been monitoring their launches as best we can.'

Natasha jumped in. 'I wasn't aware Israel had sent anything to any planets.'

'They haven't,' said Beth. 'But they are very big in the satellite business, both communications and defence, and when they said they might want a stake in Space Station Beta, we surmised that they had intentions to go further out.'

'It's worth interjecting here,' said Constance quickly, 'that the space debris that put you all into emergency mode when you were on Alpha was a result of an Israeli operation. They were in the middle of recovering a high-orbit satellite and something went wrong, causing a chain reaction of deorbits which Brad Shepperton had to avoid.'

'I bet they didn't say what went wrong,' Jim intoned almost under his breath. Almost.

'No they didn't,' Constance confirmed, 'though actually I got the distinct impression that they didn't know themselves. They seemed to be in a bit of a panic, truth be told.'

'Okay,' said Jack, his mind racing, 'so does that have anything to do with Brad Shepperton's curious announcement at the press conference about damage to the station which meant we couldn't be joined online by any of the earthside news agencies? Was that true, or was it really an exercise in damage limitation, an excuse to keep them out of the picture?'

'Ah, Jack,' said Constance. 'I see you've not lost your edge. I will confess that it was the latter. My idea. You will understand that I felt something had to be done after Miss James blew the whistle.'

Jack nodded and fell silent.

'Anyway,' Beth continued, 'our surveillance of the Israelis led us to a German breakaway group, apparently based in Berlin, who have been masking as Israelis in their attempts to develop a space suit of the highest dexterity.'

'Sorry,' said Natasha, 'am I the only one not following this?'

'Bear with me, Dr Koroleva,' said Beth. 'The suits you were wearing were, as you know, the strongest, most pliable and resilient to date. They allowed you to move about and operate machinery on the surface under massive pressure. As Dr Chandra here, Selena, will testify, the race to manufacture and test ever more resilient space suits has been highly competitive.'

'But what does this have to do with other spaceflights, before ours?' Ryan asked. 'Are you saying this German group managed to get something into space? To Venus, even?'

Beth nodded. 'Not on their own. They're too small for that. But with the help of another space agency—'

'Which one?' Jim fired.

Beth looked down the table towards Constance.

'The thing is,' said Constance, 'we don't really know.' She raised her hand. 'But we think it's Russia.'

'I knew it!' Jim growled.

'Or possibly China.'

Jim threw his hands in the air.

'Why not Israel?' asked Jack quietly. 'I mean, if the German group has been masquerading as an Israeli cell, might that not be because they are in fact working with the Israelis?'

Constance cleared her throat. 'Let's talk about it later, shall we, Jack? I know,' she said, turning to the others round the table, 'I know I said we would have transparency. But really I don't think the inner machinations of our surveillance bear on our proceedings here today.

What is important is that we did track a vessel, or some kind of craft, heading out on a similar trajectory a few days before the Resolution launched from Alpha.'

'Okay,' said Jack. 'But that would mean they had a nuclear drive as well, if we really think they arrived on Venus ahead of us.'

'That is true,' said Constance. 'However, we just don't know for sure. We lost track of it after two days.'

'Lost track of it?' said Jim. 'How is that possible?'

Beth came back in. 'That was of course my question when the WSA told us at High Command that this had happened. They didn't know then and, as I understand it, they don't know now.'

'That is correct,' said Constance, with a face as near to embarrassment as Jack had ever seen. 'All the astronomers and trackers will tell me is that the signal was never really that strong, and it might even have been an asteroid. It was hard to be sure of its trajectory in so short a time, but it could have started out on Earth and have been headed for Venus.'

'Well,' said Jack, half under his breath and half to Ariel on his right, 'this really is going to be a long meeting. We haven't even got to the start of the mission, and we've already had our first surprise. How many more, I wonder?'

7

Takeshi Takahashi faced a dilemma. Ever since he had been tasked with the investigation of the crystal after the WSA had handed it over to High Command, he had made it his personal mission to ensure the project had the best resources available. But someone else was showing too much interest for his liking. His colleague Nathan Dexter had plenty of other things to do, so why did he keep asking about it?

The three senior members of the United Nations High Command were traditionally from different nations, and this term of office was no exception. It was true that having a Japanese citizen and an

American under the leadership of an African Brit meant that there were two British citizens in senior positions at the UN at the same time, Beth Griffiths and Constance Bridlington, but that would change soon enough. More problematic was the lack of anyone from the southern hemisphere. Yet political correctness had to give way to technical competence sometimes, and no one in the South even vaguely suitable had shown interest.

The first thing Takeshi had done was transfer the crystal to a holding site. Putting his uncommonly high budget to good use, he set up a makeshift laboratory in a warehouse on the outskirts of the city. When it came to choosing scientific personnel, he had decided to go for quality rather than quantity. But before he had installed his first technician, an unwanted visitor had come calling. Takeshi wasn't one to panic, but he needed to act quickly. Fearful that Dexter was behind this act of subterfuge, he decided to neutralise the intruder and say nothing more for the time being. Having rendered the man unconscious, he tied him to a chair while he examined the head wound he had caused. It was only then that he recognised Dr Ryan Chase, world-famous astronaut. At first he didn't know whether to be worried or relieved, but either way he decided this was not something to be too troubled about. He loosened the man's bonds before removing the crystal and shutting down the equipment, leaving his unexpected victim to wake up in his own good time.

When he reported back to Beth Griffiths, she was exasperated. 'What is it with you men? First Bill pulls his commando stunt in the monastery, and now this! Anyone would think we were out to get the whole crew!'

Takeshi pointed out that the crew had not exactly been behaving professionally, and they left it at that, deciding to wait to see what Chase had to say when he resurfaced.

As for his concerns about Nathan, Takeshi decided to keep these to himself for the time being.

8

The formal review meeting was grinding on. Constance covered the selection of the crew and how they finally settled on two leading scientists with astronaut training and two astronauts with mountains of maturity and experience. She briefly rehearsed the mission's research parameters, which focused on the Venusian atmosphere and lithosphere. Then, with the help of the astronauts themselves, she went over the events on the planet's surface and Natasha's spectacular discovery of the crystal, eclipsed so soon by her discovery of Ariel.

'Okay, it's cards on the table, right?' There was menace in Ryan's voice.

'That is correct,' Constance responded.

'Well, doesn't it strike anyone else a little odd that our Russian crew member just happened to find this crystal, right before – oh, look at that – she bumps into the stowaway?'

'May I respond to that?' Jack asked quickly. 'For one thing, the crystal and the man were discovered on different EVAs. As to the crystal, who else was going to find it? You yourself know, Ryan, that Natasha was briefed to concentrate on lithosphere, while you collected all the data you could on the atmosphere and, as I recall, the interaction between the two.'

Ryan nodded.

'And as for Ariel, we were obviously all outside when he got in, and any one of us could have found him, although you, Ryan, were outside when he was discovered. Now, I don't find your being outside any more suspicious than the three of us being inside.'

'Except,' Ryan pressed, 'I have since reviewed the ship's internal audio and I distinctly heard our Russian cosmonaut here talking Russian to the stowaway. Very early on.' He sat back in his chair with the satisfied grin of a chess player who had just made a winning move.

All eyes were on Natasha. 'I can explain,' she said, clearly reluctant to do anything of the sort. She thought back to her first time alone with Ariel, when he briefly opened his eyes, so vulnerable, so helpless. 'I was trying get a response from him. I thought it was important to speak, and actually I mainly used English. But it seemed sensible to try Russian, seeing I could.'

'Well,' put in Jack, 'it clearly had no effect, and we all know that Ariel is as English as they come in how he talks.'

'Quite so,' said Constance. 'And as for how you came by those recordings, Ryan, we will not pursue that here.'

Ryan blew through pursed lips but said nothing. He had been countered successfully.

'Gentlemen,' Constance began, 'I really think it's high time we got to the bottom of this distrust of Natasha. You all trained together. I know it was over an unprecedentedly brief period, and that was in the nature of the emergency. But you seemed to be getting on well enough with one another at the start of the mission. Isn't that right, Dan?'

'Absolutely. Jim and Jack already knew each other, even if they hadn't actually flown in space together before. Ryan I'd vouch for any day. And Natasha, well, she came with the highest credentials.'

No one spoke. Almost everyone in the room knew that Russia had made a big deal in the media about their cosmonaut being the best qualified of the bunch. And what strings were pulled to place her there – who could say? There was still a whiff of politics in the air.

'May I ask a question?' said Selena.

'You certainly may,' said Constance, the relief in her voice almost palpable.

'Who actually selected the crew? I mean, we've heard a bit about the process, but who made the final decision?'

'That would be me,' said Constance, 'together with Dan here, of course.'

Selena pressed on carefully. 'And would it be fair to say there were more than aptitude considerations in each of the four appointments?'

'Yes it would,' said Constance eagerly. 'That's absolutely right. There are always political considerations, questions of funding, international co-operation, that sort of thing. Of course the demanding timetable meant we needed someone already trained in piloting the nuclear drive, which narrowed it down to a handful of people, out of whom Jim here was the most experienced. But yes, it is fair to say that we should have as much doubt around this table about all the members of the crew as we might about any one of them. Or as little.'

Jack could tell this was not going to satisfy Jim completely, or Ryan at all, but there was at least a chance it might establish a level playing field. Either way, the whole room sensed the need to move on.

'Getting back to the sequence of events,' said Constance, 'I'd like Dan to give us some perspective on what happened at this end, after the news came through about Ariel.'

'Well, to be honest we didn't know what to make of it. Obviously my first thought was that this proved someone had made it there before us, so I alerted Brad Shepperton, the Station Controller, and got on the line to Constance here. There was some toing and froing about how to contain the story, though at that point we were more concerned about the safety of the crew, the possible presence of others, and what this might mean in terms of some kind of incident or accident.'

'And this, if I may,' Constance cut in, 'is where the lack of collaboration between space agencies outside the WSA becomes critical. If someone had gone there, and got into some kind of difficulty, we needed to know who they were so we could find out where they were.'

'Surely they were somewhere nearby?' said Selena.

'Our first thought, of course,' Jack responded. 'But radar hadn't picked up any sign of another craft. All we knew was that the conditions were getting worse. And in the end – an end that came all too quickly – that was what made us leave before a full check could be made.'

'Let's get back to the surface,' said Constance. 'After Ariel turned up, there was a series of EVAs. Jim went to find Ryan, Jack went to find Jim and Ryan who later returned on their own, and finally Jack was guided back to the ship.'

There was silence as each person considered Constance's summary. Its rude brevity only served to highlight the lack of co-operation between the crew.

'All right,' said Jim at last, 'I think I need to speak to this.' He had been looking directly across the table at Ariel while Constance had been speaking, and he found himself now feeling uncomfortably exposed, almost as if his clothes had been removed. The time for honesty had come. 'As you can imagine, I've been playing these events over and over in my mind, and I am here to admit to you today that Ariel here is not the only one who was hit by amnesia. I actually think we all were. All except Natasha, actually.'

All eyes were now on Jim.

'This isn't easy for me, and I'm still not happy about the decisions that were made over my head, but... I realise now that our disorientation out on the planet's surface was far more serious than any of us appreciated at the time. We actually don't have a clue why Ryan lost consciousness, or why I did, or what those sounds were we could hear.'

'Sounds?' Constance frowned.

'Well, yes, I think so. Sounds? Impressions?'

'They were sounds.' Jack had found the opportunity he so longed for, to be on the same side as Jim once more. 'When I tried radioing you from the ship, all Natasha and I could hear were the sounds of the storm. But they weren't... normal. I don't know how else to put it.'

'They were not natural.' Natasha had found another way of putting it.

'Fair enough,' Jack smiled. 'I admit I'm now overlaying my memories with interpretations that have formed since.'

'And just what are those interpretations, Commander?' said Beth, anxious to see where this was going.

'Well, there were a lot of noises in what we could hear over the radio, but some of them sounded... intentional.'

'Like voices,' said Jim, 'though in no language I could identify.' He chuckled. 'Which doesn't mean much, by the way.'

'Well, there was no Russian, as I recall,' said Natasha more aggressively than she intended.

'Can we hear them now?' asked Selena.

'Yes, I do believe we can,' said Constance. She pressed a small tablet she had put on the table. 'Petroc, can you patch through the Endeavour's live mission records please?'

After a few moments the tablet lit up and she started to browse through the records. 'Ah, here we are. Audio. Er, what was the time frame? Yes, this must be it.' Within a few seconds they heard the intercom chat of the day, and a minute or two later there it was, Jack calling Jim and receiving only static for an answer. Only it wasn't static. It was the noise of the storm relayed through Jim's outer-suit microphones.

And suddenly the crew were back on Venus. Like hearing a pop song from the past, associated memories came flooding in. Jack and Natasha glanced at each other before quickly looking down. Ryan scratched his head, concentrating hard on the patterns in the sounds now engulfing the room. Jim felt a little dizzy and looked across at Ariel once more.

But Ariel had stood up and turned round, and was now looking out of the window. The snow-capped alps dissolved before his eyes into a fiery orange. Slow rivers of lava steamed below him, as he soared through sulphurous clouds into the mouth of the storm. Into the thick of the battle.

He pulled himself away from the window and turned to face the room. 'I think I remember something.'

Chapter 20

Puzzle

1

Alice was uneasy. She had shared in David's excitement as he entered his sabbatical. The three-month break from church would allow him to delve more deeply into the life and works of one of his great heroes, the controversial sixteenth-century church leader John Calvin. And the trip to Geneva made absolute sense, since it was where Calvin had made his base and where so much of the history was accessible. It even made sense that David should touch base with Mel while he was there, just to keep things warm.

How warm?

The relationship between the three of them had happened so naturally, and so positively, that it had never occurred to Alice there was anything more than friendship in its triangular lines. David had shown a keen pastoral interest in this high-flying investigative journalist. True, she was not like most of the people in their church congregation. Well, not like any of them, now she thought about it. But then that was part of the attraction – for both her and David. Mel kept them in touch with the wider world, and the truth was, Melody Grantley James would prove to be a phenomenal trophy of grace, were she finally to commit her life to the Lord Jesus.

And for a long time that outcome seemed almost inevitable. Intellectually she grasped things very quickly. Her questions were real, and her heart seemed genuinely open to the implications of making a commitment. Her current relationship was an issue, one that presented itself as a problem the closer she came to that commitment. Because Jack, it seemed, was not for turning, and it was surely becoming clear to Mel that she would have to give him up if she was going to make any progress in her spiritual journey and actually begin to walk with the Lord.

So why the unease? That was the problem. She didn't know where it was coming from. But she had been a Christian long enough to know that feelings like this are not usually to be ignored. So she prayed, looking for guidance on how she might talk to David about it when they next spoke on the phone.

She didn't get very far in her prayers before she realised this was not something they could discuss via electronic media. Either it must wait till she joined him in Geneva, or she must go without delay.

And suddenly the way ahead was clear. She booked the flight there and then, before firing up her electric duster and cleaning every item on the ground floor, singing as she went.

2

After the recording of the sounds on Venus had been played to the members of the Aphrodite mission review, the meeting had been adjourned. Everyone needed a break. Most decided to spend the thirty minutes allotted in the cafeteria near the main entrance. Jack, Natasha and Ariel decided on a walk in the grounds to the rear of the building.

They sat on a bench. Ariel glanced warily towards the mountains which, mercifully, had returned to their former state. Jack and

Natasha sat on either side, waiting for him to speak. Evidently he still needed to process what he had seen in his head.

Jack decided they should go first. 'So Natasha,' he said, 'what did you make of that? Was that weird or was that weird, hearing those sounds again?'

Natasha frowned. 'This may sound stupid, but I didn't know there even was a recording.'

'Aye, standard stuff,' said Jack. 'Anything on a radio goes through the system, and the system knows all. Well, records all.'

'I suppose so,' she said. 'Just as well only audio was working.' Was that a smirk?

'I'm sure I don't know what you mean,' he said. 'Actually, Ariel really won't know what we mean. The thing is,' and he turned to Ariel, 'Natasha and I both experienced, er, heightened emotions when all this was going on. Do you think that may be true for you too, Ariel?'

Natasha smiled, relieved that this was coming out in the open, if only so they could decide how to cover it up again when the meeting reconvened.

Ariel looked up at Jack. 'Heightened emotions?' he echoed. 'Oh yes, there were plenty of those. The battle was fierce.'

'That battle again,' said Jack. 'Any more details?'

'Well, I can confirm that it took place on Venus, presumably some time before you found me. I can't say precisely where, though as I was flying it may have been quite a way off.'

'Flying?' said Natasha. 'In a space craft?'

'That I couldn't say,' said Ariel.

'Well, I guess it's all cards on the table now,' said Jack. 'Jim's clearly ready to get real, so I don't think it would be right for us to hold anything back.'

'Details?' Natasha mouthed, with a sudden look of horror.

'No, no details,' said Jack. 'But I think we do have to own up to how we *felt*, even if we speak in general terms about heightened emotions.'

'I think Jim should go first,' said Natasha. 'His feelings were clearly not so warm towards his colleagues, and we don't want him to lose any momentum. We have to get to the bottom of what happened to all of you out there.'

'Well, I don't think we'll be getting to the bottom of anything,' said Jack, 'but a little more light and openness could take us some way.'

They stood up together and began to make their way back inside. Suddenly Ariel stopped. 'I wonder what you looked like from above. Can we find out where you and Captain Adamson and Dr Chase all were?'

'We can try,' said Jack. 'I for one am not totally clear on just how far I went from the ship, but my guess is, we can work it out with a fair degree of accuracy. But, Ariel, what are you getting at?'

'I don't know,' he muttered. 'I'm just wondering if I flew over you, that's all.'

3

It was raining again in Bruges, the perfect cover for three people to slip into an old clock shop without so much as a sideways look from either tourist or local. Hugh Coates led Miranda and Darlene Piper past the ceaseless tick-tocking and a small flurry of chimes to the kitchen at the back, before taking the elevator to the communications hub.

Miranda had admitted to being 'gob-smacked' when Hugh had joined her and Darlene in a London hotel and revealed his arrangement with British Intelligence. Her disappointment in Hugh's colluding with a national institution was only momentary. Within minutes she could see this relationship suited him more than it did the British government. It seemed he was left to play by his own rules much of the time, although it wasn't clear who was really calling the shots when Hugh suggested they travel together to Bruges, the centre of an operation she had assumed was known only to the inner circle. But then the formidable Ms Piper clearly qualified for that status, and what's more didn't seem inclined to escort Miranda to her own headquarters. After a quick and quiet meal, where each woman studied the other without chit-chat, they made their way to a helicopter pad on a tall building Miranda didn't recognise, and flew to a local airport where she was happily reunited with her Gulfstream. Back in the cockpit she had almost felt things were back to normal. Almost. Ms Piper was a piece she couldn't as yet fit into the puzzle. What was clear, however, was that Miranda herself now held key information about Ariel which both Hugh and Darlene wanted to fit into the fragmented picture that was emerging from the Aphrodite mission.

They entered Hugh's office and, as soon as the door was closed and the spider light on, they began. Miranda soon realised this was never going to be a real conversation, certainly not like Montagnola, nor even the sort she was used to with Hugh. He might be sitting in the chair from which he commanded so much of his clandestine empire, but it was Darlene who took control right from the start. Miranda had not taken to her, despite reassurances from Jack, and she looked her up and down with more than a hint of disdain. The short two-toned hair and straight off-centre parting were even more severe than the cut of her jacket and skirt.

Darlene's accent was posh, but not properly, as if it had been learned, and there was an unnerving grit in her voice. 'So, Miranda, you and I have talked only briefly, and while I have a fairly good picture of the set-up Jack Forrester had in Switzerland, I want to hear from you first-hand. Tell me, what was your impression of the one we're now calling Ariel?'

Such a simple question. Why couldn't she answer it?

Hugh saw the unfamiliar confusion written on his protégée's face and decided to come to her aid with a more precise question. 'Tell us about the storm, Miranda, and what happened afterwards?'

'Yes,' Darlene added, 'you went there to get a look at the space suit, didn't you?'

Miranda nodded, happy to go anywhere except her final walk in the woods with Ariel. 'Yeah,' she said, 'Hugh allowed me to go take a look. We decided that a storm should make perfect cover for getting in. Once inside, I'd have to make it up as I went along, which was fine.'

'Right,' said Darlene. 'But you got knocked out by a falling tree.'

'A branch, yes,' Miranda said. 'Though, at the time, I literally didn't know what hit me.'

'And you were tended by the monks?' Darlene prompted.

'Right, yes, good old Brother Ambrose.' Again she steered well away from any mention of Ariel and the part he may have played in her recovery. She wasn't even sure herself, and there was no way she was going to fuel speculation about healing powers. She hated not being sure of her ground and told herself off for not being prepared for an interrogation that had been totally inevitable.

'Go on,' said Darlene, clearly suspicious of the short answers she was getting. Miranda looked at Hugh who gave her the slightest nod.

'Well,' she said, 'you've obviously had access to the recordings made by the devices Hugh and I placed. What do you need me to fill in?'

'Okay, let me get to the point,' said Darlene.

'Please do,' Miranda scowled.

'Did you get a look at the suit? How did Ariel read your mind? And did you find out anything that might corroborate the, frankly, wild claims made by a certain doctor on Space Station Alpha?'

She was ready now. Be selective and don't lie. The truth, some of the truth, and nothing but the truth. 'No, I never did find the suit. Who's got it anyway? Never mind. As you know, the General turned up and gave me the third degree, before he disappeared and Jack decided to play a hunch and see if I could help stimulate Ariel's memory – though he also gave me a grilling on my industrial espionage story. Anyway, I decided to tell Ariel about the footage from the space station. Except I didn't so much tell him as show him. That's the mind-reading thing you mentioned. I'm sorry, Hugh, but that's how he knew I'd seen it in a plane... and even that your name was Hugh.'

'Ah well,' said Hugh, 'let's not worry about that. We hardly knew we were going up against telepathy when we embarked on this little adventure now, did we?'

She gave him a sheepish grin before tackling Darlene's final question. 'As for the white coat on the space station, it's hard to know what to think. It looked like something was going on. But surely that's all going to come out in the wash. Aren't they putting it all together in Geneva right now?'

'It seems to me, Darlene,' said Hugh, his tone now turning more formal, 'that we have a remarkable individual in this man called Ariel – if man he be. My guess is that he has been enhanced, though you will doubtless form your own opinion. But tell me, what happens next?'

Darlene blew out a sigh. 'That all rather depends on how the UN plays this. A lot will depend on whether Geneva decides it's a matter of international security. Or even global security, if they really do go down the ET route. If the matter goes to a further inquiry, public or behind closed doors, then we may well need you both to give evidence. Apart from that, I think we can say we're done, at least for now.'

'Why does that not reassure me?' said Miranda.

'I can't help what will or will not reassure you, Ms Freeman, but one thing's for sure. You've not told us everything that happened between you and Ariel. Maybe you'll rethink your position if things don't turn out so well for him.'

'What's that supposed to mean?' said Miranda.

'Only that you may be able to speak for him if things turn ugly, that's all. You know, personal facts, character witness, whatever.'

She stood up. 'Hugh, thank you for letting me into your lair. We'd tracked you here enough times, of course, to know that something was going on. But let this be a sign of even greater co-operation to come.'

She shook his hand, nodded to Miranda, and left the office.

'Bitch,' Miranda muttered.

'That may well be,' said Hugh, 'but an important one none the less. Pardon me a moment while I ensure she is escorted directly off the premises. We wouldn't want her taking any wrong turns.' And with that he disappeared into the outer office.

Miranda breathed a long sigh. She was still coming to terms with the fact that Hugh had allowed British Intelligence into the place. Clearly there was a mood of co-operation between them. Doubtless it would serve Hugh's purposes. She looked around. She herself had only been here a few times. On Hugh's desk there were three upright screens with their backs to her, while on the wall behind his chair she could just make out a larger one which she had seen in the background on her last two calls, currently camouflaged by featuring a picture of the surrounding wallpaper. Without knowing why, she walked round and tapped it. Instantly it revealed what he had left open. It appeared to be a mind map. She stepped back round to take a better look at the whole thing, at which point she almost backed into Hugh on his return.

'Ah, I see you have discovered my little plot.'

'Ah, sorry. Couldn't resist. What are you plotting then?'

'No, my dear girl, I mean my plotting of the events and characters in our current adventure, with their various interrelations. You know me. It's the lines between things that fascinate.'

She looked again at the wall screen, and realised that there were lines of varying hue and thickness joining the names of the people they had been monitoring. In the centre was Ariel, with lines going out in all directions. Other lines criss-crossed between various names.

'Looks like some kind of spider's web,' she remarked.

'Mm, maybe. I see it more as a pond with several fish swimming around, and one large stone thrown into the middle. I know I've drawn lines, but think of them as waves too.'

'Like light, you mean – particles and waves?'

'My, you have turned the philosopher, haven't you? Yes, that will do. Certainly our friend Ariel has sent out shock waves that have got everyone dancing. Some, as you see here, are working more or less together. Some, like here, are very much at odds.'

He remained standing behind her. 'Are we still working together, Miranda?' he whispered.

She walked over to a picture, inset in the wall where a window would once have been.

'I... I... Look, I'm sorry I meddled with your screen.'

'Now now, you know that's not what I'm talking about. Come, Miranda, it's not as if you don't owe me. Ms Piper has gone. It's just you and me. Now, why don't you tell me what's really been going on?'

4

The conference room was buzzing. It seemed every member of the crew needed 'just a few words' with Constance first, such that by the time things formally resumed she had a somewhat different running order.

'Ladies and gentlemen,' she said, 'clearly the recording we played earlier on has proved very stimulating. Specifically, it seems to have jogged the memories of the Endeavour crew. I'm going to ask Jim to speak first, and then we'll go from there.'

Jim thought about standing up but decided that may be a shade too formal. But he wanted gravitas, so he began by thanking Constance for the opportunity to speak first. Natasha was so pleasantly surprised she gave a gracious nod in his direction.

'Okay,' he began, 'you already know that the recording we heard a while ago was of sounds coming from my suit radio, switched to environmental while I was looking for Ryan. What I hadn't recalled until now was that while I was hearing those sounds, out there on the surface, it felt to me like there were voices mixed in with the noise of the air currents. I put it down to a trick of the elements, and when I lost my footing – and then lost consciousness – I guess I put it out of my mind. But hearing those sounds again today, I do recall how I felt for all the world like there were others out there.'

'What did you think they were saying?' asked Beth. 'At the time, I mean.'

'I couldn't make out any words, either then or just now,' Jim replied. 'It just sounded like people speaking. Or, should I say, shouting.'

'It sounded aggressive,' Natasha said as she stared at the table in front of her.

'Ryan, do you have anything to add?' asked Constance. 'Can you remember how far you had got in your analysis before Jim found you unconscious?'

At this Jim shifted uneasily in his seat. 'The thing is, Ma'am,' he continued, 'I don't actually remember finding Ryan. That is, I saw a stooped or slumped figure ahead of me and took it to be Ryan, but…'

'What is it?' said Constance.

'Well, I know it sounds crazy, but it seemed like he was fading out and back in again. I can only think it was my visor playing games – the readings were going crazy right in front of my eyes. Anyway, that's when I lost my footing. The next thing I remember is Ryan helping me get to my feet and walking back with me to the ship.'

No one spoke. Ariel closed his eyes. All others were on Ryan.

'Okay,' said Ryan at last. 'I'll admit those sounds have brought things back to me too… specifically, the moments just before I blacked out. To answer your question, Ma'am, I didn't really know what I was seeing on the scopes and scanners I'd managed to set up. The fluctuations were unexpected, not at all consonant with the climatic conditions.'

'What do you mean?' said Beth. 'I mean, what are you saying?'

'I try not to leap to conclusions, Ma'am,' said Ryan, 'but I guess I'm saying that I cannot explain why there were certain disturbances in the region.'

'Even with all that data?' Beth pressed.

'Data of a certain kind – atmospheric and geological. If Venus had a magnetic field, which it doesn't, I might think that that was messing with the instruments, but as it is I can only think…'

'Think what?'

'Well frankly, Ma'am, it's as crazy in its own way as the data I've been getting from the crystal. Or, at least, had been getting, before it was taken from me.'

Once more the room became silent. Beth was dismayed the crystal had come up so soon, but hardly surprised, given Ryan's recent experience. She looked to Constance for some direction from the chair.

Constance thanked Ryan and suggested they hold off discussing the crystal until they'd heard from Natasha and Jack.

'I have very little to add,' said Natasha. 'When the radio noise, and whatever else it was, came through, Jack decided to go and look for both men, leaving me in charge of our unconscious visitor. I kitted Jack out with the specialised trigs I used for distant scanning, and I used its cradle signal to help guide him back in after Jim and Ryan returned.'

Jack watched with equal measures of awe and relief when she didn't so much as flinch at any point in her report.

'Very well,' said Constance, and she turned to Jack. 'Remind us, Jack, how things looked to you out there.'

'Well, you know, I think it starts in my head. Jim has already pointed out that Ariel is not alone in his amnesia. It's clear to me now that there are holes in the memories of all three of us who went outside. I think the whole place was playing tricks with our heads. In fact, even before Jim and I went out, I had a dream which definitely included voices like the ones we seem to be hearing in that recording.'

'But... let me get this straight,' said Beth. 'If you were inside the ship, you couldn't hear the storm at all.'

'Not strictly true,' said Jack, 'but certainly it sounded different inside the ship. More in the way of rumbles and vibrations. But no, I can distinctly recall, now I've heard that recording, that my dream contained those voice-like sounds. And that's before we heard the feed from Jim's microphone.'

'So, what exactly are you saying?' said Beth.

'I'm just saying!' Jack replied. 'I have no idea what it means. But I now realise I heard those voices in my dream before we heard them in the speaker. Make of it what you will.'

Constance let Jack's words float awhile before she made to move on, at which point she was forestalled by Selena.

'Sorry, Constance,' she said, 'but there is one other person in the room who was there at that time.' She was looking across the table towards Ariel.

'Of course that's true,' said Constance, 'but we have ascertained that he was unconscious while all this was going on. Isn't that right, Ariel?'

'I believe so,' he replied. 'However, I too find these sounds familiar. I associate them with the battle that I half-remember – something I have expressed already to General Petersen and some here. So I am left wondering whether I was involved in some kind of battle immediately before you found me.'

'Yes,' said Natasha. 'That would fit.'

'Though you found us,' put in Jim.

'I suppose I did,' said Ariel.

Dan Marshall decided he had been quiet long enough. 'Okay, Ariel,' he said, finding an unexpected joy in using the name that had been given since he last saw him. 'Let's say you were injured in some kind of incident immediately before you turned up on the Endeavour. That still doesn't explain how you could be there without the appropriate environmental protection.'

'What about the suit?' said Beth.

'My own question too,' said Selena. 'I've heard some rather strange things about it. Where is it now, may I ask?'

'You may,' said Constance. 'Jack has been looking after it. I thought it best he take it with him to Montagnola because we weren't sure whether Ariel might need it at some point. It is back here now, and of course we have in you, Selena, one of the world's foremost fibre and polymer technicians. And may I say that I can think of no one better qualified to head up the team that examines it. You have my full confidence, and I hope that of everyone around this table.'

Most in the room nodded their heads in the cheap kind of agreement that flows from neutrality. Constance looked towards Beth for a sign of where she stood. She would have preferred it to come to her team, but she knew that, thanks to her trigger-happy staff, she had little equity in the goodwill stakes when it came to insisting on anything. After a moment's reflection she too nodded her agreement.

Ryan took the opportunity afforded by the pause. 'What about the crystal?' Maybe because he had been breathing the fresh air of co-operation, or maybe simply because he was tired, his tone contained less of an edge than before.

'Indeed,' Constance responded. 'We can all agree that Ariel's suit and the crystal found in the same vicinity appear to have a role in our mystery. Dan, would you like to tell us what happened on Alpha?'

Dan proceeded to relate how the crystal vibrated and glowed on his desk at around the same time as Ariel was waking up in another part of the station. As a result, when the crew left for Earth later on, he had asked Ryan to begin analysing it.

At that point he cleared his throat and took a sip of water. 'There is just one more thing I'd like to add,' he said. 'I hope Jim won't mind me mentioning this, but I was surprised by his reaction when we put the Stranger – I mean Ariel – into Jack's custody. I've known Jim for quite some time, and he's always been measured in his responses when he's been faced with, shall we say, unwelcome developments. I remember travelling with him early on, and hearing him say he's the kind of guy that expects red lights and takes green ones as a bonus.' Jim smiled at this. 'I mention it now because I think it may all be a part of the same emotional mix we've been discussing.'

This passed without further comment, so Constance chose the moment to read out a report from Dr Schlesinger, detailing his preliminary and, as it turned out, only analysis of the crew and of Ariel and his suit. After the crew had left Alpha he had been through the data and test results, such as they were, and found no abnormalities beyond the expected traces of Ryan's and Jim's black-outs. But when he came to check Ariel's medbed records he was surprised to find they had been wiped.

'Whoa!' Jack was one of several to interrupt. 'That's the first I've heard of it. Who wiped what?'

'Sorry, Jack,' said Constance. 'Put it down to the uneven contact you and I have had lately. As you know, when you put the MAG on Ariel and clipped the IV pack round his wrist, the medbed got to work—'

'Sorry,' Selena interrupted. 'I can guess that the IV pack is an intravenous drip, but am I the only one who doesn't know what a MAG is?'

When Constance hesitated Dan took over. 'Our apologies, Selena. It's an occupational hazard with space flight, I'm afraid. Abbreviations and acronyms everywhere! The IV pack is, as you rightly guessed, an intravenous device. Basically, once your sick astronaut is strapped into the medbed, the IV pack takes care of finding a suitable vein for intravenous feeding. Meanwhile the Maximum Absorbency Garment – what some of us call a diaper and Jack calls a nappy – takes care of waste. The kind we have in the medbed has extraction and self-cleaning components—'

'I understand,' said Selena as she raised her hand to signal that this was enough information.

'Jolly good,' said Constance. 'Useful clarification, of course. So, to return to Dr Schlesinger's report. This is what he actually wrote: "The medbed record shows no use. This is either due to faulty equipment or faulty application."'

'You mean, we hadn't turned the thing on?' Jim growled.

Constance pressed on. 'Patience, Jim. He then arrives at his final conclusion, that the record had been wiped, in view of the plain fact that the patient was not DOA. Sorry, dead on arrival. So it must have been working. Yet there was no record of any intravenous infusion.'

The room fell silent for several long seconds. 'Well,' said Jack, 'clearly the intrigue level has just gone up a couple of notches. Either someone was already interfering with the mission, or Ariel really did get nothing from the medbed.'

Not for the first time Beth looked like she had something to say but decided against.

'We must move on for now,' said Constance. 'Regarding the suit, Dr Schlesinger documented a change from a shimmering silvery effect that was almost impossible to focus on – a point corroborated by the crew – to a dull, silvery white. He also believed that Ariel's skin colour was 'unstable', though no one's quite sure what he meant by that.

'Why don't we test it?' said Jack. 'Let's go round the room and ask each person to say what colour they think Ariel is? Sorry, Ariel, are you okay with that?'

'Of course, Jack.'

'Okay. I'll go first. I see a White guy, basically, though well tanned... though it's not quite a tan. I think I'll stop there. Constance?'

They went round the room, and while people put it differently, the sum of it was that Ariel's face and hands were a brownish white, or yellowish, depending on how the light fell.

'Well, this is most interesting,' said Constance, 'not least because everyone bar none found it difficult to put a colour on Ariel's suit as well, at least in the early days. We all seem to see things differently.'

'To see Ariel differently,' said Selena quietly.

'Yes,' said Constance. 'That puts it well. What is true metaphorically is strangely true physically as well, it seems. Ariel, you have put us in a quandary, no question. To some you are the result of an experiment in genetic manipulation, to others the injured party in a skirmish we know nothing about. To some you are a threat to national or even global security, and to a few, it seems, a trusted friend.'

She stood up. 'Well now, ladies and gentlemen, I think we have talked enough for one day. I for one have found this most useful. Tomorrow we will get on to the decisions and discoveries, not to mention rather drastic manoeuvres, that have taken place since Ariel and the crew arrived back on Earth.'

5

Miranda sat on a wall by the river that traces a lazy path round the historic centre of Bruges, dangling her legs as though she were a child again. The rain had not long stopped, so there were few boat trips or tourists sitting outside cafés. Hugh was studying her intently.

'Well, you know most of it,' Miranda protested. 'I kept the updates going as long as I could.'

'Yes, yes,' Hugh deflected, 'but I want to hear you express it all together, now that you've had time to process it. What do you think's been going on? And why the devil did they let that journalist in there? Honestly, sometimes I wonder whether these people really know what they're doing.'

'Aw, come on,' said Miranda, eyes sparkling. 'You know very well you wouldn't want to do what they do. You'd always prefer to just watch and listen.'

He shrugged. 'Let's start there anyway. You spotted Miss Grantley James, and you befriended her.'

There was no edge to his tone, but she knew he would want details. And this was something she could cover far more easily. Unlike Ariel.

'Yeah,' she said, 'we hit it off right from the start. She relaxed pretty quickly actually.'

'Oh, do tell.'

'Well, I'm not going to satisfy your salacious interest, if that's what you want. And it may have been risky letting her drink so much. I thought I may have blown it next morning.'

'Evidently not. Do you like her?'

'No use pretending otherwise,' she said, as a single boat passed close by under a bridge with a few bedraggled passengers.

'And did you tuck her into bed? I know you, Miranda. Are you emotionally compromised? I won't mind. I simply need to know.'

Hugh's need to know had often been perplexing to Miranda, but it had never been more annoying than now. She stuck her tongue out.

He shrugged again and seemed happy to move on, apparently satisfied to have exposed this particular aspect of her adventure. They talked about the bits and pieces picked up by the various listening devices and then, when she reached the night of the storm, they grabbed a hot chocolate from a nearby vendor and began to walk along the river. The cobble stones were no match for the leafy paths of the monastery grounds, and there were few trees nearby, but even so walking in the fresh outdoor air helped her to relive that night.

'I parked in the layby near the relay we'd set up, and then did a pretty cool gate-vault, if I say so myself. It was all going swimmingly well until I was a few minutes in. I swear to you, Hugh, it was like the place had its own miniature storm going on.'

'Ah well, my dear, that's because it did. I'll show you the charts when we get back to the office. Apparently the storm got itself into some kind of vortex and dumped almost its entire might on Montagnola. Specifically the retreat centre, as far as I can make out.'

'That's weird.'

They turned a corner and walked across a low-arched bridge back over the river. Miranda was getting into her stride at last.

'Actually, it really was weird in there, you know. As I think about it now, it was like the trees were full of voices, shrieking and wailing and God-knows-what. I guess it was a trick of the wind.'

'It's odd, I'll grant you,' said Hugh. 'You'd expect an effect such as you describe to come from metal buildings or wires. Were there any?'

'Not that I saw,' she replied.

Hugh mentally filed this information away. Just as they emerged into a cobbled square the heavens opened, and they dashed for cover. When the shower turned out to be more protracted rain, they made their way back to the covert headquarters and continued their discussion there. Miranda told him about Petersen, and the animosity between him and Jack, and the role Melody played in the various sessions that Jack and even the Abbot put on. She spoke openly and freely about these, and clarified that Ariel's 'readings' of her were more than mind-reading, delving somehow into her memories and emotions. Not surprisingly Hugh's face lit up at the prospect of such intelligence-gathering. She even repeated her apology for showing him the footage she had seen on the plane.

But of the walk in the woods she said nothing.

6

The second day of the review meeting in the *Palais de Nations* felt far less tense, and by the morning break they had come much further than Constance could have hoped, so she decided this was the time to voice her desire to include Melody Grantley James at some point in the future. Jim and Ryan saw this as an opportunity to do something less antagonistic, and almost everyone else agreed on pragmatic grounds, given that the world would need some assurance that the media had not been entirely shut out when they went public again. Which had to be fairly soon. Beth was the only one to challenge the choice, but that only succeeded in provoking Jack to raise Bill's involvement.

'The room needs to be aware,' Jack began, 'that High Command's special envoy, one General William Petersen, was a bull in the proverbial china shop from day one. Our progress with Ariel had been slow, admittedly, but we were getting somewhere.' Beth made to interrupt but he pressed on. 'We were dealing with the infiltration by Hugh Coates and his able assistant,' and at this Jack couldn't resist a smile, 'an infiltration that eventually turned out to be from our side anyway, though at that point I for one did not know that he was in cahoots with British Intelligence.'

'Well now,' Jim cut in, 'that rather depends on which side "our side" is, don't you think?' Clearly the connection with British Intelligence was not going to stop rankling that easily.

Constance decided to intervene. 'Let us freely admit,' she said, 'that this has been complicated. Not even I knew that there was an arrangement of this nature with Mr Coates. Clearly General Petersen was unaware of it. I think we all were. I have dug a little deeper, and I am at liberty to inform you all that he has a similar arrangement with the Americans. And probably others. That is not something for public consumption, obviously, but I hope it helps us see that we were all equally in the dark.'

'All the more reason to have kept his assistant away from Ariel then, surely,' said Beth.

'Let's not rehearse the argument Jack and the General have already had,' said Constance. 'Suffice it to say that I was happy to trust Jack's judgement, and clearly Ms Freeman came to play an important role.'

Jack then proceeded to tell them about the discovery of Ariel's ability to read people's minds, in some fashion or other, before outlining the approach he had taken: to allow Ariel to interact with the crew and talk about whatever he wanted.

'What about this abbot fellow?' said Beth. 'What's the story there?'

'That's something I should address,' said Constance, immediately sensing the thinning of the ice beneath her feet. Yet it was a moment she had prepared for. 'I first met Leonardo some five years ago. I needed a break – don't we all? – and I found this retreat centre on the other side of the Alps. I wasn't too bothered by the spiritual mumbo-jumbo in some of its publicity material, which was clearly background rather than something you had to sign up to, and I went ahead and took my break there. Now, whether it was just good customer service and the hope that I would bring more colleagues, or something else, I don't know, but I found in the Abbot a deeply wise and... sane individual. And when I discovered just how good their electronic screening was, to facilitate a proper break from the never-ceasing demands of modern life, I knew then that it would be my regular place of withdrawal.

'As you know, I was not able to be present on Alpha when the crew returned. And I admit it was a deliberate decision on my part. I left others to face the press, and to make the preliminary assessments. I knew my task was to provide somewhere we could take stock of what and whom we had found. A safe space. And that idea led me to

Montagnola.'

'You had no right to make that call,' said Beth quietly.

'My dear, I had every right. As head of the WSA it was my call.'

'Pardon me, *dear*,' Beth retorted, 'but once you knew about the stowaway you had a duty to share that information with me.'

'Which I did,' she replied calmly.

'Immediately! Not after they'd already got back!' It was the first time she had raised her voice, and her strength of accent increased with the volume. The others looked on, so many spectators in a grand-slam final.

'Beth, this started as a mission of space exploration. Even when Ariel turned up, there was never a sign of threat or danger, not at any time, beyond the changing climatic conditions for which we had already prepared.' She decided to go for the jugular. 'As for military involvement, sending in Petersen was perfectly reasonable. Sending him back with his henchmen was totally out of line!'

Match point.

'Allow me to explain,' said Beth, more quietly now. 'It's only right that everyone here should be aware of the deal you and I made, Constance, giving you extra time at the monastery, or whatever that place really is, while we concentrated on the crystal. We all need to understand, as well, that Bill Petersen is used to taking a lead. That's why he's head of the Task Force. And yes, he certainly is answerable to High Command, and you can be sure that we have had words with him about his... nocturnal adventure.'

'Oh,' said Jack, 'you mean the attack on fellow team members?'

'I can only repeat the apology I have already made to Constance. Civilians were only taken so that Ariel would have some of the company he was used to.'

Jack looked at her, not sure whether to laugh or cry, and promptly decided both would be wasted.

Natasha noticed the assumption that Ariel himself was not a civilian, and equally felt nothing she wanted to say would help at this point.

'However,' Beth continued, 'the whole incident did at least bring to light Ariel's remarkable gift for self-preservation. The damage incurred by one of Bill's men is particularly interesting in the light of what happened on Space Station Alpha. Now I appreciate it was dark on the night in question, so we can't be sure just what happened, but we do have footage of what happened in Dr Schlesinger's laboratory.'

'That is correct,' said Constance, 'though it's inconclusive. It proved helpful in jogging Ariel's memory, but that's because he was there. To the rest of us it's not at all clear what was happening.'

Dan frowned. 'I'm not sure where you're going with this, Constance. I for one trust Schlesinger's testimony. He's not exactly given to hysteria. In fact, if I may, I'd like to suggest that this would be a good time to total up all we know, or think we know, about Ariel's... abilities.'

Natasha felt the chill of an approaching threat. She looked across to Jack but couldn't catch his eye. No doubt he was preparing himself for the inevitable processes of the military mind.

'I think that's an excellent suggestion,' said Constance, 'and I suggest we make it the subject of our next session. Let's have a break now. Then it's time we let Ariel speak for himself. It seems to me we've reached the shared understanding we've been aiming for. At least we're sharing information.'

She stood up, and the room emptied with barely a whisper. No one disagreed with her closing remarks, but it was clear the tension between the Space Agency and the military had not gone away. It seemed the match had gone to a final set, with everything still to play for.

7

Alice had never been to Switzerland, and as she landed at Geneva she forgot for a few moments the reason she was here. She always felt excited on entering another country. In this one they spoke at least three languages, although with her rusty schoolgirl French she was very much hoping that English – by force of practical necessity still the *lingua franca* of the world – would get her through.

It did. Within an hour she was standing in the foyer of David's hotel, from where she was shown to his room. When she had told him she was coming out to join him he had messaged her back to say he might be out and about, most likely in a library somewhere, but that she should make herself at home. Rather conveniently, the room already had a double bed.

The moment she stepped into the room the soft scent of an expensive perfume stopped her dead in her tracks. With the gift to memory that the sense of smell so often brings, she knew exactly when she had last encountered it. Mel had been wearing it when she visited them just two weeks before.

She sat on the bed and instantly sprang up again as though it were electrified. 'Don't be silly,' she told herself. 'There's a perfectly reasonable explanation. She just called by. As expected.'

She went over to the window. There was a chair with a new shirt she didn't recognise. She opened the blind and looked out. Were they out there together now? Had Mel called in to see him that very morning? Yes, that must be why the perfume was still in the air. But then surely he wouldn't have gone out, knowing that Alice was on her way? So did that mean she came yesterday? But then, why was such a subtle perfume still so noticeable? None of the answers she imagined bore thinking about.

She called him on her eband. It went to voicemail.

8

The late morning sun was low enough in the sky to shine directly into the conference room as the nine members of the review team filed into what just might be their last session. Tiredness gave way to fascination as together they rehearsed the remarkable happenings and abilities that had come to light with the one now called Ariel.

They began with the crew's account of the initial discovery. This time Jack made sure Natasha left nothing out – the weirdly reflective clothing, the intermittent consciousness, the blue eyes. They all affirmed Ariel's general weakness at that time, and Dr Schlesinger's report was examined again, this time accompanied by the camera footage. Beth was quick to tie this to the nocturnal altercation with Bill and his men in the forest. Both times Ariel had been more or less unconscious, and both times he had withstood serious bodily injury in ways that seemed little short of miraculous.

Next up was his apparent ability to open a locked door, once again attended by unconsciousness. And last but not least came his mind-reading abilities.

A hush now descended on the room, which Constance allowed to linger for a few moments before giving Ariel the floor.

'Ladies and gentlemen,' he began, 'it has been fascinating to witness your discussions thus far, and I thank you for letting this particular fly on the wall finally come and land centre stage. As many of you know, I have rediscovered my command of English, and while I still sense that it may not be the only language locked up in here, I am clearly very at home in it. As to land of origin, I regret we are no further forward. Nor with which company I served. For yes, I feel increasingly certain – though I know not why – that I served in a battalion of some sort. There was a rout, it was intense, we were in the ether, victory seemed close. I fell.'

Beth attended to her eband briefly.

'I have smatterings of recall in the days that followed, and I must give especial thanks here to Natasha who was like a bollard or a cleat on a jetty when you're tossed about by the waves, something to tie myself onto, to stop me being swept out to sea.'

Natasha smiled, unsure when she was last compared with a bollard. No, she was sure. This was a first.

Ariel continued. 'And I want to acknowledge the part played by Miranda in helping me to recall what happened on the space station.'

Natasha's smile faded.

'Leonardo provided me with a space to process what I was

learning... relearning, I suppose. To get my bearings. Above all, I have come to realise that Jack here has cut me an enormous amount of slack – with Constance's crucial support – which has brought me... brought us... to where we are today. I say "us" because I am as eager as everyone in this room to discover who or what I am.'

Jack smiled, delighted that this truth had been voiced so soon and so clearly.

'Regarding the "what" I might be, it is clear that I am able to do things that others can't. I can't say how I do them, any more than any of you can say how you read text or interpret the thousand-and-one signals coming at you each day. I just do it. When what I now know to be Dr Schlesinger's saw touched my flesh, as soon as it touched me, I instinctively scrunched myself together at the point of contact, not allowing the substance of the saw to violate the substance of my flesh. I think now – and this thought will be new to everyone here, including Jack and Natasha – that I was undergoing a process of change while I was on the space station. A process that had presumably begun on or before Venus. Perhaps it was the enhancement process some have speculated about, I don't know. To me it felt more as if I were becoming weaker, not stronger.'

Beth made another tiny adjustment to her eband. Jack guessed she was bookmarking the time in her recording.

'It's strange,' Ariel continued, 'but I seem to have spent the last two weeks living between faints! I can only think that I pass out because my system is going into overload. So let me say right away that I shall willingly submit to whatever medical tests you deem necessary to get to the bottom of what is going on.'

'Let's not say *whatever* tests,' said Natasha, sounding more like his legal counsel.

'Very well,' said Ariel, 'though we shall have to be a little creative if we're to find out what has been done to me... what I'm really capable of, won't we?'

Selena watched Beth's face and thought she saw signs of conflict there. She certainly hoped so. The thought of where the military might go with a compliant Ariel made her shiver. Yet she could not help but admire the confidence coming from this extraordinary man who, even now, was trying to explain what it was like to 'read' the thoughts and impressions that were open to him when someone looked directly into his eyes in a receptive way.

'How about you read my thoughts then?' said Ryan suddenly. He was looking directly across the table at Ariel.

Ariel turned his head slightly and looked straight back. Almost immediately Ryan looked away, crying out as he clutched his head. 'Ow! What was that?'

Jim was instantly on his feet, but Ryan pulled him back down. 'It's okay, Jim.'

'I believe that was an echo,' said Ariel simply. 'I'm not sure I have the ability to read you unless you want me to. But it seems this is not the first time we have met in this way.'

'I'm sorry, I don't understand,' said Beth.

'You're not the only one,' said Jim.

'Allow me to explain,' said Ariel. 'During one of my aforementioned faints I saw Dr Chase in a laboratory. Just before he was attacked by an oriental-looking man.'

'How?' Beth squeaked. 'How could you do that?' Jack noticed the colour drain from her face at the mention of the oriental figure.

'I believe that the crystal made the connection for us.' Ariel described what he saw, and Ryan confirmed that he had been looking intently at the crystal when he had been hit over the head.

Beth was eager to move the discussion on. 'Well, that rather confirms a link between Ariel and the crystal, does it not? One which you, Dan, have suspected since the thing glowed or buzzed in your office.' Dan nodded. 'I'd like to propose, Constance, that we now bring together all three parts of our puzzle – Ariel, his suit and the crystal – and see what we can find out. I've already got a lab ready where we can bring the best technical brains and equipment to bear.'

Ryan couldn't resist. 'Yeah, you sure have great equipment there.' He looked down the table to Constance, who nodded for him to continue. 'Maybe not such great hospitality,' he went on, and described his visit to the lab, carefully omitting Dan from his account of how he tracked it down, but naming the connection with Takahashi.

'Well, I'm sure I don't know what to say,' said Beth. 'Constance, you must agree this is highly irregular, going off and breaking into a secret facility.'

Before Constance could answer Jack jumped in. 'Methinks the lady doth protest too much. Something tells me, Ms Griffiths, that you were already aware of this.'

'Let's call a halt here,' said Constance quickly. 'I think we can deal with these details outside of this room. But I don't want to lose the focus we have right now on Ariel and his abilities. Ariel, what do you think the crystal is?'

'I'm sorry,' he replied. 'I really have no idea.'

9

Two floors up Beth's office was quiet. Takeshi Takahashi knocked anyway, and at first he thought he heard movement inside. He waited, knocked again and went in. The room was empty. He started to walk towards the inner chamber Beth used for a quick change of clothes, at which point a secretary popped her head round the door.

'Sorry, Mr Takahashi, Ms Griffiths is still in the meeting.'

Takeshi grunted an acknowledgement before leaving. Two minutes later Nathan Dexter emerged from the changing room, brushing small particles of ceiling plaster from the shoulder of his immaculately tailored suit.

CHAPTER 21

Taken

1

While the news about the Man from Venus had gone quiet across the world, *Exposé* had not remained inactive. Their name may have been a French word, but it meant the same in every language. It was clear to this group of men and women, highly dedicated to exposing lies and revealing secrets, that Melody Grantley James was the only person outside of the mission team who just might know who the Stranger was. It was in *Exposé*'s DNA to uncover the truth at any cost, and she was the softest target.

Lucien Barretours was the latest member of the European cell that operated behind *Exposé*. In his late thirties, blessed with the rugged looks of a Frenchman world-weary before his time, he had been recruited for his effectiveness as a climate activist in the cause of global cooling, having already demonstrated a flair for disruption. That alone would have been a valuable skill in their line of business, but what confirmed his appointment was a flair for effective interrogation.

The headquarters of his new employer was in Cologne, fronted by the European office of its online news arm which specialised in exclusives somehow obtained well ahead of the world's main news agencies. The secret behind this independent news site was a backbone of ruthless determination to give the world what it deserved to have. And secrecy was crucial. When circumstances dictated the use of violence or extortion to obtain a story, it was first released anonymously on a site with no traceable connection. So far this had worked without detection, though in the way of these things everyone knew it was only a matter of time before the front organisation drew the attention of the authorities.

When they had first made contact and discovered Lucien's interrogative skills, he was immediately assigned to the abduction and interrogation of Melody Grantley James. His plan was now well advanced, having put a tail on her since she had first arrived in Geneva some two weeks before, shortly after her return to Earth. She had disappeared almost as soon as she had arrived, though their mole in the UN soon came through with the news that she had joined the team in a monastery in the Swiss village of Montagnola. Lucien investigated but quickly decided it was way too risky to try and lift her in such confined surroundings.

But now she was back in Geneva, and the tail soon reported on her movements. She had met up with a man they could not as yet identify, apparently a fellow Brit. Lucien had been summoned to Cologne from his home, a small apartment in Lyon, to meet with two of his new associates to decide whether they pounce now or wait even longer and increase the risk of losing the advantage they hoped to gain.

As far as he could tell, everyone Lucien had communicated with so far in the organisation was using their real name. That seemed especially likely with the woman in charge of the news office, Marta Bergstrom, who made no secret of the fact that she was the sister of the Director of the European Space Agency. He wondered just how much of his sister's clandestine activities Lena Bergstrom was aware of. Marta met him now as he stepped out of Cologne's central railway station, her bright red silk scarf heralding her approach. He guessed she was ten years his senior, only a little short of fifty, but there was something young about her, playful, which he took to immediately.

They stepped out of the echo of milling crowds and travel announcements into the sun and the riverside air, soon passing under the shadow of the vast Gothic cathedral which stood next door quietly tolerating the bustle of everyday life with sublime indifference. They walked on into a busy shopping street, finally leaving behind the constant rumblings of the trains that made their way over the giant railway bridge, the Hohenzollern, which took the main line across the River Rhine.

It was a short walk to the *Exposé* office, a large ground-floor apartment close by the *Gross St Martin Kirche*, the Great Church of St Martin. No introductions were made until they went into a small room at the back. 'Welcome to the cave,' said Marta. There were no windows here, and Lucien noticed that his eband had lost signal. It seemed he had arrived at the centre of things.

Waiting in the room was a man dressed in a long black house coat, who was introduced simply as Dog. His English was better than theirs, though Lucien thought it was not his mother tongue. Unlike the workers in the front office he was unkempt. His straw-coloured hair was long and straggly, though his beard was surprisingly well-trimmed, the effect of which was to set up an appearance of someone wild but controlled. But the most noticeable feature was a fire in his eyes. Lucien decided his features and accent put him somewhere in Scandinavia.

'Hello Lucien,' he said. 'Welcome to our little operation. I trust you'll fit in here.'

'I think I will,' said Lucien in a fairly heavy French accent. 'I have a high regard for the work of *Exposé*. The world cannot go on much longer – no? – allowing its political leaders to talk us all to death.'

'Well said,' said Dog. 'So, let's get to it. Miss James – can we take her?'

'I think we may not have a better time,' said Lucien, 'now that she is separated from the others.'

'What about her new friend?' said Marta.

'We try to avoid him, but if necessary he comes too,' said Lucien. If he was on trial here – a sensation seemingly confirmed by Dog's intense stare in his direction – then the way to pass was surely through action.

'Very well,' said Dog. 'We go today. I'll send word to our man in Geneva. We have an interrogation chamber ready here in Köln. Marta will show you where.'

2

Selena stared at the suit spread out on the table before her. Beside her stood its only known owner, Ariel, while opposite them Beth was gazing at it from different angles. Nothing. It was just a white overall.

'Are you sure–?' Beth began.

'Yes, this is – or was – my garment,' said Ariel.

They were in a room adjacent to Beth's office. Ryan was standing in the corner. 'Looks about right,' he said, though his gaze kept returning to the crystal which was occupying a transparent box on a table next to him.

They were waiting for Takeshi. 'Funny,' said Beth, 'it's not like him to be late. Well, let's get on. How do we want to do this?'

Ryan didn't hesitate. 'I need a lab. The one on the outskirts of the city will do just fine. And of course I'll need access to Ariel, since his proximity may be significant, though don't ask me why.'

'What do you think, Selena?' said Beth.

'That seems reasonable,' she said. 'I have a few bits and pieces of testing equipment here, which I brought with me in case, but I can't match the kind of equipment Ryan says is in the lab where he tried to... recover the crystal. And I agree that Ariel should come with us.'

'Very well,' said Beth. 'I suggest you get going first thing tomorrow.'

The door opened. It was Nathan Dexter.

'Hello,' said Beth. 'What brings you here? Have you seen Takeshi?'

'He's not well,' said Nathan, whose eyes were already on the crystal. 'Anything I can do to help?'

'Actually yes, there is,' said Beth. 'I have a meeting I need to be in, in the Human Rights Room, and it's not going to be a short one. Would you mind checking in with Takeshi and taking these good people to the facility he's set up? It's not too far from here.'

'I'd be delighted,' he said, suppressing what surely would have been an ugly smile.

3

The *Institut de l'Histoire de la Réformation* was set in a fine-looking building in the *Parc des Bastions*, not too far from the southern tip of Lake Geneva. The man on the hotel front desk had very kindly told Alice that David had asked for directions to the park earlier that morning. He didn't mention whether he had anyone with him, and she didn't ask, even though every nerve in her body was screaming at her to do so. When she checked her eband and discovered that the Institute contained a library with access to original documents by John Calvin, she left at once.

The taxi dropped her off on the wrong side of the park as it turned out, so she had to walk right across it to get to the building. She made her way past some giant chessboards where children were moving the pieces at random. It seemed an eloquent picture of how her life was suddenly turning out. She quickened her pace and followed a path under some trees where the leaves had already announced the arrival of autumn. People were walking or jogging, and here and there couples walked arm in arm. As couples do. She shivered, and then as she emerged from the trees into a partially grassed square she saw a man and a woman coming down the steps from an arched doorway.

It took her a few seconds to register it was David and Mel.

She stood still. Half of her wanted to run towards them and call out their names, but she gave in to the half that wanted to see how they were with each other. At least they were not holding hands. They were talking. As they reached the bottom of the steps they disappeared behind a fairly large black van that was parked in front of the building. She waited for them to reappear, but there was no sign of them.

She started walking once more, quickening her pace. Suddenly the black van's tyres squealed and she had to step back onto the grass as it raced past.

David and Mel were gone.

4

Takeshi looked around the laboratory, satisfied it was fully prepared at last, just in time for the first scientists due to arrive the next day. All he needed now was the crystal itself, which he had taken back to the UN building for safekeeping after Ryan's intrusion. He locked the lab door and made his way along the corridor to the front of the converted warehouse. As he approached the entrance area some moving shadows caught his attention. He stopped. Thinking quickly he started to whistle nonchalantly, hoping that whoever it was did not know how untypical that was for him. As he stepped out into the entrance he was ready.

A man on his left grabbed him by the arm. Before another man on the right could do the same, Takeshi had already dropped to the floor and used his legs to force his first attacker to do a rough kind of somersault over Takeshi's head and into the second man. By the time they had got to their feet Takeshi was already at the front door. He could see it had been forced with something like a crowbar. Realising he would be unable to lock it behind him, and suddenly worried now for the safety of his laboratory, he turned to face his attackers once more.

As he was preparing a new manoeuvre, one he hoped would render both men unconscious, he failed to see a third figure approach from outside, crow bar in hand.

Everything went dark.

5

Jack was in the cafeteria checking messages on his eband when the name Alice Carter appeared on the small screen. It took him a moment to register that this was Mel's friend in Canterbury. Why would she be contacting him? A sense of unease began to grow even as he accepted the call.

'Hello, is that Jack Forrester? It's Alice here, Alice Carter.'

'So I see,' said Jack. 'What's up, Alice?'

She told him that she was in Geneva to meet up with David. She started calmly enough, but the words came tumbling out ever more rapidly as she described what she had just witnessed. And no, she didn't get the van's number. 'I'm sorry, Jack. I don't know what to do.'

'You've done the right thing,' he responded as calmly as he could. 'Where are you – the *Parc des Bastions*, you say? I don't know where that is. Can you get a taxi and come meet me here at the *Palais de Nations* – er, the UN building? I'll meet you at the main entrance. Message me before you go through security.'

His blood ran cold. That Melody should be with David again, and here in Geneva, was chilling enough. But then to hear an account that sounded for all the world like an abduction, in broad daylight... He marched straight to the office of Beth Griffiths, to be greeted instead by a man.

'Hi, I'm Nathan Dexter.' The accent was American. 'And you, I believe, are Jack Forrester.'

'Aye, that's me,' said Jack. 'And I've heard your name before. Beth not here?'

'Sorry, she's tied up with some human rights thing at the moment,' said Nathan. 'Can I help? I gather we both have some level of security clearance.'

Jack eyed the man, desperate to get a search started but unsure just how to go about it. He had no choice now but to wait for Alice anyway, so he decided this was not the time to bring in someone new. 'No, that's fine,' he said. 'It'll wait.'

He made his way down to Constance's office, using the delay to gather his thoughts. Petroc greeted him. 'Don't tell me,' said Jack, 'Constance is not in either.'

'She is in, sir,' said Petroc, 'but I believe she is dealing with a call right now.'

'Likely to be long?' said Jack, 'only I need to meet someone in the entrance hall soon.'

'Can I help with that, sir?'

'Thanks,' said Jack. 'Maybe.' He sat down to wait. For the next five minutes he watched Petroc field calls and speak to visitors with a high degree of competence, quickly forming the impression that this was a man to be trusted. When Alice's message came through on his eband he asked Petroc to go down and meet her. 'She's called Alice Carter, and she's a friend of a friend – well, of Miss Grantley James in fact.'

Petroc responded with ill-suppressed glee just as Constance emerged from her office.

'Ah, Jack,' she said. 'It seems we have a problem. Do come in.'

'Can I go first?' said Jack as he closed the door behind him.

'No, this can't wait,' said Constance, looking straight at him. She was shaking. 'I've just had a call from someone who tells me that he "has" Melody, and that you are to come and get her if you want her back.'

Jack sank into a chair. 'Me?' he said. 'Me personally?'

'Yes, Jack,' she said, 'you and Ariel. You are to take Ariel to them and bring Melody back. Straight swap. If we don't comply... Melody does not come back. I'm so sorry, Jack.' She sat down next to him. 'And Jack, to make matters worse, they've also taken a friend of hers, someone I've not even heard of, and they're threatening to harm him too.'

'David Carter,' said Jack. 'His wife is on her way up right now.'

6

It was a pleasant jaunt in the late summer sun for Lucien and Marta as they walked across the magnificent Hohenzollern Bridge. Just metres away, on the other side of a vast grid of heavy ironwork, trains thundered over the river as they came and went. There was a fresh breeze blowing, trying and generally failing to lift Marta's short dark hair, and Lucien soon found her company to be just as energising as the elements. She talked mainly of the stories they had unveiled to the world, blasting the lies of governments and corporations alike. She was clearly a woman who loved her job, and the passion seemed to be focused on truth-telling. When he asked her about their methods of extracting the truth, her dark eyes sparkled and she simply said, 'You'll soon see.'

When they reached the bank on the eastern side of the river they took some steps down to the water's edge. They passed under the mighty bridge, briefly engulfed by a party of tourists on their way to a river-tour jetty nearby. After a few more minutes Marta unlocked an iron gate and they disappeared into a small private residential complex. It looked brand new. And suddenly they were alone. Apart from the distant rumble of the Hohenzollern, the place was quiet. A perfect spot for interrogation.

They approached the front door of one of the select detached cottages, where she held her eband up to a keypad and then ushered him in. It looked unused and unlived-in. Everywhere was sparkling and spotless. She showed him around, taking pains to point out the cleanliness of the kitchenette 'which should be maintained at all times', before taking him upstairs to a studio room with a balcony overlooking the Rhine. Here there was also a bathroom and two bedrooms which faced away from the river.

'Very nice,' he said. 'And very expensive.'

'Ah, but the real feature is the basement,' she said with a fresh glint in her eye. She led him back downstairs and across the room to a door directly opposite the main entrance. Lucien watched as she pressed her eband and the latch slipped across. As she opened the door a light came on, illuminating stairs that took them down and round and further down, till they came to another door. Once more she pressed her eband, and this time two locks slid back. She pulled the door wide open, and they went in.

'Welcome to our lair!' she called out, and her voice died almost instantly.

'Wow, first a cave, and now a lair!' said Lucien, fascinated to hear his own voice fail to bounce off the walls. The room was about five metres square. The walls were smooth and white, though when he touched them he felt hundreds of small bumps.

Marta made a quick circuit. 'It has all the modern conveniences,' she said. 'Like this! How do you say it? *Comme ça!*' On the wall opposite she made a great show of pressing a shiny metallic pad with the tip of her finger. Instantly two pieces of curved metal shot out from either side of the pad, meeting in the middle and forming the perfect manacle. She carefully removed her finger.

'Titanium,' she said. 'Electronic pin lock. No one's going to get out of that without unlocking. You just push the prisoner's wrists and ankles against the pads – or just their wrists if they're on the floor – and they're instantly cuffed. Conscious or not.'

Lucien had never seen anything like it. 'I thought you were going to say it has a toilet,' he laughed.

'Don't be silly!' she grinned. 'It has two!' His laugh withered as with both hands she pressed two almost invisible raised points in the wall. The unmistakable smell of bleach hit him as a thick section of the wall pivoted, the top disappearing into the wall space while the bottom came forward and clicked into place. And there was the traditional shape of a toilet seat, with enough space to wash away whatever it received. 'Automatic flush,' she said. 'Someone can be left here for hours quite humanely. And no nasty smells! *Wunderbar, nein?*'

Lucien felt the definition of humane had just been stretched, but said nothing and gave a weak smile.

'And we have the same arrangement on the wall over there!' she said with glee.

'What about food and drink? Don't tell me – there's a hatch.'

'Ah, I see you catch on fast, Lucien! They can be given water here, *in situ*, or if they are not cuffed they can be fed via a small elevator which is loaded upstairs and sent down, appearing in a hatch over there.'

He walked over to what he had taken to be the only piece of furniture in the room. It looked like a bench, though by now he understood that it would be far more.

'Ah, what you might call our *pièce de résistance*,' she said. 'Similar restraints on top. Inside we have a fine collection of drugs and injectors to help in the search for truth. Oh, and it delivers a range of electric shocks too.'

She stood back, ran her fingers through her neat and tidy hair and, like an estate agent looking for a reaction, waited for his response.

He was lost for words.

'Do you think you can work with this?' she said.

'It is amazing,' he said at last. 'Clinical, but amazing.'

'Well,' she grinned, 'you did say you have a high regard for our work. You know how committed we are. Time for some refreshment?'

They made their way back upstairs, Marta locking the doors behind them. Lucien breathed deeply as they stepped back into daylight.

'*Apfelsaft?*' she said?

'Apple juice would be just fine,' he replied.

He followed her to the kitchen area. 'Tell me,' he said as casually as he could make it sound, 'what is it with the Dog? The name, I mean.'

'Dog? His real name is Sirius,' she said. 'Sirius Oksanen, I think.'

'You think?'

'Well, he didn't actually tell me himself, you understand. That's not how the cells in the organisation operate. But I saw it somewhere.'

'Is that Finnish?'

'I don't know,' she replied.

He grunted. 'You don't usually find Scandinavian types to be so...'

'I know what you mean,' she said. 'There is something unnerving about him. The thing is, if you keep on the right side of him, he's fine. He leaves me to get on with the news business, while he takes care of our role in the, ah, wider work.'

Lucien decided now was not the time to ask for details, and he had a feeling that that would be on a need-to-know basis anyway. 'And me?' he said. 'Where do you think I fit in?'

'Oh, on the wider side, for sure,' she said. 'Get the people we target, and get the truth from them so we can publish it.'

'So... I fit somewhere between the two of you?'

She shot him a quick grin. 'Drink up!' she said. 'We'll come back later.' Then she washed and dried their glasses before carefully placing them back on the shelf.

Lucien followed her out, unsure whether he had just been with a zealous company representative or a psychopath.

7

'What do we know?'

Beth was in her office chairing a hastily convened gathering of a new and unexpected mix of people – Constance, Jack, Natasha, Ariel and Nathan Dexter. No one doubted this was her territory, or that they needed a plan fast.

'I've been in touch with the local police,' said Nathan, 'and they've told us to wait till they get here.'

'I'm sure they have,' said Beth. She drummed her fingers on the desk. 'Damned inconvenient that Takeshi's not well,' she murmured. 'Jack? Any ideas on who we're dealing with?'

'Well,' said Jack, rubbing the back of his head and looking more tense than anyone had seen him, 'as you know, they've asked us to meet them tomorrow in Stuttgart. The co-ordinates are for somewhere close to the main railway station. My guess is that they're based in another German city. But it could be any one of several, considering how quickly you can get to Stuttgart by rail. Could be Berlin, could be Frankfurt, Cologne, Leipzig...'

'So we can't identify them, and we can't make a pre-emptive move,' said Beth.

'No, that won't be possible, I'm afraid,' Jack sighed.

'We could try offering them money instead, I guess,' said Nathan half-heartedly.

Only Constance bothered to respond. 'No, it's Ariel they want. He's the prize, and I don't think there's a price tag in the world that would fit.'

'I am honoured,' said Ariel.

Natasha ended the awkward silence that followed by asking if the kidnappers had said why they wanted Ariel.

'Not a word,' said Constance. 'We don't know who they are, or what they mean to do with him.'

'Sell him to the highest bidder maybe,' said Jack.

'So there could be a price tag?' said Ariel calmly.

Natasha got up and tackled a water dispenser near the inner door, hitting it hard with the palm of her hand when it hesitated to pour.

'I suppose this couldn't be your former associates we're dealing with here, Ariel?' Constance ventured. 'Those you fought with? Those who gave you your special abilities, even?'

'Or who share them?' Beth added as it dawned on her how much more complicated things could become if there were more Ariels.

'I rather think not,' said Ariel. 'I may not remember names, faces or places, but I do recall the *feeling* of being with my comrades. They would not do this.'

Jack shook his head in a mix of resolve and resignation. 'Listen,' he said, 'I think we have no option but to go and see what we find.

But if the police want to tag along, that could be difficult. I'd have thought one of our guys would be better at surveillance, or even intervention. I could talk to London.'

'Mmm,' said Beth, 'I don't know. The Germans would take a dim view if they found out. It would need to be UN personnel, I think.'

'I'd be happy to tag along,' said Nathan.

'I thought you'd had your fill of field work,' said Beth. 'What about Bill?'

'You cannot be serious,' said Natasha as coldly as she could, which was at the freezing level. She was still standing by the door.

Jack considered the options. 'There's so little time. And Nathan, while I appreciate the offer, I have to admit that Bill is probably better qualified for what I have in mind. I know, Natasha, but sometimes it takes one to know one, and although Bill's previous attempt at abduction failed, I think he is going to be highly motivated here. Let's face it, losing Ariel is the last thing he wants.'

'Well, that's certainly true,' said Beth.

'And losing Melody is the last thing we want,' said Constance.

Jack appreciated the affirmation of priorities, and was gratified to see Natasha nod in his direction. They were set to go.

8

Melody felt sick. She had been wandering through a series of suffocating dreams in which she had struggled and rolled, bumped up and down, and then struggled some more. Now she lay still, listening to her own heart racing.

It must have been several minutes before she really woke up. David! They had been coming out of the library, down some steps, when a man got out of a van and called them over. David had asked her if she recognised them from the UN, but before she could reply another man came round the van, stood behind David, and put his hand across his mouth. David went rigid and immediately slumped. Before she could move she felt what she now realised was the other man's hand over her own mouth and a pin-prick in the side of her neck. Instinctively she bit hard and stamped her foot, but it was no good. She swooned. The last thing she remembered was the sliding of a van door. The whole thing must have taken less than sixty seconds.

She tried to sit up and felt something on her wrist. Her jacket was gone, and her arm was somehow attached to the wall she was propped up against. She could just make out the figure of a man lying, much as she was, against an adjacent wall. 'David?' she whispered. 'David? Is that you? Are you all right?'

His silence only made her lonelier, so she decided to fill the space by thinking through what was going on. She could see clearly now that her left hand was manacled to the wall and her eband was gone. She looked around. It was difficult to gauge how large the room was. Everything was white, dimly lit from the faintly glowing ceiling. Having made sure it was David lying against the other wall, she focused on the other side of the room where she could just make out the outline of a door.

'Well, David,' she said, louder this time, 'we're obviously in a cell of some kind. And I have a horrible feeling you are not meant to be here.'

9

The evening before the exchange was not going to be easy for anyone. While Beth, Constance and Jack talked to the police, Natasha booked Alice into their hotel and met with her and Ariel in the lounge, having agreed that it would be unwise to leave her on her own. They talked freely about their time in Montagnola.

It didn't take Alice long to recognise what they were doing. As an experienced counsellor herself, she knew that she needed to give her mind something else to chew on, or else the fear would inevitably chew on her. 'It sounds like a very strange kind of place,' she said. 'What did you call it – the Temple of the Four Elements?'

'That's the name of the place behind it,' said Natasha. 'We were in the Elemental Retreat Centre, which I think is a Western outpost of the organisation based in Tibet.' She told her how Constance had found the place and how wonderfully suitable it had proved to be, giving them the space they needed to let Ariel try to regain his memory.

Alice studied Ariel, and as she did so her heart began to beat more slowly and her whole body relaxed. 'Amnesia?' she said. 'How extraordinary! I hadn't realised you were a mystery to yourself and not just to us.'

'That puts it well,' said Ariel.

'We haven't released anything about his amnesia,' said Natasha quickly.

'No, of course,' said Alice. 'I realise everything we discuss right now is top secret. I really appreciate you letting me know something of what David has got himself mixed up in.'

'Do you mind telling us about David?' said Ariel. 'Melody told me a little, but–'

'Did she?' said Alice. 'What? What did she say?'

Ariel hesitated.

'I'm sorry,' she said, 'I shouldn't have asked that.'

'Not at all,' said Ariel. 'I just need to be sure you really meant to.'

If anyone else had given her a chance to withdraw, to think about anything other than what had been eating her from even before David's abduction, she would have taken it. But something about this man's manner, something in his eyes, told her that she should press on.

Natasha stood up. 'I'm just going to go and get us some more water, okay?' She withdrew without waiting for an answer.

Ariel sat back in the plush armchair that quietly advertised the extravagant comfort of the hotel. 'You need to know first that I had deep and personal conversations with several people at the monastery,' he said. 'I think the idea was that this would bring things to the surface for me.'

'And did it?'

'Um, work in progress,' he said with a faint smile.

'I'm sorry,' she said. 'Do go on.'

'Naturally these conversations were confidential. I don't think they were being recorded, although...'

'What?'

Ariel chuckled as he thought of Miranda. 'No, it's nothing,' he said. 'There was an issue with secret recordings, but I don't think we need worry about that.'

'My, what a dramatic life you have had!'

'Yes,' said Ariel, 'and that's only in the last couple of weeks!'

Natasha arrived with the water and said she needed to get an early night. It seemed right to follow the model Jack had set up in Montagnola and allow them both to have a private conversation.

'Thank you,' said Alice. 'I mean it. Thank you for all you are doing.' She felt tears start to well.

'Think nothing of it,' said Natasha, and she bid them both good night.

Ariel poured some of the water into Alice's glass. 'She is a remarkable woman,' he said when Natasha had gone. 'Not that I know many women,' he added. 'At least, I don't think I do.'

One of the hotel staff came and turned up the artificial log fire nearby before silently withdrawing.

'So,' said Ariel. 'As I was saying, these were confidential conversations, and as I recall Melody even surprised herself in how frank she was when she talked about your husband, saying that you would be mortified if you could overhear it—'

'Oh well, please, go no further,' said Alice, though the tears moved closer to the surface.

'Not at all,' said Ariel. 'I think the current situation changes that, and I am fairly sure that she would want you to know what was going on in her head. What she was struggling with.'

Alice felt the tension return to her shoulders as she braced herself.

'The thing is,' Ariel continued, 'she clearly values your friendship

– that is to say, specifically yours, Alice, as well as David's. While she had learnt a lot from David about Christian doctrine, she saw in you someone who lived it. Not that David was all talk, but I think she saw in you – she sees in you – a living example of human goodness and beauty.'

Alice shook her head. 'I don't understand.'

'Sorry, let me explain. We spent a lot of our allotted time talking about truth, beauty and justice, as well as religious faith, and she had clearly benefited intellectually from what David had taught her, or, should I say, discussed with her. She got that from you too, but I think in you she saw it lived out in a way she could relate to.'

'So, let me see if I've got this right,' said Alice slowly. 'Her relationship with David remains purely platonic.'

'If you mean it has no erotic dimension, then yes, that is correct.'

The tears broke. But when she had dried her eyes relief turned to fresh concern. 'What are you not telling me?'

'I'm not "not telling" you anything,' said Ariel. 'I just haven't told you everything yet. I can, of course, speak only for Melody, not David whom I haven't met.'

She sipped her water, steeling herself once more. 'Go on,' she said. 'No, let me guess. She's got a crush on him. I know she has! I knew it! I know it, I know it.'

'Look at me, Alice.'

It took her a few moments, but eventually Alice raised her head and looked into his eyes. He said nothing, yet as she dived into the sea of blue she was drawn into the black hole at the centre. Just a pupil in a man's eye, yet there seemed no end to its depth. A black hole for sure, only it wasn't crushing like a physical singularity, or disorienting like the rabbit hole associated with her namesake. It was charged with promise.

Almost immediately she could hear Melody speaking in her head. She was saying that she didn't understand the way she felt about David, that it was all tied up with Jack's jealousy and his distaste for religion, but that she didn't want to lose Jack's love or Alice's friendship.

Alice sat motionless, pivoted on the fine edge between the mundane and the mysterious. After a while Melody's voice faded, and there came an impression, like a scent in the air, that allowed her to taste the truth in some of its complexity and subtlety. If this was a love triangle, it was not exactly what she had feared. There was desire there, unmistakably, but that desire had not been corrupted. Not yet at least. Melody was still seeking after truth, and while that was undeniably bound up with David, it was more a case of being lost in confusion than trying to undermine a marriage. All was not well, but all was not lost.

A waiter asked someone nearby if they would like to order. The artificial fire flickered.

'What just happened?' she asked.

'It's an ability I have. Call it a gift.'

They stood up, and she hugged him. 'Thank you, Ariel. I don't know who you are, but right now I can say that, for me, you're like an angel sent from God. He does that, you know. He sends people into our lives with just what we need, when we need it. I don't know where David is in all this, and obviously that's something you can't tell me, but I feel a whole lot happier than... well, than I have done for some time. Bless you, and good night.'

The firelight sparkling in her eyes told Ariel the tears were still close, but he could see that there was more than sorrow and pain there. A measure of relief and a glimmer of hope. He marvelled at the release that the truth could bring.

Might he come to know the same one day?

10

It was already late when two representatives of the Swiss and German police arrived at the UN building. Petroc showed them to Constance's office where they were soon joined by Beth and Jack. It was a tricky negotiation, but a combination of Beth's authority and practical wisdom won the day. Commander Forrester and General Petersen would make the exchange, while German police would be armed and ready in the wings, which apparently meant in the trees close by the Stuttgart opera house. Petersen was to stand in for Ariel. He would swallow a temporary tracking device, just in case he was removed from the site, but it was hoped that he could be recovered unharmed just as soon as the hostages were secured.

'Of course, Ariel will have to be somewhere nearby,' Constance said. 'He has insisted on it, and on reflection I agree with him. If for any reason they don't take Bill, we must have the real thing on hand, or Miss Grantley James and her friend could be in even worse danger.'

It was going to be a busy night.

11

Melody did not know she had been asleep until the sound of the door opening interrupted a dream in which she was selling white furniture. The lights went up just as two men stepped inside and closed the door behind them. One of the men spoke to her with a French accent. Melody had time to spot a blue cloth jacket over a lighter blue waistcoat. He had the beginnings of a beard, possibly designer stubble, and there was a hardy look about him, but his eyes were not unkind.

'Hello Miss James. First, let me apologise for the surroundings. I do hope you are not too uncomfortable. I need to ask you some questions, and then, depending on your answers, you and your friend can go. Do you understand?'

'Yes.'

'Good. First, I need to see what your eband can tell me.' He took it from his pocket. 'But it is set for opening by your voice command. Can you unlock it for me please?'

'I'm so sorry,' she said, 'but what with all this trauma – you know, being drugged and bundled into a van and all – I've quite forgotten the password. I'm sure you understand.' She attempted a smile, though it went flat as she started to shake.

The other man shook his head, spilling his long, unkempt hair. The Frenchman raised a hand, presumably to forestall any discussion on the matter, and the other went over to take a closer look at David.

'Ah now, Miss James,' said the Frenchman, 'I hope you realise that this is not helpful to me. Please try to remember.'

She waited a moment. 'No, sorry, can't.'

The other man spoke. 'Melody, isn't it?' His English was clearer. There was menace in his voice. 'Such a lovely name. We can certainly make you sing a pretty tune if you don't co-operate.'

'Who are you?' said Melody. 'And what do you want?'

'Perfectly reasonable questions,' said the Frenchman. 'However, we are the ones asking, and you answer. Now, the eband please.'

Melody sat as upright as she could, her back hard against the wall, her left hand still restrained. She eyed the two men, wondering whether this was a game of good cop, bad cop. If it was, it felt like the stakes were about to go up. The other man somehow released David from the wall clasp and proceeded to drag his unconscious form across the room. 'Here, give me a hand,' he said to the other, and together they hauled him up onto the bench, whereupon the second man stretched David out. Four sudden rapping sounds announced the strapping of his wrists and ankles. He was secure.

'Now then,' said the bad cop to David's prostrate form, 'let's wake you up, shall we?' He opened the side of the bench and turned a dial. Immediately David's body went rigid.

'Stop!' Melody shouted. 'What are you doing?'

The man ignored her, and slapped David's face a few times. 'Come on, that's it, wakey-wakey.' David stirred.

'Unlock the eband please, Mademoiselle,' said the Frenchman.

She hesitated, a move that the other man was clearly not going to tolerate. He turned the dial once more and David's body began to convulse.

'All right, all right!' she yelled, but the electric shock was reapplied.

The Frenchman pressed the eband into her left hand and she unlocked it. 'Okay!' he shouted. Melody thought she detected disapproval, even fear, in his voice.

The dial was turned back and David's form slumped back flat on the bench.

'Thank you, Miss James,' said the Frenchman, though his eyes seemed to say sorry as well.

The two men left, and Melody promptly burst into tears.

Chapter 22

Capture

1

Stuttgart had never been the most glamorous of German cities, but today the sun was shining and the opera house was doing its best, its newly refurbished fountain casting crystals in the air before the grand entrance columns. On the far side of the water from the building Jack sat on a bench with Bill Petersen. Jack could not help but find Bill's offer to stand in for Ariel impressive, both for its courage and for its cleverness. Ariel's description had not been released to the public, and, assuming neither Miranda nor Melody had leaked anything, there were no photographs.

They were an hour early, though they knew that the same could be true of the kidnappers, so they had travelled separately from Ariel. They had taken the metropolitan railway, the S-Bahn, from the airport and walked directly from the station. Ariel and Natasha were following by air a little later.

They watched a few people coming and going in the small park, some visiting the box office, others just passing through. Jack wondered if they were all police officers in plain clothing, though Bill pointed out that the police could not have removed the public without giving the game away.

They had not found conversation easy, but now that they were together in the field a new bond was beginning to form.

'It's good to be on the same side,' said Bill.

'Well now, I thought we always were,' Jack returned.

'Yes, well...'

'Let's go through the plan one last time,' said Jack.

'You hand me over,' said Bill, 'and once the hostages are safe I kick ass and run. If they're armed you cover me.'

Jack frowned.

'What?'

'We can't assume they'll make the exchange here,' said Jack. 'If you and I are separated, you may be on your own at the critical moment. Your tracker won't last more than a day–'

'Maybe more,' Bill said with a grin. 'I have excellent bowel control!'

'Och, it's no joke,' Jack protested. 'I don't know... maybe I was mad to agree to this.'

'Nonsense,' said Bill. 'I'll be okay. And your girl is hardly helpless. Stays pretty cool in a fight, as I recall.'

Jack had to smile at that.

'Anyway,' said Bill, 'they're not leaving town today, not if I can help it.'

'Hmm,' said Jack, 'we don't even know how many there are.'

'Come on,' said Bill, a note of the old impatience sounding through, 'we're doing this because you and I know how to think on our feet. Ha! What's the worst that can happen?'

As if to answer that question a man came out of the opera house and strode towards them. Jack stood up.

CAPTURE

'Commander Forrester, where is the man you found on Venus?' The accent was French.

'Well, he's seated right here,' said Jack. 'He's still not saying much, I'm afraid. So, where are the hostages?'

'Commander, please do not take me for a fool.' And with that he held up an eband and projected a photograph on to Bill's chest. There was Ariel, and behind him a building which Jack soon realised was the monastery at Montagnola.

'Oh, Melody!' Jack sighed, and sat back down. In an instant Bill was on his feet and had the Frenchman in a full-nelson. 'Bill, don't be stupid!' Jack shouted.

Then several things happened in quick succession. Melody appeared from inside the opera house, with David on her arm and Dog right behind them. Natasha and Ariel emerged from the corner of the park, having run much of the way from the station. Lucien thrust both his arms down to break Bill's grip on the back of his head, before taking a step back and flipping him onto the ground by pulling his legs forward. And a second after that an amplified voice from somewhere in the trees said, '*Polizei! Keine Bewegung!* This is the police! Nobody move!'

They all froze, Natasha panting, Melody holding onto David as firmly as she could, all the while feeling his weight drag her down. Then she heard Dog's voice behind her. It sounded like he was speaking into his eband. 'Okay guys,' he said quietly, 'take them out.'

A shot rang out from somewhere in the wood. Two bystanders quickly turned round and left the park. As before Melody's instinct was to drop to the ground, shielding David as best she could. Natasha did the same, but when she tried to cover Ariel she found he was no longer with her.

He was walking towards Jack and Bill.

Jack, suddenly noticing that the Frenchman had a gun to Bill's head, said, 'Wait. The guy you really want is coming right now.' As Lucien turned to look, Jack grabbed the gun from his hand. Bill began to scramble to his feet, only to go down again as a shot rang out from the trees and hit the bench, quickly followed by a new megaphone message: 'Pigs neutralised.'

2

Two hundred miles away Beth and Constance sat and waited. They had transferred to Constance's office as she was not one for staying away from her domain in a crisis. A tablet lay on the table between them, their sole contact with the action.

They had been told by the German police that firearms officers were in position. A new report was imminent. Neither of the two women was good at waiting, so they tried chatting, but that didn't go very well. Constance was just about to cross to her window when the tablet lit up and burst into life.

'Bad news, I'm afraid,' said the liaison officer on the radio. 'Somehow our cover has been blown. There was gunfire.'

'Anyone hurt?' asked Beth.

'We are not sure,' said the voice, 'but it seems the attackers were ready for us. I'm afraid it's all down to your people now.'

3

Marta clenched the bar on the fire door of the opera house as she watched the scene unfold before her. When she saw Lucien overcome, she squeezed harder.

Lucien had been livid when he had first been told Dog's real plan. It seemed he had never intended simply to extract information but was determined to take the Man from Venus himself. So much for being in the inner circle. Lucien had been used.

But after a while his feelings had begun to change, and Marta had been a part of that. True, Dog was out of control, certainly out of theirs, but Lucien had quickly fallen in with Marta's argument that talking directly to the Man was a far greater prize. Why ask another journalist for the story when you could go to the source direct?

CAPTURE

But Dog's agenda remained unclear. What was he planning to do with this Man? Marta knew this had to be handled carefully. But careful was plainly no longer a word that applied to Sirius Oksanen.

Her attention was drawn away to the one figure who had started moving when everyone else had stopped, apparently making for the bench where Lucien was. She heard Dog's voice in her earpiece, 'Stop shooting! Do not injure the target!' Then she watched as Forrester threw the gun he had wrested from Lucien high in the air towards the trees, before he made his way slowly, hands in the air, towards the hostages. She marvelled at the combination of sense, courage and compassion this displayed. Clearly this man knew when he was beaten, yet was not going to be deterred from helping the people he had come for.

But Dog was standing behind those people, and now, to Marta's horror, he took aim at Forrester. This had gone far enough. She burst out of the door crying, 'Dog! No!' Her voice, amplified in his earpiece, was enough to distract him, and Jack took the opportunity to kneel down and attend to Melody and David.

Dog glared at Marta before turning back to his prey, only to see a figure emerge through the heavy spray of the fountain, splashing through the small pool that encircled it. Concerned this may be the space man, he held the gun steady and hesitated. It was just long enough for the figure to fire. Searing pain went through his right shoulder. Without a moment's thought he switched hands and fired back. The figure fell back into the water.

Jack now got to his feet. 'Come on, man!' he shouted at Dog. 'We can still do this! You're holding all the cards. Put that gun down and let's do the exchange.'

Dog said nothing. Jack could see he was looking beyond him, so he turned round to see Natasha dragging Bill from the water. 'It's okay, Jack!' she called out. 'He's alive! But he needs medical attention urgently.'

'Come on,' Jack repeated to the man with the gun. 'I need to get my guy to an ambulance. We can still do this. You can't blame us for trying, but you win here. No question.'

Dog eyed the man talking for all the world as though he were still in control, and he hated him for it. But his scorn was suddenly eclipsed by the sight of Lucien approaching with Ariel in handcuffs. They had the prize they had come for. 'Marta,' said Dog icily, 'take our guest to the van. Lucien, take this gun and follow with the hostages. Both of them.'

Lucien made to question the command but Dog's eyes seared into him. 'Change of plan,' Dog said. 'They don't get to trick me and not pay for it. Now go!' Lucien waved the gun at Melody and got her to help David hobble back the way they had come. He allowed Ariel to take David's other arm. As they went Melody turned to look at Jack. A rugged defiance was in her eyes, and he loved her for it.

'Goodbye, Commander,' said Dog. 'Till we meet again.' And with that he put his eband to his mouth, said 'Exit all', and walked away as if he were on a stroll through the park.

Jack stood still as stone. He knew how close to death he had come, and he knew he could not follow. Not if he wanted to keep everyone alive for the more complex rescue plan they were now going to need. He forced himself to turn around.

'An ambulance is on its way,' said Natasha, kneeling by Bill where he still lay as she tightened his belt around the top of his leg. 'He's been hit twice. That first bullet only skimmed his head, which must be why he was able to follow you. But the second one is in the thigh. He's lost a lot of blood.'

'Okay, Natasha. Good job. Bill will be your friend for life.'

She glared at him, but only briefly.

Jack sat down on the ground next to them and sighed. 'What a mess!'

4

The police debrief later that day was a dismal affair. One German officer had been wounded, the rest simply embarrassed as they were taken by surprise and quickly disarmed. It would now be down to the security services to find Ariel and the two hostages. Beth learned that the kidnappers had quickly taken control of the whole park, including the opera house, so it was clear that they were dealing with a highly organised and well-equipped foe. 'The fact that they could get the better of the police is impressive enough,' she said to Jack. 'But to have taken Melody first, and to get that unauthorised photo of Ariel, shows we're not dealing with amateurs.'

Jack felt the edge in the word 'unauthorised', but he knew Beth was not in the frame of mind to blame Melody right now. 'I can only think she took it when she had some time alone with him,' said Jack. 'I take full responsibility.'

'Well, you can tell her off when you next see her,' said Beth. 'That's our priority right now.'

'Aye, thank you,' said Jack. 'How's Bill doing?'

'He'll live,' Beth replied. 'Thanks to Natasha.'

They were sitting in Beth's office after the police had gone, both trying to process what had happened.

'The thing is,' said Jack, 'while they do seem very organised, and they managed to anticipate the police involvement, it seems to me they have a loose cannon.'

'Like ours, you mean?'

'What?' said Jack. 'Oh, you mean Bill. Well yes, it's true, neither Bill nor this guy called Bob or Dob, or something like that, were acting according to script. Which I guess is why they ended up shooting each other.'

'Well,' said Beth, 'at least there were no other casualties.'

'No,' said Jack, 'though I have to say David Carter didn't look to be in great shape.' He smacked his forehead. 'I almost forgot – where's Alice?'

'Natasha is with her now,' said Beth. 'Jack, how are we going to find these people? We don't know who they are, and now they have no reason to get in touch.'

'Well, let's review the recordings – our own and the police

footage,' he said. 'I know the names they used were probably not real, but...'

'What?'

'I don't know. There was something unhinged about that guy. I wouldn't be surprised if he used their real names out of spite. I could see he hated it when the woman he called Marta interrupted him. I probably owe her my life for that.'

'Marta, you say? Did she have an accent?'

'Hard to say really. Let's have a listen.'

Beth called for Bill's eband recording. In all the fuss it hadn't been uploaded yet, but Nathan helpfully brought the eband itself in. 'May I join you?'

'Sure,' said Beth, and they set to it.

'You know, I'm pretty sure that's "Dog" she's calling him,' said Beth, as they were reviewing Jack's recording. Surely that's code, a field name?'

'Well, if it's not, then we're looking for a Dog, a Marta and a Lucien,' said Jack. 'I'll contact Darlene in London. They're already on the case.'

'And I'll get on to my contact in Washington,' said Nathan.

'Great,' said Jack. 'Tell me, Beth, where's the crystal now?'

'After we agreed to let Ariel go, I sent Ryan and Selena off to Takeshi's pop-up lab to start work on it. And on the suit. Too bad we don't have Ariel there as well.'

'Ah, but that may be where you're wrong,' said Jack. 'I have an idea. Nathan, can you take me there please?'

Nathan looked mystified. 'Of course,' he smiled.

5

Lucien placed Melody's eband on the table. He was in the Cologne apartment, which had become his base, waiting for Marta to come and debrief him. After the debacle in Stuttgart she had left with the wounded Dog – a thought that made him chuckle and chilled him at the same time. Lucien had decided to take the train back to Cologne immediately, rather than risk giving the authorities time to put out some picture of him doubtless taken from the trees. Whatever 'neutralising' the police had meant, he could not be sure one of them hadn't already uploaded a telephoto shot of him. Marta, meanwhile, was to take another route, which she had presumably done after securing the hostages in the van with Dog and a number of their field agents.

He went upstairs and looked across the Rhine. The Hohenzollern was so close that it blocked the view of the twin spires of the landmark Gothic cathedral. He guessed that might have taken something off the price. Even so, this was a high-ticket pad, and he shuddered to think where the money came from.

He went back downstairs. The door to the basement was locked. He couldn't resist the urge to press his ear up against it, though he expected to hear nothing. To his surprise he could just make out a dull thumping sound. He couldn't be sure if it came from the interrogation chamber, or was just a sound from somewhere outside. Either way there was nothing he could do about it. He had no means of unlocking it.

He went to the kitchen, just in time to see Marta arrive. 'What took you so long?' he said.

'I decided a change of trains was prudent,' she said. She poured herself a glass of water. 'Dog's not going to be happy.'

'Dog is a maniac,' Lucien replied. 'Is he hurt bad?'

She detected the note of hope in his question and gave him a weak grin. 'It appears not,' she said, nodding towards the front window. Lucien turned, to see the man himself approaching. Marta opened the door, and in he walked, arm in a sling, followed by Melody and her friend who he had learned was called David Carter and was now walking unaided. Two armed guards brought up the rear, escorting Ariel who was still handcuffed. 'Take them upstairs,' the wounded leader barked.

When they had gone he turned to Marta. 'What do you think you were doing, breaking out like that? Showing yourself? And using my name!'

Marta knew better than to apologise. 'And why do you think I did?' she asked. 'Of course I didn't mean to give anything away, but I had to stop you. You were going to shoot Forrester! That was never part of the plan.'

'Plans have to be flexible,' said Dog calmly. Lucien found the sudden calm in his voice unnerving. 'Let's all sit down and have a drink, and a think,' Dog continued. 'How do we want to deal with our friends?'

Lucien looked at the man before him, seemingly all the more dangerous for being wounded. How could he work with such a man, knowing his life might depend on him in the field?

Marta fetched a carafe of water. Since they were talking about the hostages, and that was supposed to be his area of concern, Lucien decided to take the initiative. 'Okay,' he said, 'we look at the logistical problem first. We have three hostages and one holding cell that accommodates two.'

Just then Dog's eband signalled a priority incoming call. 'I have to take this,' he scowled, and disappeared upstairs. After a few moments Lucien began to follow.

'What are you doing?' Marta asked.

'Oh, just seeing where the plans might be flexing next,' he said. 'Stay there. I'll be discreet.'

He climbed the stairs, quiet as a mouse, and came to a halt just before his head showed above the upper floor. As he listened to the various movements he decided that both the guards and the hostages were in the large studio space. He knew that the stairs came out directly there, so going any further was impossible. Dog must be in one of the bedrooms, or possibly the bathroom at the top of the stairs. He realised now that if the bathroom door had not been closed, any occupant would have seen him coming. Resolving to run up the remaining stairs if it should suddenly open, he stayed put and went on listening.

Melody was nearby, talking softly to her friend David. The target he could not hear. The guards appeared to be looking out of the window and wondering whether they should go out onto the balcony, until they discovered the door was locked. But then everyone went quiet as the sound of a single raised voice came from one of the bedrooms. Clearly their leader was in the doghouse. How many more plays on his stupid name could Lucien find? Doubtless loads. He had a suspicion that whoever was on the other end of the call had a lot more authority than both Dog and Marta, and was almost certainly venting their anger over the way the exchange had been handled.

Lucien continued to listen, straining to hear all the words and trying to guess what was being said on the other end of the line. He was concentrating so hard he failed to see Melody walk to the bathroom. As she opened the door with her back to him, he froze. She saw him as she was closing the door. He put his finger to his lips and instantly wondered why he had done that. Surely she would interpret it as a sympathetic gesture. Even conspiratorial.

Of course she would. So why did that idea not bother him?

6

Jack studied the crystal. He realised he had not done that before. Although he had shared in the initial excitement back on Venus, the discovery of Ariel had all but eclipsed it. It had all but eclipsed everything.

He was sitting with Nathan in a shiny new laboratory situated in a gloomy old warehouse. It was only a matter of hours since the bungled attempt at a rescue in Stuttgart. While Takeshi remained off sick Nathan had brought Ryan and Selena, as requested, to work on the crystal and Ariel's suit respectively, though they had now left for the day. Ryan had not yet succeeded in disrupting any part of the crystal, contenting himself for the time being with scan results instead.

But Jack wanted to test his idea.

He gazed at it, adopting a way of observing which a teacher had shown him in his childhood when looking at the Moon, first taking in the telescope's whole field of view before allowing his fine-detail vision to move from crater to mountain peak. And now as he looked, really looked, at the crystal, he began to discern what seemed like whiter pools on its surface and threads of light running through it. At first he put it down to the effects of too much staring, recalling the famous story of Percival Lowell's sighting of Giovanni Schiaparelli's *canali* on Mars. These channel lines that only some could see turned out not to be actual features at all, and certainly not the mistranslated 'canals' which he speculated had been built by Martians.

Next Jack tried another observational technique, looking away from the crystal, then coming back to it, looking askance, averting his eyes and using only his peripheral vision.

Finally he held it in one hand while pressing and poking it with the other, unsure what he thought it would do, but obeying some inner voice, half-heard, that this might get him somewhere.

And then he heard something. It was a rumbling noise. At first he took it to be someone moving around outside, but as soon as he took his eyes off the crystal the noise stopped. He looked at Nathan, but he was checking his eband and seemed totally unaware.

He looked again. There it was, a faint rumbling. And then he heard what he most wanted to hear, Ariel's voice. 'You're looking much better, David.' Then another voice. 'I'm just glad I'm not back in that room.' Then the rumbling stopped suddenly and everything went quiet.

The crystal looked dull once more, and there were no *canali*. He said nothing for the moment and handed it over to Nathan for safekeeping.

7

Takeshi awoke with a sore head. His pride didn't feel much better. He massaged his neck and then tried to sit up. That's when he noticed that one of his legs was somehow attached to the wall.

The light level was low. He was in a curious white room with no windows. The whole place was clinically sparse.

He bent his knees and drew himself close to the wall. With both hands free he was able to pull hard at the smooth white manacle just above his ankle. It didn't give. He examined its connection to the wall, admiring the seamlessness of the whole thing. Well, almost seamless. Looking closely, he could just make out a line at the half-way point over his shin. He tried to trace it with his thumbnail, deciding it was a powerful magnetic lock. When he went to press his eband, to see if he could deliver some kind of counter-magnetic pulse, he found his arm was bare.

There was nothing for it. He would have to try the old-fashioned way of calling for help. Immediately he started to hit the wall with the karate-hardened edges of his hands. After five minutes he gave up. Closing his eyes, he began to breathe deeply until his heart rate lowered and he entered a state of calm. The minutes passed, possibly hours.

Presumably whoever had brought him here would show themselves in due course.

8

It was late. Jack was back in Beth's office, struggling to recall what the voices he had heard through the crystal had said, and to describe to Beth and Nathan the faint rumbling noise. 'It was a rumble with a clatter in it. I think it was coming from somewhere in the distance.' He scratched his head. 'The funny thing is, it puts me in mind of one time I was based in London. Sometimes I'd forgo the Underground and cross the Thames by walking over the Hungerford Bridge. The trains used to make just that kind of sound.'

Nathan leant across to Beth and whispered something. 'That's okay,' she answered out loud. 'Jack has clearance. Go ahead.'

Nathan crossed to the water cooler and poured a drink. He was frustrated. Since his recruitment by person unknown to a secret organisation called the International Front he had been told to work with just one other person, Sirius Oksanen. At first 'Dog' had seemed a cool and calm character, patient and determined like Nathan himself. But it had soon become clear that his was the quietness of a dormant volcano, and now the lava was pouring out and Nathan had to do something to stem the flow. In his last call to Dog he had warned of the consequences of using real names in the middle of the operation in Stuttgart. That had been bad enough. But when Dog had taken it upon himself to keep the hostages, things had become far more dangerous, for now the search was bound to be intensified. Nathan felt he had no choice. Dog may be one of the organisation's pets, but now was the time to show some initiative of his own.

It had worked. It was agreed he should take Dog out of the equation.

Nathan had told the Finn that, while he would try to point the authorities in another direction, if push came to shove it would be critical that his own double-agent status remain secure. Even to the point of actively assisting the search for the hostages.

Push had just come to shove. 'The Hungerford Bridge,' he said to Jack. 'That's a railway bridge, right, with a sidewalk running parallel to the tracks?'

'Correct,' said Jack.

'Well, that is interesting,' said Nathan, sitting back down, his mind now made up. 'Only Washington is interested in a guy like the one you described, a Finn named Sirius Oksanen.'

'What makes you think that it's him?' said Jack.

'Because,' he replied slowly, 'they have established links between him and a radical news site called *Exposé* based in Cologne. Not far from the cathedral.'

'The Hohenzollern Bridge!' Jack shouted.

'Precisely,' said Nathan. 'If the crystal has some kind of radio link to Ariel, then it may be that they're holding him somewhere in the city. Somewhere close to the station.'

'Or on the Deutz side of the river,' said Jack, recalling a time in his teens when he had stayed in a hostel near the bridge on the east side.

'Well,' said Beth, 'it seems like it's our best shot.'

'It's our only lead!' said Jack. He turned to the American, wondering if he had misjudged the man. 'Nathan,' he said, 'I think you've just given us hope.'

Beth asked Nathan to get the details Washington had on Oksanen and put out an alert.

'Great,' said Jack. 'Let's get going first thing tomorrow.'

'Absolutely,' said Nathan. 'I suggest we take the crystal with us, in case we can use it again.'

'Good idea,' said Beth, as Jack shook the hand of the man who may just have saved the love of his life.

9

The door to the balcony was finally open, and the ever present sounds of trains rumbling on the bridge were carried in on the welcome breeze. Earlier on Dog had come storming out of the bedroom shouting, 'Who does he think he is?' before muttering something in what Melody took to be his own language. Once he'd unlocked the balcony door he had hurried back downstairs, taking one of the guards with him. The other one went out on to the balcony to have a good look around. Determined not to waste this opportunity for two of the men in her life, Melody followed him out, leaving Ariel and David sitting on the sofa. If the holstered gun the guard was wearing worried her, she didn't show it.

'It's nice out here, isn't it?' she said, holding firmly to the rail and looking for any landmarks she might recognise. All she could see was a large bridge over a river. It reminded her of the Forth Bridge near Edinburgh, which promptly ushered in memories of meeting Jack's father.

The guard did not return her conversation, but he seemed happy enough to look at her. She backed into the corner of the balcony rail as if she were posing for a picture. And in a way she was.

David and Ariel watched fascinated as Melody lingered outside, the guard happily co-lingering. 'I think Melody has given us an opportunity to talk to each other,' Ariel said. 'Freely.'

'Well, I know Melody wanted us to meet,' said David. 'But I don't think this is what she had in mind.'

'Indeed.'

'She clearly thinks a lot of you,' said David, keeping one eye on the balcony. 'You've made quite an impact.'

'It has been mutual,' said Ariel, now also looking towards Melody. 'You know that she is in a quandary?'

David sighed. 'I'm not sure what she's told you,' he said. 'But yes, I think I've let things get out of hand. For my own part, I hasten to add. Melody hasn't done anything.'

'Have you?'

'Ah well,' said David, 'that rather depends on what you mean by "done". I've not broken my marriage vows as such, but in my heart... well, it's difficult.'

Ariel looked at the man before him, and not for the first time tears filled his eyes. There was something familiar here. Not something about David personally, but something familiar about the situation. Could this be an echo of his previous life? 'I spoke to Alice,' he said simply.

David sat up. 'When?'

'Yesterday.'

'I guess you spoke to her in Geneva,' said David. 'She was due to arrive yesterday when... Well, you know what happened. How is she?'

'Very upset,' said Ariel, 'but very calm, considering.'

They both watched from their position on the sofa as Melody tried talking some more with her unresponsive conversation partner.

'It's interesting,' said David, 'how close you seem to have become to Melody. And now, it seems, to Alice.'

'Yes,' said Ariel, 'I suppose I have. I'm sure you of all people will understand how that is possible.'

David gave a low laugh, hanging his head a little. 'There really is something about you, isn't there? The thing is, while you were in the UN building doing whatever it is you were doing, Melody and I had several hours together. And while we didn't talk about you the whole time, it became pretty clear to me that you've become very important to her, and I can only think you're the reason for her growth in spiritual understanding.'

'I had the distinct impression that you were the one to thank for that,' said Ariel.

'Impression, you say? I gather from Melody that you are very good at gathering impressions... reading people.'

'What did she tell you?' asked Ariel, surprised at his own question. He did not normally sound so defensive.

'Do you want to do your thing now?' said David impetuously. 'Only we are rather pressed for time.'

'If you are sure,' said Ariel, though he was already looking straight into David's eyes. He saw the cathedral and felt the embrace... saw the café and noticed the flirtation... saw the lake and felt the jealousy. Then they were having dinner at David's hotel, before the two of them were standing by the lift, unsure whether they were saying goodnight.

David turned away suddenly. 'Hold on,' he said. 'What's that guy doing? He's hemming Mel in there a bit, don't you think?'

Immediately Ariel turned away and stepped out onto the balcony. 'May I take the air now?' he said. The guard waved his hand at Melody, and she stepped back indoors.

'You all right?' said David as she sat next to him.

'Of course,' she said. 'How did you two get on?'

He felt uneasy about the way she seemed to be brushing aside the trauma they had been through only that morning, but he decided to put it down to a coping mechanism. 'Well,' he said, 'he is as you say remarkable, though not just for the reasons I think these guys want him. Even without the mind-reading thing, he's very perceptive.'

She nodded. 'So, what do you think about *him*?'

'I don't know. I began to get a feeling as we talked.'

'Good,' she said. 'Go on. What did you feel?'

'Well, I know I'm the one who's been wounded, but you know what? I think he has been too.'

10

The other guests had left the bar of the Eden Hotel when Jack took his last sip of single malt before turning in at the end of what felt like the longest day of his life. A priority call came through on his eband. It was Nathan Dexter.

'Jack, sorry to call so late, only I thought you should know. The crystal has gone missing.'

'What!' The longest day just got longer.

'Yes, and that's not all. We can't find Takeshi. He's suddenly disappeared.'

'Oh man,' Jack breathed, wishing he knew more about the missing member of the High Command triad. 'Okay, Nathan, thanks for letting me know. We'll have to chase that particular hare after tomorrow. First we go to Cologne.'

'Sure thing,' said Nathan. 'I'll be ready.'

11

The talk in the kitchen-diner of the house in Cologne was quiet but tense. Marta was taking the moral high ground by storm. 'But now we're stuck with them! Just what do you propose we do with them?'

Dog leered as he looked towards the stairs. 'Well, I know what I'd like to do with the journalist.'

Marta shot him a look of disgust. 'Sometimes, my friend, I think you are more animal than human.'

Lucien was amazed at her temerity. But then Marta hadn't yet ceased to amaze him.

'Well, you know...' the Finn intoned. 'Dog by name...'

Marta found the rather loose response out of character but said nothing. Dog might have different methods from her, and was of course involved in the messier side of the work, but she had never yet had reason to doubt his self-control. The change was unsettling.

Lucien turned round as the door to the basement opened. The other guard reported on 'the Jap' down below. 'Looks like he's meditating or something,' he said.

'Well, let him meditate,' said Dog. 'The Client hasn't told me what to do with him yet.'

'What's this?' said Marta. 'We have another guest downstairs?'

'We do,' said Dog.

She frowned. 'Don't you think it's getting a little crowded round here?'

'Oh, but Marta, you love a party!'

Lucien, still unsure of his ground, decided to make the most of Dog's slightly improved humour and speak up. 'Can we use the fact that we still have the hostages to our advantage?'

'Go on,' said Dog, looking at Lucien as if he'd only just entered the room.

'Well,' said the Frenchman, 'I guess a lot depends on what we want from the one they are calling Ariel.'

'You needn't worry about him,' said Dog, 'I've just received instructions from the Client. It seems he has found a buyer. He won't be our problem for much longer.'

'Excellent,' said Marta. 'Frankly, I wasn't sure your call had gone that well.'

'Ah, my dear Marta, you mustn't be alarmed by a few angry remarks. Everything is in hand.'

'So what about the hostages, then?' asked Lucien. 'That means they really are superfluous to our needs.'

Lucien felt a chill as Dog responded with a crooked smile. 'You know, my friend, you're absolutely right. It's time we were rid of them.'

Chapter 23

Degradation

1

The early autumn sun streamed across the Rhine, teasing out the greys and browns of the dark Gothic cathedral and tingeing with gold the green iron veins of the Hohenzollern Bridge. Over the bridge came Jack Forrester, striding into the sunlight, his collar turned against the Rhine's chilly breeze, leaving Nathan Dexter and a surveillance team parked on the western bank near the cathedral. Marching from the other side, a flash of red round her neck and the sun warm on her back, came Marta Bergstrom, accompanied by the two guards who had been with them in the house.

She was wearing sunglasses, so by the time Jack recognised her coming towards him she was already studying his face and deciding this really was the same crazy, courageous man she had observed only yesterday in Stuttgart. 'Hold on, guys,' she said to the guards, 'I've just remembered something back at the house. You go on to the office. I'll catch up with you later.'

Jack watched her turn around while the men came towards him. They walked straight past him, clearly unaware of who he was. He quickly called the team and asked them to arrest the two men they could see even now coming towards them. Then he picked up his pace in an effort not to lose Marta, but slowed down again when she stopped to look out over the water. Had she recognised him? As he approached her she confirmed the fact by speaking while looking out across the river. 'Lovely morning for a walk, don't you think, Commander?' The accent was German.

He came and stood beside her. 'I'm afraid you have the advantage,' he said.

'Marta Bergstrom,' she said, and shook his hand.

Jack nodded. 'I believe I may owe you my life.'

'You're welcome.'

'How can I repay you?' said Jack, trying to feel his way into the surprise conversation. An early tour boat chugged below them, disappearing under the bridge.

'Oh, a little forgiveness would be nice,' she said. The sun was bright behind her, conspiring with the sunglasses to hide the expression on her face. 'In fact,' she went on, 'how about a little immunity from prosecution?'

Jack gave a low whistle. 'Anything else?'

She didn't miss the irony. 'I know it's a lot to ask,' she said, 'but there is more I can give you. Tell me, Commander, do you know where your walk is taking you?'

Jack stepped round her and studied her face. She was probably approaching fifty. Her skin was a pale white, her hair short but shaped with neat, dark triangles in front of her ears, and these framed a well-worn but lively countenance. Obligingly she took off her sunglasses, and he could see at once that her eyes were deadly serious.

'All right,' he said. He was aware this may be a dead end, but something in her look told him that the woman who had stopped this Dog once may do so again. As such, she was the best key he had to unlocking and maybe even resolving the crisis. Perhaps the only safe one, for he had heard details of armed raids in hostage situations before, and they seldom seemed to have ended well. 'Tell me what more you can give.'

'And the immunity? No, don't tell me, you'll see what you can do.'

'Marta,' he said, 'if you deliver the hostages unharmed, I'm sure there's a lot that I can do.'

She looked down at the water ceaselessly flowing under the bridge. How much time did they have? And just how much could she deliver? And what about the new boy? Lucien was still something of an unknown.

'I'd like to sound out one of my colleagues,' she said, 'if you can give me time.'

Before Jack could answer, a priority message alert beeped from her eband. It was Lucien.

2

Marta and the guards had left for the *Exposé* office at Dog's behest. Initially troubled by his words about the superfluousness of the hostages, she had been reassured by his dismissal of the guards and only too pleased to return to the world of information, where her inspiration lay. Lucien began to hope that things might calm down now, and maybe they could all do some clear thinking.

He sat in a comfortable chair in the upper lounge, trusted to watch Ariel and David. He was tired, having shared a bedroom with Dog the previous night, next door to Marta and Melody. The Scandinavian hadn't talked much, but Lucien had heard enough to glean that Dog was a committed pleasure-seeker, believing that man's basic desires should be indulged. Especially his own. He had said that the quest for pleasure was the only way to find some semblance of meaning in this life, and if it turned out to be nothing more than an illusion, so be it – at least he would get something from life before he lost it. It sounded to Lucien almost as if he had managed to convince himself he was part of some great cause for the improvement of humanity.

Ariel and David had been left to sleep in the lounge, Ariel happily taking the floor and offering the sofa to David. The guards had taken turns on night watch down in the kitchen-diner.

Once Marta and the guards had gone, Dog had disappeared downstairs with Melody, leaving David very uneasy. Melody had told him not to worry, a sentiment Ariel echoed after she had gone. She was surely too valuable to be in any real danger.

Lucien could not agree but held his counsel, repeatedly sighing as he played nervously with the gun in his hand, fitting and removing and refitting the silencer. Still, what could he do? It was clear now, though hardly surprising, that Dog was just a higher link in a chain that extended beyond him, who knew how far? Turning on the guy would simply invite more problems. Unless Marta had had enough and wanted out? Sadly, she had given him no reason to believe she was ready to break ranks.

He heard Dog talking with Melody downstairs. It sounded like they were making a drink. Perhaps his fears were unfounded.

He came away from the stairs and turned to Ariel who was sitting on the sofa with David once more. It occurred to him now that this was a chance to talk directly to the man at the centre of all this trouble. Maybe he could shed some light on what to do.

'So tell me, man from the heavens, what do you make of all this? Have you come to the earth to tell us we're all doomed? That we've messed up, and soon our planet will be like the hell-hole where they found you?'

Ariel found the question both surprising and refreshing. 'Well, Lucien – I'm sorry, I only know your first name – I rather think that you know all that already, without me having to tell you.'

Lucien happily conceded the point and adopted the more personal approach he had intended anyway. 'So what were you doing there in the first place? How did you even get there?'

Ariel looked at him, standing in front of the window. He could see that, although the gun was in his hand, it presented no threat, and that this was a man who didn't really know where he stood right now. He decided being his usual straightforward self remained the best way to respond. 'I'm afraid I can't answer that,' he said.

'No, of course not,' said Lucien. 'All very classified, I am sure.'

'It's not quite that simple,' said Ariel. 'I actually have no memory of anything before I was found on Venus. We've been trying to put that right for the last three weeks.'

Lucien let out a long, low whistle, sensing the man was neither lying nor joking. 'So that explains all the secrecy, and why there has been nothing on the news for so long.'

David picked up on the change of mood in the conversation. 'Lucien,' he said, 'may I ask you a question? What are you going to do with us?'

'Well, Ariel has been open with me,' said Lucien, 'so I will return the favour. I'm rather new to this organisation, and still learning how, er, extreme it is in certain parts.'

'What attracted you to it in the first place, if I may ask?' said David.

'*Bien sur*. I've been involved for some years now in challenging governments and big business to be more... transparent with the people they claim to serve. When *Exposé* asked me if I would come help them, it made sense. A good move, no? And I think it was. At least, it would be if I could work with only Marta – you know, to get the real stories behind the façades. I think it could have worked...' He gazed out towards the balcony.

'I see.'

'So,' said Lucien, turning abruptly to Ariel, 'how far have they got, my friend? Have you been interrogated? Drugged?' Even as he asked the question an image of the basement came to mind.

'Nothing like that,' said Ariel. 'Not so far.'

'It strikes me, after what I saw in Stuttgart, that Jack Forrester is a good champion to have. Would I be right?'

'The best,' said Ariel.

David, realising his eyes had not left Lucien's gun, turned to Ariel. 'How has Jack been? I mean, has he been in charge of your time in...? Well, I'd better not say. Mel has told me a little – nothing classified, of course.'

Lucien smiled. Already some of the fault lines were appearing. Clearly David was not part of what had been going on, even though he and the journalist were obviously close. How useful such an understanding would have been, if he were to continue to work for the man who had hired him. A man who even now was carrying out who knew what methods to extract information from his prey. Lucien shivered. The Dog-man seemed to have a predilection for hurting people.

He put the gun down on a small table. 'Gentlemen,' he said as he stretched his arms behind his head, 'I think it's time for me to decide which side I am on. And I don't think it's with the madman downstairs. It seems to me that you, Ariel, do not belong with him either. I'm going to make a call to my associate, Marta. I do not know for sure, but I'm hoping that she is also unhappy with the way things are going.'

He pressed his eband a couple of times, and Marta's voice came through on speaker. 'Marta,' he said, 'I have an idea I want to discuss with you. Is now a good time?'

'Go ahead,' she said.

He heard the sound of rumbling in the background. 'You are still on the bridge?' he asked.

'Yes. Go ahead.'

'*D'accord*,' said Lucien. 'I think you and I need to take over this project. We need to get Ariel and the hostages away from here. I am hoping that you share my, er, doubts about our senior colleague.'

There was a moment's delay before Marta responded. 'Well, for one thing, Lucien, although Dog acts like he is everybody's boss, it's not really so simple. He may have access to people I do not, but he is not my manager. And yes, I think the same. In fact, I have someone here who may well be able to help us achieve our goal.'

'Oh?' said Lucien. 'Who is that?'

'Jack Forrester.'

Another low whistle. This was better than he could imagine, not least for gaining Ariel's trust. But was Marta really in cahoots with the authorities? Had he been taken in by a double agent?

'Marta, what is going on?'

'Hello Lucien.' It was Jack. 'Marta and I are walking towards you now. Let me assure you that she and I have only just met... if you don't count our brief encounter in Stuttgart yesterday. Lucien, if you really want to help Ariel, then we are on the same side.'

Lucien scratched his head. 'I don't know...'

'Lucien,' Jack pressed. 'Where are the hostages? Is Melody okay?'

The question was the slap in the face he needed, and only now did he notice that all had gone ominously quiet downstairs. 'No, Mr Forrester, I do not believe she is. She is with the mad Dog as we speak.'

'Then we're coming in,' said Jack. 'And if we're smart, we'll do this together. There's no SWAT team about to descend on you. You have my word.'

'That is good,' said Lucien. '*À bientot.*'

He ended the call and looked at Ariel and David. 'Wait here,' he said, and taking the gun he made his way quietly down the stairs. The room was empty, but he could hear a voice coming from the kitchen area on the right. Carefully he looked round the corner, but there was no one there. He stepped into the kitchen and approached what he had previously taken to be a climate control panel in the wall but which was now revealed as some kind of intercom. It was Dog's voice coming through the speaker. It seemed he was playing with his food. But who was his victim? The unknown Japanese prisoner, or Melody?

His question was answered by the chilling sound of a woman's muffled cry.

3

'Natasha, can I ask you a favour?'

'Of course, Alice. You can ask.'

They were sitting in the busy 'canteen' of the *Palais de Nations*, having talked a while about their backgrounds which couldn't have been more different. Whereas Alice had enjoyed a largely happy childhood and a stable upbringing based around family and church, she could not detect the presence of any sustained home life in Natasha's past. In fact, though it was hard to believe, there seemed to be no significant others in her life at all.

Eventually they had come round to what was really on their minds – what the others were doing. They knew Constance was busy fending off the military departments of the member nations of the WSA. Selena had managed to persuade Ryan, bereft once more of the crystal, to join her in the lab as she tried to identify the composition of Ariel's strange suit. And Jack had gone off to Cologne with Nathan and a surveillance team, having persuaded Beth to hold back on a SWAT team at this stage. Nathan had surprised them by agreeing with Jack. Maybe he wasn't so typical of the military types after all.

Alice sipped her herbal tea and requested her favour. 'I'd like to go and see Bill.'

'He's in hospital.'

'I know. That's why I want to go and visit him. But he'll be under guard, and I don't think they'll let me in on my own. Whereas you... you're one of the team. Plus, you helped save his life.'

Natasha took a long swig of the glass of water she had been nursing. She knew that her actions in the park in Stuttgart were as much a result of her training as anything. But she also recalled the desperation she felt as she staunched Bill's wound and kept him awake, imploring him to hang on. 'You know I'm not his biggest fan,' she said simply.

'No, I didn't know,' said Alice. 'But then, if I'm honest, Natasha, it's not easy to know what you think about anyone. You're something of a closed book.'

'Sorry,' said Natasha. 'Just the way I am, I guess – hard to read...' She paused, her mind clearly elsewhere, before carrying on. 'General Petersen did not take too kindly to me when we first met. Well, before we met, I think. He tried to take Ariel by force, not to mention paralysing me with a stun gun.'

Alice gasped.

'But I admit that I was surprised, moved even, by his recent offer to stand in for Ariel. Even then, in the park, some of his actions were still rather inflammatory, but I have to say he was very determined. And in the end he only got himself shot.'

'Precisely,' said Alice. 'So, shall we see if we can go?'

Natasha's eyes only managed to say, 'If we must,' but it was enough for Alice.

They made their way up to Beth's office. When they arrived, they were surprised to find Bill there, sitting in a wheelchair.

'Well, this is amazing!' Alice exclaimed. 'We were coming to ask Beth if we could come and visit you. We thought you'd be in a military hospital or something.'

'He was,' said Beth, eying the neat and respectable-looking woman in front of her. 'They stitched him up last night. Apparently no vital organs were damaged, though he's lost a lot of blood.'

'Then what's he doing here?' asked Alice. She had caring eyes, something Beth couldn't recall seeing in the workplace lately.

'He was determined to come in and see a certain person,' said Beth, nodding towards Natasha.

Natasha looked at the figure half-slumped in the chair. She didn't know what to say.

Alice waited a moment before deciding to follow her instinct. She went over and took Bill's hand. 'I'm honoured to meet you, General Petersen,' she said. 'I know we didn't get the outcome we had hoped for, but we're all so very grateful for your sacrifice. And I'm so pleased you'll soon be on the mend. And I'm sorry that sometimes I talk too much.'

Bill smiled. He couldn't remember when he last did that. 'You are very kind, Mrs Carter–'

'Alice, please.'

'It's very sweet of you to say those things, Alice, and I could say that I was just doing my duty.'

'A bit above and beyond, don't you think?' said Alice.

'Well, that's as may be. A more cynical person might say I stepped out of line when I drew my gun on one of the kidnappers. Or,' and with this he turned to Natasha, 'when I fired a stun gun at one of my colleagues.'

'Well, I'm sure I wouldn't have anything useful to say about that,' said Alice, 'but it has been an honour to meet you. And we're all hoping that Jack and Mr Dexter will be successful in Cologne.' She turned to Beth. 'Well, Ms Griffiths, this has been very nice. I'll leave you now, if I may. Lots to pray for.'

'Well, she's different,' said Beth when Alice had gone. 'Take a seat, Natasha. I know Bill may have things he wants to say to you, but as he's taken the trouble to come to us, I'd like to have a wider discussion. Before you came in we were talking about how best to handle the situation if – sorry, when – we get Ariel back. We feel it may be prudent to remove Ariel from the spotlight a little longer, while at the same time bringing in a different mind.'

'Another Selena?' said Natasha.

'If you like. Only this time we go to him. Bill, do you want to take it from here?'

'Okay,' he said, before coughing for a few moments. 'Sorry about that.' He wiped his mouth with the back of his hand. 'Back in the day, when I was training, I knew a guy called Sean MacEvoy.'

Natasha's eyes instantly lit up. '*The* Sean MacEvoy?' she said. 'Director of SETI?'

'The very same,' Bill said.

'Well,' said Beth, 'actually the former Director, but still very much involved.'

'He'll be well into his seventies by now,' said Bill.

'Why would you know someone like him?' The question was out before Natasha could smooth the edges off it.

'Simple really,' said Bill. 'As you know, Sean finally got SETI integrated into the WSA, as well as strengthening its political muscles, and I was on a placement to see how the UN might organise a proper global military response in the event of an alien invasion. Sean and I hit it off. I guess neither of us would let people stand in our way if we could see how to make something happen.'

Natasha shook her head. 'We actually did that? Took it seriously, I mean... the possibility of an invasion by an extra-terrestrial race?'

'Well, that was the thing with Sean. He got *everybody* to take it seriously. Though, as you'd expect, he was far more interested in communicating with aliens than fighting them.'

'Anyway,' said Beth. 'He's based in his native Ireland now. He retired to Cork, though we might find him in Dublin where he's a professor emeritus or something at Trinity College. The thing is, Bill and I believe he'd have a different angle – whatever we think or don't think about Ariel. And it would take Ariel away from here for a while.'

'And you don't mind that?' Natasha's question was directed to both of them.

Bill sat up straight and said, 'Truth is, Natasha, I'm pretty sure Ariel will continue to be the focus of further kidnap attempts – if not from idiots like me, then from other quarters.'

Natasha recognised the apology, and she took Bill's hand exactly as Alice had done. He started to cough again.

'Look now,' said Beth, 'when Bill arrived here a couple of hours ago, his chair was in the reclining position, more like a gurney. So he had a great view of my ceiling.'

Natasha let go of Bill's hand and looked at Beth, wondering whether she had suddenly lost it, or whether her Welsh accent had finally proved too much for a Russian to understand. Seeing her perplexed look, Beth took something out of a drawer. 'Perhaps this will explain,' she said and placed what was clearly some kind of monitoring device on the desk. Stuck to one side of it were flakes of what looked like plaster. 'It seems we have a mole,' she concluded.

Natasha took a closer look at it. 'Do we have any ideas who?' said Natasha. 'Is this something Hugh Coates might be involved with? Only he does seem to have ears and eyes everywhere.'

'No,' said Beth, 'I've already checked with Constance. He says he has nothing here.'

'And we believe him?'

'We don't have to,' said Bill. 'We just need to be on our guard.'

'That's right,' said Beth. 'We're going to put the device back where we found it and use it to feed useless and even false information to the mole.'

'Good idea,' said Natasha.

'There's more,' said Beth. 'One of my senior personnel, Takeshi Takahashi, has disappeared.'

'Okay,' said Natasha. 'I can see what you are saying. It is not safe here. So if Ariel does come back to us, how do we get him to MacEvoy?'

'That's where you come in,' said Beth.

4

Lucien examined the console on the kitchen wall for any sign of door-openers. He swiped and pressed the controls, but only succeeded in turning the thing off and sending it back into the wall. Desperately he ran to the door that led to the basement. It was locked. He had no idea where the lock or the bolts were, but he had to try something, so he raised his gun and pointed to the slight gap near the door handle. His hand was on the firing button when a voice stopped him.

'Wait a moment.' It was Ariel, coming down the stairs with David close on his heels.

'It's that madman!' Lucien shouted. 'I don't know what he's doing to her, but it does not sound good.' He explained about the secret monitor that he'd found and then accidentally lost.

Ariel responded swiftly. He strode to the door and grasped the handle. Lucien watched as Ariel's eyes half-closed and the door opened.

'How...?'

'No time to explain now,' said Ariel.

'Okay, let's go!' said Lucien. 'There is another door down there. It's the interrogation room.' Gun at the ready, he led the way to the chamber of horrors now filling his mind, while Ariel and David followed. When they arrived outside the door Ariel stepped forward and quietly set a hand on it. Instantly and very noisily the bolts shot back into the door. As Lucien stepped inside he was assailed by a waft of bleach and sweat. Dog had already turned to see why the door had opened.

'How did you get in?' he barked.

Lucien halted and took in the scene before him. Sitting on the fold-out toilet slightly to his left was an oriental-looking man. His arms were stretched upwards, manacled firmly to the wall. In front of the far wall stood Dog. The fire in his eyes was stoked to boiling point. His entire countenance had the menacing look of a hyena that resented any disturbance to its messy business. Lucien could just make out Melody's bare left arm behind him. Her blouse was on the floor.

'Animal!' Lucien roared, and broke into a run, raising his gun to strike Dog with the butt. He never made it. His legs gave in as Dog rugby-tackled him to the floor.

David ignored the fight and rushed to Melody. Sweeping up her blouse in his hands he tried awkwardly to put it across her, but with her arms still manacled to the wall all he could do was hold it there, at which she began to shake her head from side to side and pull wildly at her bonds.

Ariel attended to the man on the floor. He took both of Takeshi's manacles in his hands, but just as he was about to release them he faltered. His vision became blurred, and a great shadow began to envelop him. He was falling through swirling clouds of a suffocating darkness thick with angry voices. Summoning all his strength he forced his eyes to open wide and found he had just enough time, just enough focus, for one final push. And then he collapsed.

It was enough. The manacles sprang from Takeshi's arms. He didn't wait to find out how. His tormentor had already wrested the gun from Lucien as he forced him to the floor, and was on the point of blowing his brains out. Takeshi made his move, hurling himself on top of both men.

The gun went off.

5

Across the river Nathan had left the surveillance van as soon as the two guards had been handed over to the local police. He walked the short distance to the *Exposé* office, announcing himself as a UN inspector who had been in discussions with Marta Bergstrom and one of her colleagues – a Finn, he thought. When they didn't look convinced he played his trump card: 'I was told to wait in the cave, if that means anything.' They led him through.

It was Dog who had boasted to him about this particular room and the high level of electronic shielding it carried. Nathan was hoping it would provide the privacy he needed, but also that it would allow him to test a theory. He wanted to see whether the crystal would work no matter what electronic blocking mechanism was used. He checked the time. Marta hadn't showed, so unless she had gone on an unplanned shopping trip, she was almost certainly with Forrester. Dog was in the house.

He was eager to get on and get gone. Declining a coffee, he quietly closed the door of the small room and sat down at the table. He took out an old piece of cloth from his jacket pocket and unwrapped it. And there it was, a small ball with a dozen faces.

He had been waiting to use the crystal for nearly three weeks, after receiving a message from an unknown caller whom he had come to think of as Mr X. The nickname was as good as any, and the simpler the better when it only had his own mind to occupy. Mr X had said he represented the International Front, which Nathan had never heard of, committed to defending the earth from outside forces. At first Nathan didn't buy it. But the guy seemed to know a lot about Nathan and, far more interestingly, what had just docked on Space Station Alpha.

The call had come to his eband on a highly secure and so far untraceable channel. As further messages ensued Nathan gradually became convinced that these people really did know things no one else knew – and they were insistent that the Stranger had actually come from 'outside forces' and was not the result of human biological enhancement. Ariel was not human and never had been. By this point Nathan was more thrilled than disturbed. They claimed to know Ariel's origins, though they wouldn't say what they were, but they assured Nathan that this was sufficient knowledge to bring the accolades, and the power, he so deserved. If he followed their instructions.

If he didn't, then his wife would know about his extra-marital liaisons. Even the one his best friend didn't know about.

It was a case of carrot and stick, and if he was honest it was the carrot that pulled him in. Did he want to know? Yes he did. Mr X told him about the Stranger's sudden and mysterious appearance in the Endeavour's lounge long before he heard it from Beth Griffiths. That had felt good. He was in a secret inner circle, while Beth had to wait for the stuck-up Constance Bridlington to get round to sharing information. Later came the alarming yet delicious news that Ariel was part of an elite fighting force that posed the greatest threat there had ever been to global security. In fact the continuing dominance of the human race was quite possibly at stake.

Yet this was not everything. Mr X told him about the crystal that had come back with the crew. Nathan was to find a way to secure it. Since Beth was sending him to take notes on behalf of High Command at the meeting of WSA directors on Space Station Alpha, he should try to acquire it there. He soon located it in Dan Marshall's office, where he witnessed first hand that it was anything but inert, but getting it off-station had proved completely impossible. So he had waited patiently for the next opportunity. They emphasised that no one in the UN could be trusted, and he must make every effort to keep the information secret and the crystal safe. In the crystal he would come to possess a valuable weapon in the fight against the enemy, and the time would soon come when he must use it.

That time was now. He needed to get Ariel out of the hands of his self-appointed guards and protectors. Taking the crystal in both hands, he positioned his thumbs and fingers in such a way that he was touching ten of the twelve pentagonal faces of the crystal – any ten, his secret mentor had said – and pressed. Then he put it down again, gazing intently as it slowly revealed its tell-tale patterns of connection. Connection with Ariel. He watched lines and colours take shape, just as he had been promised. After a few minutes every facet of the crystal had a white shape forming in its centre, and he placed his finger on one of these at random. Instantly he heard a commotion, voices coming from the crystal itself. He wanted to listen longer and work out what was going on, but he had to work quickly. So, still following the meticulous instructions he had been given, he took the crystal in both hands once more and pressed ten of the faces. After a split second of a noise like feedback the crystal went quiet, and the lines and shapes disappeared. Now he must trust it had done its work.

Across the river Ariel swooned under a cloud of darkness.

6

Ryan let out a deep sigh. 'We're getting nowhere.' He was standing next to Selena, poring over Ariel's suit spread out on a bench in front of them. She was happier than she had been for a long time, delighted with the high-tech lab that the curiously absent Takeshi Takahashi had set up. And she was enjoying the company of a colleague who was more interested in the project at hand than in her – a refreshing change after three years of reporting directly to Conway Box. In one morning Ryan had restored her faith not only in men but even in Americans.

He was side-stepping left and right now, looking at the object of their attention from various angles. 'Is this even the right suit?' he said. 'I mean, I know it became this dull, white colour while we were still on Alpha. But Schlesinger said he couldn't even saw through it. And we've just managed to cut it.'

'Perhaps the good doctor simply meant that his saw blade got caught in the fibres,' said Selena.

'No, he said the thing skidded off it, as if it became hard for an instant and then went back to normal. Kinda like our space suits, only more so.'

She shook her head. It was a conundrum. Idly she began to stroke the material with the back of her hand. 'Of course,' she said after a few moments, 'Ariel was wearing it at the time.'

They looked at each other. It felt as if their eyes had just been opened.

7

Nathan came out of the cave saying he'd come back another day. By the time he had left the *Exposé* office, at least two suspicious journalists had furtively taken his photo, with a deft stroke of the hair, eband at just the right angle, or both hands over a convenient yawn.

He was over the Hohenzollern in minutes and managed to catch up with Jack and Marta as they were going through the iron gate into the private residential area. Jack brought him up to speed with the plan, such as it was.

When they got to the house Marta held back while the two men slowly approached the front door. It was locked.

'Boy, we could do with Ariel right now,' said Jack. 'He'd save us some time.'

'What?' said Nathan, puzzled by the remark.

'Oh, some other time,' said Jack. He listened with his ear close to the door. 'I can hear voices,' he said. 'It's a bit of a commotion. They're shouting. Come on, we need something to break the door down!'

'Or we could use this.' Marta stepped forward and raised her eband arm. She quickly unlocked the door and stood aside, while Jack stepped over the threshold.

The first thing he saw was the basement door facing them. It was open.

Forcing his personal angst to submit to his training, Jack crossed the room and raced up the main stairs. Moments later he reappeared, shaking his head to indicate there was no one up there. Still without a word both men now made their way down to the basement, Nathan leading the way with gun in hand. As Jack turned the second corner, his ears were assailed by something they had never heard before, wretched and inconsolable. It was the sound of a woman sobbing.

He followed Nathan into the dimly lit room, a realm of whiteness spoiled only by the dark pool of blood that had formed next to an oriental man lying on the floor. To the right two men were wrestling frantically on a bench. But Jack's eyes were drawn to David and Mel standing against the opposite wall. Immediately he ran towards them, tripping over Ariel whom he had completely failed to see lying in the way. He fell forward and landed at Mel's manacled feet.

At the same time one of the wrestlers on the bench went rigid as a paralysing electric current went through his body. Satisfied his last opponent was neutralised, Dog turned, only to see Nathan's gun pointing directly at him. Dog raised his own, but with a satisfied sneer Nathan fired two bullets into his chest. The Dog was put down.

Nathan now attended to the man on the bench. 'He's still breathing,' he shouted, 'whoever he is.'

'Lucien!' Nathan and Jack both turned to see Marta at the door. She hesitated.

'It's okay,' said Jack, 'I think the shooting's over. No, wait. There's no signal in here. Can you go upstairs and call an ambulance?'

She disappeared.

Jack didn't know where to look next. He ached for Mel, yet he could see that David was doing all he could. But he didn't know whether Ariel was dead or alive. And there was a man right in front of him with a bullet somewhere in his abdomen.

Happily Nathan stepped in. 'Takeshi!' he called. 'Takeshi, stay with me, man!' Jack watched as Nathan carefully lifted his colleague's head onto his lap.

Jack scooted across the floor to Ariel. 'Well, I think he's alive,' he said. 'I don't know if it's one of his faints, or something they've done to him. I suggest we leave him be for the moment.'

He turned back to Mel who now seemed more delirious than hysterical. 'Right,' he said, sounding as calm as he could, 'how do we get these wall-brace things off?' He noticed that there were two sticking out of the wall near the door, above a toilet of all things, but he could see no obvious sign of a release mechanism. Frustrated, he charged back up the stairs, calling for Marta, and as he did so Nathan seized the opportunity to take the crystal from his own jacket, wipe it with the cloth and place it one of Dog's pockets. It would make highly suggestive evidence that the madman had taken it from his Japanese prisoner, leaving Nathan completely unconnected to it. He then went back to Takeshi, so that when Jack and Marta returned he was busy trying to stem the flow of blood in his colleague's stomach, using an old cloth he said he had found on the floor. Seconds later Marta pressed the wall and Melody was released. She slumped into David's arms, spent and silent, and together they slowly sank to the floor.

Jack looked at the carnage around him. David was holding onto Mel, the manacles having somehow disappeared into the wall. Nathan was applying pressure to Takeshi's abdomen. Marta was attending to Lucien on the bench. And Ariel was on the floor, hands outstretched close by the manacles that had been protruding near the door. It occurred to Jack, in the light of what Marta had just done, that the manacles shouldn't still be visible, but there they were, wedged in an opening in the wall. It looked like they had been forced apart somehow. 'Well, my old friend,' he said as he placed Ariel in the recovery position, 'it looks like you've been up to your old party tricks again.'

Nathan frowned. Clearly there were things he did not yet know. His job was far from done.

Chapter 24

Trauma

1

Everyone knew that Constance Bridlington was not an emotional person, but today that fact seemed to have eluded her own body. After Beth had visited in person to give an account of the casualties – one kidnapper dead, another electrocuted but alive, Takeshi seriously wounded, Ariel unconscious, and Melody the victim of a sexual assault – she had closed the all-too-transparent door of her office and sobbed uncontrollably. Eventually the tears became intermittent, and when Petroc called she was able to brush him off with a request for tea. 'Not the tea here in my office. Right now only the blend they serve in the canteen will do.' That bought her another fifteen minutes to sit disconsolate and alone and let the awfulness of the human cost wash over her.

How could she possibly have prepared for this? She knew she could not, and she told herself as much. Nearly all the planning had been in the mission itself. The aftermath was meant to be all about the pressure they could bring to bear within the political machinations of the global cooling movement. She couldn't possibly have known this would happen.

Or could she? As soon as Ariel had been discovered on board the Endeavour everything had changed. Even before Schlesinger's report she must have known that. Was that the real reason she didn't attend the press briefing on Alpha, or even the meeting of the WSA directors? Yes, she had to mastermind Project Icarus, which meant finding somewhere for them to interview the stowaway, which in turn sent her to Leonardo. Yes, she had to deal with the government heads who wanted to know what it all meant. And yes, she still had to assure their experts that there would be critical data for the global cooling agenda. But was that it? Or did she already know by then that this was going to be too much for her?

She thought back to those early days after the Resolution had docked. She had congratulated herself for the brilliant move of bringing Melody Grantley James further in. But now? Would Melody ever recover? And whose fault was it? Why was it not the fault of one Constance Bridlington?

Petroc brought in the tea. 'Are you okay, Ms Bridlington?'

'Yes thank you, Petroc. I'm fine.'

He went back to his office.

I'm fine. Words that seemed to define her. I'm fine with the uncertainty, the danger, the subterfuge. Of course I am. I'm fine that people have nearly died, have died, may still die. And I'm fine with being nowhere nearer the truth of who on earth Ariel is or where he's from.

I'm fine.

She sipped the tea, wondering whether its comfort came from the liquid itself or the simple act of drinking it. She decided it was probably both. And at least one thing was certain. She had sent

Melody to the ideal place to recuperate. A place that was friendly, secure and familiar. And Leonardo would make sure she had all the time and space she needed.

Petroc came through on the intercom. 'Commander Forrester is here, Ma'am.'

'Send him in.'

She couldn't think of a better person to see right now. All through this series of impossibilities Jack had been her mainstay, her bridge between the space exploration industry she knew so well and the treacherous pathways of military intelligence.

The thought of him brought a well-timed smile to her face just as he entered the room. 'Tea?'

'Aye, I'd love a cup.'

They sat together near the window. 'You don't have the view we get in the conference room, do you?' said Jack. 'I often wonder why you look out of it so much.'

'That's precisely the point,' said Constance. 'The view is just right for thinking while I'm listening. No distractions from natural beauty.'

No distractions from natural beauty. The phrase rolled around in her head. Is that what happened with Ariel's abductors and Melody? But how could beauty inspire such wickedness? She kept her thoughts to herself, and they sipped their tea.

'So,' she said, eyes on her teacup. 'Where do we begin?'

'You've seen my report?'

She nodded. 'But tell me what you think. Where do we go from here? In your opinion.'

'Well,' he said, topping up his cup from the silver teapot, staring at the pale liquid as if that might make it stronger, 'Ariel is back at the hotel. His room is next to Natasha's, so I think all we can do there is wait for him to wake up.'

'You think he will?'

Jack shrugged. 'I think we should give it a day or two. Obviously if this turns out to be more than one of his episodes, we'll need to get the medics in. But I'd rather leave him be for now, if that's all right.'

'Absolutely,' she said. 'And, horrible though it is, this awful business has made all the military departments step back a little and give us space.'

'One good thing then.'

She watched him closely. 'Has Beth told you of her plan?'

'Natasha taking him to Sean MacEvoy, you mean? That's fine by me.'

Constance looked at him. His change of focus was plain to see. Not that Ariel mattered any the less, but Melody had to be his number one concern now. Even so, Constance didn't want to go there just yet. 'And what about Takeshi?' she said. 'It's good that we got the crystal back. It appears the Finn took it from him when he abducted him. But do you think Takeshi planted that listening device in Beth's office?' She looked over her own shoulder even as she asked the question.

'I can't see why he'd do that,' said Jack, 'not now we know he was their prisoner. Unless they had a hold on him. Either way, we can't quiz him on it. He's not come round yet, even though they say he's even tougher than Bill. But then he was shot at very close range. According to David Carter he saved the life of one of the kidnappers, Lucien Barretours, by launching himself into the fray unarmed. Straight out of being manacled.'

'And we think Ariel got him out of those dreadful things?' said Constance.

'Must have been him,' said Jack. 'They hadn't been properly retracted, just forced opened somehow, even though the magnetic lock hadn't been switched off. Marta said that was impossible.' He smiled. 'So I guess it was Ariel.'

They sipped some more. Still not the moment to talk about Melody.

'Marta Bergstrom,' said Constance. 'Who'd have thought it? Lena's sister...'

'Aye, well, I'm not sure they're so far apart,' said Jack. 'Sure, Lena is more respectable, and she's done wonders for ESA. But my impression of Marta is that she's trying to make a real difference too, even if she does use unconventional methods. In a way she's just a journalist with a conscience—'

He broke off and his cup hit the saucer with a crack. Now was the moment. 'I'm so sorry, Jack. I'm so, so sorry.'

2

Alice followed David into the hotel room. The scent had gone, but her desire to talk about the one who had been wearing it had only grown. That seemed so much harder now.

David flopped onto the bed, while Alice chose an armchair in the corner. She looked around the room, wrestling with her own imagination. This was stupid.

'I've heard from Cop,' she said. 'She says the church is flourishing without you.' Gentle sarcasm felt safe just now.

He sat up against the bedhead. 'Ah well, they say it's a mark of a good leader if he can leave the flock healthy and find they remain healthy. How did last Sunday go?'

'Gordon did fine. They're used to him after all.'

'True,' said David. 'He's fine when all he has to do is preach. A bit of fire in the pulpit doesn't go amiss once in a while. Though I do sometimes think he'd offer Old Testament sacrifices given half a chance, if you know what I mean.'

She nodded. 'Which he won't be!'

'Indeed not.'

'How are you, David?'

'I don't really know, love. Physically a lot better...'

'Come here and let me give you a hug.'

She held onto him more tightly than for a very long time, as if she might squeeze back into him the love and life they shared up to a week ago. With her next question she released him. 'Where are you?'

'It's been difficult,' he said, and they sat together on the bed. 'We both knew when I came to Geneva that I might see Mel, but this...

Oh Alice, it was awful!' His lips began to quiver. She laid a hand on his shoulder, and the floodgates gave.

When he had fallen quiet they lay down on the bed together. But before long she grew restless again and went back to the armchair. 'Do you want to talk about it?' she said. She hadn't been prepared for this. For David and Melody to go through a trauma together. Now anything that had happened before would be eclipsed by it.

Before. How she wanted to know what had happened before.

'Alice, I know you're tougher than people think you are, but I'm not sure you really want to know what we've been through.'

The 'we' was like a dagger. 'I think I need to know.'

He sighed, then nodded. 'Yes, I suppose you do. I know I would if it had been you.' Without moving he told her about the kidnap at the steps of the library, and she didn't ask him why Melody was there, or if that was the first time they'd met up. He told her about some dim memories of being manacled to a wall, and she didn't ask what he and Melody said to comfort each other. And he told her about the journey in a van, conscious this time, to a park that he had since discovered was in Stuttgart. 'That was the first time I've ever seen anyone shot,' he said as he stared at the wall on the other side of the room. 'But we thought we were going to be set free. We'd been told by the woman who seemed pretty high up that this was an exchange. That's when things changed. Mel didn't want them to have Ariel, even though it would mean we might not go free.'

Alice just listened, unable to get the measure of her own pain.

David was talking more freely now. 'By the time we got back to what turned out to be Cologne, we could tell that there were divisions among the kidnappers. The woman – Marta, her name was – seemed to have gained the moral high ground, while the chap called Dog really was in the doghouse! I don't think his boss was very pleased with how it went.'

'Dog?'

'Yes, that's what they called him. It makes me shiver to think of him. I know we go on about how unpleasant people can be at church sometimes, but Alice, honestly, this felt like evil.'

She walked back across the room and sat on the bed beside him.

'Anyway,' he continued, 'soon we realised it wasn't just Marta. There was a French guy, Lucien, and it turned out he was having doubts as well.' He turned and looked at Alice, enjoying the closeness of her. 'I think Lucien felt he'd been duped.'

'A house divided against itself,' said Alice softly.

'Yes,' said David. 'And no, it couldn't stand. But the trouble was, I for one was starting to realise they really didn't know what to do with us.'

'That must have been frightening.'

He nodded. 'The situation was volatile. They'd got Ariel, and I couldn't for the life of me see why they needed to keep us.' He shivered. 'And of course, they didn't.'

'Did you think they were going to kill you?'

'You know, I honestly didn't dwell on it at the time... just the thought was paralysing... at least, not until things got so bad that any one of us could have been killed.'

Alice shivered. 'But... don't you think this man Dog might have been saved? I mean, might he not have seen reason?'

'Who can say?' said David. 'The Lord alone knows the answer to that question. But one thing's for sure. His feet were firmly set on the path of destruction, and as we know, that so often means self-destruction.'

He hesitated, but she couldn't let him stop there. 'So how did it all end?'

He took a deep breath. 'There's no nice way of saying it. He decided to take Melody down to the basement, which is where we'd been at first, only I hadn't been terribly with it then. We thought he wanted to interrogate her, give him something that would help him understand Ariel more – his value maybe, I don't know. The thing is, Alice, he was pretty cool most of the time, cool as in clinical and careful. He wouldn't strike you as the kind of guy to lose control.'

'But with Mel he did?' Just saying the name was a struggle, never mind the thought of losing control.

'I'm afraid so.' He ran his hand back through his hair. 'The Frenchman, Lucien, he was left with Ariel and me, and we got talking, and that's when we knew he was really unhappy about the way things were going. And I think he was worried about Mel too, though none of us dared say it out loud. And that's when he contacted Marta, and she came soon after that, with Jack and an American guy from UN High Command.'

'Do you need a break?' she said softly.

'No, let's get this done.'

He sounded like he did when a sermon wasn't really cutting it and it was almost time to deliver it. But it struck her that it had to be like this, that when we put things into words we have to reduce the event or the feeling somehow and box it up. Never more than with trauma.

David kept his eyes on the wall while he continued. 'Lucien crept downstairs when he knew help was on its way. Ariel and I decided to follow, and our worst fears were soon realised.' He swallowed hard. 'The trouble was, we could hear what was going on, that he was assaulting Melody, but the room was securely locked and Lucien didn't know how to get in there.'

'Then how—'

'Ariel did his thing. He just opened the locked doors! I tell you Alice, I wouldn't have believed it if I hadn't seen it with my own eyes. I don't know if he had some kind of hidden technology, or...'

'Or?'

'Well, there's something about him.'

'Yes, there is.'

He looked at her, surprised. 'You know?'

'We had some time together when you were... away. But go on.'

'Right. He did mention that.' He stood up and walked over to the window, before turning back to carry on. 'There was a lot of scuffling and fighting. There was another man, a prisoner who I've since learned Ariel managed to set free before he passed out, and he tried to help Lucien get the better of this Dog chap. That's when the gun went off, though I didn't really know where it was or if anyone was hurt. I tried to cover Mel as best I could... and then Jack appeared and there was more shooting... that was the American. He had to, it was self-defence. It all happened so fast. There were bodies on the floor, and Mel was crying – wailing actually – but eventually things calmed down and we were escorted out of the building.'

Alice sat still a while. 'And how is Mel now?'

David's face began to crumple. 'I don't know. They've taken her somewhere, I don't know where.'

She got up and held him close. There was a way to go, but this had to be good. Didn't it?

3

Lucien didn't know which was worse, recovering from electrocution or being held in custody, but he broke into a smile when Marta walked into the small hospital room, her signature red scarf set off by a royal blue trouser suit. Dog had not had time to deliver more than the default level of the 'workbench' in the basement, so Lucien's paralysis had been temporary and his symptoms were likely to be less severe than David's. And because the bench delivered the shock in a way that was designed to impose maximum discomfort with minimum show, his burns were not severe.

'Does it hurt?' said Marta, stooping down and kissing him on both cheeks, before putting some flowers on his bedside table.

'Not as much as having the guard on the door,' he said.

She sat down on a chair by the bed. 'I'm sorry.'

'Why? Why would you need to be sorry?'

'I'm sorry you got bitten by our fancy equipment, I'm sorry you got dragged into this, and I'm sorry I didn't act sooner.'

The guard poked his head round the door and then withdrew again.

'But I'm not sorry I met you.' She leant forward and kissed him on the forehead and then pulled a miniature bottle of red wine from an inside pocket. 'I thought we might share this. Are you allowed alcohol?'

'We won't ask,' he said, delighted with the choice. She unscrewed the cap and put it to his lips. He allowed her to administer the soothing liquid, and as his body relaxed she joined her lips to his.

'Tastes good,' she said.

He grunted.

She sat down at the bedside and downed the rest of the bottle.

'You know,' he said, 'I thought you were strange when we first met.'

'And now?'

'I think you're *wunderbar*!' He coughed and groaned. 'But tell me,' he said. 'What's going to happen to you now?'

'I believe Jack described it as assisting with their enquiries. I don't think they've decided how to charge me, or even if they will.'

'I'm glad,' he said. 'And what about the others? No one is telling me anything in here.'

'Well, Dog is dead. That's official. They're asking me who his phone call was with, but I told them that's not how it works. I keep out of the subterfuge network. Although...'

'What?'

'Well, it's strange, but over the last couple of weeks I've seen this latest contact really get to him, under his skin as they say in English. What you don't know is that, until recently, he hardly ever lost it – you know? He always struck me as very disciplined, and he carried out his job with clinical precision. What we saw in there...'

'A different animal?'

'Yes, exactly so.'

Lucien sat up and she adjusted his pillows, affording him the opportunity to take her hand and stroke it gently. 'You think there's a connection between his change of behaviour and his new client?'

'Maybe,' she said, clasping his hand in both of hers. 'But the whole affair has been crazy.'

He laughed. 'I'm glad it's not normal *Exposé* life!'

She sat back down.

'While I've been lying here I've been thinking,' said Lucien. 'This man they are all interested in, Ariel – he really is something else, no?'

'To be honest, I don't understand any of it,' she said.

'Ah, but Marta, you should have seen it! He just strode in there as if the doors were not locked!'

She shook her head. 'It makes no sense. I mean, he did not know the house and had no access to the controls. And he can't have had eband access.'

'Well, that's just it,' said Lucien, pulling himself higher against his pillows. 'Did you not notice? The guy wears no eband.'

Marta shook her head again. 'According to Jack, it's some kind of trick he can do. Something he does with his mind, I think.'

'Hmm,' said Lucien, 'maybe he overstretched himself, and that's why he passed out.'

'Maybe,' she said.

'Do you think he is from outside space?' said Lucien. 'Sorry, I know that sounds crazy.'

She smiled, partly at his English but mainly because of the new ease and intimacy between them. 'Who knows?' she said. 'But if we were visited by aliens, I do not think it would happen this way, do you? My guess is, he was part of a secret mission. Something happened... and now he can't remember.' She looked at her eband. 'Hey, I have to go.'

'Will I see you again?' he said. 'You can visit me in prison if you like.'

She blew him another kiss. 'In that case, my friend,' she said, 'either I must learn French, or you must learn German!'

4

She had only been away four days, but it felt like a lifetime. Another life. Melody was back at the Elemental Retreat Centre.

Summer had ripened here on this side of the Alps, but it still felt as though autumn was being held back. Leroy was attending to his leaves, but there were plenty more on the bough. The ever present backdrop of birdsong was a soothing balm, and she took comfort from knowing it had gone on long before she had arrived and would surely continue long after.

Leonardo's warm smile was more welcoming than ever, Ambrose's concoctions were gently calming, and the aroma of the refectory's distinctive fresh coffee recaptured so much of what had gone before.

But Ariel was not here.

Jack came just in time for the evening meal that she had agreed to share with Leonardo and her trauma counsellor in a corner of the lounge next door to the refectory. Hannah Sommer had been chosen by Constance to stay with Melody and help her talk things through. A trusted friend of the Director, qualified counsellor and psychiatrist, it was down to her to decide when to medicate, when to talk and when to listen, all within the healing environment provided by the retreat centre.

As the meal progressed Jack tried to find Mel's eyes, but when her head wasn't down she was looking out of the window. Dr Sommer seemed well chosen for the role she had to play, content to step forward when required but equally happy in the background. Her first session with Melody alone would take place as and when the patient felt ready, though Hannah implied that tomorrow morning would not be too soon. Jack spent most of the time bringing Leonardo up to date with recent events. The Abbot listened in attentive silence.

After coffee Leonardo disappeared and Hannah stood up to go to her room. 'Remember, Melody, I am here for you 24-7. You just call – I mean knock.' Melody had been put in her old room in the hope that the familiar surroundings would help her sleep, and Hannah had been given the room next door. 'I hadn't realised we'd be quite so cut off here,' Hannah whispered to Jack as she tapped her eband in the vain hope that this might somehow restore connectivity.

'Oh, aye,' said Jack, 'nothing gets in or out of here. Well, that's the theory anyway!'

She looked puzzled.

'Long story,' he said. 'Why don't you go and catch up on the mountain of work you're bound to have, or even take some time off? If you really need to get connected, just walk out of the main gate and down the road a ways. We know where you are if we need you. And let me say I'm glad you're here. Mel and I are just going to take a wee walk around the cloister, and then we'll be up.'

Hannah decided on the walk to the gate before retiring, taking gulps of the fresh evening air as she went. Soon its invigorating woodiness was infiltrating her very pores. Already she could see why Constance had chosen this place, even without the personal significance it had for her client.

After she had gone Jack helped Mel into a light coat and took her arm in his. 'Let's walk, shall we?' They made their way slowly round the courtyard, stopping at each elemental shrine. 'Interesting counsellor we have there,' said Jack. 'German?'

'Swiss, I think,' she said limply.

When they got to earth she put her hand in the stone basin and let the soil run through her fingers. 'We're dust, you know,' she said so quietly he barely heard it. 'We come from stuff, and we go back to being stuff. And on the way, some people treat us like just so much stuff—' She broke off and wept.

'It's all right,' Jack soothed, elated that he had at last found the moment to put his arms around her. 'Better out than in, lass. It's okay.'

But he knew it was far from okay.

5

Natasha called David on her eband. 'It's Natasha. Ariel is awake, and he's eager to talk to you.'

She was content with the white lie. In fact Ariel was only just starting to make sense, having woken an hour earlier, but she felt that

David's presence could only be beneficial, as one of those who was with him before he passed out. He and Alice were in the process of changing hotel, at the suggestion and expense of Constance, and soon they would be just along the corridor.

Natasha was in the main lounge area of a suite which had a communicating door to her own room. Ariel emerged from his room, now fully awake.

'Where are we, Natasha?' he asked as he looked out of the window. 'I see trees. And a lake. And there are the mountains! Are we back in Geneva?'

'We are,' she beamed. 'We're in our hotel, not far from the UN building. We're in different rooms from before – I'm just next door. We weren't sure when you were going to wake up.'

'How long have I been gone?'

'Only since yesterday,' she said as casually as she could.

'Yesterday? That's the longest since...'

'I know,' she said softly. 'Can you remember what happened?'

'It came out of the blue, Natasha. Very invasive. Like a great heavy cloud came over me, blinding me, rushing in my ears, suffocating.'

She grimaced. 'Sounds terrible. What do you think caused it? I hear you had done quite a bit of... door-opening up to that moment.'

He chose a large and luxurious leather armchair that seemed to swallow him up as he settled into it. He looked smaller.

'I don't know. The doors had not proved troublesome. Nor had the restraints on the wall.'

Her eyes widened. Jack had told her very little before he had left for Montagnola.

Her eband flashed. It was David saying they had arrived. She told Ariel that David and Alice were neighbours now. 'Would you like them to join us?'

'That would be nice.'

She called them in and very soon agreed with Alice that a strategic withdrawal, aka shopping trip, would be appropriate.

When they had gone David sank into an identical armchair on the other side of the window. 'Quite a place, this,' he remarked. 'Certainly out of my price bracket.'

They talked a while about the traumatic events in the house in Cologne, but David felt they were skirting around the real issues. For himself, the pressing problem was his relationship with Melody, and therefore with Alice. But for Ariel? He decided to quiz him further on the sense of suffocation he had felt. 'Tell me about this invasiveness you sensed – you know, just before you passed out. If you can.'

'I shall try,' said Ariel, 'though it is hard to put it into words.'

'I understand,' said David. 'It's a pity I can't read your mind!' He ran his fingernails lightly across the leather. 'But then, maybe I could.'

'What do you mean?'

'Well,' said David, 'couldn't we try it in reverse, so to speak? Might we be able to open our minds to each other, only reverse the direction of reading? To put it in computing terms, could you write to my mind rather than read it?'

'Well now, that is an interesting notion,' said Ariel. 'Though I'm not too sure what it would be like for you. It could be dangerous.'

'I think you're careful, and caring,' said David. 'I'm willing to take that risk.'

'There's something else you should be aware of,' said Ariel. 'I doubt that it would be easy for you to control the flow of your own thoughts. You may remember that, when we were in the house in Cologne, you were sharing with me what happened during the evening that you and Melody spent together. I can't promise that won't come through to me again.'

'Don't worry about that,' said David. 'I'm relying on it.'

6

Hannah and Melody had been allocated the discussion room, but Melody asked to go into the chapel. She said the associations there would be conducive, though really all she knew was that she felt more at peace there. Or at least further from the doubt and the dirt.

They sat in the chancel, and not for the first time she wondered what the present incumbents did with this part of their monastery. 'I mean, it's not as if they come here to pray, or even sing,' she said to Hannah.

'Do we know they don't sing?' Hannah asked.

'Well, no, we don't,' said Melody, 'now that you come to mention it. But I've not heard anything.'

Hannah let her talk about the place, the woods and the refectory where the Brothers were sometimes silent but usually conveniently abuzz with conversation, making it easier for Jack and Leonardo and the others to talk freely there. And she watched Melody start to come alive when she talked about Ariel. 'The time we had in the woods was wonderful,' she was saying, 'but quite honestly it was all wonderful. Even when he didn't say a word, somehow his presence made a difference.'

'He does seem quite special,' said Hannah, confining herself to affirmation and containing her own curiosity.

They talked some more, until Hannah felt the time had come to prod, ever so gently, in a certain direction. 'Still,' she said, 'clearly not everybody is so warm towards Ariel.'

'Well, that is interesting in itself,' said Melody, sitting up straighter. 'I was thinking about that a bit before... when I was starting to draft my next article. I want to write about perspectives and their place in building a cohesive narrative. And about recall. You know, the way most of our recollections dim, except a few.'

'Go on,' said Hannah.

'Well, it seems to me that the clear memories we have, going right back to childhood, are like anchors, or perhaps I should say small islands, in a sea of fairly muddled impressions. We may not remember all the details of where we were when someone said something memorable – whether positive or negative doesn't matter – or what happened before and after, but it has found a place in our minds so deeply rooted nothing will shift it.'

'And how does that relate to perspective, do you think?'

'Silly me,' said Melody, 'this stuff must be your bread and butter.'

'Not at all,' said Hannah. 'I'd love to hear what a writer has to say.'

'A journalist's perspective on perspective, eh?' said Melody, though today the smile could only be a grin. 'Okay. I think those core memories create a kind of scaffold, or network – think islands in the sea again. And that helps us to make sense of the tons of stuff that comes at us every day, the vast bulk of which we soon forget.'

'You mentioned childhood memories,' said Hannah. 'We know that people's basic beliefs, their worldviews, are shaped in the early years.' She studied Melody's face as she thought for a few moments. She still couldn't read what was going on inside.

'Maybe,' Melody said. 'Though surely that doesn't mean your perspectives can't change later in life. Your childhood gives you the equipment to formulate views. The views themselves don't have to stay the same.'

Hannah nodded her respect.

'Anyway,' said Melody, and to Hannah's surprise she looked her squarely in the eye, 'if anyone's changed people's perspectives around here, it's Ariel.'

'Though people do see him differently,' Hannah pressed, gently building on the show of strength.

'Yes,' said Melody, 'but only a few of us have really got to know him. The forces that have come against him – the military, and whatever drove the kidnappers–' She broke into a series of coughs, retching at times.

'Take your time,' said Hannah. 'Shall we go and find some water?'

'What? No, I'm fine. Sorry about that. Where was I? Those forces that have come against Ariel don't know him. They've not known anything about him. Which is the point, of course.'

'Man of mystery.'

'Yes,' said Melody. 'And yet, when they have met him, and got to know him even a little, they've changed. Some quite quickly – I think of the man called Lucien who was involved in the whole business. And some have taken longer. Unbelievably, I hear that even the military man who first came to us here in this very place – even he's come round. Big time.'

'What do you think they have come round to? If you don't mind me asking.'

'Well now...' said Melody, welcoming the current train of thought like a fresh breeze, 'that is a good question.' She got up and started to walk around the chancel. She wanted to touch the stone yet wanted to touch nothing. Be touched by nothing. She looked up at the stained-glass windows and their pictures of the garden and the rainbow. They felt wrong. She turned her back on them and returned to where Hannah was sitting, right where Ariel had sat so long ago now, as it seemed. 'I think they appreciate his transparency,' she said at last.

'Ironic, don't you think?' said Hannah, 'given that no one knows who he is.'

'Yes,' Melody nodded, 'it is ironic, but totally fitting. If he doesn't know who he is, he isn't going to show it or hide it.' She clasped her hands together. 'Perhaps that's it – people can see that he has nothing to hide, not deliberately.'

'Anything else?' said Hannah.

Melody began to wonder where this was going, and whether Hannah was recording it. She could see no equipment for making notes and concluded that she was relying on her eband. 'Simplicity,' she said. 'I think they warm to that. I'm not saying he's simple, you understand, and his origins and story may be complicated. But he is straightforward. Disarmingly so.'

A door opened at the far end of the chapel, the one that led to Leonardo's office. Jack popped his head round. 'Everyone all right?' he called. 'Need some coffee?'

Hannah looked to Melody to answer.

'We're fine, Jack, honestly.' She put her hands through her hair as nonchalantly as she could, though not without a shiver. 'I tell you what, why don't you meet us in the refectory in half an hour?'

'Fine.' He withdrew.

Hannah leant her head to one side and stared at Melody. 'What was that about?' she asked.

'What do you think?' said Melody.

'Well, ordinarily I'd be tempted to think that you might have asked Jack to interrupt us at a certain point, just in case you needed saving.'

'Ordinarily?'

'Yes.' Hannah smiled. 'But then, instead of just dismissing him, you effectively gave us half an hour to do something.'

Melody returned the smile. 'Respect,' she said. 'I might have known Constance would give me someone good.'

Hannah continued to look straight at her, undeflected.

'Okay,' said Melody. 'I want to talk about *it* – you know? And I want to do it before coffee! Is that all right?'

'Melody, it's very all right.'

'First, can you tell me what you know?' said Melody. 'I'd rather that, if you don't mind.'

It was as good a plan as any, avoiding the need for Melody herself to go over events, doubtless hoping she would be able to pick up on what Hannah said.

'Very well,' she said. 'You must understand that, the minute you were abducted in Geneva, you lost your freedom. Whatever else happened, whether there were more relaxed times and then more tense ones, you remained a captive. You were drugged from the very start, held in a room that had been carefully designed to render people powerless and vulnerable, and then you were subjected to the emotional trauma of a release that proved a sham.'

'You've been well briefed,' said Melody. She didn't know whether she felt shocked or relieved by Hannah's summary so far, but decided she was happy to feel both.

'I don't know all the details,' said Hannah, 'and obviously cannot share your perspective. But I can give you some facts, purely on the basis of the medical report I have been given. You were originally drugged with a concoction of fast-acting non-opioid drugs.'

'Would that be David as well?'

'I'm not privy to that information,' said Hannah, 'but it would seem likely. You were both rendered unconscious almost immediately, I gather.' She paused, wondering whether Melody wanted to talk about David Carter.

'Please go on,' she said.

'At some later point,' Hannah continued, 'you were drugged with two more chemicals, which seem to have been administered with one clear intent.' She noted Melody's expression of concentrated attention before continuing. 'The effect of one of the drugs would, in the case of someone who was not on any other medication, be to stimulate or enhance the emotions. In a context such as your own, that would most likely be fear.'

Melody shuddered. 'And the other?'

'The other one was quite the opposite. It was a relaxant, something that would be intoxicating and... encourage sociability.' Hannah was suddenly struck by the need to swallow.

'I don't understand,' said Melody. 'Does that make any sense to you?'

'I'm afraid it does,' said Hannah, 'judging by the amounts that were administered. My guess is that you would initially have shown great resistance, before this was overcome by a relaxed and compliant attitude.'

'I don't understand,' Melody repeated.

'Your attacker wanted to feel your resistance, Melody, and then see you cave in and give yourself... almost willingly. Or at least resign yourself to your fate.'

Melody still looked more perplexed than shocked.

'It's about his own sense of power. Specifically power over you, as the one he had chosen to assault.'

Melody sat in silence, her shoulders gently rising and falling as she breathed deeply.

'Does any of this resonate with you?' asked Hannah. 'Let me emphasise, you don't need to understand your attacker's motivation. But does this in any way fit with your recollections, such as you may have? We must bear in mind that trauma can cause a certain level of amnesia.'

'Don't we know it?' said Melody. The connection with Ariel was just what she needed, and she decided to press on. 'I remember now. I thought it odd that he made me a drink in the kitchen, as if all we were going to do was have a friendly chat. That must be when I was drugged. And then he forced me downstairs at gunpoint!' Her hands began to shake. 'It's absolutely true that I felt much more fear after that. And then anger, once I'd been manacled and started to resist. I remember now, after he'd said some rather puerile things about my physiology – stuff I'd heard before, but only from teenagers – he produced a pair of scissors from somewhere and proceeded to cut through my sleeves. He did it so calmly, so precisely, cutting around the manacles. But then he grabbed the front of the blouse, at the top, and pulled so hard the buttons went flying. And then...'

'Take your time... if you want to go on.'

'Trust me, I do. So then he started to... well, slobber over me. I don't know how else to say it. But then... he stood back and he looked at me. I tell you, Hannah, it was not the sort of look any woman wants to see, no matter how desirable she thinks she'd like to be. I don't mean to boast when I say that I've had to deal with unwanted advances for most of my life, but honestly, at that moment, all the clever things I would normally say just drained away. He looked at me like I was... I don't know, like I was a fly caught in his web. The more he relished it, the smaller I felt. Insignificant. Like nothing really mattered any more.'

'That would fit with the drugs,' said Hannah, 'though it might also have been a defence mechanism on your part. You knew there was nothing you could do. You needed to shut down. You may not have been thinking that way consciously, but the brain is a wonderful and complex thing.'

'Fearfully and wonderfully made,' Melody whispered.

'Sorry?'

'Oh, it's nothing. Just something David used to say.'

'He clearly means a lot to you,' said Hannah.

'Well, yes, let's not go there,' said Melody. 'Hannah, thank you so much for this. I don't think there's anyone else who could have helped me start to crawl out of the hole I've been in these past hours. At least, no one who's available.'

'You mean...?' She wasn't sure if it was Jack's name coming next, or David's.

'I mean Ariel.'

Hannah hesitated. 'I think you may have found it very hard to talk to a man in these circumstances,' she said, trying not to sound defensive. 'Especially a man you admire so much, or... have feelings for?'

'What? No!' said Melody. 'I told you, Ariel is different. He's not like any other man I've met.'

Hannah looked unconvinced, but didn't want to press it, especially having come so far. 'Well, look at that,' she said, checking her eband. 'I think it's time for that coffee.'

7

David was looking at Ariel. He realised he'd not properly studied his face before. Even now that wasn't easy, as the deep-blue eyes pulled him in. The features were well defined, chiselled even, yet soft and unthreatening. Perhaps that was more down to the expression in his eyes. Those eyes.

'Thank you for trying to help me with this,' said Ariel. Or did he think it?

'You're welcome,' David returned. 'You've done so much to help us.'

'Yes,' said Ariel, 'but only because you were in danger, and that danger was caused by my presence. If only we knew what all this was about.'

David was pretty sure that they had left speech behind now, and that to any onlooker they would look like they were daydreaming. He sensed Ariel's reluctance to expose him to what happened in the white room, and so he offered some of his own pain instead. Ariel felt the horror slam into him as David was once again confronted by the immediate aftermath of Melody's assault – the manic look in her eyes, the bruising round her neck, the weals and bite marks as he glanced further down. The sense of horror was attended by a surprising mix of disgust and desire, before the whole concoction of emotions became infused with an agonising sorrow.

An image arose of a flower, which turned into a whole scene, a meadow. A young David was picking a beautiful blue-and-white flower, and his parents were gently arguing over whether it was right to pick a flower that was so beautiful, knowing that its beauty would be irrevocably damaged in the act of plucking. The scene changed as a stream became an aisle and hills became arches, and there was Alice walking slowly up the aisle, light from her purity radiating in all directions. The light became dazzling, before melting like a cloud and revealing a white room, a broken flower, an almost overwhelming desire to pull the flower close, curtailed by distaste at the bruises and marks, the shaking and shouting.

He was picking up a blouse now, one he had wanted to remove himself but which now was all he had to cover the hurt and the shame. He was so angry. For this was a flower he had not picked, though he had wanted to. A body he had not possessed, a soul he had not joined. And ruination was upon her.

Ariel let the cocktail of desire and distaste filter down and settle, until he found a place where he and David might meet. Sensing the time had come, and keeping his gaze steady, he took David by the hand and began to lead him to the other side of the white room.

David resisted, shaking Ariel's hand off. He wanted to stay here on this side of the room. But something deep down told him to go with it, to trust this man, and so he came to where a Japanese man was sitting, hands raised awkwardly, manacled to the wall. Suddenly David felt the urgency, and the surge of compassion, as he glared at the bonds, expecting them to spring open. But maybe they wouldn't this time. Why should they? How could he possibly expect to open them just by willing it?

He looked more closely. The manacles became huge, filling his vision, and now he could see a space between the two halves. Soon the gap was enormous. Easy to reverse the polarity. To tell the molecules to flee from each other. To prise the halves apart.

Just when it seemed they were about to fly from each other, it all ceased to be inevitable. The doubt returned, and with it the giddiness. He was falling back, tumbling, over and over, driven down by a weight of darkness, drowning in a sea of voices. All was lost, and he was falling from the battle. He saw the thought, identified it as alien, fought it, and once again saw his own feet standing firm on the floor. From here he stretched upwards till he thought his body would burst, and glared one last time at the bonds. They sprang apart. And now he readily succumbed to the weight of the darkness, letting its waters pull him down, fill his mouth and throat and lungs, and plunge him into the abyss.

8

Nathan Dexter was a patient man. He had spent years on the margins of action, just outside the limelight, feeling secure yet wanting more. As an analyst with US intelligence he had lived the life of a spy through the surveillance reports of others, vicariously indulging in their influence over individuals and even nations. With experience had come cynicism, but he masked it well, and so at last he had come to the nearest thing there was to a centre of it all, UN High Command.

Or so he had thought. All that changed when his unseen contact upped the game. He could find nothing in any files about the International Front. All his skills and training told him he must find out who was feeding him this privileged information. But for now he would have to let events unfold.

Doubtless there would be unforeseen obstacles in the role he had to play. The crystal had worked, but getting Ariel away from his protectors was never going to be easy. Still, whoever this source was, they were sure to have more up their sleeve. And he was clearly important to them. Right now prudence dictated that he wait for further instructions. Sooner or later they were sure to come.

9

Alice and Natasha tumbled into the hotel room in a whirl of laughter and shopping. 'This has been so much fun,' said Natasha as she tripped over one of her bags on her way to the inner door.

'Ssh! Wait!' Alice put her fingers to her lips in the time-honoured fashion of a pastor's wife used to a home-working husband. 'Sorry,' she whispered as Natasha frowned with curiosity. 'It's just, they may be in the middle of something. You know.'

Natasha gave a nod of acknowledgement and slowly opened the door. 'I think they're asleep!' she giggled. But when she looked again her smile suddenly disintegrated before she quickly disappeared into the room.

Alice dropped her bags and rushed in after her. Natasha was already on her knees directly in between David and Ariel, studying their faces. They were sitting upright in their armchairs, looking at each other, totally still.

Alice placed her hands on David's shoulders and began gently massaging them, whispering his name. Natasha decided to follow suit with Ariel. And so, gradually, both men emerged from their stupor.

'You gave us a bit of a fright there, my friend,' said Natasha as she sat herself on the arm of Ariel's chair.

'Are you all right, my love?' Alice patted the giant cushion behind David who began to blink rapidly, as if he hadn't been able to do that for some time and was now catching up.

'I'm okay,' he said at last. 'That was intense.'

'I'll make a cup of tea.' She crossed to the small bar where there were drink-making facilities and set about putting the world to rights.

Ariel stood up and stretched. 'Well, I must say, I don't think I've ever done that before. David, are you really all right?'

He nodded, stood up and looked out of the window. 'Well, we're still here to tell the tale.'

'And it's a tale we'd like to hear. Wouldn't we, Natasha?' said Alice as she laid out cups and saucers on a coffee table. Natasha brought two chairs and, while the tea brewed in the cups and Alice apologised profusely for not having a teapot, they settled down to hear what had happened.

David shifted the cushion behind his back. 'I can only describe it as a most intimate connection,' he said. Natasha gave a muted yelp as she poured hot tea on her hand.

'At first it was like before,' David continued, 'when we did this in Cologne. I was aware that Ariel could see what I could see, feel what I could feel, as we were back in that awful basement.' Alice fumbled with her cup and it rattled as it landed on the saucer. 'But after a while it was as though Ariel took me by the hand and led me to his experience of what was going on. I felt the surge of power as I... he... broke open those manacles.'

'Oh my!' breathed Alice, as the thought of Ariel eclipsed everything else hammering at her heart. 'The Spirit of the Lord is upon me, to set the captives free.'

'Absolutely,' said David, 'and this was so literally true, Alice, so real and concrete. How often we spiritualise what the Lord did, and what he tells us to do, and that's right of course. But this was physical – you know? It was amazing. Straight out of the book of Acts, like Peter breaking out of prison.'

Ariel said nothing.

'Why were you both still locked into each other?' Natasha asked. 'Because that's what it looked like.'

'Because,' said David slowly, 'that amazing feat had happened in the middle of what I can only describe as an attack.'

'Really?' said Ariel.

'Really,' said David. 'It was intrusive, invasive. Oppressive.'

'So, maybe it was a spiritual thing after all,' said Alice, gingerly sipping her tea.

David sighed. 'Yes, but of course! You're right as always, my love. A physical act can also be part of a spiritual battle, as we well know.' As I should know, his thoughts alone continued.

Natasha stood up. 'So, what are you saying?'

'I'm saying that I think Ariel was attacked in the spiritual realm. And maybe not for the first time.'

'But what does that mean?' said Natasha, a note of desperation creeping into her voice.

'I, I don't know,' David stuttered.

'It means,' said Alice, rising to her feet, 'that we need to pray. Just as soon as we've got that shopping in.'

Chapter 25

Intelligence

1

Autumn was further along in Ireland, and Ariel made the most of every moment as he and Natasha walked through one of the brightly flowered parks of Dublin's fair city, each dragging a small case behind them. They had taken a bus from the airport, Natasha keen to let Ariel mingle with 'normal people' for a while at least. As they walked into Trinity College, Ariel noticed precious few trees spaced around the tightly cropped grass of the main square. Natasha got the impression there were as many tourists and passers-through as there were students, all coming and going through the various squares that lay within the grand grey-stone buildings.

They stood in the Library Square, looking up at the tall tower of the Campanile. The open spaces dwarfed the intimate cloisters of the monastery in Montagnola, and Natasha began to feel somehow exposed by the buzzing crowds. Happily, just seconds after the appointed hour, she saw the unmistakable figure of Professor Sean MacEvoy striding towards them. He was wearing a knitted pullover with no jacket, which told her he had not walked far. He had a good head of hair for a man of his years, which shone silvery white in the sunlight, and as he drew closer she could see an unmistakable glint in the eyes that flashed behind the silver-framed spectacles.

He stretched out his right arm as he sped to a stop and shook them both firmly by the hand. 'Natasha, Ariel, I'm Sean. So pleased to meet you both.'

'I'm honoured,' said Natasha, acutely aware not only of his legendary status but also that he would naturally be far more interested in Ariel than in her. As the man credited with moving SETI from the scientific to the political mainstream, there was next to nothing he didn't know about the search for intelligent life beyond planet Earth, not to mention within the governments of Earth itself.

'Now then,' he breezed, 'let's see if we can't find somewhere better than here for a cup of coffee.' He chuckled. 'Shouldn't be difficult. I tell you what, why don't you come back to my place and we can talk for as long and as openly as we like? I know a nice little restaurant where we can have lunch first, not far from my house. I've taken the liberty of getting your hotel bookings cancelled by the good folk at the UN.'

'Oh, thank you,' said Natasha. 'I didn't know you had a house in the city here.'

'I don't,' he chirped. 'I live in Cork. But if you follow me to the College Park just over there, our transport awaits.'

2

Alice put her brand new teapot down and sighed. 'It's no good, David. We're going to have to talk about it.'

'Of course, love,' said David, taking his place in the armchair where, just yesterday, Ariel had sat and shared devastation with him. 'But obviously we must keep Ariel's confidence, just as we would with anyone in the fellowship back home.'

She began to shake her head. 'No, darling, that's not it. I mean Mel. Before I arrived in Geneva.'

'Oh. Yes, of course.' He sank back into the chair. 'Sorry, love, is something bothering you?' He knew it was a coward's question, but it was all he could manage.

Alice knew that the moment had arrived. She desperately wanted this to be a consultation between two hearts, not a confrontation between two jousters, but she could see it was not really in her power to determine which it would turn out to be. 'Well yes, something is bothering me,' she said. 'You remember when she came to see us at home, not long after they'd all landed back on Earth?'

He nodded. His mouth was dry.

'Well, she was wearing a certain perfume. I think it's called Mind Mist. Anyway...' David looked at her hands. She was squeezing her wedding ring between her thumb and forefinger as she fought to find the next words. 'Well, the thing is, it has a very distinctive smell. I quite like it, actually... well, I used to. Only I detected it in our room, your room, in the other hotel. You know, when I first arrived.' There, she thought, I've said it. It's out now.

But it brought her precious little relief.

'Oh, is that all?' said David, following a script he had rehearsed many times in his head. 'Well, that's because she did come to my room. Before we went to the library. You know, for my Calvin thing.'

She felt the evasion, and the pain level rose accordingly. And now the tears started to swell, tears she'd so hoped would stay away. But they seemed to have a life of their own, and if it looked like emotional manipulation, then so be it. What could she do? It was all or nothing now.

David saw her eyes glistening, and he crossed to her chair and knelt before her. 'Alice, sweetheart, don't be silly.'

'I'm not!' she wailed. 'But I need to know!'

'Of course, of course. And I'll tell you everything. Come on, let's have a cup of tea—'

'No!'

He inched away from her, still on his knees. 'All right,' he said quietly. 'We'd had dinner, as we were both in town and the others didn't need her at the UN building. She came back, and we just got talking... you know how it is. She's always been so stimulating–'

Alice grunted.

'Sorry, no, wrong word. Oh, come on, you know what I mean! And honestly, love, she's changed since meeting Ariel. She's even closer now.'

'Closer to who?' She hated herself for the tone of her question, but she felt trapped in the slipstream of the whole conversation.

'To the Lord, of course!' he said, privately congratulating himself for not correcting her grammar.

She looked at him, and his gaze did not drop. He looked like the same David. Perhaps he was.

'Okay,' he said at last. 'I admit it was probably unwise to carry on the conversation in my room. Our room.'

'Unwise? You think? Honestly, David, what were you thinking? No, don't answer that.'

He knew they had reached the nub of it. More than what had happened Alice needed to know what had been going on in his heart. In the heart that belonged to her.

He got back on his feet and returned to the armchair. How he wished that they could join minds now, as he and Ariel had done. Or did he? Maybe words were best. They were not as immediate, but their very mediation provided the buffer that was sometimes needed when two people communicated. And anyway, hadn't there been a kind of mediation even with Ariel? David himself had had to re-experience the event and interpret the feelings coming across from Ariel. Truly, everyone's perspective was their own.

He realised he was breathing fast. 'Okay,' he said, 'let's go back. When I was still building up the typesetting firm, when we first moved to Thanington, you remember how hard that was?'

She nodded. 'Yes, but they were good times.'

'Yes they were,' he said. 'But with the business so young, and the church needing so much attention, it was – to be frank – a bit of a slog. Not that I begrudged it, not for a moment. But there it was.'

'Okay... So?'

'So, when Melody came into our lives, I admit that I was flattered. And I don't just mean by the fact that she was an attractive woman showing an interest.'

The word 'just' pierced like a dart. He was still talking.

'She was sophisticated. And she was so hungry, spiritually – you remember, don't you?'

'Yes, I do,' she spluttered.

He wanted to put his arms round her, but he knew that would be fuel on the fire right now. 'And that really gave me a lift,' he said. 'You know, that someone was genuinely interested in following the Lord, someone like her. I mean, she was hardly typical of the people we were dealing with day by day, was she?'

'No.' The tears did not stop.

'And she really did become our friend, didn't she? Isn't she?'

'I hope so.' She knew she owed David that much of a confession of faith, even now. She thought of the mind-to-mind gift that Ariel had given her in the hotel lounge by the fire, and all the things he had said about Mel's love for Jack and how she prized Alice's friendship.

'Well then...' He climbed out of his chair but she was up and across the room before he could get to her.

'I think I'll go for a walk,' she said, drying her eyes with her hands. 'I need the fresh air.'

'Okay. But are we okay?'

She nodded very quickly and left the room, still none the wiser about just how much of the night Melody Grantley James had shared with her husband.

3

Sean's 'transport' turned out to be a private helicopter. 'This is great!'

Natasha shouted into her cheek microphone. 'It's funny, I've been to Venus and back in the world's most sophisticated flying machine, but I've never flown in one of these!' The G-force was nothing compared to orbital and escape velocities, but here she had a proper sense of flying upwards as they swooped away from a city that she could actually see shrinking beneath them.

She was seated with Ariel opposite Sean MacEvoy in the back of an old Twin Squirrel. It had been decommissioned by the military some years before, but he had managed to acquire it 'at a fair price'. Although his piloting days were over, he was reluctant to let it go. One of his old flying buddies was standing in as chauffeur.

They came down near the centre of Cork in an area of green that turned out to be called Shalom Park. And the peace certainly was palpable after the helicopter had dropped them off and flown away. With all the noise there had been precious little conversation, and Natasha began to wonder whether Sean was ignoring Ariel. Perhaps he was saving something up.

Less than twenty minutes later they were seated outside the front of a riverside restaurant, breathing in the cool autumn air.

'Is your house really somewhere near here?' asked Natasha. 'Or should we be expecting another flight?'

Sean responded immediately with a great belly laugh. 'No, no, sorry to disappoint you, lass! It's just a short boat ride from here.'

She eyed him carefully, unable to tell if this was for real or a joke. She decided time would tell. They ordered, and at last Sean turned his attention to Ariel.

'So, my friend, you've been causing a lot of trouble, or so I hear.' It was hardly the opening she had expected.

'Yes,' said Ariel, unfazed and apparently in complete agreement. 'I do appear to have been something of a provocation for some people.'

'Hmm,' Sean mused, 'a provocation. Well, yes, that's good, that is. I like that.' Natasha enjoyed the soft Irish tones as they floated across the table. A carafe of white wine arrived, a mouthful of which the waiter poured into a single glass. Sean seemed fully focused on Ariel now, so Natasha tasted it. It was perfectly chilled and sumptuously dry. She nodded and the waiter began to pour. She stopped him halfway on the third glass, realising Ariel had not drunk alcohol before. 'Sorry, Ariel, do you...?'

'I don't know,' he said. 'But I'm willing to try.'

Sean laughed again. 'My, this is going to be fun. What an enigma you are, my friend! But then, that's entirely appropriate.'

'Why do you say that?' Ariel asked, tentatively sipping the cool liquid as the waiter withdrew.

'Ah, put it down to Fermi!' he said as he took a sip.

'Fermi's paradox,' Natasha explained, without explaining.

'What's that?' said Ariel, after sipping a little more deeply.

'I should probably let the master tell you,' she said.

'What? Me, you mean?' said Sean with affected surprise. 'Well, you know, I've never actually thought of it as a paradox. More as a puzzle. The funeral paradox – now that's a paradox!'

'I've not heard of that one,' said Natasha.

'Oh, it's simple enough,' said Sean. 'The older you live, the fewer people you have at your funeral.'

She raised her eyebrows.

'And it works the other way too,' he said nonchalantly. 'The younger you die, the more turn up at the wake.' He took a larger mouthful of wine. 'But enough of that. To Fermi's so-called paradox. It's a reality that was supposedly first articulated by the physicist Enrico Fermi over a hundred years ago. Basically, it asks us to face a harsh reality in this business of finding intelligent life out there in the vast universe – nobody's talking to us! I mean, we have a lot of space and time out there, so where is everybody?'

He drew his chair closer to the metal table and turned his collar against the chilly breeze. 'Let me put it a little more clearly. If there are millions or even billions of planets that could potentially support life, and there do seem to be... and if they've been around for billions of years, which we believe many have been... then why haven't at least some of them evolved civilisations that can cross those vast distances as easily as we just flew from Dublin? Why aren't they calling in to see us? Or at least sending us a message? With all the billions of years available, you'd think some of the messages would have crossed a few light years of space by now.'

Natasha had grown up with this conundrum, yet she never tired of letting its force hit her afresh. 'It certainly is a mystery,' she said.

'Right,' said Ariel. 'So, just checking. We are sure, are we, that there really are so many planets like this one?'

'Sure, sure, sure,' Sean echoed. 'Now what a lovely thing that is – certainty. Doesn't it just warm your heart to be sure of something?' He smiled, and winked at Natasha. Slowly she was beginning to get the measure of the man's use of irony. It was not a small measure.

The day's catch arrived on platters, and they tucked in. Between mouthfuls Sean continued to air the various theories on extra-terrestrial intelligence. 'Of course,' he said, 'there is a school of thought that, even though other races may not survive long enough to figure out how to cross the vast distances of space, their robots may do better.'

'Robots?' said Ariel.

Sean nodded. 'That's right. Artificial intelligence may be more robust. It could last a lot longer.' He tapped Ariel on the hand, testing it. 'Seems like flesh and blood!'

Half an hour later, with Fermi's paradox and Drake's equation thoroughly explored, and a second carafe standing empty, Sean declined the waiter's offer of a third on the grounds that he could live with being found drunk in charge of an equation, but not in charge of a boat, so they began to make their way to a nearby quay where a small craft was moored. When Natasha saw the name on the side she didn't wait for confirmation before jumping on board. It was Voyager.

Sean cast off and they made their way downstream, the river ever widening as they went. Natasha left Ariel in the stern happily looking out at the birds and the bushes floating past, and joined Sean at the helm. Tugging the wind-strewn hair from her eyes, she asked him the question that had been surfacing in her mind since lunch. 'So, Professor, how have you lived with the paradox – the puzzle – for so long?'

'Oh now, that's not so hard,' he said. 'There's no paradox at all if there really is no one out there.'

'No,' she said, 'but what are the chances that we really are alone in the universe?'

He noticed her look quickly back over her shoulder at Ariel, and his heart raced. He had been asked that question many times over his long career, but never had it been so personal.

4

'Hello. This is Coppelia Swanson. Please leave a message. You never know, I may get back to you.'

Alice didn't want to leave a message, but talking to her best friend was now her number one priority. 'Hi Cop. Do you think you could call me as soon as you hear this? Or when you've got a moment.'

David was out when she had returned to the hotel room. She needed to think, and talking to Cop was often the best way of doing that. Mercifully, Cop called back within five minutes.

'Alice? What's up? You don't sound right.'

Alice placed her eband on the table in front of her and switched to video. As soon as she saw her friend's troubled face, a torrent of words and sighs came gushing out – Mel's visit and the perfume, the kidnap, Ariel's assurances about Mel, and even David's sense of the oppression that had overcome Ariel in the horror-filled basement. Cop listened to the end, and Alice was glad just to feed off her friend's compassion as she garbled and groaned her way through the previous four days.

Finally she came to a halt. 'I'm sorry to land this on you, Cop, and I expect I've told you things that you shouldn't know. But I just had to talk to you about it.'

'Of course you did, silly,' said her friend, mustering her best unshocked look. 'So, er, where's David now?'

'Not sure. I went out for some air, and I suspect he's done the same.'

'And Melody is gone, you say?'

'Yes. Don't worry, it's not really that bad.'

'No. Good. Do you want to come home though?'

Alice pressed her hands to her face and slowly drew them down. 'I don't know. I guess we'll both be coming home soon. Oh, Cop, I hope we're going to get through this!'

'Of course you are, sweetie. You and David have an incredible relationship.'

'Do we?'

'You do. You both enjoy an intimacy and honesty that's rare. And that's why you're hurting right now.'

'I suppose you're right,' said Alice, though there was little belief in her voice. 'Thanks, Cop. I really needed this.'

'Sure thing,' said her friend. 'I'm glad you called, and you know I'll be praying for you.' She leaned nearer to the camera. 'But before you go, help me to pray for this Ariel chap too. What do you make of him? And that business with the oppression? Doesn't sound good to me.'

'No, it's not. But I don't know what to make of it all really. Only... I sense it's really important that we help him, even if we never find out who he is.' She sighed. 'Which makes this whole business with Mel so incredibly annoying, apart from anything else!'

'Well,' said Cop, 'it seems to me you've got three options on the space man. He's most likely some guy mixed up in something he's suppressed – hence the amnesia – and no one's admitting they sent him to Venus. Or he's a bona fide alien. Or...'

'Yes?'

'Or might he be an angel?'

'What, you mean literally? I don't know. Can an angel lose his memory?'

'No, I suppose not,' said Cop. 'It's just... the way you talk about him... the effect he has on people. I don't know.'

'Well,' said Alice, 'that much is true. We really don't know.'

They ended the call. Listlessly Alice put her eband back on and stared at the wall. After a while she noticed a small collection of generic paintings, insipid portrayals of misty scenes – a mountain, a city street and a lakeside jetty. Her eyes came to rest on the last one, a short pier leading out into the water. There was no boat there, so it was in effect a pathway to the deep, a way through the mist to forgetfulness. And to peace? No, she knew better than that. Peace came not from giving in to fear or exhaustion, but from pushing through to resolution. She would not let this pain defeat her. Hers was the way of truth, whatever the cost. That was the Master's way, and so it must be hers too.

She turned away from the wall, picked up the tea tray and made for the kitchen.

5

Sean unlocked his front door and led his guests inside. 'Well,' he said, 'I'm thinking you must be very tired. Natasha, your room is upstairs, first on the right. Ariel, you're opposite. Let's meet back down here in about an hour, in the kitchen where all the best conversations are to be had!'

Natasha looked around. The main downstairs room was large, open plan, with wide see-through stairs going up to a mezzanine. On the walls were photographs and paintings. She recognised one or two of the scientists, and asked if the watercolours were of local places. 'Oh absolutely,' he said. 'There's nowhere more peaceful under heaven than round here at Cork Harbour and the mouth of the Lee.'

'It is a lovely place for retirement,' Natasha observed.

'Retirement? Well now, let's see... to retire, to withdraw. Yes, I suppose I've done a bit of that. But Natasha, there's so much still to do!'

She smiled. She felt invigorated by the sheer focus and willpower of the man. She tried to remember if he'd ever been married, but she couldn't and didn't like to ask. There were no family photographs in sight.

She got Ariel installed and then crossed to her room where she flopped onto the bed. The travel and the wine soon had her asleep.

It was nearly two hours later when she woke. Splashing water on her face from a sink in the corner, and effecting the quickest change of clothes since she'd been on Venus, from jacket and cargo trousers to polo neck and jeans, she flew out the door. But she needed the bathroom, so she turned back from the top of the stairs and looked around. There was one more bedroom between her room and the bathroom. Hearing Sean's loudness and laughter coming up the stairs, punctuated by Ariel's quieter voice, she poked her head inside. It had to be Sean's room. There was a depiction of the Milky Way on the ceiling, and a poster of a typecast green alien on the wall. By the bed was a fairly large constellation globe, and under that a photograph in an old-fashioned frame. A much younger Sean with dark hair was smiling out, his arm round a woman holding the hand of a young child. A daughter?

Curiosity gave way to embarrassment at the prying, and she withdrew to the bathroom. Minutes later she strolled down the stairs to face the inevitable hearty greeting.

'Well, look who it is now! If it isn't Sleeping Beauty herself. Why don't you come and join us?' Sean was standing next to the dining table, where a magnificent orrery was set in pride of place at the centre. 'I can't believe it,' he continued. 'Ariel here tells me no one has bothered to check out his knowledge of the planets. Although he tells me you are the one responsible for his current name. Sadly this gizmo doesn't stretch to the moons of Uranus... but well done, girl! It's a good name. The lion of God.'

'Or altar, I believe,' she said.

'Ha! Even better. Did you know that it's also the name of an old exoplanet analyser? So it couldn't be more appropriate.' He placed a jug of water on the table. 'And of course Uranus is Greek for the heavens, which is where you found him.'

'Are you a believer?' asked Natasha, as she sat at the table and helped herself to some of the savoury bites that had already been laid out in small, hand-painted bowls.

'My, your friend is good at asking questions now, isn't she, Ariel? Well, let me tell you, lass... when I'm asked that question, it's nearly always in the context of intelligent alien life. But I'm guessing you're not asking me that just at the moment.'

'No, sorry, I didn't mean to pry.'

'Not a bit of it! I don't mind telling you that I'm a better Catholic today than I was when I was working full time. We have a priest here locally who's actually got a brain – can't think when they started to fit those – and, well, it all seems to make a lot more sense than it used to.' He grinned. 'Nothing to do with my age, of course.' He poured a small amount of red wine into three large glasses. 'So, Nastassia – are you Orthodox?'

She smiled, suddenly overcome with joy that the question had not made her angry. Nor had the use of her Russian name.

'How did you know?' She tasted the wine. Predictably perfect.

'What, that you're not a Natalia but an Anastasia? Well, girl, I'm hardly going to be inviting a cosmonaut of your pedigree into my home and not do a little research first, now, am I?' His eyes were positively alight.

'I'm flattered, I think.'

'Ah, you shouldn't be. And while we're on the meaning of names, that makes you an Easter girl rather than a Christmas one. Am I right?'

'I suppose so,' she said.

'This is intriguing,' said Ariel.

She had actually forgotten for a moment that Ariel was there. That was a first. 'Sorry,' she explained. 'You see, Natasha (she spelt it out) is an informal version of Natalia, which means you're born at the time of the Nativity – you know, Christmas. Whereas Nastassia is a shortened form of Anastasia.'

'Resurrection,' said Ariel.

'Ah, good,' said Sean, 'I can see we're going to be firing on all cylinders tonight. Right. Let me get this pasta bake out of the oven. Natasha, there's a salad on the kitchen counter that needs a few finishing touches. And Ariel, while we're doing that, why don't you tell me what on earth you've made of all this hullabaloo?'

Sean's good humour and quick wit were irresistibly infectious, and soon he and Natasha were trading views on the origins of the universe. The fire was alight and they'd made it to the dessert wine when Sean asked Ariel what he thought about the soul of man. 'Or do I have to say, human spirituality? Though that doesn't have quite the same ring, now, does it?'

Ariel looked at the fire, seemingly fascinated by the flames darting up like tongues around the logs. 'Let me start by saying that I don't think I've ever drunk this much wine before. Of course, I may never have had any before, so I suppose there's no comparison there.'

'Exactly,' said Sean. 'Comparison isn't easy when you've only got one of something. A bit like the universe really.'

Natasha was beginning to wonder whether Ariel had met his match in this towering intellect deviously disguised as a harmless, funny old man. But her fears were soon allayed.

'Precisely,' Ariel was saying. 'There is surely only one cosmos.'

'Is that cosmos as in the Greek, meaning the world?' said Sean. 'Or cosmos in the modern cosmologist's sense – the universe?'

'That's a fair question,' said Ariel. 'I have learnt from our friends in the retreat centre that in times gone by the earth was all there was to know for mere mortals. The heavens were up there, out of reach, certainly in this life.'

'Right,' said Natasha. 'The earth was all we could inhabit, and the heavens, or heaven, was a world of perfect ideals, untouched by the shifts and changes of physical reality as it is lived on earth.'

'So what now?' said Sean. 'Has heaven moved up a notch? Now that the universe is part of our study – part of our back yard, thanks to people like you, Natasha – has heaven had to move back a bit, beyond the curtain so to speak?'

'Until we pull that curtain back, perhaps?' said Ariel as he traced the firelight shining through his wine.

'What, you mean on God's very own dwelling place?' said Sean.

Ariel continued to stare through his glass. 'You asked me earlier about the human soul, or perhaps the spirit of the human race,' he said. 'I understand some have taught that humanity will one day draw back that curtain, and while for many today that has come to mean mapping and understanding the entire universe, in bygone eras it meant piercing the very heavens.'

'The kingdom of God,' said Sean in an uncharacteristically quiet voice. 'Of course, in the Bible, that's not so much something we're aiming for as something that's heading towards us.'

Natasha and Ariel both looked at Sean in surprise. He didn't respond but continued in the same vein.

'That's the thing about so much religious talk,' he said, 'and scientists are no better. We make man the measure of all things. It's all about us. One darn great universe and still we act as though we're all that's in it... as if we really understood more than a trillionth of what there is to know. Understanding cosmic evolution, even the biological variety... ach, we're still just children in the play room.' He drained his glass. 'As I often tell my students, the more we know, the more we know we don't know.'

They sat quietly for a while, listening to the hiss of the logs and the flutter of the flames.

'I don't want to be over-defensive,' said Natasha at last, 'but in a sense it couldn't be any other way. I mean, as a species with both curiosity and spirituality, we are going to be at the centre in one way or another.'

'Isn't God meant to be at the centre?' said Sean.

Natasha tried to recall some of the conversations she and Ariel had had in the monastery, but the wine and the fire pulled a veil over it. She wanted to hear what Ariel had to say. And she knew Sean did too. 'Ariel,' she said, 'what do you think? Is humanity the measure of all things? Or are we back to hunting the Little Green Men like the one in the poster on the wall?'

As soon as the words were out, it was as though they turned round and slapped her in the face. She had just told Sean she had been in his bedroom. Her cheeks burned. She didn't dare look up.

He made no comment.

'Well,' said Ariel, 'if we're thinking about aliens, you do have to ask why they haven't visited. As Sean was saying earlier.' He burped.

'Well now,' said Sean, volume rising once more, 'there are of course accounts in human history of strange encounters. Perhaps nothing like yours on Venus, but yes, visits to this planet. Tall figures coming in flying machines. Miracles that read now as advanced technology.'

'But surely that kind of view was hit on the head by serious archaeology back in the last century,' said Natasha.

'Yes, yes,' said Sean. 'But you and I are good church-going folk, Natasha. I'm guessing we've both been taught the Bible, even if we haven't read it all. Don't you recognise any alien activity there?'

'What?' she stammered. 'You mean... Jesus?'

'Well, no, I wasn't going there actually,' he said. 'But right back at the beginning you've got flaming creatures keeping human beings out of Eden, whatever that was. We'll forget the serpent for a minute. But what about the giants, the nephilim, as well as the cherubim and the seraphim? Or just plain old mystery men standing in the road, brandishing a sword, or slaying whole armies, or talking to shepherds on a hillside?'

'You mean angels?' said Natasha.

'Aye, I mean angels! Whatever you may think about them, real or imaginary, or a case of mistaken identity, they're not usually described as your regular human being. Well, not always. Apart from when they're looking all nice and innocent, like Ariel here.'

Once more they sat in silence for a while, which Natasha found surprisingly easy in the surroundings Sean had cultivated. She thought there was a clock ticking somewhere, but then realised it was the fire grate contracting as it cooled.

'So, let me get this right,' she said at last. 'You're saying these beings in the Bible are aliens?'

'Aliens! Angels! Who's to say? Either way, they're recorded as visitors to this planet. This world is not their home. But I'm prepared to entertain angels as a possibility.' He winked at Natasha, but her level of biblical literacy did not extend to spotting the reference to entertaining angels unawares.

'But, but...' She was fighting to clear her head. 'But angels come from God. They're often God's spokesmen.'

'So?' said Sean. 'As I say, who's to say?'

A priority message came through on his tablet.

'Oh,' said Natasha, 'you're not wearing an eband. Don't tell me – you don't own one!'

'Ah, I don't trust anything that doesn't really delete,' Sean said.

He read the message. As soon as he had finished he went straight to the table and started clearing up. 'Best get some sleep, my friends,' he said. 'That was Constance Bridlington, no less. It seems we'll have to continue our discussion another time. We've been called to some little village I've never heard of in Switzerland.'

6

Alice was asleep, but David turned this way and that, until his gaze came to rest on a picture on the wall. He hadn't noticed it before. Dimly lit by the light of the alarm clock and some other kind of alarm on the ceiling, it slowly revealed itself to be a jetty leading into water. He shivered.

Five minutes later he got up. Alice barely stirred. Dressing quickly and throwing on a coat that hung by the door, he left the room, following some kind of lead which he barely recognised but which in his half-sleep seemed irresistible. He trotted down the stairs to the lobby and out into the night. If the night clerk behind the desk saw him go, he showed no sign.

The street was quiet. He crossed over and slipped into the park that led to the lake. The Moon was bright and seemed to beckon him on towards the water. As he came out from under the trees he followed a path towards a small quayside where a few boats were moored. Nothing stirred.

What was he doing here? He turned to walk along the water's edge but decided against it when he thought he could make out a lone figure sitting on a bench a little way away. Approaching the small quay he walked round and sat down on the wall, his legs dangling on the lakeside. For a few minutes, perhaps longer, he watched the moonlight shimmer and shift on the water.

He was fully awake now, or thought he was. Yet it was a strange wakefulness, for he was soon losing himself in the sparkling moonlight. And then a dam seemed to burst, as he felt a great and terrible wave of love wash over him. Inside a fountain of feelings welled up in response. Awe, pain, terror and the weight of glory. He groaned, his thoughts too deep for words.

At once he was besieged by a desire that wouldn't let go. No, that wasn't right – he wouldn't let it go. How long had he longed for Melody? When had it begun? Why was the desire so strong? What to do?

There was only one thing he could do. There had always been three in his marriage, and the third person was Jesus. There could be no other. He must yield to the wave of love, holy and terrible, that even now cascaded over him, body and soul. 'No, no, no,' it said in time with the water lapping gently but insistently at his feet. This was a baptism like no other he had known. A positive baptism of no. No to each yes to which he had so often succumbed.

His perspective began to change. Every exhilarating desire he had experienced for Melody began to show its dark side, one after the other, like hidden thorns on a sweet-scented rose. As a black hole was supposed by some to flip itself into a white one, spewing forth its trapped energy on the other side of space-time, so now the thoughts and feelings he had told himself were innocent revealed the danger and pain they had inflicted for so long.

He could not move. Didn't want to. Time seemed to flow back and forth, past and present, fluttering on the soft breeze over the water and the moonlight.

A change in the wind brought him back, and the sound of footsteps. The figure on the bench had gone. Were those tears on his face, or beads of sweat? He stood up and slowly made his way back to the hotel and up to the room. Within minutes he was ready for bed again as, strangely warm despite the chill night air, he lay next to the gently sleeping form of the love of his life.

7

From the top of Bruges' landmark Belfry Tower the houses and shops of the old city looked like toy models laid out in a playroom. Miranda looked down on the warm colours and shivered in the chilly sunlight. She just wasn't right, and that bothered Hugh. 'What are you thinking?' he asked.

'That we don't do this often enough,' she said. 'You know, take in the sights.'

'I suppose not,' he replied. He turned away from the city far below and pulled gently on her arm. 'Miranda, my dear, I have a mission for you.'

She squinted in the sunlight. 'What?'

'I want you to take a break.'

'Hugh, I've told you, I'll be right as rain before you know it.'

He ignored her. 'And I want you to get to the bottom of the mystery of our times.' She cocked her head to one side and frowned. Her heart rate increased. 'Not single-handedly, you understand. But I can think of no one better placed to represent my interests. No, my interest.'

'Go on.' She had stopped shivering, and even now a warmth was running through her body not unlike the glow of the brandy Hugh kept on the plane for post-deal celebrations.

'Petroc informs me that there is to be a gathering, bigger than before. And they're having it in your favourite place.'

'They're hardly going to invite me.'

'Maybe not. But it is, after all, a public facility,' said Hugh, turning his collar against the swelling breeze.

'You know they'll take the place over,' she insisted. 'Close it to visitors.'

'Maybe, though Leonardo has to keep his customers satisfied. Anyway,' he smiled, 'he has a soft spot for you.'

'You've spoken to him?'

'Of course. He remains friendly, even though he knows my real name now. He was very amenable to the idea in fact. My guess is, he'll face any consequences with our Ms Bridlington afterwards.'

She turned back to look at the city below. 'But Hugh, in all honesty, what can *I* do?'

'I'm sure I don't know. But you'll find your feet when you're there, of that I have no doubt. There's still too much in the dark, Miranda. Why was Forrester on that mission? What did they really expect when they got there? Did Koroleva know something might happen? And anyway...'

'Yes?'

'From what you've told me, and from what you haven't, I'd say you're more likely than most to get Ariel to come clean.'

'What do you mean, come clean? The guy has amnesia!'

'Yes, of course. What I'm saying is, I'm sure if anyone can help him, you can. Now, off you go. You can send me a postcard.'

And with that he took a plane ticket from his inside coat pocket, placed it in her hand, turned on his heels and headed for the staircase back to solid ground.

8

Petroc knocked and opened the office door he had been through a thousand times. 'Mr and Mrs Carter, Ma'am.'

David and Alice entered to find Constance waiting by the window at the end of a table. She was wearing a light floral house jacket, and with her was an Indian woman in a loose bronze-coloured satin trouser suit. 'David, Alice,' said Constance, 'I'd like you to meet Selena Chandra. Selena is involved in this whole business. She's an expert in textiles, and works for Box Industries which developed what our astronauts now wear.'

Greetings exchanged, they sat down together.

'Now then,' said Constance, 'I want to extend an invitation to you both. I would love it if you would accompany Selena here to Montagnola.'

'You mean the retreat centre?' said Alice in surprise.

'The very same. I know you've heard about it, and I rather think you deserve an all-expenses-paid stay there.'

David looked nonplussed. 'That is a very generous offer,' he said. 'But why?'

'No such thing as a free lunch, eh?' said Constance. 'Well, no, you'd be right. Though I do actually think the place would do you good. I've personally found it most restorative.'

David half-wondered whether she had picked up something about what he and Alice were going through, until he surmised she was thinking of his ordeal in Cologne.

'But I also think that you have something to bring to the table,' she continued. 'Time is running out. We are soon going to have to let the crew go back to their own countries and face the media. As it is, Washington and Moscow are eager to have their darlings out on the celebration trail.'

She walked back to the window and turned towards them.

'Now obviously you, David, have been through an intense time with Ariel. I feel we owe it to you to get some well-earned therapeutic rest. The UN has recently tripled the budget on the current investigation, bringing in the best minds and so forth, so it's honestly not a problem. And the least we can do is include your dear wife.' She smiled at Alice who returned the gesture.

'So... what is it that you think we can "bring to the table"?' said David.

'I was coming to that,' said Constance. 'It seems clear to me at least that we need a range of perspectives brought to bear on this whole business. And while you can be sure that all manner of intelligence agencies and investigation bureaus are on the case, trying to find who sent Ariel to Venus and why, I feel increasingly that we need to cast the net wider.'

'In what way?' said David, his engagement clearly growing.

'By considering the logical – and not wholly unlikely – alternative,' said Constance.

'Which is?' said Alice.

'That Ariel is not from this world.'

David looked across the table to Selena, whose dark eyes sparkled in the light from the window. She gave no sign of an opinion.

'Now, I realise that you are not here in a professional capacity, and I do have someone from SETI coming who will cover that. Mind you, I'm even open to prayer as a solution!' She attempted a laugh, but they could see she was more than half serious. Evidently that was no longer a ridiculous notion either. 'But you have become an important part of Ariel's experience, so... well, there it is. What do you say?'

David looked to Alice for confirmation, which came in the slightest nod. 'We'd be honoured.'

9

The journey from Cork to Montagnola was conventional in both its method and its duration. After an early start and two airport changes, by the time they arrived at the small terminal in Agno Sean and Natasha were feeling quite hungry and even more tired. Ariel was quiet, and the day itself looked weary as night drew in. Jack met them and drove them to the monastery. They came in by the front gate.

Unpacking was the usual brief affair, and within minutes they made their way downstairs in search of something to eat. As Natasha emerged onto the cloister she was surprised to hear a buzz of conversation emanating from the refectory. Its source turned out to be an even greater surprise. At one table sat David, Alice and Selena. At another Jack, Melody and a woman she didn't recognise. And in the corner Leonardo sat talking to a young woman with dark, auburn hair. It took Natasha several seconds to recognise Miranda sitting there with the Abbot. 'Excuse me, guys,' she said to Sean and Ariel, 'I'll join you in a minute.'

She crossed the room. Instantly Leonardo was on his feet, gushing a welcome. 'I don't understand,' she said. 'What are we doing here?'

'Ah, did Constance not tell you?'

'Not really,' said Natasha. 'I'd only just got Ariel away, and all of a sudden we're back here again. Which is very nice, but confusing.'

Miranda sensed the need to explain herself. 'I'm not really here,' she said. 'That is, not officially.'

Natasha shook her head and smiled. 'Miranda, I don't think any of this is official, do you?'

10

It was cold in the stationary car as Nathan listened to the latest recording from the device he had planted in Beth's office, yet within minutes he felt a warm glow, and the semblance of a smile began to iron out the frown that had been creasing his brow. It seemed there was going to be another get-together, only this time in the retreat centre in Montagnola. After that? Since they couldn't hold Ariel any longer they planned to pass him on to a social-services department in an English-speaking country. No one really knew when his memory might return.

Surely now was the time to make his next move.

But how to communicate with his unknown contact? As he sat in the darkness of the car park outside Takeshi's laboratory, he could think of only one way he might be able to do that. And that meant getting the crystal back.

Ryan Chase had left an hour ago, along with the few other scientists and technicians working there. Wrapping a short scarf around his neck, Nathan got out of the car, walked across to the door and entered the code. Within a few minutes he was in the lab. Relieved that Selena had convinced Ryan not to keep taking the crystal back to his hotel, he unlocked its transparent container and took it out.

It felt good just to hold it again.

'Well now,' he said out loud, 'I don't have the instruction manual, so it's time to experiment!' Convinced that it was a high-tech communications device, he could think of no better strategy for getting in touch. He would sit down with it, touch all the sides as before and wait to see what happened. Perhaps he would hear something. He knew it was impervious to electronic jamming, and he guessed it had a good range on it.

Suddenly he hesitated and shook his head. What did he really know about it? Next to nothing. Then again, so far his secret mentor had been proved right. Those promised rewards of knowledge and power must by now be just around the corner. And surely they were going to be pleased when he took the initiative and warned them to intercept Ariel before he was lost to them both.

Taking a lab stool, he called for lamp light only, turning off the main lights. The crystal looked different in the gloom. Charged by his secret knowledge, he took it in both hands as he had done before and placed his thumbs and fingers on ten of the twelve pentagonal faces. He decided to keep them there longer this time, before releasing them and putting it down. As the crystal began to glow he peered at it, and very soon it was the only thing in his vision. In his mind. Lines began to trace their way throughout the crystal as they had done before, and eventually white patches formed at the centre of each face. Last time he had pressed just one of those to be linked with Ariel. He still had no idea how he might link with his secret mentor, but he had to try something. Anything. Maybe he should touch two of the crystal's faces, both at the same time.

But it was so beautiful. Why touch it and risk damaging it? Leave it be. And it must surely be dangerous. Who knew what might happen if he strayed from his instructions?

He struggled for a while, until timidity finally gave way to curiosity. He positioned it in the palm of his right hand and placed his left thumb and index finger simultaneously on opposite sides. Instantly there was a loud crack and a jolt up both his arms. He fought to stay on the stool.

He managed to hold it tight between his finger and thumb. Or was it holding him? Images flashed across his mind. There was a strangely shaped room with boxes and screens... a building like a temple on a mountainside... and now a silhouetted figure on a steep slope. He forced his finger and thumb off the thing. After a moment a clear picture of the strange room appeared in one face of the crystal, while the silhouetted figure could be seen in the opposite side. Then came a voice, seemingly in his head. At least, he thought it had to be speech he could hear and not just growling, though he couldn't identify the language. He thought back to some of the dialects he had heard in his surveillance and analysis days. There had been nothing like this.

His body began to shake. Must be the shock. Had he short-circuited the thing? But that voice, it didn't sound happy. In fact, it was angry. One might almost say malevolent.

This was getting him nowhere. He reapplied his fingers and tried to move them around the many faces, hoping to turn it off as he had done before, but they seemed almost stuck to the thing till finally they wouldn't move. Pain returned to his hands and arms. He couldn't let go. His scarf felt tighter about his neck.

He decided to concentrate on the voice. Was it sneering? Maybe, but threatening too. He felt exposed. Much more of this and he would feel violated. A sense of helplessness came over him like a deluge.

He swayed on the edge of consciousness, feeling the stool start to slip from beneath him. Just before he fell he thought he heard a different voice, one that rang clear. This time it was not a lot of words, one on top of the other, but a simple phrase, though once again he couldn't identify it.

He descended into darkness and silence.

When he got up off the floor he could see from his eband that an hour had passed. The crystal had rolled into a corner. He approached it warily, but it seemed to be inert once more, so he forced himself to pick it up. There were no lights or lines, no sounds or images, no stings or shocks. And no voices.

He locked it back up in its box, turned out the lights and left the building with a brooding sense that he was in more danger now than he had ever been in his life.

Chapter 26

Temptation

1

The Atlantic tide was gently washing the whitened sands of Cape Canaveral as Jim Adamson chewed on a long, wiry strand of grass and looked out to sea. With the autumn mist still heavy in the air it was impossible to see where the sky ended and the ocean began.

He had just come from the Space Command Base on Merritt Island, where he had undergone a follow-up medical examination, and was now standing just a few steps from his own backyard. His holiday home had become his own private retreat centre, a fine base for sketching. And brooding. Jackie was back in Wyoming, keeping in touch with the girls who had both made college the same year. He knew his place as husband and father was with her in the empty nest, and he would be there soon enough. But not yet.

Just minutes ago he had taken his unshown and unkind caricature of Natasha and burned it in his garden incinerator. He watched closely as the long face with angular cheekbones and stretched nose curled in the flames, relieved to see his travesty turn to ash. He knew he had got the eyes wrong. Strong brow line yes, even a haughty look, but sinister? To see them blacken and disappear now seemed to clear his own vision.

How long had he been in the wilderness, that place of testing and trial? Forty days? Forty years?

Ever since he had blacked out on the Venusian surface he had felt like he'd been sitting on a bomb. Repeated medicals had given no clue as to why. Physically he was as fit as ever, and mentally there was nothing a rest wouldn't sort out. Given the delay with the celebratory tour, he was advised to make the most of the hiatus.

But the bomb was still ticking. It may not have shown up in a scan, but he knew it was there. How he had struggled to defuse it! First it had been little more than disgruntlement when Jack had been put in charge of the Stranger. This had been given time to grow into a smouldering resentment during the long ride home. Understandable enough. But once they had returned to Earth and more and more fuss was made over the mystery man, it had become so bad that there was only one thing for it: to put a distance between himself and Jack. It was as if he had become hazardous material in need of isolation.

Then came the review in Geneva, and those recordings. The bomb had gone off and he had survived. He had swallowed his pride, and for the first time he could see that there was a real enemy, however invisible to the ordinary equipment of human vision. Call it spiritual, call it psychological – either way, relief had come. For a while.

Yet here before the ocean mist it seemed the struggle was not yet over. The urge to get to Ariel, even to foil those who were protecting him, was not put down. And surely his grievances were just. Why wasn't he there, wherever they were right now, forcing Ariel to remember and so solve the mystery of his appearance on the Endeavour? He should be there, finding out once and for all whether the Stranger was friend or foe.

Of course he knew the reason why he had been excluded. Almost from the start he had shown himself to be no friend to Ariel. And, as he had been sketching the crew from memory these last few days, he had slowly admitted to himself that he had allowed that enmity to infect his friendship with Jack. How long had he secretly envied the man? He still couldn't say for sure, but with every stroke of his pen his thoughts had been coaxed back to the storm on Venus, and those voices, and his fall when he lost the will to stand.

But stand now he must. It was time to come out of the wilderness.

2

Sean woke early and went outside. He missed the sea. The sky was dark and heavy with cloud, with a fine drizzle just getting going, so he stayed inside the cloister round the main courtyard. He saw the shrines and soon concluded he didn't have the right kind of mind to make any sense of them.

Natasha's voice startled him. 'Another early riser?' she said, coming in from somewhere outside the building. He saw the cream-coloured tracksuit and guessed she'd been out for a run, though she was neither panting for breath nor sweating.

He saw no need of small talk and fired off the questions that were knocking on the door of his mind. 'What are we doing here, resurrection girl? And what is this place? No, you know what, I don't even want to know. But what's the game plan? Any ideas?'

She returned fire. 'Well, alien boy, I think we're here to finish what we started before people got abducted and assaulted and killed. We're here to find out who Ariel is – who sent him, what he is a part of.'

'And I'm here because somebody has the crazy idea he may be an alien?'

'You think it's crazy?'

'Don't you? Come on, girl, use your wits. The guy's plainly human.'

'But... what you said in Ireland... about visitors in past times? Was that just theory?'

He sighed. 'All right, let's unpack it a bit.' He shivered. 'Is there somewhere we can talk in the warm?'

They made their way into the refectory, where they found Leroy powering up the kitchen before the day began. His face lit up when he saw Natasha, and she didn't have to ask twice before hot coffee was on its way. The aroma seemed to settle the Irishman.

'Right,' he said, as they sat in a corner with their hands wrapped around steaming mugs. 'I've spent my life working with cumulative evidence.'

She nodded.

'We look at stars, we detect planets around them, we analyse their atmospheres and chemical make-up – you know the sort of thing. And in my particular line of work we pay special attention to radio signals – actually signals across the entire electro-magnetic spectrum. Signals that have any kind of pattern that might be seen as logical, deliberate, intelligent. We've had a few false alarms there in recent decades, as you know. But gradually, tentatively, we build up a picture. It's a picture of where stable and, God willing, intelligent life could develop. Right?'

'Sure.'

'Now, I've done my damnedest, as you know, to get SETI taken seriously by politicians as well as scientists, and today the grid of radio telescopes around the globe, in countries that are prepared to talk to aliens even if they won't talk to each other, gives us better eyes and ears than ever before. At the same time I've dared to look into the cooky stuff – you know, UFOs, close encounters, messages from space. And, yes, accounts from the past, whether that's cave drawings or documentary evidence.'

'Like the Bible.'

'Just so,' he said, 'and Hesiod and Homer and Cicero, and that's just the Western guys. And yes, yesterday I was allowing for the possibility – possibility, mind – that appearances by angels did not preclude alien encounter. In fact, you could say that's how the texts are meant to be read. Angels are a different race after all. They're not human.'

'So then,' said Natasha, 'why can't Ariel be such a being? After all, in the accounts angels are often taken – or mistaken – for human beings. So these aliens are clearly humanoid, wherever they're from.'

She paused, and the quiet was interrupted by the smash of crockery on stone floor. 'Don't worry,' she said. 'It's probably Leroy. He's not regular kitchen staff.'

'Okay,' said Sean, draining his mug, 'let's say Ariel is one such. The questions don't go away. How did he get here? Where are his friends?'

'Well,' said Natasha, 'we can answer your first question. He got here by hitching a ride on the Endeavour.'

'Very funny, but that won't do now, will it?' said Sean. 'You picked him up from one of the unfriendliest environments in the solar system! If he's alien, he's hardly a local boy. How did he survive the environment? And – what? – did he just walk through the walls to get on board your ship, walls so tough they could survive seventy-two hours of Venusian squashing and pounding? And yes, I'll grant that the conditions were less severe than normal, but we all know they were still lethal.'

They sat and sipped in silence for a while.

'Tell me about the trip home,' he said suddenly. 'Were there signs that he wasn't human? Did he eat? Go to the toilet? Listen to the news?' His eyes were sparkling.

'All reasonable questions,' she happily conceded. 'And I'm surprised more people haven't asked about our journey home. In fact he was out of it for almost the whole time, plugged into a medbed. But when we arrived on board the Resolution we fed him a mix of glucose and protein—'

'Ah,' said Sean, 'astronaut juice, the most delicious food known to humanity. Funny, I thought the cuisine had improved in space.'

'Oh it has,' said Natasha, 'but we keep some of the old stuff. For emergencies.'

'And what about what comes afterwards?'

'Yes,' said Natasha, catching his meaning, 'Jack did take him to the toilet.'

'How did that work?' said Sean, not quite believing what he was asking.

She smiled. 'The toilets are strictly one person at a time. They're sealed units. As for how they work, well, when you don't have gravity it's all down to momentum and the movement of air from a carefully placed fan. Everything is sucked away into the recycling system.'

He chuckled, delighted at the ease with which Natasha answered the question, even though it wasn't quite the answer he was looking for. He still wondered if anyone had yet witnessed Ariel going to the toilet... going in the second sense, and not just making the journey to the little room.

'There was one other thing,' she said. 'We noticed that his muscle tone was very good.'

Sean nodded. 'No evidence of a long stay in zero-G, you mean? That is curious,' he said, 'though hardly conclusive.'

She finished her coffee. 'I don't have conclusive answers,' she said as she got to her feet. 'But I do know that Ariel has remarkable... abilities, including the ability to resist physical harm.'

Sean moved his head from side to side, stretching his neck muscles. 'Does he now? Well, that is a little more interesting. And I guess it's enough to justify me being here – enjoying your highly agreeable company.'

She smiled at the flattery. 'I'll see you back here in an hour,' she said. 'You won't want to miss the breakfast.'

3

Two hours later Sean and Natasha had disappeared to the rear building, along with Ariel, Jack, Leonardo and David who was still curiously disappointed that he wasn't in a real monastery, though its apparent paganism opened up some exciting evangelistic possibilities. Miranda had taken off for the woods, while Alice had not yet appeared. That left Selena, Melody and Hannah alone in the refectory.

'Well, if you don't mind, I'd like to leave you two ladies together,' said Hannah. 'There is some work I really must catch up on.'

'I thought I was your work,' said Melody. 'Just kidding. We'll be fine.'

Hannah hesitated. 'You know where I am. Just call in if you need me.' And with that she stepped out into the cloister and turned back up the stairs.

'Now,' said Melody, relishing the opportunity to have a normal conversation, 'can I say how glad I am to meet you, Selena? Your work sounds fascinating.' She poured them some water. 'Selena... that's a beautiful name.'

'My father chose it. You see, while my mother was in the hospital giving birth to me, he was viewing a piece of moon rock at an exhibition. Apparently he had no other opportunity.'

'Ah,' said Melody, fighting hard not to react to the melancholic tone in Selena's reply. 'So you're a moon girl.'

'I'm not surprised you know my name is based on an ancient word for the moon,' said Selena, 'what with you being in astronomical journalism.'

'Space journalism, strictly speaking, and any kind of exploration really,' she said. 'My concern is who goes where, not the latest theories in cosmology! Selena is based on the ancient Greek word, isn't it?'

'Yes, and Chandra means the same, only in Sanskrit.'

'Wow,' said Melody, 'double moon girl.'

Selena gave half a smile. 'So are you interviewing me now?' she asked cautiously.

'If you like,' said Melody. 'But no, I'm just interested to meet someone like you at the top of her field.'

'Someone like me?'

'Sorry,' said Melody. 'I should be clear. I'm aware of Box Industries, and of its chief executive. Conway Box does not strike me as a man committed to equal opportunities.'

'Oh, I don't know,' said Selena. 'He's invested heavily in India, and Indian labour.'

'Right,' said Melody. 'Sounds a bit colonial to me.'

'Well, I have a great deal to thank him for,' said Selena. 'With his... encouragement I have risen to the top of my department.'

Melody noticed the hesitation. 'Seriously, Selena, how do you work for the man?'

'What do you know?' Selena whispered.

The truth was, Melody knew nothing, but she sensed something. 'I'm not sure I should say,' she whispered back. 'I don't want to imply any impropriety, least of all on your part.'

Selena's eyes began to fill.

'Oh, I'm sorry, Selena, I didn't–'

'It's all right,' she said. 'Heaven knows, it's nothing compared with, you know, what you've been through. I mean, usually it's nothing more than suggestive comments.'

Melody noted the word 'usually'. 'It's so unfair,' she said, 'that there are still cultures where men take advantage.'

'Well,' said Selena, 'at Box Industries I'd say our corporate culture is simply American. As for the workers, they are drawn from all over.'

'Well then, perhaps it's a man-woman thing,' Melody said. 'It seems almost universal anyway. Not that men take advantage everywhere all the time, but that you can never be sure when it will break out.'

'You make it sound like a disease,' said Selena.

'Oh, but it is,' said Melody. 'But enough of that.' She drew her chair closer to the table. 'I gather you got to play a key role in giving Jack his space suit.'

'I suppose you could say so,' she said. She lowered her eyes.

'Something to be proud of, I'd say,' Melody probed.

'Well, we are a team, you know. My part was–'

'Selena! Tell me the truth.' Melody could sense the mask was starting to loosen.

'It's nothing, really,' said Selena quietly.

'Now listen to me,' said Melody, glad to be engaged in something like her old job once more, 'humility is a wonderful thing. But credit is due where credit is due.'

'Well, yes, it's true that I was the one who saw that, if we could combine two polymers we were working on, we'd potentially have the toughest flexible clothing known to man.'

'Thanks to woman!' Melody cried.

'Yes, I suppose so,' said Selena, allowing a smile to surface.

'Mind you,' said Melody, flicking her hair (when had she last done that?), 'I'm not sure it held the top spot for long.'

'What?' Selena frowned. 'Oh yes, Ariel's suit. Now that is quite remarkable.'

'Do you have it here?' Melody asked.

'I couldn't possibly answer that!' said Selena, and they both enjoyed a moment of innocent laughter.

'What makes it remarkable to you?' said Melody. 'As an expert, I mean? You know, beyond the obvious indestructability thing?'

'Ha!' said Selena. 'Yes, that does take some explaining. Although… Ryan and I have actually managed to cut it.'

'Wow!' Melody sat back. 'What did it take to do that?'

'Well, that's what's so interesting,' said Selena. 'It was finally cut by a blade similar to the ones that had failed before.'

'And what do you make of that?' said Melody.

'To be honest,' said Selena, 'that's been the most remarkable thing of all. The reports from Endeavour and Alpha both referred to it as constantly changing in the way it appeared, yet that gradually diminished over time. And now, well, it looks like the resilience of the fibres is diminishing too.'

Melody thought of Ariel and began to wonder.

4

The discussion room was lively. If Ariel had proved to be a stone dropped in their pond, Sean was a boulder that had landed with a mighty splash. Was it really impossible for Ariel to stow away in the Endeavour's engine department? What level of trauma could cause such extensive amnesia? Could proximity to the nuclear drive on the Resolution be a cause? Yes, the liquid propellant was meant to screen them from the effects, but maybe something went wrong. And how sound was the evidence that he had resisted a saw and a gun butt, especially given his propensity to faint?

'It strikes me,' said David, 'that you are determined to prove Ariel a fake.'

'Then you don't understand me at all,' said Sean. 'I deal with evidence. I have to deal with evidence. Lost without it. As for fake, that rather depends on what he's claiming.'

'I claim nothing at all,' said Ariel.

'There you go,' said Sean. 'And what about testing? Prick me, and do I not bleed? Who said that?'

'Shylock, more or less,' said David, 'when he was speaking as a representative of the Jewish people.'

'Well then,' said Sean, 'this pen should do the job.' Taking a slim silver stylus from his jacket pocket, he leant across Jack and grabbed Ariel's hand, placing it flat on the table. He was fast, but not quite fast enough. As he brought the pen down towards the back of Ariel's hand, Jack caught Sean's arm, halting the blow in mid-air.

Leonardo and David leapt to their feet. Natasha put her hand over her mouth. 'Okay, okay,' said Sean, dropping the pen on the table and putting his hands in the air. 'But you get my point!'

'Aye, but I don't think we like your humour,' said Jack.

'Put it down to my teaching method,' said Sean, as Leonardo and David sat back down. 'I'd have pulled short if you hadn't intervened.'

No one looked convinced.

Sean pressed on. 'Honestly, when did anyone last test these amazing properties our friend here is meant to have?'

'You must feel free to do that,' said Ariel. 'We know that I have been able to protect myself so far. You can try the pen if you wish.'

Natasha felt she was finally beginning to understand Sean's methods and how his mind worked. 'I have a suggestion,' she said. 'Why don't we apply the point of the pen slowly, gradually? That way Ariel can do what he does, and maybe we'll observe something.'

'Good girl!' Sean boomed. 'I suggest you be the one to do the deed.'

Ariel nodded, and Jack vacated his chair. Natasha sat down next to Ariel and picked up the pen. Turning his hand palm-up she gently applied the nib to his skin. 'Okay,' she said. 'Here goes.'

'How fascinating,' said Ariel as she began to press. 'I do believe it hurts.' Instantly Natasha stopped. 'No, please go on,' said Ariel. She started again, but when bright red blood began to appear, she stood up and cried, 'Where's the first aid?'

Jack disappeared out of the room and returned seconds later with a metal box in his hand. Natasha rummaged inside till she had found some antiseptic. She dabbed Ariel's hand and applied a small plaster, before wiping the pen clean.

'Well,' said Leonardo. 'I wasn't expecting that.'

'I don't think any of us were,' said Jack. 'Apart from the professor here.'

'QED, my friends,' said Sean. 'Though I'll have the pen back please.'

5

Miranda knew she could not recreate the walk in the woods she had shared with Ariel, but even so her heart missed a beat when she saw the clearing with its tall upright trunks. More leaves had fallen to the ground, and the low sun cast longer shadows than before. She kept walking, and when she came to the wall she turned left, content with the memories as she basked in the afterglow.

When she reached the fallen bough she knew she had to stop. She sat down on it, idly rubbing her ankle, now safely protected from thorns, at least, by a thick pair of jeans. She smiled. Why had she felt so safe here? Was it even real?

She thought about their conversation, and how she had said that he and Hugh were the only ones who understood her enough to let her be herself. But already back then she had begun to see that Ariel had taken things to a new level.

As for the woods, well, they were just woods. It was so clear now that Ariel had made all the difference. The place was undeniably a great place for a retreat, but that was all. She could see why it might be popular, although, as she thought about it, she had no idea whether it actually was.

A twig cracked some distance away, and she looked up. Coming round a slight bend in the path ahead was one of the Geneva party she didn't really know. 'Hello there,' the woman said. 'I'm Alice. I hope I'm not disturbing you.'

Miranda decided brutal honesty was not appropriate. 'No, of course not,' she said. 'I'm Miranda. I used to be with your lot.'

'Really?' said Alice. 'How fascinating. Though, to tell you the truth, I don't think they are my lot. I'm not really a part of things. But my husband was, um, involved in an incident with... You know Ariel then?'

'Er, yeah, just a bit,' said Miranda.

'Ah, sorry if that was a dumb question,' Alice returned. 'I don't really know all the ins and outs of it. May I?' She sat on the fallen branch next to the forlorn-looking girl.

'So we're both outsiders then?' said Miranda.

'Perhaps we are,' said Alice, 'though I suspect you're not really. Why aren't you in the meeting with them now?'

'Long story!' said Miranda. 'One involving subterfuge, spying, trespassing, getting hit on the head by a tree struck by lightning, followed by a grilling by a soldier who was way too up himself, followed by... Ariel.'

'Oh goodness!' said Alice. 'I'm happy to hear the longer version if you have the time.'

Miranda looked at the woman next to her. There didn't seem to be a complicated line in her sunny face. Though perhaps a shadow. Light and shade – there they were again. She let out a little laugh. 'Tell you what,' she said at last. 'I'll tell you mine, if you tell me yours.'

The next hour seemed to evaporate into the musky air between bark and leaf, as first Miranda and then Alice talked and talked about the tumultuous days that had led them to where they were now. They couldn't cover everything, but they enjoyed putting so many things into the safe box of a good story well told.

At no point did either of them say anything personal about Melody.

'My limbs are getting stiff,' said Miranda at last. 'Let's walk.'

'So, let me see if I understand correctly,' said Alice as they passed under the trees. 'You work for one of the richest men in the world. In fact you work closely with him, and you think he's a voyeur.'

'Whoa, girl!' said Miranda, coming to an abrupt halt. 'I didn't say that.'

'You said he likes to watch people without interfering. Isn't that the classic definition of voyeurism?'

'Okay...' said Miranda. 'So then, you're married to someone who spends all his time interfering with people's lives!'

'Touchée!' said Alice. 'Perhaps I was falling into caricature.'

Miranda picked up a stick. 'Still,' she said as she tapped it against a tree. 'I suppose it is kind of true. Hugh has often said that I'm his action girl, and he'd rather stay on the sidelines and watch. For him it's all about information-gathering.'

They walked on in silence for several minutes. Miranda was weighing something up. She decided to go for broke. 'So I suppose...' she said, as she cast her branch away, 'I suppose Hugh's a bit like God.'

'Sorry?' said Alice. 'I don't follow.'

'Well, from what people say, and even some of the things you've said, God seems to like to watch from the sidelines, or even behind the scenes altogether. You know, while his servants do the biz?'

'Well, I–'

'In fact,' Miranda continued, 'you could say God's a bit of a voyeur.'

Alice was about to protest when she remembered herself, and the things she taught others about counselling. She decided to look deeper.

'Has that been your experience, Miranda?'

'Oh boy, now you're starting to sound like him!'

'Who?'

'Ariel, of course!' She said no more.

'What is it, Miranda?'

Miranda looked again at her new-found friend, if she was a friend. 'Oh well,' she said. 'Why not? The thing is, Alice, when I was last here, I had what I'm pretty sure you would call a religious experience. At least, Leonardo certainly would.'

'Leonardo?'

'The Abbot here. An interesting guy.'

Alice decided to deflect the potential distraction. 'Would you like to tell me about your... religious experience? Can you even put it into words?' Her evening in the hotel lounge with Ariel came to mind.

'Actually,' said Miranda, 'I think I can. I was with Ariel back there, under the trees, where you and I just met... and then I wasn't. I was in a walled garden, dressed in a long, green, flowing dress – don't laugh – and holding hands with the gardener, I think he was. And I felt safe. I mean really safe.'

She stopped and looked at Alice. She wasn't laughing.

'And you say this was with Ariel?' Alice asked evenly.

'Yep, we were walking right here,' said Miranda. 'Although... I don't think he was the guy in the... dream, or vision, or whatever it was.'

'Oh, Miranda, I think this is tremendously important. Don't you? I mean, you and I have both known what it is for Ariel to... affect our minds. And our hearts, if you'll allow me to use the term.'

'Use away!' said Miranda.

'Well, whoever was in your garden experience wasn't being a voyeur, was he? He was there with you. Right alongside.'

Miranda shook her head.

Alice couldn't tell if this was a signal of disagreement or some kind of awakening. 'The thing is,' she pressed, 'David and I have been wondering whether Ariel is in fact... now it's your turn not to laugh... an angel.'

The expletive was out before Miranda could retract it. 'Oops!

Sorry, Alice. But... you're serious, right? What? Like an angel who's lost his wings?'

'I don't know about that,' said Alice. 'But maybe an angel who's lost his memory.'

6

Hannah was trying to work, but something kept gnawing at her mind until she gave in and left her room. It was Melody. Something in her recovery process was not right. Or perhaps it was too right, too okay. At times like this, and with someone presenting as strong as this, Hannah knew it was better to talk it out.

She opened the door, looked out into the corridor and shivered. This was a strange place. In so many ways it looked the perfect venue for recuperation, and yet its resident brotherhood set up a maleness in the air that unsettled her.

Time to find her patient. She left her room and trotted down the stairs.

She passed Selena on the way down and was soon given directions to Melody's last known destination, the observatory. She made her way through to the covered way before turning right and making for the trees. She was just beginning to upbraid herself for her lousy sense of direction when she saw the signpost. A few minutes later she was on the observatory steps.

'Hello!' Melody emerged from the interior of the round building. 'Fancy meeting you here.'

'Yes, well,' said Hannah, 'I'll admit it. I'm not here by accident. I wanted to give you the opportunity to talk some more. I thought it might be helpful.'

Melody shrugged. 'Take a seat,' she said, indicating the top step. The sun was warm on their faces, but not shining directly into their eyes, and Hannah quickly approved the choice.

They talked a while about Melody's privileged upbringing and her career as a journalist, her need for affection and attention and her ability to use her wits and female charms to get things out of people. All this seemed admirably self-aware, but after a while Hannah decided to home in on something more recent and specific. 'I know earlier on you said not to go there,' she said tentatively, 'but, well, you might have known I wouldn't ignore a comment like that. Can we talk about David? You were probably as surprised as I was when he and his wife turned up yesterday.'

Melody looked blank. Had they arrived yesterday? She knew it was true, but it was like a buried memory, something far off in the distance. Yet now it came rushing up to meet her, assailing her with a host of associated memories that broke out in a series of loud sobs interspersed by agonising gasps and gaps of pregnant silence.

The sun shone. The birds sang. A faint breeze stirred the trees.

'Sorry,' said Melody at last. 'I don't know where that came from.'

'Do you want to talk about it?'

'Goodness me, yes. I don't want to leave it after all that!' She wiped her face and blew her nose. 'David. Where do I begin?'

'How did you meet?'

She told Hannah about their meeting in Canterbury Cathedral and the developing relationship with him and his wife Alice on and off over the years. She felt it was coming to an end when she had come to Geneva, and was confused when David turned up. 'It was like he wanted to regain the initiative, I think,' she explained. 'Like he was afraid of losing control.'

'How did he behave towards you?'

'What do you mean? There was no impropriety.'

'An interesting word,' said Hannah. 'It's just that, when someone wants to turn the balance of a relationship around, sometimes they do things they wouldn't normally do when things are going their way. Do you think it was significant that he chose to meet you in a cathedral in Geneva?'

Melody raised her eyebrows. 'I suppose it might be,' she conceded. 'But he did want to show me something connected with his sabbatical project. I don't think it was a territorial thing. He's not generally a manipulative person.'

Hannah said nothing.

'No, really. I genuinely think he's been responding all along to my interest in what he calls spiritual things. Well, at the start at least.' She paused. 'I'm digging a hole for myself here, aren't I?'

'Not at all,' said Hannah. 'We may even find we can dig you out of one. Tell me why you reacted so strongly when I suggested we talk about David.'

'Oh, because I've got it all wrong with him. I know you'll say it takes two to tango, and it does, but I've not really been very careful, or caring, towards him. It's not that I've flirted with him or anything.' She looked up at the trees. 'Well, maybe sometimes.'

In the silence that followed Hannah decided this was not a time to hold her counsel. 'Melody, this man is a pastor. The onus of propriety – to come back to the word you used just now – is on him.'

'I know,' said Melody. 'And he knew that. He was careful to do things right. But you know how it is... the unspoken feelings, the looks... the enjoyment of each other's company.'

'You said you got to know Alice as well. Did the two of you often meet without her?'

'No,' said Melody limply, 'not often. I think maybe we both knew it wasn't a good idea. Which is why I was surprised he decided to meet up while we were both over here and Alice was back in England.' She sighed.

'Still,' Hannah prompted, 'you only met in public places.'

Melody got to her feet and looked along the path back to the retreat centre. It wasn't completely straight, but she could just see a hint of the building in the distance. She thought of Ariel, and her next words were out almost before she knew it.

'We spent the night together.'

She turned round to face Hannah, who remained glued to the step. 'It's not what you think,' she added a moment later. 'I meant the words literally. We didn't have sex, but I was in his hotel room for half the night and... and...' She buried her face in her hands.

Hannah stood and faced her, checking only just in time the reflex reaction of giving her a hug. 'Look at me, Melody. Breathe. Now, when you're ready, tell me what it is that's upsetting you.'

Melody turned and looked up at the observatory sitting there under the dome of the sky that was its reason for being, and at the trees that reached up towards the same sky with all the life and connection that Ariel had sensed. 'You want to know what's upsetting me, Hannah?' she said at last. 'I'll tell you. It's me. I'm upsetting me. I'm selfish. Not self-obsessed, you understand – I love people, generally speaking, and find them fascinating. But I can't seem to escape me, myself.'

They sat back down on the step together. Hannah waited for Melody to continue.

'We'd looked around the city. We'd been on the lake. We had a relaxed evening together, talking, not talking. And then it came to saying goodnight. There was a moment, standing in front of the lift. Oh, Hannah, as I look back at that moment now, here with you, it looks like a great big crossroads, with massive traffic lights. Those lights were amber.' She made a brief sound of derision. 'No, they were red. And I jumped the lights.'

'But Melody,' said Hannah, 'at the risk of sounding like a cracked record... David was on the same road, the same position at your crossroads. The lights were red for him too.'

'I know, I know,' said Melody. 'But the truth is...'

'Yes?'

'The truth is, I knew he would say yes if I made it clear that I didn't want our evening to end right there. He'd already got in the lift and pressed the button when I jumped in with him. Neither of us said a word. I don't know what the poor guy thought was going to happen. All right, don't look at me like that. I know he wasn't a poor guy. But there it is, don't you see? I know I can have power over a man. And I haven't... I haven't always taken responsibility. I can blame the increasing closeness we felt as the day drew on. I can blame the alcohol. And yes, I can blame him. Blame will come to rest on every one of those doorsteps. But it sure as heaven rests on mine as well.'

Hannah looked at her. 'Melody James, you are a remarkable woman. And I'm done arguing with you.'

'Good!' said Melody, and this time there was no grin, but a real smile. 'And, for the record – though there had better not be a record of this conversation! – we talked through the night, till I called a taxi and left at some unearthly hour. But I meant it when I said we spent the night together. We were close, it was intimate, and it would have been embarrassing if Alice had turned up. Alice... his wife, my friend.'

They both sat a while longer, before a cloud drifted over the sun and they decided to walk back. As they emerged from the trees not far from the building, Melody stopped. 'I'm a bit of a phoney, aren't I?'

'What do you mean?'

'Well, you know, Miss ever-so-confident, achieving, glamorous... mess! I mean, look at me. Emotions all over the place. I've had what many would call a charmed life, and here I am talking to a shrink. No offence.'

'None taken,' said Hannah. 'But you've just been through a major trauma, and that's after everything else you've clearly been struggling with.'

'But that's just it,' said Melody. 'I wasn't really struggling, was I? Not even before... And even that feels like too much fuss. I mean, it's not as if he actually raped me.' She shook her hair. 'There, I've said it.'

Hannah scowled. 'Melody, listen to me. You may not have been raped in any of the technical senses we'd use in a courtroom, but what you experienced was a sexually motivated, sadistic violation. Don't you ever try to suggest it was anything else.'

Melody's eyes filled. She stretched out her arms, and the two women held each other. And as they did so a series of faces began to sweep across Melody's mind. First she saw Jack, followed by David. Then it was Miranda. Surprising, but she let it pass. Then, with frightening clarity, she saw Dog, but this apparition also melted away, dissolved in the strong comfort of her present embrace, so different from all others. Only the fifth face lingered. Good and pure, honest and true, with no pretence and no desire, it was the thought of Ariel that brought her peace at last.

7

'Oh, hi Petroc, can you put me through to the boss lady?'

Jack was alone in Leonardo's office. Constance came on the line.

'I think we have a wee problem.'

'Jack,' said Constance, 'why is it that every time you use the indigenous wee, it's anything other than small?'

'Ah, that's pure Scottish irony, that is,' he replied. 'But here it is. Ariel bleeds.'

'I'm sorry?'

'He bleeds. Sean stuck a pen in him. Well, no, Natasha did actually. But the thing is... well, I don't know what the thing is. I don't get it at all. I mean, I was there when Bill's henchman got his arm shattered. And we've all heard what Schlesinger had to say, and seen the footage, such as it is.'

'Hmm,' came the voice from the other end of the line, 'such as it is. I wonder.'

'What do you wonder?' pleaded Jack.

'Well, just think now,' she said with something ominously like excitement in her voice. 'It was dark when that thing happened with Maddox.'

'Your point being?' Jack didn't like where he thought this was going.

'Well, we don't know that he actually hit Ariel's head, do we? It may have been a tree stump.'

'We were in the middle of the path!'

'Well, a stone then. But Jack, we can't be *sure*, can we?'

'What are you getting at?' asked Jack. 'Just where are you going with this?'

'You know, Jack, this might actually leave us in the best place we've been since this whole funny business began. Although...'

'What?' He was not used to Constance Bridlington thinking out loud.

'Well, there's more to it than just Ariel, isn't there? We have to deal with how people react to him, don't we? And that can be a problem in itself.'

'Aye. And how is that a problem right now? Do you think there's going to be another kidnap attempt?'

'Quite possibly,' said Constance. 'I fear something's afoot. I don't know... it may be nothing. Only, well...'

'What is it, Constance?'

'Nathan Dexter has gone missing.'

CHAPTER 27

Gathering

1

Jack sat alone under the statue. The sun was about as high as it was going to get. The air was still, and he could hear the gentle sound of water playing nearby. The disappearance of Nathan Dexter was worrying him, partly because it potentially signalled a fresh threat, but also because he didn't really know what it meant. With Ariel safely back, he could see no advantage to any would-be kidnappers, unless he had been taken in order to set up another hostage-swap for Ariel.

He looked around the courtyard. This place no longer felt safe. In truth, had it ever been? A slight breeze wafted into the cloister. They needed a change of tack.

He got up and went to see who was in the other building. As soon as he had crossed the small courtyard he could hear raised voices coming from the discussion room. The loudest, of course, was Sean's. He was apparently attacking the notion of metaphysics, making some kind of distinction between discovering meaning in the universe and bringing meaning to it by who and what we are. As Jack entered the room, David was talking theology.

'But Sean, I thought you were a believer.' He sounded gentler than in their previous discussions, muted somehow.

'A Christian, you mean? Aye, so I am.'

'Then I don't understand your reluctance to believe that the world has already been made by a greater Mind than our own.' He paused. 'Why are you smiling?'

'May I?' Natasha interrupted. Jack waited unseen in the doorway.

'Be my guest, if you think you can,' Sean sparkled.

'I think, David,' said Natasha, 'that Sean tends to attack the things he believes in. He wants to know they will stand up to it.'

'You know, I wish you'd been one of my students,' said Sean.

'So do I,' Natasha replied.

'Okay,' said David. 'I think I get that – and thank you, Natasha. But surely we have to ask *why* we would bring meaning to the universe if we didn't find meaningful patterns in it to start with – you know, the laws of nature, that kind of thing. Laws which may be different where the angels live, in the heavenly realm. Which, by the way, is why I'd rather not call them aliens, as that makes it sound like they live in the same part of God's creation as we do. Which, generally, they don't. I think. Not all the time, at any rate.'

Sean chuckled and gave David a hearty pat on the back. Probably too hearty, Jack thought, considering the guy must still be feeling a tad vulnerable after his ordeal in Cologne. As Sean congratulated David on putting things so clearly while at the same time seeing what wasn't clear, Jack decided to dive in.

'Sorry to interrupt, guys, but I've just been talking to Geneva and it looks like we have another missing person. I think we need to prepare for a new phase of our operation.' He checked his eband. 'And it's coffee time.'

2

There were days when Constance wished she could be in two places at once, and this was one of them. How she would love to be in Montagnola right now. But she knew she must stay put, a fact confirmed by the call she had recently received from Jim Adamson. He and Ryan were on their way to meet her.

She'd been surprised it had taken this long.

Once they had been installed by Petroc she let them have their say. Ryan was convinced someone had entered the lab the previous night, because the crystal was slightly askew in its box, not exactly how he had left it. Constance told them about Nathan's sudden and unexplained disappearance. Given there were no signs of forced entry, they concluded it must have been him.

'Another mystery to add to the pile,' said Constance with a sigh.

'Well Ma'am,' said Jim, who had left the uniform at home, 'much as I have no wish to add to your pile... I think it's time I came clean.'

Constance joined them at the table.

'Not that I've been deliberately withholding, you understand,' Jim continued. 'At least, I don't think I have. But these past few weeks have given me time to mull over what on earth happened to me – or should I say, what on Venus happened to me – when I went out looking for this guy here.'

Ryan stared at the table.

'As you know,' Jim continued, 'after the review we had here with everybody I flew back to the States for a medical. There's nothing, Constance, no sign of what happened to me, of what they did to me.'

Constance frowned. 'Who, Jim? Who did something to you?'

'You remember the recording we all listened to?'

'Of course. It got quite a reaction!'

'Well,' said Jim, 'that's who I'm talking about. The people, beings, whatever they were... behind those voices. Somehow they got to me. Now, I know you all think I've been grumpy since the mission, and so I have. But honestly, Constance, it's far, far worse.'

'I believe you,' she said. 'For a start, you've never used my first name twice in the same conversation before! And I can see for myself how... disturbed you are. Ryan, have you felt the same?'

He looked up. 'Well, Ma'am, I've been very busy, as you know, with the crystal and all.' Jim cleared his throat and Ryan felt the nudge. 'But I agree with the Colonel here that the time for excuses is over, and yes, I know that my own mental state has not been... I don't know... as I would wish it, given my level of training.'

'Well now,' said Constance, 'that is a relevant point. You've both had previous experience in space. Jim, you've been to Mars twice already of course. And Ryan, I know you've had extensive experience in micro-gravity labs in orbit. All that to say, I am taking your words most seriously. Most seriously indeed.'

'So what do we do now?' said Jim. Constance felt no sharp point on the end of the question.

'Gentlemen, I think it's time you both went to Montagnola.'

3

Two floors above the domain of Constance Bridlington Beth sat at her desk with her chin resting on both hands. Takeshi was in hospital, no longer critical but off duty for weeks to come. Bill had suffered a setback – hardly surprising after resurfacing so soon. And now Nathan was gone. It had been important to draw the mole out, but how she wished it hadn't taken so long.

Her intercom beeped. 'They're here, Ma'am.'

She stood up as Marta came in with Lucien on her arm. 'He got bail,' she said drily. Beth noticed how gently she placed Lucien in a chair before taking a seat herself. 'He is taking German lessons,' she said with a lift in her voice. Beth also noticed it was a while before she let go of his hands.

'Even harder than English!' he complained. 'All those cases! And the word order – pah!'

Beth smiled. 'Well, you two look like you've found something good in all this, and I'm pleased about that.'

Refreshments arrived.

'Now,' said Beth, looking at them both. 'I have a proposition for you, and actually I think it could make your lives even better – especially yours, Lucien, what with all the investigations going on into your past exploits.'

'We are listening,' he said.

'Right,' said Beth. 'First of all, you need to know that several of our member states have been talking to each other.'

'Isn't that a good thing?' said Marta.

'Not when I don't know exactly what they're saying!' Beth quipped, though she didn't smile. 'What I do know is that they're following the line of "the enemy of my enemy is my friend". They're cooking something up.'

'Who is the enemy?' said Lucien, taking Marta's hand back.

'Ariel.'

'*Merde!*' said Lucien. 'They don't know who they're dealing with!'

'You make him sound like a threat,' said Beth.

'He's no threat – *pas du tout* – unless you threaten him!'

'Well, that would be just dandy, wouldn't it?' said Beth. Marta and Lucien both looked blank. 'Dandy... er, just lovely, helpful. I was being ironic!'

'Ah! So what do you propose?' asked Marta.

'I want you to abduct Ariel. Again.'

'Whoa!' shouted Lucien. 'Too much irony!'

'I'm deadly serious,' said Beth. 'Except this time, of course, we'll know exactly where Ariel is. He'll be somewhere safe.'

'And how does that make things better for me?' said Lucien. He wanted her to spell it out, and he made sure his eband was recording.

'Do this, and your past indiscretions will melt away.'

They both began to nod. 'Is Jack part of the plan?' said Marta.

Lucien grunted. 'Sorry, still a little sore.'

'No,' said Beth. 'But then there is no plan as yet.'

They conferred briefly. 'Okay,' said Marta. 'Tell us what you want us to do.'

4

With the scent of change in the air Jack decided to talk with Natasha and Ariel apart from the others. The chapel was empty. Jack told them that, with Nathan gone and Jim and Ryan on their way, it felt like the whole rehab plan had just about stumbled to a halt. It looked like Constance felt that Ariel's powers could be explained away. But what of his presence? They were going to need a story about how he had managed to stow away on both the Endeavour and the Resolution. 'It seems to me,' he said to them in little more than a whisper, 'that we have two basic choices on that front. Either we say that we got him on board somehow–'

'But that would be a lie,' said Natasha. 'And not a very believable one either.'

'Right,' said Jack. 'The alternative, then, is to say that he managed to hide somewhere on the Resolution, and succeeded in getting into the Endeavour unseen before we separated, and then got out when we weren't looking.' He sighed. 'Okay. That sounded even more stupid when I said it out loud.'

'Unless,' said Ariel, 'I managed to get to my ship. Or I went in my own ship?'

'Sure,' said Natasha, 'but you say that as someone trying to remember, not lie.' She turned to Jack. 'Surely you can't be serious about this?'

'Nah,' he said. 'Not serious. Just desperate.'

Ariel and Natasha walked towards the stained-glass windows at the far end of the chapel. The tree was still there, and the serpent. 'I don't think lying is a good idea,' said Natasha. The serpent didn't move.

'Jack wandered over to join them. 'No, you're right, of course,' he said. 'But how do we get Ariel away from all this... this fuss and nonsense?'

'Maybe we don't,' said Ariel. 'Maybe it is what has to be. Think about it, Jack – Melody's breaking story can't be taken back. The media interest is, I understand, stoked and ready to boil over. And while Constance has done an admiral job in fending off the military might of who-knows-whom, and Beth has helped us foil our abductors, I can't see how we can escape. It is, after all, a small planet.'

Natasha looked at Jack. 'It's true, hiding is difficult, and causing him to disappear would probably just fuel speculation anyway.'

'Maybe,' said Jack, a new note in his voice, 'though he appeared out of nowhere, and you know what they say... easy come, easy go.'

5

Darkness had begun to settle when the taxi turned up at the front of the Elemental Retreat Centre with yet more visitors. 'Well, this wasn't exactly what I expected,' said Jim as he took his baggage from the trunk. Ryan didn't know what to expect. As far as he was concerned, the whole notion of a monastery was covered in craziness.

They were shown to their rooms by a young English monk who was way too talkative. Ryan checked the crystal was safe in an inner zip pocket of his jacket, where it would stay close to his heart until it was safely under his pillow later on. Then, with no time to unpack, they went downstairs. As soon as they emerged into the main cloister they heard sounds of an evening meal in progress, but Ryan wanted to look around. 'Come on, Cap,' he whined. 'Just a quick look round this part.'

There was enough light from the cloister lamps to reveal the four shrines. Ryan scratched his head as they went round, wondering what they meant and why they were so familiar. Every now and then one of the monks would appear. He noticed one who didn't appear to be wearing a habit, though in the shadows it was hard to be sure.

Eventually hunger won the day and they went inside. Ryan's spirits lifted immediately. This was clearly where it was all happening! As soon as he stepped into the light and the warmth, he relaxed. Maybe this wasn't such a bad idea after all.

Jim followed cautiously and looked around. To the right was a large table where several monks were seated, talking fairly loudly over the background noise. Behind the monks was a bar of some description, where two more were busily employed. One he recognised as the talkative English fellow. Directly in front of him were a man and two women, none of whom he recognised, and beyond them a table with two more women, one of whom was Melody James.

As he looked to the left he was surprised to see Sean MacEvoy, the famous SETI scientist. That gave him hope. Seated with him were Jack and Natasha and Ariel.

An older monk with silver hair approached, shaking them both firmly by the hand. 'Welcome, my friends. Great timing, no? You are of course Colonel Adamson and Dr Chase. I am Abbot Leonardo. Welcome to my home.'

6

Leroy couldn't sleep. He was excited by the arrival of so many guests, but also troubled by the fact that he couldn't account for one of them. He had seen someone outside shortly before dinner, though they had kept to the shadows and so Leroy couldn't be sure who it was. Later, when he had checked the room roster before everyone retired for the night, he realised that all the guests had been in the refectory.

Most of the rooms on the first floor were now occupied, and everyone was abed. Nearly all the Brothers occupied the rooms to the rear of the building, where Miranda had returned. The Endeavour crew plus Hannah were on the side of the building furthest from the chapel, with Sean just around the bend – 'where I belong!' – at the front, along with Leonardo and a few more Brothers. Jim and Ryan were in the rooms between the front stair well and the door that led to the attic.

Leroy was finally dropping off to sleep, having decided that the shady visitor must have been one of the last two arrivals, most likely Dr Chase, when he heard a noise above him. It sounded like footsteps, only that was impossible, as he was on the top floor.

The realisation that the attic was of course really the top floor woke him like a wet flannel in the face.

Donning his habit, he left his room quickly and quietly. The corridor was bathed in the dull green hue of the emergency exit lights. He turned right past the inner stairs and the guests' rooms, before coming round to the front of the building, where he knocked gently on the Abbot's door. Within seconds Leonardo was there, and together they decided to investigate. 'No need to wake Brother Josef,' said Leonardo.

They were just about to ascend the stairs to the attic when Jim emerged from his room, fully dressed.

'Colonel Adamson,' said Leonardo. 'I'm sorry – did we wake you?'

'No, I was already awake,' Jim stammered. 'In fact, I'm not feeling very well.'

'I'm sorry to hear that. Can we get you anything?'

In response Jim swayed, and he only remained on his feet because Leroy caught him. As the two men began to escort him back into his room, Jack came round the corner. 'Everyone all right?' he said in a loud whisper.

Jim brought himself upright, though Leroy maintained a steadying hand. 'Jack,' he croaked, 'what is it with this place? Can you hear those voices?'

Jack looked to Leonardo but could not see his expression in the dim light. 'What voices, Jim? Bad dream?'

'That's what I thought at first,' said Jim, 'but it can't be. Not unless I'm still asleep!'

'That is entirely possible,' said Leonardo.

'Can we have some light here?' said Jack.

Leonardo, concerned not to illuminate the whole corridor and disturb anyone else, opened the door to the attic stairs and called for light. It was enough to see that Jim was wide awake.

'Can you still hear the voices?' said Jack. Jim nodded.

'Jack,' whispered Leonardo, 'Leroy here has just reported sounds coming from the attic. Would you mind ever so much joining us to investigate? After we get Colonel Adamson back to bed?'

'No need,' said Jim, whose ears were clearly alert. 'I'll come with you.' And before anyone could respond he started up the stairs.

7

Miranda couldn't remember when she had felt so excited. To be back in this place, in this room. It would be criminal to sleep it all away. So she decided to sit awhile by the window and look down at the cloister below. She tried to make out the statue in the middle, fascinated by the way it seemed to change its shape in the gloom. In fact she soon realised that her eyes couldn't properly resolve anything she was looking at. The very arches of the cloister seemed to be made of mist.

She looked back at the statue. Ever since she had first planted the listening device underneath it she had been intrigued by it. It was a human figure, but she had never been able to make up her mind whether it was male or female. Perhaps that was deliberate.

She thought of Ariel, and decided he was not likely to be asleep yet. She wouldn't get ready for bed yet herself either.

She began to dose. A few indeterminate moments passed, before she was roused by a sound that seemed to be coming from the ceiling. Then she heard a door closing nearby. And so, once more, she set off barefoot into the hall after dark.

She turned the first corner, realising that this time she had no idea who was in which room. Was that a shadow at the end of the corridor? She pressed on, heart thumping. Just before the next corner she stopped. Voices. It was Leonardo whispering to someone. She waited. Now a third voice, an American. That had to be Chase or Adamson. Definitely Adamson.

'Miranda?'

She started, then quickly turned round. It was Jack in sleeping attire, which as far as she could see amounted to tee shirt and shorts.

'Still on surveillance duty?' he whispered.

'If you like,' she said. 'There's something going on, Jack.'

'Right,' he said. 'I can hear Jim's voice. Wait here, will you?' And with that he ducked back in his room, reappeared in shirt and trousers, and went off in the direction of the voices.

Now what? she thought. Am I supposed to just stand here and wait?

8

With every stair Jim ascended, the voices in his head got louder. A storm was swirling around him. The stairwell light turned from white to yellow, before resting in an orange he had not seen since he was on Venus. He staggered to the attic door, to be caught and held once more by the young English monk.

Leonardo sat them both down in the corner before pressing his ear to the solid oak door. 'I can't hear anything,' he said.

'Where's Ryan?' said Jim. 'I need to find Ryan!'

'Shout any louder, my friend, and you will,' said Jack. 'Though he's clearly sound asleep.' He frowned. 'Which I must admit is unusual. He was always a light sleeper on the mission.'

Leonardo nodded to Jack and, checking that Leroy had made Jim comfortable, tried the door handle. Jack was expecting it to be locked as before, when he and Ariel had last come this far, but to his surprise Leonardo was able to turn the handle. Equally taken aback, he opened the door.

'Wait up,' whispered Jack. 'Let me go first.'

'Very well,' replied the Abbot, 'but please be careful.'

The room was much larger than Jack had expected. There was a low light. Directly opposite him was the back of a console which he dimly perceived to be part of an array of screens, some of which must be activated as they were casting a glow onto the seat beyond. On his right, running under a pair of small dormer windows along the foot of the slanting ceiling, was a large white conduit which looked like heavy-duty trunking.

His eye was drawn to a second light source, this one from the other side of the room. As he approached he saw a man sitting with his back to another dormer window, hunched over something that was glowing and very slightly pulsating. Jack turned to Leonardo and beckoned him in.

To Jack's surprise Leonardo made straight for the other side of the console, muttering something in Italian. One by one the screens went off.

Jack turned back to face the seated figure. He didn't recognise the face lit up in the glow, but he could not mistake the crystal in the man's hands. The fellow was mumbling as he stared into it.

'Leonardo!' Jack called, done with whispering now. 'Have you any idea what's going on?'

Before Leonardo could respond Jim came stumbling through the door, followed by an agitated Leroy. Leonardo called Leroy over to the console, while Jim headed straight towards the man sitting hunched over the crystal. 'Ryan! Is that you?' Jim shouted. 'Wake up, Ryan!'

'Jim, Jim,' called Jack, shaking him by the shoulders. 'Jim, look at me!'

'He can't see you.' The voice was Ariel's, and Jack turned to see him coming through the door, with Miranda hot on his heels.

'Will somebody tell me what's going on?' said Jack. 'Jim seems to think this is Ryan, but he's still downstairs. As far as we know! Is anyone else joining the party?'

'I don't know, Jack,' said Ariel calmly. 'But let me try something.'

'Be my guest.'

Ariel bent over the man and placed his hand under his chin, slowly lifting his face. Lit from below by the crystal it looked more like a gruesome mask than a human face, but as he looked on Jack was suddenly back in the steel-grey briefing room with its harsh lighting on board Space Station Alpha. And now he knew he was looking at the unnamed man who had sat next to Brad Shepperton at the meeting of WSA directors. He stepped back, shaking his head, more bewildered than ever.

Ariel looked into the crystal and, as he did so, Jim bent double, clutching his head. 'Get away!' he shouted, and then stood up straight and began to flail his arms around as if he were swatting a swarm of invisible flies.

Ariel went down on his knees, still holding the man's chin and gazing into the crystal. He began to sway. 'Oh no,' said Jack, 'not again!' He reached out to catch him, but before he even got close Miranda rushed past and caught Ariel as he dropped to the floor.

Leonardo and Leroy looked on in horror as the unknown man finally tore himself away, screaming, taking the crystal with him. They saw Jack try to restrain him and gasped when he was flung back on top of the now prostrate Ariel and Miranda. The young monk went to assist, but Leonardo caught hold of his habit and pulled him back. 'No, Brother, we must keep our distance!'

Leroy pulled himself free, only to freeze when for a fleeting moment he looked into the unknown man's wild eyes. They were filled with fear and rage. And was that regret? A second later the crazed figure turned away. Holding the crystal before him, arm outstretched, he rushed headlong through the dormer window, disappearing in an eruption of splintered glass.

Light

Interlinking lines of light in ever finer fractals.
Voices vie to strangle the stranger or save.
Ears enveloped in sounding fury, pressed hard by hammers on anger's anvil. Too late! the cry. The line is broken. What now for those in nature's night and the fearful fog of oblivion?
There shivers the repentant, spurred on by duty's call, destined to be saved through weakness.
But oh, the gall of greed and gain in this, the hopeless! Too late the remorse, to try to right the wrongs,
when wrong has long since wrought its doom, and hope is lost.
Here lie the fallen.
Is there no way back? Back to the beginning?
See now, love comes, her arms outstretched, the heart that aches,
too soon to lose what's only lately found.
Rest. The time is soon. Rebellion trounced again, for now.
So take the time to say goodbye.
The fight goes on, and not alone.
Rest.

Chapter 28

Investigation

1

No one slept much that night. By the morning the local police had cordoned off the broken body that lay sprawled beside the path behind the main building. In the daylight it became clear that he had been dashed against the tiled roof of the covered way as he fell and was likely dead before he hit the ground.

When the inspector arrived she asked to see Leonardo. Almost immediately after that she called for Jack.

'How can I help?' said Jack, only half awake and feeling so much the worse for having caught a little sleep. With nothing more than a jacket thrown over his nightwear, he shivered in the morning chill.

'Commander Forrester?' An elegant woman held out her hand. She was on the cusp of middle age, maybe, with laughter lines just showing round her deep-brown eyes before they disappeared on their way to her long dark hair which was tied back in a loose pony tail. 'I am Inspector Olivia Bandalucci from Lugano Police. Commander, can you tell me how one of your colleagues came to die in this way?'

'My colleagues? I don't understand. Do you know something I don't?'

'*Certo*,' she said under her breath, shaking her head and taking a step closer to him. 'Commander, are you saying you did not know this man?' They were standing out on the grass on the other side of the covered way from where the corpse still lay shrouded by a sheet hastily fetched from the infirmary. The crystal had been recovered a short distance away. 'It is my understanding that you also were working for the intelligence service.'

'Okay, slow down a moment,' said Jack. 'What's with the also? Perhaps you'd like to tell me just who this man was.'

A pair of impeccably groomed eyebrows rose in response. Jack studied her face and saw a hint of classical Italian glamour softened by an apparent absence of make-up on her olive skin. There was a scent of the Mediterranean about her, and a gleam of playful intelligence in her eyes. He was fully awake now.

'You need to understand,' he pressed, 'I only got a brief look at the face of our man in the attic, and it was, well, contorted. And it was lit from below – you must know what that's like. And yes, of course I searched the body afterwards, but there was nothing on him to identify him. And as for his face, well, to put it bluntly, after the fall there wasn't really much of it left to see.'

'*Va bene*,' she said and stepped back again. 'We have reason to believe the man is called Nathan Dexter. Is he not known to you?'

Jack smoothed the top of his head with his hand and exhaled slowly. 'Nathan Dexter? The chap who works for the UN High Command?'

'*Sì*,' she nodded. 'We received word from them.' She checked her eband. 'A Beth Griffiths... she said she had reason to believe he might be in the area. And she sent us this picture. As you say, it is not easy to make an identification, but–' She held up her eband.

'Sure, yes, that's him,' said Jack. 'I've only met him a couple of times, and I certainly didn't recognise him last night. And actually, Olivia – may I call you Olivia, only I can't remember the rest of your name – things start to make some sense if this is Nathan Dexter. At least, it may go some way to explaining a few things.'

She looked at him. 'Very well, *Jack*,' she reciprocated with a wry smile. 'I imagine you need to sleep. My colleagues will be taking witness statements throughout the day, and I may need to talk with you again later. My guess is that the information I have given you will mean you need to talk to your people.'

'Olivia, you are a star,' said Jack. 'I'm glad we're in your hands.'

As he turned to go back inside, his hip accidentally brushed against the inspector's hand, although as he approached Leonardo's office he began to wonder just how it had come to be there.

He yawned. He was finding it hard to process the new information, and unsure whether to make the call to Geneva before getting more sleep. The matter was decided when Leonardo beckoned him in. 'Jack, I have Constance on the line.'

Jack took the phone, and Constance confirmed that Beth had been in touch with the local police. Based on a hunch of Takeshi's they had put Nathan under surveillance, all the while feeding information via the listening device they had discovered in Beth's office.

'So you knew he was involved in the kidnap?' said Jack.

'We didn't know anything,' said Constance. 'Not for sure. But Beth always did trust Takeshi's judgement. In his hospital bed he went over everything that had happened and began to formulate a theory, with Nathan very much at the centre. We weren't sure, but it was the nearest thing we had to a lead. Oh, and by the way Jack, you can expect a visit from Lucien and Marta in a while. Probably after the police have finished their preliminary investigation.'

'Lucien and Marta? Whatever for? Don't you think we have enough people here already?'

'Probably, but Beth has a plan to get Ariel away, and they're part of it. Anyway, listen to what they have to say. But tell me, Jack, how is everybody? Did anyone else get hurt? How did it happen?'

Jack related the events as he recalled them, even though they seemed more like a weird, bad dream that he couldn't shake off.

'Ariel's out for the count, again. Jim's getting over it – no more voices, and he's sleeping soundly. Talking of which, Ryan is getting over a headache brought on by what we believe to be a knockout drug of some kind. Apparently he dreamed someone was trying to suffocate him.'

'Hmm,' said Constance. 'Doesn't that sound a little similar to the abduction here in Geneva?'

'Could be,' said Jack. 'Let's see what toxicology reveals. As for Miranda–'

'Yes,' said Constance, 'What was she doing there anyway?'

'You tell me,' said Jack. 'Maybe ask your friend Leonardo? Or Hugh Coates?'

'All right. Well, how is she?'

'She's more comatose than asleep. As I think about it now, I reckon the timing of her intervention will have a bearing on her injuries. As I say, she caught Ariel just before Dexter – I still can't believe it was him – just before he flung himself out the window.'

'How on earth did he manage that?' Constance asked. I thought the whole place was equipped with high-tech security. Surely the window was made of toughened glass.'

'It was,' said Jack, 'but it shattered when the crystal hit it – whether it was just because it hit the glass first and was so much harder, or whether it broke it through some other kind of force, I wouldn't like to say. But there's clearly a lot more to this crystal than we understood. I know Ryan and some other top brains have been looking at it, but I can't help feeling we're missing something there.'

A sigh came from the other end of the line. 'Jack, I think we're missing rather a lot, don't you?'

2

The morning floated by in a thin haze, as though the previous night had drained the life out of it. But by the afternoon everyone was up and about, with many paying visits to the reception room at the front of the building which had become the police incident room. Melody felt relieved that they had picked the one room none of them had ever been in. Somehow it left the place less sullied.

But she knew that was not really true. The horrific suicide had shaken everyone, not least the small crowd of Brothers and guests that she had joined in the night outside Ryan's room at the foot of the attic stairs. No one could forget that agonising scream and the heart-stopping crash that followed.

She decided to add Hannah to her list of people to avoid. There was no point in going over any more today, and trying to process the trauma of the previous night seemed hopeless. Far better to let her journalistic instincts kick in. She wanted to know about the man who had died, and so she persuaded Jack to visit the observatory one more time. Donning their coats, they walked out into the crisp autumn air.

'Oh, this is better,' she said as they followed the path through the trees. 'Doesn't it just do you good?' And she let him take her hand.

'Aye, it does,' said Jack. 'It's invigorating. More like back home.'

'Oh, Jack, let's go there when this is all over. I'd love to see Edinburgh again. And your dad.'

They reached the observatory steps and sat down. From time to time a shy sun peeked out through the blanket of clouds.

'When this is all over, you say?' Jack mused. 'I wish I knew when that might be. Or even what it might look like.'

'Yes. Poor Ariel. What do you think will become of him?'

'Well, there are plans afoot,' he said. It seemed pointless now to withhold anything from Mel, not least because she was sure to be writing it all up in the not-too-distant future. 'Your friends from Cologne are coming.'

She shivered.

'Ah sorry, lass, I didn't–'

'It's okay, Jack. Honest. So Marta and Lucien are coming here? Why?'

'Apparently they are now the left and right hands of Beth Griffiths, colleague of the late Nathan Dexter. They're coming to take him away – Ariel, I mean. That is, assuming we can think of somewhere safe to take him.'

'But... how are we going to explain his disappearance?'

'I like the "we" in that question,' said Jack. 'Because I'm thinking you may be a part of it.'

'Oh,' she said as she caught his meaning. 'Always happy to use my writing talents in the service of the truth.' She smiled, and Jack's day became a little warmer. 'But this Nathan Dexter. Did you know him?'

'Not really,' he said, 'though we were in a couple of meetings together, and then we joined up at the last minute when we went in to... get you back. To be honest, I wasn't really looking at him then. But last night, with his face in that harsh light, I finally realised where I'd seen him before. He was actually on board Alpha with us. I think there's a whole lot more to come out about our boy Nathan.' He called up a picture on his eband. 'What were you up to, Mr Dexter?'

'Is that him?' said Mel idly, but a second later she grabbed Jack's arm. 'Wait a minute,' she said. 'I know that man! He was the guy I saw watching David and me, that day in Geneva.'

It was Jack's turn to shiver. Mel lowered her eyes.

'Ah well,' he said eventually, 'it strikes me we'd best go talk to the inspector again. We've got a lot of pieces to put together.'

She looked up, a playful grin already banishing her guilty face as she thought about the sophisticated woman she had met earlier in the day. 'Jack,' she said, and gently stabbed his chest with her forefinger. 'It's not like you to involve the police any more than you have to!'

'Ah well, you know... she's quite a bright spark. For a police officer.'

They sat a while in the waning light until it became too cold, and then walked arm in arm back to the Centre.

3

Leonardo was deep in thought as he escorted Jim from the incident room to the infirmary next door. As they entered they passed Brother

Josef on his way out. They found Brother Ambrose standing between two beds, studying some equipment that was chirping away quietly. On the beds Ariel and Miranda lay quite still, although when Leonardo saw Miranda's fingers twitching he went and stood next to her. There was movement under her eyelids as well, and he wondered out loud just what her dreams would tell them. Ambrose confirmed there was a great deal of neural activity going on in both patients, though he was finding it hard to interpret Ariel's monitor.

They sat down in a corner and Ambrose shone a light into Jim's eyes and asked him a series of questions. He could detect no sign of lingering psychosis, and that was good enough for the Abbot. Jim needed no such reassurance. The voices had gone.

The two men left the infirmary and walked slowly round the cloister, stopping at the shrines, half-heartedly comparing notes on being an abbot and captaining a ship, talking about anything other than recent events. Jim stopped at the door to the chapel. 'May I take a look?'

Leonardo was delighted to oblige. Just as he opened the door, Jack called to them, fresh from the refectory where caffeine had done its work. 'Jim, would you mind going over last night? I'd love to hear your perspective? I'm guessing there are things you may not have mentioned to the police. As not relevant, I mean.'

Jim made as if to speak but then simply nodded, realising he was actually pleased Jack was playing a leading part in the investigation.

The three men filed into the chapel. 'Why is it always empty in here?' said Jack.

'Well,' said Leonardo, 'I think you know by now, Jack, that we are not a conventional sort of monastery. We do not keep the hours – at least, not through prayer and singing. We do in fact make use of the chapel, but not every day. And anyway, I wanted this space to be available during your visit. Both your visits!'

They sat themselves down in the chancel and let Jim talk. He no longer cared whether Leonardo was allowed to hear what he had to say. His need to let Jack know what he had been going through trumped everything else.

'I need to start at the beginning,' he said. 'Ever since we were on Venus, I've not been right.' The Abbot showed no sign of surprise. He pressed on. 'I guess we were all out of sorts, and yes, I put it down to the advent of the Stranger... of Ariel... but the review in Geneva made it clear to me that the trouble began outside the ship.'

'Those sounds, like voices,' said Jack.

'Exactly right,' said Jim. 'And while I've been back in Florida I've been going over it all in my mind. The distrust, the suspicion... and, if I'm honest, the jealousy.'

Leonardo nodded, as if to affirm the notion as equally unsurprising.

'Sure,' said Jack. 'I think all our senses were heightened, and our hackles raised – mine too.'

'Maybe,' said Jim. 'All I know for sure is that I was out of line. Anyway, last night I was back there – not in the suspicion or the jealousy, you understand, but on Venus. I could hear those damned voices again. I could feel the disorientation. And then, there he was! Ryan, crumpled up on the ground. Leastways, I took it to be Ryan, just as I did back on Venus. Only this time you were there, Jack, telling me it wasn't Ryan.'

'Aye, that I was.' He described the waking dream Jim had apparently been having.

'Well,' said Jim, 'the voices got louder and more menacing. They seemed to be all around me. And then... Ariel was there, grappling with the mysterious figure. Or was that you? I don't really know even now. But what I do know is that Ariel snapped something.'

Leonardo and Jack looked at each other, genuinely surprised. 'Say again,' said Jack.

'Hard to explain,' said Jim. 'Sorry if I'm not making much sense. I think Ariel broke a connection, or a bond, or something. The voices just went off. Period. Silence. I don't remember much else. Next thing I know, I'm waking up in my room.'

Leonardo began tapping his lips with his finger. 'Captain, I mean

Colonel...'

'Jim,' said Jim.

'Jim,' the Abbot echoed, 'I want to thank you for that. It is beginning to make sense to me now.'

'Well, I'm sure glad it makes sense to someone,' said Jim. 'What are you thinking?'

'That the crystal is a channel for emotion. Perhaps also an amplifier.'

'Well, I'm sure I wouldn't know how you begin to test that,' said Jim. 'Nor would I want anyone else to go through it!' He stood up and stretched. 'Now, if it's all the same to you guys, I'd like to take a walk before dinner.'

'But of course,' said Leonardo.

When Jim had gone, Leonardo looked Jack straight in the eye. 'I'm guessing, my friend, that you have other questions, not just about Jim's experience.'

'So true,' Jack nodded. 'It's time we talked about the attic.'

4

It was not easy for Hugh Coates to return to Montagnola, and harder still to enter the monastery alone and undisguised. His car swept into the front drive, followed immediately by a private ambulance. He had come to take Miranda home.

Where was home? He had decided it was Bruges. Until she came back to us, back to him, that is where she would stay, attended day and night by a committed and well paid team of nurses, under the care of the only doctor Hugh could countenance, his own private physician.

He rang the front door bell, to be greeted by a monk who at the sight of the stranger with an ambulance ran straight to Ambrose in the infirmary.

Natasha was sitting under the fountain in the middle of the courtyard. She peered through the front corridor and studied the silhouette of the new visitor. Even now, with all this upset, all this coming and going, the buildings around her seemed very still. Unruffled.

When Ambrose ushered the visitor through to the infirmary Natasha realised it must be the man who had brought Miranda to them. The man who would now take her away.

She sat and waited a while. Something told her it couldn't end like this, that if she was going to see Miranda again she would need to know her mentor and protector. Driven by a sudden intuition, she leapt to her feet and dived into the infirmary.

It took a moment to find him. He was standing in the corner of the room, almost invisible in his long dark coat, watching the ambulance team checking her vitals, transferring her drip and then rolling her away to the ambulance.

The man shook Ambrose by the hand and began to follow them out towards the front drive. Ordinarily Natasha would respect his obvious need for privacy, but this was not ordinary.

'Mr Coates?'

He stopped and turned. 'Yes.'

'I'm Natasha Koroleva.'

Hugh signalled the ambulance crew to continue loading their precious cargo. 'Dr Koroleva, it is an honour.'

'It's very kind of you to do this.'

'Kindness doesn't come into it.'

'I see,' said Natasha. Perhaps this was more like family, a father collecting his child. 'Sir, I would like to visit Miranda, if that is possible.'

'It may be some time before she wakes,' he said. 'Maybe ne—'

'I'd like to come anyway. Soon.'

'Of course,' he said. He walked across to the ambulance to oversee the installation. 'It's Hugh, by the way,' he said without turning.

And then he jumped inside.

5

As Leonardo and Jack reached the top of the stairs to the attic, the police inspector was just emerging. The door was kept open by a heavy-looking box.

'Olivia.'

'Jack.'

As she went for the stairs on the small landing they brushed past each other. Leonardo stood back. It looked for all the world like a smirk on his face.

'What?' said Jack.

'Nothing, my friend. Nothing at all.'

Jack gave a disingenuous shrug, as if he had no idea what Leonardo was talking about. Anyway, right now he had more important things on his mind. He led Leonardo inside. Another police officer was there, apparently making an inventory. 'Okay,' said Jack to Leonardo. 'Let's start with the conduit right here. It looks like it's coming in from the stair well, and I know that goes over the chapel. What's it hiding?'

'Ah, Jack. That is the nature of conduits. They hide cables. These run from the satellite link station in the grounds, and they come in through my office by the chapel.' With an uncharacteristic frown on his face he sat down on a small swivel-chair in front of the console where he and Leroy had stood in the night. 'This is very difficult.'

Jack watched the officer making his list, and slowly it dawned on him why Leonardo might be struggling. Could it be that, because of Nathan's incursion, they had pierced into the very heart of this peculiar place? Jack chose a chair close by and kept his voice down. 'I'm sorry, Leonardo, but you must see that we're going to have to investigate all of this very thoroughly.'

'*Sì, sì,* of course. And I have told Tibet as much. And I am glad it is you I am talking to.' His eyes darted in the direction of the officer who had worked his way to the other side of the room.

'Yes, well,' said Jack. 'The police will need a complete

understanding of the place so that they – we – can work out what Nathan Dexter was doing here.'

'I may be able to help there,' he said. The officer stopped writing.

'Go on,' said Jack. 'And don't worry about him. I'll be sharing information with the inspector anyway, as she will with me.'

'Good, good,' said Leonardo, wiping his brow.

'Are you all right?' said Jack.

'Of course,' said Leonardo. 'It must be coming up two flights of stairs. I'm not as fit as I used to be.'

The officer left, nodding briefly to the two men as he went.

'Very well,' said the Abbot at last. 'This is, as I have implied, the control room for the communications we have with the outside world.'

'Including Tibet.'

'*Precisamente*. The land line comes through here, and the satellite links also.'

'So you can talk to them in your office. And in the attic?'

'Yes, and I also have a small tablet that allows me to talk to them if I am elsewhere on site.'

Jack nodded his appreciation of Leonardo's new-found transparency. 'Actually,' he said, 'I remember now. Early on Ariel said he saw you talking on some kind of hand-held device. He said you were talking about a shell.'

Leonardo frowned. 'Curious,' he said, but after a moment he broke into a smile. 'Ah, *si*, that would be when they asked about the crystal – it is *shel* in Tibetan. The *shel rdo* is the crystal rock they have at the Temple.'

'I see,' said Jack. 'At least, I'm beginning to. You've been interested in the crystal ever since Constance told you about it.'

Leonardo seemed to consider his next words carefully. 'I may have hidden things from you,' he said, 'but I won't lie to you, Jack. It was actually Tibet that first told me about the crystal. And no, I do not know how they knew. That is something I want to find out.'

Jack scratched his head. The level of subterfuge did not really surprise him, but its location certainly did. How could a Himalayan monastery be first in line for state secrets? But then, who said they were state secrets? Space exploration had long been first and foremost a genuinely international endeavour. It had to be the Chinese Space Agency. He filed the thought away.

'And these screens?' he said. 'I noticed some of them were on last night.'

Leonardo took a deep breath. 'This is because I think our unwelcome visitor was checking on the rooms.'

Jack pulled his chair closer to the Abbot. 'I see. Can we take a look now?'

Leonardo hesitated, clearly in doubt, but succumbed at last to the inevitable prospect that sooner or later he would have no choice in the matter. Again he comforted himself with the thought that it was better to reveal secrets to a friend, at least in the first instance. He pressed three small areas on the glass console in the centre of the desk. Jack was surprised that there was no biometric or other key to unlock, until he thought of the attic door. That was deemed enough of a security measure, though they clearly hadn't reckoned on someone like Nathan Dexter turning up.

As Leonardo pressed, three screens sprang into life, each with an image that was split in two. Jack quickly recognised them as rooms from the floor below. They were all currently unoccupied. On the left of each screen he could see almost the whole room from above. On the right a view of some furniture. It didn't take him long to work out that he was looking through a light in the ceiling and through the camera that powered the digital mirror.

'Is there sound?'

Leonardo nodded.

'Oh, Leonardo! Why, man? What's the game plan here?' He thought of the hotel scandals earlier in the century, when 'security' cameras had become commonplace in guestrooms. And he thought of himself, with Melody, in one of these very rooms. 'I must say, I didn't have you down as a peeping tom.'

'Good,' said Leonardo, 'for I am not. Let me show you the rest.' He pressed and swiped more of the console, and now one of the split screens changed, revealing various numbers and lines. 'These are monitors,' he said.

'And what precisely do they monitor?' said Jack.

'Neural activity,' said the Abbot.

'I don't understand.'

'Basically, we have a sleep monitoring system in place here,' Leonardo explained.

'Does Constance know about any of this?'

'No.' He looked down, and there was sorrow in his voice. 'Try to understand, Jack, that this is a centre of learning and discovery. More than one of the Brothers has a degree in neuroscience.'

'And you provide the lab rats,' Jack whispered.

'What can I say? If it helps, I did not know about this when I arrived. It is very much Brother Josef's project. He deals direct with Tibet and I don't get involved more than I have to.'

'Actually,' said Jack, 'it does help – a bit.' Clearly attention would need to turn to this Brother Josef and his direct access to Tibet.

There had to be plenty more Leonardo could reveal, but Jack felt they had gone far enough for now. Others would follow and investigate precisely what the equipment was designed to do. He turned his attention to the other side of the room and the shattered window that was now boarded up. 'And what about that console over there? Spare me the detail – just the highlights will do.'

'Of course,' said Leonardo. 'While what you see here is for internal monitoring, over there is for outside. It is mainly weather-tracking equipment, linked to the four shrines and the sculpture down in the courtyard.'

'I see,' said Jack. 'Makes sense. You said "mainly". What else does it do?' He was almost afraid to ask.

'It picks up spy drones, prying satellites, that sort of thing.'

'Wow,' said Jack. 'And what do you do when you've picked them up?'

'We can neutralise them if we wish. A simple microwave burst is usually enough.'

The military overtones confirmed beyond all doubt that this place was going to be examined in minute detail.

He looked at the storage boxes behind him, wondering what they might be hiding. Again he decided not to go there just yet. He returned to the internal monitors and stared at them for a while, Leonardo looking on, apparently embarrassed into silence. Jack began to wonder whether the connection with each room was entirely passive, or might they be capable of active interference too, like the ones that went after spy drones? Invasive manipulation, even? Were the Brothers interfering in people's dreams? What about Tibet? They clearly had access. Why stop at sleep? Might they even be able to manipulate waking perceptions? And what did that mean for the experiences they had all had here during the last month?

He struggled to reinterpret the place that had become such a haven for the crew, and for Ariel. And then he recalled the obvious fact that not everything strange had happened in this place. Ariel's mysterious arrival had taken place on another world. Doctor Schlesinger's saw had been resisted in space. A locked door had been opened in Cologne. All verifiable and potentially repeatable. And that was to say nothing of the mind-melding exercise David had described in Geneva.

Leonardo saw the signs of anguish on Jack's face. 'Jack, I want to assure you, we take privacy very seriously. I am sure you can see that none of our devices are open to the prying eyes and ears of hackers.'

Jack shook his head, his heart still unable to catch up with what his brain was busy processing. Doubtless all this was secure from the average hacker, but Hugh Coates had found a way in. And so had Nathan Dexter.

Not for the first time Jack felt that things were getting away from him. Wearily he trudged back down the stairs, leaving Leonardo to his dark machines and even darker regrets.

6

The refectory welcomed three more diners that day. Marta and Lucien arrived escorted by an underling in Beth's team. They were just in time to show Inspector Bandalucci their authorisation for moving the body before she left for the day. The late Nathan Dexter would now be in the care of UN High Command. And yes, his family had been informed.

The escort left soon after. Later that evening Jack and Natasha met with Marta and Lucien in the hitherto little-used lounge, where a fire was burning to stave off the chill of evening. They quickly agreed that Ariel should be removed to a safe location, if necessary even while he was unconscious. In which case transferring Dexter's body might provide the cover they needed.

They mused together over where Dexter fitted in with all the clandestine activity surrounding Ariel. As Marta told them about the mysterious client Dog had been in touch with, she and Jack both began to wonder whether he or she (no one ever heard the client's voice) could be the one behind Dexter's latest and last move. Or whether the client was even Dexter himself.

'After all,' said Marta, 'Beth says we know he has been working against Project Icarus, as she called it, for some time. You say you remember him back on the space station. And we've recently received pictures from my colleagues on *Exposé* of a man who called into the office not long before we arrived at the house over the river in Deutz. It was Dexter.'

'I can't make much sense of it yet,' Jack admitted, 'but it sounds like getting Ariel away from everyone – and so getting him away from here – is the best plan we've got. Though what happens after that, who knows?'

'I understand there was some kind of crystal someone found in the basement,' said Lucien. 'What is that all about?'

'Honestly, if I could tell you I would,' said Jack. 'I mean, it's something we brought back from Venus – that's simple enough. But its significance is beyond me. Dexter must have stolen it from Ryan's room for a reason. He clearly thought he could use it in some way.'

'Maybe he already had,' said Marta.

Jack nodded. 'Interesting thought,' he said. 'Well, there's a whole bunch of other stuff that's been going on, but I'd best report back to Geneva before I say any more.'

'*Ah oui*,' Lucien grunted. He wasn't expecting them to be taken into Jack's confidence any time soon.

Marta decided this was a good time to unveil the rest of the plan Beth had given them. 'I have a note on my eband that I can share with you. It's from Beth Griffiths and Constance Bridlington. Apparently it's not easy to make direct contact with you when you're here.'

'Well, that may be about to change,' said Jack. 'Another long story. Sorry, I'm tired.'

She transferred the message from her eband to his.

Jack smiled as he opened the written message that Constance so often preferred over audio or video. 'Okay,' he said after a few moments. 'We're to find a way to get both Dexter's body and Ariel to a medical facility not far from here. But maybe you knew that already. Apparently it's only used for mountaineering accidents, so it's often unstaffed. But it has full body-scanning equipment. Beth will rendezvous with us there, and she'll bring a technician to run some full body scans on both of them. The crystal is to be handed over to Ryan who will recommence his analysis.'

Natasha went and stood by the fire. 'Scans. Here we go.'

'Well, yes,' said Jack, 'I guess it was only a matter of time. But then, we really are running out of options here, and it's not as if these will be invasive.' With that he said good night and left for his room. Marta soon followed.

Natasha stared at the fire.

'What is it?' asked Lucien.

Natasha studied the Frenchman. He was probably her age, late thirties, with the rugged looks of a man who had been through the mill yet was at home in his own body. 'You've met Ariel,' she said. 'What did you think of him?'

He came and stood on the other side of the fire. 'He is remarkable. I don't know... there is something about him.'

Natasha wasn't sure if he was just saying what she wanted to hear. 'So,' she said, 'you abducted him and then had your doubts?'

Lucien smiled as he shook his head. 'Natasha, my brief was very simple. Bring Melody Grantley James in for questioning. Find out from her who or what they had really found on Venus. As for doubts, I had plenty of those as soon as I saw the interrogation chamber I was supposed to use. By the time that animal took over, I had already changed my allegiance.'

They sat down. Natasha sensed Lucien's genuineness, something she had been less sure of with Marta who seemed altogether more calculating. What he said made sense. Melody had been an obvious target. She was not part of the proceedings in the UN building, yet she had been with the key people in Montagnola. And Nathan Dexter's involvement provided the answer to how the kidnappers knew about the monastery in the first place. 'It's ironic,' she said. 'If you'd taken only Ariel, you wouldn't have found out much at all.'

'Ha! We didn't know about the amnesia, of course. Or, when we had him, whether he was telling the truth about that.'

'That's been a bit of a theme actually,' she said, smiling.

'I do believe that is the first real smile I have seen in this place since I got here.' He put another log on the fire.

'So, tell me,' she persisted, 'what made you join *Exposé*?'

'I don't know if I ever did join,' he said. 'I was offered this mission as a kind of test, a probation. I liked the connection with global cooling, I wanted to play my part. If they had found out something important in the fight to save the planet, no matter how distasteful to governments, then the world deserved to know. And the mystery man could well be a part of that. Eh, for all I know, he still could be.'

Natasha realised she had not really given this much serious thought. She had no doubts about the genuineness of Ariel's amnesia, but his past remained obscure. Could he have been part of some other secret mission trying to get ahead in the cause of global cooling? It was obvious how popular – and powerful – anyone would become if they learnt how to change the earth's climate on the scale they had seen on Venus. And the commercial gains would be vast.

She put her hands over the fire. 'I assume you know about Ariel's... abilities,' she said.

He nodded. 'A little, yes. He got us into the basement, and somehow freed the oriental guy as well. I tell you, Natasha, those locks were highly advanced. And I have heard he can get into your head as well as through a door.' He looked at her. 'Heart too, perhaps?'

'So what now?' she asked, ignoring the question. 'How are we going to get him to this place in the mountains?'

'I am not sure,' he said, and yawned. 'But I think Marta and Jack are working something out.' His eyes sparkled in the firelight.

'Well,' said Natasha, 'it seems a pity to waste this last log, but it's been a very long day, so if you'll excuse me...'

'But of course. Sleep well, Natasha. And sweet dreams.'

7

Jack's first task the next day was to inform the inspector that an item of evidence from the attic was about to leave the country. He wasn't sure quite how he was going to convince her to let the crystal go, but when it came to it she was most compliant.

'Not to worry, Commander,' she said as she ducked into the front door of the monastery from a sudden shower. 'I have already been told of this. Please go back to your breakfast.' As he turned to go back to the refectory, she caught hold of his hand. 'But thank you for letting me know. I appreciate the courtesy.'

He made his way around the cloister, wondering whether it really was time to shut down the electronic screening over the whole place, at least for a while. Right now the line of communication between

Beth and Olivia was a lot more efficient than the one between him and Constance.

The thought of Constance slowed him down. He was worried about her. It was almost as if she wanted to cast doubt on Ariel's special abilities. But how could they doubt what they had experienced? Then again, what had Constance actually experienced herself? For whatever reason, she had always kept her distance. She had seen nothing with her own eyes, felt nothing in her own head. It wouldn't surprise him if even the voices on the Endeavour commlink recording sounded to her like so much static noise, though he realised now that no one had actually thought to ask her.

As he stepped into the refectory, Jack began to wonder whether the same might not be true of him too. After all, what had he actually experienced first hand? It was true that doors had been opened surprisingly, but there could be other explanations. What had he actually seen with his own eyes? Even out on the surface of Venus all he got was confusion.

He joined Jim and Ryan at the breakfast table where the delicious aromas and buzzing conversation soon drove such thoughts from his mind. And he was delighted to see that both Americans were starting to enjoy the place, in spite of recent events. Or maybe because of them.

The toxicology report had come through. It confirmed that Ryan had fallen foul of the same drug as the one used to abduct Melody and David – another strong suggestion that Nathan was involved all along. It seemed beyond doubt now that he had made sure Ryan would not wake up while he removed the crystal from under his pillow.

Breakfast was already drawing to a close when Jim revealed that their stay was going to end earlier than expected. The pressure was mounting to give NASA something to get its teeth into, not to mention Washington. And with so much of the air cleared, he felt they had no reason to stay longer. They were booked on a flight later that day, and the crystal was to go with them.

'I assume the necessary clearance has been given,' said Jack. 'For security and customs, I mean.'

'You bet,' said Ryan. 'I'm not letting this baby out of my hands again. No sir, not anytime soon.'

'Well, I hope you have better luck this time,' said Jack. 'Just be prepared to think outside the box.'

He took a swig of coffee from his mug, while Ryan gave him a puzzled look, but Jim smiled. 'Okay, my friend,' he said as he rose from the table. 'This is where we part company again. But on better terms, I trust.'

'Aye, that's for sure,' said Jack, and the two men clapped one another in a cautious transatlantic bear hug.

'And the crystal?' said Ryan eagerly.

'Oh right!' said Jack. 'Ha! Almost forgot. We need to go to the incident room, where our friendly police inspector is keeping it warm for us.' He drained his mug. 'Which is more than I can say for this coffee.'

8

The morning brought most of the residents a welcome lull. Melody decided to visit the Hermann Hesse museum in the village at long last. She was unsure when Hannah suggested they go together with Alice, but eventually accepted if only to soften the sharp stab of regret that she had never made it there with Miranda. And at least a public place would prevent them talking about anything personal.

With Ariel still lying unconscious in the infirmary in Ambrose's care, Natasha took Lucien and Marta on a tour of the grounds.

Selena went to her room, where she spread out Ariel's suit on the bed and gazed at it. It simply didn't accord with those early accounts from the Endeavour and Alpha – no shining, no shimmering, no confusing the concentrated gaze. Taking the small piece of material Ryan had already removed, she placed it in a sampling chamber connected to her tablet and started to run more tests.

Leonardo vacated his office so Jack could call Constance. The Abbot intended to have some time in the meditation room but was drawn by voices in the adjoining discussion room. There he found David Carter locked in a lively discussion with Sean MacEvoy. As Leonardo entered the room, the young pastor was chapter and verse on the unique role Jesus Christ played in saving humanity from a fate worse than death. 'There is no other name under heaven,' he urged, 'by which human beings must be saved.'

Sean looked unconvinced. 'What if we do find other races out there, with intelligence, with spirituality? Are they "under heaven"? And what if, for the sake of argument, we were to allow that Ariel is such a being? Are we to assume he too is in need of a Saviour?'

'Why not?' said David. 'Jesus told us to go everywhere, to the ends of the earth.'

While Sean gleefully pointed out that outer space was somewhat beyond those parameters, Leonardo sat down quietly beside them. 'But I take your point,' Sean conceded. 'Ariel has come within our purview. He's here on planet Earth. Even so, again assuming for the sake of argument he's from some other planet, have we the right to take a human message to him? To his race?'

David stroked his chin. 'Well, I don't really know the answer to that. But the gospel is God's message, attested by angels, entrusted to human beings.'

'Ah,' said Sean. 'So you think the Gospel of Mark's young man at the empty tomb, and Luke's two men in shining clothes, were angels?'

'Well yes,' said David. 'Even if you don't think that Mark and Luke are strongly hinting at that – which I personally do – we have Matthew's account which clearly refers to an angel of the Lord.'

'A messenger, I believe it says in the original Greek text.'

'Yes again,' said David, 'because that is what an angel is.'

'Why are they always men?' said Sean without so much as a pause to blink. 'I mean, didn't Jesus say that angels weren't male or female?'

'Er, not exactly,' said David, thrilled to be back in the heat of debate, far from the angst of self-examination. Somehow theology seemed so much easier than confession, and certainly more straightforward than counselling, even with a sparring partner as tricky as Sean MacEvoy. 'When Jesus told some people there would be no marriage in the age to come, he did say this was because we would be like the angels. But whether that means they're two genders or one, or none, I don't think we can say. What we can say is, individual ones are always referred to as male by those who encounter them. In the Bible.'

Sean raised his bushy eyebrows but said nothing.

Leonardo seized the opportunity afforded by the pause. 'Gentlemen, I must say this is very fascinating. Even to me, as one who has not really given the Bible much credence.'

David started at Leonardo's voice. 'Ah, Leonardo. Yes, it is all rather weird, I know, having a conversation like this. When we're talking about someone we know, I mean.'

'Aye,' said Sean, 'but doesn't it just give the whole issue some bite!'

'And there is some urgency,' said Leonardo. 'For the Centre will not remain open to the public for much longer, and we are tasked – or should I say, you are tasked – with getting our beloved teacher and friend, Ariel, to a new place of safety. Apparently one has been chosen that lies in the mountains. So time is short.'

'In the mountains?' said Sean. 'Why there? Why not Geneva?'

'I think there is a desire for continued secrecy,' said Leonardo.

Sean nodded. 'What's happening with the dead man?' he asked. 'I mean, where are they taking the body?'

'To the same place, I believe,' said Leonardo. 'They now have clearance from the local police to remove the body.'

'Though we may have a problem there.' It was Jack, who had obviously finished his call to Geneva. 'It seems our helpful police inspector has assured us of officers on the route we'll be taking, but Beth Griffiths is far from reassured by that. She wants Ariel's move to be as secret as possible.'

'So, what, are we talking about hiding him in the vehicle somehow?' said David. 'Is that the plan?'

'I suppose so,' said Jack, frowning. 'It's all we can do, short of flying him there, and I don't see how we're going to do that. Asking for a local helicopter would draw too much attention, as would flying one in from Geneva.'

'Ah, this is most frustrating,' said Leonardo. 'We have a helicopter here in one of our outbuildings, but currently no pilot. Miss Miranda may have been able to do it, I don't know, but that is of course not possible now. Most annoying. We have the ideal mode of transport, but no one to fly it.'

'Well now,' said Sean with a glint in the eye, 'that may not be strictly true.'

Chapter 29

Intimidation

1

It was time to execute the plan. Still unsure of Geneva's wisdom, Jack could see no better option than spiriting Ariel away, to disappear as mysteriously as he had come. He knew that the air would become even thicker with conspiracy theories, and he accepted that some of them might well strike near the truth. But he could not help feeling more than a twinge of disappointment that Constance was so ready to believe less of Ariel.

Sean had tried to reassure him that she had taken a leaf out of his book, questioning before believing, preferring to live in the honest shadows of uncertainty rather than evangelically proclaim truths that beggared belief. But Natasha encouraged him more with the thought that this might be a manifestation of Constance's more maternal side, choosing the most practical way to protect Ariel.

Today was therefore to be a day of goodbyes. David and Alice had booked an early flight to start their journey home. After a short stay in Geneva, when David would complete the research that had been so violently interrupted, they would both make their way back to Canterbury. Cop had assured Alice that on their return they would be left in peace for as long as they needed.

David didn't know how to tackle the farewell to Mel, and was relieved when she strolled up to him and Alice outside the front door. Hannah was waiting in the wings. Mel tried to assure them both how much she still valued their friendship. All three agreed they needed time to go away and process the events of recent days. 'If I ever get finally debriefed, or demobbed or whatever,' said Melody, 'I think I'll lie low for a while... maybe join Jack on a trip to see his father in Edinburgh.'

When David and Alice had gone, she turned back to Hannah. 'Did I gush too much? You know, overdo the let's-stay-friends thing?'

Hannah took her by the arm and led her back towards the cloister. 'You did just great,' she purred. 'And anyway, everyone's feeling sad right now, or awkward, or just plain anxious about what's going to happen.'

They had scarcely crossed the courtyard when Selena appeared from the stairs. Melody greeted her. 'How's it going with the suit?'

Selena shook her head. 'To be honest I am quite mystified,' she said. 'Its molecular structure seems very straightforward now, almost like it's settled down to normality. I'm keeping a tiny sample for further research, but I've decided to give it back to Jack. We both feel that it should go with Ariel.'

'Oh Selena,' said Melody, 'that is so amazing!' With tears welling up she stretched out her arms, and Selena gladly accepted the hug. 'Right,' said Melody, 'sorry about the emotion. Bit wobbly at the mo.'

'Then I am sorry I must say goodbye to you,' said Selena. 'Only I shan't be stopping long in Geneva. It's time to get back.' They hugged once more amid earnest promises of mutual visits in the future.

Less than an hour later Jack, Natasha, Melody, Hannah and Sean gathered by the statue in the centre of the main courtyard and waited for Leonardo to appear. Natasha couldn't resist running her hand under the sill around the base of the statue. She was surprised when she encountered the rough patch again.

'Jack!' she cried. 'It's still here – Miranda's listening device!'

Jack gave a low whistle. 'Yikes, I'd completely forgotten about that. Still, best leave it. It's in my report, and I guess Beth will see to it, along with the attic and any other surprises lurking behind closed doors.'

'Talking of which,' said Sean, 'where do you keep a helicopter around here?'

'It's in one of the outhouses.' Leonardo stepped out from the corridor behind them. 'It is at your disposal, insured and ready to fly.'

Jack was still nervous about a man Sean's age taking it up, but the advantages were too great to resist. Sean was in the know, and that meant no one else need be brought in. And it felt like time was of the essence. No one knew who Nathan Dexter had been working for, or what their next move might be.

Lucien and Marta emerged from the infirmary. 'We're ready,' said Lucien. 'The body is in the back of the car Beth provided.'

'Very good,' said Leonardo. 'And Brother Ambrose tells me that Ariel will be ready for you very soon.' He looked up at the statue with its familiar depiction of the four elements – the flowers, the panpipes, the firebrand and the bucket of water. He gazed up at the stars depicted on the cloak, which he had long suspected were a subtle nod to the fifth element. He gave a wistful sigh as he recalled Ariel's jest about element number four-point-five.

He turned to address his friends. 'Now I too must say goodbye. Not just to you wonderful, fascinating, magnificent people, but to this place.'

'What!' Melody could not contain the shock.

'Only for a while! At least, that is my hope,' he said with a smile, though somehow its usual warmth seemed to drain away all too quickly. 'I have been recalled to Tibet where I must answer for recent events face to face.' He waved a hand in Jack's direction before he could say anything. 'Please, do not worry. It is what it is, as people so often say. None of us could have expected things to turn out this way, and all of you really have enriched this place more than you know.'

With much shaking of hands and further words of farewell they slowly dispersed, leaving Leonardo gazing up at the motionless figure of stone.

2

Three hours later Sean was singing in full voice as he guided the small chopper south-east towards Lake Lugano on the ten-mile flight to the medical outpost. In the back Ariel was strapped in, a cushioned collar round his neck, while Natasha watched him intently from the other seat. They had decided to give Ariel headphones as well, just in case he awoke mid-flight in need of rapid reassurance. For her part Natasha was not convinced that Sean should be enjoying himself quite so much. But it seemed that a return to the cockpit was proving to be quite a thrill.

But that was not the truth of it. Underneath the song Sean was doing battle with both present and past. For the present, although it was only a short flight, he was keenly aware that with only one engine his options were severely limited in the event of mechanical failure over this terrain. On top of that, it occurred to him only now that his licence did not extend to Switzerland. The whole idea seemed crazier with every passing minute.

He sang louder.

The lake came into view. Flying as low as he dared, he swept over the road and railway that intersected the water like a low-level dam. Then he hugged the shoreline, only ending his song when the navigation screen indicated they were nearing their destination.

There were trees everywhere, and the further he flew from the lake the closer these came to the bottom of the small craft. The ground was rising relentlessly. When Natasha turned on a light to get a better look at Ariel, Sean saw her reflection in the curved glass of the cockpit. Only it wasn't Natasha, it was Imogen, and she was calling their daughter's name.

The past had struck a paralysing blow.

Natasha's voice came through on the com, shattering the vision. 'Sean! Slow down!' He pulled back on the controls and the craft lurched upwards and sideways. For the first time Ariel groaned. Natasha's heart was in her mouth.

The manoeuvre was enough. The trees receded and suddenly they were above the hill. Between them and the next rise was a church, and behind this Sean could see a road with a modern-looking building at the end of it. On its flat roof was a large circle with a red cross, and he knew it to be his destination.

3

Jack squeezed into the back of the makeshift hearse. Nathan's coffin was carefully covered with a tent and other camping equipment. This mission was so far off the radar that no one outside of a few at the UN must know. Plus one Inspector Bandalucci, whose discretion simply had to be a matter of trust. Jack didn't expect problems on the way, though if they were stopped he wondered whether a Frenchman, a German and a Scotsman would seem likely camping companions, outside of a joke. They spent the first five minutes of the journey sketching a story just in case.

Lucien was at the wheel. At first they followed the car's navigation system, plotting a discreet way through local streets that would bring them out onto the southbound carriageway of the autostrada. Jack couldn't help feeling he should be travelling with Ariel, who had not been unconscious for this long since their return from Venus. But the chopper was too small, and he was quite sure that Natasha remained the best protector Ariel could have. That and being several hundred metres above another potential abduction.

But who were they protecting him from? If Nathan had been behind the attempt to abduct Ariel, who was behind Nathan? And what about other parties with the same idea? The best he could hope for now was that Nathan represented the only well-informed attempt. Success now lay in secrecy.

The car was slowing down. 'Toll,' said Lucien. Jack tried to shake off the unfamiliar anxiety. The dashboard indicated toll paid as they began to cross over Lake Lugano. The minutes passed. All was well.

As they passed a sign saying they were in Melano Lucien switched the car's navigation and drive systems to a pre-programmed setting. He kept his hands near the wheel, but the car negotiated the exit and the local traffic before it turned left up towards the Sanctuary of the Madonna. Steadily they climbed the hillside. All other traffic was gone now, and they were soon in thick woodland, the autumn leaves reflecting browns and golds on every side, while the low sun flashed continuously through the trees as they passed. Jack sighed as he thought of the view Ariel must have missed as he had flown overhead, fast asleep. 'They should be there by now,' he said.

The car twisted and turned further up into the foothills. Then, as it came out of a sharp bend, it slowed unexpectedly. They all looked ahead at the cause. Emergency vehicle lights were flashing red and blue, and a police officer was waving at them to stop.

'Okay guys,' said Jack, 'we might need that story yet.' Time to test the Inspector's discretion.

Lucien lowered the window for the approaching officer. He was wearing a blue jacket, and as he got closer Lucien thought he had a vaguely oriental look about him. He began talking in Italian, until Lucien asked for French, but when the man shook his head they both decided on English.

'You need to turn around,' said the officer, gesticulating. 'Accident here.'

Lucien found Jack's eyes in his mirror and gave him a what-do-we-do-now look.

Jack decided to use his UN status. He got out of the car and walked round the front of the vehicle, keeping the attention away from the back. The first thing he noticed was the officer's hand straying close to a holstered gun on his utility belt. Aware he needed to speak sooner rather than later, Jack held up his hands and said, 'Military – we're military personnel. We need to get through to an important meeting at the mountain hospital.' Carefully he pointed his eband at a small tattoo-like stamp on his left forearm and scanned it, before sharing it with the officer. It confirmed he was with British Intelligence, seconded to the United Nations.

The officer seemed to relax. 'Wait please.' He walked back to his patrol car, leant in through the open driver's door and talked with someone inside. Jack couldn't be sure if there was anyone else there or if he was using the radio. Moments later the officer beckoned to him to come closer. As Jack reached the car he was surprised to see the officer draw the gun from his holster and point it straight at him, shouting something in Italian. It sounded like a warning – one that could only be meant for the benefit of the car radio. Whatever it was, it gave Jack enough time to roll forward on the ground and sweep the officer's legs from under him.

Instantly Marta and Lucien were out of the car. While Lucien rushed to assist Jack, Marta went to the other side of the patrol car, a small pistol stretched out before her in both hands. She tried to peer through the front passenger window, but all she could see was the reflected glory of autumn leaves. Quickly she opened the door and stepped back, still pointing the gun straight ahead. A man's body slumped out, his head hitting the ground with a dull thud. He was wearing a police shirt.

Checking that no one else was in the vehicle, she rushed round to the other side, firing into the air. The three men stopped their tussle instantly. Jack and Lucien hauled the fake officer to his feet.

'Where did you get that?' said Jack, staring at the gun in Marta's hands.

'A girl has secrets,' she said. 'What do we do now?'

'We get this car out of the road,' said Jack, and take our friend here with us to the facility. You can keep an eye on him if you sit in the back with the gun, and I'll come behind in the police car.'

'Jack, we have a problem,' said Marta.

'Another one?'

Stepping back while keeping her gun trained on their attacker, she showed them the dead police officer on the other side of the car. Jack groaned.

'I think I see,' said Lucien. 'He kills the cop, then he kills you... us... and leaves one of us here as the dead killer in a shooting.'

Jack nodded. 'Aye, a shoot-out that happened after he conveniently called out a warning. Marta, keep him in your sights. We need to look at that radio now. If police headquarters heard that warning then we're going to have to explain. I can mention our friendly Inspector Bonder...

'Bandalucci,' said Marta.

While Lucien carefully heaved the police officer's body back into the passenger seat, Jack got in the other side and started to examine the radio. He was just about to speak when Marta suddenly came crashing onto his lap. The twenty seconds it took for Lucien to get round the car, and for Jack and Marta to disentangle themselves, was enough. The man had disappeared into the woods.

The radio crackled into life. '*Angelo! Angelo! Stai bene?*'

Jack hesitated.

'Let me,' said Lucien. '*Si, si, va bene. La radio–*' He clicked the radio off.

'Well done,' said Jack. 'I thought you couldn't speak Italian.'

'It was not exactly advanced, eh?' Lucien shrugged.

'I'm all right, by the way!' called Marta, who had chased after the man and was now emerging from the trees at the roadside. 'I think he fell over there. It's pretty steep.'

The two men poured out apologies for ignoring her, which continued for quite some time until Marta kissed them both on the lips, Jack first and then Lucien, where she lingered.

'Er, right,' said Jack, still unnerved by Marta's unpredictability, to say nothing of her coolness in a fight. He turned back to the car. 'I don't think we can go chasing anyone in the woods right now. The police will have to do a search. Talking of whom... I wouldn't be surprised if another patrol car turned up pretty soon. We need to get to this facility. It can't be far away. I'm just hoping there hasn't really been an accident. I'll drive the patrol car and the lately departed officer. You two bring up the rear.'

Lucien raised his eyebrows.

'Follow on!' said Jack. 'It means follow on behind.'

'*Ah oui.*'

They returned to their makeshift hearse while Jack fastened the seatbelt across the dead police officer. He started the engine, but before he could pull away Lucien came running back up the hill, calling Jack to stop.

'What is it?' asked Jack through the open window.

'It's Dexter!' he cried. 'He's gone.'

4

Sean worked hard to control his breathing as he gently lowered the helicopter towards the landing pad. He knew he was turning too fast, and the flashing of bright sunlight soon told him he was in a spin. He pulled up again. 'Sorry,' was all Natasha heard.

He began the descent for a second time. Now there were crosswinds to contend with. Where had they come from? He put it down to flying in the Alps and cursed himself for ever thinking he could do this. Clutching the main control stick he pivoted the craft as close to a hover as he could manage. 'Okay, everybody!' he shouted. 'Brace for impact. We're going down!'

He took stock of the situation as they hovered a few metres above the roof of the medical station. The winds were definitely coming from both sides and were totally unpredictable. Steadying the craft as level as he could, he eased the throttle and brought her down. It felt like now or never, and he cut the power. The chopper slumped on to the pad with an enormous thud, followed by a cracking sound. Immediately the whole craft began to slide. They were down, but the winds kept coming.

'Hold tight!' Sean shouted again. 'We may be going over!' And with that the landing skids screamed across the concrete until they went over the edge of the roof.

Natasha felt her seatbelt burn into her shoulder as the craft rolled onto a lower part of the hospital roof. As they continued to slide, upside down, she thought she could hear the sound of scraping even through her headphones, though it seemed to be mixed with a primal scream somewhere in her head. She looked in horror as the edge of the roof came rushing towards them. One more flip and they were off the roof entirely. Sudden weightlessness, then a teeth-crunching thud.

The craft was almost still now, though it felt like some giant hand was still tugging at it as the winds howled. It had come to rest more or less up the right way. Dazed but driven on by the adrenalin of fear and guilt, Sean unbelted himself and clambered into the back, only to find Ariel tugging at his seatbelt in a frenzy, saying, 'I'm sorry, I'm sorry,' over and over again.

'All right, old chum,' Sean soothed. 'Calm down now. We're okay, but we need to get out of this mess. All right?'

'I'm sorry, I couldn't hold it!'

Ignoring Ariel's ravings, Sean turned to Natasha. He retracted her safety belt and smoothed her hair from her face. 'Talk to me, Natasha!'

His frown turned to a grin as he saw the light dawn in her eyes. 'That's my resurrection girl. Come on, now. We need to get out. Ariel's ready. See?'

At the sound of Ariel's name she started to climb out of the seat.

'Okay now,' said Sean, 'we've had a bit of a prang, and our position is a tad precarious. I'm going to climb out of my door, then I need you to guide Ariel out through his. And you follow. Are you with me?'

She nodded, and Sean carefully climbed out of the craft. 'There's a bit of a drop!' he shouted over the wind's fury. 'Just slide him down and I'll make sure he lands on his feet.'

Natasha removed Ariel's headgear and then her own, before twisting him out through the door feet first and lowering him from the shoulders down towards Sean. At that moment she felt Ariel tense and almost jump from the copter, landing right in front of Sean.

She looked out of the door for the first time and gauged the situation. The craft had rolled over the stepped roof on to the higher ground behind the building, which meant it had dropped by only one storey, probably no more than three metres. Mercifully it was wedged against the back wall of the building, one of its long rotor blades partly buried in the leafy soil of the hillside that rose steeply behind the hospital. Yet she could see that it might not hold for long, so with the wind screaming angrily in her ears she jumped from the craft. Taking Ariel by the arm, she started to pull him away, leaves lashing against her face. Sean joined her on Ariel's other arm, and together they half-led, half-carried their patient around the corner of the building.

They waited for the sound of twisted metal as the helicopter would surely be torn from its temporary mooring, but it didn't come. The winds dropped in a heartbeat. Ariel sank to the ground, followed by his two guides, backs to the wall, and together they watched the sunlight dance through the trees once more.

'I'm sorry,' Ariel gasped. 'I couldn't hold it. I don't know—'

'*You're* sorry,' said Sean. 'That really was not my best landing ever!'

'You were brilliant!' said Natasha. 'A bit rusty perhaps...' They both succumbed to an irresistible urge to laugh. 'Though honestly,' she went on, 'that wasn't right.'

'I know. It must be the type of controls. I'm not used to them all being in one central stick.'

'No,' she said, 'I don't mean you! I mean the wind. What on earth made it behave like that?'

Ariel looked up at her. 'Nothing,' he said simply. 'Nothing on earth did that.'

5

Jack pulled into a small car park in front of the two-storey building that sat snugly in a hollow on the steep wooded hillside. It looked like a cross between a mountain rescue post and a cottage hospital. After a few seconds he realised his hands were still firmly clenched round the wheel. He had some explaining to do. There was a figure in a dark red winter coat with black fur-lined collars standing at the front door. When he saw it was Beth Griffiths, his whole body relaxed. He let go of the wheel and got out of the car just as Lucien and Marta drove up behind him.

'I was wondering why a police car had come calling,' said Beth, leaning against the doorpost. 'Now I'm wondering why you're the one driving it!'

'Long story.'

She looked across to the other car. 'Have you got a body for me?'

'Well,' said Jack, 'about that. I do have a body. It's just not the one we set out with.'

Beth's hand went to her forehead. 'You'd best come in,' she sighed. 'It's turning out to be rather an eventful day.'

'Will do, but first I'd like to move the body, if that's okay.' As he walked back to the car she saw the unexpected passenger slumped inside.

'What about Nathan?' she called out.

Lucien joined them. 'Gone, I regret to say it.'

Parking her fast multiplying questions, Beth prepared the front room for the body. They carried it on the stretcher that had originally been used for Nathan's body and laid it on the floor before covering it with a sheet. Beth called Inspector Bandalucci.

'I'm afraid I couldn't stop her coming,' she said after the call.

'Hardly surprising,' said Jack. 'So tell me, why has your day been eventful already? And where's the helicopter? Surely they've arrived by now?'

'They have,' she said, 'though the chopper's a wreck. I've never seen a storm like it.'

'Storm?' said Jack. 'What storm? It was pretty quiet on the way up here.'

She led them all up some wide stairs to the top storey and through to a room at the back where, because of the steep gradient, they were now back at ground level. As she opened the blinds Marta gasped at the sight of the mangled wreck jammed up against the building.

Lucien whispered something in French.

'Okay,' said Jack. 'I'm guessing they're okay, or you'd have said something by now.'

'Oh yes!' Beth replied breezily. 'In fact, the whole business woke Ariel up. So that's a result, isn't it?' Jack couldn't be sure whether it was relief he was detecting in her voice or some kind of manic resignation.

'Jack!'

He turned to see Natasha standing in the doorway. When she marched over and hugged him he knew all was not well. 'Where is he?' he asked as she quickly unclasped herself. 'And how's that mad Irishman?'

They filed into an adjacent room where Sean was sitting at a low table. Ariel was lying on a flat bed, on the point of going into the body scanner. When he saw Jack he sat up. Jack looked across to the operator who nodded his approval, and he sat down beside him.

'Ariel, you don't look so good.'

'Oh Jack, I've failed.'

'How's that, old friend?' Jack put his arm around Ariel's shoulders. Something had changed.

'I couldn't stop it. I couldn't hold them back, and I couldn't hold us up.'

Natasha sat down by Sean. 'He's been talking like this since we... landed.'

'Crashed,' said Sean.

'Crash-landed,' Natasha persisted. 'The conditions were terrible, frightening. Sean was amazing.'

'Well, you're all in one piece,' said Jack.

'More than you can say for the helicopter,' said Sean drily.

'I'm sure the Temple of the Four Elements has adequate insurance,' said Beth.

'I wouldn't be so sure,' said Sean. 'I'm not licensed to fly here.'

Natasha's eyes widened. 'But... I thought...'

'Oh, I'm a qualified pilot,' said Sean, 'but I'm not registered with the local authorities.'

'Leave that with me,' said Beth. 'There's someone at Locarno I can talk to. Now, shall we get on with the business? It's why we're here, after all.'

They went back downstairs, leaving the operator to his work. Ariel lay down and looked up at the ceiling before he was slowly swallowed up by the machine.

6

Olivia Bandalucci knew how to play the long game. Clearly the suspicious death in Montagnola was part of a bigger picture, and it would take time for other aspects to emerge. But the death of a fellow officer took it to a different level. Everyone in her department would soon be all over it, and the media would be only two seconds behind. None of her colleagues, however loyal, would keep a lid on this for long. In fact their very loyalty would send them in search of justice for their fallen colleague. She knew she could not contain this much longer, even for the security services.

Beth Griffiths had said little on her call – just enough to lead Olivia to tread carefully. She had already recalled one patrol car just before it had climbed the hill to investigate an interrupted call. Then she had told the officer on radio duty at headquarters that she was going to carry out a preliminary investigation, and that they should wait before sending anyone else out. She knew that uniform would be finding this difficult, not to say downright suspicious, and the forensic team would want to know why the car had been moved. It was only a matter of time before the truth was out.

All of which was why, when she arrived at the medical station, Beth could only agree: the situation would be very hard to contain for long. 'Maybe we shouldn't try,' said Jack, after Beth had called him into the front office to join them. While Beth frowned, Olivia looked hopeful. 'I mean, we're not the criminals here,' he added, 'and we can't go on hiding Ariel much longer. Everything is going to have to come out sooner or later.'

'Quite,' said Beth, 'and it's my job to make sure it's later.'

Jack smiled. 'Usually, yes, I grant you. But look, we're all officers of the law here. We need to catch the people who stole Nathan's body.'

'*Che?!*' Olivia exploded.

'Ah,' said Jack. 'Has Beth not mentioned that?' He cleared his throat. 'I'm sure she was just about to.'

Beth sighed.

Jack proceeded to give a full account of what had occurred on the journey, taking care only to talk about what happened on the ground and leave Beth to say as much or as little as she wanted about the helicopter crash.

Olivia listened carefully, interrupting only for minor points of clarification. Although her eband was sure to be recording, Jack noticed that she occasionally scribbled something with a pen in an antiquated-looking notepad. From where he sat he couldn't be sure whether she was writing or drawing.

When he had finished, Olivia tossed a surprisingly warm and natural smile in Jack's direction. 'Thank you, Jack. I really appreciate your candour. Now then, I hope you will both understand that I will have to bring a full investigative team here. I think some of that can wait until tomorrow, but what cannot wait is the transfer of the officer's body.'

'Of course,' said Beth, pleased to be relieved of at least one responsibility.

'And,' said Jack, 'my colleague Marta Bergstrom should be able to help you in the search for the killer. She saw where he scuttled away. Probably fell.'

'Hmm,' said Olivia. 'This also cannot wait. I will get a team up with search equipment and dogs. And I'll be back in the morning.'

And with that she left the building, already giving instructions on her eband.

Beth turned to Jack.

'Before you say anything,' he pre-empted, 'I rather think that our beloved leader will welcome this.'

'Constance, you mean? She's not my leader, Jack. But what are you saying?' Tiredness was creeping into her voice.

'Well, I've detected a certain desire to play down Ariel's special abilities, and it wouldn't surprise me if she welcomed the opportunity to shroud the whole of Project Icarus in a mist of confusion and conspiracy theories.'

Beth nodded slowly. 'Right. I think I see. And a disappearing body might be very handy.'

'It might,' said Jack, 'though obviously anyone looking into things carefully would soon be questioning the body count. But there could be possibilities here, with certain media at least.'

'Well, whatever happens, it's out of our hands now,' she said as she flopped into a nearby chair. 'It's all a bit of a puzzle, though, isn't it, Jack? I mean, I for one have favoured the bio-enhancement theory all along, you know. But it's not as if anyone's popped up anywhere claiming the poor guy. If he's someone's asset, why aren't they coming to collect? And where are they hiding? We've looked for them, believe you me.'

'We?'

'High Command, British Intelligence, Washington and a few others I'll not mention. But no credible operation has been found. Even Conway Box has tried to find them in his own ham-fisted way!'

'Box?' Jack exclaimed.

'The very same,' said Beth. 'Like a bull in the proverbial he's probably singlehandedly shut down any hope we have of finding them – if they exist.' She sighed. 'No, if Ariel was working for someone, they seem to have cast him off, whoever they were.' She hauled herself out of the chair. 'Come on, let's go and see how our scan technician is getting on.'

Jack revisited the bio-enhancement idea in his mind but remained unconvinced. Even if the enhancement was only temporary, surely those responsible would be desperate to find him and examine him. If they did exist, they must be very patient, waiting for the dust to settle.

He followed Beth back upstairs, followed by Natasha and Sean. Lucien and Marta had stepped outside to look at the helicopter.

The operator was just coming out of the scan chamber. He was smiling. 'All normal,' he said in a strong German accent. 'I think our patient is fine.'

Jack went in and sat down next to Ariel who was drinking a cup of coffee in the recovery chair. 'Hello Jack,' he said. 'It seems I'm normal.'

While Sean and Beth hovered around the doorway, Natasha came and sat down with Jack and Ariel. 'I don't understand,' she said.

Jack turned to Beth. 'Are we sure this thing is working properly?'

Beth called the technician back in. 'It is all good,' he said. 'Some of the neural pathways looked unusual at first–'

'Unusual?' said Jack.

'*Ja*. But I checked the calibration, and the second time it all looked perfectly normal.'

'Okay,' said Beth. 'Thanks. Can you get the results sent off to Geneva? Then you can go back if you like. I'll follow on tomorrow.'

When the technician had gone, Jack looked long and hard at Ariel. 'Well, my friend,' he said at last, 'you've been called a few things in the past few weeks, but normal has never been one of them.'

'I know, Jack.' he replied, 'It is bemusing, isn't it?'

'Well,' said Beth, 'I can only think that whoever... enhanced you, has either lost interest or, more likely, wants to keep their distance. Clearly the effect doesn't last.'

'Maybe it went wrong,' said Sean in a voice that Natasha took to be more sarcastic than serious. But there was disappointment and resignation there too, as if yet another 'proof' of alien identity had collapsed under a heap of actual data.

Lucien and Marta came running up the stairs. 'Has she gone?' said Lucien as they stepped into the crowded room.

'She has,' said Beth, 'but she'll be back, and a whole lot more police besides. And I'll need you both to co-operate fully with her investigation.' She raised her hand. 'It's okay! Jack and I have decided honesty might be the best policy on this occasion.'

Lucien nodded. 'And the helicopter?'

'Ah,' said Beth. 'I think that's outside the bounds of honesty just at the moment. You know nothing about that.'

'*Mais oui,*' he shrugged. '*C'est vrai, non?*'

'Now then,' Beth continued. 'There's not enough room for all of us to stay here tonight, unless we want to sleep on stretchers. Jack, can you stay here with Ariel? We're going to have to sort out this helicopter business in the morning. Meanwhile, I suggest the rest of you join me in a hotel down in the town.'

'I'd like to stay,' said Natasha.

'Of course you would,' said Beth drily. 'Assuming we agree that Ariel should have a proper bed, I'll leave you and Jack to fight it out for the other one.'

7

Two hours later Jack and Natasha were clearing away paper plates and food packaging. 'This brings back memories,' said Natasha. 'It's almost as bad as cosmonaut food!'

'Aye, it's true, I've had better,' said Jack. 'But the company is perfect.'

They were sitting in the front room of the medical facility, watching the twilight seep into the forest around them. The police had removed the officer's body, and Ariel was outside, looking up at the trees.

'We've come a long way,' said Natasha.

Jack nodded. 'I wonder who's come the furthest. Ariel seems different now. And I don't just mean what the scans are telling us.'

'If we know what they are telling us,' said Natasha. 'I'm not sure that technician really knew.'

'I've been thinking about that,' said Jack. 'About what he didn't record – the first scan.'

'The one that made no sense? The... unusual neural pathways?'

'The very same. Let's take a look, shall we?'

They climbed the stairs and went into the scan chamber. Natasha booted up the machinery. 'Password-protected, of course,' she said. 'Pity we don't have physical records, like the old days.'

'Hold on a mo,' said Jack and promptly disappeared into the neighbouring room. A few moments later he returned with a triumphant grin on his face, holding up two transparent sheets. 'What you said made me wonder if the operator made a hard copy. So I went to the printer, called up recent items, and hey presto!'

They sat down and looked closely at the records. They couldn't make much sense of them, but they could see the earlier one was different. They were dated and timed, though no name or context was given.

'Well,' said Jack when they had finally decided they could get no further, 'let's put them away safely. You never know when they might be useful.'

'Talking of safety,' said Natasha. 'Where's Ariel?'

They hurried back down the stairs, only to see him coming in through the front door. 'There are a number of police down the road,' he said. 'I thought it wise to come back inside. Anyway, it's getting cold out there.'

Jack and Natasha looked at each other. They couldn't remember ever hearing Ariel mention the cold, or come to that any kind of discomfort.

'How are you feeling now?' Natasha asked.

ARIEL

'Oh, a bit lost, I suppose.' His voice was flat. 'I'm afraid that helicopter ride rather did me in.'

'Can you tell us about it?' said Natasha. 'And what you meant about the turbulence we experienced when we got here?'

'Didn't you hear the voices?' he asked. 'They're gone now.'

'You almost sound disappointed,' said Jack.

'Yes,' said Ariel. 'I feel... disconnected. Things are very quiet in my head.'

'I'm glad you have some peace,' said Natasha.

'Oh, it's not peace,' said Ariel. 'Something's brewing. I just can't quite access it. I just feel very let down.'

Natasha dropped her gaze.

'Not by you!' Ariel added quickly. 'Never by you. I think I'm talking about those I used to be with.'

'Makes sense,' said Jack. 'Beth says we've received no claims on you. No one's owning up to anything.' He showed Ariel the scans. 'I think what we have here may document some kind of change. I suspect that, whatever the reason for your special abilities, the process may be wearing off.'

'I think so too,' said Ariel. 'I have never felt so weak. When I woke up in that helicopter I found I had practically no influence on the descent of the craft. No real strength against the wind. I knew we were going to hit the ground. And Jack, I was afraid.'

'No shame in that,' he said.

Ariel looked unconvinced. 'I suppose not. But it didn't feel right. I even wonder now whether I would be able to protect myself against attack.'

'You mean physical attack?' Natasha asked.

'I'm not sure what I mean,' said Ariel. 'Yes, physical attack, if I had to face another gun butt. Or pen nib!' He allowed himself a brief smile. 'But it's as though I've lost myself, like a beached whale, or a grounded bird. I feel so... helpless.'

Natasha took his hand. What she said next took Jack by complete surprise. 'Why don't you come and stay with me for a while in Russia?'

648

Ariel looked at her, eye to eye. 'I'd like that very much.'

They decided to call it a day. Ariel retired to a small ward room at the back of the building. There was no window, but it was cosy.

Jack and Natasha returned to one of the front rooms. 'Well, I've made up a bed here,' he said, pointing to the place where they had previously laid the murdered police officer. When Natasha began to object he raised a hand. 'No, I'm fine here. You take the room next to Ariel.'

As she turned to go, he called her back. 'Natasha, did you really mean that? That you'd set up home with him?'

'As a lodger, yes,' she said.

'Right,' said Jack. 'Though you need to face the possibility, lass, that Ariel won't be free for a while.'

'That's okay,' she said. 'Nor will we.'

'How d'you mean?'

'We have the world tour to do... you know, to celebrate our historic trip to Venus. Jack, had you forgotten?'

'Ah, right. Of course.' He yawned. "One other thing. I've been in touch with Constance, now we're getting messages again, and it seems Miranda is awake.'

Natasha's eyes lit up. 'We should go and see her.'

'That we should,' said Jack. 'We surely need something to cheer us up.'

8

Once they leave the narrow streets of Melano and climb steadily into its dramatic backdrop of forested hills, the cobbles of the *Via alla Madonna* become rough and spaced out as the road snakes its way heavenward. Olivia was glad of the wire fence that afforded some protection against what might fall from above, but she could see that the drop on the other side was marked by nothing more than the occasional wooden post and a flat ridge of stone running between them. With the light fading she knew an accident might be just one false step away. She recalled the search team.

She met with her lieutenant where they had parked outside the Sanctuary of the Madonna, a level haven in this land of steep inclines and perilous drops. He had examined the point at the roadside indicated by Marta and seen evidence of a fall, or possibly a slide, down through the forest, but there were no other traces. As for Dexter's body, they decided it must have been wheeled back down the road and into a car.

When the officer had gone Olivia leant against her car and thought about her witnesses. Every bone in her detective's body told her that Lucien Barretours and Marta Bergstrom were not to be trusted, and yet she had no reason to doubt their story. Jack Forrester was even trickier. He actually did seem trustworthy, a regular boy scout, but as an intelligence agent he was surely accustomed to withholding the full story, not least from the police.

Then there was Eucabeth Griffiths. She had checked her out online and in police records. High up in High Command at the UN. What was she up to? And why was she transporting her colleague's body here? It made no sense. Unless, of course, secrecy was the issue. Secrecy from other colleagues. And so a picture of internal intrigue and deception began to take shape in Olivia's mind.

She slipped into the church. The contrast was immediate. Gone the simplicity of forest and sky. Here white fluted columns led her eye to sumptuous paintings overhead, while below these an ornate altar of white and gold stood proud and tall. More paintings decorated every wall.

She sat down on one of the wooden pews, which seemed to be the only objects of simplicity here. The fuss all around seemed to mirror her own thoughts. What she needed was perspective.

How long was it since she had been to mass? She couldn't say. And what would she confess? She realised she wouldn't know where to start. Nothing to declare.

She thought about the man in the middle of it all, the one they called Ariel. She hadn't been able to interview him because he was in a coma. Same went for the mysterious Miranda Freeman. Was she a harmless bystander? Unlikely, given who she worked for.

But Ariel. This was the stowaway they brought back from another world. By any reckoning he was interview candidate number one. She made up her mind to insist she be given access to him as soon as he awoke.

As she stood up to leave, Jack Forrester came back into her mind. She smiled. Maybe there was something to confess after all.

Chapter 30

Revelation

1

Ariel was going down again. Sean wrestled with a snake coiled around the flight console, while Natasha sat motionless, her head back and her milk-white throat exposed. Ariel couldn't move. The snake was around Sean now, crushing him. The trees were ever nearer, no longer friendly but reaching out with jagged limbs that threatened to crumple them all.

He tried to get out of the bonds that fastened him, but they would not give. The snake was nearer now, drawn by the soft, smooth throat. This was not acceptable. He could not let Natasha die.

One supreme effort and his bonds broke. He was free.

He was still falling.

The snake dissolved into a fiery orange as the ragged mountainside opened its volcanic maw, ready to receive its prey. There was not a tree or lake in sight – no green, no blue. Just endless yellow and orange, acid rain and choking sulphur.

The surface of the planet rose up to strike him. Yet, even as he braced himself for the collision, a white light shone out of the mountainside. Held aloft now by Natasha, who stood glorious in her suit of glass and gauze, it blazed. And he gazed into its glory.

They were calling his name. The voices of friends.

No Stranger. No Icarus. No Ariel. Another name. His name.

The light exploded in her hand.

He awoke.

2

It took less than two hours for Jack to realise that his camping days might be behind him. Sleep in his fleece top had been patchy and his back was sore. He rolled out of the makeshift bed, stood up and stretched. The room was cold now, the only light a dim wash of insipid yellow coming from some sort of medical equipment in the corner.

He walked to the window and prised open a couple of slats on the ancient-looking blind. It was so dark he could barely make out a single tree. He was just about to remove his fingers when something like a long flash of lightning lit up the forest.

No thunder followed, but it took several moments for the imprint of the scene to fade from his vision. And as it did, he began to see it more clearly. Imprinted on his retina he could make out individual trees and, across the car park, standing between two of them, the silhouette of a human figure.

He looked out of the window again. Too dark. Dressing quickly, he went to the front door. It was locked. Perhaps Ariel had got his old tricks back, though it occurred to him now that Ariel had never been one to relock anything he had opened.

He turned the key and heard the bolts slip clear. Gingerly he opened the door and stepped outside. No point in shilly-shallying. 'Ariel!' he called in a loud whisper. 'Ariel? Is that you?'

'Hello Jack.'

To his surprise the voice came from behind. He spun round to see Ariel standing in the dim light of the hallway inside. 'Ah,' he said, 'there you are. Ariel, I think we've got company.'

'Yes,' said Ariel. 'But she's asleep.'

'Natasha?' said Jack. 'Aye, good, then let's not wake her. But I mean out here. I just saw someone.' He didn't wait for an answer, but stepped inside and grabbed a large torch that he had seen hanging near the front door. Ariel stayed put as Jack rushed back outside and swept the area, shining the powerful beam into the trees and bushes, and even under his car. He was about to check round the back of the building when Ariel spoke again.

'It's all right, Jack. It's a friend.'

'What?'

'A familiar face. Jack, listen to me. It's time to go.'

'Go?' said Jack, as annoyance began to give way to fear. 'Go where? What do you mean? Where are we going?'

'It's all right,' Ariel said again. 'Don't be alarmed. Come with me. I'd like you to come with me.'

Only now did Jack shine the torch in Ariel's direction, taking care not to shine it into his face. The light of the torch seemed to be absorbed before it was released in a shimmer of silvers and whites.

'The suit! You're wearing your suit!'

'I took it from your bag, Jack. I trust you don't mind.'

'Ariel,' Jack stammered, 'what's going on?'

'Take my hand, Jack. I don't think we have much time.'

'But...'

Ariel held out his hand. 'Trust me, Jack.'

Jack sighed. Sensing the renewed confidence in Ariel, and welcoming it, he took his hand. 'Okay, my friend. What now?'

Instantly he felt a rush of air on his face, and he dropped the torch. He looked down and saw it shining far below on the fast-receding ground. Instinctively he grasped both Ariel's hands and looked for safety in his eyes. A soft light bathed them both. Jack risked one more glance below. All he saw was treetops rushing away down the mountainside below.

3

Natasha was restless. She tossed her head this way and that, but was unable to escape the dream. If it was a dream. She was in a strange bed, and over her head a thick darkness loomed like a mountain in the night.

A noise came from outside. Awake now, if dimly, she got up, automatically donning her tracksuit before quietly walking along the hall to the front of the building. She looked through the clear glass of the front door and peered out into the woods. Was somebody there? It looked like there was a torch on the ground, still turned on. Her eye was caught by a hint of a movement to the left, in a small corner. With little reflection in the glass she could make out a hungry fox nosing around a bin that had toppled over.

The sense of relief was short-lived. Some sixth sense told her someone, or something, was behind her. And now she felt intense heat, although she could see no reflection of a fire and her back turned icy cold. She froze. Sweat began to trickle into her eyes, but when she went to wipe it away her hand wouldn't budge. The only thing to move were the hairs on the back of her neck. She tried to call out for help, but all she could summon was a squeak of a whisper.

Memories surfaced. But the helplessness she felt just then surpassed even the silent ache of an orphan girl waking up in yet another institution.

She shivered as she began to imagine claw-like hands reaching out towards her neck, wanting to clasp her round the throat. Paralysed by fear, she tried to look round, but her gaze remained glued to the window. A whisper. 'Do you want to know?' She closed her eyes and opened them again, releasing small torrents of sweat that ran like tears down her face. Her vision cleared. Gradually the trees across the car park began to take shape, each one silhouetted by a glow that seemed to approach from the slope beyond. Was someone coming, bringing a light?

The fox scudded across the tarmac and disappeared into the

woods further up the hillside.

She blacked out, or so she thought, for now she must be dreaming as she found herself in the chapel at the retreat centre. She was standing with her back to where the altar should be, looking down the aisle towards the bit of ceiling that seemed to jut out more obviously than ever. She imagined the stained-glass windows behind her, the garden... the tree. The claws were now fangs in her mind, and once more she tried to turn round, desperate to see if the serpent was coming down from the tree. But still she couldn't move. She imagined it now, slithering out of the stained glass, down the wall, across the stone floor, ever nearer.

'Ariel!'

Her scream broke the paralysis and she turned to face her enemy, but there was no one there. Like a frightened child she ran back to her bed and pulled the cover over her face. Hours passed, or was it minutes? And Ariel was there, sitting on the bed by her side, telling her it was all right, everything was all right.

She let the soothing words infuse her like warm milk. Now she had no desire to move, or even open her eyes. She knew that he was there, protecting her, knowing her, loving her.

Yet already he was saying goodbye, and she knew it was right. 'Goodbye, Natasha. My friends have come for me. All is well.'

She woke in a sweat. Casting off the bedclothes she crossed to a handbasin and threw water over her face. The place was completely quiet.

She needed to think. Best not wake Jack. She went back to bed.

4

They touched down just below the topmost ridge above Melano. As Ariel released him Jack was hit by a wave of nausea, until the cool night air chased it away.

He looked around. They were above the tree line. Stars shone brightly through gaps in the clouds, and he knew that dawn would not break for an hour or more, even up here. There was a good deal of mist coming off the trees below, and he guessed the lake must be about a mile further down. Somehow he had been swept up the mountainside in a matter of seconds. There was no road, no cable car, no helicopter.

'We don't have much time,' Ariel said again.

'To do what?' said Jack.

'To say goodbye.'

Jack felt a cold chill across his back and pulled his jacket around him. He touched his cheek. It was cold, but not as cold as he thought it should be. He tried to recollect what happened after he saw the treetops below, but all he could recall was a twisting sensation before finding himself on solid earth once more.

He decided to sit on a flat piece of rock that offered some measure of level seating. 'What just happened?'

Ariel joined him. 'I'll try to explain, Jack. I really want to. But it's difficult.'

'Aye, and we don't have much time – so you keep telling me.'

'I think we have an hour. I will try to use terms that make sense to you.'

'That would be nice,' said Jack, annoyed at his own tone. Was this really the end?

Ariel didn't seem to mind. 'Imagine, if you will, a spatio-temporal matrix, a network of crossings and avenues that intersect your world without exactly being a part of it. This is something I and my... associates can usually navigate without too much trouble. It allows me to move about in your world rather freely, as you have just witnessed.'

Jack slowly shook his head, forcing his brain to catch up with his ears. 'Right. I see. And I guess it helps you go through locked doors as well.'

'Yes. Though in that case it's more a matter of realigning atoms, changing the molecular structure, keeping things apart, just for a moment. But it has also meant I have been able to protect myself, either by phasing out of your dimension – to use a term I know you're familiar with, even if it is misleading – or by briefly altering my presented molecular make-up, changing my body's density.'

'The saw! The gun butt!'

'Just so,' said Ariel. 'And while I am sorry for Corporal Maddox's splintered bone, I have to say there seemed little alternative. It was an unconscious reaction – an automatic protective response on my part.'

'I wouldn't worry,' said Jack. 'He'll soon mend.'

'Yes, I'm only sorry I can't stay to apply the molecular rearrangement process in a more controlled way.'

'As with doors and manacles,' said Jack.

'Yes. I could probably speed up the healing process, as I did with Miranda's ankle.'

Jack wondered what that was about, but decided to say nothing now he could ask Miranda direct.

'But since Venus this ability has been all but lost,' Ariel continued. 'Jammed, if you like.'

'And you know this how, exactly?'

'My friends. Two of them finally managed to reach me.'

'What kept them so long?'

Ariel sighed. 'Do you remember that I thought I'd been in a battle before you found me? Well, that was the echo of a real situation, buried deep somewhere in my mind. I was hit. Hurt. I fell, and I was lost.'

'Ariel, I–'

'It's okay, Jack. There's so much you couldn't know. And you and your friends have been so, so kind. You've given me space, and time…'

'Like a matrix,' Jack remarked.

'Indeed, a little spatio-temporal matrix all my own! Very good, Jack.'

'Go on.'

'As I say, I was lost – not just in myself, but lost to my comrades. So they developed a device that could track me.'

'What, like a homing beacon?'

'Yes, I suppose you could call it that, though it was a two-way device. It was something that could make a kind of bridge to me, after my spatio-temporal matrix was jammed.'

'Ariel, it's perishing cold up here, and to be honest I'm not getting much of this.'

'No, sorry. Come with me a moment.'

'Whoa there!' said Jack. 'We're not going flying again, are we? I don't think my stomach could take it. I know I'm an astronaut, but I'm usually in a plane or a spacecraft when I go into a dive. EVA is normally such a gentle thing, you know?'

'Do not fear,' said Ariel. 'I simply thought I might demonstrate what I'm talking about and warm you up as well. I can leave out the flying sensation this time.'

They stood up, and Ariel held out his hands as he had done before. Gingerly Jack took them, first one and then the other, hoping very much they were not about to jump. The twisting sensation returned, but only briefly. Within a heart's beat they were standing outside a door in a warm, dark corridor. Carefully, quietly, Ariel opened the door and went inside. Jack couldn't see clearly, but he could hear the sound of breathing. He peered in and gradually made out that someone was sleeping. He watched as Ariel sat down on the bed. Something made him stay back at the door, fearing to interrupt the gentle intimacy. After a few minutes Ariel returned. Jack was about to speak when Ariel put a finger to his lips, before closing the bedroom door.

'Now,' Ariel whispered, 'grab that snow coat over there, and those gloves and boots. They all have thermal linings. You'll feel much better with those.'

Once he had put them on, Jack began to look around. The place seemed familiar.

'Okay, Jack. Hold on.'

Reluctantly he obeyed. A twisting sensation, and they were back on the flat piece of rock overlooking Lake Lugano. The mist was beginning to clear, and Jack thought he could make out the outline of the Alps in the far distance. He pulled the hood over his head. As he did so, he noticed the logo of the mountain rescue facility on his glove. 'Hold on!' he said, still whispering. 'Were we just...?'

'In the hospital? Yes, Jack. They were the nearest warm clothes available, and I did rather rush you earlier. Also, I wanted to check that Natasha was safe.'

'Natasha?' As the penny dropped, so did Jack. He sat down on the rock once more. 'I don't know what to say.'

'I'm sorry, Jack, this is a lot for you to take in. Still, you will have time to process it after I have gone. But if you want to understand anything at all, I think I had better get back to my story.'

Jack huddled into his coat, and as its warmth enveloped him he felt his mood shift to one of acceptance. 'Just hit me with it,' he said. 'You've always been a patient teacher, and I will try to learn.'

Ariel smiled. 'Wonderful. You remember the bridging mechanism I was talking about, the homing beacon? Well, if you haven't already guessed, this was found by Natasha when you visited the surface of Venus.'

'No,' said Jack with a sigh of resignation, 'I hadn't guessed. The crystal, of course! Weirdly, that makes a kind of sense now. Pray, continue.' He put his arms behind his back and looked out across the valley below, still shrouded in mist and darkness. Even so, the clouds seemed to be receding, and he knew that the night was preparing to give way.

Ariel sat down next to him. 'The crystal was meant to keep a point of contact with me. You need to understand – or rather, accept, because I can't explain it in the time we have – that although my friends knew where I was, they were not able to make direct contact. During the battle several of us had phased in and out of your dimension. Again, I'm using words that might mean something to you. It may even be that Jim caught a glimpse of one of my comrades when he was out in the storm and the enemy was surrounding us. From what I have learnt, I think my friend may have been stooping over Dr Chase, making sure he was all right.'

Jack nodded. Clearly he would need to revisit everything in the light of these revelations.

'The battle was intense,' Ariel continued, 'at times almost chaotic. All in all I rather think we played havoc with the environment.'

'The Window!'

'I believe so, yes,' said Ariel. 'So in all the confusion the crystal was a way of keeping a potential channel open. It was a channel I had to find from my side of the chasm, except I didn't know that. I'm sorry, this isn't very clear, is it?'

'You're doing just fine.'

'Thank you, Jack. So Natasha found the crystal not far below the surface of Venus, and she brought it back to the ship. I rather think that may have determined where I finally crashed out. And where my matrix jammed.'

'Why we found you in the ship's lounge, you mean?' Gradually it was beginning to make more sense. Ariel had not used doors to come aboard the ship.

Ariel nodded. 'Now, my colleagues' strategy was sound as far as it went, but it was risky too.'

'How so?'

'Because they were not the only ones who might use the crystal to try to get to me... or be there to meet me if and when I found a way back. They knew they could not hide it from the enemy. Even so, they judged it worth the risk. And, once you took off from Venus with both me and the crystal on board, you left the immediate influence of the enemy. For a time.'

Sitting on the mountainside, looking across to the distant mountains, Jack couldn't help feeling this was all very far away. Yet the word 'enemy' brought a chill that his survival coat could not keep out. 'I see,' he said. 'So the enemy has been trying to get to you through the crystal ever since.'

'It would appear so.'

'And where does Nathan Dexter fit in?'

'I don't know,' said Ariel. 'My friends say they managed to secure his release from the crystal's influence shortly before the end. One of them even risked showing himself. But clearly their success was short-lived. After that, I tried to help him in the attic, but by then he was already surrounded. And I myself was becoming increasingly... grounded, my body almost completely in this space-time arena. What you saw as my extraordinary abilities were failing fast, though at that moment I was more aware of the enemy than of my friends. And then I blacked out.'

'As you often do,' Jack remarked, with no hint of blame, thinking it remarkable that Ariel had been so stable for so long. 'I can't imagine what it's been like for you, not knowing where you belong, or where those friends were that you instinctively felt you'd once known. We've never really understood.'

'In a sense, how could you?' said Ariel. 'Although... I think some have shown great understanding. You don't always need words.'

They sat a while in the stillness. The inky smudge of the distant horizon was starting to crystallise into a mountain range.

Ariel broke the silence. 'Do you know, Jack, there was one black-out that I am sure the enemy played no part in. In fact, I don't think it was even down to my weakness, not exactly. More a heightened sensitivity. As I sit here now, above the trees, I have something closer to my usual perspective on your world. But down there, *among* the trees... oh Jack, the sense of upthrust, of life exploding, of earth reaching for heaven... it was almost more than I could bear. There was no way I could stand up straight, not at that moment. Please don't ever underestimate the treasures you have on this planet, will you Jack? Don't miss the beauty!'

Jack's ears took in what Ariel was saying, but his mind was still focused on the tactical weakness of the crystal device. 'So... this enemy,' he said. 'Could they be responsible for the voices we heard? Is it possible that some of us heard your enemy?'

'I've been wondering about that,' said Ariel. 'Bear in mind I myself am still processing these explanations, such as they are, and my friends have had very little time to communicate with me. And Jack, you need to understand that our enemy, as you call them, is your enemy as well. They followed us from Venus, of course, but they are already very active here on Earth. Have been for millennia. I haven't learnt very much as yet about how they have been trying to get to me, though my friends did mention one early attempt – the time when those satellites nearly made holes in the space station.'

'That was the enemy?' Jack shivered at the thought of an attack in space, with so many people so vulnerable.

'Apparently – they think so anyway,' said Ariel. 'Both sides were busy around and about us at that time. My friends were the ones who made sure your ship's external cameras failed on Venus... to keep the options open for explaining how I came to be on board. But the enemy has certainly been making far more use of the elements. So, as far as those voices in the wind are concerned, I suppose it's possible you picked something up, but... I tend to think that all you would have been able to hear was the wind itself. I was already out of it on Venus, so I can't be sure, but I did hear the recordings in Geneva.' He looked down the hillside in the direction of the medical station. 'And I heard them again when Sean made that heroic landing. I myself could tell they were the work of the enemy, but I'm guessing that most people would simply put them down to a freak storm.'

'Most people, maybe,' said Jack. 'But I think I heard them in a dream, back on the Endeavour.'

'Yes, you did mention that in Geneva,' said Ariel. 'And this doesn't altogether surprise me now I think about it. Perhaps what you call your subconscious mind is far more adept at perceiving such things than I realised. Even if it was only the wind you picked up with your physical hearing, maybe you perceived the angry powers behind it, almost as if the wind itself were angry.'

'Now you're sounding like Leonardo!' said Jack.

'Ah, Leonardo... so near and yet... so open to the enemy, for all his walls of software and stone. Thinking about it now, I can see that the storm we had the night Miranda joined us was almost certainly the result of enemy activity, but...'

'But what?'

'Well, in many ways I suspect Leonardo's closed view of the world has done more damage than any of the enemy's more direct activity.'

'But if he thinks the world is closed, he's hardly going to be open to outside forces, is he?'

'Ah Jack, I see there is so much you still don't understand.'

'Doubtless,' said Jack.

'The enemy forces are not from *that* Beyond. You and I and the enemy are all very much a part of this elemental universe – yes, even though I usually move about in another realm. The openness, the beyondness, I spoke about in Montagnola... that is something far, far greater. More glorious.'

Jack looked at Ariel. There was almost no ambient light, yet his eyes were alight.

'We all work within our own limited capacities,' Ariel continued. 'And there are certainly limitations on what the enemy can do. In your world I suspect their most powerful weapon is human influence.'

'Wait,' said Jack. 'Do you really mean human influence, or their influence on humans?'

'Both. And while Leonardo may be an unwitting tool in their hands, I fear Nathan Dexter was more aware of what he was doing. Yet even he did not know who he was really dealing with. And by the way, it may help you to know that, according to my friends, his body was removed by two men who were helping the false police officer.'

'Your friends saw that?' said Jack.

'Yes, they were watching from the trees.' For a moment Jack wondered why they hadn't intervened, but he guessed that was not their standard procedure, nor something they wanted to risk while they were so close to restoring Ariel.

'So why take Dexter's body?'

It was Ariel's turn to shiver. 'I don't know, Jack, but they told me that the man impersonating the police officer was almost certainly the one who first drew Mr Dexter in. They think he does not normally operate in Europe, but they are quite sure he is a servant of the enemy.'

'Wow,' Jack said, suddenly recalling the man's non-European features. 'I wonder if we'll ever catch him now.'

'I do not know,' said Ariel. 'As I say, the enemy's usual line of attack is more subtle, more through human institutions than individuals. And that too has been evident these last few weeks.'

'In what way?'

'I'm thinking of the Temple of the Four Elements,' said Ariel. 'Leonardo is a remarkable man, but he has been shaped in large part by the people in Tibet, and now he is shaping others. There is nothing inherently wrong with blending scientific research and a veneration for creation, but there is a subtle line between icons and idols.'

'Excuse me?'

'It is not a fragile line,' he continued as though Jack were still following him, 'but it is hard to discern which is which if your heart is not in the right place and you are not really open to the truly transcendent.'

'So who's right and who's wrong?' said Jack cautiously. 'In your opinion.' He wished he had set his eband to record so that he could process all this later, but he decided to leave it now. Every word Ariel uttered was being firmly imprinted on his mind.

'Not a bad question,' Ariel conceded, 'and certainly not an easy one to answer. Right and wrong often appear as shades in your world, though trust me, they are still very different from each other. Jack, your species seems to be doomed – or blessed – to stand apart from nature, though not from creation, which means you can both wound and heal in a way other creatures and natural processes do not, and that is very useful to the enemy. Add to that the fact that Leonardo's monastic order has responded to your global environmental crisis with fear as well as wonder, and it is no surprise he has opened the gates to elemental forces far beyond earth, air, fire and water.'

Jack thought of the attic, but there was something else on his mind. 'You talk about influences,' he said. 'Right from the start, even on Venus, we've all exhibited our fair share of strange behaviour. Perhaps we were coming under these influences.'

'I honestly don't know what to say about that,' said Ariel, 'though if you mean what I think... my guess is that you and Natasha were already close, and you and Jim already uneasy with each other, before those feelings became heightened to a degree you felt was out of character. I might say the same thing about Melody and David too. But yes, I do think these feelings were amplified by the enemy and became harder for you all to deal with.'

Jack stood up. Ariel needed no special powers to know that the mention of David had unsettled his friend.

'Jack, let me say one more thing about David.'

'Sure. Shoot.'

'You should talk to him. Up to now you have left all the talking to Melody, and you need to ask yourself why. What is it you dislike, or fear, about his beliefs... his view of the world?'

'Well...' Jack began, but was quickly interrupted as Ariel got to his feet.

'As I say, you need to ask yourself. But I would be grateful if you could pass a message on to David when you speak to him. Tell him I was with him at the quayside and he should keep praying and not give up. There are forces in the cosmos that will hinder his prayers and use his desires against him, so he must be vigilant and never give up.'

'Perhaps you should tell him yourself,' said Jack. 'Somehow I think he'll take it better from you.'

'There is no time. But I hope I have shown *you* enough, Jack, this very night, that the world is not as tightly closed as you have believed. Or as Leonardo believes, for that matter. Though I think Sean may get further with a man like Leonardo than David is likely to.'

'That's if he ever comes back from Tibet,' said Jack. 'I rather think we did for him.'

'Yes,' said Ariel. 'Who can say whose paths will cross now?'

They both looked down at the valley below.

'Mel will be devastated,' Jack said at last. 'She didn't even get to say goodbye.'

'I am sorry about that,' said Ariel. 'You will be there for her.'

A prediction or a question? Jack gave both a nod.

A meteor drew a line of light across the sky. In an instant it was gone, its only trace a rapidly dimming streak beneath his eyelids.

'So tell me, what are these enemy forces trying to do?' said Jack, guessing he had just broached a subject too vast for the time available.

'Ah, Jack. They have been sowing confusion, but more than that I cannot say.'

'You mean you don't know?'

'I mean it is not for me to say.' He stood up. 'Now, the time approaches. In a little while you will see me no more.' He pointed up the mountainside. 'When I am gone, walk over the ridge in that direction and you will come to a mountain railway. Wait there, and eventually a train will arrive and take you back down to the lake. After that, you must decide what you will say to your friends, and what you will say to the world. I cannot explain fully what has happened. And I don't know if I am answerable for any of it. But this much I will say, Jack. I am very much hoping these few weeks with you all will be a time I shall never forget! Though I now return to what I was, I shall never be the same.'

They began to walk towards the summit. Jack wanted to ask Ariel what it was like where he came from, and whether there were others like him still left on Earth, but he could see the moment had passed. When they reached a scrub bush that had found a way to live on the bald mountainside, Ariel asked Jack to go no further.

'Jack, I can confirm this has not been the first time I have walked on this planet, or spoken this language. We are the ancient ones. I don't know when or even whether I shall return, but I want you to know I have gained so much by this unexpected taste of human life, and the fleeting friendships I have known.'

He gave a brief bow and turned. Jack watched as he trudged up the remaining slope to the top of the mountain. As he walked his suit began to shimmer, though there was no light on this side of the mountain to cause any reflection. Just after he disappeared over the ridge there came a flash similar to the one Jack had seen earlier through the blind in the window.

He walked to the top, knowing full well he would not see Ariel. When he reached the summit, he found himself on a long ridge. He looked back towards the mountains where the peaks were already tinged with pink by the imminent sunrise. Overhead a squadron of birds in neat formation flew into the west. He looked to the east, and there, heralding the dawn and shining like a jewel in the brightening sky, Venus blazed in reflected glory.

PART THREE

LIFE ENDURES

What is this face, less clear and clearer
The pulse in the arm, less strong and stronger –
Given or lent? more distant than stars and nearer than the eye

T S Eliot
Marina (Ariel Poems)

CHAPTER 31

Publicity

1

Natasha awoke to the sound of a priority call on her eband. 'Jack, what is it? Why are you calling me? You can knock on the door, you know.'

Jack thought about his nocturnal visit to her bedroom, albeit in the manner of some kind of guardian angel, and immediately decided that was never going to be part of his report. 'Good morning, Natasha. I wonder, could you be a dear and drive down to Capolago? I'll be arriving by train in about half an hour.'

'Sorry? You're not making any sense, Jack.'

'I know,' he said cheerfully. 'See you in a bit.' And with that he was gone.

She clambered out of bed and stumbled around for a few seconds as she shook off the effects of what to her surprise had eventually become her best night's sleep in a long time. She splashed water over herself and dressed quickly. It didn't take long to check the entire facility. She was alone.

She replayed Jack's message, then asked her eband to let her know what and where Capolago might be. It was down at the end of the lake. Not too far. The trains turned out to be the mountain variety, rack and pinion, used for climbing steep gradients.

Something about Jack's call was gnawing at her subconscious, so she played it again. There it was – I'll be arriving. I, not we. Panic started to rise like a kettle coming to the boil. Where was Ariel? What had Jack done? And why didn't she know?

She called Beth. 'Sorry to call early.'

'Early? What makes you say that?' said Beth. 'We'll be with you in five.'

Natasha looked at the time. It seemed she had slept too well. 'Okay,' she said, 'though you'll pass me on the way. I need to go and get Jack. I'll explain when I can.'

But she never really could. She picked Jack up and plied him with questions on the way back, but all she could get was that Ariel had really gone, though he had made a special goodbye to Natasha while she was sleeping. That helped a little, especially when she remembered a dream about Ariel and Jack, both dressed in some kind of armour and smiling at her. It was a long time before the chilling heat returned to her memory, drained of its terror.

When she and Jack got back to the mountain hospital, Beth, Marta, Lucien and Sean were all gathered. Jack related the night's events as plainly as he could, leaving out the return for the winter wear and the message for David. He talked about the crystal and the enemy, and the jamming of Ariel's spatio-temporal matrix, though he made no real claim to understand what that actually was.

When he had finished there was silence.

'Well,' said Beth at last, deciding this was not the time to question anything Jack had said, 'I don't really know what to make of all that, and I doubt that anyone else here does. But I think you're right that Constance will welcome Ariel's disappearance. As for this enemy he kept talking about, did he really say nothing about how we might prepare to defend ourselves?'

'No,' he said, 'not really. But I didn't get the impression that we should be bracing ourselves for invasion, or anything like that.'

'Well, that's all right then,' said Sean with a brazenly sham sigh of relief. He had been studying Jack's face while he had been speaking, trying and failing to detect signs of deceit.

'Well,' said Beth, 'I guess the priority now is to come up with a story. Starting with that police inspector. But Jack, I hope you won't mind if I send Marta and Lucien up the mountain to take a look.'

'Be my guest,' said Jack. 'I'd expect nothing less. In fact, depending on the story we settle on, you can get our tenacious inspector to put out an alert for him. We have Melody's photograph.'

'I want to go up there too,' said Natasha.

Sensing this was more a search for connection than for Ariel, Sean offered to go with her.

Beth stood up. 'That leaves you and me, Jack, to tackle Inspector Bandalucci. Then I think we'd all best be getting back to Geneva, don't you? It seems our work here is done, if not quite in the way we expected.'

Nothing like we expected, thought Jack.

Lucien had just loaded his passengers for the short trip to Capolago when the Inspector arrived. He didn't wait to say hello.

She went inside and wasted no time in asking to speak to Ariel.

'I'm afraid that won't be possible right now,' said Beth. 'It seems our man did a runner in the night. We've not been able to find him, so I've sent my colleagues back to Geneva. You may have seen them leaving as you arrived. In fact, we'd love it if you could put out an alert. Jack can send you a picture, can't you Jack?'

Olivia looked at them both closely. 'What makes you think he has run of his own free will? Have there not been attempts already to abduct him?'

'That is true,' said Jack. 'And it is a possibility, though Natasha and I were here and didn't pick up any kind of trouble.'

Olivia looked at her eband. 'Very well,' she said. 'Send me the photo. I assume, then, that you will be leaving Lugano soon.'

'That's right,' said Beth. 'There's nothing for us here now. But I will be telling your superiors just how helpful and conscientious you have been, Inspector.'

Don't overdo it, thought Jack. He noticed Olivia looking at him. She said nothing about the fact that she had already spotted him in a car with Natasha Koroleva earlier that morning, driving north along the autostrada.

It made no sense. At least, not yet.

2

Constance had also slept well. She felt the mists were clearing. She had always suspected that dear Leonardo was not quite what he had seemed, even if she was disappointed in the level of skulduggery that seemed now to have been uncovered at the monastery. She could hardly be blamed for her choice of the place, though that didn't stop her blaming herself. Yet even now this might serve them well. A plan was forming in her mind, and although sketchy she felt the full picture would be revealed soon. Beth's call about Ariel's disappearance was surely part of it. There were plenty of possibilities.

She decided to call a second review meeting. With Jim and Ryan back in the States, Dan in space and Selena on her way to India, it would be a smaller affair. No bad thing.

But there would be one new person, and she was now key. Melody Grantley James should write a second article. Of course it would not be the last word – who ever got to be so privileged? But it would be a clear statement. Ariel had disappeared as mysteriously as he had arrived. They would need to deal with a number of loose ends, but she was confident her team would soon have it covered.

That night she slept even better.

3

The coffee was flowing in the conference room at the UN. Hannah had returned to her surgery to deal with a mounting backlog of cases, leaving a determined Melody to begin to rebuild her life, on the proviso she call day or night when the darkness closed in.

Melody knew why she had been included in the select gathering, and it had nothing to do with Jack wanting to make her feel better after missing Ariel's sudden departure. The truth was, it was time to talk to the world and she was the obvious choice. The vista from the conference room window seemed to her an ever present reminder that there was a world out there, vast and uncontrollable, and she had agreed to do her best to set the opening parameters of the conversation that was bound to rumble on in the weeks and months to come. Maybe even years.

She took a seat next to Jack at the large oval table, her back to the window. Opposite her were Natasha and Sean. As before, Constance and Beth were seated at either end. Constance formally started the proceedings. This had begun as a World Space Agency matter, and so it would end.

'Good morning, ladies and gentlemen. Welcome back, and thanks especially to Professor MacEvoy and Miss James for joining us, as together we seek to make sense of recent events and, crucially, to agree the basis of two documents – an official statement by the WSA, and an article by the journalist who first... ran with the story of the unexpected find on Venus.'

Melody walked over to the small refreshments table near one of the doors and made herself a peppermint tea. Jack watched her closely, hoping this was the last time she would be reprimanded, however subtly, for breaking the story so early on.

Beth pitched in. 'Yes, I think it's an excellent idea to get Melody to write the first well-informed article after the lifting of the embargo. Well, it's been more of an outright ban really, as far as the news agencies of the world are concerned, which of course has got a lot of people making stuff up – some bits predictably cooky, though not all of it. Several agencies have done some good rooting around to see who might have got to Venus before the WSA mission, and that's actually been quite useful in our own intelligence-gathering. You'll be interested to know that the unidentified flight we tracked shortly before the Resolution left Alpha was almost certainly an unauthorised mining expedition to the Moon.'

Jack noted the 'almost' that put a small dent in Beth's certainty, but he decided to keep quiet. He was still basking in a sense of relief that Hugh Coates was not behind Ariel's presence on Venus.

'And even the alien stories haven't all been totally crackpot,' Beth continued. 'We've had one or two from your own neck of the woods, Professor.'

'To be sure,' said Sean. 'The ones I'm aware of have for the most part been pretty speculative and hypothetical – nothing too fanciful. They all seem to amount to "aliens called by and dropped someone off". He shook his head.

'What about theories of enhancement?' said Jack, surprising himself at how unready he was to talk openly about the idea that Ariel was not human. 'Has there been anything from the bio-engineering world?'

'Not really,' said Beth. 'But then, why would there be? We haven't said anything at any stage about Ariel's special abilities.'

'Quite,' said Constance. 'And let me underline that last point. You've all done an amazing job in keeping that side of things under the hat. As have the Brothers at Montagnola, doubtless for their own reasons. There have been rumours about what an alien might be capable of ever since the first story broke, but nothing based on anything anyone saw. Obviously the death of Nathan Dexter may just possibly change that. The police have already interviewed everyone at the monastery, and while I understand everyone kept their testimonies very much to the actual events as they saw them, it is possible some anomalies were picked up.'

'Don't doubt it,' said Jack. 'But, in the end, what have they got in terms of hard evidence? A bizarre business run in a retreat centre, an intelligence agent who dies in suspicious circumstances, and the man of the moment gone missing? As far as I can tell, there's nothing there to suggest that Ariel was anything other than human.'

'Very good,' said Constance. 'And I can report that the photo that

Melody took of Ariel has been deleted from the system at *Exposé* – a condition of Marta Bergstrom's immunity from prosecution – and the only remaining copy will be archived in the confidential part of the final report on Project Icarus.'

Jack sighed. Maybe that was the last reprimand. But it was good to know. And he comforted himself with the thought that, in the end, he had only sent a verbal description of Ariel to the police.

'Do we know what Nathan Dexter was up to?' said Melody with a sudden flick of her hair. 'Who he was working for, and why?'

'We're still piecing it together,' said Beth, 'but since Washington unlocked his video diary we've learnt quite a bit.'

'Such as?' Jack's interest was piqued at the mention of a diary, though he wondered just how much of it Washington would have shared.

'Well,' said Beth, 'as you know, we'd already worked out that he was passing on information. His diary confirms it was to the kidnappers.'

'But why?' Melody pressed.

'I think we're building a profile of a man who felt he had been overlooked in his service with American intelligence agencies,' said Beth. 'And who'd had enough of the relentless neutrality demanded of him here at the UN. But you need to understand, I didn't know him very well – that's the nature of the job, I'm afraid, where the three of us are chosen for limited periods before the rota changes. We only get to overlap for a couple of years.'

'So what more have we got from the diary?' said Jack.

'Well, there's quite a bit of ranting in there, disgruntlement about for ever monitoring and never intervening, and clearly a chip the size of a tree for being passed over for field work.'

'Until someone offered him some,' said Jack.

'Exactly,' said Beth. 'He talks about an organisation called the International Front and, I kid you not, a "Mr X" who contacted him and told him things about Ariel no one else knew.' Jack thought of his mountainside conversation with Ariel but said nothing as Beth continued with the story from Dexter's point of view. 'They put him in touch with a hit-man.'

'Or maybe Mr X was the hit-man,' said Jack.

'Maybe,' said Beth. 'Either way, they managed to convince Nathan that Takeshi was a danger to his world-saving mission—'

'Sorry?' said Natasha.

'To save the world from Ariel, of course!' said Beth. 'And the army that was presumably following him.'

Sean nodded. 'It's so frustrating,' he said quietly. 'If only we'd known what was going on in Dexter's head. If he'd only told us... we could soon have ascertained whether there was a real threat, and just who was threatening whom.' He sighed. 'Well, maybe.'

Jack was still thinking things through, revisiting events after the kidnapping. 'So Nathan was the reason the Stuttgart operation failed so spectacularly. They already knew about Bill standing in for Ariel.'

'Yes,' said Beth, 'And about the police presence, of course.'

'So, where was it all going?' asked Melody, still trying to work out what Nathan thought he was doing.

'As far as we can tell,' said Beth, 'his plan was to hand Ariel over to this Mr X, but of course it all got a bit complicated because of the Finnish chap.'

Melody sipped her water.

'Okay,' said Jack, eager to steer them away from this particular part of the discussion. 'So... things start to get out of control, and Nathan – with or without his new boss's say-so – eliminates the guy and covers his own tracks into the bargain.'

'Right,' said Beth. 'In fact, it does look like he received a pretty direct command to "neutralise" him. Though he clearly despised the guy anyway. There's quite a bit in the diary about Oksanen's strange philosophy and even stranger lifestyle. That said, in the end it looks like the murder was what started to tear Nathan apart – the guilt, I mean. At the end of the day, he was an analyst not a field agent. I don't think he'd shot anyone before, not in cold blood.'

The room fell silent.

'Let us return to the matter in hand,' said Constance, 'the official WSA statement. I have drafted something which will now appear on the panel in front of you.'

She touched her tablet and a moment later a series of rectangular screens embedded in the table lit up. It was not a long piece, and after a couple of minutes everyone was looking up. No one spoke. Natasha wondered if she was the only one already questioning the ethics of it. Yet, seeing no better alternative, she joined the unanimous agreement on its basic approach. The conditions on Venus had been unsurprisingly disorienting, a fact that could be bolstered by psychological assessments of the crew, and a stowaway had either got there before them or just possibly found a way to remain hidden on the flight out (to be discussed). He had been injured because he was not properly equipped, and when questioned during convalescence turned out to be even more disoriented than the crew. The proposal suggested further discussion on just how much to say about the monastery and its 'unconventional' or 'questionable' approach to hosting a retreat.

It did not take long to agree that the official statement should be brief, offering a minimum of information. It was a good idea to play on the universal sense of disorientation, but hints of other things could be saved for Melody's article. That was the place to fuel conspiracy theories which, it was hoped, would distract people from what really happened. The facts were far too complicated and inconclusive to share.

They took a break from the coffee and reconvened after it had been replaced with water.

'Very well,' said Constance. 'Now that we have an agreed statement, let's turn to the article.'

Natasha raised her hand. 'Before we do,' she said, 'can we just revisit the other option?'

Constance tilted her head ever so slightly. 'What other option?'

'The truth,' said Natasha. 'If not all of it, at least that we had a special person among us.'

With Constance untypically lost for words, Jack stepped in. 'I totally get where you're coming from, Natasha – you know I do. But if we go down that route, and actually say what kind of impact Ariel had on us, and on others – including some very unsavoury characters – then we risk opening up a whole can of worms... the two squirmiest of which would most likely be theories of human enhancement and alien invasion. Either one of those would cause a lot more than speculation and conspiracy theories. More like outright panic.'

'If I may,' said Sean. 'Jack's right, and you know how it pains me to say it, Natasha. But let's remember, we ourselves don't know who or what Ariel was... is. Far better to take time to process what we do know. If he turns up again, or any of his friends do–'

'Or his enemies,' said Beth.

'Or his enemies,' Sean echoed in acknowledgement, 'then we'll have some idea what to expect.' He turned to Beth. 'Shouldn't this really be treated as a matter of national security anyway?'

'Sort of,' said Beth, 'except that it's already international. As owners of the Aphrodite mission the WSA is in the best place to guard the data. My guess is member states will want access to anything we've held back, but beyond that we should leave people to come to their own conclusions, or guesses, about the whole story.'

Jack shook his head. 'The WSA member states may be a smaller can of worms, but they could still be all over us if we're not careful. I mean, they may be buddies when it comes to the exploration of outer space, but national security is a different thing.'

Sean nodded. 'Who are we really talking about?'

'As things stand,' said Jack, 'there's a triangle of distrust in the east – Russia, India, China. It's better than it has been, but I wouldn't want to predict how they'll react if we tell them everything – or, conversely, if they think we're withholding.'

Constance reactivated her tablet. 'But we are agreed, are we not, that a well-informed article is the best way to proceed for the time being?' She looked around the room, halting at each person until she received a nod of acquiescence.

'Very well. Now, I fully realise that the article must be your own, Melody, and not written by a committee. So I suggest you now seek the clarification you need to write a first draft. And then, would tomorrow be too soon to reconvene to discuss it?'

'No,' said Melody, 'tomorrow will be fine. I've already had some ideas, and frankly there aren't that many ways to serve up this particular dish.'

'Excellent,' said Constance. 'In the meantime I will contact Dan Marshall and keep him up to date. He is probably best placed to liaise with Jim and Ryan.'

The discussion that followed proved straightforward, until they got to the question of how Melody was to handle the monastery and the somewhat enigmatic Temple of the Four Elements.

Sean floated a suggestion. 'We're all a bit worried about what happened there, isn't that right? Somebody dying is bad enough. And, sure, we'll keep a lid on it for a while. But my guess is, sooner or later, some monk or police officer is going to blab. And when they do, something will get out about those toys in the attic and the potential to mess with people's heads. So, I wonder, should there be a hint of something about that in the article?'

Jack was the first to respond. 'I'm not sure. Why raise interest in the place? If we need it, we can fall back on it in the future.'

'I agree,' said Beth. 'And there's no harm in having a contingency plan.'

They had come to an uneasy agreement. Each person in the room was keenly aware that there would be many unpredictable challenges ahead. Jack made a mental note to contact Darlene Piper in London, just in case Hugh Coates turned out to be the first one.

4

Melody had not got far into the outline of her article before she encountered not one but two dilemmas. If she omitted all reference to the monastery, there was always the risk that someone would leak the information anyway. *Exposé* was still very much in business, and they knew that she had actually been there herself. And it wouldn't take them long to discover the monastery had closed. Any investigative journalist worth their name would soon find out about the 'toys in the attic', as Sean had dubbed them. And all this was to say nothing of what certain intelligence agencies might find out, and what their governments decided to do with the information.

The second dilemma concerned Nathan Dexter. Should she really keep quiet about the snatched body? She had discovered that he had a family. Even if the local police were trustworthy, which was far from certain, his wife deserved to know that there was no body at his funeral. She was more likely to keep the secret, but once again there was a risk. Far better, surely, to pre-empt the revelations and start to control them now.

But how might she control them? She thought of Dexter, who had followed her and David and then betrayed them all for reasons that they had hardly begun to understand. And she thought of Ariel, the one who had shown them a glimpse of something better, something to reach for, both in themselves and in the unseen world of the spirit. Two characters in their midst, so different, both now gone.

And then she had an idea.

5

The next day they met early. The blinds were angled against the dogged infiltration of the morning sun, and the aroma of coffee was noticeably absent. They had all read Melody's piece.

'Good morning, everyone.' Constance's voice was croaky, and as she cleared her throat and took a sip of her water Petroc sidled in and whispered something in her ear. When he had gone she addressed them once more. 'As you know, we're here to discuss what Melody has written, but first I'd like you to view the screen in front of you, as Dan Marshall is ready to join us. He recently returned to Alpha to do a little digging for me in their medical files.'

She didn't elaborate, and no one asked. Jack admired her consistent thoroughness in getting her hands on all the data that had ever been logged about Ariel.

As Dan came on and began to speak from his office on the space station, Jack ran his fingers through his hair. It was little more than a month since he had been in that very room. It seemed more like a year.

'I've spoken with Jim and Ryan,' Dan was saying. 'Jim is more than happy to keep silent about the whole affair. He's read Mel's article and will read whatever revisions you may come up with today, though he did say he would be happy to go with it as it is.'

Melody's eyes widened.

'As for Ryan,' Dan continued, 'he's just happy to be back on American soil and doesn't really care what you do!'

They laughed, but Melody decided to push a little. 'Hi Dan. Can't say I'm not surprised at the slack you're cutting me today – so thank you! Just one thing on Ryan. He has the crystal at the moment. How does he think we should handle that?'

'Well, I was coming to that, Mel, but there you go, one step ahead as usual.' He laughed and she relaxed. 'The thing is, the crystal seems to have changed.'

Natasha broke in. 'Dan, hello. To clarify, do you mean its molecular structure has changed?'

'Hey, Natasha. Nice seeing you. Apparently, it's a bit more complicated than that, but then, that's Ryan for you. But in lay terms, he's not picking up any weirdness, and it's now in pieces.'

The buzz around the room was electric, though Dan could only guess what this might mean for them all. 'Sorry, guys,' he said, 'gotta go. I'll be back earthside by the end of the week, if you need me. Constance, I've nothing to add to my last report which, taking my lead from others, now includes the dream I had in this very office. But I would just warn you of one thing, unofficially you understand. Schlesinger is on leave, and I think he's got it in his head that he needs to examine Ariel again – not that he knows him by that name, and you can be sure I've told him everything's classified until it isn't. Bye now!'

The screens went back to their nondescript grey, with just the WSA logo in the centre, a globe with the three letters worked into it and arrows streaming outwards.

'We didn't talk about the crystal going into the article,' said Jack. 'And maybe now we don't need to.'

'I agree,' said Beth. 'It sounds like Schlesinger might be a bit of a loose cannon, mind. We may need to ensure we have the only copy of those medbed records – you know, the ones that weren't there but should have been!' She sighed. 'But can we talk about what *is* in the article, particularly the bits we didn't agree yesterday.'

'Of course,' said Constance. 'Melody, over to you to explain.'

Once more Melody wasn't sure if Constance was upbraiding her or just giving her enough rope to hang herself with. But she was eager to air her two major dilemmas, and this she did to a silent audience. She finished by justifying her creative idea, which was to affirm in the strongest terms that the stolen body was not Ariel's. 'So you see, I'm suggesting, recommending, that we pre-empt the leaks and conspiracy theories that are bound to come.'

'And by expressly denying that the stolen body was Ariel's,' said Jack, 'you actually fuel the suspicion that it was.'

'How does that help?' said Natasha. 'Honestly, I'm asking, not arguing. I'm not very good at this kind of thing.'

'No shame there,' said Melody. 'I think it was the disfigured face that gave me the idea. It's just the kind of thing conspiracy theorists thrive on. You know, whose body was it really? Was it Nathan Dexter, or was it the man from Venus? In the end I suppose what I'm hoping is that people won't think Ariel is still out there somewhere. And that should discourage any false messiahs popping up claiming to be him. Which would be ghastly.' She flicked her hair from her face. 'And of course it might prevent interested parties looking for him.'

'Interested parties?' said Natasha.

'Other Nathan Dexters,' said Melody. 'And the ones who work for them.' She lifted a glass with a shaky hand to quivering lips.

'I'm sorry,' said Natasha. 'Yes, I see.'

Constance looked at Melody. 'Would you like to leave the room, dear?'

'No, I'm fine. Honestly.'

'Very well. But we have now all been reminded of two things that need a contingency plan – not only the crystal but the abduction of yourself and David Carter and Ariel, which was not limited to this city but witnessed publicly in Stuttgart as well. I'm sorry to have to ask, but I think you should say something about that, given that you were there. Not to speak would, as you've already argued, raise suspicions.'

While Melody took another sip of water Jack took the chance to respond. 'May I refine that idea a little? Why not say that it was too traumatic to write in detail? Hopefully then the worst you'll get is publishers calling you with book contracts.'

This was agreed, and the discussion did not go on much longer before the wisdom of Melody's approach was taken as sound, if not without risk.

Just as they were expecting Constance to close the meeting, she surprised them by asking Melody to step outside for a moment. Seconds later Petroc slipped through the door at Beth's end of the table and beckoned to Melody. She went willingly enough, although she felt the sting of exclusion.

Constance addressed them once more. 'I hope we all agree that Melody has done a splendid job here, not only in writing things up so readably, but in the thoughtful approach she has taken, helping us to think ahead.' There were nods and murmurs of agreement. 'But I asked her to leave because I am concerned about her. I believe absolutely that she is the right person for the job. But if we go with this, she is going to be bombarded with questions and become the object of a great deal of scrutiny.'

When no one responded immediately, Sean decided to voice his thoughts. 'Well, you're right of course, Ma'am, and we could spend the next half hour weighing up the pros and cons of going with this, our best way forward, or compromising with something that does a similar job but doesn't involve Melody. But I'd just like to say two things about that. First, I think we owe it to her to see this thing through. Heaven knows, she's been through a particularly nasty mill, and that's precisely why I think she should see some fruit from her suffering.'

No one spoke, so he pressed on.

'The second thing I want to say is that I am happy to whisk her away to Ireland if a little disappearing act of her own is called for. If she wants that, and if we think that's appropriate.'

Jack smiled. 'I don't think I want to comment on your second point either way, Sean, but as to your first – well said. Very well said.'

'Good,' said Constance, 'that's agreed then. Thank you, all. Let's go and rejoin our beloved colleague before she starts to think we're talking about her!'

Jack filed out with the others, wondering whether the formidable Ms Bridlington had known full well what Sean was going to say. Whether she did or not, one thing remained clear to him. Right now, for such a time as this, she was the best director the WSA could have.

6

'I'd like to talk about loose ends.' Constance was standing in her office with her back to the window and her hands on the sill. Jack and Natasha sat on either side of the table, while Beth took the other end. 'Jack, Natasha, once the article has gone out tomorrow, I shan't have a reason to keep you here any longer. So, assuming you don't wish to pick up the tabs on your hotel, it is my happy yet sad duty to dismiss you both.'

She joined them at the table. 'So, to those loose ends. Beth has asked to talk about Nathan, and about Hugh Coates as well. And I would like to have a brief discussion about Selena.'

'Selena?' said Jack, mystified.

'I think you know that I was impressed with Dr Chandra,' Constance explained. 'It seems to me she's a bright spark in a dark Box. Pun intended.'

'Well, that's true enough,' said Jack. 'From the little Mel has told me, she's the real brains behind fibrogenotex. And as we all know, without that... without her... we wouldn't have got to the surface of Venus, Window or no Window.'

'I'm hardly surprised,' said Constance. 'I think, if we'd asked her to join us before she came to Geneva, she'd have said no. But now...'

'Join us?' said Jack. 'Wow.'

'Think about it,' said Constance. 'A move to the Indian Space Agency would be good, but coming here, to headquarters? She'd be terrific.'

'In what capacity?' said Natasha.

'I'm thinking of developing a small team to work exclusively on relations between the member states. I'm not sure it's full time, and she would want to continue her research anyway. Something tells me she won't be satisfied until she can get us to the surface of Venus at any time, even with normal conditions. Or to the subterranean seas of Titan and Europa, more likely. I think Ariel's suit made more of an impact on her than we realised. And anyway, I simply can't abide the idea of her working for that dreadful man another month!'

'Sounds good to me,' said Jack.

'Excellent,' said Constance. 'You know I value your opinion. Now, Beth, what about Nathan?'

'Well,' said Beth, 'it's the who, the where and the why, I suppose. Who do we think took the body? Where did they go? And why on earth did they do it? The answers must lie with whoever he was mixed up with. We need to start somewhere. Takeshi's convinced it's all to do with the crystal.'

'Sounds like you may need some help from Washington on this one,' said Jack. 'Though I'd be happy to talk to London too. Who knows, we may get to work together on this.' He smiled warmly. 'Part time, of course.'

'Well,' said Beth, 'I won't deny I could do with your help. I have my own contacts, of course, but I need someone on the ground. And Takeshi's not back to full strength yet.'

'Very good,' said Constance. 'That just leaves us with Hugh Coates.'

'Right,' said Beth. 'The man has more power than you know. I mean, they talk about a mine of information – we haven't found the bottom of this particular one yet, I can tell you. His grip on the communications industry is legendary, of course, and now he has a leading position in nuclear-drive technology he's going to be right at the heart of the next wave of planetary exploration. I can't help thinking that to have a man like that involved in Project Icarus has not scared us enough. If you get my drift.'

'What do you want to do?' said Jack.

'I want to keep tabs on him, at the very least,' said Beth. 'It's probably all we can do anyway.'

'I may be able to help with that,' said Natasha.

They all looked at her in surprise.

'I've just had a message from Miranda,' she beamed. 'She's feeling a lot better. I've promised to go and visit her.'

Jack smiled. 'Careful, Natasha, or you may find Selena's not the only one switching career today! We'll make a secret agent of you yet.'

'I'm sure I can be as *fatale* as any *femme*,' she riposted.

'I don't doubt it for a minute,' said Jack.

Beth studied Natasha. 'Can we meet up later and talk about this?'

Natasha shrugged. 'Sure. Why not? But if we're being serious, I should declare that I really will need to be part-time. Only Sean has offered to help me find funding for some research.'

'That's great!' said Jack. 'What kind of research?'

'The next step in global cooling, of course,' she said, 'using our data from Venus. Up to now we've only scratched the surface. What Ryan and I brought back from Venus – which is a lot more than the crystal, I might remind you – will keep us busy for a while. Until we return! And the news about Selena gives me hope that that might be sooner than I thought, so I am eager to get started.'

'Talking of data,' said Jack, smoothing his chin, 'may I ask what's happening with the records we have on Ariel and the crystal? Schlesinger's, Ryan's, and whatever the tekkies find in the attic?'

'You may ask,' said Beth. 'Let's just say it's as secure as we know how.'

'Very good.' Constance went over to her desk and called Petroc. 'I think it's time,' she said simply.

They all looked at each other, equally perplexed. Seconds later Petroc came in with a silver tray, four fluted crystal glasses and an unopened bottle of champagne.

'Jack, would you like to do the honours?'

Petroc withdrew as Jack released the cork.

While the bubbles rose to kiss their faces Constance explained. 'I think it is clear that Ariel has impacted your lives in ways you do not yet know the full nature of. I propose a toast. To Ariel.'

'To Ariel!'

Chapter 32

Believers

1

The small square outside the cathedral gate seemed to contain half the population of Canterbury, except they were clearly drawn from all over the world. European students jostled with Asian tourists in the ancient Buttermarket, some sampling the local fudge while others grabbed a selfie under an imposing statue of Jesus that looked down upon the throng from above the arched entrance to the cathedral precincts. Alice always said he looked slightly sad, as if he were silently imploring the crowds to come and taste something more lasting.

David and Alice were standing at his feet, quite relaxed even though they were waiting to see Melody for the first time since they had returned home from Switzerland. She was coming with Jack and

Natasha, breaking off from their world tour while in London. She had sounded almost excited on the call, eager for them to learn what the public didn't know.

They had read Mel's article of course, and seen the first interviews with the Endeavour crew, and they knew what others only suspected – that there was a lot left unsaid. No surprises there, more a sense of relief. They themselves had told a very sketchy story to the church, though Alice had told Cop everything she knew.

A large party of tourists came past, taking their noise with them through the arch towards the historic cathedral. As they cleared away, Alice pointed up the Burgate to where three people were striding arm in arm towards them. Jack looked like a king between consorts.

The reunion was warm enough, once they had got past the stilted remarks on the weather and the crowds. David was not in favour of meeting in the cathedral, and a café was certainly not the place for a confidential chat, so they walked to David's car and drove up the hill to where the university looked down on the city below. They walked for a while, but the chill north-easterly soon put paid to that.

'Come on,' said Alice, 'let's go back to our place. We'll take you to your car – Mel knows where we live.'

'That's very kind of you,' said Jack nervously. 'Actually my car is not far from here. The only thing is... we're expecting to be joined by someone else in a little while. And I'd really like us to be together.'

'How many are we talking?' said David.

'One, maybe two.'

'Oh, Jack,' said Natasha, 'enough of the cryptic talk. It's Miranda. You met her at the monastery.'

'Well, that's wonderful!' said Alice. 'Why don't you wait for her here on campus, and then bring her down? That will give me time to get some things ready.'

'Thank you,' said Natasha. 'And there's a call I need to make in the meantime. But please, don't go to any trouble.'

'Of course not.' It was Alice, so you could hardly call it lying.

2

Jack and Melody waited in the car while Natasha left the car park and found a quiet spot shielded from the prevailing wind under some trees next to the university library. She called Sean.

'Well hello, and how's my favourite cosmonaut?'

She had decided not to use video, preferring to warm her hands in her pockets. The sound of his voice in her earpiece, with its avuncular tone and insuppressible vitality, lifted her spirits immediately. 'I'm okay,' she answered. 'Just about to go into a meeting at David and Alice's house with Melody and Jack.'

'Ah. I see.'

'I wanted you to know about it. I can only think you weren't invited because you came into our story so much later.'

'Ah, but my dear, I was invited. Jack told me about it. I declined.'

'Why?'

The wind whipped up some leaves and she faced another way to reduce the noise in her earpiece microphones.

'Well now, I think it's going to be a gathering of believers, don't you? And anyway, I did hear Jack's account the very next morning, if you recall.'

'Okay.'

'Cheer up now,' said Sean. 'Isn't your friend Miranda going to be there too? You wanted to see her again.'

'Yes,' said Natasha. 'And stop worrying about me. I just wanted you to have the chance to tell the others about... you know, the crash landing.'

'Ah.' He paused for a second, which in Sean's case was a long time. 'Tell you what, I'll tell you now, if you've got time, and you can pass on as much of it as you like.'

She agreed, sensing it was probably easier for him to talk from a safe distance.

'For a start, I did hear some voices. No idea if they were the same ones you guys reported hearing on Venus, but there it is. But I've got to say, Natasha, that the whole thing was a bit stressful.'

She sensed the Celtic understatement. 'Do you want to say more about it?'

'Yes I do,' he said. 'You're a clever girl. I know you well enough by now to have looked me up. You know I lost my wife and daughter in a helicopter crash.'

She hesitated as the guilty memory of her intrusion into Sean's bedroom surfaced in her mind.

Some students ran past, laughing.

'Yes,' she said.

'Did you know I was the pilot?'

'I wasn't sure,' she admitted. 'It's hard to find details on it, and I thought you'd tell me if we ever got to know each other that well.'

'Which is precisely why we are going to know each other very well!' said Sean. 'You are an extremely smart and sensitive individual, Natasha Koroleva. But there it is – the memories that assailed me in that copter... I was a fool to fly you there, and we nearly paid for it with our lives. I don't know why I did it. Pride, maybe – trying to see if I still had it in me? But maybe demons too...'

Natasha waited for the explanation.

'Maybe I thought I could exorcise something... you know, atone for the guilt of the past.'

'But it wasn't just the elements we were up against,' said Natasha, 'or, if I may say so, your memories. You heard what Ariel told Jack. There were forces–'

'Well, maybe there were,' he said. 'But it needs thinking about. What you won't know from looking me up is that I had an auditory-nerve enhancer fitted a couple of months back, and for a while that causes all kinds of sound effects, I can tell you. So who knows what I heard? But what I do know is, it was windy, it was stressful, and I was stupid.'

'I have to go,' she said. 'But we must talk some more soon.'

'Of course,' he replied. 'Now, get yourself gone and give my love to all the faithful.'

3

Less than an hour later the conservatory at the back of the surprisingly sumptuous house was filled with chatter and the clinking of plates and cups. David was explaining to Natasha that Alice's parents had gifted them the house early on, as both home and equity for building up a business. Jack was praising Alice for the finest cup of tea he'd had in weeks. 'It's all very well,' he said, 'touring the world like some kind of celebrity. But for a decent cup of tea you have to come home.' Melody became subdued quite early on, happy to simply watch everyone catch up with each other.

The biggest surprise had been the arrival of Hugh Coates. He had offered to leave once he had delivered Miranda, but Alice wouldn't hear of it, and this was her domain. She soon found the great man to be delightfully ordinary, and she noticed how whenever he lost sight of Miranda he was asking where she was and how she was. She liked him.

Miranda she was less sure of. But the effect that Ariel had had on her was clearly profound, and she could only think that was a good thing.

Jack's inevitable doubts about Hugh being there soon began to evaporate. He even wondered whether it might be for the best. After all, this was a chance for the arch-secret-keeper to hear things honestly and openly. His attachment to Miranda was plain to see, and if ever there was going to be a time to test his loyalty, this would be it.

A brief shower pelted the conservatory roof before allowing the low autumn sun to return and warm things up. Everyone relaxed into a natural pause. Jack took this as his cue to address the gathering, and taking a silver teaspoon he tapped gently on the fine china. All eyes were on him.

'I'm very grateful to Alice and David for providing us with this space – and feeding us so well!' Soft but heartfelt laughter. 'All the people here deserve to know the truth – aye, even you, Hugh!' More laughter. 'Miranda, I gather you awoke on the very night that Ariel left us. If you think that's amazing, well, it is. But I don't think we should find it surprising. We none of us understand, yet, the full nature of the link between Ariel and the crystal, and certainly not what happened in that attic when you so efficiently pushed me out of the way and got to him before I could. We'd all love to hear your account of that, and anything since then, if you're willing.' Miranda nodded. 'But first, let me share what happened at the end, and in particular what Ariel told me before he left.'

With that he took them back to the night in the small mountain hospital under what he now knew to be Monte Generoso. He had decided this was the time to tell the whole story, even if he never told it again, now that he had had some time to reflect on its many enigmas. He described the light in the trees and the mysterious figure he had first taken to be Ariel but now believed to be one of his former associates, and then the flights (he didn't know what else to call them) up and down the mountainside above the trees. Because these were almost instant yet without any real sense of momentum or G-force, he said he was satisfied that Ariel could move from one set of spatial co-ordinates to another without going through the intervening space.

He even told them about the visit to check on Natasha. It seemed so right to share it now, and although her quiet tears worried him for a moment, when she looked up her face was radiant and her eyes shone with approval and reassurance.

He kept going. 'Back on the mountain, Ariel told me a little about his new perspective on what had been going on since we found him. It was only a little of a little, because clearly his memory was just returning and his mysterious friends had not had time to tell him much. He also gave me the distinct impression that he wasn't actually allowed to tell me everything he now remembered. He spoke of an enemy, something some of us had picked up on before, when he half-recalled a battle before we found him on Venus. He implied that this enemy was used to operating in the part of the universe that's native to Ariel, and that they're more limited here.' At this, David whispered something to Alice. 'But the crystal provided them with a way to get to him. It was actually a device planted on Venus by his comrades after he was lost, to keep some kind of link open, but it was that very link which proved so useful to the enemy.'

Once more he looked across to Natasha, and she silently nodded. He had already urged her not to blame herself for giving the enemy access, even though she was the one who had found the crystal, since without it Ariel's friends might never have found him. It had been their strategy, and her part in it was unwitting.

Hugh asked where the crystal was now. Jack, surmising he probably knew already, said it was in California where Ryan was still studying it. And since it was not as if Dan Marshall had proved himself secure where Hugh was concerned, he even decided to pass on what Dan had told them, that it now seemed inert and had broken into pieces. Even as he said this out loud Jack was comforted by the realisation that both Ariel (with his suit) and the crystal (in its active state) were already beyond the reach of any more interference, at least where human beings were concerned.

He went on to share Ariel's theory that some of the storms they had been through, both on Venus and in Switzerland, had been whipped up by the enemy, and that when some of them had heard voices on the wind, or even in dreams, they may have been picking something up from the alien forces.

Natasha saw this as the moment to share what Sean had said about his new ear implant playing up.

'Well, there's not a lot we can say, really, is there?' said Jack. 'I mean, Sean is a complicated chap, and he's not going to believe without more evidence.'

'More complicated than you know,' said Natasha, and, sensing the burgeoning intimacy of the group, she told them about the loss of his wife and child in a helicopter accident. She decided they didn't need to know that he was the pilot. 'It's not something I really want to argue with him about.'

'Absolutely not,' said Jack. 'And we're not here to argue – not now and, for my part at least, not in the future either. I just want you folks to know the truth as I experienced it. Now, where was I?'

'You were talking about voices on the wind,' said Natasha. 'But, before you go on, tell me, did Ariel say there might be other ways we may have sensed this enemy of his? Only when you were speaking just now I suddenly remembered the stained-glass window in the monastery chapel. The one with the tree and the serpent.'

'We need to talk,' said Alice, all smiles gone. 'But Jack, don't let us stop you.'

The room was still cosy, and he still felt he was among friends, but Jack felt the mood had just changed. He sighed. Perhaps he could expect nothing else from their hosts.

'Okay,' he said, 'just before he went Ariel told me to pass on a message.'

They all looked up expectantly.

'Actually, it's for only one of you, so I guess I should save it for now.'

'Was it private?' Alice asked. 'I mean, do you think the person would mind if you shared it publicly?'

'It's for David.'

Alice looked shocked, Melody and Miranda crestfallen, Hugh mildly amused.

David shifted uneasily in his chair. If this was going to be advice about his marriage, it was definitely for another time. 'Best save it,' he croaked. His mouth had gone dry.

'Okay,' Jack said with just a tinge of guilt for doing it that way. 'Let me finish here, then,' and he went on to describe Ariel's final departure over the summit and quite literally into the wide blue yonder.

It was Hugh who eventually broke the silence that followed. 'Allow me to thank you on behalf of everyone here, Jack. I feel honoured to be among present company, though you will understand when I say I shall be keeping an open mind.'

'Of course,' said Jack. 'No arguments, remember?'

'What's going to happen to the monastery?' said Miranda quietly. 'I gather they've shut it down.'

'For the time being,' said Jack. 'It's not clear when Leonardo will return from Tibet, or where he'll go.'

'I think that's sad,' said Melody.

'What about the Brothers?' said Natasha.

'Er, not sure,' said Jack. 'I expect it will reopen eventually, when it's no longer the scene of an investigation and they've finished deactivating or removing the equipment. I would imagine some of the Brothers will stick around to look after the place.'

'I can't imagine it without Leroy,' said Natasha.

'No,' said Jack, 'some days he did seem to be everywhere, didn't he?'

'Perhaps he's got a spatio-temporal matrix,' Hugh joked.

Jack laughed, though he cut it short when he realised he hadn't used that precise term in his talk. Nor in his report to Darlene Piper. As far as he could recall, it was only in his confidential report to Constance. Was nothing out of this man's reach? Ah well, he thought, keep your friends close and your enemies closer, especially the ones that refuse to be put in either category.

4

With Jack's update to everyone over, he and David went through to the kitchen, while Alice led the others out for a tour of their large garden, still bursting with flowers in what had become the typical twenty-first-century autumn. The rose garden was putting on a spectacular show. As they all meandered between the various shrubs and flower beds, Miranda and Natasha lagged behind.

'How have you been?' asked Natasha.

'Awful,' said Miranda. 'I was really hot. Apparently I had a fever, Hugh tells me. Boy, but he's been brilliant, you know?'

'I think that's wonderful,' said Natasha.

'Anyway,' Miranda continued without reaction, 'let me tell you about that crazy crystal you found. I remember making the dive in the attic. But... and this will sound crazy... it was like I'd jumped into the crystal and was trapped inside! It was... oh, I don't know... it was like the light from outside was diverted somehow, and I was cut off from it. Ariel was worse than useless – no, don't look at me like that, Natasha. I know it wasn't his fault. I soon realised he'd overstretched himself. It was all very weird, though. But then, that's dreams for you, right? If it was a dream.'

They sat on a bench under a climbing floribunda while Natasha waited for Miranda to continue.

'So, I'm trapped inside, not sure what's going on. I think I see Jack, but in an instant he's gone. Then these two bright shining guys turn up and smash the walls of the crystal. I don't know if they've come from outside the crystal or have been in there already, but they start pulling me out. "Hold up!" I shout, but they take no notice. Then I see Ariel lying in the rubble.'

'Oh.' Natasha was relieved she had not shared her own very different vision-dream when Ariel came and said goodbye, especially now that she knew it had been real. It couldn't have been more different from Miranda's experience. She had already come to realise that all her envy for Miranda's relationship with Ariel had drained away. Miranda may have been 'read' by Ariel, and even trapped with him in the crystal somehow, but Natasha's relationship had been much closer to conventional, and all the better for it.

'It's a bit hazy now,' Miranda went on, 'but I remember reaching out to Ariel and pulling him out of the rubble. Or at least trying to. It was like a wall had fallen on him.' She shivered. 'And then he looked at me, and d'you know what he said? "Miranda, don't be afraid. This wall needed to collapse, but remember the wall around the garden. And remember the gardener."'

Natasha looked mystified.

'Oh sorry,' said Miranda, 'I forgot. It was Alice I told before. You see, when Ariel and I had our walk in the monastery grounds, well, I had a bit of a fall, and I passed out.'

Natasha still looked mystified.

'I'll explain,' said Miranda. 'While I was out of it, lying on the forest floor, I had a dream about an amazing garden, a walled garden. And the gardener... well, I didn't get to see who he was, but I just felt so safe. So safe.'

'So, in your crystal dream experience,' Natasha suggested, 'Ariel was telling you the dream in the forest was important.'

'Right,' said Miranda, 'but I already knew that, as soon as I'd had it. But the thing is, Natasha, I never told Ariel about it! So, explain that to me. How does Ariel get to remember a dream I had?'

Natasha slowly shook her head. 'I don't know. Do you think...?'

'That Ariel was the gardener?' Miranda said. 'I don't know. None of it makes any sense. At least, not so far.'

But then it did. For now, as they sat on the bench in such a beautiful garden, Miranda remembered that she had briefly re-entered the walled garden immediately after Ariel had looked into some of her darkest memories. Maybe something had crossed over from her to him as they were briefly joined together.

They sat in silence for a while, listening to the birdsong and the gentle breeze in the trees. Within moments Miranda was back in the monastery woodland, and Ariel was catching her as she fell, even though he had been on the other side of the fallen tree just a second before. She smiled as she thought of Jack's account of his night flight up the mountainside. Was it possible that, even back then, Ariel might have been able to get through or past that tree and catch her in an instant? Why not?

'Your other dream experience,' said Natasha, 'how did that end? You know, when you were in a coma? You mentioned two shining figures.'

'Right, yes,' said Miranda, struggling to regather her thoughts as the harsh memories of the crystal wrenched her away from the walled garden. 'I got the strong sense that they were going back to the rubble to fish Ariel out. And I think that's when I woke up, because Hugh says I was shouting "Get him out! Get him out!" over and over again.'

'And they did, didn't they?' said Natasha. 'Get him out, I mean.'

Miranda smiled. 'I suppose they did.'

They stood up to join the others. 'I've been thinking about the timing,' said Natasha as they walked. 'I think you and Ariel both woke up around the same time. He came round in the helicopter, and soon after that we heard you'd woken up. So I wonder. Do you think that when you caught hold of Ariel in the attic you got dragged into whatever the crystal was doing at that point?'

'Yeah, I reckon so,' said Miranda. She stopped walking. 'And that would explain why I caught a glimpse of Jack. I brushed past him but he never got a hold on Ariel.'

'Right,' Natasha continued. 'After that, you went into a coma, or something like it, and a fever. And then, as you came out...'

'Yes?'

'I believe you witnessed Ariel's friends finally breaking through the hold the crystal had on you both. And probably, if we talk to Ryan, we'll find out that's when the crystal became breakable.'

'Wow!' said Miranda. 'You're good.'

Natasha smiled and said nothing about where else her thoughts had been going. If the enemy had been using the crystal to get to Ariel, who knew what terrible danger Miranda had been in? But surely she was safe now.

They caught up with Alice, Hugh and Melody, who had been round the garden and were now lingering outside the kitchen window. Seeing Jack and David still talking inside, Alice became suddenly eager to tell them all about her kitchen garden, though not before she had quietly reassured Miranda that she had said nothing to anyone about their conversation in the monastery grounds.

5

On the other side of the window the two men saw their time alone would be mercifully brief.

'Okay,' said Jack. 'The message was quite simple. I wasn't running record on my eband, believe it or not – I know, call myself a spy, eh? – but things were moving fast that night. Still, I think I memorised it word for word. It's not exactly what I'd call a normal message. He told me to tell you that there are forces in the universe – no, actually he said cosmos, but I guess that's the same thing – there are forces in the cosmos that will hinder your prayers and use your desires against you, and you should be more, er, vigilant, and never give up. Oh, and maybe you'll understand this bit, he said he was with you... at the quayside?'

David stood by the sink, gazing through the window into the garden. At the mention of the quayside he breathed in sharply, seized by the sudden memory of the figure on the bench nearby when he had crept out of the hotel at night... the night of his baptism of 'no'.

'Do you want me to say it again?'

David shook his head. 'No, that's absolutely fine, thank you, Jack. I think I got every word.'

6

Melody and Natasha let Miranda go only after promises of swift reunion.

As they walked back to the car Miranda asked Hugh what he was thinking.

'Oh, lots,' he said. 'You may not realise it, Miranda, but I too have a sense of great loss. I know it's not as personal as yours, but when I think of that man's abilities...' He sighed. 'What I wouldn't give, eh?'

He unlocked the car but slowed down as they approached.

'What?' said Miranda.

'Oh nothing,' he mused. 'Well, I think it's nothing. This "enemy" Jack talks about. It doesn't appear to amount to much more than voices on the wind. It's not as if anyone's tried to apply rigorous analysis to them.'

'So, what are you saying? That it was all in our heads? In Ariel's head, even?'

Hugh could not miss the forlorn note in her voice. 'I don't know. Maybe that's where it all began – in his head.'

'Okay,' said Miranda, 'knowing better than to end the conversation by dismissing his words outright. 'But might his head not have been a window into something real?' She thought about the strange dreams of her coma, if that's what they were.

They reached the car doors. 'Hugh, you need to understand something.'

'Of course I do.'

'Ariel's mind-reading thing. It wasn't the moral equivalent of bugging people's thoughts.'

'But Miranda,' he said as they climbed in. 'How can you know that?'

'Because it was such an open thing! Open and honest and good. And loving.' She strapped in. 'It's not like he was a voyeur or anything!'

'Meaning I am?' He started the engine.

'No,' she grinned. 'You're whatever the listening equivalent of a voyeur is! But seriously, it wasn't an intrusive thing.'

'Nor is voyeurism,' he said as he checked his rear-view screen.

'No, but it's not exactly done with consent!' she objected. 'I mean, when I think about those mirrors in the monastery...'

'Ah well,' said Hugh, pulling away. 'That did all seem rather silly, don't you think? Although... there are some interesting results from their neuro-scanning equipment.'

'What? No, don't tell me.'

'I shan't, he said. 'Not until you're back at work.'

7

Alice was keen to speak with Natasha about the picture in the monastery chapel window and they quickly decided to return to the garden.

This left David with Jack and Melody. He offered them tea, but they had all had more than enough. They sat back down in the conservatory. 'I suppose we should have met together before now,' said David, his words falling to the floor somewhere in the middle of the awkward triangle. Jack decided enough was enough. It was time to lance the boil, mess or no mess.

'Aye, you're right there,' he said. 'And you can hardly blame yourself, or your extraordinary wife for that matter. I'll admit I've been less than keen to come and see you. Recently... or before.'

David could see this wasn't easy for him, but for once he had nothing to say. No pithy piece of counsel, no Bible quote, no warm words of wisdom.

Mel looked out into the garden, wishing she was with Natasha and Alice. Knowing she was where she must be.

Jack continued. 'My mother was religious, God rest her soul. I think you'd have to say she had a simple faith. Although she passed it to me I didn't take it any further than childhood. For better or for worse.'

Mel had not heard him talk about his mother to anyone else before, and certainly not any kind of attachment to the Christian faith. She found herself praying that this small window of transparency would open wider, even now, before Alice and Natasha came back inside. But then she didn't know that Alice would be making very sure that she and Natasha stayed well away till the time was right.

David considered where to take the conversation. Should he ask Jack about his teen years, or maybe his scientific training? But personal questions didn't feel like an option now. Jack was neither a friend nor merely an acquaintance. The awkwardness hampered the usual methods.

He needed to find common ground. What united them? He didn't want to go there. But there was someone else important to them both, someone who in a way had been with them all day, even though he was gone.

He cleared this throat. 'I gather you all had quite a bit of quality time with Ariel when you were first in the monastery,' he said. 'Did you find any links there with your childhood faith?'

It was a dumb question, and he knew it. For the first time he looked across at Melody. She was seated in a cane chair with her back to the garden, the late afternoon sun turning her fair hair to gold. He couldn't read her face, but his plight must have been sufficiently obvious, for now at last she joined the conversation.

'It's slightly awkward,' she said. 'Only, Ariel and I spoke about spiritual things rather a lot.' She hesitated, but decided it was all or bust. 'You remember our conversation in Geneva, David, before... well, you know. You said I'd come a long way spiritually, and we both knew who was responsible for that.' She turned to Jack. 'But when you gave us those hours with Ariel, Jack, I don't think you ever allotted any time with him for yourself, did you?'

'Well, yes and no. It's true I didn't schedule any long conversations. Somehow I thought it was more other people's kind of thing, I suppose.'

'You even let Miranda have a large chunk of the day,' she persisted. 'I must say, I thought that was amazing. We all know how much that meant to her, but I think you picked up on it first.'

'Mel, you know I get suspicious when you flatter me,' Jack replied. 'Are you saying I was scared to have time with Ariel myself?'

'Were you?' She was in full silhouette, but he could imagine the wide eyes flashing.

Jack sighed. 'You know what?' he said, 'I really don't know and I really don't care. I guess if I learnt anything from Ariel it was to forget the personas we so often assume.'

David sensed an opportunity to be sympathetic and spiritual at the same time. 'Well, we all have to adopt personas from time to time,' he said. 'And not just professionally – to our families and friends too. But I do agree with you, and with Ariel it seems, that there is a time to drop them all. And I think that's what I do before God.'

'Okay,' said Jack without much reflection. 'I'd love to know how you do your job. Your pastoral one, that is. Does that require a professional persona?'

The word 'professional' hit home, knowing he had been nowhere even close to that where Melody was concerned. He considered his next words carefully. He needed to address himself to the issue behind Jack's question, just like his Master would do. Not that He ever had to do that from such an awkward position, one that right now felt more like compromise than concern. 'You're right,' he said at last. 'And I'm really, really sorry. It's not enough to say that, I know, but—'

'It's something,' said Jack, who felt David had squirmed enough for one day. 'Look, David, we don't really know each other, not directly, and I've no doubt that's a big part of our problem. I've already said it's my own fault that I stayed away from you when Mel started to get interested. And, if you want to know, Ariel and I did have proper conversations. He was like that – if he didn't have long, he didn't take long! So...'

'So?'

'So let's put the past behind us. Just... no hugs or promises of undying friendship, okay?'

'Of course.'

'And as for you, my love, let me say right here and now – ha! in front of a man of the cloth – that I want us to stay together.' He stood up. 'I mean, really together.'

She rose from her chair straight into his arms. He couldn't see her tears, but he felt them as they ran warm on his cheek in the full embrace she had been dreading and craving for so long.

8

'You have a lovely garden,' said Natasha. 'Sorry I missed a bit of your tour earlier.'

'Not at all,' said Alice. 'You and Miranda had some catching up to do. And I'm sure you'll be doing plenty more in the coming days.'

They walked past the roses and under a willow to what seemed to be the bottom of the garden. Natasha looked over the low hedge.

'That's the River Stour,' said Alice.

'Ariel would have liked it here,' Natasha said in a half-whisper.

Alice looked at her. Feelings of compassion and envy swirled together inside her. 'You loved him,' she said, before quickly turning aside to unlock a gate in the hedge. They walked through. There wasn't much of a path on this side of the river, but an old log had been deftly chiselled out to act as a bench for two. Natasha imagined Alice and David sitting on it at the end of the day. 'It must be nice to grow old with someone,' she said. 'Not that you're old!' she added hastily.

They laughed together.

The minutes flowed by, as if carried by the fallen leaves on the water.

'Tell me about this enemy Ariel talked of,' Alice said at last. 'If you don't mind.'

'I can't really,' said Natasha. 'It was only ever a dim memory of his. At least, until he spoke to Jack on that last night.'

'How wonderful that he came and checked in on you,' said Alice. 'A real guardian angel.' Natasha offered a brief smile, and Alice sensed her desire not to dwell on that. She switched to the source of her new-found concern. 'Can you tell me more about the chapel? And that stained-glass window?'

'Oh, it was weird,' said Natasha with renewed enthusiasm. 'I'm Orthodox, you know, and I've seen a few churches in my time. But this. It was all wrong.'

'In what way?'

'To begin with, although the chapel seemed old, when you looked more closely you could see it had been built quite recently – in the past fifty years, I would say. There was no cross, no altar...'

'Wouldn't you expect that though,' said Alice, 'given it wasn't a Christian set-up? I mean, wasn't it some kind of eastern religion?'

'Yes, I suppose so,' said Natasha, 'though I think it was originally a Catholic school, one that didn't last long for some reason. Some whiff of a scandal, as far as I've been able to tell. After that it was taken over by an organisation called the Temple of the Four Elements. It looked like they only made changes to the details, but kept the religious feel.'

'Important details,' said Alice.

'Yes,' said Natasha. 'They say the devil is in the detail, don't they?'

'They do,' said Alice. 'So what's this about a picture with a tree and a serpent?'

'It's something Ariel and I studied in our... scheduled time together.' Alice noticed the hesitation which seemed to imply that a good deal of their time together had been anything but scheduled. 'We were able to have a proper look at the stained-glass windows over where the altar would have been. That's when we noticed the changes. A rainbow had been added to the great flood, and there was a camp fire in the garden of Eden.'

'Well, I get the rainbow,' said Alice. 'But a camp fire?'

'Yes,' said Natasha. She broke into a smile. 'Ariel made quite a bit of the fact that in the Bible story the only fire in the garden was there to keep people out, not warm their feet!'

'Did he?' said Alice. 'How interesting.'

'Yes. We worked out that the alterations were made to reflect the four classical elements – earth and fire in one window, air and water in the other. It was as though they didn't want to erase the famous biblical stories, so much as adjust them.'

Alice nodded. 'So that's why you thought of the serpent when Jack was talking about the voice of the enemy.'

Natasha tilted her head slightly. 'Well, yes. But there was more to it than that. You know how, when you look at some pictures, they draw you in? That happened when I looked at the serpent. It was very intense. I lost Ariel's voice for a moment.'

She looked up at Alice and saw she was studying her face. 'But that's not all,' she added.

Alice waited.

'When I read some of the original Bible story out loud, Ariel had one of his episodes. I should explain, he used to fall unconscious, or semi-conscious, at times. It made me think the story meant more to him than he himself knew.' She gazed out across the stream to a tree growing right on the water's edge. 'I may be wrong, because he did have an episode after he was overwhelmed by the... upsurge of life in the trees outside.' She smiled at the memory. 'I think he had an unusually sensitive awareness of life.'

'But you think there was more to it on this occasion?' Alice prompted gently.

'I do, yes,' said Natasha. 'I don't know... it almost seemed he was trying to recall something.'

The river kept flowing. A memory surfaced as Natasha thought of her chilling episode in the mountain hospital, and the hands around her neck, but perhaps it had only been a dream. She decided not to mention it here where the sound of the wind in the trees and the trickle of water over stones seemed to soothe her very soul. Away in the distance church bells rang. Both women remained still, at rest on the solid log.

'I remember now,' she said at length. 'As we talked about the tree of life and the tree of knowledge, I think I finally understood something. Why we might need to be forgiven.'

'Do you need to be forgiven?' Alice asked.

'I think we all do,' said Natasha, and Alice sensed no deflection. 'At least, I think that's what the story is saying. It is about the whole human race, after all. Somehow we all get to the point when we know we've followed the wrong... promptings in life?'

'The voice of the serpent,' Alice whispered. Her eyes were fixed on a broken branch that was floating past. Some of it was above water, though much of it lay below the surface.

'Yes,' said Natasha. 'The serpent seems to be the focus of disobedience. I guess over the years I had begun to believe that we had just lost our way – you know, as a human race. But that day with Ariel this story came back to me so powerfully. It seemed to be telling me our problem was disobedience, that perhaps that is the reason we are lost. Sorry, I'm not making much sense, am I?'

Alice looked at her. 'Natasha, you are making so much sense. You do understand, don't you, that David and I are part of a church here in Canterbury.'

'Yes, of course,' said Natasha. 'Melody has talked quite a bit about you.'

Alice looked back to the river. 'Yes, well, Melody has come at this via a different route.'

'You mean, via Jesus?'

Alice smiled, her conflicted emotions dissolving before the miracle that even now seemed to be occurring in front of her. 'Natasha, if you don't mind me saying, it seems to me you are not far from the kingdom of God.'

Natasha's smile was radiant, until suddenly a frown darkened her whole countenance. 'Alice, do you think I need to be exorcised?'

The question caught Alice off guard, even though it was not far off the reason she had wanted this conversation in the first place. She prayed quickly, automatically, before answering.

'No, Natasha, I don't think you do. Somehow I think your guardian angel has made that unnecessary.'

9

Later that day the goodbyes proved much warmer than the hellos, and Natasha said she would like to spend more time with Alice. That prompted an unexpected pang of envy in Melody who wondered whether she would ever feel at ease with Alice again. But she drew encouragement from the knowledge that Jack and David had at least drawn a line, if not exactly reached an understanding.

When they had gone David and Alice automatically headed for the kitchen. As they cleared away the leftovers of a day that was always going to be difficult, they slipped with accustomed ease into the kind of talk they so often shared after entertaining visitors. David said little about his conversation with Jack and Melody, but enough for Alice to know that there had been a new level of honesty and reality between the two men. They decided Jack was a closed book that was just starting to open its pages. Melody had survived a horrendous ordeal, her faith seemingly intact despite the snares of the enemy. And the Lord was clearly reaching out to Miranda in ways that even they couldn't yet comprehend.

That left Natasha. 'Do you think she's close?' said David. 'Close to believing?'

'I think she's been on quite a journey,' said Alice. 'And yes, she is close.'

'What did she say about the serpent?'

'Darling, do you think we oversimplify things sometimes?'

He put down the cloth and the teapot that he had already polished to an unnatural shine. 'What do you mean?'

'Well, we make a great deal of being soundly converted. And that's right of course. But do you think we sometimes push too hard, or even in the wrong direction? I wonder, do we always trust God to work beyond our own work?'

'Of course,' he defended. 'That's why we commit people to God in prayer. Only he can change their hearts. And then there's Ariel's message to me... which I notice you haven't asked me about, doubtless for all the right reasons.'

'Well?'

'He said I should be vigilant and pray and not give up. Never give up.' That was enough to share for now.

Her eyes widened. 'Maybe he really was... is an angel,' she said, her mind expanding with the very notion. 'Which means, even if I've not entertained an angel unawares, I've certainly conversed with one!' She dried her hands. 'So... not an alien then?'

'Well, said David, 'I guess that depends on your definition of alien. As an angel Ariel would rightly be categorised as a member of an intelligent race – the only non-human one we already know about, now I think about it.'

They looked in silence across the kitchen sink into the garden, sifting through their separate memories of the 'stranger' they had entertained unawares. Alice thought of her first and only in-depth conversation with Miranda, and whether God might be open to the charge of voyeurism. It seemed so obviously off the mark now. Whoever and whatever Ariel was, she had been reminded through all this that God had agents everywhere. He was a God of action, not simply observation.

'So, then...' said David at last, 'we do need to keep praying for Natasha – right?'

She forced her mind back to her recent conversation with Natasha at the bottom of the garden. 'Of course we must pray for her. It's just, well, she's made me wonder whether the Lord changes hearts in more ways than we recognise. I mean, don't you often say that we're all being reformed, re-formed, all the time, changed from one degree of glory to another?'

'I do,' he said. 'And I don't doubt God is working in Natasha.'

'He definitely is,' she said. 'And I'm sure there was a lot more going on in her life before Ariel came along. But I think he's really helped her to find her faith again... you know, in a way that's right for her now. I'm not sure she'd put a tick by every doctrine in the creed, but I can't help feeling the Lord's been protecting her, and that she knows it.'

'That's good to know,' said David, who trusted his wife's judgement even more than his own in such matters. 'And do you think he's been preparing her as well as protecting her?'

'I suppose he must be,' she said. She started on the dishes again.

'What is it?' David asked, recognising the signs of unfinished business.

'Well, don't you find it strange? I mean, if we're right about Ariel, how on earth could he not know it himself? How does all this fit in with our views?'

'Our theology, you mean?' said David. 'Honestly, I really don't know. And somehow I don't think we have to have it all worked out in a day.'

'Wow,' she said. 'I can't remember if you've ever said that before.'

He looked at her, hoping he would never stop learning from this woman. She was more beautiful now than ever, outshining every flower he could see through the window behind her, every other woman he knew. Every one.

'I love you,' he said. 'And I love that we do this together – this exploring, this serving, this journey.'

They held each other a long time, as slowly they backed into the draining board. Alice felt the moisture on her back. 'Darling... I'm nearly in the sink!'

'Sorry,' he said, 'didn't realise I was pushing you.'

'You weren't,' she said. 'We were moving together.'

He gently pulled her away from the offending worktop, closer to him. 'Are we okay?'

'You know, I think we are.'

CHAPTER 33

Unknown

1

It was common knowledge in the astronomical community that the earth was not close enough to the sun to be in danger of becoming another Venus, but the prospect of a world ravaged by climate change still loomed large. And the mystery of the temporarily open Window persisted. It was always going to take several weeks before the initial findings of the Aphrodite mission data could be shared with the press in any meaningful way, but the day had finally come when Constance could smile at the sight of a press briefing room filled with science correspondents. Ariel was off the agenda at last.

So she had hoped, and so it might seem as long as photos, results and graphs lit up the display screen for all to see. But then came time for questions.

'Harry Kingston, *Astronomer's Horizon* magazine in Sydney. Ms Bridlington, a question for you, if I may? It's nothing very technical.'

'Jolly good.' Gentle laughter rippled across the room, some instant, some delayed by the translation process.

'Forgive me, but has the last twenty-five minutes of stunning photos and colourful graphs shown us that we're no wiser than we were before we sent astronauts to the surface of Venus? That we still don't know why the localised cooling took place?'

'Thank you, Mr Kingston,' said Constance. 'It may not be a technical question, but it is a very good one. And, while my eminent colleagues here on the panel with me are doubtless very eager indeed to dig into the data for you, it is perhaps appropriate that we begin by looking at the big picture. So yes, I can assure you – though perhaps not reassure you – that none of the initial data can give us an unambiguous reason, or set of reasons, why the temperature and pressure dropped. As for the acidity levels, the data is still being processed and models run. One of the astronauts' suits is proving useful in that regard. I hope that answers your question for the time being. Perhaps now more detailed questions can be put to my colleagues.'

'Thank you,' said Mr Kingston. 'But Ma'am, might it not have something to do with Icarus?'

Constance hesitated, panic rising beneath the even-minded persona she had assumed. She referred them to the official statement, but it clearly didn't satisfy. When she saw a familiar figure in the back row wave his hand, the sudden relief prompted her to let him come and take the question.

'Ladies and gentlemen, I'd like to invite Professor Sean MacEvoy to come and address you all.'

Sean made his way to the front, seating himself in Constance's chair while she stepped back. The few in the room who didn't know him were quickly informed by a whisper from their older neighbours.

'Ladies and gentlemen, I am one of the team that was brought in to assess the extra passenger who came back from Venus. As you are aware, that person did not stay with us for very long, but I can assure you that nothing in the data we have – either from the planet Venus or from our interrogation of this man – points to any connection between him and the Window. Now, I'd be lying to you if I didn't admit that how he got on board the Endeavour is a bit of a mystery.

But wherever you think he came from, whichever theory you want to sign up to, I can assure you that there is no clear evidence that the localised cooling was caused artificially. There are no extra chemicals, no trace of other spacecraft, nothing. Not so much as a drop of phosphine! All indications are that this was a natural phenomenon, and of course a God-given opportunity to study sudden climatic change in an intense environment. An opportunity that I'm proud to say we lost no time in taking.'

As several of the more serious publications and websites kick-started a wave of applause, Constance leant over and whispered in his ear. 'Sean, I don't think anyone could have done that better. Thank you so much for putting us back on an even keel.'

'Ah, no problem,' he said, as he got up from the chair. 'Choppy waters ahead, though, don't you think?'

He returned to the back of the room, leaving Constance to steer her way through questions about barometric pressure and temperature, fielding her experts along well-prepared lines, and even giving some grounds for hope with the first results from the CO_2-munching airborne microbes that the Endeavour had left in the upper atmosphere of the greenhouse planet.

The waters were calm for now.

2

If anyone knew a cover-up when he saw one, it was Petroc Naismith. While the boss was busy in the briefing room, he took the opportunity to call Bruges. To his surprise he was put through to the Chief.

'Petroc,' said Hugh smoothly. 'How may I help?'

Petroc knew by now that this was not a friendly question, but a way Hugh had of saying, 'You should be helping me – why are you asking for my help?' And sadly Petroc had no intel to give right now. He simply wanted to float an idea.

'Float away,' said Hugh distractedly.

'Sir,' he said. 'What are we going to do? I mean, things are moving on, and no one knows the truth!'

'Truth?' said Hugh. 'Which truth are we talking about, Petroc?'

'The truth about Ariel, sir! I don't know everything, and I'm sure you and Miranda know much more...'

'Yes.'

'But I know enough to know there's a story to tell! Aren't we going to go public? Doesn't the world have a right to know?'

'Let's unpack those questions one at a time, shall we?' said Hugh. Petroc buried his disappointment, only too pleased to be granted an audience of more than one minute. 'First of all, who is "we"? If you mean your primary employer, the WSA, then you already have gone public. If you mean, as I take it you do, some aspect of Infostructure, then I cannot see what possible benefit there would be. You are asking me if we are going to kill our unique surveillance capabilities. I think you know the answer.'

'Sir.'

'As to your second question, and the right to know, I fear that may be beyond the both of us. Does the world have a right to hear the gossip about an amnesiac? Questionable. Does someone, somewhere, have a right to know that an enhanced soldier popped up on a space mission, only to disappear in highly suspicious circumstances a few weeks later? With no questions asked by Russia, or is that China, or everyone's favourite, Israel? Well, my young friend, I think that is a very good question. And you can be sure that I am giving it my utmost attention.'

'That is really good to know, sir. And I shall of course be here, should you need me in the course of any... moves you may make.'

'Duly noted.'

'Thank you, sir. And I'd be very happy to work alongside Miranda, sir. If that's considered helpful at any stage.'

'Goodbye, Petroc. Carry on the good work.'

The call ended. Petroc hit the desk in frustration, although what hurt more was the predictability of the Chief's attitude. There was nothing else for it. He would have to do some digging of his own. Clearly there was much that had gone on in Switzerland he still didn't know, not in detail. And he was sure it was the detail that would reveal the truth. And only when he had the full picture could he to go back to the Chief. Or maybe even take matters in his own hands.

He considered his options. He already had access to all the WSA files, but the ones in High Command were beyond his reach. Maybe it was time to make a friend over there. Isn't that how it worked out here in the field? That's how Miranda had done it, after all, getting to know Grantley James the way she did.

His frustration evaporated in a surge of excitement. And what about other avenues? Hadn't Hugh taught him to think about connections, and connections to connections?

Constance returned. He hadn't seen her so happy. He busied himself archiving and tidying files, until the standard request for tea came through. He was just about to go and fetch the boiling water when one of the files on his desk screen caught his eye. It was a report by the Stuttgart police. Now that was a whole different set of potential connections. What about that couple in Cologne, the Frenchman and the German woman from *Exposé*? Surely there was something to hack there, 'by wire or by wiliness' as his training motto had gone.

He duly filed the report, only to spot another reference to the police, this time in Lugano. His heart raced. Hadn't they actually penetrated the retreat centre? Talked to people? Weren't they around at the very time Ariel disappeared? And Mr Dexter's body?

He tried to open the Lugano report and hit the desk again when it wouldn't open. All the Lugano information was held at High Command. Oh well. Another reason to make a friend there, as soon as possible.

The intercom beeped. 'Petroc, how's the tea coming on? Are you sending off to India for it, perhaps?'

'Sorry, Ma'am. Coming right up.'

He went to the water boiler down the hall, wondering how much longer he could stand being a glorified tea boy.

He reached the boiler. India... wasn't that where Dr Chandra came from? Another bunch of potential connections, a new doorway to information! The possibilities now seemed endless. Take your time, he thought, as he carefully filled the pot with fresh boiling water. Give it a year, and Hugh Coates just might have a new right-hand man.

3

'Bill! How are you? You're looking much better.' Beth welcomed Bill Petersen into her office at UN High Command. They chatted for a while, and Bill confirmed that he was back on full duties once more and would soon be out and about again.

'One thing,' he said. 'I just got back from visiting Ed Maddox – you know, the poor unfortunate who managed to get his arm shattered on my little escapade at the monastery.'

'Yes,' said Beth. 'Don't remind me.'

'Well, the thing is, Ed has no idea why he suffered that injury.'

Beth stiffened. 'What did you say to him?'

'I am ashamed to admit that I went with the whole "you must have hit the ground" thing. But Ed's not stupid, Ma'am. He knows he hit Ariel.'

'But does he know where he hit him?' Beth said.

'Well, he's pretty sure he hit him on the head, but he's prepared to believe Ariel may have had a weapon of some kind that he couldn't see in the dark, something to block the blow.'

'Good,' said Beth. 'In that case, that's what he did!'

Bill nodded. 'Okay. Got it.'

They said their goodbyes, and Beth left Bill with an underling to archive his eband footage from the disastrous manoeuvre. 'Thank you, sir,' said the underling. 'Don't forget to clear the local memory on your eband.'

'Of course,' said Bill.

He left the building. Maybe he'd delete the files later.

4

Ryan poured Jack another Chardonnay as they sat talking on the balcony of his apartment next door to his lab. Both men were taking time out of the world tour and had just made the speedy journey from Los Angeles to Ryan's modest abode.

'Well,' said Jack, sipping the cool nectar, 'it's good to finally see where you do your thing. I'm not sure when I'll be back in the States. And I guess we all need to move on now.'

'Too right,' said Ryan. He sounded and looked deflated.

'So,' said Jack, 'I gather the crystal is no longer quite so interesting.'

'Oh, it's interesting all right,' said Ryan, 'but only because it isn't, not any more, if you see what I mean. How a piece of rock can go from resisting anything I can throw at it to cracking under a simple laser, I do not know. Looks more like a simple piece of selenite now.'

'The timing is interesting, though, don't you think?' said Jack, his tone as dry as the wine.

'What? Oh, right, yeah, with Ariel gone and all. I think that may be outside my area of expertise.'

'Yours and mine,' said Jack. 'Maybe there was something in what Leonardo had to say.'

'Shoot, what do I know?' said Ryan. 'But here. Talking of the old guy, I've got something for him. I'm pretty sure I'm never gonna see him again, but maybe you will.' With that he took a small box from his hip pocket. 'It's not something I'd want to put in the mail, if you get my drift.'

'The crystal!' Jack said. 'Ryan, that's a brilliant gesture, but I'm not sure it's in our gift. It will have to go with the rest of the stuff we brought back.'

'Oh, it will... mainly!' said Ryan, who seemed to be making even less sense than usual. 'What I'm giving you is the centre. It's no different from the rest, but I thought he'd like it, given the geometry.'

Jack looked as nonplussed as he felt.

'Maybe this will help,' said Ryan, projecting an image from his eband on to a napkin. 'If you cut down a dodecahedron, what do you get?'

'Ah,' said Jack, 'a smaller doe-decker-whatnot. Right. But how are you going to explain the fact that some of it's missing?'

'Don't you worry about that,' said Ryan. 'There are several pieces now, and I've lost some of the mass anyway through chemical testing. It won't be difficult to account for the missing material.'

They sat in the late afternoon sun a while longer, before Jack voiced the question he had come to ask. 'So, Ryan. What do you really think? Is it possible it could be... could have been... some kind of communication or tracking device?'

Ryan felt the alcohol working its slow, delicious magic on his brain, and thought, What the heck? 'Yes,' he said out loud. 'Theoretically, I would think it's possible to arrange the molecules in the crystal in such a way that they become a form of nanotechnology. Bearing in mind we don't even know what element those molecules are. Hey, for all I know, you could program it to boil you an egg!'

'Or send a message,' said Jack. 'Relay a voice, or voices?'

'Like when you used it to try to link up with Cologne, you mean?'

'Yes,' said Jack, 'but I was thinking more about those other voices.'

Ryan thought for a moment. 'Was it always in the vicinity when someone said they could hear them?'

'Good question,' said Jack. 'Let's see. Obviously it was on Venus. But in Switzerland? In the helicopter crash? No, I don't think it works. You were on your way back here by then.'

'Okay,' said Ryan, downing his glass, 'let's go with it, for the moment. You say the crystal is supposed to be some kind of link with Ariel.'

'Right,' said Jack, 'and he definitely was nearby during those times. But how does that work? I mean, how come Natasha could hear the voices during the crash-landing?'

'Don't ask me,' said Ryan. 'I'm not the alien expert here.'

They opened another bottle and watched the Californian sun sink lower in the sky. It looked like it was aiming for a gap between two houses across the road.

'I'd still like to know what you think,' said Jack quietly, now wondering whether Ariel himself had been some kind of conduit.

Just as he began to think Ryan had fallen asleep, his answer came back. 'Maybe it was association.'

'Sorry?' said Jack, his head now distinctly less clear. 'Which association?'

'No, association!' said Ryan. 'Maybe she associated the voices with the last time she'd been in a stressful situation with Ariel, which of course was the first time. On Venus. That may be the origin of it.'

Jack nodded. 'Could be,' he said. It was beginning to feel less important now. Zipping the crystal safely in his inner jacket pocket, he stretched out on the chair and watched the sun take its final bow.

5

Days came and went. Soon the crew had appeared on every television channel in every country, visiting a good many of them in person courtesy of a private jet provided by none other than Hugh Coates. No charge to the WSA, just so long as the TV cameras regularly got to see the Nuclear Aerospace name and logo on the side of the plane. Jim's pride in his crew was evident to all, which gave Jack no small amount of satisfaction. The world got to see an international crew, all soundbites and smiles, and actually none of it was a lie. Again and again they regaled their audiences with vivid descriptions and well rehearsed summaries. The phenomenal conditions on Venus, the endless explanations of why they could survive there, the storms, the experiments, the data. And the stowaway.

Always Icarus, now Ariel, eclipsed everything else, no matter the occasion. Even the nerds and astronomical aces couldn't hide the fact that this trumped what should really have been the talk of the world, the amazing fact that human beings had walked on the surface of a planet that had for over a century been considered off limits. Even when they reminded their audience that Venus had been so much less unfriendly than normal, it wasn't long before they had to admit that those conditions had ended just as mysteriously as they had begun. And that soon got people talking about Ariel again. He must be the reason the Window opened up in the first place.

Which was why they were so glad they had Melody's back-up story, for this was the moment to unleash the revelations about the retreat centre in Montagnola. These served to pour just enough cold water on the ET theories. In the end most people arrived at the same conclusion. China (or some other favourite) had tried to do it their way, and one man had got out before it all went horribly wrong. Just a man. A man who by now was either dead and his body stolen, or debriefed and back among his people. The rest had been so much smoke and mirrors, courtesy of a Chinese cult with a base in Europe.

And so it was that even the conspiracy theories contributed to the tour's resounding success.

It was all wrapped up in a matter of weeks. Weeks without any new dramas or revelations. Every conspiracy theory needs oxygen, and when the invasion didn't come, people grew weary, and the spotlight finally settled where it belonged – on the data that gave life-saving ammunition to the global-cooling cause. And, more than the data, the stories. It seemed the crew's graphic accounts of a thick, boiling atmosphere linked to a volcanic lithosphere began to melt even the hardest hearts. Global cooling was cool again, and the passion had returned to the politics.

When the last interview with the whole crew was in the can, Jim and Ryan returned to the States, while Natasha disappeared on a 'brief holiday' in central Russia, taking with her something she had found in her bag the day after Ariel's departure. Something she did not feel she could share with anyone. Not yet. It was a small notebook containing handwritten poems. The one who had remained closed almost the whole of the time he had been with them had left some clues to the inner workings of his mind. And he had left them with her.

Jack took the leave he was long overdue. British Intelligence confirmed that he was on standby but no longer on call. That left just two more things he wanted to do before going home.

First he made enquiries and discovered that Abbot Leonardo was back at the retreat centre. It was not the place for a holiday, but a day or two wouldn't hurt. After that, with his travel budget now very much a private affair, he would make his own retreat in Ireland somewhere, taking the opportunity to visit Natasha who by then would be staying with Sean.

He took a train to Paris and from there to Lugano. The long journey was just what he needed to change mental gears and ready himself.

As the taxi pulled away from the front of the Elemental Retreat Centre, Leonardo stepped out to welcome him. 'Jack, this is a most agreeable surprise. When I heard you were coming I was delighted. To what do I owe the honour? You can hardly be passing through, yet I understand you are not planning to stay.'

They walked through to the cloister, drawn by the aroma of what Jack now considered some of the finest coffee in the world.

'To be honest, I wasn't even sure that anyone could stay here at the moment,' Jack said as they sat down together in a corner of the empty refectory.

'Ah well,' said Leonardo, 'it is not long that we have been open for business.'

'Business as usual?' Jack asked, knowing the answer.

Leonardo sighed. 'How can it be, my friend? But Brother Ambrose has done an excellent job keeping the place in shape. And now that the authorities have left us in peace, we can start to rebuild.' He sipped his coffee. 'I say "we", though...'

'Are you not staying?' said Jack.

'It seems not,' the Abbot replied. 'You have done well to come now. Soon I shall be returning to Tibet. For further training, you understand.'

'I think I do,' said Jack sadly. 'They can't have been very happy, what with the exposure and all.' He managed to stop himself offering an apology, even though he felt sorry for the abbot.

'Well,' said Leonardo with a mischievous grin, 'at least they have recalled Brother Josef as well! He may not have to face Italian justice, but he will have to give an account to our superiors. And they still have plans for this place and the work we do here. They said we remain an invaluable bridge between East and West. But they are no longer sure I am the one to take the Centre where it should go next.'

'And where might that be?'

'They wish to see a greater connection between the meteorological work and the cause of global cooling.' He smiled. 'At least Brother Leroy will be happy about that. Though I worry for him. He doesn't want me to go. I have told him I should be back within the year.'

'And will you be?'

'Who knows? You are kind, Jack, but do not worry that you can't help me.'

'Maybe I can,' said Jack, removing a box from his pocket. 'I have a present for you.'

'Oh?'

'From Dr Chase.'

Leonardo's eyes lit up as, without ceremony, Jack handed the box to him.

'So small,' Leonardo whispered.

'It's not the whole thing,' Jack explained, 'but Ryan thinks you will like it. And not just because of its origin. This piece is from the centre, so it's kept its shape, more or less. Think of it as a smaller version.'

Leonardo opened the box and carefully removed what had now become the most exquisite jewel. 'And this is for me, you say?'

'That's what the man said,' said Jack. 'Though you might want to offer it to the Order.'

Leonardo smiled. 'Jack, this is a gift beyond value. What can I say?'

Jack decided to take the question literally. 'You can tell me more of what Tibet had to say. If you're allowed.'

Leonardo searched Jack's face. Ever the man on a quest. 'Very well,' he said. 'They were naturally unhappy about the publicity, though I think I understand why Miss Melody decided to name us.'

'I hope you do,' said Jack. 'It was not primarily to shame you. She was actually carrying out what all of us on the team decided was for the best – to tell people where we had been before they found out for themselves. It was hardly the best kept secret in the world anyway. And yes, the, er, equipment you had here was always going to help us spin a yarn – sorry, tell a story – to protect Ariel.'

Leonardo nodded slowly. 'I see. Yes. And I think you were right. I appreciate very much you coming to tell me this in person.'

'I also wanted to tell you what happened on that last night,' said Jack. 'I felt we owed it to you, after everything.'

As they started on some freshly baked cookies Leonardo found behind the counter, Jack described the journeys by road and by air to the mountain rescue facility. Leonardo knew about the fate of the helicopter, but the details brought him unexpected encouragement. 'This explains so much,' he said. 'And Ariel thinks this was some kind of psychic attack?'

'That was his suspicion, yes, if you want to call it that. Maybe more than a suspicion. But that wasn't the sum of the drama. On our journey in the car, we had to deal with an enemy very definitely made of flesh and blood. A police officer was killed, and we narrowly escaped being shot ourselves. And we lost Nathan's body.'

Leonardo did not react. Jack had been unsure just how much Leonardo had already discovered, and this certainly didn't appear to be news to him.

'You asked me about Tibet,' Leonardo said at last. 'And I will tell you this much, because I feel I owe it to you. I first heard about Mr Dexter's body being taken the day I arrived at the monastery in the Himalayas.'

'What?' said Jack. 'But... how is that possible?'

'That is something I have been asking myself ever since,' said Leonardo. 'Clearly someone told them, someone close to the event.'

'Any suspects?' asked Jack.

'I'd rather not say.'

'Of course,' said Jack. 'Well, it remains a mystery for now, although with its connection to the murder of a police officer, I'm sure plenty of resources will be allocated to solving it.'

They talked a while longer, Leonardo now comfortable to share more. 'Another surprise I had in Tibet was their reaction to Ariel's suggestion that we should have a mixed community of men and women. They said they were trying this out already, though they didn't tell me where.'

Jack brought him up to date on the others. Leonardo was particularly pleased to learn of Miranda's recovery. 'A lively girl,' said Leonardo. Because of his accent Jack wasn't sure whether the word was actually lovely, but lively was certainly true.

'What will you do with the crystal?' Jack asked as they left the refectory. 'Or should we call it the jewel now?'

'The jewel, yes – I like that. *Il gioiello*. No, *la gemma*! It is, as you say in English, a real gem, no?'

'Yes it is,' said Jack. 'And tomorrow I'm off to see the person who unearthed it, or more precisely, unvenused it. You'll be interested to know that Natasha is going to be at the forefront of the drive to increase global cooling.'

'That is wonderful!' said Leonardo. 'Perhaps her connection with the Temple of the Four Elements is not yet broken after all.'

'Or is that Five Elements?' said Jack.

Leonardo laughed, and it was good to see. 'Certainly our little gem will help me gain an audience with some of the more conservative elements in Tibet!' he grinned.

'Well,' said Jack, 'I hope so. As for Natasha, she has a lot of work ahead of her. The data we brought back has been welcomed, but it hasn't given up anything particularly revolutionary as yet.'

'Oh, I'm sure it will,' said Leonardo. 'Just keep digging!'

And with that they departed, Leonardo to his office, and Jack to the library. He had been wanting to spend time with its curious range of volumes ever since they had arrived, and at last he could look forward to a few hours' reading without interruption. And there was something else he needed to ponder. Was it really a chance coincidence that Constance Bridlington had chosen for Project Icarus a place that was connected to an organisation that knew things even before they did?

6

Early in the morning three days later the squeak of polish on metal could be heard coming from the monastery's woodland observatory. When he had to think, Leroy liked to clean. This was for the kind of thinking that you came at sideways, when the thoughts weren't really looking and you could catch them unawares.

It also helped with disappointment and confusion.

It can't be true, can't be true... so the cloth intoned as he rubbed vigorously on the handrails under the telescope. There was no way he could believe that the world's great champion, come to save us, would leave so soon. After all, who ever heard of a saviour coming to talk to a few friends and then beetling off again before the work had hardly begun?

He had said as much to the nice police inspector. Her English was very good, and she liked to listen. He had never expected to tell anyone about the conversations he had overheard, or even the proper ones he had had with Natasha and Ariel. But he could hardly withhold anything from the authorities, and the inspector had been most attentive and obviously grateful.

And now, what was there to do but wait? Either the enemies of this man had triumphed, or he was busy working on our behalf. He had to be the reason that the Centre was now going to work in a more focused way in the cause of global cooling. That was something at least.

There was talk of a new abbot. We would have to see about that. But for now, he would keep busy.

7

Olivia Bandalucci leant back on her sofa in her one-bedroom apartment, pulled her bathrobe tighter around her and rubbed her neck. It was late. Or rather, early. In her accustomed manner she had printed out the key files and spread them all over her floor, occasionally promoting some to the coffee table for closer inspection.

Right now she had in front of her the statements of three of the Brothers. The first one was not really her concern, as others were looking into the antics in the attic. In the second statement the medic Ambrose had provided valuable information on the one they called Ariel. The man was clearly an amnesiac, prone to fits, with signs of abnormal neural activity. But nothing Ambrose had said was helping her determine why he had disappeared, or where he had gone.

The final statement had ideas on that, but these were no real help either. The young monk called Leroy, in her judgement naïve but no liar, had been able to supply several pieces of a puzzle that continued to make little sense.

Leroy's had not been a predictable testimony. A lot of it seemed to derive from his ability to be out of sight and within earshot at the same time. It seemed his alien had fairly low-level superpowers, amounting to little more than the ability to open unlocked doors and resist serious wounding. And possibly heighten emotions. But the real reason he thought this man, or alien, was going to save the world was through his intellectual powers. Leroy – and all the Brothers in fact – had been impressed by what they called his spiritual vision.

She decided to call it a night. Her empty bed was calling. Her brief was not to go hunting for aliens but to catch a killer, a cop-killer at that. And it looked like nothing she had learnt at the monastery was going to help her in her quest.

Tomorrow she would drive back up to the scene of the crime one more time. And then she would have to turn her attention to the UN agents. There had been no help there from her superiors, which was as predictable as it was disappointing, but something told her the

British spy might be her way in. She would have to go outside the official channels, but not too far outside. And where better than Jack Forrester?

She took off her bathrobe and draped it neatly over the back of a chair. As she pulled up a sleeve of her silk pyjamas to remove her eband she noticed a message that had come earlier that evening. It was from an unknown number which, when she checked it, turned out to belong to someone called Petroc Naismith.

Epilogue

The grey buildings of Auld Reekie struck a bleak note in the weak sunlight as Jack and Melody looked down over the city he called home. Arthur's Seat had long been a place for significant moments here in the heart of Scotland's capital, and this was going to be one of the biggest in his life.

His leave was coming to an end, and tomorrow he would be travelling to Geneva to discuss his role in a possible follow-up mission to Venus. This time no one expected them to get further than the usual thirty miles from the surface, so Natasha and Ryan were not on the list of candidates. Jim had no desire to return. So it seemed that Jack, if he went, would be the voice of experience in a new team.

'I thought your dad might join us up here,' Mel said as they sat on a convenient crag.

'Well, no,' said Jack, zipping his all-weather jacket up a little higher against the wind. 'He knows I've got something to say to you.'

'Oh.'

'Mel, it's been a crazy time these past weeks, months, since I stood in that impossible place and brought back that impossible man. And you've borne so much!'

She brushed the hair from her face, but the wind would have none of it. 'I'm okay.'

They looked across Leith to the Firth of Forth.

'This is an extinct volcano, you know,' said Jack.

'Okay,' said Mel. 'I like the word extinct.'

'Aye, a bit of a contrast from where we found our friend.'

'I know. What a strange place to find him!' She looked up into the cloudy sky in the general direction of where the sun must be, knowing that Venus was up there too in the same region of sky. 'I still wonder who he really was. Is. Still, he walked among us. That's the thing.'

'Aye,' said Jack. 'And now we have to move on.'

'Yes,' she said, 'but not forget. We need to remember the things we felt – and the things he said, even though we don't really know who he was.' She turned into the wind and let it pull her hair behind her in a flurry of gold. 'Perhaps he was a messenger. Though, if he was, I'm not sure we received the message. Apparently that can happen, even when God sends the messenger.'

'Aye,' said Jack, 'and I'll admit it's no so easy for me any more to dismiss that idea.' His accent was always stronger when he was back in Scotland. 'If anything is clear to me now, it's that some messengers are themselves as important as the messages they bring.'

She turned and looked at him. Her man was changing.

'It's strange,' Jack said, 'almost the whole time we had him he didn't know who he was.'

'But he seemed to understand the world, though, don't you think?'

'That's true,' said Jack. 'And whichever world he came from, he certainly made us all think. Maybe he and his friends are from somewhere that managed to get through the kind of global meltdown facing us right now. I like to think of him as a friendly visitor, wherever he's from.'

She noticed he had slipped into the present tense. 'Sounds good to me,' she said. 'I wonder if we'll ever see him again. Perhaps he'll come back.'

'What?' said Jack with a faint smile, looking around. 'Like King Arthur?'

'Oh, I don't know,' she said. 'He's a bit too much of a legend. Maybe more like King Jesus.' She pulled the hair from her eyes and watched Jack's face, expecting a frown or some other comment, but none came. 'Still,' she said, 'I'll need to mull it all over some more, especially the things he said in Montagnola. I'm going to see Miranda soon. She wants to meet up, and I'd love to compare notes with her properly. The more perspectives the better.' She sighed. 'I know he said nothing about coming back. We don't even know if they'll let him. Whoever "they" are.'

They held each other's gaze for a while, each wrestling with the notion that humanity might genuinely not be alone in the universe, and wondering whether that was a cosmological question or a theological one. Or both.

She turned back into the wind and raised her voice. 'Whatever it all means, we really do need to get on with our lives!'

'Aye,' said Jack. 'Talking of which...' He got down from the crag and looked up at her as she turned to face him, her hair wild in the wind. Then he took a small box from his pocket. 'The last time I did this—'

'The last time?' she said, horrified.

'Aye, let me finish... the last time I took a gem from my pocket, it was the heart of a great mystery given to a man of great heart, our friend the Abbot.'

'Oh, Jack. I knew it!'

'What?' he asked. 'What did you know?'

'That you're a romantic!' She leant forward to kiss him, and he accepted it graciously enough, but his mind was clearly now on the task.

'Melody Grantley James...'

'Yes, Alexander John Forrester?'

'Will you marry me?'

She covered his face with kiss after kiss, yes after yes. Then she took out the ring and set it on her finger. It was a silvery white gem, like nothing she'd ever seen. Almost.

'Wait a moment,' she said. 'This looks familiar. Jack? No, it can't be!'

'Well, yes actually, it can. Ryan assured me they wouldn't miss it. After all, it's only a small shard. He polished it up for me. It was a hoot, as neither of us was particularly sober at the time.'

'But you are now.'

'Oh yes,' he said. 'I had it mounted here in Edinburgh, but you can change the setting if you want.'

'I wouldn't change a thing,' she said. A few last rays of sunlight made it beneath a bank of cloud and set her moist eyes sparkling.

They both sat in silence on the crag for a while, till the cold wind prodded them to their feet. 'It's funny,' she giggled, 'I was only thinking this morning how the retreat centre in Montagnola would make a great setting for a wedding.'

'Aye,' said Jack, 'that's true enough. But so would the church on your father's estate.'

She hugged him, praying that she would always be able to know him this close, with nothing and no one between them. 'I can't wait to tell the others!' Then she danced off the crag and held out her hand, and together they made their way back down the hillside to the city below.

Poems of Ariel

These poems are the ones Natasha made available to us from the notebook Ariel gave to her. The titles are ours, not his. Three of them were used in the main text. All throw a little light on what was going on in Ariel's head at certain times.
[MF/MF]

Who am I?

Who am I?
To be, now, is to have been, then. Before.

Where am I?
In a story? Whose? Those of my friends?
The scent of a melody, soft siren seeking harmony.
The riddle of a miranda, to be wondered at.
I wonder.
She swims well, out of her depth, guarding her story.
What is my story?

But first there was you.
You were there when the world was new
again.
Risen again.
Eyes locked, hearts joined.
Your song soothed its way in.
Into me.
Who is me?

They say I am a mirror, yet
reflections of others illumine my soul.
But they do not make me me,
Who I am.

Who am I?

Lapse

We used this early on in our account, as it clearly relates to his arrival.

Down and down he flew, falling fast in fear and fury. Eight became four became two became one, then fractioned over two, over four, over eight. He was slowing. Closing. Landing. Bright light shifted into dark matter.
He froze. In two hundred degrees of boiling sulphur he lay cold as a corpse. Swirling clouds of angry orange licked his limbs and fingered his face. Yet he knew nothing of it. He dreamed.
In the thick of battle comrades cried, cheered by the scent of victory, bracing themselves as one for the onslaught to come. We're going to push forward. We're going to push back the enemy. Today will be a day to remember.
To remember... Remember the sound of fear in your enemies. Remember the look of dread in their eyes. Remember what you do. Remember who you are.
Location.
A new face. She looks worried. Questions crease her brow. Compassion crowns her eyes. Beautiful eyes.
New voices. Angry.
Must sleep. Sleep and remember.
Remember.

Life

We took this to be a vivid description of his sense of life in the trees outside, before he lost consciousness after opening the French windows at the retreat centre.

A rush of air, mossy and moist.
Grass. Dirt. Stone. Leaves rustling, shadows dancing.
Life.
Upward thrust, root to shoot, sap in the stem, trunk of the tree,
bark through to branches, brimming to twigs, filling the leaves.
A leaf.
Veins flood with food, humming with light.
Life.
The leaf is green, throbbing translucence.
It fills all things. All things are the leaf. The light.
Where does it end? Look askance for the spaces between. Averted vision. Interstices.
Brain on fire. Eyes water. A rush of air. The earth swoops up.
Darkness.

Light

This one appears to be an account of his clash with the enemy – we think with obscure references to Jim and Nathan and Miranda. If so, it must have been written (or finished) after he had heard from his friends, yet in time to be included in Natasha's notebook.

Interlinking lines of light in ever finer fractals.
Voices vie to strangle the stranger or save.
Ears enveloped in sounding fury, pressed hard by hammers on anger's anvil. Too late! the cry. The line is broken. What now for those in nature's night and the fearful fog of oblivion?
There shivers the repentant, spurred on by duty's call, destined to be saved through weakness.
But oh, the gall of greed and gain in this, the hopeless! Too late the remorse, to try to right the wrongs,
when wrong has long since wrought its doom, and hope is lost.
Here lie the fallen.
Is there no way back? Back to the beginning?
See now, love comes, her arms outstretched, the heart that aches, too soon to lose what's only lately found.
Rest. The time is soon. Rebellion trounced again, for now.
So take the time to say goodbye.
The fight goes on, and not alone.
Rest.

Undivided

Borne on a sea of music
Carried on currents of shining cloud
I plumb the boundless depths within my soul.
A universe within a universe.
Ever deeper, lifting layers of misted past,
Towards the pointless point.
I am person, whole,
Undivided
I am.

Trees

wood winding
        life stretching
                earth-rooted
                        heaven-reaching
cathedral arches
        top temple columns
                in effervescent glory

Ariel

And here I am,
Right where I should not be. Or should
I?
Everything sings with life, while I go on
Looking for before.

Printed in Great Britain
by Amazon